Praise for *The Best of Manhunt*

"... provides rich insights into the history

"This book comes most highly recommended to all readers of classic and contemporary crime fiction. In fact, if you read only one anthology of republished crime stories this year, it should be *The Best of Manhunt*."
—Alan Cranis, *Bookgasm*

"...may be the greatest short story compilation... The stories are brutal and filled with final-page twists—or in other words: essential reading. Highest recommendation."
—*Paperback Warrior*

"This compilation of forty stories, most taken from the early years of the magazine, is a gold mine. Some of the stories are so good they are masterpieces in their own right, there are writers here at the top of their game ... These stories are a reflection of the angst and concerns of the time they were written, they are often prescient and trailblazing ... also relevant for today's world too... A must for noir/hardboiled fans."
—Paul Burke, *NB*

"The most important crime fiction anthology maybe ever published."
—*Paperback Warrior* Podcast, Episode 4

"Forget some time in the pokey: maybe some time with this book'll teach young readers some respect for decent genre writers."
—Nell Beram, *Shelf Awareness*

"A convincing argument for the value of the magazine, *The Best of Manhunt* is essential reading for anyone interested in the history of crime writing, and an excellent collection of stories."
—Matthew Surridge, *Splice Today*

"For 14 years, 1952 to 1967, Manhunt published the best crime fiction in the United States. This excellent volume collects several of those classic Manhunter stories with their suspense, thrills, and menace. This wonderful anthology is the best anthology of the year! GRADE: A"
—George Kelley

"Talk about getting a lot of bang for your buck, this book is guaranteed to provide that in spades!... a virtual Who's Who of crime fiction."
—Hank Wagner, *Mystery Scene*

"Most of the stories are tight pieces about violence or its aftermath, whether from the perspective of perpetrator, victim, or witness. The prose is usually strong, terse and blunt, typically locked tight on the perspective of a single character even when not in first person. Plots are almost always sharply constructed and dramatic without simple twist endings."

—*Splice Today*

"…39 tough and relentless gritty stories from the legendary digest published in the 1950s and 60s by plenty of writers who were pretty legendary themselves…"
—Kevin Burton Smith, *Mystery Scene*

"Get your hands on Stark House Press' new *The Best of Manhunt*: A Collection of The Best of *Manhunt* Magazine edited by Jeff Vorzimmer, even if only to read the editor's excellent introduction, 'The Tortured History of Manhunt,' which almost reads like a crime story itself!"
—*The Stiletto Gumshoe*

"This collection is an excellent representation of what readers could easily find back in the day. Filled with tense stories often with catchy titles, this volume showcases the best of the best."
—Amazon.com

Praise for *The Best of Manhunt 2*

"Short stories are a complex art form, every word has to count, the message has to be clear and sharp, and the tale perfectly encapsulated. The stories here are taut, lean, and pacy, they are dark, erotic, psychological, cynical, gritty, and action driven. A must for noir fans."
—Paul Burke, *NB*

"*The Best of Manhunt 2* is another masterpiece of short fiction that will be an essential part of any hardboiled library… Highly recommended."
—*Paperback Warrior*

"*The Best of Manhunt 2* and its companion volume, *The Best of Manhunt*, are the most important books Stark House has published to date."
—Ben Boulden, *Mystery Scene*

"… a perfect masterpiece of short stories…"
—*Paperback Warrior* Podcast

THE MANHUNT COMPANION

Peter Enfantino • Jeff Vorzimmer

STARK HOUSE

Stark House Press • Eureka California
www.starkhousepress.com

THE MANHUNT COMPANION
Published by Stark House Press
1315 H Street
Eureka, CA 95501
griffinskye3@sbcglobal.net
www.starkhousepress.com

The *Manhunt Companion* ©2021 by Peter Enfantino & Jeff Vorzimmer
The History of *Manhunt* ©2019 by Jeff Vorzimmer

ISBN: 978-1-951473-44-0

Book design by *jcaliente!design*, Austin, Texas

PUBLISHER'S NOTE:
This is a work of fiction. Names, characters, places and incidents are either the products of the author's imagination or used fictionally, and any resemblance to actual persons, living or dead, events or locales, is entirely coincidental. Without limiting the rights under copyright reserved above, no part of this publication may be reproduced, stored, or introduced into a retrieval system or transmitted in any form or by any means (electronic, mechanical, photocopying, recording or otherwise) without the prior written permission of both the copyright owner and the above publisher of the book.

First Stark House Press Edition: March 2021

Table of Contents

Preface ....Jeff Vorzimmer.. 7
The History of *Manhunt* ......Jeff Vorzimmer.. 9
Manhunt Story Reviews ....Peter Enfantino....................1953 17
....1954 50
....1955 79
....1956 107
....1957 139
....1958 165
....1959 184
....1960 197
....1961 212
....1962 224
....1963 238
....1964 250
....1965 264
....1966 278
....1967 290
Indices ....Stories and Articles by Issue........................ 295
....Alphabetical Index by Story 333
....Alphabetical Index by Author 365
....Alphabetical Index by Series 405
....TV Episodes based on *Manhunt* Stories 409

Preface

Peter Enfantino and I first appeared together in conjunction with *Manhunt* on the pages of *The Digest Enthusiast*. He was writing an on-going series in which he was reviewing every story to appear in the magazine over its 15-year history and I was being interviewed about my recently-published collection, *The Best of Manhunt*.

I had accumulated a lot of information while doing research for the two anthologies I produced of *Manhunt* stories, which I collected in a database. I thought the information might be of interest to fans and collectors of the magazine. I envisioned a reference book with which one could look up authors who had appeared in the magazine or particular stories or series to find which issue and on what page a story had appeared.

I thought Peter's summaries would be a great fit for such a reference book. For example, if you remembered a particular story you read in *Manhunt* by a certain author, but couldn't recall the name or the issue in which it appeared, you could look up in the index the issues with that author's stories and skim the reviews to identify it.

Fortunately, when I approached Peter with the project, he was as enthusiastic about the idea as I was. I'm sure you'll find his story summaries as delightful and entertaining as I have. I found myself laughing out loud while reading some of them. To his reviews I have added a brief blurb about each issue on the covers, page count, first and last appearances of certain authors or circulation. I was writing these simultaneously and separately from Peter, so you might find some repetition in the reviews that follow. The indices were generated from the database.

Which brings to mind something else I should say in this preface and that is, while Peter has made an effort not to spoil a story for you if you've not read it, it's inevitable that a summary might reveal an important plot point you might find to be a spoiler. We're sorry, you've been forewarned, but we sincerely hope it won't detract from the pleasure of reading the story.

Another point I should make is that while Peter and I are both fanatical in our love for *Manhunt*, we don't always agree on which stories are the best, or the worst, for that matter. You will come across stories he rated as only worthy of two stars, but that I thought highly enough to include in one of the *Best of* anthologies. So, if you find yourself disagreeing with Peter's assessment of a story, well, keep in mind he's read all the stories and you haven't (unless you're Bill Pronzini). Even I can't make that claim.

—Jeff Vorzimmer
Austin, Texas

The History of Manhunt

The first issue of *Manhunt* appeared on newsstands in late 1952 and within two years became the widely acknowledged successor to *Black Mask*, which had ceased publication the year before. The stories in *Manhunt* captured the noir of Cold War angst like no other fiction magazine of its time and paved the way for television anthology shows such as *Alfred Hitchcock Presents* and *The Twilight Zone*.

Manhunt can best be described as a joint venture between publisher Archer St. John and literary agent Scott Meredith, both based in New York. In 1952, St. John published comic books and had recently ventured into and, in fact, developed 3D comics and graphic novels. His company, St. John Publishing, produced what is considered the first graphic novel, *It Rhymes with Lust*, in 1950, which was part crime, part romance, and followed that, later the same year with *The Case of the Winking Buddha*. Neither book sold very well and the line, dubbed "Pictures Novels," was discontinued after the second title.

Archer St. John, always an admirer of *Black Mask*, the premier pulp magazine from the 1920s through the 40s, felt that since that magazine's demise there was a void in the world of crime-fiction pulps and an opportunity. Of course, comic book publishers don't usually have big editorial staffs nor do they solicit manuscript submissions. For help, St. John approached Scott Meredith, a literary agent who was beginning to turn the publishing world on its ear with practices such as charging would-be writers reading fees and submitting manuscripts to publishers simultaneously, creating an auction system of competing bids.

For Scott Meredith it was an opportunity to get his stable of writers in print and create another stream of income. St. John served as the front man to avoid any ethical questions or conflict of interest charges that Meredith might otherwise face. St. John would manage the production of the magazine from editing, layout and illustration to the printing and distribution of the magazine while Meredith's office would ensure a steady supply of fiction from among the manuscripts that crossed their transom.

Of course, it was not a very well-kept secret within the publishing business. Those in the business, with even a passing familiarity with the roster of the Scott Meredith Literary Agency, would notice a preponderance of his clients on the pages of *Manhunt*. In fact, all ten of the most prolific contributors to the magazine were Meredith authors who, between them, contributed over one-fifth of all stories that appeared in *Manhunt* over the course of its fifteen-year run.

Manhunt has often been referred to, then and now, as a closed shop, only available to the Meredith stable of authors, but that's not entirely true. As often as not, writers not represented by an agent would submit stories directly to *Manhunt*. These were forwarded to the Meredith office and occasionally published in the magazine, though the authors were not usually signed to a publishing contract on the strength of a single story. This would at times create awkward moments when a producer from a television studio such as Screen Gems or Revue—

Peter Enfantino • Jeff Vorzimmer

producers of *Alfred Hitchcock Presents*, *M Squad and Studio 57*—would call up the agency looking to secure the rights to a story they read in *Manhunt*. The Meredith agent would stall the producer, scramble to locate and sign the author then make the deal.

Archer St. John originally wanted to call the magazine *Mickey Spillane's Mystery Magazine* to compete with *Ellery Queen's Mystery Magazine*, albeit with grittier, more hard-boiled stories. Having Spillane's name on the masthead would have been appealing to both St. John and Meredith in that, by 1952, Spillane's first six books had combined sales of 20 million copies. His first book, *I, The Jury* had sold 3.5 million copies by 1953, when it was adapted for the screen.

When Scott Meredith checked Spillane's contract with his publisher, Dutton, he found a clause that gave the publisher total control of Mickey Spillane's name in conjunction with any books *or periodicals*. If they were to use Spillane's name on the magazine they had to get Dutton's permission. However, Dutton balked at the idea.

Dutton felt that short stories were a distraction for Spillane, and they wanted him to get back to the business of writing novels. At that point, it had been over a year since Spillane had delivered his last novel to them (and it would be ten years before he delivered his next one). The name of the magazine was changed to *Manhunt*, a named borrowed from a then-defunct crime comic book.

St. John intended to kick off the magazine with a Mickey Spillane story. He had heard that *Collier's Magazine* had turned down a novella Spillane had written, "Everybody's Watching Me," and offered to serialize it in the first four issues of the new magazine and pay Spillane $25,000 (equivalent to $237,000 today). If Spillane's name could not be on the masthead, it would at least be on the cover of the first four issues.

The print run of the first issue, dated January 1953, was 600,000 copies and sold out in five days. It was digest size (5½"x7½"), 144 pages and priced at 35¢ and $4 for a year's subscription. In addition to the lead story by Spillane, the issue also included stories by Cornell Woolrich under the name of William Irish; Ross Macdonald, under his real name, Kenneth Millar; and Evan Hunter, later known by the pen name Ed McBain. It also included a story featuring Richard Prather's detective Shell Scott, featured in six novels of his own over the previous three years, and, who rivaled Spillane's Mike Hammer in popularity, and another featuring Frank Kane's Johnny Liddell. Stories by Floyd Mahannah, Charles Beckman, Jr. and Sam Cobb (Stanley L. Colbert) rounded out the issue.

St. John surrounded himself with a staff of talented young people. His Managing Editor, who appeared on the masthead simply as E. A. Tulman, was 24-year-old petite brunette Eleanor Tulman. His favorite artist, 32-year-old Matt Baker—a black man in the predominantly white world of comic books—did the illustrations for *Manhunt*. Baker was the artist who had drawn the panels for the two graphic novels St. John had published. He brought an entirely new look to *Manhunt*, with heavy ink drawings highlighted with a spot color. Each story had one illustration on the first page in a style not unlike *Black Mask*.

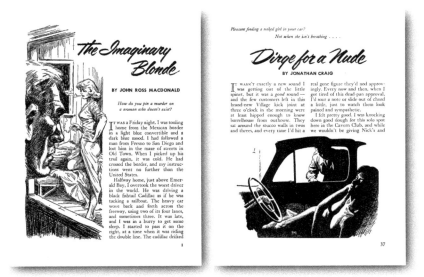

Pages from the February 1953 issue of *Manhunt* with illustrations by Matt Baker

Baker himself would do most of the illustrations for the first nine issues thereby setting the style used for the entire 15-year run. Up-and-coming young artists such as Robert McGinnis, Walter Popp and Robert Maguire, as well as older, more established artists, such as Frank Uppwall and Willard Downes, painted the covers.

The editorial note on the contents page of the second issue stated that the press run of the first issue probably should have been closer to a million copies. St. John apparently split the difference and ran 800,000 copies of the second issue. In addition to the second installment of "Everybody's Watching Me," the lead story was another by Kenneth Millar, a Lew Archer story titled "The Imaginary Blonde" under his new pseudonym John Ross Macdonald. There were also two more stories by Evan Hunter under the pseudonyms Richard Marsten and Hunt Collins, a Paul Pine story by John Evans, as well as stories by Jonathan Craig (Frank E. Smith), Fletcher Flora, Richard Deming, Eleazar Lipsky and Michael Fessier.

In addition to the contributors of the first two issues, the third issue was notable in that it included stories by older, more established writers such as Leslie Charteris with a Saint story, Craig Rice (Georgiana Craig) with a John J. Malone story, as well as stories by William Lindsay Gresham and Bruno Fischer.

The third issue also contained another two stories by Evan Hunter, one under the pseudonym Richard Marsten. In fact, Evan Hunter contributed 16 stories to the first 9 issues of *Manhunt* under his own name and various pseudonyms and 46 stories over the entire life of the magazine, making him the most prolific contributor by far. For a magazine that was supposed to be all about Mickey Spillane, it was turning out to be all about Evan Hunter.

Peter Enfantino • Jeff Vorzimmer

By mid-1953, St. John, with Meredith's help, started a campaign to lure big name authors to *Manhunt*. They approached James M. Cain, Raymond Chandler, Rex Stout, Erle Stanley Gardner, Nelson Algren and Erskine Caldwell. They offered as much as $5,000 (about $47,000 today) for a 5,000-word story. This was the kind of money writers could expect from the slick magazines, but not from the pulps.

Many writers like Erle Stanley Gardner initially balked at the idea of publishing in *Manhunt*, but eventually succumbed. Gardner's first response to his agent was, "I hate to turn down an offer of $5000 for a story, but, confidentially, I don't like this magazine concept with which *Manhunt* started out. I think it is a definite menace to legitimate mystery fiction."

By the end of the decade all those big-name writers, including Gardner, had agreed to publish stories in *Manhunt*, though many appeared only once, the last being the only appearance by Raymond Chandler. His story, "Wrong Pigeon," previously published only in England, appeared posthumously in the February 1960 issue.

The year 1953 would be the peak year for St. John Publications. *Manhunt* was turning out to be its biggest-selling title, spawning spin-off magazine *Verdict*, which specialized in reprinting classic crime stories; *Gunsmoke*, featuring westerns; and *Menace*, a *Manhunt* clone, and its 3D comics were selling millions of copies. The company had 35 different comic book titles with several lines of romance comics, Mighty Mouse and Three Stooges comic book lines, for a total of 169 issues published that year.

Another of Archer St. John's projects was a men's magazine that would include articles of interest to men, photos of women in various stages of undress and quality fiction. However, he was concerned about the post office not allowing the mailing of what they would certainly deem pornographic material to subscribers. After *Playboy* appeared in December 1953, he was emboldened to move ahead with the project.

In 1954, Archer brought in his 24-year-old son Michael to help run the business, while he focused on the new men's magazine, *Nugget*. Again, he turned to his favorite artist, Matt Baker, to do the illustrations for the magazine. Although that year would turn out to be another good year for St. John Publications, there was trouble on the horizon.

In the spring of 1954, there was a backlash against sex and violence in comic books that were clearly aimed at children. The crusade was led by New York psychiatrist Fredric Wertham who published the now-infamous *Seduction of the Innocent*, a book-length study of the adverse effects of violent comic books on young minds. The book ultimately led to a Senate investigation, which issued its own *Comic Books and Juvenile Delinquency Interim Report* that included a list of comic book titles it deemed inappropriate for children. There were, of course, some St. John titles on the list.

It was also apparent in early 1954 that 3D comics were just a passing fad. Sales of 3D comics plummeted to the point that, by March of 1954, 3D titles had all but disappeared. The sales of comic books in general were in a slump, brought on in large part by the scare created by politicians and PTA groups after the Wertham study.

Other forces were coming to bear that would have a personal effect on Archer St. John and the fate of St. John Publications. In August of 1954, President Eisenhower signed *The Communist Control Act*, which outlawed the Communist Party in the United States. Anyone who had ever been a member of the Communist Party could face imprisonment or even the revocation of citizenship. Archer's brother, the famous journalist Robert St. John, living a self-imposed exile in Switzerland and doing research for books on South Africa and Israel, was determined by the FBI to have been a member of the Communist Party. On September 24, 1954, Robert St. John was summoned to the American Consulate in Geneva and stripped of his passport. When Robert asked why his passport was being taken from him, the reply from the Consul-General was that it was because of his Communist Party activity.

Robert turned to his brother Archer back in the States for help to get his passport reinstated and get the necessary affidavits for the appeal. Over the following months Archer, who was very close to his brother Robert, became increasingly frustrated by the stonewalling he got from the U. S. government on his brother's case.

Adding to his personal turmoil was the fact Archer was separated from his wife and living at the New York Athletic Club. His employees at St. John Publications also suspected he was addicted to amphetamines, in addition to being an alcoholic. By mid-1955 Robert's case had still not been decided, though he had submitted numerous affidavits from noted citizens that affirmed that he was never a member of the Communist Party.

In August, Archer told family members that he was being blackmailed, but didn't give anyone specific details. His son Michael told him not to give in to the blackmailers. Archer told his son that he was staying at the apartment of a friend but wouldn't tell him where.

On Friday night August 12, 1955, Robert St. John got a call in Switzerland from Archer in New York who told him, "Never in my life have I felt so frustrated. I feel like I'm banging my head against a stone wall. I see no possibility of getting your passport back. I've done everything in my power to help you, but I've failed. I'm sick over this." The next morning Robert got a call telling him that his brother had overdosed on sleeping pills, an apparent suicide. He was 54 years old.

At times, Archer St. John's life resembled a story from the pages of *Manhunt*—Al Capone's gang once kidnapped him, in 1925, when he was young newspaper publisher—and his death was no different. The apartment where Archer had been staying was a duplex penthouse owned by an attractive, redheaded former model and divorcée named Frances Stratford. She had been sleeping in an upstairs bedroom and had found Archer downstairs lying next to the couch, unresponsive, at 11:30 a.m. that Saturday morning.

A couple had been seen leaving the apartment the night before, and the police began an investigation. The following Monday, the *New York Daily News* reported, "A couple of shadowy West Side characters, a man and a woman, suspected of feeding dope pills to magazine publisher Archer St. John, were being hunted . . . by detectives investigating St. John's mysterious death in the penthouse apartment of a former Powers model."

After St. John's death, his wife, Gertrude-Faye, known as "G-F," pronounced "Geff," showed up at the offices of St. John Publications and promptly fired the entire staff, including Matt Baker. Apparently, she hadn't wanted anyone around who knew about her husband's affairs. The irony was that none of the staff knew anything about St. John's private love life, not even Baker who was probably as close to him as anybody.

Despite the failure of the previous *Manhunt* clones, *Verdict*, which lasted only four issues in late 1953 and *Menace*, which lasted two issues, the following year, Michael St. John decided to expand his own editorial staff and to introduce yet two more titles, *Mantrap* and *Murder!* in 1956. Unfortunately, the new titles suffered from the same lackluster sales of the first two spin-off titles and were discontinued just as quickly.

Undaunted by the failure of four new titles in as many years, Michael kept searching for a formula that would repeat the success of *Manhunt*. What Michael and his business manager, Richard Decker, came up with was an opposite, more genteel, direction. They approached Alfred Hitchcock with an offer to license his name and image for a mystery digest.

Alfred Hitchcock's Mystery Magazine was an immediate success and, in fact, sales would steadily increase throughout the rest of the decade while those of *Manhunt* were in steady decline, down to 169,000 by 1957. Its digest size, with two-column layout and heavily inked spot color illustrations, were identical to *Manhunt*'s.

In an effort to boost sales of both *Manhunt* and *Alfred Hitchcock's Mystery Magazine*, St. John and Decker decided to increase the size of both magazines from their current digest size to regular magazine size to get, what they hoped would be, more attention on newsstands. What it got *Manhunt* was the unwanted attention of the Federal District Attorney.

After only the second issue at the bigger magazine size, Michael St. John, Richard E. Decker, Charles W. Adams (the Art Director) and Flying Eagle Publications (a subsidiary of St. John's Publications and holding company of *Manhunt*) were indicted on March 14, 1957, for "mailing or delivery copies of the April, 1957, issue of a publication entitled *Manhunt* containing obscene, lewd, lascivious, filthy or indecent matter" in violation of United States Penal Code 18 U. S. C. §1461.

In District Court in Concord, New Hampshire, St. John's lawyers moved to have the charges dismissed on the grounds that the complaint didn't identify what article was specifically being charged in the issue as "obscene, lewd, filthy or indecent." They argued that "the indictment is so loosely drawn that it would not afford them protection from further prosecution." District Court Judge Aloysius J. Connor agreed and threw out the indictments on August 7, 1957.

Federal prosecutors promptly refiled charges with specific complaints: "All six of the stories have definitely weird overtones and can certainly be characterized as crude, course, vulgar, and on the whole disgusting. But tested by the reaction of the community as a whole—the average member of society—it seems to us that only the feature novelette, 'Body on a White Carpet,' and the illustration appearing on page 25 accompanying the story entitled 'Object of Desire,' could be found to fall within the ban of the statute as limited in its application by the important public interest in a free press protected in the First Amendment." The defendants faced a fine of $5,000 ($43,000 in today's dollars) and up to five years in prison.

The offending illustration by Jack Coughlin accompanying the story "Object of Desire" on page 25 of the April 1957 issue.

In March of 1957, Jack Coughlin, the freelancer who did the illustration for "Object of Desire," was called into Art Director Charles Adams' office. Adams handed Coughlin a copy of the latest issue of *Manhunt* and asked him to turn to page 25, saying there was a problem with the illustration there and asked him to explain. Coughlin looked at it, focused on the woman in the illustration, and said he couldn't see a problem. Adams told him to look at the man's crotch. It was then that what appeared to be a penis seemed to almost leap off the page. "Once you see it, you can't *not* see it," Coughlin said.

Apparently an employee of the printing company in Concord, New Hampshire had called Adams attention to it. Adams eventually brought Coughlin to a New York City courtroom where Coughlin gave a deposition before a judge claiming that the illustration wasn't intentionally obscene, but rather a fluke of the scratchboard engraving process used in *Manhunt* illustrations. Coughlin, who was paid $35 for the illustration was never asked to do another for the magazine. He was told sometime later that the judge had believed him and the case was never tried in the State of New York.

However, on December 1, 1958, the final verdict of the District Court jury was that Flying Eagle Publications and Michael St. John were guilty and fined $3,000 ($26,000 today). Judge Connor gave St. John a separate fine of $1000, a suspended sentence of six months in jail and two-year probation. Richard E. Decker and Charles W. Adams were acquitted. Michael St. John immediately appealed the verdict and the case went to Federal Appeals Court.

On January 21, 1960, the Federal Appeals Court in Boston set aside the verdict of the District Court and ordered a new trial. Chief Judge Peter Woodbury found that the prosecutors had erred in their instructions to the jury by telling them that two defendants, Decker and Adams, originally listed on the indictment had 'been separated from this action" rather than that they were acquitted.

The new trial was scheduled to begin March 28, 1960, but Michael St. John's lawyers requested that the case delayed until the next court term later that year.

Early the next year the Court of Appeals concurred with the decision of the Circuit Court. On January 10, 1961, Judge Bailey Aldrich upheld the original conviction and fine of $5,000. After three years and nine months of litigation, St. John Publishing was financially drained. The circulation of *Manhunt* had dropped to 100,000, and Richard Decker had split with St. John in the summer of 1960, taking *Alfred Hitchcock's Mystery Magazine* with him to Palm Beach, Florida.

Scott Meredith had always been annoyed with what seemed to be chronic cash-flow problems at St. John, and it only got worse. The magazine limped along for the next six years, and fewer of Meredith's writers appeared in the magazine. Only 26 stories by the top ten Meredith contributors appeared in the 1960s.

No new Evan Hunter stories appeared in *Manhunt* in the 60s, although three stories from 1953 were reprinted under different titles, one of which appeared in the last issue of April/May 1967. By then the circulation had dropped to a little over 74,000 copies. Michael St. John decided to get out of the publishing business entirely and sold off all the assets of St John Publishing, including *Nugget*.

Vol. 1 No. 1 Jan 1953

The magazine's debut. Issues started appearing on newsstands in December of 1952. The first three issues would contain just fiction. The newsstand price was 35¢ and subscriptions were $4 for a year—prices that would remain in effect through 1963.

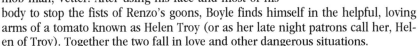

"Everybody's Watching Me" by Mickey Spillane (a serial in four parts) (29,500 words total)★★

Joe Boyle stumbles into big-time trouble when he delivers a message to mobster Mark Renzo from fellow mob man, Vetter. After using his face and most of his body to stop the fists of Renzo's goons, Boyle finds himself in the helpful, loving arms of a tomato known as Helen Troy (or as her late night patrons call her, Helen of Troy). Together the two fall in love and other dangerous situations.

In the 1950s, no one sold more gritty, hardboiled fiction than Mickey Spillane (1918–2006). *I, The Jury* (1947), *My Gun is Quick* (1950), *The Long Wait* (1951), *The Big Kill* (1951), *Vengeance is Mine* (1951), *One Lonely Night* (1951), and *Kiss Me, Deadly* (1952) all sold millions of copies while pushing the boundaries of violence and sex in mainstream fiction. The American Booksellers Association reported that only the Bible outsold Spillane in 1952. His character Mike Hammer ("hero" of all the aforementioned novels, except *The Long Wait*) bedded women and broke teeth like no other popular creation before him. Hammer's translation to the big screen was equally popular (Robert Aldrich's version of *Kiss Me, Deadly* with Ralph Meeker, is regarded by many as the greatest noir film of all time), with new movie and TV adaptations popping up every couple years.

Without Spillane's massive popularity, it's unlikely that publishers like Gold Medal and Lion would have taken a chance on such hardboiled writers as Gil Brewer, Vin Packer, Jim Thompson, and David Goodis and even more unlikely that Flying Eagle would have launched *Manhunt*. It's appropriate that Spillane should lead off the premiere issue

Despite his popularity, Spillane had many detractors (most of them literary critics) who decried "the Mick's" blend of blood and bosoms. Spillane is definitely an acquired taste, one that either hooks you immediately or turns you off. Whatever it was he had, it appealed to an enormous amount of readers, as Spillane quickly became the biggest-selling hardboiled author of the first half of the 20th Century.

"Die Hard" by Evan Hunter (7000 words)★★★

Matt Cordell, ex-P.I., current drunk, is asked by Peter D'Allessio to save his son Jerry, whose life has become a nightmare of heroin addiction. Cordell initially turns down the request but reconsiders when the elder D'Allessio is gunned down in front of him. Cordell finds that there's a hell even worse than the one he occupies.

Cordell is an ex-private investigator who lost his license after beating his wife's boyfriend and now finds his solace on a barstool. All seven of the Matt Cordell stories have basically the same framework: Cordell is either drunk or in the process of becoming so when someone approaches him to take on a case. At first he refuses, then relents, usually after a drink. He makes love to, or assaults, every woman that crosses his path, depending on their intentions. He gets shot a few times. He has a few more drinks. He solves the case. He heads for the next bar.

Though written under the Evan Hunter byline, the Ed McBain style and trademarks show through in his Cordell stories. The graphic violence (particularly in "Dead Men Don't Dream," where the reader discovers Cordell's fondness for breaking bones), the "you are there" feel to his descriptions of the city, and the staccato dialogue all could have been lifted from any one of the novels set in the famous 87th Precinct. Because the set-ups are so similar, it is probably a good idea for the reader to space these stories out rather than read them in one sitting. Perhaps this is why Hunter abandoned the Cordell character after just a handful of short stories and one novel (*I'm Cannon—For Hire*, published by Gold Medal in 1958, wherein Cordell, renamed Cannon, is hired to protect a man from a killer). Cordell's descent into a bottle full of Hell is not pretty and probably wasn't a lot of fun to write about.

"I'll Make the Arrest" by Charles Beckman, Jr. (4000 words) ★ ★

Well-known actress Pat Taylor is strangled, and the cop investigating the murder happens to be the corpse's old beau. This cop is determined not to take prisoners. Charles Beckman wrote nine stories for *Manhunt* in the first two years of the magazine's existence, as well as stories for *Pursuit* ("A Hot Lick for Doc"), *Double-Action Detective, Trapped, Mystery Tales* ("Nymph in the Keyhole") and Popular's pulp *Detective Tales* (with wonderful titles such as "Die-Die Baby" and "Doll, Drop Dead!"). He also wrote the novel *Honky Tonk Girl*, which would probably be forgotten if it hadn't been published by the notoriously collectible Falcon Books in 1953. Falcon published digest-sized paperbacks and *Honky Tonk Girl* would prove to be their last.

"I'll Make the Arrest" was adapted (by scripter Mort Shaw) for the television anthology series, Celebrity Playhouse, starring Phillip Carey and Jan Sterling, and aired on May 22, 1956.

"The Hunted" by William Irish (10,000 words) ★

A woman is falsely accused of murder in a geisha house and is aided in her pursuit to prove her innocence by a sailor on shore leave.

William Irish was a pseudonym of Cornell Woolrich, the highly regarded mystery writer who found major success in the 1940s in print and on radio. Woolrich's dramas became a mainstay of such radio shows as *Escape* and *Suspense*. "The Hunted" is not a very good story. It's rife with dull, clichéd dialogue and inexplicable plot twists and *deux ex machinas*. The entire story reads almost like a radio drama: the events occur only long enough to get to the end of an hour. It's also (in these PC times) insanely racist:

Character to his Chinese landlord: *"How do you find an address in a hurry?"*

Landlord: *"You ask inflammation lady at telephone exchange."*

Then again, Frances M. Nevins writes in his book-length biography of Woolrich (*First You Dream, Then You Die*) that the story is "a fine action whizbang." An interesting subplot to the story is that in 1953, when the editors of *Manhunt* were putting together the premiere issue, they solicited a story from Woolrich and received "The Hunted," purported by Woolrich to be a brand new story. It was only after the publication that a reader wrote in to Flying Eagle to report that the story was actually a reprinting of a story that appeared in a 1938 issue of *Argosy* with the title of "Death in Yoshiwara." Nevins writes that the editors of *Manhunt* "were not amused."

"The Best Motive" by Richard S. Prather (5500 words)★★★
One of our favorite P.I.s, Shell Scott, tackles the case of the stalker and the stalkee. Luscious newlywed Ellen appeals to Scott's good Samaritan side (and his libido as well) when it appears she's being stalked by a crazed ex-boyfriend. A couple of really good highlights in "The Best Motive" illustrate why Shell Scott was such a popular P.I. in the P.I.-infested 1950s: After Shell is forced to abandon his car as it's ripping through a guardrail over a cliff and into the sea, he remembers locking an unfortunate thug in the trunk; and the bar that Scott frequents, "The Haunt," is populated by waiters dressed as skeletons.

Shell Scott not only starred in 35 novels, but several short stories (collected in the Gold Medal paperbacks, *Three's a Shroud, Have Gat-Will Travel, The Shell Scott Sampler*, and *Shell Scott's Seven Slaughters*) and achieved what only a few other P.I.s can brag about: their own magazine. *Shell Scott's Mystery Magazine* presented (albeit briefly, issuing only nine issues from February through Nov 1966) such *Manhunt* authors as Jonathan Craig, Hal Ellson, John D. MacDonald, and Henry Kane, as well as spotlighting a Shell Scott "short novel" each issue. When *SSMM* went belly-up (due to poor sales), creator Richard Prather (1921–2007) was not even informed that the magazine had been discontinued and was not paid for quite a bit of the fiction that he had written for the digest. A tenth issue was prepared but never released.

"Shock Treatment" by Kenneth Millar (5000 words)★★
Evelyn, the wealthy heiress and Tom, her newlywed husband (the requisite gigolo) enjoy a weekend in the woods until Evelyn goes into diabetic shock. Will Tom show his true colors or true love? Told entirely in dialogue, an interesting experiment, with Evelyn coming off as a shrewish Lucille Ball.

Kenneth Millar (1915–1983) later went on to acclaim as Ross Macdonald, creator of Lew Archer. His wife was the successful mystery writer, Margaret Millar. Author Bill Pronzini writes that MacDonald's *Lew Archer, Private Investigator* ranks with Hammett's Continental Op collections and Chandler's *Simple Art of Murder* as "the finest volumes of so-called hard-boiled crime stories."

"The Frozen Grin" by Frank Kane (8500 words)★★
Private eye Johnny Liddell helps the D.A. investigate the murder of a prosti-

tute. Really nothing special, "The Frozen Grin" is a typical tale with dumb heavies, broads with big breasts, and henchmen who can't shoot (or stab) straight. That said, I have a special fondness for Liddell, due mostly to his Dell paperback series of the 1960s. With titles like *A Real Gone Guy*, *Trigger Mortis*, *Bare Trap*, and atmospheric covers (by artists such as Bill George, Victor Kalin, Harry Bennett, Robert Stanley, and king of the noir, Robert McGinnis), these books are a collector's treasure.

Frank Kane (1912–1968) had a freewheeling style of writing. It seemed to be all over the place at the same time. He could write dark:

> *There was a dull, crunching sound as the man's nose broke. Liddell chopped down at the exposed back of the other man's neck in a vicious rabbit punch. Sammy hit the floor, face first. Didn't move.*

or light:

> *She slid out of his arms, shrugged her shoulders free of the gown. It slid down past her knees, and she stepped out of it. Her breasts were full, pink tipped; her waist trim and narrow. Her legs were long, tapering pillars; her stomach flat and firm.*
>
> *Her eyes dropped down to her nakedness, rolled up to his face.*
>
> *"I'll do my best to make sure you're not bored, Johnny."*

Frank Kane's famous creation didn't dip his toes solely in the *Manhunt* waters. In addition to the 18 stories published in *Manhunt*, Liddell starred in 29 novels from 1947 (*About Face*) to 1967 (*Margin For Terror*) and several short stories in that same span. Liddell stories could be found in *Ed McBain's Mystery Book*, *Mike Shayne*, *Accused*, and *Crack Detective Stories*. Sixteen of Liddell's cases (Six from Manhunt) were collected in *Johnny Liddell's Morgue* (Dell, 1956) and *Frank Kane's Stacked Deck* (Dell paperback, 1961). Kane wrote two books under the pseudonym of Frank Boyd: *The Flesh Peddlers* (Monarch, 1959) and *Johnny Staccato* (Gold Medal, 1960), the latter a TV tie-in of an offbeat series starring John Cassavetes as Staccato, a private investigator who moonlights as a jazz pianist. Kane cut his literary teeth in the pulps and on radio, where he wrote over 40 scripts for *The Shadow* from 1945–1950 (with wonderfully pulpish titles such as "Etched With Acid," "Unburied Dead," and "Scent of Death"). The author also created, wrote, and produced the TV show *Claims Agent*, based on his own character, Jim Rogers.

"Backfire" by Floyd Mahannah (22,000 words)★★✔

Pete Mavrey meets a beautiful, but troubled, woman named Bernice Falkner. Bernice has been harassed by an ex-boyfriend and, attempting to escape him forever, fakes her own death. She then contacts Pete and drags him down into her web of deceit, murder, blackmail, and other general nasty stuff. "Backfire" has an interesting premise well executed during its first three quarters, but then suffers from way too much expository and a ludicrous wrap-up. Mavrey's one of those likable characters that always seems to be in the wrong place at the wrong time. Floyd Mahannah (1911–1976) wrote five crime novels: *The Yellow Hearse* (1950), *The Golden Goose* (1951), *Stopover for Murder* (1953), *The Golden Widow* (1956), and *The Broken Angel* (1957). His first published short story appeared in the June 1949 issue of *Ellery Queen* ("Ask Maria").

"The Set-Up" by Sam Cobb (1500 words)★★
Short-short about a crime beat reporter and his financial woes. Answering a strangulation murder, he discovers a way out of his monetary mess. Sam Cobb was a pseudonym used by writer Stanley L. Colbert, who dabbled a bit in the slicks (two appearances in *Esquire* in 1952), and then went on to a career in television production. He also has a story credit on the film, *Hornets' Nest*, a 1970 World War II action film starring Rock Hudson.

Vol. 1 No. 2 Feb 1953
First appearance by authors Richard Deming, Fletcher Flora, Ross Macdonald and Jonathan Craig.

"The Imaginary Blonde" by John Ross Macdonald (10,000 words)★★
Famous P.I. Lew Archer stumbles across his latest case when he stops for some shuteye at a motel in California. Archer awakens to the screams of a hysterical woman covered in blood outside his room. Later, after Archer checks out, he finds the owner of the blood parked in his car along a beach highway, very dead. When the motel manager hires Archer to find the murderer, the trail leads him to Palm Springs and a web of double identities and bone-crushing thugs.

"Sex Murder in Cameron" by Michael Fessier (3000 words)★★
The town of Cameron buzzes when wealthy, handsome bachelor Cass Buford marries homely Linda. They buzz even more when Linda buries a hatchet in Cass' head. Michael Fessier (1907–1988) was a San Francisco reporter when he began writing short stories in the 1930s. His novel, *Fully Dressed and In His Right Mind*, was published by Knopf in 1935, but his claim to fame was the several movies he wrote and/or produced, including *The Merry Monahans* (1944) and *Red Garters* (1954).

"Dirge for a Nude" by Jonathan Craig (5000 words)★↓
Swingin' piano player Marty Bishop is harassed by his ex-girlfriend, the beautiful and bountiful singer Gloria Gayle. The harassment stops when her vivacious nude body is found by Marty in the front of his Caddy. It's up to Marty to piece together the puzzle of "who killed the babe" before the cops come calling. Ding-Dong-Daddy-O dialog has never done anything for me and Craig's hip dialog sounds phony even for its time.

"Stabbing in the Streets" by Eleazor Lipsky (5000 words)★★★
District Attorney David Wiley investigates the stabbing of a young seaman by a Spanish-speaking man, claiming self-defense. A good cast of supporting characters builds this into a well-done crime drama. The climax provides no real answers to the puzzle, but I think that makes it even more satisfying. Eleazor Lipsky is best known for writing the novel *The Kiss of Death* (1947). The movie version made a star out of Richard Widmark who, in a memorable scene, tosses a wheelchair-bound woman down a flight of stairs. *Kiss* was remade in 1995 by director Barbet Schroeder and starred Nicolas Cage and David Caruso. The remake was unjustly savaged by critics and largely ignored by the public but the original (which starred Victor Mature and Brian Donlevy) remains a high point in noir cinema. "Stabbing in the Streets" was Eleazor Lipsky's only story for *Manhunt* and the sole *Manhunt* story selected for David C. Cooke's *Best Detective Stories of*

the Year 1953.

"Carrera's Woman" by Richard Marsten (4500 words)★↗
Jeff McCauley has his hard-earned ten grand ripped off by an obese Mexican bandit named Carrera, but Jeff holds an ace card of his own—Carrera's beautiful, but equally dangerous wife. Harlequin Romance done *Manhunt*-style. Comes off like one of those Grade-Z 1940s mystery flick quickies.

"Attack" by Hunt Collins (1500 words)★★↗
A cop on his honeymoon comes back to his cabana to find his wife beaten to death and the perp making tracks in the sand. About as noir and violent as the 1950s got. Too bad the story's rushed and the characters thin (we never even learn the name of our hero) but the literal bang at the climax saves the day.

"Everybody's Watching Me" by Mickey Spillane
(Part 2 of 4) (see Vol. 1 No. 1 for details)

"So Dark for April" by John Evans (7500 words)★★
A dead body with no socks, in his office in the dark part of April, gives P.I. Paul Pine a big headache. Convincing the cops he had nothing to do with the murder, Pine begins his own investigation to find just who did in the nattily dressed corpse. Stolen collectible stamps and greedy in-laws provide the whys and whos. Not a lot to get excited about and I hate two-page expository detailing scenarios our narrator couldn't possibly know.

Paul Pine starred in four highly regarded novels, *Halo in Blood* (1946), *Halo for Satan* (1947), *Halo in Brass* (1949), and *The Taste of Ashes* (1957). A fifth novel, unfinished because Browne had become bored with detective fiction, was later published, still unfinished, as *The Paper Gun* (1985).

The pulp *Mammoth Detective* was a favorite stomping ground to John Evans, who also wrote under his own name, Howard Browne, and the pseudonym William Brengle. In addition to the Pine stories, Browne also created a real estate troubleshooter named Lafayette Muldoon and the department store detective Wilbur Peddie. Max Allan Collins has said that "among the post-Chandler private eye novels of the 1950s, there is no finer example than Howard Browne's *The Taste of Ashes.*"

Howard Browne had a fascinating life and career. He was editor of the science fiction digests *Amazing* (1950–1956), *Fantastic* (1952–1956), and *Fantastic Adventures* (1950–1953), and later went on to a successful television career, writing for such shows as *Maverick* (the classic episode "Duel at Sundown" co-starring a very young Clint Eastwood), *The Virginian, Ben Casey, Mission: Impossible, Mannix*, and *The Fugitive.*

"The Lesser Evil" by Richard Deming (7000 words)★★
Three wise guys want Manville Moon to take over as faux-Godfather to scare off a big syndicate that's muscling in on their territory. Moon agrees for a price but then regrets it when guns start blazing. One-legged detective Manville Moon

shot his way through many short adventures and three novels, *The Gallows in My Garden* (1952), *Tweak the Devil's Nose* (1953), and *Whistle Past the Graveyard* (1954). Richard Deming (1915–1983) also ghost-wrote at least ten novels as Ellery Queen and his name can also be found on several *Mod Squad* and *Dragnet* TV tie-ins. He wrote competent, enjoyable mysteries but today is unknown, even to vintage mystery fans.

"As I Lie Dead" by Fletcher Flora (5000 words)★★★★

Cousins Cindy and Tony muse on their grandfather's artificial beach how nice Acapulco would look if only they had the old man's money. Being a take-charge kind of guy, Tony sees to it that Grandfather meets a watery demise. Unfortunately, for the kissin' cousins, their crime is witnessed by a rich neighbor. Being wealthy means this blackmailer wants something a little warmer: Cindy. Excellent cross-double-cross story with a literal big bang climax.

Fletcher Flora (1914–1969) wrote dozens of short stories for such high class digests as *Alfred Hitchcock, Ellery Queen, Mike Shayne,* and *Hunted*. Flora's novels include the superb *The Hot Shot* (1956), which explores the seedy world of high school basketball betting, and *Skullduggery* (1967), a novel that, much like "As I Lie Dead", involves money-hungry relatives.

Vol. 1 No. 3 Mar 1953
First appearance by Bruno Fischer, Craig Rice and Harold Q. Masur. This issue also includes the only appearance of a Saint story by Leslie Charteris. Cover by Willard Downes.

"The Sleeper Caper" by Richard S. Prather (7500 words)★★
Our man Shell Scott investigates the murder of a jockey in Mexico. Seems some local Mexican mafia boys are fixing horse races and this jockey won't play their game.

"Dead Men Don't Dream" by Evan Hunter (4500 words)★★⤴
Matt Cordell is invited to the funeral of an old friend. At the funeral, he's approached by a young woman who tells Cordell that his friend was murdered by a shakedown crew and the next victim is her father. That doesn't sit well with Cordell, who puts his bottle down long enough to bust up the ring pronto.

As usual, Evan Hunter loves to play with the usual conventions of the P.I. story. In most stories, the private dick would be surrounded by hot and cold running dames. In "Dead Men Don't Dream," Cordell hits rock bottom when he rapes a prostitute. No sympathetic characters here.

Frank Kane, creator of Johnny Liddell, crafted a faithful adaptation of "Dead Men Don't Dream" for the 1958 *Mike Hammer* television series, starring Darren McGavin as Hammer. It's hard to buy Carl Kolchak as Mickey Spillane's wrist-busting P.I. (and the prostitute rape, of course, is nowhere to be seem) but the show is entertaining and profits from Frank Kane's snappy dialogue.

"Stop Him!" by Bruno Fischer (4500 words)★⤴
Roy Kester breaks out of jail to find his wife remarried, while Roy was doing time. Roy finds and terrorizes the woman and her new husband. Nothing here you haven't read time and time again. The "shock ending" is telegraphed pages before. Certainly doesn't clue you in on why Bruno Fischer (1908–1992) is such a respected noir writer. Fischer wrote over 20 crime novels, seemingly always tagged with a title torn from the pulps: *The Bleeding Scissors* (1948), *The Restless Hands* (1949), *House of Flesh* (1950), and *So Wicked My Love* (1954) among them. Fischer also wrote dozens of stories with equally provocative titles for the pulps: "I'll Slay You in My Dreams" (*Dime Detective*), "The Lady Grooms a Corpse" (*Black Mask*), "Silent as a Shiv" (*Detective Tales*), and "The Hour of the Rat" (*Dime Mystery*).

"Triple-Cross" by Robert Patrick Wilmot (3500 words)★★
A P.I. and his assistant are hired by a hussy to frame her husband. At one point, according to a blurb in the Feb 1953 issue of *Manhunt*, The New York Times called Robert Patrick Wilmot "the best in the tough tradition since Raymond Chandler." Their estimation came before this lackluster tale was published.

"The Loaded Tourist" by Leslie Charteris (6000 words)★

Simon Templar, aka The Saint, is vacationing (or whatever he does) in France when he witnesses a mugging. The victim is a shoe salesman carrying a suspicious suitcase. The case is recovered by The Saint and inside is revealed a selection of rare stamps and jewelry. Why was the shoe salesman carrying such a heavy load? Why were bad guys ready for him? Why was The Saint so popular?

Of course, Charteris' character became famous after hitting it big on the small screen, making Roger Moore, if not a household name, at least a name on the lips of mystery followers. It was a direct result of Moore's success as Simon Templar that led to his taking over the James Bond role after Sean Connery stepped down. I never saw the attraction in either Saint fiction or TV show.

"Payoff" by Frank Kane (5000 words)★★

Johnny Liddell is contacted by a nightclub owner who's convinced he'll be murdered that evening at midnight. He's absolutely on the money and, right before Liddell's eyes, the man buys the farm. Losing a client never sits well with Liddell and he sets out to find the bad guy (or in this case, the bad girl). Tough guy Johnny knows how to handle the hardware and the women...

> He stood there looking at the beauty of her face, counted off the men whose deaths already lay at her door.
> He raised his hand, hit her across the cheek with the flat of his palm, knocked her sprawling. She lay there quietly, a thin trickle of blood on her chin, while he phoned the police.

"The Tears of Evil" by Craig Rice (3500 words)★★★

Super lawyer John J. Malone is invited to a shindig at pals George and Kathy Weston's pad. Before the party can begin to swing, Kathy is found dead, her neck broken. Malone knows that the murderer must be one of the partygoers, but he can't convince George of that. Craig Rice's John J. Malone starred in 11 short stories published in *Manhunt*, and nearly a dozen novels published from 1942 up to Rice's death in 1957. The novels co-starred The Justuses, Jake and Helene, a married couple who always seem to find trouble and look to Malone to get them unstuck. Malone was also featured in short-lived radio and TV programs. Craig Rice was born Georgiana Ann Randolph, made the cover of *Time Magazine* (January 28, 1946), and wrote scripts for radio and movies. Her final novel, *The April Robin Murders*, unfinished at the time of her death, was later released as a collaboration with Evan Hunter. Many of the Malone short stories can be found in two collections, *The Name is Malone* (1957) and *Murder, Money, and Malone* (2002).

"The Mourning After" by Harold Q. Masur (4000 words)★★

Scott Jordan, another lawyer who never seems to spend time in a courtroom, is asked by a jewelry store owner to track down a young jewel thief. When Jordan confronts the girl, she tells a long and sordid tale of multiple marriages and deceit. Jordan would appear seven more times in *Manhunt*. According to his *Man-*

hunt bio, Masur was a "successful lawyer until he decided he'd rather present case histories in stories than in court."

"Everybody's Watching Me" by Mickey Spillane (Part 3 of 4) (see Vol. 1 No. 1 for details)

"Teaser" by William Lindsay Gresham (4000 words)★★★
The short life of Gerry Massingham, who is a woman divided into two separate identities—Warm Gerry and Cold Gerry. Warm Gerry loves to lead the men to the precipice and the Cold Gerry takes over to shatter the men's dreams. Then the two of them meet Joe McCallister. The shifts between Cold and Warm Gerry can be annoying, but the vicious payoff is worth the wait.

"Prognosis Negative" by Floyd Mahannah (4000 words)★
P.I. Jim Makin tries to save sexy señorita, Revita Rosales, from the paws of mobster Ernie Fidako and his main goon, Big Sam Cannon. Revita and her husband were smuggled over the border by Fidako, but the deal turned sour and Revita is on the run. Another P.I. with a gimmick: Makin is dying and wants to make his last days count for something, so he does good deeds.

"Against the Middle" by Richard Marsten (1500 words)★★⌐
Charlie and Gene are being played for saps by the vivacious Deirdre, who believes in not spreading herself too thin. Just before dueling, the boys come to their senses and dole out some manly justice to the wanton hussy. Richard Marsten was yet another pseudonym for the prolific (let's get this right) Salvatore Lombino/Evan Hunter/Ed McBain/Hunt Collins/Dean Hudson/Richard Marsten/Curt Cannon/Ezra Hannon/John Abbott. Under the Marsten name, Hunter wrote the crime novels, *Runaway Black* (Gold Medal 1954), *Murder in the Navy* (1955), *So Nude, So Dead* (Crest 1956), *The Spiked Heel* (Crest 1957), *Vanishing Ladies* (Perma 1957), *Even the Wicked* (Perma 1958), and *Big Man* (Perma 1959). Also as by Marsten, the two scarce juvenile science fiction novels, *Rocket to Luna* and *Danger Dinosaurs!*, both published in 1953 by John Winston.

Vol. 1 No. 4 Apr 1953

First appearance by David Goodis and Henry Kane. The last of four installments of "Everybody's Watching Me," which began in the first issue.

"One Little Bullet" by Henry Kane (11,500 words)★✔

Peter Chambers, P.I., finds trouble in the Long-Malamed Cocktail Lounge. More deadly but desirable dames, seedy bars, damaged noggins, shady men with guns, and expositories worthy of a few yawns.

Henry Kane's version of Mike Shayne, Peter Chambers appeared in nearly 30 novels, including *Hang by Your Neck* (1949), *Death of a Hooker* (1961), *And Kill for the Millions* (1972), and even his own short-lived radio show, *Crime and Peter Chambers*. Chambers also starred in several short stories, six of which appeared in *Manhunt*. Kane adapted the Ed McBain first 87th Precinct novel, *Cop Hater*, for the screen in 1958, starring Robert Loggia as McBain's Detective Steve Carella.

"Big Talk" by Kris Neville (2500 words)★★✔

Two newspapermen, working the night crime beat, check in on a battered woman at a hospital. Gritty little short-short is somewhat diminished by a predictable (and rushed) finale.

"Be My Guest" by Robert Turner (3000 words)★★★

Punch-drunk ex-boxer Rocky and his beautiful wife Janie retire to the hills of Maine after Rocky's last fight. Trouble in the form of mobster Mr. Calligy comes calling. Seems Rocky was supposed to take a fall during his last bout but it didn't work out that way. Calligy has come to take out his lost 50Gs on Rocky and Janie. Nicely done. Author Robert Turner gets us into the deteriorating brain of Rocky much like Jim Thompson did with Collie in *After Dark, My Sweet*.

Robert Turner was a prolific writer in several genres. He wrote three crime novels (*The Tobacco Auction Murders* (1954), *The Girl in the Cop's Pocket* (1956), and *The Night is For Screaming* (1960)), wrote for pulps such as *The Spider*, scripted comic books, and sold stories to TV (including "Hooked" from the Feb 1958 issue of *Manhunt* to *Alfred Hitchcock Presents*). In 1970, Powell paperbacks published *Shroud 9*, a collection of short Robert Turner/Ray Carroll stories that included eleven culled from *Manhunt*.

"Fan Club" by Richard Ellington (3000 words)★

Private dick Steve Drake only got to meet the lovely but bitchy Evelyn Lanier a short time before she was murdered. The prime suspect will be Evelyn's ex Charley Boxer, an old friend of Drake's, unless the P.I. can find the real killers before the cops get wind of her untimely death. Rest assured Drake saves the day. One of the most abrupt endings I've ever read, but that's not a bad thing since I don't think I could have stayed awake more than a couple more pages. In the Hall of Fame of P.I.s, Steve Drake doesn't merit much discussion. The creation of Richard Ellington (who supplemented his writing career with stints in radio (*The Fat Man*) and TV (*Man Against Crime*)) starred in five novels (*It's a Crime* (1948); *Shoot the Works* (1948); *Stone Cold Dead* (1950); *Exit for a Dame* (1951); and *Just Killing Time* (1953)) and two more short stories (both in *Manhunt*) before disappearing into obscurity. This character should not be confused with Earl Drake, the tough guy of Dan J. Marlowe's long-running Gold Medal series.

"Shakedown" by Roy Carroll (3000 words)★★★
When his beautiful girlfriend Vera tells him she'll be gaining a little weight over the next nine months, eternal bachelor Van tells her he's not the kind to bounce a Van Jr. on his knee. Smelling some free big money, Van talks Vera into sidling up to their rich boss, Mr. Harry Owen. The plan is to get Owen to bed Vera, pin the pregnancy on him, and make Vera Mrs. Owen. When Vera follows through with the plan, the boss snaps, kills Vera, and buries her body in the woods. Unfortunately for Owen, he does all this while Van is keeping an eye on him. Van sees the murder as nothing more than an even bigger payday. Good twist ending when Mr. Owen shows Van a thing or two about villainy. Roy Carroll was a *Manhunt* house name, used here for a Robert Turner story.

"The G-Notes" by Robert Patrick Wilmot (7500 words)★★
Bad guy Joe Carlin botches a jewelry job, irritating his employer. His boss pays him his cut in two one-thousand dollar bills, making it very difficult to make change. Overlong, "The G-Notes" meanders almost as much as Joe Carlin.

"Mugger Murder" by Richard Deming (3000 words)★★★
A cop suspects that a man who has killed a mugger in self-defense may actually be a thrill-killer, baiting potential muggers. A fascinating look at a coroner's investigation. An antecedent of Brian Garfield's novel *Death Wish*.
Adapted for the second season of the TV show, *The M Squad*, starring Lee Marvin and Paul Newlan.

"Kid Kill" by Evan Hunter (2500 words)★★★↩
Two cops investigate an accidental shooting involving two young brothers. One cop is convinced the shooting was no accident and that a ten-year-old boy is a cold-blooded murderer. Chilling short-short with the usual Evan Hunter touches. As an interesting side note, because *Manhunt* published two similar-themed stories back to back ("Mugger Murder" and "Kid Kill" in which the murderers escape justice) in the same issue, the editor had Shepherd Cole "of the prominent law firm of Kole and Kole" write an afterward on the feasibility of "getting away with murder."

"The Blue Sweetheart" by David Goodis (6500 words)★★
Clayton wants his old flame Alma back from mobster Hagen but it may cost him more than the massive sapphire he's been flaunting around town. Microwaved *Casablanca*. Hard to believe this came from the pen that wrote *Shoot the Piano Player* and *Street of No Return*.

Peter Enfantino • Jeff Vorzimmer

"Everybody's Watching Me" by Mickey Spillane
(Part 4 of 4) (see Vol. 1 No. 1 for details)

Vol. 1 No. 5 May 1953

Debut of the true crime feature *"Portrait of a Killer,"* *"Crime Cavalcade"* and *"Manhunt's Movie of the Month."* *"Portrait"* Will run through the Jul 1955 issue, *"Cavalcade"* through Dec 1955, but the movie review would be discontinued after the next issue.

"The Guilty Ones" by John Ross Macdonald (8000 words)★★

Lew Archer is hired by Reginald Harlan to find his sister, who has run away with an artist. Seems there's quite a bit of money in the family, and Reginald wants to keep it that way. Not much in the way of excitement here and the tell-all climax is rushed.

John Ross Macdonald (1915–1983), no relation to fellow mystery writer John D. MacDonald, found huge success with Lew Archer, headlining the P.I. in *The Moving Target* (1949), *The Drowning Pool* (1950), *The Zebra-Striped Hearse* (1962), and fifteen other well-received novels. Several of the Archer short stories were collected in *The Name is Archer* (Bantam paperback, 1955). Paul Newman portrayed Archer (renamed Harper) in two successful films, *Harper* (based on *The Moving Target*, 1966) and *The Drowning Pool* (1975). Archer was also the star of his own short-lived TV show, this time fleshed out by Brian Keith.

"Services Rendered" by Jonathan Craig (3500 words)★★★★

Bad cop Henry Callan is using Carol Hobart as his private whore. She's desperate to have her husband released from prison and cleared of murder charges and Callan has promised her his cooperation in exchange for hers. Henry Callan is not just a bad cop, he's evil, a character trait that Craig seemed to adore and surely excelled at.

"Stakeout" by Robert Patrick Wilmot (4000 words)★

Denham is hired to be a bodyguard by Audrey Ganns and her blind husband, Wade. Unbeknownst to the couple (or is it?), Denham is in cahoots with a couple of bad guys who plan to steal the blind man of the jewels stashed in his safe. Lifeless story, devoid of thrills, good characters, and a middle act. It's also stocked with a dopey, clichéd climax right out of a bad EC Comics story. Robert Patrick Wilmot's minor claim to fame is the series of novels published in the early fifties (*Blood in Your Eye*, *Murder on Monday*, and *Death Rides a Painted Horse*), all starring Steve Considine, "ace private eye and crack trouble-shooter" for Confidential Investigation Services, Inc.

"Graveyard Shift" by Steve Frazee (4500 words)★★

A gang of thieves attempts to knock off a gambling joint while one of their female members holds a gun on a police dispatcher. She attempts to manipulate the flow of police traffic to divert the patrol cars away from the gang's target. A little too detailed, the action gets lost in the technical dispatcher jargon.

Steve Frazee wrote a handful of crime stories in addition to "Graveyard Shift" ("My Brother Down There," which Frazee later expanded into the novel *Running Target*. He won First Prize in the *Ellery Queen* Story Contest in Apr 1953), but was known primarily for his superior action and western tales found in such diverse publications as *The Saturday Evening Post, Adventure*, and *.44 Western*. Many of his western novels were actually crime dramas with western curtains and trim (*He Rode Alone*, simply one of the best westerns ever written, was actually a revenge yarn with desert settings and new spins on the old western character clichés). About Frazee, writer Bill Pronzini said "During the 1950's, no one wrote better popular western novels and stories." As a Frazee completest, I can't disagree.

"Now Die In It" by Evan Hunter (9500 words)★★★
Matt Cordell is hired to find the killer of a pregnant teenager. He's drawn to a world of juke joints and pool halls. Hunter peppers the story with more 87th Precinct-type passages such as "The streets were crowded with people seduced by Spring. They breathed deeply of her fragrance, flirted back at her, treated her like the mistress she was, the wanton who would grow old with Summer's heart and die with Autumn's first chilly blast." The story was adapted for the second season of the *Mike Hammer* show in 1959 by frequent *Hammer* writer, Steve Thornley. For the most part, Thornley sticks to Evan Hunter's plot until the climax. In the story, the murderer's fate is ambiguous; not so with the Hammer episode. The plot of "Now Die In It" was also later used for the third 87th Precinct novel, *The Mugger*.

"Cigarette Girl" by James M. Cain (3500 words)★★
The working girl in the title is in a lot of trouble, but tough guy Cameron comes to the rescue.
James M. Cain (1892–1977) wrote two blockbuster crime novels, *Double Indemnity* and *The Postman Always Rings Twice*, the latter of which, author Max Allan Collins says, "set the standard for tough, lean writing." Both were made into classic noir films in the 1940s. Black Lizard (certainly the preeminent noir publisher of the 1980s), published three of Cain's lesser-known novels, *The Root of His Evil, Sinful Woman*, and *Jealous Woman* (the latter two were originally published together in one volume in 1948 by Avon) in 1989. Cain's short stories were collected in *The Baby in the Icebox* (1981).

"Nice Bunch of Guys" by Michael Fessier (2000 words)★★
Slow-witted Marty just likes to sell his newspapers and keep to himself, but that's not good enough for the neighborhood toughs, who have other ideas for Marty.

"Old Willie" by William P. McGivern (2000 words)★★★
Who is the old man known only as Old Willie? He's protective of a Danish girl named Inger Anderson, and a local mobster named Cardina better watch his step around her. Good surprise at the climax when we find out the true identity of Old Willie.

"Build Another Coffin" by Harold Q. Masur (4500 words)★

Lawyer Scott Jordan is hired by a beautiful young woman who stands to inherit a boatload of dough from an institutionalized aunt who suddenly stops answering the girl's letters. Jordan throws the usual quota of punches and spends the average three to four pages on an expository (half of which is action he couldn't possibly have insight on) that draws yawns from not only the reader but perhaps the supporting characters as well. This story definitely needed an editor's pencil, as witnessed by this awkward paragraph:

Denney went up in the air and flew backward, crashing against the wall. I scrambled to my feet and reached him in a single jump. His eyes were glazed and I picked one up from the basement and threw it at him with all the strength I had.

This would have to be the first instance I've come across where an assailant is dispatched with one of his own eyeballs.

"Don't Go Near..." by Craig Rice (8000 words)★

Craig Rice's John J. Malone is hired to find out who's killing the lions at a small carnival. Some readers may take "Don't Go Near" as a parody of tough guy stories. Parodies only work if they're funny or interesting. This story is neither.

"Assault" by Grant Colby (1000 words)★

A woman's fears about her husband become real. Nothing more than a fragment, it's hard to judge stories like "Assault" that have no real beginning or end, but the fragment here is neither startling nor interesting.

Vol. 1 No. 6 Jun 1953
The last issue to have a movie review (A review of The Hitch-Hiker).

"Far Cry" by Henry Kane (11,000 words)★
Other than a change of scenery (this bar's handle is "The Raven"), this is the same ol' song and dance as Peter Chambers' previous escapade. More sleep-inducing head trauma, bedded broads, and double-crosses than you can shake a shot glass at.

"Small Homicide" by Evan Hunter (4000 words)★★★
The strangled body of a baby girl is found in a church pew. The detectives of the 37th Precinct attempt to track down her killer.

"Ybor City" by Charles Beckman, Jr. (4000 words)★★
Our nameless protagonist witnesses the murder of a blackmailer and pieces together the whereabouts of his murderers. When we finally find out who our narrator is, it's not much of a surprise.

"The Loyal One" by Richard Deming (4500 words)★★★
A mortally wounded racketeer holes up in a snowed-in cabin with his wife Cynthia and their bodyguard. When it becomes apparent the mobster won't make it, the loyal henchman sees Cynthia in a different light. Nasty climax.

"The Faceless Man" by Michael Fessier (4000 words)★★
Farmer Henry Rankins hires ex-con Claude Warren to help him tend to the farm. This angers the townspeople and, when Rankins is found dead, they become a brutal mob (the "faceless man" of the title) out for blood. The only thing standing in their way is Sheriff Ben Hodges. Not much in the way of an original plot.

"The Double Frame" by Harold Q. Masur (4500 words)★
Lawyer Scott Jordan's third *Manhunt* adventure finds him stalked and confronted by an ex-con who's convinced Jordan has stolen his stashed loot. The reader will know the identities of the real looters before the slow-witted lawyer.

"The Caller" by Emmanuel Winters (5000 words)★★★
Some foul-mouthed brute has been calling Miss Turner and reading her the works. Miss Turner, being prim and proper, is properly disgusted and goes to the police to file a complaint. When the police nab the Lothario, he tells them he's been hired by one of Miss Turner's work associates. The true identity is a mild surprise.

"Hot-Rock Rumble" by Richard S. Prather (14,500 words)★★
Shell Scott is hired by wealthy Jules Osborne to recover his mistress's stolen

jewelry before she makes trouble for the man. Scott engages in his usual romantic antics and his noggin suffers the requisite blows, all wrapped up tidily in a novelette. The Scott character is a fairly well written character, but I guess my problem with the lesser Scott stories (this being one of them) is that they're not tough enough for *Manhunt*. They're lightweight à la formula crime shows like *Mannix*, *Ironside*, and *Barnaby Jones*. There's no sense of danger to the lead or his trusted supporting cast.

"One Down" by Hunt Collins (1000 words) ★★
Adele hates Ben's job and the fact that it keeps him away from home so much. Ben's decided to keep the job and rid himself of Adele.

Vol. 1 No. 7 Jul 1953
The first appearance of Fredric Brown. Cover by Lou Marchetti.

"The Wench is Dead" by Fredric Brown (8500 words)★★✓

A motley assortment of humans: Howard Parry, ex-Bachelor of Arts in Sociology, now a stinking drunk; Wilhelmina Kidder, aka Billie the Kidd, exotic dancer, hooker, and Parry's drinking partner; Mamie Gaynor, heroin addict and soon a cooling corpse and a royal pain to our two drinking buddies. Add to this several junkies, whores, and alcoholics and you have a perfect picture of life in Los Angeles in the 1950s. Brown's unrelenting gloom rivals that of the king of depression, Davis Goodis, in bleakness if not in quality.

"Quiet Day in the County Jail" by Craig Rice (4000 words)★★

For her own protection, a State's witness is kept locked in a cell under constant watch. Though she's protected by several guards, the woman seems convinced she'll be killed by the mobster she's set to testify against.

"I'll Kill for You" by Fletcher Flora (4000 words)★★

A very short and unaffected tale of love, adultery, and murder. An early line: "A last whimper of regret at the doorway to Hell," sounds like something George Chesbro would cook up for one of his Mongo novels a few decades later.

"Day's Work" by Jonathan Lord (1000 words)★★

Short-short about two hitmen, on the way to a job, who witness a hit and run.

"Good and Dead" by Evan Hunter (5500 words)★★ ✓

Skid row bum Matt Cordell puts his old gumshoe skills to the test when one of his drinking buddies is found with a hole in his head. One of the weaker of the Cordell entries, "Good and Dead" became one of the better *Mickey Spillane's Mike Hammer* episodes (re-titled "So That's Who It Was"). The episode opens with Hammer finishing off a six-week undercover stint in Chinatown, which then segues into a faithful reading of the short story.

"Say Goodby to Janie" by Bruno Fischer (8000 words)★

Paul Sherman, head of the City Crime Commission finds himself in all manner of bad ways—he's convinced the mayor is accepting bribes but can't prove it just yet; he's having an affair with the mayor's wife; then, to top it all off, he's accused of murder. A meandering, unmemorable mess that reminds me of the Grade-Z noir melodramas that sometimes find their way onto late night cable; the kind of tale where the protagonist holds a gun on the bad guys at the climax and explains (to the audience and the patient police) how he came up with his suppositions (often in an unbelievable way).

"The Follower" by Hunt Collins (2500 words)★★
Ella Brant is convinced someone is following her home from the bus stop every night but her husband thinks she's got an overactive imagination. She doesn't.

"I'm Getting Out" by Elliot West (3500 words)★★★★
Farm hand Tom has finally had enough of his boss Jake's bullying and murdering ways. He leaves the farm, but before he can get on the bus, Jake's wife Poppy begs him to take her with him. Tom wants no part of the soulless woman but decides to go back to the farm to get wages owed him. When he gets there, Poppy convinces Jake that Tom assaulted her, and murder follows. Lots of interesting twists to the clichéd "love triangle" warhorse, in that Tom can't stand the sight of the beautiful woman and wants only to get the money owed to him. Topped off with a nasty climax.

"Evidence" by Frank Kane (4000 words)★↗
Swingin' dick Johnny Liddell's hands are full again. This time, a beautiful redhead enlists Johnny's help when she's blackmailed. You'll never guess what the babe uses as her retainer.

"The Double Take" by Richard S. Prather (11,000 words)★★
Bad guys are using Shell Scott's good name and his office to bilk unsuspecting folk out of large quantities of money. Shell doesn't take this lying down. At least not until he gets the girl in the end.

"Heirloom" by Arnold Marmor (1000 words)★★
Hired gun Del only has to steal a necklace to earn his hundred bucks. The boss warns him not to touch the beautiful owner of the jewelry but Del is his own guy. Lurid ending is right out of *Tales from the Crypt*.

Peter Enfantino • Jeff Vorzimmer

Vol. 1 No. 8 Aug 1953

First appearance of James M. Cain and the first and only appearance of Donald Hamilton, with a science fiction story, "Throwback."

"The Collector Comes After Payday" by Fletcher Flora (5500 words)★★★★

Brutalized his entire life by a sadistic drunkard father, Frankie is resigned to a life of bad luck until, one night, he's pushed too far, Frankie murders his father and begins a life filled with good luck. Money and women suddenly become easy as wishing for it, but Frankie soon tires of it and wants more. Flora tells the story of Frankie with dirt and grime, illustrating just what a heel this guy becomes. We, as the witness to the transformation, see Frankie go from sympathetic victim to the brutalizer his father was, climaxing with Frankie getting just what his father got.

"Still Life" by Evan Hunter (4000 words)★★

Homicide detectives Hannigan and Knowles investigate the rape-murder of a beautiful sixteen-year-old who, by the account of those who knew her, was a saint and a virgin. As the cops dig deeper, they discover that the girl was neither. With its clipped dialogue and straightforward narrative, this would have been a perfect script for Jack Webb's *Dragnet* show. One of Hunter's lesser crime stories.

"The Little Lamb" by Fredric Brown (3500 words)★

Hans is missing his wife Lamb, who's gone down into the village. He's afraid she's seeing a rival artist on the side, so he grabs his gun, visits the rival painter, and zzzzzzzzzz...

Certainly one of the most acclaimed fantasists of the twentieth century, Fredric Brown was also very adept at mystery and crime stories and novels. Among his most famous crime novels are *The Fabulous Clipjoint* (1947); *Night of the Jabberwock* (1950); *The Lenient Beast* (1956); and my personal favorite, *The Screaming Mimi* (1949), a classic obsession tale that was made into a decent noir flick in 1958 (directed by Gerd Oswald and starring Anita Ekberg and Gypsy Rose Lee). In the 1980s, publisher Dennis McMillan began an impressive series of reprint volumes titled Fredric Brown in the Detective Pulps, collecting hordes of long-forgotten Brown crime stories from the crumbling pages of *New Detective*, *Phantom Detective*, *Dime Mystery*, and dozens more. Unfortunately, these were done in low print runs, went out of print, and are now very collectible. A little more accessible may be *Mostly Murder* (Pennant paperback 1954), 18 stories that, according to Bill Pronzini, make the argument that "Brown was a better short-story writer than a novelist."

"Slay Belle" by Frank Kane (4000 words)★

One of Johnny Liddell's men is murdered and the trail leads to the woman he was protecting. Sub-par Liddell feels like a small piece of a larger story. Of course, the reader's lucky it's a short snore and not a long snoozer.

"The Crime of My Wife" by Robert Turner (3000 words)★★
Earl breaks it to his new bride, Norma, that he's a confidence man and his new angle is to pimp her out to rich married men. Earl will take incriminating pictures and blackmail the men and all Norma has to do is look pretty and spread her legs. Norma tries it and decides that she doesn't need Earl anymore.

"The End of Fear" by Craig Rice (7000 words)★★
John J. Malone helps an heiress accused of murder. Rice's long, slow story might have fit better in the pages of *Ellery Queen*.

"Less Perfect" by Frances Carfi Matranga (1000 words)★★
As a woman poses nude for artists, her crippled husband sits and simmers until he can't take it anymore.

"Two O'Clock Blonde" by James M. Cain (2500 words)★
Serious bachelor Jack Hull attempts to get a date with the voluptuous Mademoiselle Zita and inadvertently hooks up with her maid Maria instead. Turns out Maria is running a scam with her hubby Bill, and Jack is their latest mark. A little manhandling of Maria by Jack, but other than that this could very well be James M. Cain's version of *Three's Company*, but not as funny.

"The Ripper" by Richard Ellington (4000 words)★
P.I. Steve Drake investigates the mutilation murder of a young showgirl. While interviewing one of the girl's colleagues, he stumbles into the path of what Drake believes is the original Jack the Ripper, or maybe not, or yes, maybe. But then, who knows? "The Ripper" could very well be the worst of the two dozen-plus Jack the Ripper stories I've read (and I've read some bad ones), with an ending so absurd and contrived, it cries out for an Ed Wood adaptation to screen. If you've just got to have a "Jack" fix, look past this "Ripper" and seek out the collections *Ripper* (edited by Gardner Dozois and Susan Casper, published by Tor paperbacks in 1988) and *The Harlot Killer* (edited by Allan Barnard, published by Dell in 1953). Together they feature 32 "Jack" tales, with only one story overlapping (that being the classic "Yours Truly, Jack the Ripper" by Robert Bloch) or the full-length novel, *Terror Over London* (Gold Medal, 1957), by Gardner F. Fox.
However, there are still several problems with the plot (for one, why would reporters make an immediate connection between the killing of one showgirl to the murder of several prostitutes six decades earlier?), "The Ripper" makes for a better half-hour of visual suspense than reading material. Frank Kane adapted the story for *Mickey Spillane's Mike Hammer* in 1958, under the title, "Final Curtain." Ironically, Darren McGavin, who starred as Hammer, also tackled Jack the Ripper (the real thing) in an episode of *Kolchak: The Night Stalker* in 1974. The two series share a very similar narrative style.

Peter Enfantino • Jeff Vorzimmer

"Kayo" by Roy Carroll (1000 words)★★★

A good little bit about a punchy ex-boxer who kills a man who'd been taunting him. A fragment, but a well-written fragment.

"Rhapsody in Blood" by Harold Q. Masur (9000 words)★★

The most boring P.I./lawyer in crime literature, Scott Jordan (or maybe the second most boring next to Craig Rice's John J. Malone) is hired by Phil Elliott to handle his impending divorce. Elliott's wife is loaded but she'll be giving him trouble rather than a handout. Things turn dicey when Elliott's accused of passing phony money. "Rhapsody" actually holds the reader's interest (itself a miracle considering how I've felt about Masur's Jordan stories) until the obligatory expository. This monologue lasts four pages and the revelations Jordan declares could only have been cooked up by a screenwriter.

"Throwback" by Donald Hamilton (3000 words)★★★★

Thirty years before *The Day After*, Donald Hamilton tells the tale of survivors of the final war. After bombs drop on their idyllic life, George and Ellen Hardin must fight to survive among a band of roamers. A unique non-genre story (there is murder and fighting in the story, but they are incidental to "the big picture"), "Throwback" is more than just a good cautionary science fiction tale, but a well-written story of a married couple trying to beat the odds and continue what life they have left despite heartbreaking loss (their children were in town when the bombs fell, and now she's pregnant with a third). Donald Hamilton is best known as the creator of Matt Helm, possibly the most popular American literary assassin of all time, star of over two dozen novels with titles such as *The Revengers*, *The Detonators*, *The Ambushers* and *Death of a Citizen*. The latter is Hamilton at his peak and perhaps one of the finest crime novels of the 1960s. Matt Helm was "glamorized" in a series of Dean Martin movies, each entry worse than the previous.

"The Innocent One" by Richard Marsten (1500 words)★★★

Miguel stands, tending to his field, as men from the village pass, commenting on Miguel's hot-blooded wife, Maria. A sharp first line becomes a grinning last line.

Vol. 1 No. 9 Sep 1953
The first appearance by Erskine Caldwell and the first and only appearance of Ray Bradbury.

"The Death of Me" by Evan Hunter (9500 words)★★
Matt Cordell is surprised when he picks up the morning paper (which is stuffed inside his shoes) and finds out he's been murdered. In between trips to his favorite dive for a few belts, he attempts to discover who's behind the obvious mix-up. By the fifth entry in the Cordell series, you can tell that Hunter is pretty much dried up (even though his protagonist very definitely is not). Ho-hum plots and padded descriptions mar these later entries.

"Fair Game" by Fletcher Flora (3500 words)★★★
Ray Butler, strong-arm for mayor Dixie Cannon, is burning bridges all around him. He's roughing up anyone who stands in the corrupt mayor's path to wealth and power while at the same time keeping Cannon's wife company when her husband's off running the town. When Cannon finally puts two and two together, Ray finds he's on his own.

"What Am I Doing?" by William Vance (4500 words)★★﹀
Detective Dick Sanders is a cop facing what might, these days, be considered a mid-life crisis: his wife is irritable and pregnant, which leads him into the arms of wealthy and lonely babe Kit Cord. Deciding he has to have his new play toy at any cost, Sanders plots to set up Kit's husband, a successful MD, by planting drugs in the doctor's car. After his son is born however, he sees the light and reconsiders. A rare happy ending in the *Manhunt* universe.

"Accident Report" by Richard Marsten (4000 words)★★
When a street cop is run down, two detectives attempt to find a needle in a haystack and apprehend the killer.

"Bonus Cop" by Richard Deming (9000 words)★★
For most of his career, Homicide Captain Michael Train has been a cop on the take. Taking bribes, ignoring the prostitutes, and looking the other way when it comes to syndicate murder. Then one of his own cops is gunned down, a young man Train had thought of as his son, and the Captain goes on a rampage.

"The Motive" by Erskine Caldwell (2500 words)★★
Every few months, Kathy meets up with Van for a weekend of wild lust. Van's married and Kathy's biological clock is ticking. She's decided to marry another man but Van won't have any of that. The author of *God's Little Acre* and *Tobacco Road* fills seven pages with "I'm getting married" and "No, you're not."

"Chase by Night" by Jack M. Bagby (2500 words)★★

Steve's wife Nancy is attacked by three punks in a hot rod. Steve decides that jail's not good enough for these punks and doles out his own brand of justice.

"The Millionth Murder" by Ray Bradbury (6500 words)★★

An American couple, vacationing in South America, discover the United States and Europe have been destroyed and they could very well be the last white people left on Earth. This leaves them in a precarious position since the locals, after years of bad treatment by tourists, are uprising and would like nothing more than to see the couple gutted and hoisted.

Ray Bradbury, who has found success in just about any genre he's written in, be it science fiction, horror, fantasy or mystery, dips his toes into the political fiction arena and leaves this reader wanting less rather than more. "The Millionth Murder" doesn't just remind us that we are "the Ugly Americans," it smears it in our faces.

Bradbury wrote a screenplay based on "The Millionth Murder" in the late 1950s, retitled "And the Rock Cried Out," that remains unproduced. Oliver Stone should give Bradbury's agent a call.

"The Molested" by Hunt Collins (1000 words)★

A woman is molested on a subway train. A one-note joke that's not very funny. Not a good issue for Collins/Marsten/Hunter.

"Life Can be Horrible" by Craig Rice (6000 words)★

Chicago lawyer John J. Malone has his work cut out for him. Two dimwits come to his office and tell him a sob story: they'd been hired by an estranged wife to break into her house and steal her $10,000 from the husband who's hidden it from her. When they enter the house, they find no money and a very dead husband. Since the men are the sons of a good friend, Malone takes their case. He's amazed when, only a short time later, he's approached by the wife to accompany her to her home. When they get there, they find the $10,000 and no corpse.

It's a wonder, since Malone has all the trappings of a P.I., that Rice chose to make her character a lawyer. No lawyer would do the foolish things Malone does and certainly no lawyer would ever give the deadly dull expository that ends this yawner.

"The Scrapbook" by Jonathan Craig (3000 words)★★★

Charlie Stevens is known to his co-workers as the slightly creepy, but harmless old maintenance man. Behind the façade, Charlie is a serial killer. The psycho elements will be old hat to today's reader, but Craig throws in a curve you have to admire: Charlie murders *then* rapes his victims. That's a twist not seen much in 1953.

Vol. 1 No. 10 Oct 1953

First issue that doesn't have a single story by Evan Hunter, but he would contribute, under various pseudonyms, five stories in the next two issues.

"The Girl Behind the Hedge" by Mickey Spillane (3500 words)★★★
Walter Harrison's suicide is explained by his good friend Duncan. Decidedly un-Spillane-ish with an ending that would not sit well with today's politically correct crowd.

"Squeeze Play" by Richard S. Prather (4500 words)★★★
Ann Crane's husband Leroy has gone missing. She's concerned because Leroy was an accountant for bigtime Mob man Wallace Hackman. Enter Shell Scott. Though the plot revolves around Leroy and Hackman, the emphasis is on the brutal exchanges between Scott and Hackman's right hand man, Pretty Willis.

"Balanced Account" by Richard Deming (4000 words)★★★
Gerald Mason is accused of rape by the beautiful teenaged girl next door. After his name is dragged through the mud by the press, the girl admits Mason never touched her. Mason decides that since he's had to pay for his new rep, he may as well earn it.

"Dead Heat" by Robert Turner (4500 words)★★
Sadistic horse owner Lew Winters blackmails his jockey into fixing races.

"The Idiot" by Harold Cantor (3500 words)★★★
The occupants of Happy Dell Resort play a sick joke on a retarded young man. This is one of those rare stories that leads the reader to believe it's going down one path but effectively veers down another. Though I've read stories very similar to this in the past (the obvious being Steinbeck's *Of Mice and Men*), the author gets extra credit for making his main protagonist both likable and loathsome. "The Idiot" has all the earmarks of an *Alfred Hitchcock Presents* episode.

"Professional Man" by David Goodis (8500 words)★★★✓
Elevator operator by day, hit man by night, Freddy Lamb is the best at what he does. He's got the best girl in town too, but his boss has his eyes on her. When Freddy's gal gives the cold shoulder to the chief, Freddy gets his next assignment: wipe out the dame. If written by an optimist, "Professional Man" would find Freddy offing his boss but, since this nasty little tale is penned by David Goodis, there's no happy ending waiting on the last page. Downbeat slices of criminal life like this are what made Goodis such a hit in the 1950s and a favorite among hardcore crime readers to this day. Filmed by acclaimed director Steven Soderbergh for the Showtime series *Fallen Angels* in 1995, starring Peter Coyote and Brendan Fraser.

"Summer is a Bad Time" by Sam S. Taylor (4500 words)★↲

Walt only wants to make his wife Della happy, so he lets her accompany him on a business trip. Turns out that Della only wants to meet up with her side guy in one of Walt's towns. Nothing new here, but the story is slightly redeemed by an overly sadistic revenge finale. Sam S. Taylor (1903–1994) wrote five stories for *MH* and four novels in the 1940s and 1950s, three originally in hardcover for Dutton (*Sleep No More* (1949), *No Head For Her Pillow* (1952), and *So Cold, My Bed* (1953)) and one in paperback for Gold Medal (*Brenda* (1952), under the pseudonym Lehi Zane).

"Response" by Arnold Marmor (1000 words)★★

Jose Abrardo, police chief on a small island, is constantly feeling pressure from mobsters to allow gambling on his island. He's not one to bow to pressure. It's tough to appraise stories that are only a thousand words long, but "Response," like most of the other short-shorts has nothing new to add to crime literature.

"Where's the Money?" by Floyd Mahannah (4000 words)★★

When he was a young man, Joe drove a getaway car for a bank job gone wrong. After he and his partners do twelve years in the stir, the partners want to know what Joe did with the money. Joe insists he never had it but the bad guys aren't buying that and they kidnap Joe's daughter.

"The Beat-Up Sister" by John Ross Macdonald (12,000 words)★ ↲

Lew Archer's third *Manhunt* case is also his worst. This time he's hired by a girl who's not only beautiful but also broke (am I the only one who wonders how these guys made a living when they never got paid?). She's trying to find her sister, who may be the victim of foul play. Long and boring, "The Beat-Up Sister" is redeemed only by an explosive climax.

"The Bobby-Soxer" by Jonathan Craig (1000 words)★

A cute little bobby-soxer is pulled into an alley and attacked until a crazed mob rescues her and beats her assailant.

Vol. 1 No. 11 Nov 1953
Evan Hunter returns with a story under the Richard Marsten byline.

"The Big Touch" by Henry Kane (14,000 words)★
Peter Chambers handles a blackmail scheme, with the beautiful showgirl Annabel Jolly as his prime suspect. Tedious and clichéd, even at this early stage of hardboiled P.I. fiction.

"The Watcher" by Peter Paige (1500 words)★★★
For years Marcia Smith has been known as something of a "tease." When her main tease happens upon Marcia being raped by two thugs, he considers letting the crime continue and teaching Marcia a lesson. Nasty twist ending.

"The Bells are Ringing" by Craig Rice (3500 words)★
Super-Attorney John J. Malone is in the wrong place at the wrong time (as usual): he witnesses a prisoner blasting his way out of a jailhouse. Turns out the guy is wedding a dying woman. John J aids the felon on his journey. Ludicrous.

"Case History" by Charles Beckman, Jr. (3500 words)★★
P.I. Nick Scotch (of the Scotch Detective Agency) is attempting to find who's blackmailing lovely Evelyn Rose. Slow read builds to a climax right out of left field.

"The Right Hand of Garth" by Evan Hunter (5000 words)★★
Gunman Ed is tired of sneaking around with his kingpin boss's gorgeous girlfriend. When the boss hires a new gun, Ed sees a perfect way of getting out from under the mobster's shadow.

"Six Stories Up" by Raymond J. Dyer (2000 words)★★★
Paul threatens to jump off a ledge and a police chief attempts to talk him down. The kid claims he didn't murder his employer. He ends up jumping and afterwards they find the boy's boss with plenty of Paul's fingerprints on the body.

"Classification: Dead" by Richard Marsten (5000 words)★★
A woman is shot dead hours after having an illegal abortion. Very reminiscent of Hunter/McBain's 87th Precinct mysteries, complete with his stylized staccato dialogue and police form reproductions.

"A Long Way to KC" by Fletcher Flora (4500 words)★★★
Escaping a two-thousand dollar debt, Dickie Cosmos flees to the high country and stumbles onto a veritable goldmine: a beautiful girl and her hillbilly husband who make their own moonshine and hoard the huge profits. Sensing a way out of his debt, Cosmos plans the mountain man's quick demise. Familiar plot enlivened

by good writing.

"Coney Island Incident" by Bruno Fischer (8500 words)★★
Ray Whitehead chances on the beautiful Cherry Drew on the beach at Coney Island. Thinking he's in for a good time, he accepts her invitation back to her hotel room, only to find out that Cherry was involved in an armored car holdup and her partners are searching for her. Seems she's got the loot and is being selfish with her cohorts' slice of the pie. She uses Ray in an attempt to get her and the money out of town but she's not fast enough. "Coney Island Incident" drags on far too long and is told so matter-of-factly that it most resembles a bad 1950s cop show episode. The following year Fischer turned it into a novel titled *So Wicked My Love*.

"Kid Stuff" by Jonathan Craig (2500 words)★★
Chris is upset that his girlfriend Laurie has dumped him for an older, more experienced lover. He decides to stalk and kill them both. The "shock ending" is telecast so far in advance that it would have been a shock if it was a different ending!

Vol. 1 No. 12 Dec 1953
Cover by Frank Uppwall.

"Black Pudding" by David Goodis (8000 words)★★
After serving ten years in prison for boss-man Riker, all that Ken wants to do is forget. Forget that he served the time, forget that Riker set him up, and forget that the boss stole Ken's wife, Hilda. Unfortunately, Riker and his boys didn't forget Ken and they hound him until Ken is forced to strike back. Not a great story, "Black Pudding" does work up a few exciting moments in its climax. Certainly doesn't stand with Goodis' best work. The third and last of Goodis' *Manhunt* stories, "Black Pudding" was dramatized on the short-lived USA Network series, *The Edge*, in 1989, starring Patricia Arquette.

"Switch Ending" by Richard Marsten (4000 words)★★★★
Danny does time for big man Nick. When he's released, he goes to Nick to collect the fifty grand Nick had promised to pay for Danny's silence. When Danny gets there, he finds, to his dismay, that Nick's new bodyguard is Danny's J.D. son. Just as Donald E. Westlake saves his nastiest stuff for his Richard Stark pseudonym, it would seem that Evan Hunter allows his dark alter ego Richard Marsten to drain the brake lines. Hunter's most violent, no-holds-barred, novel in my opinion is *Big Man*, written under the Marsten name. *Big Man* (Perma, 1959) has a mob storyline much like "Switch Ending" and an ending just as downbeat.

"Killing on Seventh Street" by Charles Beckman, Jr. (2000 words)★
Stereotypical pantywaist Charles Leighton murders a mugger who's attempting to rape Charles' wife. Suddenly, weak-kneed Charles is the town hero. Only problem is, he needs to fantasize the murder to keep impotence at bay. This escalates to more murder.

"Murder Marches On!" by Craig Rice (4000 words)★★
The inimitable John J. Malone must infiltrate a marching band of funeral workers to receive a list of names and a grand. Murder and yawns follow. This is 1950s cookie cutter: the tough protagonist (P.I., lawyer, cop, etc.) who's thinking about the stacked beauty he's meeting that night (blonde, brunette, redhead, etc.), who happens into danger, and then gets put under suspicion by the chief detective on the case (who really knows the protagonist is innocent but busts his balls anyway). Heard enough?

"Sucker" by Hunt Collins (2000 words)★★★★
Harley is accused of raping and murdering his kids' babysitter, so he gets the best lawyer he can find: his friend Dave. Hotshot lawyer Dave is convinced his friend is innocent and defends him in court. After Harley is found innocent, Dave is startled to realize that he did the wrong thing. "Sucker" precedes by a couple of

decades the Matthew Hope series of novels Evan Hunter wrote under the Ed McBain pseudonym. "Sucker" reminds me of the Hope series. By the end of 1953, *Manhunt* had become an Evan Hunter story factory.

"The Wife of Riley" by Evan Hunter (7500 words)★★
Mr. and Mrs. Steve Riley just want a room to crash in after a long, grueling road trip. Unfortunately, they happen onto a dangerous bordello masquerading as a roadside motel. The proprietor has just murdered his prize redhead and, lucky for him, Mrs. Riley is a dead ringer for the corpse.

"Richest Man in the Morgue" by Harold Q. Masur (4500 words)★
Scott Jordan opens his door to find a man in a Hindu costume with a knife in his back. What did the man want with Jordan? The intrepid lawyer, who never seems to practice law, puts on his cape and tights and becomes Scott Jordan, Private Op to find out. I've often wondered, while reading these Jordan stories, why Masur went to the trouble of making Jordan's profession law (other than for the gimmick, that is). His tired plots contain all the trappings found in P.I. stories: the attractive but troubled girl who falls instantly for our hero; the blunt object used (often repeatedly) on our hero's titanium steel skull; the police detective pal who's always giving our hero a hard time (but in a jovial way); and, of course, the two page expository used to tie up all the loose ends we hadn't guessed at.

"The Quiet Room" by Jonathan Craig (3000 words)★★★★
Bad cop Streeter and his partner have a great thing going: they roust prostitutes, get lists of their johns, and then blackmail the men. Darkest, bleakest 1950s noir you can find, "The Quiet Room" is capped by the one of the most downbeat finales you're likely to read. Craig would have fit in well with the dark crime writers of today. Obviously, the producers of the Showtime TV anthology, *Fallen Angels*, agreed. "The Quiet Room" was very effectively and faithfully adapted in 1993 by director Steven Soderbergh, starring Joe Mantegna as Streeter and Bonnie Bedelia, deliciously evil as his sadistic partner. The episode was released on video as *Fallen Angels, Volume Two*. "The Quiet Room" evokes the equally bleak "Services Rendered" by Craig from the May 1953 issue.

"The Coyote" by David Chandler (2000 words)★
A sadistic father forces his son to shoot a coyote. Clichéd story with predictable outcome. "The Coyote" does have an opening line that might bring a leer: "Mama told me to see Beaver..." Though he only wrote one story for *Manhunt* ("The Coyote" was reprinted under another title in the August/Sep 1966 issue), David Chandler also saw stories published in *Collier's* during the 1950s.

"Wife Beater" by Roy Carroll (3000 words)★★★
Patrolman Tom Rivas and his partner answer a domestic dispute call to find a huge man beating his wife Cherry. Having a history with wife beaters, (his mother was brutally murdered by his father when Tom was a child); Tom reacts violently before arresting the man. When Cherry refuses to press charges against her hus-

band, Rivas takes the law into his own hands and guns down the brute. Tom then tries to change Cherry's life from bad to good but discovers it's not all that easy. Perhaps ahead of its time in its treatment of a very controversial subject (the idea that some women can't find sexual satisfaction without being abused), "Wife Beater" is a tough read.

"The Icepick Artists" by Frank Kane (5500 words)★★★
P.I. Johnny Liddell is hired by the Seway Indemnity Company, a firm losing a lot of money through fraud on the piers. Their main investigator has just turned up minus eyeballs. Liddell's job is to find out who's behind the murder and, further, the mastermind behind the fraud. Well-paced, humorous, and gory as all hell:

> *The thin man aimed for the right eye, jabbed. The blade sank almost to the handle. Shields' body jerked as the icepick bit into his brain, slumped back. The thin man held the body erect, sank the blade into its chest a dozen times.*

Pretty graphic stuff for 1953. Interesting note: following the story there's a note from the editor informing readers that author Frank Kane deliberately ended the story with many questions unanswered, as the sequel to "The Icepick Artists" would be appearing the following month.

"The Insecure" by R. Van Taylor (2000 words)★★
Kay panics when her husband doesn't come home from work. Panic turns to terror when she finds her son is missing as well. Seems rushed but 2000 words doesn't leave a lot of room for the characterization this sort of psychological suspense needs.

The Best Stories of 1953

"As I Lie Dead" by Fletcher Flora (February)
"Kid Kill" by Evan Hunter (April)
"Services Rendered" by Jonathan Craig (May)
"I'm Getting Out" by Elliot West (July)
"Throwback" by Donald Hamilton (August)
"The Collector Comes After Payday" by Fletcher Flora (August)
"The Professional Man" by David Goodis (October)
"The Quiet Room" by Jonathan Craig (December)
"Switch Ending" by Richard Marsten (December)
"Sucker" by Hunt Collins (December)

Vol. 2 No. 1 Jan 1954
First Anniversary Issue. A 160-page issue. Cover by "Michael"

"Guilt-Edged Blonde" by John Ross Macdonald (4500 words)★★
Lew Archer is hired by Nick Nemo to be his bodyguard, but Nick is gunned down before Lew can guard his body. Not one to turn a blind eye to a paying customer (even if that customer is a corpse), Lew sticks around to see if he can smoke out Nemo's killer.

"The Six-Bit Fee" by Richard Deming (4000 words)★
Manville Moon investigates the murder of a crime writer.

"Finish the Job" by Frank Kane (6000 words)★★
Johnny Liddell muscles and guns his way to the man who killed Barney Shields. Not nearly as riveting as its prequel, "The Icepick Artists" (Dec 1953), "Finish the Job" is redeemed by a refreshingly nasty climax. When Liddell decides the police won't bring Barney justice, Johnny runs over the bad guys in his rented Buick.

"Over My Dead Body" by Harold Q. Masur (4500 words)★★
Lawyer Scott Jordan comes home from a fishing trip to find out one of his girlfriends, Delia Harley, has been murdered. It turns out the girl had recently found out she was adopted at a very young age and her biological parents, now both dead, had been very wealthy. One of the surviving relatives wanted to make sure no one discovered that Delia would be next in line for the inheritance,

"The Wrong Touch" by Henry Kane (13,000 words)★★
P.I. Peter Chambers is hired by an underworld figure to prove the murdered man in his study is not his handiwork. Overlong, but a nice double twist at the climax.

"... And Be Merry" by Craig Rice (500 words)★
Billed as "a John J. Malone story," this is nothing more than a fragment. Malone is called to the apartment of a woman who's been poisoned with cyanide but the cops can't find a trace around the apartment. Eventually, the path leads to the woman's psychiatrist who spills the beans: the woman loved to lick her wallpaper. Yep.

"Pattern for Panic" by Richard S. Prather (27,500 words)★★★★
Shell Scott's in Mexico helping the wife of an army general. Seems the beautiful Senora has inadvertently made a blue movie and her co-star is back to blackmail her. But is blackmail the real story here? Meanwhile, Shell becomes mixed up in a subplot involving an eccentric scientist who has invented a deadly nerve

gas and has been kidnapped by men who would use that nerve gas to further their political futures. A delirious cocktail of snakes, mad scientists, torture, two-timing babes and a rollicking action-filled climax that sees Shell Scott doing his best Count Dracula impersonation. Author Prather's hatred of communism is driven home time and again throughout the story.

Shortly after "Pattern for Panic" appeared in *Manhunt*, it was submitted to Gold Medal, who turned it down. Not wishing to miss out on a sale, Prather changed Scott's name to Cliff Morgan and sold it to Berkeley, who published it in 1955. It was later reissued in 1961 (with the Scott name re-inserted) by Gold Medal.

Peter Enfantino • Jeff Vorzimmer

Vol. 2 No. 2 Feb 1954

Debut of The Murder Market, book reviews by Anthony Boucher, which would only run two more issues, the last was written by Hal Walker. All appeared under the pseudonym H. H. Holmes.

"Runaway" by Richard Marsten (9500 words)★★

Johnny Trachetti is the suspect in the murder of gang member Angelo (The Wop) Brancusi. Johnny didn't do it, but he knows the cops will pin it on him so they can close the case early. So he runs... and runs... and runs from mishap to mishap. If it seems like a condensed version of a longer story, especially in its rushed climax, that's because it is. A few months after "Runaway" appeared in *Manhunt*, Gold Medal released an expanded version, retitled *Runaway Black*.

"The Rope Game" by Bryce Walton (5000 words)★★★

Larry used to have a way with the gals but now spends his time at the bottom of a bottle. Ten thousand dollars gets him to clean up his act for at least enough time to run a con on a beautiful woman. He needs to get her in compromising positions for some photos her husband can use against her in divorce court. Great character study. Larry seems to be on the brink of redeeming himself, but can a guy this far in the gutter really change his ways?

"Deadlier Than the Mail" by Evan Hunter (5000 words)★↓

By his sixth outing, the "solve crime and hit the bottle" routine is growing weary not only for Matt Cordell and *Manhunt* readers but also, I believe, for Evan Hunter himself. "Deadlier Than the Mail" is a lazy tale about the theft of welfare checks during Christmas. There's not a lot to it and the "snappy patter" between characters is forced and embarrassing:

> "How old are you, Fran? Sixteen?"
> "Nineteen, if you're worried about Quentin Quail. Hey, boy, what is it with you? You still got eyes for that bitchy wife of yours?"
> "Can it, honey."
> "Sure, so carry the torch. Let me help you burn it brighter, boy. I need the dough."
> "Because your old man's checks have been lifted?"
> "Sure, but that don't cut my ice, boy. The old man never gave me a cent anyway. The holidays are coming and I use what I've got to get what I want." She cupped her breasts suddenly, reaching forward toward me. "Come on, boy, it's good stuff."
> "I'm on the wagon." I paused. "Besides, I'm broke."
> "Mmm. Well, I ain't Santa Claus."

That kind of awful dialog (so awful that, if I didn't know better, I'd suspect that Hunter was farming out work to beginning writers as he did with the soft-core novels he wrote for Greenleaf) and a ludicrous expository damn this entry to the bottom of the Matt Cordell bottle.

"The Disaster" by Emmanuel Winters (1500 words)★★
Steve Obel tries to cope with the fact that his cowardice led to the death of 28 men in a mining accident.

"I'm a Stranger Here Myself" by Craig Rice (9000 words)★
Charlie Bekker wakes from a night of drinking and whoring (or so he thinks from the evidence) and finds himself in the company of a dead model. Running from the scene, he happens into the bar frequented by one John J. Malone. The lawyer is a bit upset since he's just discovered that the star witness in one of his big cases has been found dead in a motel room. Yep, that's right. In the small, coincidental world of J.J. Malone, everything ties together and the news gets out fast (though Rice notes that Bekker stumbles into the bar just a few hours after he finds the dead girl, Malone is already reading about in the paper!). Once Charlie confesses his innocence to Malone, the lawyer does what any lawyer would do: he puts the man up in a hotel, gets him a job, and tells him to lay low, all on pro bono. John J then devises a plan of coincidences and ludicrous twists and turns. Surely this story could have been told in half the space.

"Heels are for Hating" by Fletcher Flora (6000 words)★★
Jackie Brand just wants a little dough so that he can retire from boxing so that he and his wife can start their own business. When Jackie is offered ten grand to take a fall in his next fight, he greedily accepts but then finds himself trapped in a war between underworld goons. As Flora states towards the end of the story: "…he's learned of my double-cross. Or is it a triple-cross? It's getting too damn complex to follow." Indeed. Flora again enters the world of sports betting that he excelled at in his novel, *The Hot Shot*, but this time the results are a bit too talky.

"The Onlooker" by Robert Turner (1000 words)★
Blake's world comes apart when he witnesses his woman making love to a soldier. No surprise ending here.

"Comeback" by R. Van Taylor (3000 words)★★★★
Six years after being involved in a hit-and-run accident that left him an amnesiac, Fred Stevens is living the good life with his wife Marge and son Billy, until he notices a strange man following him, appearing wherever he goes. Finally the man presents his case: he claims Fred was actually a vicious gangster named Johnny until he lost his memory. Now the man wants his half of the cut of $150,000 they stole on their last job. Fred pleads with the man that he knows nothing about the money but the goon's not taking "no" for an answer. A tense little short story that reminded me a bit of David Cronenberg's excellent film *A History of Violence*. "Comeback" and *History* share an equally brutal climax.

"Mr. Chesley" by Robert Zacks (1000 words)★★
Mr. Chesley is about to pay dearly for his heroin trafficking.

"Shadow Boxer" by Richard Ellington (5500 words)★↗
P.I. Steve Drake is hired by ex-con Jack Cordello to find his sweetheart, missing since he went into the stir three years before. Drake discovers the girl is alive and very well off. Ellington manages to avoid most of the usual P.I. trappings that I've moaned about before but he just can't help himself when it comes to the big finale, an expository I'm still trying to figure out.

But for a few minor alterations, "Shadow Boxer" made a comfortable transition to television when Frank Kane adapted it for *Mickey Spillane's Mike Hammer* under the title, "A Detective Tail."

"The Man Who Found the Money" by James E. Cronin (2600 words)★★★★
William Benson finds a money clip containing 92 thousand dollar bills and, after thinking it over a couple times, does what any good Sam would do: he goes to the police. He soon finds he should have done what 98% of the planet would have done. Well-done, with a nasty bite in its climax. Faithfully adapted in 1960 for *Alfred Hitchcock Presents*, starring Arthur Hill as the hapless Benson.

Vol. 2 No. 3 May 1954
First appearance of Jack Webb with an "Airport Detail" story.

"The Blonde in the Bar" by Richard Deming (6700 words)★★

Sam's far from the most attractive guy and so he is, to say the least, a bit surprised when a doll named Jacqueline picks him up in the bar. His suspicions become founded when the dame drops her scam on him post-coitus. She pleads mercy for her sister, who's been arrested on prostitution charges and Sam just happens to be a cop. Sam's new girl promises a payday of $500 if he comes through, but this man is made of sterner stuff. When later he finds that the woman is the front for a mafia hood trying to buy local cops, Sam goes to his boss and sets up a sting. Not much in the way of excitement here, "The Blonde in the Bar" is populated by molls in sheer negligees and hoods who talk tough as channeled through a long-winded Oxford professor ("When we have helped into office the officials we want, we'll be in a position to dictate appointments and promotions in the police department" says one Monk Cartelli!). I do have to say I enjoyed this final exchange between Sam and Jacqueline after Sam lowers the boom:

> "Sam, you liked me a lot that-that other night. Can't you—isn't there some way you can give me a break?"
> "Sure, babe, sure ... I can give you a break. I'll take you down to the can just the way you are, instead of stopping first to kick your teeth down your throat."

"Murder of a Mouse" by Fletcher Flora (4000 words)★★

Charles Bruce murders his wife and stages suicide, not knowing that the woman had plans of her own. A dull story, enlivened a bit by its twist.

"The Woman on the Bus" by R. Van Taylor (4000 words)★

A man and his young son offer shelter to a very strange woman. Laughable climax.

"Broken Doll" by Jack Webb (6000 words)★★

An airport cop catches the strangest case of his career: a beautiful corpse, clad only in a coat left aboard a plane. A slow-paced whodunit with a bizarre wrap-up. One year later, Webb wrote a novel with the same title but otherwise no similarity to the *Manhunt* tale. One-half of the team from the novel, Detective Golden makes a brief appearance in the short story.

"... Or Leave It Alone" by Evan Hunter (5000 words)★★★

Back in 1954, this harrowing tale of Joey the hophead, and the troubles he encounters while trying to recover his stash, would probably be considered cutting edge fiction. Today it's still good writing (albeit a padded) from the master of dark crime but its impact is obviously lessened by our everyday exposure to the horrors of drug addiction. Would I still recommend the read? Certainly. However, it's not among Hunter's best and you can tell the man was paid by the word at times.

"Lead Ache" by Frank Kane (11,000 words)★★

Johnny Liddell is hired by *The Dispatch* to investigate the murder of their ace reporter, Larry Jensen. The writer was working on a story involving dance clubs and white slavery. Liddell is aided by (beautiful) reporter Barbara Lake, who evidently looks just as good in a skimpy dress as behind a typewriter.

When Frank Kane landed a job writing teleplays for the *Mickey Spillane's Mike Hammer* TV series for Revue Studios in 1958, he didn't have to look too far for inspiration, using his Johnny Liddell short stories and novels as bedrock for several episodes, including "Lead Ache," which aired on March 14, 1958. Liddell's snappy one-liners translated perfectly for Darren McGavin's Hammer character. In all, Kane wrote 24 *Hammer* teleplays.

"The Right One" by Jonathan Craig (2000 words)★★★

Bizarre little short-short, about a stripper and the man she picks up at her club, that contains a nasty climax that isn't telegraphed one bit.

"The Old Flame" by James T. Farrell (5000 words)★

Arnold Benton has a tryst with his ex-sister-in-law and spends 4500 words feeling guilty about it. Literally page after page of "It's nice to see you, isn't it?" and "Yes, it's nice to see you too." I have no idea why this would be considered for publication in *Manhunt* as there is not one line of suspense or criminal activity (unless adultery qualifies) whatsoever. James T. Farrell (1904–1979) was the author of the famous Studs Lonigan Trilogy.

"A Clear Picture" by Sam S. Taylor (1500 words)★

A man tries to set up his wife and her lover with tickets to a boxing match.

"You Know What I Did?" by Charles Beckman, Jr. (3000 words)★★★

Joe Allen comes home from work to find his young son missing. Effective tale of violence and revenge.

Vol. 2 No. 4 Jun 1954
First appearances of John M. Sitan and David Alexander.

"Skip a Beat" by Henry Kane (16,500 words)★↲
P.I. Peter Chambers is summoned to the home of famous columnist Adam Woodward and hired on as the writer's bodyguard. Woodward is about to out someone very famous as a communist and he's sure that violence may follow. Before the commie ratbastard can be named though, Woodward is plugged full of holes. Since the corpse is all paid up, Chambers decides to investigate. "Skip a Beat" is yet another P.I. story that takes way too long (about 16,500 words too long, actually) to state the obvious. The only saving grace here is a nasty bit of carnage during a fight between Chambers and a hired gun:

> *I knocked the gun out of his hands, yanked him up, swung from the bottom and it caught him on the mouth. It ripped the skin off my knuckles but it knocked his teeth clean through his upper lip, and he looked like he was smiling some sort of ghastly unearthly smile, the blood all over him, before he went down. I put a finger in his collar and got him up. I grabbed the lip between my thumb and forefinger and grabbed it clear.*

"Points South" by Fletcher Flora (3500 words)★★
After losing thousands in a poker game, Andy Corkin loses his cool and belts a connected man. He's told he has 24 hours to live, so he starts living.

"My Enemy, My Father" by John M. Sitan (1500 words)★★
A nasty short-short about a teen warring with his domineering father.

"The Choice" by Richard Deming (5000 words)★★★↲
Climbing the political ladder, three or four rungs at a time, George Kenneday began clean and, naively believes, he remains clean despite "little favors" he grants to the local syndicate. Through the years, those favors become bigger and Kenneday's excuses become exponentially bigger. A strange, fascinating study of political corruption, with just a bare minimum of dialogue, topped with a slap in the face climax. Selected by David C. Cooke for his *1956 Best Detective Stories of the Year* (Dutton)

"Double" by Bruno Fischer (7000 words)★★↲
Detective Gus Taylor is a particularly violent cop when he needs to be. Right now he feels the need. He's convinced that actress Holly Laird killed her producer John Ambler, but can't get the girl to confess. So he harasses her, beats her and, when that doesn't work, he goes after her boyfriend. "Double" is a strange case: it

goes way out there with its subject matter but then pulls back and softens its stance with its cotton candy climax. Too soft for my tastes.

"Butcher" by Richard S. Prather (4000 words)★★★

Shell Scott stumbles his way into the serial killer known as "The Butcher" when he's driving home one night and happens upon a dismembered leg. He then aids the police to find the killer when it's revealed the limb belonged to a young girl Shell knew. Extremely graphic for its time and tackling a subject that wasn't addressed much (yet) in the sexual predator/serial killer, "Butcher" has a harder edge than we're used to seeing in a Shell Scott story. Prather would have never gotten away with his final line in today's "politically correct" climate.

"No Vacancies" by Craig Rice (6000 words)★

John J. Malone, lawyer for the people, is hired by a man accused of murdering his social butterfly wife. J.J. instinctively knows the man is innocent. How does he know? The coffee he drinks? The air he breathes? He just knows. I could go on about the telecasted plot devices, the wildly irrational coincidences, the "with-it" hip dialogue, and the obligatory expository, but it would just read like I was re-running my last review of a John J. Malone story.

"Die Like a Dog" by David Alexander (4000 words)★★

Skid row bum Jack drinks his days away until he meets an interesting man with a blind old dog and a story about a faded starlet.

Vol. 2 No. 5 Jul 1954
First appearance of Jack Ritchie.

"Chinese Puzzle" by Richard Marsten (5000 words)★★

A young Chinese girl goes into convulsions while doing her job as a phone solicitor and dies in front of her co-workers. Detectives Parker and Katz know strychnine poisoning when they see it. With the staccato dialogue and detailed procedural descriptions, it must have been easy, for those paying attention back in 1954, to discern that Richard Marsten was another pseudonym, like Ed McBain, for Evan Hunter.

"My Game, My Rules" by Jack Ritchie (2000 words)★★✔

Johnny takes a job from three desperate men. Since Johnny is an assassin, someone's going to die, but the hit man's mind may not be entirely on the target, but rather the target's moll.

"Association Test" by Hunt Collins (1000 words)★

Silly short-short about a psychiatrist and the word association test he conducts with his disturbed patient.

"Two Grand" by Charles Beckman, Jr. (3500 words)★✔

Doug Wallace flees L.A. after landing big debts with the mob. He heads for the hills where his brother, Jim, and wife, Sadie, live. Doug soon finds there's quite a bit of sexual tension in the air. In an amusing conversation with his brother, Doug finds out why:

> "The war was rough on a lot of guys," [Jim] mumbled. "I guess I got no call to bitch. But why couldn't I have gotten it some other way? I wouldn't have minded losing an arm or a leg, Doug. You can still be a man with an arm or leg missin'. But not with—"
> It gradually dawned on Doug what the hell his brother was talking about. His eyes opened wide. So—now he understood it.
> He remembered vaguely that Jim had gotten the Purple Heart for being shot in Korea. But now he knew where Jim had been shot.

"Two Grand" reads like the outline for one of those countless "Hill Tramp" backwoods novels that permeated the stands in the late 1950s. It's rushed and ultimately unsatisfying.

"The Judo Punch" by V. E. Theissen (1000 words)★

A bent cop's wife suspects a man is following her and asks her husband to instruct her in the deadly art of judo. Nonsensical climax asks the reader to fill in all the blanks.

Peter Enfantino • Jeff Vorzimmer   59

"Sanctuary" by W. W. Hatfield (1500 words)★★
Joe Varden has killed a prison guard and fled into the swamps to hide out with his cousin Pete and Pete's wife, Ginny. After Joe falls for Ginny, he devises a plan so he can have freedom and the beauty as well. This and "Two Grand" make for two very similar and very similarly lackluster tales.

"Return" by Evan Hunter (5000 words)★★★
Matt Cordell is giving blood so he can raise booze money when he runs into old friend Sailor Simmons, who tells Matt some news: Matt's ex-wife Trina is back in town. He would have found this news out sooner or later because, right after he returns to his homeless shelter, Trina shows up, begging Matt to take her back. After a three-paragraph hesitation, Cordell takes her back only to find that there's something up the ex's sleeve.

A good, solid entry, the penultimate in the Matt Cordell series. The "Return' in the title could refer to the return of Trina, the return of Matt's self-respect (albeit briefly), or the return of his sobriety since, as we take leave of him, he's still dry. However, there is one more story to tell...

"Return" was adapted for the *Fallen Angels* Showtime series in 1995, and starred a badly miscast Kiefer Sutherland (who also directed) as Matt "Rocky" Cordell, here re-imagined as a punch-drunk Irish boxer. "Love and Blood" (the new title) is a truly wretched thirty-one minutes of missed opportunities, with the only bright spot being the beautiful Madchen Amick as Trina.

"I Want a French Girl" by James T. Farrell (4000 words)★↲
Lawrence has come from America to Paris because he wants a French girl. He finds them, fat ones, skinny ones, dull ones, but not the one he's looking for. He's convinced that French girls are better lovers but he's finding it hard to get proof. But for one throwaway final paragraph, this has no business being in a "Detective Story Monthly." The "In This Issue" blurb on the back cover touts this as "the story of a man with a single ambition, and of the way he was forced to fulfill it.'

"The Innocent" by Muriel Berns (1000 words)★
Richard Leaman is brought up before a judge for rape and assault but Richard's mother refuses to believe her son is anything but an angel.

"Confession" by John M. Sitan (3000 words)★★★★
John Egan is a murderer. Not just any murderer. He takes his business seriously, with lots of preparation. His only motivation is "to insure the inclusion of my name in man's history and memory." Brutal serial sniper story is innovative, long before the film *Targets* covered such ground. Sitan holds back no punches, here describing our first look at Egan's handiwork:

John Egan adjusted the rifle's telescopic sight again. It was quite easy to pick out the circle of light from the single lamp over the theatrical announcement plaque. The spot was a good target point. It was ten minutes after eleven and no one was about on the apartment house roof. He had counted eight persons crossing the circle of light. They had all been men. The ninth person was a woman. The white shoes and dress under a dark coat indicated she was a nurse. There was a young couple walking behind her. A policeman turned the corner.

When the nurse reached the circle of light her head flew apart.

Or this bit where Sitan pulls us, whether we want to be pulled or not, down even farther into Egan's twisted world:

He sighted on the junction again when he saw a woman and a little girl coming along. The girl was about five years old and wore a pink frilly dress. She was skipping a little ahead of the woman when she reached the junction. At that moment John Egan squeezed the trigger of his rifle. He watched the convulsive sideways jerk as the bullet thudded home. At his distance it appeared as if the child had stumbled. John did not look back until he had broken the sniper rifle down and put it in the trumpet case. When he did look back the woman was on her knees and screaming.

I must admit while I was reading that passage, I fully expected that action would be halted in some way or that he would take out the mother. I never expected Sitan to go the distance. Obviously, with snipers a part of our everyday world, "Confession" is even more relevant now than when it was written over sixty years ago. But, further, the story examines the popularity of murder and the celebrity of evil. David C. Cooke selected "Confession" for his *1955 Best Detective Stories of the Year.*

"Find a Victim" by John Ross Macdonald (20,500 words)★★★

Fifth and final appearance of Lew Archer in *Manhunt*. This time, Lew's on his way to deliver a report on drug trafficking to legislation in Sacramento when he happens upon a bleeding man on the side of a deserted highway. The man dies soon after Archer delivers him to a hospital. Before long, the P.I. discovers that the town has quite a few skeletons in its familial closet. The plot feels second-hand (or even third-hand) but the writing crackles and keeps those pages turning, making even the obligatory conk on the head dazzling:

His fist came out from under the windbreaker, wearing something bright, and smashed at the side of my head.

My legs forgot about me. I sat on the asphalt against the wall and looked at his armed right fist, a shining steel hub on which the night revolved. His face leaned over me, stark and glazed with hatred:

"Bow down, God damn you… Bow down and kiss my feet"

Another passage, after Lew takes a nasty tumble:

Peter Enfantino • Jeff Vorzimmer

It was a long fall straight down through the darkness of my head. I was a middle-aging space cadet lost between galaxies and out of gas. With infinite skill and cunning I put a grain of salt on the tail of a comet and rode it back to the solar system. My back and shoulder were burned raw from the sliding fall. But it was nice to be home.

I still have problems with the clichéd P.I. expository ("Suddenly I knew everything that had happened so I gathered everyone in one room and told them how it went down"), but this one has enough dazzle to make me overlook the trappings. That same year, Knopf released an expanded version of "Find a Victim" in novel form.

"Helping Hand" by Arnold Marmor (1000 words)★★✦
   The D.A. can't get to mob boss, Gomez, unless O'Hara sings but O'Hara says he'd rather fry in the electric chair than rat out Gomez. Nice twist elevates this above most short-shorts.

Vol. 2 No. 6 Aug 1954
"What's Your Verdict?" debuts, will run through Dec 1955.

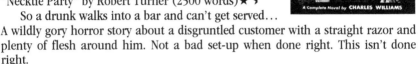

"Identity Unknown" by Jonathan Craig (4500 words)★★
The identity of a dead woman is traced through her fancy shoes. Very reminiscent of an 87th Precinct story.

"Necktie Party" by Robert Turner (2500 words)★ ↲
So a drunk walks into a bar and can't get served…
A wildly gory horror story about a disgruntled customer with a straight razor and plenty of flesh around him. Not a bad set-up when done right. This isn't done right.

"The Old Man's Statue" by R. Van Taylor (3000 words)★ ↲
What is the secret behind the young man who, day in and day out, wipes the profane graffiti away from a statue in the town square? The new owner of the town paper is determined to get to the bottom of the mystery. *Peyton Place* pathos in a small Mississippi town with a climax right out of *Friday the 13th*. Two gory horror stories in one issue.

"Effective Medicine" by B. Traven (4000 words)★
An American doctor practicing in Mexico has a problem on his hands. A local villager wants the doctor to find his adulterous wife or the doctor will feel the sharp edge of the man's machete.

"Accident" by John M. Sitan (2000 words)★★★
James Merrill has a strained relationship with his girlfriend, Gladys. They fight a lot. After one such argument, Gladys rushes out of the coffee shop they're both in and into traffic. Merrill spends the rest of the story making life a hell for the unfortunate woman who ran down Gladys.
After hitting a home run last issue with "Confession," I doubted author Sitan could come up with another, but "Accident" is a solid thought-provoker with a wallop of a climax. It gets the job done but I'd have liked to see it a bit longer. That may be because I enjoy the author's prose. This is the last of the three stories Sitan wrote for *Manhunt*.

"I Don't Fool Around" by Charles Jackson (3000 words)★★
George Burton is in love with the "new girl in town," Lynette McCaffrey, a lovely little tart who thinks nothing of revving up George's engine and then shutting it off at a moment's notice, with a smile. Much like "I Want a French Girl," this has no place in *Manhunt*. There's only a threat of violence hinted at in the final paragraph; nothing else makes this a crime story. I suspect it's simply because Jackson was a "name author" at the time (as author of *The Lost Weekend*)

and *Manhunt* would have taken anything from the author.

"Frame" by Frank Kane (9000 words)★★★
Johnny Liddell finds himself in a bit of a pickle once again. This time, an aging starlet his P.I. company has been body-guarding has been found murdered and all clues point to Liddell. Johnny had been helping the woman to cash in several thousands of dollars' worth of diamonds and the jewels are MIA. The private dick has his work cut out for him as all his business associates in the case are looking out for No. 1 and denying any knowledge of the diamonds. Non-stop action, snappy dialogue, good and hardboiled:

> *"This is for the kid, Murph." He slammed his fist against the big man's mouth. There was the sound of crunching teeth. The big man went staggering backward and fell across a table.*
> *"You won't be needing teeth where you're going."*

"And Share Alike" by Charles Williams (21,000 words)★★★★
Our narrator is hired by Diana James to steal a large amount of money from a woman named Madelon Butler. Mrs. Butler is married to a bank president, who has mysteriously disappeared after embezzling $120,000. Diana is convinced she can dig up the money before Madelon. First rule of noir: never trust a woman. Both females have so many double-crosses up their sleeves they need larger gowns. Williams ends it on a beautifully downbeat ending as the guy gets nothing but a jail cell. We find ourselves rooting for this guy even though the majority of his actions are immoral. He just happens to be a little *less* immoral than either of the female cast members.

Perhaps best known for the sea thriller *Dead Calm* (1963), Charles Williams was, according to Ed Gorman, "line for line, the best of all the Gold Medal writers ... quiet and possessed of a melancholy that imbued each of his tales with a kind of glum decorum." Writer John D. MacDonald said that Williams was "one of the two or three best storytellers on the planet."

Here are a few lines from Williams himself, taken from "And Share Alike":

> *I stood there on the corner under a street light just holding the paper while the pieces fell all around me. It was too much. You could only get part of it at a time.*
> *And when I tried to tell them that I couldn't be suffering from any sense of guilt for killing Madelon Butler because I hadn't killed her, and not only that but if I had killed her I still wouldn't feel guilty about it because if I could only get my hands on her I'd gladly strangle her slowly to death right there before a whole courtroom full of people, including standing-room, and even pass out free refreshments if I had the money, it didn't help any.*

"And Share Alike" was expanded to novel form and released by Gold Medal later that year as *A Touch of Death*.

After his brief stint with *Manhunt* (three short novels), Williams went on to write several more suspense novels (among them, *Man on the Run* (1958) and *Aground* (1960)). Like many of the classic Gold Medal crime novelists, the acclaim and notice didn't come until decades later when reprints and movie adaptations awakened a new generation to these "hidden treasures." Williams took his own life in 1975.

"Yard Bull" by Frank Selig (1000 words)★★
Security guard for the railroad recounts his early days as a train-hopper.

Vol. 2 No. 7 Sep 1954
First and only appearances of Basil Heatter ("The Empty Fort") and Jerome Weidman ("A Moment's Notice"). Cover by "Michael."

"The Witness" by John Sabin (3000 words)★★
Mark Hagan begins to question the merits of being a good Samaritan. He witnesses the murderous Earl Splade gun down a man in cold blood and reports it to the police. Now, it seems the police can't protect Mark from the murderer, who's back on the streets in no time. Abrupt but satisfying climax. This was Sabin's only appearance in *Manhunt* or any crime magazine for that matter.

"Bedbug" by Evan Hunter (1000 words)★
A paranoid husband interrogates his mad wife. Or is it the other way around? When does a 1200 word short story feel like a 120,000 word novel? When it's filled with dreadful dialogue and a story that is going nowhere. This story and "Association Test" (from July's issue) prove that Evan Hunter needs a few more words to get his groove going.

"State Line" by Sam S. Taylor (6500 words)★★★
Linoleum salesman rolls into Vegas and is immediately smitten with a rich beauty. Like most *Manhunt* dames, this one's got something up her sleeve. She's got an old hubby who's become a burden and now she's searching for a way to become a rich widow. What seems to be heading down the path of a Fred Mac-Murray film veers down a dirt road to something completely different. This would have made a nice episode of *Alfred Hitchcock Presents* (it *is* slightly reminiscent of the classic "One More Mile to Go" from the second season of *AHP*).

"Night Watch" by Jonathan Craig (4500 words)★★
Sergeants Sharber and Curran, Homicide, 9th Precinct, catch a strange case: the man's been shot in the head and when they dig further they find kiddie porn and heroin. Luckily for the detectives, the murderer falls right into their hands and confesses. This has the most abrupt ending I've ever come across. I literally searched the magazine for a "Continued from page 42" but my copy is lacking any such closure.

"Tin Can" by B. Traven (4000 words)★★★↙
Natalio Salvatorres is looking for a wife and finds her in Filomena Gallardo, a young peasant whose father is only too happy to sell her for a new pair of pants and a few bottles of tequila. Moving to a mining town to find work, Natalio's happy in his new life until one day he finds his wife has run off with another man. Seeking revenge, Natalio crafts an explosive in a tin can and heads for the hut where his wife is attending a party. Unfortunately for Natalio, the only person killed in the blast is a friend of Filomena's:

The occupants of the hut saw the bomb and jumped out of the hut without even taking the time for a shout of horror. This took them less than half a second. At once a terrific explosion followed, sending the hut up a hundred feet in the air.

Of the six people who had been inside, five escaped without so much as a scratch. The sixth, the young woman of the couple that owned the hut, was not so fortunate.

This woman had, at the very moment the bomb made its appearance at the party, been busy making fresh coffee in the corner of the hut farthest from the door. She had neither seen the bomb nor noted the rapid and speechless departure of her guests. Consequently she accompanied the hut on its trip upward. And since she had been unable in so short a time to determine which part of the hut she would like best to travel with, she landed at twenty different places in the vicinity.

As you can tell from that passage, this is a dark comedy. "Tin Can" gets even wittier when Natalio faces trial for his crime.

B. Traven was the author of *Treasure of the Sierra Madre* (1927), *The Rebellion of the Hanged* (1936), and several other acclaimed novels. His life and identity were something of a mystery. According to his *Manhunt* bio, not even his agent knew his identity.

"Ambition" by Patrick Madden (1500 words)★★★
The cops have a cold-blooded killer dead to rights but the murderer seems almost happy they do. For such a short story, this is an effective commentary on what someone will do to achieve that "15 minutes."

"A Moment's Notice" by Jerome Weidman (9000 words)★★★★
Dr. Holcomb, eighty years old, realizes he hasn't much time left but before he goes he must atone for a sin his son committed ten years earlier, an evil act Dr. Holcomb helped cover up for fear of scandal. When a similar situation rears its ugly head and his son is again the villain, the doctor finds a way to make peace with himself. Or does he?

Though I have problems with the logic, the doctor shows in solving his problem at the climax, this is a riveting story. Too often, I've found when a big name drops in to the *Manhunt* headquarters, they seldom deliver. Here's a case of the big name delivering and then some. A passage, referring to Holcomb's son, Robert, might well have been prescient of today's celebrities and their various foibles:

How did one deal with the wicked who were ignorant of the meaning of wickedness, with the sinner who had no conception of sin?

The only occasion on which Robert seemed to be aware that he had done anything the world condemned came at the moments when he was caught.

Peter Enfantino • Jeff Vorzimmer

Jerome Weidman (1913–1998) is best known for his Great Depression novel, *I Can Get It for You Wholesale* (1937) and for co-writing the Joan Crawford vehicle, *The Damned Don't Cry* (1950).

"Every Morning" by Richard Marsten (1500 words)★★

A governess plays cruel games with her hired help every morning until he can take it no more and violence ensues.

"Some Things Never Change" by Robert Patrick Wilmot (2500 words)★

Kerrigan flies back to England to reclaim the love he lost during the Second World War. She's got other plans for the sap. But is he a sap? A first: 500 words of set-up, 2000 words of expository. Outrageous and clunky expository to boot!

"The Empty Fort" by Basil Heatter (14,500 words)★★★

Flake, captain of the Jezebel, is hired by Mangio to haul in tons of shrimp. Flake is the best at his business, he knows it, and demands a larger cut from Mangio. Not one to take insubordination, Mangio hires shipmate Cutter to kill Flake and make it look like an accident. Cutter knocks Flake overboard during a nasty storm but the captain is from the "die hard" school and survives long enough to be rescued by a passing boat. Exciting sea adventure, reminiscent of Charles Williams' novels, with a violent finale at the titular structure.

The son of radio broadcaster Gabriel Heatter, Basil Heatter was the author of several novels including *The Dim View* (Signet, 1948), *Sailor's Luck* (Lion, 1953), *The Mutilators* (Gold Medal, 1962), *Virgin Cay* (Gold Medal, 1963), *Harry and the Bikini Bandits* (Gold Medal, 1971) and two adventures of Tim Devlin, marine insurance man, *The Golden Stag* and *Devlin's Triangle* (both Pinnacle, 1976). The Mugged and Printed feature this issue mentions an upcoming Lion novel called *Powder Snow*. This was retitled *Act of Violence* for publication in 1954. Heatter's novels accentuated the adventure, whether it be icy mountain tops (*Act of Violence*), ships wrecked (*Virgin Cay*), or gun smuggling in Europe (*The Mutilators*).

"The Promise" by Richard Welles (1000 words)★

Nothing more than the outline for a short story about a cop who goes after his brother, wanted for murder.

Vol. 2 No. 8 Oct 1954
First appearance of C. B. Gilford and the first of Jonathan Craig's "18th Precinct" Stories.

"The Beatings" by Evan Hunter (3500 words)★★★★
"Men can become good neighbors when their common mortar is despair." Another visit to the hell populated by ex-P.I., current drunk, Matt Cordell. This time, Matt's helping out his fellow winos, who find themselves under attack by a pack of violence-hungry teenagers. Interestingly enough, "The Beatings" starts with one of Evan Hunter's patented soliloquies of the city: *"the city wore August like a soiled flannel shirt."* Eighth and final Matt Cordell story is also the best of the bunch.

"The Bargain" by Charles Beckman, Jr. (3000 words)★★★
Frank and his wife Mavis are vacationing at their mountain cabin when a murderer, hiding from the police, takes them hostage. To win their freedom, Mavis must give the man what he wants. Nice twist when we find that Mavis might have other reasons for going along with this killer's demands.

"Clean Getaway" by William Vance (5500 words)★★★
Police chief Mark Nadine closes in on a couple of murderers at a roadside inn. The pair make a getaway but not before Mark makes a startling discovery: the woman of the pair is his wife, long gone but not forgotten. A well-written noir, cut from the same cloth as Jim Thompson's fiction, but a few too many questions left unanswered for my tastes. Second and final *Manhunt* story for Vance (although this story would be retitled "Lust or Honor" for the Dec 1966 issue). William Vance wrote westerns, under his name as well as the pseudonym George Cassidy, for such pulps as *Star Western, 2-Gun Western, Dime Western,* and *Best Western,* as well as crime stories for *Trapped, Terror Detective,* and *Mike Shayne.*

"Laura and the Deep, Deep Woods" by W. B. Hartley (2000 words)★★
Teenaged Eddie gets his first glimpse of "what sex really is" when he happens upon cute little Laura in the deep, deep woods. By no stretch of the imagination, a *Manhunt* story, "Laura and the Deep, Deep Woods" reads more like an excerpt from a Twain novel. This was the only story Hartley wrote for *Manhunt.*

"Second Cousin" by Erskine Caldwell (2000 words)★↲
Pete Ellrod comes home to find his wife's second cousin, once removed, has moved into his house and the wife is being a bit stubborn about the situation. Pete doesn't want the cousin around, as second cousins, once removed, historically have a tendency to want favors granted. Second story by Erskine Caldwell to see print in *Manhunt* (with three to follow) has the same problem I had with its predecessor: it doesn't belong in a "Detective Story Monthly." It would be better

served in *The Saturday Evening Post* or one of the other slicks of the 1950s.

"Love Affair" by Richard Deming (2000 words)★
This homophobic tale of two cops and the "woman" they pick up in a sleazy bar is about as subtle as the bar's name: The Purple Dragon. You can see the "twist" coming at you two pages in. Deming is so much better than this would lead one to believe.

"Lady Killer" by Richard Marsten (2500 words)★★
Charlie Rawlings is the best hit man money can buy. Now George Manelli, mob boss, needs Rawlings to silence an old moll of George's. She's about to sing to the cops about his organization and she knows enough to bring his comfy world crashing down around him. No relation to the 87th Precinct McBain novel Hunter would write in 1958.

"The Dead Darling" by Jonathan Craig (5000 words)★★↲
Detectives Rayder and Selby are called in to investigate what appears at first to be a suicide (a girl with her head in the oven) but it quickly becomes apparent that what they're actually dealing with is a murder. This girl spent a lot of her free time bedding married men.

Though the Ed McBain 87th Precinct novels became world famous and sold in the millions, Jonathan Craig's Pete Selby and Stan Rayder stories (aka The 18th Precinct) actually pre-dated the 87th by two years. "The Dead Darling" was expanded into the first Pete Selby novel of the same name in 1955 (nine more would follow). Craig wrote three 18th Precinct stories for *Manhunt* before turning his attention to the novels. The Selby series morphed into a second set of procedurals Craig wrote for *Manhunt* (the Police Files) but more on that later.

"That Stranger, My Son" by C. B. Gilford (3000 words)★
Paul and his father are grieving the drowning death of Paul's brother. The boy's father is convinced that Paul could have saved his brother's life. There's something to those suspicions, of course. The first appearance by prolific short story writer C. B. Gilford in *Manhunt* (he would contribute 12 stories throughout the run). Gilford became a staple of *Alfred Hitchcock's Mystery Magazine* (seeing 80 stories published between the Jul 1957 issue and his last appearance in Oct 1980) as well as most of the other crime digests of the 1950s and 1960s. Five of his stories were dramatized on *Alfred Hitchcock Presents/Hour*.

"One of a Kind" by Ben Smith (1000 words)★
Sordid short-short about rape and the degrees of evil.

"The Famous Actress" by Harry Roskelenko (1500 words)★
Wandering the streets of Paris, a man picks up a woman he later finds is a well-known actress, researching a role. Unfortunately for the lady, the man is a bit of an "actor" himself.

"Candlestick" by Henry Kane (16,500 words)★★

Peter Chambers is enlisted by police lieutenant Louis Parker to help solve the murder of publicity mega-agent Max Keith. The agent has been clobbered with a gold candlestick and the lieutenant is up to his neck in suspects. One of the suspects is the victim's sister, who stands to inherit a big chunk of the family inheritance once her brother is dead. Chambers knows the girl is innocent (well, innocent in *Manhunt* is a relative term) since, in a laugh out loud coincidence, he was bedding her when he got the call! Not really as grating as the other Chambers novellas but still double the length it needs to be.

Vol. 2 No. 9 Nov 1954
*First appearance of Hal Ellson, who would write a
total of 23 stories for Manhunt.*

"Pistol" by Hal Ellson (4000 words)★★★
To impress his fellow gang members, Dusty must come up with a gun in order to rumble. Written much like a diary, "Pistol" is an impressive debut for Hal Ellson, who would contribute 23 stories throughout the run of *Manhunt*. According to Ellson's bio, his stories are "based on his experience with these teenage gangs and have gained the praise of critics and readers not only for their excitement and realistic pace and tone, but for their obvious authenticity." Ellson's other contributions to gang-related fiction included his million-seller *Duke*, about a gang of Harlem youths.

"Replacement" by Jack Ritchie (3000 words)★★
Max Warren wants to move up the chain of command in the local organization. Once he gets there, he decides he wants all that goes with the job, including the boss' woman. Interesting story marred by a bad last line.

"Shy Guy" by Robert Turner (3000 words)★★★
Della, now employed and feeling free, tries to push her husband Aryie into her new-found world of alcohol and business parties. When the parties turn to wife-swapping, Artie's had enough and cracks under the strain. Years before this fiction became famous in the hands of Jacqueline Susann and her ilk, "Shy Guy" was a daring little story. It's lost a lot of its punch, of course, but it's still effective.

"Man from Yesterday" by Jonathan Craig (5000 words)★★★
Detectives Lew Keller and Burt Ogden must solve the intriguing case of a man found in a car, murdered. Their trail leads to a married woman the man had been seeing. Though "The Man from Yesterday" can be very dry at times (Craig has that *Dragnet*-style dialog down pat), I still found it an enjoyable read. Halfway through the story, Ed Seibert, a P.I. makes a brief appearance. This reminded me of the crossover shows that populated such seventies TV shows as *Cannon* and *Barnaby Jones*. A nice touch, and Seibert seems to be a character that Craig should have spun off.

"A Bull to Kill" by Richard Marsten (4000 words)★★★
Reardon, a rare American bullfighter has had everything taken away from him: his beloved Juanita, lost to fellow toreador Gomez; his nerve, to a recent goring; and the crowd that once cheered his name and now favors the upstart Gomez. Driven to madness, Reardon decides he will fight one more bull and then kill Gomez. Evan Hunter again proves he can't be pigeonholed. "A Bull to Kill" is as far removed from an 87th Precinct mystery as you can get.

"The Stalkers" by Grant Colby (1000 words)★
Ben is released from the sanitarium and presumed sane. He acts sane until he imagines his parakeet and puppy are stalking him.

"The Wet Brain" by David Alexander (7500 words)★↲
A "wet brain" is a derogatory term for an alcoholic so far gone that he loses all sense of reality and place. This particular "wet brain" is convinced he's killed someone but can't convince anyone of that. He's wandering the Bowery with a pocket full of money and attracting the attention of fellow boozehounds.

According to his *Manhunt* bio, David Alexander "insures the accuracy of his stories through study of actual police procedure and graduated at the head of a recent class in Criminology given by a former New York police inspector." Alexander was the author of several crime novels, among them: *Murder Points a Finger* (1953), *Murder in Black and White* (1951), *Paint the Town Black* (1956), *Die, Little Goose* (1956) and the b/side of Robert Bloch's *Spiderweb* (Ace Double, 1954), *The Corpse in My Bed* (a reprint of his first novel and *Most Men Don't Kill*, 1951).

"The Man who Had Too Much to Lose" by Hampton Stone (23,500 words)★★↲
Assistant District Attorney Jeremiah X. Gibson happens to be in the right place at the right time when he witnesses portly Jason Gracie fall ill from what appears to be poisoning. Gracie, a belligerent and pompous individual, refuses to believe this theory until his chef is found dead, poisoned. It's up to Jeremiah to sort through the motives and alibis of the cast of characters that surround Jason Gracie. Very much in the Perry Mason tradition, "The Man Who Had Too Much to Lose" is not a bad read, despite its length and its "cozy" atmosphere, which I usually find detrimental to a story published in *Manhunt*.

Published in hardcover by Simon and Schuster in 1955 and reprinted by Dell in paperback in 1957. Eighteen novels featuring D.A. Jeremiah X. "Gibby" Gibson and his helper, Mac, were published between 1948 and 1972. More interesting is the reprinting that took place in 1972 as part of the "Hampton Stone Mystery" series of paperbacks published by Paperback Library. Seventeen of the novels were reprinted in the series ("The Man Who Had Too Much to Lose" was #16). Strangely enough, the 18th, published in 1972, was never reprinted in paperback (in the series or otherwise). Hampton Stone was the pseudonym of prolific author Aaron Marc Stein, who wrote over a hundred novels under his own name, as Stone, and as George Bagby. "The Man Who Had Too Much to Lose" would be Gibby Gibson's only appearance in *Manhunt* but Gibson would later pop up in "The Mourners at the Bedside", a short story in *Ed McBain's Mystery Book* #3 (1961).

Peter Enfantino • Jeff Vorzimmer

Vol. 2 No. 10 Dec 1954
The first of two issues published in December of 1954.

"Pretty Boy" by Hal Ellson (3000 words)★
What I could make out between from all the hip jive-talk, is that this is about a young man caught up in gang life. I'd have preferred to read the translated text.

That night I bought me some reefers. I got crazy high quick and sent Zelda home for my pistol. Then I picked up the rest of the boys, cause we got a "war" on with the Pelicans. We taxied into foreign territory, fired a few wild shots and flew, cause the cops was hot in the streets.

Ellson's bio in "Mugged and Printed" touts this as "another tough and realistic picture of teen gang life."

"Two Little Hands" by Fletcher Flora (2000 words)★★
Big, brawny Obie's not right in the head and everyone around takes advantage of him, including our narrator, Jake. What Jake convinces Obie to do will haunt both of them the rest of their lives.

"The Red Tears" by Jonathan Craig (5000 words)★✔
Detectives Fred Spence and Jake Thomas of the 18th Precinct catch the murder of a pretty girl, shot and robbed of her engagement ring, the titular "red tears." Not much more than a novel outline, "The Red Tears" goes from Point A to Point B very quickly and without much substance

"To a Wax Doll" by Arnold Marmor (1000 words)★★★
Very good short-short about a cop tracking down a heroin pusher. Last little bit adds a nice, nasty bite.

"A Bachelor in the Making" by Charles Jackson (2000 words)★★
Yet another of the "slice of life" stories offered up by respectable authors outside the crime genre and ballyhooed in *Manhunt*. "A Bachelor in the Making" concerns a boy growing up and experiencing life while working in a grocery store. He doesn't witness a murder. He doesn't commit a murder. He just works and observes.

"A Life for a Life" by Robert Turner (2500 words)★★★
Three cops stake out a maternity ward, awaiting an escaped convict whose wife is giving birth. One of the cops is a trigger-happy sadist, who shows the con how good he is with a gun. Grisly climax when the con shows the cop how sadistic

he can be.

"Twilight" by Hal Harwood (1000 words)★★★
A man remembers a violent incident in his childhood. Brief, but powerful.

"For a Friend" by Bob McKnight (1000 words)★★★
Joe Rossotti's not a bright guy, but he *has* to have Carmen, a high-priced neighborhood "lady." Carmen suggests that if Joe had a grand, he'd get a grand time. She recommends the horses and even picks a horse for Joe to bet on. Since Joe's not that bright, it takes him a while to realize he's been played. Unfortunately for Joe, his epiphany doesn't occur until after the race. However, Joe concocts his revenge pretty quickly thereafter. Sly fun.

"The Hero" by Floyd Mahannah (5500 words)★★
Mel Karger, just out of the pen, wants only a fresh start. Unfortunately, that fresh start may mean dealing with the rat who framed him.

"Diary of a Devout Man" by Max Franklin (3000 words)★★★
Our titular character suddenly begins receiving messages from God telling him he has to wipe the world clean of sinners. He buys a gun and the first sinner to fall is his girlfriend. Max Franklin is a pseudonym for Richard Deming.

"Opportunity" by Russell E. Bruce (500 words)★★
A newspaper reporter comes across evidence he can use to blackmail a mobster. Proof that not all short-shorts are bad.

"The Housemother Cometh" by Hayden Howard (1500 words)★
Beau and Fred sneak a woman into their dorm. A rare (and unwanted) excursion into comedy for *Manhunt*.

"Manslaughter" by Henry Ewald (1000 words)★★
John Madden has lost his job and is facing tough times. When he goes to see his ex-boss, some hope arises. When that hope is dashed, he hits the bar and winds up in trouble.

"Hit and Run" by Richard Deming (16,000 words)★★★★
Barney Calhoun steps out of the Happy Hollow Bar one night and witnesses a hit and run. Being a P.I. in a small town doesn't bring in a lot of dough, so Barney gets it into his head he'll act as middleman for the evil deed doers. He goes to Helena Powers, the passenger in the car, and offers a deal: he'll go to the victim (who's in intensive care) and offer to pay for his silence for a fee. Helena agrees, but unfortunately, things get complicated for Barney when the victim dies. A whole new plan comes into effect, including another murder, Helena's frightened lover, and an elaborate scheme to keep Helena and Barney out of jail. Deming crafts a wonderful short novel, filled with blind curves and capped off by a riotous climax. Later expanded to a novel (Pocket paperback, 1960).

Peter Enfantino • Jeff Vorzimmer

"No Half Cure" by Robert E. Murray (1000 words)★

Doctor Kleist is helping socialite Mrs. Clinton overcome her annoying and embarrassing habit of kleptomania. Of course, he cures her but it's revealed that the doctor himself is a kleptomaniac and has stolen Mrs. Clinton's expensive cigarette case. A one-note joke extended to 1000 words.

"Judgment" by G. H. Williams (1000 words)★★★

In an issue filled with too many short-shorts, there are a surprising number of bright lights. This is one of them. Two punks are giving a bartender a hard time unaware that he's got an itchy trigger finger.

Vol. 2 No. 11 Dec 25 1954
Special Anniversary Edition.

"Crime of Passion" by Richard S. Prather (3500 words)★★

Shell Scott goes to a beach party where the host's later found on a spit, cooking like a pig. Unpleasant off day for Shell.

"The Purple Collar" by Jonathan Craig (6000 words)★

An 18th Precinct short mystery starring Pete Selby and his partner, Ben Muller. This time, the boys must solve the riddle of a hanged man who didn't die by hanging. Various characters are introduced, but the story never seems to be populated by real people. Again, this just reads like a knockoff of *Dragnet*, and though the 18th Precinct stories and the 87th Precinct tales of Ed McBain ran concurrently, the Craig stories come off as nothing more than weak imitations.

"Flowers to the Fair" by Craig Rice (6000 words)★★

John J. Malone's latest client is a mousy accountant who's been embezzling money from his boss. The boss offers to loan the mouse enough money to pay him back and the next day the accountant is found dead. Smelling something fishy, John J. investigates the killing. Not a very entertaining read. John J. seems to be able to take many of his cases on for little or no money (because the client is a sympathetic character), much like the good guy P.I.s of TV like *Mannix* or *Barnaby Jones*.

"The Scarlet King" by Evan Hunter (3500 words)★★★

Our narrator has a problem with his temper. Whenever something irritates him, he thinks of the King of Hearts (from a deadly poker game he played in the Korean War) and dispatches anyone unlucky enough to be nearby. Another minor Hunter gem with a trademark kick at the climax.

"The Pickpocket" by Mickey Spillane (1000 words)★↙

Willie's worried that his past will come back to haunt him.

"Big Steal" by Frank Kane (8000 words)★★

Johnny Liddell becomes involved in a stolen diamond racket when a woman asks him to hold a small package for her. When the woman ends up dead, her throat cut, and thugs rough up Johnny, Liddell enlists the aid of Inspector Herlihy to catch the "big man."

"Dead Issue" by Harold Q. Masur (4000 words)★

Scott Jordan (in his 10th *Manhunt* appearance), the lawyer who thinks he's a P.I., investigates the murder of a nice old woman. The case involves the upcoming reading of a multi-million dollar will, a will that has mysteriously disappeared. A

Peter Enfantino • Jeff Vorzimmer

judge, admonishing Jordan in our opener, says "The Assistant District Attorney tells me you have a tendency to take the law into your own hands." Indeed.

"Death Sentence" by Richard Deming (4000 words)★★

Isobel Banner has a strange substance she wants analyzed strictly on the q.t., so she hires Manville Moon to take the "strange white powder" from her. When he arrives at the party she's invited him to, he finds her dead. What was the curious substance and why did she feel the need to keep it a secret? Moon never likes it when a potential client ends up dead before he's paid, so he takes it upon himself to find out what the mystery is. This brings up a problem with several of these P.I. stories—why do so many of Moon's, Jordan's, Liddell's (etc.) clients seem to end up on a slab by the third page, yet the P.I.s known throughout their respective towns as guys who get the job done. Nice twist ending though!

"Precise Moment" by Henry Kane (11,000 words)★★↲

Peter Chambers becomes the target of repeated gunfire after he takes part in a midnight graveyard delivery of $750,000 in ransom money. The kidnapee, the newly-wed husband of multi-millionaire Florence Fleetwood Reed, may have had something to do with his own kidnapping.

For thirty minutes one night in 1958, Peter Chambers hit the big time when he was transformed, via *Manhunt* stablemate Frank Kane's teleplay, into *Mickey Spillane's Mike Hammer*. Retitled "A Grave Undertaking," the nicely atmospheric episode was a faithful adaptation of "Precise Moment."

"Six Fingers" by Hal Ellson (2000 words)★★

The appropriately named "Six Fingers" is a very shy boy but his friends want him to grow up fast so they involve him with a girl named Cissie.

The Best Stories of 1954

"Pattern for Panic" by Richard S. Prather (January)
"Comeback" by R. Van Taylor (February)
"The Man Who Found the Money" by James E. Cronin (February)
"The Choice" by Richard Deming (June)
"Confession" by John M. Sitan (July)
"And Share Alike" by Charles Williams (August)
"Tin Can" by B. Traven (September)
"A Moment's Notice" by Jerome Weidman (September)
"The Beatings" by Evan Hunter (October)
"Hit and Run" by Richard Deming (December)

Vol. 3 No. 1 Jan 1955
Cover by "Michael."

"The Killer" by John D. Macdonald (5000 words)★★★

A fishing club called "The Deep Six" becomes witness to a nasty bit of violence when macho man John Lash won't leave Croy Danton's wife alone. A discussion of how John D. MacDonald changed and popularized the crime story during the late 1950s through to his death in 1986 would take up an entire book. I'm also the wrong guy to write that essay. I've only read four J.D.M novels (*The Executioners, Slam the Big Door, April Evil,* and *One Monday We Killed Them All*) but I considered each of them to be top-notch and one is firmly ensconced in my "Top 10 Favorite Crime Novels of All Time" list (that would be *April Evil*). I've read dozens of J.D.M's short stories and was equally floored by the variety and uniqueness of them. Several of his "slick" stories (those found in *Saturday Evening Post, Collier's*, etc.) could have been expanded into novels. Of course, MacDonald is probably best known for the creation of Travis McGee, a character MacDonald fashioned 21 novels around.

"You Can't Trust a Man" by Helen Nielsen (4000 words)★★★

Years after taking part in a robbery, Crystal Coe has changed her name and married into money. Her real husband, meanwhile, has been rotting in jail for seven years, having taken the fall for Crystal. But, as he tells his wife after he tracks her down, his hands have not been idle in the pen. The story's not new (though it might have been in 1954) but the writing's just dandy:

> *They were a couple of very special jobs—the convertible and the woman. Blonde, streamlined, and plenty of fire power under the hood. The convertible was a later model, at least twenty five years later, but it didn't have any more pick-up and not nearly as much maneuverability in traffic.*
>
> *She came across the parking lot like a stripper, prancing out on the runaway, a healthy, old-fashioned girl who believed that whatsoever the Lord hath cleaved asunder no Parisian designer should join together.*

Helen Nielsen wrote dozens of short stories for *Ellery Queen, The Saint, Mike Shayne,* and *Alfred Hitchcock* magazines (among the 22 stories she wrote for *AHMM* is "Never Trust a Woman," proving that Helen couldn't trust anyone) as well as novels such as *Detour, Obit Delayed, Sing Me a Murder,* and *Borrow the Night*. Several of her stories were adapted for television, including "You Can't Trust a Man" for *Alfred Hitchcock Presents,* starring Polly Bergen as Crystal. The show aired May 9, 1961. The story was selected for the *1955 Best Detective Stories of the Year.*

"May I Come In?" by Fletcher Flora (2000 words)★★★
A man is pushed to the brink by a personal tragedy. Another mini-near-masterpiece by Fletcher Flora, this has a stunning kick in its climax.

"The Blood Oath" by Richard Deming (4000 words)★★★
Manville Moon must protect his beautiful girlfriend, Fausta, from the mafia when they target her for not paying her monthly "tribute." Manville Moon continues to be a solid and fun character.

"Panic" by Grant Colby (1500 words)★★★
A woman riding a streetcar is terrorized by a man with a sickle. Viciously nasty ending. I loved it!

"The Floater" by Jonathan Craig (6000 words)★★★
Lucille Taylor is found dead, floating in the Hudson. Detectives Paul Brader and Jim Coren try to piece together who put her there. Though there's really not much difference in style between this Craig police procedural and his last (or the one before that), there's a good enough story to carry the reader past the "Yes, ma'am's" and "We're just doing our job, sir's" that these stories come equipped with.

"Green Eyes" by Hal Ellson (3500 words)★★
Jim Withers and his wife Kathy are vacationing at an Acapulco resort. Jim begins to suspect that Kathy is stepping out on him with a servant named Juan. This could have been a decent read at half the length but all this story does is recycle the same image of a "white shirted image jumping from the balcony of the Withers room and running into the forest." There's no mystery to what's going on.

"Morning Movie" by Muriel Berns (1000 words)★⅃
Carol hears several juvies talking about a candy store heist while she's waiting for her matinee to begin.

"Epitaph" by Erskine Caldwell (2000 words)★
Amelie has been carrying on an affair with Walter while married to Ray. Now she's pregnant and she's unsure who the father is. *Peyton Place*-esque drivel totally out of place in *Manhunt*.

"The Drifter" by Robert S. Swenson (1500 words)★★★
Joe and Pete are waiting for their ride when a fellow drifter named Manny comes walking up, holding a toad. Manny is a simpleton à la Lenny from *Of Mice and Men*. Pete sadistically stomps on the toad and then tries to get Manny to off himself. Instead, in a scene that would have made Stephen King proud, Manny disembowels Pete:

> *... he stared down at the wound watching the blood flow like a river*

through his fingers.

He began sagging to the ground almost at once and his white shirt and pants were already red with blood. When he had sagged almost to the ground, he dropped suddenly into a sitting position, it was only a foot or so, but he dropped with enough force so that his intestines spilled out into his shirt, and he sat holding his insides and staring at his hands. He was like a man stealing sausage.

1950s splatter. The mind boggles!

"The Death-Ray Gun" by Evan Hunter (15,000 words)★★★

TV producer Cynthia Finch is found burnt to a crisp and the weapon suspected is the Death-Ray Gun used in her hit science fiction show, *The Rocketeers*. But how could a harmless prop be turned into a killing machine? *Rocketeers* head writer Jonathan Crane turns amateur sleuth to get to the bottom of the mystery. Whimsical (albeit violent) change of pace for the usually very straight and sober Evan Hunter is thoroughly enjoyable fluff.

"Kiss Me, Dudley" by Hunt Collins (1500 words)★★★

Evan Hunter's parody of Mickey Spillane has quite a few laughs in its brief word count. Hunter was obviously having a good time at the expense of another writer:

The pulse in her throat began beating wildly. There was a hungry animal look in her eyes. She sucked in a deep breath and ran her hands over her hips, smoothing the apron. I went to her and cupped her chin in the palm of my left hand.

"Baby," I said.

Then I drew back my right fist and hit her on the mouth. She fell back against the sink, and I followed with a quick chop to the gut, and a fast uppercut to the jaw. She went down on the floor and she rolled around in the fish scales, and I thought of my sea captain father, and my mother who was a nice little lass from New England. And then I didn't think of anything but the blonde in my arms, and the .45 in my fist, and the twenty-six men outside, and the four shares of Consolidated I'd bought that afternoon, and the bet I'd made on the fight with One-Lamp Louie, and the defective brake lining on my Olds, and the bottle of rye in the bottom drawer of my file cabinet back at Dudley Sledge, Investigations.

I enjoyed it.

Vol. 3 No. 2 Feb 1955
The first appearance of Sam Merwin, Jr. Cover by "Michael".

"The Revolving Door" by Sam Merwin, Jr. (4000 words)★★
Marty embezzles 50 grand from the mob and has to hide out in a fancy hotel, waiting for a way out of town. Well-written story with a predictable outcome.
This was Sam Merwin, Jr.'s first *Manhunt* appearance (with three more to follow). Son of writer Samuel Merwin, Sam Jr. dabbled in both crime and science fiction. His science fiction included *The House of Many Worlds* (1951) and its followup, *Three Faces of Time* (1955). Crime novels included *Murder in Miniatures* (1940), *Knife in My Back* (1945), *The Creeping Shadow* (1952), and *Killer To Come* (1953). In addition, Merwin was omnipresent in the pulps (just a few of the titles he appeared in: *Detective Novel, Thrilling Adventure, Fifteen Sports Stories, Phantom Detective*). His short story, "The Big Score" (from *Manhunt*, July 1955) was adapted for *Alfred Hitchcock Presents* in 1962.

"Hot" by Evan Hunter (4500 words)★★★
Life aboard a Naval ship in Guantanamo Bay ain't all it's cracked up to be even if you're on the good side of the skipper, which Peters definitely is not. His commander has it out for Peters, but Peters is determined to make him pay.

"Return Engagement" by Frank Kane (8000 words)★
Johnny Liddell is hired by Abel Terrell, a man who believes he murdered someone months before. Problem is, the victim's body turns up and police say the man died within the past few days. Terrell doesn't know what kind of scam is being played but he's pretty sure there's one and he's been the target. So, how did the corpse get a second life (and death)? Johnny knows that the answers to all difficult questions are usually found in a nightclub and the answer usually has something to do with a beautiful girl. The weakest of the Liddells, thus far, is lackluster and lazily written with a lame payoff. Frank Kane adapted his own story for the *Mike Hammer* show (the teleplay was retitled "Death Takes an Encore"), which starred character actor Lou Krugman as Terrell. One of the rare instances where the filmed adaptation is better than the source material.

"The Pigeons" by Hal Ellson (2000 words)★
At a home for boys, Hop is constantly picked on by Al. Hop's only consolation is the pigeon nest next to his window. When Al finds this out, he sabotages Hop's happiness.

"The Competitors" by Richard Deming (4000 words)★★★
Sam and Dave find that business is less than booming at their mortuary. When Dave comes up with the bright idea of buying a combination

hearse/ambulance to branch out, things get a little rosier. That is, until their only competitor, Harry Averill, of Averill's Funeral Home, gets the same idea. That's when Dave comes up with a novel way to drum up more business for the funeral home: murder their riders on the way to the hospital. Dark comedy is absurd at times (well, it would have to be, wouldn't it?) but ultimately entertains. Would have made a great episode of *Alfred Hitchcock Presents*.

"Rendezvous" by James T. Farrell (5000 words)★★↲

Annabelle lives the good life; nice house, rich husband, no job, everything money can buy. But she's not happy. She feels she can find happiness in one night stands. To that end, she contacts an old college acquaintance (the boyfriend who never was), now a big shot newspaper writer living in New York and asks him if they can meet and talk about old times. So they meet and talk, and talk, and talk. A nice enough slice of life story but here comes my "this does not belong in a Detective Story Monthly" speech. I'd like to know how readers at the time reacted to stories in *Manhunt* that had no criminal elements whatsoever (other than imagined adultery).

"Self-Defense" by Harold Q. Masur (5000 words)★★↲

George Richardson fears his adopted son will be kidnapped in the near future so he hires attorney Scott Jordan to handle the ransom drop if the boy is snatched. Sure enough, his son is taken. Better-than-average Jordan tale (the 8th of 9 to appear in *Manhunt*) is almost ruined by its Perry Mason-esque wrap-up wherein Scott tells us all about how the kidnapping went down—even though there's no way he could know this information. Interesting side note: in the Mugged & Printed column this issue, the editors mistakenly title this story "Dead Issue," which is actually the title of the previous Scott Jordan mystery (December 25, 1954).

"Classification: Homicide" by Jonathan Craig (17,500 words)★★

A woman is found stabbed to death on the top of her brownstone apartment in New York. Detectives Walt Logan and Steve Manning catch the case and eventually get to the bottom of the brutal murder.

The first of Jonathan Craig's "Police Files" stories, "Classification: Homicide" tends to get bogged down by Craig's love for technical terms and police lingo and doesn't spend enough time developing characters. I can tell there are some good characters sketched in this novel, but unfortunately they're hinted at rather than fleshed out.

Peter Enfantino • Jeff Vorzimmer

Vol. 3 No. 3 Mar 1955

The page count increases to 160 for several months, peaking at 192 pages in mid-1955. The one and only appearance of Erle Stanley Gardner ("Protection").

"I Didn't See a Thing" by Hal Ellson (4500 words)★★

Dip keeps pigeons and deals with the everyday hip lingo of Hal Ellson. It's a tribute, I guess, to Ellson's grasp of street language that I had no idea that Dip actually raised pigeons until well into the story. I thought we might be discussing drugs or girls but, no, they're birds. Ellson's definitely an acquired taste. He pretty much cornered the market on pigeon noir between this story and "The Pigeons" (from the Feb 1955 issue).

"The Punisher" by Jonathan Craig (5500 words)★★★

Second in the "Police Files" series by Craig is an improvement over the first (see Vol. 3 No. 2). Craig uses a different set of cops to tell the story of a man burned to death in his bed. At first, the thought among the detectives is that the man fell asleep while smoking, but quickly that idea is replaced with homicide. The resolution and identity of the killer is handled well.

"First Case" by David Alexander (3500 words)★★★

Miss Petty takes an unusual interest in the first case of young attorney Winston Knight, Jr. The interest can be traced back to the affair she had had with Winston, Sr. years before. Though there's not much to the story, it's still fairly effective.

"Moonshine" by Gil Brewer (3000 words)★★★★

Jim has a particularly adulterous wife and things have gotten a bit out of hand so Jim does what any loving husband would do: he starts eliminating his competitors. "Moonshine" shows the same kind of skewed world view that infested the novels of Gil Brewer.

Brewer was one of the fabled Gold Medal authors, writing such classics as *A Killer is Loose* (1954), *The Red Scarf* (1958), *The Three Way Split* (1960), and his biggest seller, *13 French Street* (1951). *Manhunt* readers were fortunate enough to visit Gil Brewer's hellish world eleven times over the course of the magazine's life.

"Welcome Home" by G. T. Fleming-Roberts (15,500 words)★★

Norb Bailey returns to his hometown to get to the bottom of the shooting death of his brother. Well-written but could have been told in half the word count.

"The Jury" by Kenneth Fearing (3500 words)★★

Thorndale knows everything about the syndicate's business and now he's to take the stand. That obviously doesn't sit well with the mob and so they make Thorndale an offer he can't refuse.

"The First Fifty Thousand" by Jack Webb (6000 words)★★↓
Airport cops Mace Prouty and Don Wells have their hands full when a woman enters their office to claim her husband took out a fifty thousand dollar life insurance policy and hopped on a plane with a briefcase rigged to blow. On the same day, a mobster that Prouty had run out of town is set to get off a plane at Prouty's airport. Interesting angle to the cop story is soured a bit by that Ring-Ding-Daddy-O lingo that also populated most of Frank Kane's fiction.

It should be noted that, even to this day, many sources erroneously identify *this* Jack Webb, (John *Alfred* Webb, 1916–2008) as *the* Jack Webb (John *Randolph* Webb, 1920–1983) who created and starred in *Dragnet* (Allen J. Hubin, in *Bibliography of Crime Fiction*, gives Webb the author's birthdate as 1920, which is actually the actor's birthdate). According to Webb's bio (published on the inside back cover of Vol. 2 No. 3), the author is "no relation to the Jack Webb who directs and stars in *Dragnet*" (in fact, his portrait actually makes him look more like the late mystery author Ed Gorman!). Jack Webb, the author, wrote many novels in the 1950s starring the crime-solving team of Catholic priest Father Joseph Shanley and Detective-Sergeant Sammy Golden, including *The Broken Doll* (1955),*The Brass Halo* (1957), and *The Deadly Sex* (1959). The bio in *Manhunt* also notes that MGM was about to begin filming a series of Shanley/Golden flicks, but I can find no reference to these films being produced.

"Memento" by Erskine Caldwell (2000 words)★★★↓
When Nellie Stoddard, a wonderful woman from all accounts, passes away suddenly, her husband, a no-good bastard from all accounts, makes a trip down to the county courtroom to attend to some unfinished business. As I've stated before with some of the "high-calibre slick" fiction contributed by Caldwell, there's not a lick of *Manhunt* blood in "Memento." That doesn't make it a bad read, Quite the contrary, it's a fabulously written tale, one that would fit nicely in the pages of *The Saturday Evening Post*.

"Sweet Charlie" by Henry Kane (4500 words)★
Stop me if you've heard this one before: a beautiful, but troubled, woman comes to Peter Chambers' office to hire him as a bodyguard. He consoles her, admires her great figure and accepts the job. She goes home and her body is found there later on. She'd paid Peter a ten thousand dollar retainer and he doesn't believe in free money so he digs into her murder.

"Incident in August" by G. H. Williams (2000 words)★★↓
Poor Mal is about to be strung up by some country hicks for a crime he didn't commit. Author Williams pulls no punches in his climax. *The Ox-Bow Incident* meets *Manhunt* noir.

Peter Enfantino • Jeff Vorzimmer

Vol. 3 No. 4 Apr 1955
The first and only appearances of Ira Levin ("Sylvia") and Rex Stout ("His Own Hand").

"Blood Brothers" by Hal Ellson (8000 words)★★★↵

The escalation of a J.D. named Speed from simple punk to accessory to murder is a tense, tough read. Ellson's staccato, jumpin'-jive style of writing can be off-putting and hard to circumnavigate at times (*Pops is up now. Got the strap in his hand. His eyes is red. I've been fighting again. That's what he figures.*) but there's a gripping tale hidden behind the gimmicky delivery. Ellson manages to concoct characters that seem very *real* despite a lack of much detail in the background.

"The Movers" by Bryce Walton (3000 words)★↵

Hiney rises from one of his benders and can't find his wife. A tedious short that's capped off with an effective but out-of-left-field reveal.

"The Day It Began Again" by Fletcher Flora (2500 words)★★↵

Our nameless narrator describes a day visiting his friend, Carlos, in prison and how worried he is that Carlos will remain there the rest of his life. Carlos's crime, which isn't explained until the closing paragraphs, is strangling women but it's just not that simple. After visiting his friend's attorney, the story-teller explains, there's only one way to exonerate Carlos. Though the build-up is slow and purposely ambiguous, the pay-off is an unexpected and effective twist.

"His Own Hand" by Rex Stout (4500 words)★★

Actor Adam Nicoll (who has immortalized the character of Kevin Kay on TV) is dead and the police suspect foul play. So, the first man they question is disbarred lawyer/private dick Alfred "Alphabet" Hicks, who had been keeping company lately with Nicoll and some of his acting acquaintances. The cops want insights into the actor and possibly a motive for the crime but Hicks keeps his theories close to the vest until he can get the actor's "friends" in a room together and sweat them. The murderer, Hicks believes, is amongst them.

Ironic that much of the drama in "His Own Hand" revolves around a play Nicoll is due to launch, since the story itself is much like a two-set stage play. Unfortunately, the murder and mystery is not allowed time to "breathe" before we arrive at the obligatory Christie-esque climax. "Alphabet" Hicks suffered a short career, no doubt due to the fact that his creator, Rex Stout, had bigger fish to fry with the massively popular Nero Wolfe mysteries. Hicks only appeared in one novel (*Alphabet Hicks*, published by Farrar & Rinehart in 1941), the events of which are mentioned by Hicks in the opening paragraphs, and this one story. His nickname (not even explained here) is due to the long nonsensical listing of letters after his name on his business card. This was Stout's only appearance in *Manhunt*.

"Mug Shot" by George Bagby (20,500 words)★★

The tireless Inspector Schmidt (Schmitty to his friend and chronicler George Bagby) finds himself the center of his latest investigation when he is mugged and assaulted by a hophead on the street one night. When Schmidt and Bagby follow the clues, they lead to the wealthy and attractive Beryl Tucker and the shady men she keeps time with. There are a lot of words here but not a lot of excitement, unfortunately, as the same details seem to be pored over endlessly. This was the first appearance of Bagby's Schmidt in the pages of *Manhunt*, but the author had seen his work find favor with the editor under the name, Hampton Stone ("The Man Who Had Too Much to Lose" in the November 1954 issue) and would also place fiction in *MH* under his real name, Aaron Marc Stein. Inspector Schmidt was the hero of over fifty novels, beginning with *Murder at the Piano* in 1935, and will return to *Manhunt* one more time in October 1957.

"The General Slept Here" by Sam S. Taylor (7500 words)★★⌐

P.I. Neal Cotten is hired by the lovely Vivian Lindsay to find the woman's long-lost aunt, Eunice Sigsbee. Cotten questions a former neighbor of Sigsbee's but when the private dick makes a return visit to the man's apartment, he discovers him dead. The same fate befalls the poor Ms. Sigsbee when Cotten finally tracks her down. Why is a kindly old woman murdered and what did she have to do with a payroll heist the year before?

The *Manhunt* debut (and only appearance) of Sam. S. Taylor's Neal Cotten, who previously had appeared in three novels written by Taylor: *Sleep No More* (Dutton, 1949); *No Head for Her Pillow* (Dutton, 1952); and *So Cold My Bed* (Dutton, 1953). "The General Slept Here" is a genuinely enjoyable, if predictable, thriller containing a very likable lead character who mouths humorous one-liners and observations (*He finally managed to say, "you… dirty little—" The rest was blue-pencilled by eternity*) that actually *are* funny. This was Taylor's swan song for *Manhunt* and, aside from a short story appearance in *The Saint Mystery Magazine* and a pseudonymous novel for Gold Medal (*Brenda*, as by Lehi Zane, 1952), Taylor seems to have dropped out entirely from the writing business soon after.

"Sylvia" by Ira Levin (3500 words)★★★

Sylvia's father is only looking out for his little girl's interests when he pays off the gigolo Sylvia has married and forbade her to see him. But, after all, Sylvia is 33-years-old and should be able to make her own decisions and mistakes so she writes her love a letter and begs him to meet with her. When papa finds a gun in Sylvia's desk drawer he jumps to conclusions. Could his sweet daughter commit murder? Perhaps but perhaps not in the way papa thinks.

Just as the name Robert Bloch was inescapably followed by the four words "the author of *Psycho*," so will Ira Levin forever be known as "the author of *Rosemary's Baby*." Most readers are unaware that Levin had any kind of career prior to his devilish mega-seller, but in fact Levin wrote one of the greatest crime novels of the 1950s, *A Kiss Before Dying* (1953). Winner of the Mystery Writers of

America award for Best First Mystery of the Year, Levin's novel of an intelligent, scheming psychopath invades territory frequented by David Goodis, Jim Thompson, and Shane Stevens. Filmed in 1956, with Robert Wagner and then later remade in 1991, starring Matt Dillon.

After *Rosemary's Baby*'s huge success, Levin turned the small town paranoia of *The Stepford Wives* into another bestseller, before returning to crime fiction with *Deathtrap* (1976), which became one of the longest-running plays of all time. His other bestsellers include *The Boys From Brazil* (1976), *Sliver* (1991), and the sequel to *Rosemary's Baby*, *Son of Rosemary* (1997). "Sylvia" was dramatized on *Alfred Hitchcock Presents* during its third season

"The Imposters" by Jonathan Craig (1000 words)★★

A man wakes up one morning, realizes his wife is aging and believes her body has been taken over by an impersonator. He murders her, convinced he's freeing his "real" wife from her captivity.

Vol. 3 No. 5 May 1955
The first of eight consecutive covers by Robert Maguire.

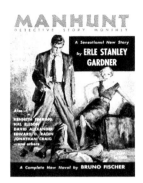

"Wrong Way Home" by Hal Ellson (3000 words)★↲

The very short saga of J.D.s Chiller, Knife, and Bomber and their gang-related violent actions. As with most Hal Ellson short stories, "Wrong Way Home" is filled with J.D. lingo and staccato sentencing and, as with most Ellson stories, the whole feels like a vignette within a novel about 1950s street life. Unfortunately, the eight pages here do not constitute a satisfying reading experience.

"I'll Never Tell" by Bryce Walton (4000 words)★★↲

Anna's been stepping out on Glenn with Igor, the farmer down the road, but Glenn's stayed quiet for the most part. One day, when Anna brings Igor home for dinner, Glenn has had enough. A tough and violent little adultery story, with a satisfactory twist in its tail. The title refers to the mute narrator, a farm aide who witnesses and profits from the carnage.

Bryce Walton was one of those rare writers who managed to survive on a steady diet of short story sales, be they western, science fiction, or crime, and a few TV scripts. Walton was a regular contributor to *Ellery Queen, Alfred Hitchcock,* and *Mike Shayne.*

"Mama's Boy" by David Alexander (6000 words)★★★

Crowley is a muscle-bound sociopath who loves to ogle himself in the mirror while daydreaming about beating women. With the rent due, Crowley hits the Village with older marks in mind and an itching to do more damage than he's ever done before. At no time does this relentless peek inside the mind of a misogynistic psycho look away from its brutal violence but, rather, holds it up proudly in front of the reader. That's not a slam on David Alexander though, who perfectly captures Crowley's insanity through his thoughts:

> *Oh, sweet Jesus, this is good, thought Crowley. She's the one. She's the one I've been waiting for all my life. I'm going to kill you with my fists, Katie. I'm going to show you how a real man kills. He doesn't need a gun. I'm going to smash and break and keep on pounding until you're dead.*

"Shake-Up" by Kenneth Fearing (4500 words)★★★

Stenner and Frolich discover a pair of their fellow detectives are dealing in stolen goods and committing murder to hide their tracks. As Stenner and Frolich see it, the only way to make this situation right is to take the bad cops out.

Kenneth Fearing's second and final *Manhunt* story, "Shake-Up" is an intricately plotted (if a bit unbelievable with some of its coincidences) thriller complete with car chases and a bang-bang finale. Fearing was acclaimed for his poetry but is, perhaps, best known to crime aficionados as the author of *The Big Clock* (Harcourt, 1946), basis for the classic film of the same name starring Ray Milland (and later remade as *No Way Out* with Kevin Costner and Gene Hackman).

"Tex" by John Jakes (3000 words)★★↙

Dishonorably discharged from the Army, "Tex" is wandering, a powder keg ready to blow and today might be the day. Though he would go on to pump out best sellers (*North and South*, The Kent Family Chronicles), writer John Jakes cut his writing teeth on the crime digests of the 1950s and 1960s, contributing two short stories to *Manhunt* and several more to the likes of *Terror Detective*, *Mike Shayne*, *The Saint*, and *Guilty*. "Tex" is suspenseful but feels incomplete, as though it was a small part of a bigger project.

"I'll Get Even" by Michael Zuroy (2000 words)★↙

Sam is tiring of the bully next door but he can't find the nerve to deal with it. So he considers murder… over and over again.

"We are All Dead" by Bruno Fischer (11,500 words)★★★

The payroll heist went off without a hitch until one of the guards ventilated Wally Gordon, leaving Wally on the edge of death. To avoid capture and the reveal of their identities, the rest of the crew had no choice but to finish the job. Oscar, Georgie, Tiny, Johnny, and Stella now each have a bigger piece of the pie. That is, until Wally's widow shows up, demanding her slice. Oscar manages to talk the girl into becoming his moll, so drama is avoided but then, after a dinner party, the entire crew gets deathly sick from food poisoning (in fact, Georgie succumbs from the foul chopped liver) and the thought occurs to Johnny that Wally's widow might not have gotten over his death just yet.

"We Are All Dead" is a fabulous caper "novel," but without most of the caper novel trappings. For one thing, the story begins in mid-robbery; we get no long descriptions of how the heist will go down or unnecessary character background. Fischer fills us in on what we need to know as the tale progresses. The finale is a nice (if overly expository) twist and double-twist that satisfactorily answers the question of who's knocking off the crew.

"Protection" by Erle Stanley Gardner (4000 words)★★↙

A life of crime and a prison stretch in the rear-view mirror, George Ollie reinvents himself as the owner of a successful diner. Engaged to his head waitress, Stella, life is looking pretty darn good. Or it looks that way until Larry, one of Ollie's former crew comes calling, putting pressure on George to cut him in on the profits from the diner. This con has some info on a job Ollie pulled years before, a bank robbery with fatalities, that the cops know nothing about. Turns out that maybe Stella has a history as well. A very good thriller with a nice change of pace climax; turns out that some of these hardboiled dames have more backbone than their men.

"Hold Out" by Jack Ritchie (1000 words)★★

Pete Harder's been kidnapped by two thugs out to blackmail Pete's boss. They want fifty large to give Pete back to the boss. But the scenario might not be as simple as it seems.

"The Lady in Question" by Jonathan Craig (8000 words)★★

Third in the "Police Files" series, with Steve Manning and Walt Logan returning after a one-story hiatus. The detectives must investigate the death of singer Bonnie Nichols, a woman who had no shortage of beaus. "The Lady in Question" sees the series evolving (for this episode at least) into more of a *Dragnet*-type format. What will strike the reader funny is how many times, in this series, these cops are heading out for something to eat or drink. There's also some good "beat" dialogue from one of the chief suspects: "*I cut her off cold after I met Bonnie. She flipped forty ways from the middle.*"

"The Goldfish" by Roy Carroll (3000 words)★★★

Night club owner/bad guy Joey Manisetti has never forgiven Dolores for running out on him but when he discovers she's shacking up with his business manager, Maxie, Joey swears he'll treat her better. Well, what's Maxie to do?

"El Rey" by William Logan (1000 words)★★⸝

After climbing the treacherous El Rey, two lifelong friends discover they've forgotten to bring a marker to prove they've reached the top. "No problem," says one man, "I know the perfect marker!" A short-short with a very humorous twist.

Peter Enfantino • Jeff Vorzimmer

Vol. 3 No. 6 Jun 1955
A 192-page issue. Cover by Robert Maguire.

"The Reluctant Client" by Brett Halliday (3500 words)★★
Mike Shayne gets a call from a terrified Mrs. Laura Jensen, who insists her jealous husband is going to kill her for the affairs he's conjured up in his head. Laura begs Mike to come to her beach house but, when Shayne arrives, the woman decides it was a bad idea and Shayne should leave. As the dick is leaving, he hears a gunshot and races back into the house, finding Laura Jensen with a bullet hole smack dab in the middle of her forehead. But was it her jealous hubby who ventilated her?

Mike Shayne is a guilty pleasure (like Shell Scott and Johnny Liddell) but I find the shorter cases much less satisfying. The action just starts kicking in and it's time to turn out the lights. Also, the usual P.I. tropes are evident: Shayne never thinks to call the cops before he heads for Laura's place even though he, himself, had urged her to do the same; and every gumshoe has to have his disbelieving cop and Shayne has his Sgt. Peter Painter, who automatically assumes Mike has offed the gorgeous dame lying on the rug.

"Interrogation" by Jack Ritchie (2500 words)★★★
Two detectives question a man for stealing lingerie from a clothes line but they suspect the guy's been up to nastier things with little girls. Jack Ritchie is one of those crime writers who can take a simple idea and turn it into a complex and substantive short story. Here. the two detectives let their Q&A devolve into something sinister and dangerous.

"Body Snatcher" by George Bagby (2000 words)★★
To keep up with the other women in the neighborhood, Yolanda has created a phony husband named Harry, who's on a stint in Korea. When the Korean War comes to an end, Yolanda finds she'll have to either live with egg on her face or find a Harry. A corpse in the river with a tattoo reading "Yolanda" tilts her decision.

"Code 197" by Richard S. Prather (5500 words)★★
Shell Scott finds himself dodging bullets and evading danger when one of his friends, writer Jim Brandon, is murdered just after finishing his scorching exposé on communists in America. Evidently, the Commies figure Brandon told Scott what (and who) was in his manuscript and they attempt to tie up all loose ends. Some of the Shell Scott adventures can come off very dated and "Code 197" (which refers to the Penal Code definition of self-defense) is one of those stories. There are still enough eccentricities to keep a reader's interest (the opening action sequence, set in a pet store, is really quite exciting) but the wrap-up is a letdown.

"Decoy" by Hal Ellson (1500 words)★

Another of Hal Ellison's vignettes about street kids and the mischief they get up to, with the requisite staccato "beat" lingo (*I'm looking for Woody. He's a wino from way back. I got use for him. He ain't around. I don't see him in the cellar. He ain't laying in the yard. I go to the alley where the bums sleep. He ain't to be seen.*).

"The Careful Man" by Max Franklin (17,000 words)★★★

Sam has a great scam going: he and his "sister" Mavis move from town to town setting up women. He scours the want ads for lonely women, determining if they have enough (but not too much, to avoid scrutiny) money to tide him over, marries, and then dispatches them soon after. With the help of Mavis, he makes thousands until he meets up with Helen, a shy, matronly farm girl who Sam quickly falls in love with. A good solid read, but the reader will see the payoff coming about halfway through the story.

"The Makeshift Martini" by Jack Webb (5000 words)★★

Wells and Prouty, airport cops, have a dead blonde on their hands. Further, it turns out the woman was poisoned. But with an airport full of travelers, how does the pair whittle down the suspects? Other than the terminal background as a gimmick, the "Airport Detail" series is nothing more than another 87th Precinct clone.

"The Dead Grin" by Frank Kane (1500 words)★★↲

Johnny Liddell is asked by an insurance company to investigate a fatal shooting. Was it an accident or was it murder? No one can fool Johnny Liddell. Quite a bit shorter than the usual Liddell but this one's very enjoyable and has a nice twist in its final paragraphs.

"Everybody's Watching Me" by Mickey Spillane
(Reprint of the entire story. See Vol. 1 No. 1)

"The Vicious Young" by Pat Stadley (1000 words)★★↲

A nasty short-short about a woman terrorized in a diner by a group of young thugs.

Vol. 3 No. 7 Jul 1955
First appearance of Davis Dresser, writing as Brett Halliday. Cover by Robert Maguire.

"See Him Die" by Evan Hunter (5000 words)★★★
A gang converges on a high rise apartment to watch the police battle a trapped killer in an apartment across the alley.

"Solitary" by Jack Ritchie (2500 words)★★★★
An ex-con floats between reality and the fantasy he concocted while in solitary confinement.

"The Baby-Sitter" by Jonathan Craig (6000 words)★★
Fourth entry in Craig's "Police Files" series is more of the same. In this episode, Steve Manning and Walt Logan investigate the strangulation of Doris Linder, part-time babysitter, part-time teen-age trollop. Seems Doris babysits middle-aged men as well and one of them might have killed her to keep her quiet about her impending motherhood. Still nothing but cookie-cutter writing: the cops catch a murder, they interview suspects, they favor the most likely suspect, and the perpetrator turns out to be the guy the reader suspects all along. Either these are cops who have no life outside the badge or Craig chose not to dwell on that aspect of a continuing series. But by ignoring the background, these characters stay one-dimensional.

"Scarecrow" by David Alexander (4000 words)★★
When Andy Tevis comes tearing into town, exclaiming that surly ol' Jeff Purdy done fell into the Winding River, Sheriff Estes and his deputy head up to interview Jeff's widow, Martha. After suffering abuse from her husband for twenty years, could Martha have pushed Jeff over the cliff into the Winding River? And what about that misshapen scarecrow up on the cliff? Could that have something to do with Jeff's "accident?"

"The Watch" by Wally Hunter (1000 words)★★★
A creepy short-short à la *The Bad Seed*.

"Juvenile Delinquent" by Richard Deming (20,500 words)★↲
When his "foster nephew" is arrested for murdering a fellow gang member, Manville Moon hits the street to find out what really happened. Moon discovers that the J.D. gangs are now backed by the mob and the gangsters are peeved that a private dick is sniffing around in their affairs. In the end, it's not the mob at all but, coincidentally, one of Moon's old flames who's been working a welfare scam for extra dough.
The worst of the five Manville Moon stories to appear in *Manhunt*, "Juvenile Delinquent" is a bloated and boring waste of space and time, redeemed only by a brief but exciting action scene in its midsection, where Moon must use his wits to

get himself out of a basement filled with hopped-up J.D.s. The finale, with its contrived and unbelievable climax, is good for a few chuckles but nothing more.

"The Big Score" by Sam Merwin, Jr. (7000 words)★★★★

A quartet of over-achieving teen punks rips off and murders an old man in his own home, ignorant of the fact that he was mob-connected. "The Big Score" resembles Merwin's first *Manhunt* story ("The Revolving Door" in Feb 1955) in that it involves the mob but contains much more unscripted dialogue and page-turning suspense. A fabulously tense drama, with four well-delineated characters and compelling twists and turns.

The story remained, for the most part, the same when adapted by mystery writer Bryce Walton for the seventh season of *Alfred Hitchcock Presents*, but the TV drama doesn't have the same impact due to some sub-par acting by the actors playing the J.D.s.

"You Can't Kill Her" by C. B. Gilford (4000 words)★⌐

The bottle means more to Van than his wife, Sarah, and whenever he gets liquored up, Sarah receives a nasty beating. Their handyman, Jassie, knows Sarah's about to boil over and use that shotgun on Van, so he handles things himself. Tedious backwoods drama.

"The Death of Arney Vincent" by C. L. Sweeney, Jr. (2000 words)★★⌐

Arney Vincent needs a new face after his latest bank heist so he goes to the Michelangelo of the plastic surgery industry and is very happy with the outcome. The doc has another idea how to make a quick ten Gs and Arney's listening. "The Death of Arney Vincent" is a very compact thriller, with a surprising (if a bit far-fetched) climax, that might actually benefit from its brevity.

Peter Enfantino • Jeff Vorzimmer

Vol. 3 No. 8 Aug 1955
Page count is reduced to 144 pages. Cover by Robert Maguire.

"Red Hands" by Bryce Walton (4000 words)★★
The local hoods always made fun of "Red Hands," a brutish man-child who earned his nickname by nearly killing two men with his bare hands. Ed finds a way to profit on the half-wit but the plan backfires.

"The Happy Marriage" by Richard Deming (4000 words)★★★
When George finds a piano wire stretched across the top of his staircase, he becomes convinced his wife, Nora, and his best friend, Tom, are out to kill him. His suspicions are confirmed when he tapes the two making plans for an encore assassination attempt. But, rather than go to the police, George plans an elaborate scheme to rid himself of Tom but keep the wife in her place. Almost everything goes as planned. An amiable tale with a very satisfying twist in its final paragraph.

"Make It Neat" by Frank Kane (5000 words)★★
Judge Carter is murdered in his study and the gunman is spotted by the judge's wife as he makes an exit. After the woman IDs the killer down at the precinct, she herself is shot down on the building's steps. Weeks later, Johnny Liddell is called in by Citizen's Committee to look into why the police have been dragging their feet. No surprise, Liddell discovers the police department is headed by a rotten apple. Good set-up is marred by a hurried finale and unsatisfying answers.

"Pass the Word" by Jack Sword (3000 words)★
Luke Caron has a worry-free strategy to smuggle 25 pounds of heroin in from Mexico and he's sure the mafia will want to hear his plan. He's right but the deal goes wrong. Subtitled "A Casebook Story," Jack Sword's gimmick is that the crime, and its aftermath, is told though a series of statements by participants and witnesses but the bits don't add up to a cohesive (or interesting) whole.

"Shot in the Dark" by Craig Rice (9000 words)★⌿
Manhunt's favorite lawyer/wanna-be P.I. John J. Malone is parked with his love, Dolly Dove, when a shot rings out and a man stumbles through some bushes. Upon further investigation, Malone discovers a female corpse, ventilated five times. The body in question belongs to one Violet Castleberry, a very well-to-do matron with a yen for expensive jewelry. Who stands to gain from Violet's murder? Her best friend, Avin? Her step-daughter, Olive, next in line for the family fortune? Or is it the poultry man down the street? After an interminably long time, we get our answer in a silly expository near the rushed climax. "Shot in the Dark," like the worst P.I. fiction of the 1950s is cluttered with inane one-liners and situation comedy straight out of a B-film.

"Nudists Die Naked" by Richard S. Prather (21,000)★↲
Shell Scott is approached by a woman who believes she's been targeted for murder. To his horror, Shell soon discovers the dame lives in a nudist camp and for the dick to go undercover, he'll have to take off more than just his gun. An interminably long and unfunny Scott episode packed with lame one-liners (...*never in my life had I seen so many naked women all at once. I didn't mind though: I'm broad-minded.*) and a sense that Prather (who could do so much better) was cruising with this one. Later expanded into the Scott novel, *Strip For Murder* (Gold Medal, 1956)

"Try It My Way" by Jack Ritchie (2000 words)★★★
A tense prison stand-off ends with a surprising climax.

Vol. 3 No. 9 Sep 1955
First appearance of Richard Deming's series character Clancy Ross.

"Uncle Tom" by David Alexander (5000 words)★★
A tale of race relations in the deep south, narrated by an African-American boy facing integration and a cloudy future.

"Cast Off" by Jonathan Craig (4000 words)★★
Steve Manning and Walt Logan investigate the bludgeoning death of an antique dealer. Was the murderer his mistress or the rival antique dealer who wanted to buy him out? The fifth episode of the *Dragnet* clone offers little in the way of action or plot.

"The Big Day" by Richard Marsten (5500 words)★★★★
Three men plan the perfect bank robbery. Staking out the building for weeks, they track the employees' movements daily to the minute. It's the perfect caper. Until it isn't. As in most heist stories, "The Big Day" for Carl, Anson, and Jeremy unravels due to the tiniest unplanned incidents. As with most stories written by Evan Hunter, the minutiae is detailed (but never boring) and captivating; though no background is given for the three masterminds, all three are engaging characters.

"Pickup" by Hal Ellson (2000 words)★
A rare non-J.D. tale by Hal Ellson about a man who becomes obsessed with a young girl who hangs out at a candy store. Though it's thankfully void of Ellson's J.D.-lingo, the story is, nonetheless, equally annoying due to its monotony.

"Side Street" by James T. Farrell (1500 words)★★
Tommy Brandon waits outside the apartment he and his girlfriend live in as she has an abortion inside.

"The Muscle" by Philip Weck (1800 words)★★⁄
A short-order cook eyes the three goons who have walked into his diner and ponders who in the restaurant they've come for. The answer is very predictable.

"The War" by Richard Deming (10,000 words)★★★⁄
Gambling entrepreneur/playboy Clancy Ross is visited at his nightclub/casino, The Club Rotunda by Janice Talbot, the wife of his close war buddy, Jim. Janice explains that Jim witnessed a mob murder committed by mafia big-wig Bix Lawson and was, himself, murdered in their apartment only a week before. Now the mafia has pinned Jim's murder on Janice and fronted money for her bail, with an eye on killing the girl and framing it as a suicide.

Clancy Ross might be a cut-throat businessman but no one, not even the mob, messes with his best friends. After one of Lawson's bent cops threatens Clancy (and leaves the casino with a busted nose), it's all-out war that climaxes with thrown grenades and a truly surprising twist.

"The War" is our first look at the charismatic Clancy Ross, who holes up in the third-floor office of The Rotunda like a slightly-darker version of Bruce Wayne, using his vast wealth and cunning to right wrongs. The most interesting aspect of Ross is that Deming avoids the usual traps of the P.I. story by giving Ross a different vocation (but with the hardboiled sentiment of a P.I.) and, as we discover in the end, a mean disposition. Ross will appear five more times in *Manhunt* and get the full-length treatment with *She'll Hate Me Tomorrow* (Monarch, 1963).

"Flight to Nowhere" by Charles Williams (20,500 words)★★★

A boat, the *Freya*, is found drifting in the Gulf of Mexico, unmanned. The only clue left aboard is the captain's journal. It tells the story of professional scuba diver Bill Manning and his meeting with the beautiful blonde, Shannon Macauley. The woman hires Manning to recover an antique shotgun from the bottom of the lake. When Manning finds the weapon, his suspicions are aroused when he notices that the gun has been in the water only a few hours. Turns out the woman is looking for a diver to help her and her husband retrieve millions in diamonds from a downed plane in the Gulf of Mexico.

When a band of thugs turns up looking for the same plane and Mr. Macauley ends up a corpse, Manning starts questioning the honesty of the beautiful blonde. This leads to an exciting climax when the thugs force Manning to pilot his boat to the supposed crash site.

Though there's a solid plot in here that keeps you turning the pages, I couldn't help the feeling that this was a Reader's Digest Condensed novel. That's really not far off the mark since "Flight to Nowhere" was expanded and released in hardcover by MacMillan the same year as *Scorpion Reef*. The following year, Dell paperbacks released it with a beautiful Robert Maguire cover as *Gulf Coast Girl*. "Flight to Nowhere" seems rushed. Passages are missing, action scrimped on (though its downbeat ending retains the power of its big brother). Think of it as a warm-up to the main event, the novel, *Scorpion Reef*. Much like a short feature that's sculpted into a major film.

There's still a lot of good writing here, as the memorable final passage in Manning's journal shows:

> *"... that last, haunting flash of silver, gesturing as it died. It was beckoning.*
> *Toward the rapture. The rapture..."*

Peter Enfantino • Jeff Vorzimmer

Vol. 3 No. 10 Oct 1955
First appearance of Stephen Marlowe.

"The Spoilers" by Jonathan Craig (7000 words)★
Mel Traynor has his head caved in with a camera and there's no shortage of suspects. Could it be the teenage girlfriend? The jealous wife? The wife's boyfriend? Steve and Walt try to run the various suspects through the strainer (as they do in every entry of the "Police Files" series) and see what happens. Craig continues his formulaic series with wearying results. The *Dragnet*-style chitchat (Manning repeats his "It would be easier if I asked the questions" mantra to suspects in every PF story), the rote, mechanical writing and plot, and the interchangeable cast of suspects. I'll repeat—a little characterization never hurt *any* story. After six episodes, you'd think a *Manhunt* editor would raise the issue with Craig.

"Field of Honor" by Robert Turner (2000 words)★★★
Robert Turner ventures into Evan Hunter country in this J.D. tale of two rival girl gangs, highlighted by a bloody showdown. The story's a good one, told at a fast pace, but a bit too preachy at times for my taste. When it comes to giving sermons, Hunter can hit the ball out of the park, Turner can't.

"In Memory of Judith Courtwright" by Erskine Caldwell (3000 words)★★
Why did 18-year-old Merle Randolph kill himself with his father's shotgun, and what does it have to do with school teacher Judith Courtwright? It's a slice of Southern life told the Erskine Caldwell style but, this time, the author doesn't have anything new to say.

"I Saw Her Die" by Gil Brewer (2500 words)★★↲
Hewitt claims he saw the brutal killing of a woman in a new development of homes but more importantly the killer saw him. Two detectives take him out to the site but there's no body or even a sign of violence. But Hewitt saw *something*.

"Blonde at the Wheel" by Stephen Marlowe (5500 words)★★★
Fred wakes up in the passenger seat of a convertible driven by a beauty named Petey. How did he get there? No idea. Fred has a rare form of amnesia that strikes with no warning and can last for days. The blonde at the wheel isn't as alarming as the dried blood on his Polo. The blood, the girl explains, came from some kind of a fight the night before, a tangle she has no info about other than from the limited mutterings of an amnesiac. Fred insists they turn the Buick around so that he can face the music but, after stopping at a roadside cafe and reading the headlines of the morning paper, Fred doesn't know what to do. Did he murder the wealthy Fred Pearson at the Buena Vista Motel? Is it only coincidence that this dive is where Petey has a room? And why does Petey have a man's suit in her closet?

Those questions and more will *not* be answered by Stephen Marlowe in the maddeningly ambiguous climax. Well, maddening for some but not for *this* reader. Sometimes the best mystery is the one unsolved. Marlowe keeps the pace at breakneck speed, constantly teasing us with clues that might be answers but sometimes end in dead ends and crisp dialogue between the frightened Fred and the seemingly-golden-hearted Petey.

"Tell Them Nothing" by Hal Ellson (8000 words)★★
The dynamic of a street gang changes when one of the J.D.s finds a gun. Suddenly, he's a big man on the street. The tense situations and interplay between the four youths is lost within the usual Hal Ellson staccato and silly street lingo.

"The Hunter" by John A. Sentry (2000 words)★★⌐
A serial rapist sits in a bar sizing up his next "conquest," not realizing he's about to meet his match.

"A Stranger in Town" by Brett Halliday (19,000 words)★★⌐
Just finished with a case and heading back to Miami, Michael Shayne stops in a roadside bar in Brockton for a well-deserved drink. His placidity is interrupted when a gorgeous gal stumbles into the bar and whispers "I'm sorry" to him just as three goons lay into him. Beaten unconscious, Shayne just misses becoming Brockton's latest hit-and-run with a well-placed knee. The private eye manages to escape, with one goon left behind as roadkill, but the big question is: why is Mike Shayne the target of this attack?

As Shayne digs deeper, he discovers the town has a dirty little secret, something hidden deep in the walls of the sanitarium located on the outskirts of Brockton. Thoroughly engaging despite the padding (Halliday tends to repeat himself quite a bit) and a contrived finale. "A Stranger in Town" was expanded into the novel of the same name and published by Dell in 1961.

Vol. 3 No. 11 Nov 1955
First and only appearance by W. R. Burnett ("Vanishing Act"). Cover by Robert Maguire.

"Big Frank" by Bryce Walton (4500 words)★★
Big Frank Connel is a traveling salesman who has a side job when he can pull it off: strangling female hitch-hikers and burying their bodies along the roadside. But Frank gets sloppy and the latest hitcher is standing on the road for a reason.

"I'll Do Anything" by Charles Beaumont (3500 words)★★
If Julio wants to join the Aces, he'll have to stick a switch-blade into a man who disrespected the Aces' leader. No one in the group believes Julio has the stones to commit murder but he may just surprise them yet.
Known primarily for his fantasy and science fiction, Charles Beaumont was known to dabble in the mystery field a time or two as well. He is, of course, famous for his *Twilight Zone* teleplays and the circle of equally famous writer friends (Richard Matheson, Robert Bloch, William F. Nolan, and Ray Bradbury, to name a few) he traveled with.

"Time to Kill" by Richard Marsten (10,000 words)★★
Hal Thompson has had enough of the Navy and so, while on a mountain-climbing excursion in a small village in Japan, the sailor deserts and takes refuge in a house owned by a kindly old man, his wife, and their attractive daughter. Thompson convinces the trio he's surveying a local volcano and manages to evade the ensuing search party. Thompson falls for the lovely young Nara but danger rears its head when he discovers that the old man plans on blowing up the destroyer anchored in the harbor.
A very average adventure redeemed only by a (literally) explosive finale, "Time to Kill" has the feel of a condensed novel; it's rushed and lacking in characterization. The 13th (and final) Marsten story to spear in *Manhunt*.

"Fat Boy" by Hal Ellson (3000 words)★
Character study of Ronald, a bullied obese boy and his day at the beach with "friends." I'm not sure what the point of this story was other than to inflict nastiness upon this mentally and physically challenged teenager. The climax, where Ronald heads to the house of one of the girls in his group, with murder on his mind, seems tacked on in order to be picked up by the editor of *Manhunt*.

"Vanishing Act" by W. R. Burnett (8000 words)★✓
Ex-police reporter Bob Stuart runs into taxi driver Lou Jacks, who tells the man a strange story about Dan Polling, a mob lawyer he gave a ride to recently. Something just wasn't right about the man's demeanor and it doesn't sit well with Lou. With a bit of prodding, Bob goes to the man's apartment with Lou, and the

lawyer's wife answers the door. She has no idea where her husband is and this intrigues Bob enough to agree to investigate. The next morning, the police arrive and haul Bob off to the precinct. Eventually, after much interrogation, Bob learns that Lou is dead and the Pollings have disappeared.

A very long and arduous read, "Vanishing Act" is like one of those 1940s bottom-billed crime movies with smart-alecky Bob and the tough-but-fair lieutenant who doesn't actually believe for a moment that Bob is responsible for Lou's murder but puts on a charade anyway. The climax is the obligatory expository (something about an armored truck heist years before) and showdown between Bob and the bad guys.

"Woman Hater" by Sam Merwin, Jr. (5000 words)★★★

Captain Mike Conway is called to the Grand Plaza to hush up a killing. Seems local boy made good Lyon Wister (nee Willy Lyons) has beaten a man to death in his hotel room and that won't look good on the front page of *Variety*. Wister is the hottest star in Hollywood, so his PR man asks Mike to haul the body away and forget he ever saw it in the room. Since it looks like the dead guy was pilfering Wister's room, Mike agrees but something picks at his brain. When the dead man's wife turns up missing, Conway digs deep into Lyon Wister's background and discovers that delivering beatings is number one on Lyon's list of hobbies. Gripping with a great hardboiled lead character and a climax that delivers.

"The Trap" by Robert Turner (1000 words)★★

Two teen hoods attempt to rob a gas station but the manager is waiting for them.

"The Man Between" by Jonathan Craig (10,000 words)★★

Detective Steve Manning investigates the murder of a sporting goods manager and discovers there's no shortage of suspects. The seventh installment in Craig's "Police Files" series, "The Man Between" is no better or worse than the previous six; the pacing and dialogue remind one of a mediocre 1950s detective TV show.

"Low Tide" by Cole Price (1500 words)★★★

Harry discovers that his business partner, Chuck, is sleeping with Harry's wife. Harry concocts a revenge plan but, too late, learns that his wife is one step ahead of him. For such a short story, "Low Tide" is enthralling and ends with a nice kick in the teeth.

Peter Enfantino • Jeff Vorzimmer

Vol. 3 No. 12 Dec 1955
Cover by Robert Maguire.

"First Offense" by Evan Hunter (5500 words)★★★
A cocky teen faces his first police line-up and becomes less self-assured as the process unfolds. One of two 1955 *Manhunt* stories selected by David C. Cooke for *Best Detective Stories of the Year* (Dutton, 1956), "First Offense" was effectively filmed as "Number Twenty-Two" for the second season of *Alfred Hitchcock Presents* (airing February 17, 1957). Directed by Robert Stevens (who would helm over 40 AHP episodes), the show starred a very young and charismatic Rip Torn as Steve Morgan, the arrogant punk who hits a home run on his first offense.

"My Son and Heir" by Stephen Marlowe (4000 words)★★★★
Ex-FBI turned P.I. Chester Drum is rudely awoken by Senator Ohland, mad with worry about his son, Roy. Seems the young man took a girl up to the family cabin and may have hurt her. The Senator will pay Drum five hundred bucks to accompany him to the cabin. Drum agrees but, upon arriving at the cabin, discovers the situation has not been properly explained to him. Roy has strangled the girl and now the Senator wants the P.I. to dispose of the body and help him save his political career. No wisecracks, no luscious dames, no happy ending; this P.I. story is quite unlike any other.

Stephen Marlowe's Chester Drum was a very popular character, the star of 20 novels published by Gold Medal (one co-written by Richard S. Prather and co-starring Shell Scott) between 1955–1968, and a handful of short stories published in the crime digests.

With a bit of tinkering, "My Son and Heir" was transformed into a *Mike Hammer* episode carrying the same title. Hammer is hired by wealthy Eugene Ohland to beat some sense into his son, Drummond, who's fallen in love with a "common girl." As in the story, Hammer accompanies Ohland to the cabin but there he finds Mrs. Ohland and the dead girl. Turns out Drum called his mother when the girl fell and hit her head, knocking her unconscious. Taking advantage of the situation, Mrs. Ohland kills the girl and prevents her son making any mistakes. Hammer must use his head rather than fists to sort out the truth. With excellent source material, writer Lawrence Kimble helps crafts a crackling half-hour filled with high tension.

"Custody" by Richard Deming (3000 words)★★★
When Harry Maddon is summoned to the home of his ex-wife, Hazel, by police, he fears harm may have come to his son, Tommy, by the hands of Hazel or her new husband, both violent alcoholics. His son is safe but the cops explain that Hazel has fatally shot her husband during an argument; the woman claims she doesn't remember. Harry takes Tommy home but once he begins questioning his

son about the incident, he realizes his ex-wife may not be the shooter. Also selected by David C. Cooke for *Best Detective Stories of the Year* (Dutton, 1956).

"Outside the Cages" by Jack Webb (4500 words)★
The cops have an animal trainer stashed away in order to keep him safe before he testifies in a big mob trial. His boss is having a problem with his tiger at the zoo, so he appeals to the cops to let him borrow the State's witness for a little while. Meandering and silly.

"The Jokers" by Robert Turner (2500 words)★★★
A group of college boys think it would be a whole lot of fun to play a gag on Georgie Grootch, the religious custodian at their university. Since Grootch has never "gone out" with a woman, they hire exotic dancer Lillie Lamar, the Snake Dancer to show Grootch what he's missing. Lillie steals into Georgie's room one night while the boys listen at the adjoining wall. A woman's scream sends the group scrambling for the exit but, later, after Lillie fails to emerge, they return to the scene of their crime just in time to bump into Grootch exiting the furnace room. When pressed as to the whereabouts of the dancer, the custodian only mutters that he's sent the woman to the fiery pit she deserved. The set-up has been used before but the grim finale makes the trip worthwhile.

"The High Trap" by Floyd Mahannah (8000 words)★★★
While driving down the desolate road that leads to their ranch, Tom and Kay Lander come across a man parked by the side of the road, across from a deserted Air Force runway. When a jumbo jet makes a surprise landing, the man forces Tom and Kay by gunpoint to the tarmac. They learn that the man is a member of a group of hoods who have hijacked the plane and its millions in diamonds. A host of passengers, including the owner of the ice, exits the plane and are ordered to start walking across the desert. Tom and Kay, however, are taken hostage and loaded onto the plane as insurance. Very soon, Tom learns that the men are going to parachute off the plane with Tom and Kay as sacrifices. A suspenseful edge-of-your-seat adventure thriller made all the more intriguing when the thugs begin to turn on each other and Tom must devise a way for him and his wife to escape.

"Kill Me Tomorrow" by Fletcher Flora (11,000 words)★★⤙
Peter Roche, the Senator's son, comes home for Christmas to discover dad has married a woman half his age. A real head-turner, Etta immediately catches Peter's fancy and the two become "really good friends" almost overnight. Etta shares Peter's disdain for the Senator but they both enjoy his money and decide that three's a crowd. Etta lets on that the Senator is in financial straits so there's only one way for Etta and Peter to cash in; the gorgeous but devious gal concocts a complicated plan wherein she fakes her own death and then "comes back from the dead" to kill the elderly Roche.
Peter murders a prostitute and runs Etta's car off a cliff with the corpse in the front seat. Etta hides away for a spell and, when they feel the time is right, the duo proceed with the finale of the plot. Things go fine until a nosy inspector figures

Peter Enfantino • Jeff Vorzimmer

out the con and slaps the bracelets on the murderous pair. What is, essentially, one of mystery fiction's oldest plots manages to work here through snappy dialogue and effective characterization. Oddly enough, the focal point of the crime, the Senator, is only discussed and never actually materializes amidst the action.

"Surprise! Surprise!" by David Alexander (4500 words)★★★✔

All the boys down at the Eighth Precinct know that Joe Bacci's wife is stepping out on him; the worst part is that the guy-on-the-side is a detective in the same squad room. Joe just ignores the catty comments but, eventually, the lid is going to blow. It's a testament to David Alexander's writing that a story as choppy as "Surprise! Surprise!" is so effective. Alexander slows the narrative down now and then to let us know about the atrocities committed in the precinct:

> *A couple of lovers on West Third made a suicide pact and turned the gas on and they were lying in each other's arms deader than the mackerel in the Fulton Fish Market when we found them. That wasn't all. They hadn't stuffed the cracks in the doors too well and the gas had seeped through to the next flat and asphyxiated a three-months-old baby that was sleeping in its crib.*

Joe Bacci's adulterous wife meets with a grim fate but these interludes are what makes this story click.

The Best Stories of 1955

"Moonshine" by Gil Brewer (March)
"Memento" by Erskine Caldwell (March)
"Blood Brothers" by Hal Ellson (April)
"Solitary" by Jack Ritchie (July)
"The Big Score" by Sam Merwin, Jr. (July)
"The Big Day" by Richard Marsten (September)
"The War" by Richard Deming (September)
"Flight to Nowhere" by Charles Williams (September)
"My Son and Heir" by Stephen Marlowe (December)
"Surprise! Surprise!" by David Alexander (December)

Vol. 4 No. 1 Jan 1956
Last appearance of the regular non-fiction columns, which will be discontinued after this issue.

"Who Killed Helen?" by Bryce Walton (4500 words)★★★★

Helen and Jimmie are out of work actors, hungry for any part that comes along, so when Helen gets a call from a slimy, misogynistic producer to come over to his place to test for a part, Helen demurs and Jimmie pushes her. Helen calls hours later, terrified, begging Jimmie to come get her but he's too drunk to make it out the door. The next morning, the police come calling. Gripping and grim, with one of the bleakest finales I've ever read, "Who Killed Helen?" is perhaps the poster child for noir crime writing of the 1950s.

"Dangerous" by Hal Ellson (6500 words)★

Monotonous claptrap about a gigolo named Domino who takes advantage of all the young girls in the neighborhood until (in the only scene that could be deemed *Manhunt*-worthy) one of his regulars gets fed up and puts a knife in his belly.

"Fight Night" by Robert Turner (2000 words)★★

Two men having a drink in a bar are accosted by a burly nitwit. More of a fragment than an actual story, "Fight Night" exists only to hammer home the point that fighting is bad. Turner makes his argument: "In the movies, you see guys wallop each other all over. It almost looks like fun ... Only there's something wrong, something missing.... It's the sound of bone hitting more bone and flesh. There is nothing else like the sound of a driven fist hitting into a man's face."

"It's Hot Up Here" by Arnold Marmor (1000 words)★★

Scorned by the gorgeous prostitute downstairs, a young man gets his revenge.

"The Cheater" by Jonathan Craig (5000 words)★★⤴

Jonathan Craig's "Police Files" detectives, Steve Manning and Walt Logan, try to find the guy who pushed bookkeeper Edward Macklin in front of a subway train. What was the motive?

"Breaking Point" by Eleanor Roth (2000 words)★

The trials and tribulations of Mrs. Gunheim's maid.

"Spectator Sport" by Roy Carroll (1000 words)★

Ken follows Pink Shirt into the park to watch him murder a young girl. Carroll has the same annoying scatter-shot approach to prose as Hal Ellson (*Pink Shirt walks faster toward the arbor. Trees thicker there. Vines growing over the arbor. During the day it's gloomy around there.*).

"The Dead Stand-In" by Frank Kane (21,000 words)★★★

Johnny Liddell is hired by an anonymous woman to look into the death-by-cop of a hit man named Larry Hollister. Seems like an open and shut case to Liddell but he needs the dough so he has a look-see. Hollister was an out-of-town contract killer whose last rub was a nobody named Lorenzo; Liddell's interest is piqued when the cops hang a robbery motive on Hollister. Why would a well-known assassin suddenly become a small-time hood? As the puzzle pieces fall into place, everything points to Louis Carter, the owner of the Club Cameo, a guy who Liddell has dealt with in the past. Did Carter have Lorenzo rubbed out because of a deep, dark secret and then have the hatchet man killed as well?

Fair warning: the meandering plot and silly wrap-up are secondary to Frank Kane's lively sentences (*Her breasts were big, alive, made their presence known through the housecoat*), corny dialogue ("You do a lot of talking, peeper. How would you like to try it with no teeth?"), and memorable supporting cast (ace reporter Muggsy, tough cop Ryan, and especially the jocular waiter at the Club Cameo). Liddell was certainly one of the most charismatic dicks in 1950s crime fiction.

"You Want Her?" by Pat Stadley (1000 words)★★

Sparrow and the Rodders head out into the night looking for trouble.

Vol. 4 No. 2 Feb 1956

N. F. King replaces Scott Meredith (who appeared on the masthead as John McCloud) as Editor. Archer St. John's widow, G. F. "Geff" St. John appears for the first time on the masthead as Associate Editor. First and only appearance of Robert Bloch ("Terror in the Night"), who three years later would write the blockbuster novel Psycho.

"Block Party" by Sam Merwin, Jr. (4000 words)★★★★

A page-turner about a botched hotel vault heist and subsequent murder, very reminiscent of the work of Jim Thompson in its grim view of life amongst criminals.

"Sauce for the Gander" by Richard Deming (10,000 words)★

With his bookkeeper ventilated right outside the Club Rotunda, Clancy Ross makes it his personal mission to hunt down the murderer. Unlike "The War" (Sep 1955), the previous Clancy Ross thriller, "Sauce for the Gander" is tedious and overly long.

"Dead Soldier" by Jack Sword (3500 words)★★★

When his wife and son are killed by a drunk driver and the man is let off with a slap on the wrist, soldier-of-fortune Robert Mayne uses his skills in order to seek justice. A very intriguing read told entirely with police reports and witness interviews.

"Fog" by Gil Brewer (3000 words)★★★

Bill Calders arrives at the house of his old friend, Art Thompson, a man he hasn't seen since Thomson got married. Art isn't home but his gorgeous, semi-clad wife, Sarah, certainly is. When Bill becomes uncomfortable about Sarah's advances, he excuses himself and heads back to his hotel. Later that night, Bill gets a call from an excited Sarah, claiming Art had entered a foggy forest across from the house and never came back.

"Fog" is deceptively simple; it builds to a climax we're almost certain is inevitable from the beginning. And yet, like the Gold Medal novels it most closely resembles, the story isn't simply a PG-13 sex drama. Its denouement is actually quite chilling.

"Marty" by Robert S. Swenson (1500 words)★★

Eva answers a knock at the door and it's her old beau, Marty, one big bundle of bad news. Eva tries to tell Marty her husband is due home soon but Marty isn't concerned. In fact, he seems to know everything there is to know about Eva's lifestyle these days.

"Cool Cat" by Hal Ellson (8500 words)★

Cookie wants to take over the gang; in order to do that he has to get rid of their leader, Twist, so he sets up a bad robbery designed to get Cookie nabbed. The plan goes awry and Cookie is suspicious.

Exactly what's expected from a Hal Ellson *Manhunt* story: short, staccato sentences; cool gang monikers (Peaches and Twist); with-it dialogue; and at least one rooftop scene. What you also get here is padding, lots and lots and lots of padding, designed to fool the reader into thinking there's actually something going on here.

"Terror in the Night" by Robert Bloch (1500 words)★★

Bob and Barbara wake to find Marjorie Kingston, hysterical and dressed in hospital gown, babbling on their front porch. Marjorie claims that she's been committed to the local asylum and has just made good her exit, with bloodhounds hot on her trail. Naturally, Bob and Babs are a bit skeptical, but in the end they hear the baying of the hounds. Slightly expanded and revised when it was included in Bloch's collection *Terror in the Night* (Ace Double paperback, backed with the Bloch-penned *Shooting Star*, published in 1958). The insane asylum was a place that Bloch would gravitate back to through the years in both short stories ("Lucy Comes to Stay" and "A Home Away from Home") and novels (*Night-World* and *Psycho II*). One of the author's anthology screenplays took place in an *Asylum* (1972).

"Handy Man" by Fletcher Flora (3000 words)★★★⅃

Campan's right-hand man, Carey, has a lot of initiative; in the mob, that can be dangerous for both parties. Fabulously grim and twisty, "Handy Man" has a suspenseful scene at the climax between the two men, leading to an unexpected conclusion.

"They're Chasing Us" by Herbert D. Kastle (4000 words)★★★

A grocery store robbery goes wrong and bad brothers Mel and Sid are on the run. A compact but very effective heist story that never dwells on the crime but, rather, on the after-shocks.

"The Watchers" by Wally Hunter (1500 words)★★⅃

A woman is stabbed to death in front of several witnesses, watching from their bedroom windows. Eerily close to the circumstances surrounding the murder of Kitty Genovese nearly a decade later.

"Killer" by William Logan (2000 words)★★

Tommy is tasked with finding the leak in the "organization." The story is far too short but Logan hints at what might have been, had he more space to work with.

"Job with a Future" by Richard Welles (1500 words)★
Out of work and the mother's nagging him, Tommy needs to find a job. Luckily, local hood Fats wants to hire Tommy.

"Sleep Without Dreams" by Frank Kane (4500 words)★★
Hal Lewis, director of the *Phantom* radio show and another of Johnny Liddell's seemingly endless supply of good friends, asks Johnny to tail Libby, Lewis's wife while the director is out of town. Lewis is sure Libby is carrying on an affair and will soon drop the axe on their marriage. Liddell refuses, citing his disdain for "keyhole peeping" and tells Lewis to find another man.
A few weeks later, Libby comes to Liddell, confessing she's in love with another man and asking for advice. While Johnny is mulling his answer, the phone rings and it's Hal confessing he's just murdered the "other man!" A thread-bare plot and sparse action mar this Johnny Liddell thriller.

"Shot" by Roy Carroll (1500 words)★★
Why has Renick been shot while shuffling his way through a crowded street en route to meet his wife? A violent vignette written by Gil Brewer under the Carroll house byline.

Vol. 4 No. 3 Mar 1956
First and only appearance of prolific pulp author Walter Kaylin. Cover by Tom O'Sullivan.

"The Temptress" by Jonathan Craig (7000 words)★★
A girl is found nude and murdered. A bible salesman claims that God told him to murder her. In the end, God tells him to leap out of a window. A Police Files story starring Manning and Logan.

"Split It Three Ways" by Walter Kaylin (2000 words)★★★
Paulie, Sal, and Willie plan a small heist: rob a barkeep one night after closing. Sal decides to cut his girlfriend, Gertrude, in on the action. Bad idea. She ends up kicking the barkeep to death and then wants an even share. Unfortunately for Gertrude, it turns out that Paulie's got a tough girlfriend of his own.
Walter Kaylin was a mainstay of the "Men's Adventure Magazines" such as Male, Stag, For Men Only, and True Action, with "true adventure" yarns such as "Trapped in the Bayou's Pit of a Million Snakes," "The Army's Terrifying Death Bugs and Loony Gas," and, most famously, "Weasels Ripped My Flesh" (immortalized by Frank Zappa and the Mothers of Invention in 1970). Several of Kaylin's tales were collected in He-Men, Bag Men & Nymphos (New Texture, 2013).

"Lend Me Your Gun" by Hal Ellson (3500 words)★★
After a bad rumble, members of the Ramblers are arrested and interrogated with old-fashioned police tactics: beaten, hosed, etc. One of the Ramblers, Zootie, takes exception to this kind of treatment and asks our narrator, Nick, to lend him his private gun to off the cop. Suffers from a very abrupt ending.

"An Eye for an Eye" by Phillip Weck (2500 words)★★★
A blind man travels the country, searching for a prostitute named Angela. He's convinced that the local whore, Gladys, is his girl, living under a new name. Could this be a case of mistaken identity? Good twist ending.

"Madman" by Roy Carroll (4000 words)★★★★
A mesmerizing and beautifully-written tale of murder and madness in the deep South, as told by a teenage boy, reflecting on his "last good day."

"His Own Petard" by Daniel O'Shea (2000 words)★
Johnson's having an affair with his buddy's wife and decides that he's tired of his own wife. He decides to rid himself of her but finds out she's having an affair with his mistress' husband!

".38" by Joe Grenzeback (1000 words)★
A man decides to off "the other guy" but decides to off the two-timing wife at the last second. Two bad adultery/murder stories in one issue. This should be

avoided at all costs.

"Hunch" by Helen Nielsen (5000 words)★★★★

A grizzled, pessimistic cop looks for suspects in a series of murders involving teenagers. He sees suspects everywhere, eyeing even his own son. Good twists and turns. It's the victim's boyfriend. It's the next door neighbor. It's his own son. Nielsen never tips her hand.

"Suffer Little Children" by De Forbes (3000 words)★

Famed pianist Rudy Kleinman also happens to be a psychopath who gets his jollies by talking little kids into murdering their parents. Story alternately should have been shorter *and* longer. There's no payoff, but one huge hoot of a last line.

"Two Hours to Midnight" by Brett Halliday (21,000 words)★★

A bit of excitement down at the Hibiscus Hotel. A woman calls the switchboard to report a dead man in room 316. The hotel dick heads up to the room but finds nothing. Several minutes later, a hysterical woman is telling her story to Mike Shayne. She found the dead body of her brother in the Hibiscus Hotel, phoned it in from a different room (to avoid smudging fingerprints, she claims), then returned to find the corpse vanished. Is the hysterical girl off her rocker? And what's with the attractive dame in the lobby, insisting that Shayne take *her* case first? As bodies pile up, Mike Shayne discovers that all the sub-plots in his life that night are merging into one violent story.

"Two Hours to Midnight" begins as a fast-paced, exciting thriller (told in "real time") but meanders and loses its way halfway through the running time. There are confusing twists and turns, switched identities, whopping coincidences, and a two-page expository that kills any momentum the first act set up for the reader.

Dell published an expanded version of "Two Hours to Midnight" as the novel, *The Blonde Cried Murder*, in 1957. Six months after this story appeared in *Manhunt*, Mike Shayne got his own digest magazine, effectively killing any chance of seeing Shayne in *Manhunt* again. A new Shayne novel (written by several different writers under the Halliday pseudonym) appeared every month for 29 years in *Mike Shayne's Mystery Magazine*.

Peter Enfantino • Jeff Vorzimmer

Vol. 4 No. 4 Apr 1956

Cover by Tom O'Sullivan—the first issue to credit the cover artist. *"WORLD'S BEST-SELLING CRIME-FICTION MAGAZINE"* replaces *"DETECTIVE STORY MONTHLY"* on the masthead.

"First Kill" by Helen Nielsen (5000 words)★★
After a separation of years, Vern shows up at his brother's ranch but the two have an immediate dislike for each other. Vern is the delicate one while his brother, Kirby, is into guns and hunting. When a cougar starts killing off Kirby's livestock, the two head out on a hunting expedition. Slow and uninvolving, with a plot we've seen before.

"Strictly Business" by Hamilton Frank (1500 words)★★★
A blackmailer finds himself being blackmailed. Short-short with a genuinely funny finale.

"Pat Hand" by J. W. Aaron (5500 words)★★✓
Johnny turns to murder when he discovers his old girl friend is being blackmailed by her own husband.

"Widow's Choice" by Cole Price (2500 words)★
Nan's husband committed suicide while in the service and now she's moved to Isla Blanca to start over again. Dud Graham sure seems like a nice guy but he's always hitting on Nan and there's something very... off about the guy. When he takes Nan to his beach shed to show her his spear guns, she knows she's in for trouble.

"The Better Bargain" by Richard Deming (3000 words)★★✓
King Louis Indelicato, mob boss, discovers his wife has a little something on the side. The only thing he had ever asked of her was fidelity, so naturally he's a bit peeved. The mobster calls the highest-paid hitman in America into his office to paint a picture: he wants his wife and the boyfriend *defunto* ASAP. The assassin agrees to the sum of 20 grand to pull off the hit but changes his mind when he sees a picture of Mrs. King Louis. As he flicks open his switchblade, he smiles and Indelicato realizes the hitman is his wife's lover.
"The Better Bargain" was adapted very cleverly for the second season of *Alfred Hitchcock Presents*. Much of Deming's story works because the identity of the hitman is not revealed until the final paragraph even though we "see" him in the intro during a motel tryst with King's wife. Obviously this scenario would never work in a visual medium so teleplay writer Bernard C. Schoenfeld eliminated the motel scene altogether. A rare case where the adaptation is better than the source material.

"Come Across" by Gil Brewer (3500 words)★⯪

Runyan becomes obsessed with the pretty girl living across the alley from his apartment; he ogles her through his blinds, watches her walking the streets, and follows her to restaurants. He finally gets up the nerve to ask if he can see her and, to his amazement, she agrees and gives him her apartment number. When he arrives, the girl is sexily dressed and a man is leaving her bedroom. His fantasy shattered, Runyan loses what grip on reality he had maintained and murders the woman. Every now and then, even a great writer like Gil Brewer can type out a dud and this would be that dud. There's an underlying tension about Runyan (we're never sure exactly what his intentions are), but Brewer opts to dispose of the subtlety and finishes with a sledge hammer.

"Line of Duty" by Fredric Brown (18,000 words)★★★★

John Medley is a deeply-disturbed man who believes God has given him the job of "delivering mercy to those in pain." His latest salvation lies in Medley's yard with a bullet to the back of his skull, but the police are convinced a kindly old man like Medley couldn't possibly be involved.

"Line of Duty" is a chilling read, with most of the violence taking place "off stage" and an emphasis on psychological horror and superb character development. The author achieves much of the development by switching point-of-view from chapter to chapter. This is a "condensed version" of Brown's novel, *The Lenient Beast,* published the same month as this issue of *Manhunt.*

"Room Service" by Robert Turner (1000 words)★★★

Short-short about a sniper and his target: a beauty queen in a parade. This rifleman seems like nothing more than a teenage psycho until Turner shows his hold cards. Very short but very effective.

"Dry Run" by Norman Struber (5600 words)★★

A hitman is sent by his mobster boss to ice a rogue assassin but, too late, discovers his boss is only testing him. Another *Manhunt* story filmed for *Alfred Hitchcock Presents,* this time adapted for the fifth season by mystery writer Bill S. Ballinger. Walter Matthau and Robert Vaughn star as the two hitmen. Author Norman Struber had dozens of short stories in the crime digests (*Off Beat, Trapped, Guilty, Mike Shayne,* among others) of the 1950s but, surprisingly, never graduated to novels.

"One Way Or The Other" by John R. Starr (1000 words)★

Silly short-short about a man trying to catch his ex-wife with her new lover.

"A Trophy for Bart" by James Charles Lynch (3000 words)★

Bart Owens's neighbor, Charley, is always bragging about his Geiger counter but when Charley runs the gizmo over one of Bart's wife's souvenir rock fragments and discovers it's uranium, Bart sees red. His ire is further stoked when Charley exclaims that the two of them are going to be millionaires. Why should Bart share the wealth?

Peter Enfantino • Jeff Vorzimmer

"Open Heart" by Bryce Walton (1000 words)★★★

A brutal short-short about a single mother hoping she's found love with the new man in her life, unaware she's let a psychopath into her home. An unusual story that Bryce Walton could have taken in several directions but opted for what might have been, at the time, the most daring.

"One-Way Ticket" by Duane Yarnell (3000 words)★★

Humorous tale about a con man who answers a lonely hearts letter and prepares to take a pretty young lady for all she's worth.

Vol. 4 No. 5 May 1956
First and only appearance of pulp writer, Frederick C. Davis.

"Squealer" by John D. Macdonald (3000 words)★★↙
When Dick Reilly is viciously beaten and his girl, Bettie Lee, is raped, there are plenty of witnesses but none want to squeal to the cops. It takes a little bit of inventiveness on the part of two detectives to crack the case. By the time "Squealer" was published, John D. Macdonald was one of Gold Medal's superstars, with an even dozen thrillers placed in the spinner rack. This J.D. short feels strangely out of place alongside MacDonald's more "serious" material.

"The Man who Never Smiled" by Robert S. Swenson (2500 words)★★
After a man watches his wife killed in a hit-and-run, he spends most of his time saying nothing and watching for the criminal car. A story that begins with an eruption of violence but settles for a somnambulistic closure.

"Preacher's Tale" by Max Kane (2000 words)★
A school teacher is raped and beaten by a member of the Zeets but, rather than go to the police she plots an elaborate revenge. Very sleazy and portly-written (I'd say Max is probably the least of the three *Manhunt* writers surnamed Kane), "Preacher" is so far below the quality of story *Manhunt* was publishing; it might better have fit in one of the lesser digests like *Two-Fisted* or *Off-Beat*.

"Kill Fever" by Rey Isely (4500 words)★★↙
Sam Pippet didn't like mob boss Vic Malone from the moment he met him; he did, however, take to Malone's wife, Estelle. When the gal with the gorgeous gams lets on that she wants her husband out of the way, Sam comes up with (some would say a too) elaborate plan to kill the big man. There's a good pay-off if you wait long enough but Pippet's contrived booby trap really does defy logic. Isely's only *Manhunt* story.

"The Unholy Three" by William Campbell Gault (5500 words)★★
Joe Puma's had some interesting clients before but eleven-year-old Johnny Delavan takes the prize. Johnny is convinced his sister is dating the wrong sort and he wants Joe to investigate. He's willing to pay him part of his paper route money for the job. Joe looks into the case but finds nothing out of the ordinary until he's introduced to the "wrong guy" and the case turns dangerous. One of the weakest of the Puma stories, "The Unholy Three" seems either rushed or truncated, especially in its climax, which happens mostly "off-screen."

"Ten Minutes to Live" by George Fielding Eliot (4000 words)★↙
An accountant is sent into a high-security prison compound to perform an

audit when the notorious criminal, Tiger Tolland, stages a prison break. Standard adventure-thriller with a ludicrous finale.

"Lenore" by Frederick C. Davis (11,000 words)★★↲

Attorney Webb Bowers has always been obsessed with the gorgeous Lenore Collister but never had a chance, since Lenore was a member of the upper crust and Webb just a good guy. One night, during a party, Lenore shoots and kills a local man, claiming self-defense, and Webb is assigned to defend her. Lenore turns on the charm and Webb becomes ever more convinced she's innocent until an incident on a fishing boat opens his eyes to what really happened that night. An old-fashioned Floridian thriller, laced with sex and subterfuge, that does just enough to hold interest but not much more. Frederick C. Davis was one of the busiest writers during the pulp era, contributing hundreds of fast-paced murder mysteries to such magazines as *Black Mask, Dime Mystery*, and *New Detective*.

"Devil Eyes" by Jack Ritchie (2000 words)★★

Phil Gillespie is madly in lust with Mrs. Brosnan but he loves her money. Now what to do with Mr. Brosnan?

"Oedipus" by Walt Sheldon (4500 words)★★↲

Ponderous study of a photographer, slowly going mad, who plans the murder of his wife.

"The Strangler" by A. I. Schutzer (5500 words)★★

Tied to a job that pays nothing and a husband dying of emphysema, masseuse Frieda wonders if the good life can somehow be obtained by imitating the murderer terrorizing the city, the Strangler. Frieda gives it a try and discovers that not only is it rewarding monetarily but that she also gets a kick out of it. With money to burn, she leaves her husband and sets off to start a new life but then accepts a ride to the train station from a stranger who might just be the real killer. There's a thread of a good thriller running throughout but "The Strangler" is too padded to hold interest.

"City Hunters" by George Lange (1000 words)★

Everyone in town knew that Clem hated Abner but when Ab turns up dead, shot in the forest, the Sheriff can't match the bullet to Clem's gun. That's because Clem didn't use *that* gun.

"The Red of Bougainvillea" by Grove Hughes (3000 words)★↲

Marge just loves to undress in front of the uncurtained bedroom window; it's driving her husband Wiil nuts but what can a man do? Then Marge spots a peeper in the bushes outside the window and Will decides he needs to take action. He's convinced it's Dingo, the guy down the street who's constantly ogling Marge in the supermarket but the true culprit, brought to light in the very predictable last paragraph, is a little closer to home.

"The Pigeon" by Claudius Raye (2000 words)★★↗

J.D. thriller about a mobster sent from Chicago to train a youth gang into becoming a well-oiled machine. A cut above the usual J.D. fare in that author Raye sends us traveling down a different road than we had expected.

Vol. 4 No. 6 Jun 1956

The year appears on the spine for the first time. Cover by Walter Popp.

"Circle for Death" by Pat Stadley (3000 words)★★★
A beat cop breaks up a gang battle and then must weather the inevitable storm as the gang harasses the cop and his wife.

"A Helluva Ball" by Jack Q. Lynn (2000 words)★★
Anne and Jackie, two teenage addicts, truck on over to Fixer's pad for a fix. Fixer's ... well, a fixer. With a little flesh and lovin', he'll set you up with a right nice needle full of H. Only problem is, Jackie's not hep to the man's mojo needs and gives him the old knee-to-the-cajones treatment. The two girls must flee before Fixer can gather his wits and git his mitts on 'em. Back in 1956, this kind of prose probably came across as very timely and realistic:

> "It gets worse, doll," Anne says. "You get horrors inside. Ice and fire. Somethin' eatin' out your guts. Then you gotta get the fix, Jackie-baby. Skin-pop to the big pipe. Yeah."

These days it just sounds hopelessly dated in the same way *Ozzie and Harriet* drew laughter.

"Hitch-Hiker" by Roland F. Lee (1000 words)★✓
Baylor takes a very disturbing drive with a very disturbed young man.

"One More Mile to Go" by F. J. Smith (2500 words)★★★
Mr. Jacoby murders his wife and dumps her body in his trunk. On the way to the swamp, his taillight fails and he attracts the attention of a state trooper that won't take "No" for an answer. Rather funny comedy of errors that was filmed in 1957 for *Alfred Hitchcock Presents*. Directed by Hitchcock himself, the episode starred David Wayne as Jacoby.

"Addict" by W. E. Douglas (1500 words)★★
A teen addict, arrested for possession and checked into a hospital, goes through withdrawals. The prose is harrowing but "Addict" is nothing more than a vignette, a pamphlet detailing the horrors of heroin addiction and the cycle that curses those who can't kick it.

"Dead Man's Cat" by Sylvie Pasche (3000 words)★★✓
Did Ed have to too much to drink and take an accidental header off the Third Street Bridge or was he pushed? And did his beautiful young wife (the one who married Ed for his money) have anything to do with it? It takes a very smart cat to get to the bottom of the mystery. An amiable enough "cozy" with a very funny last

line.

"Three, Four, Out the Door" by Robert S. Swenson (1500 words)★★
Two hoods rough up the patrons of a small diner.

"The Canary" by Jack Ritchie (2000 words)★★★
An old con is pressured into a prison break he doesn't want to make.

"Lipstick" by Wenzell Brown (2500 words)★★★
Carlo's stumbled into a good thing. He's found a badge and he uses it to gain access into the apartments of pretty women. The latest, Mrs. Cortele, has become something of an obsession with Carlo but she's not going to give in to him easily. Absorbing little tale ends on a chilling note.

Wenzell Brown is best known for J.D. novels such as *Gang Girl* (Avon, 1954),*The Big Rumble* (Popular, 1955), *Cry Kill* and *Teenage Mafia* (both Gold Medal, 1959). Though a frequent contributor to *Alfred Hitchcock*, this was Brown's only appearance in *Manhunt*.

"The Squeeze" by Richard Deming (7000 words)★★★
Casino man Clancy Ross has always had mobster Bix Larson to worry about but now there's another mafioso who wants Clancy's prize possession, the Club Rotunda. Tony Armanda intends to be the big man in town but he knows that he has to wrest control of the Rotunda from Ross if that's to happen. Clancy is perfectly happy to stand to the side and watch as Larson and Armanda annihilate each other but, before too long, he becomes the focus of the war.

After the disposable "Sauce for the Gander" (Feb 1956), Deming finds himself back on high ground with "The Squeeze." There's not much plot to speak of but Deming's prose is exciting and the Clancy Ross character is original and dynamic; so much more so than the private eyes he's meant to be clumped with.

"Vigil by Night" by James W. Phillips (1000 words)★↲
What appears to be the musings of a late night peeper becomes something else entirely.

"The Prisoners" by Evans Harrington (23,500 words)★
An assistant warden takes an interest in Johnny, a young convict, determined to show he can rehabilitate the man through kindness rather than the whip. Through a series of misfortunes, Johnny digs his grave deeper and deeper. One pictures "The Prisoners" performed at some off-off-Broadway dive with a cast of self-important actors, spouting lines concerning the inner good. Certainly unlike any other *Manhunt* story in that sixty pages are spent with nary a focus in mind, the novella was an abridgment of a novel published by Harper the same year. I haven't read the novel but it's apparent where the cuts take place in the shorter version.

Peter Enfantino • Jeff Vorzimmer

Vol. 4 No. 7 Jul 1956

Last Appearance by Charles Williams who contributed three novellas to the magazine. Cover by Walter Popp.

"Still Screaming" by F. L. Wallace (2500 words)★★★

Savage short about a man searching for the thugs who raped and murdered his wife. Though written over sixty years ago, "Still Screaming" is as grim and violent as anything contemporary; think Liam Neeson as the lead.

"Terminal" by William L. Jackson (4000 words)★★★✓

There's a madman loose in the city and Detectives Anderson and O'Rourke hit the streets before blood can be spilled. The two cops have never gotten along and when Anderson disobeys a direct order from his Captain, tragedy strikes. A white knuckler from start to finish, "Terminal" is a fabulous read and it's a shame author Jackson only had this one contribution to *Manhunt*.

"Pal with a Switch Blade" by Norman Struber (4500 words)★✓

Ex-gang member Danny has moved out of the city to stay away from trouble but one day he emerges from school to see his past leaning on a dirty car door. Luis has a score to settle and seeing Danny as a successful student (on the football team!) doesn't help matters. A padded street gang tale with almost comical dialogue, "Pal With a Switch Blade" adds fuel to the argument that the J.D. sub-genre has not aged well.

"Rumble" by Edward Perry (1000 words)★

The Ravens rumble with the Seminoles. Edward Perry hits all the same beats (odd monikers, clipped sentences, rumbles) that Hal Ellson uses and achieves the exact same effect.

"Stay Dead, Julia!" by Peter Georgas (2000 words)★

After murdering his wife and tossing her body into a lake, a man has an insane dialogue with himself. Psychological thriller misses the mark by a wide margin.

"Office Party" by Austin Hamel (3500 words)★★

An office party gets out of hand and young Mr. Warren accidentally kills a belligerent co-worker when the man attacks a sweet young girl. Mr. Warren later discovers, to his chagrin, that there's more to the backstory.

"Terror in the Night" by Carl G. Hodges (3500 words)★★

A young couple is held prisoner in their home by a wounded murderer.

"Fall Guy" by Joe Grenzeback (5500 words)★★

Junior tough guy Tim is tricked into a jewelry heist by his elder partners, Pug and Joey. When the robbery goes South and the store owner killed, Tim is left to fend for himself. His ace in the hole (and albatross) turns out to be the jewelry he's held on to and stashed at a local newsstand. But Pug and Joey come looking for Tim and the blind newsstand owner. An intriguing premise gives way to the obligatory showdown and rote fisticuffs.

"A Date with Harry" by George Lange (1500 words)★★★

Very funny quickie about a man who meets "Harry" in a bar and is promised a wild night in a hotel room with dames. The dames don't show and our guy is left with… Harry… which is exactly how Harry had planned it.

"Change for a C-Note" by Jerry Sohl (2000 words)★★

Jelson used to do emergency clean-up for bad guys who took a bullet, but now the doc is no more than a stinkin' drunk. The thugs who come calling on him tonight don't care that his hands are shaking or that he's barely coherent; they need a surgeon right now. Jerry Sohl had a very successful career as a science fiction writer but found time to craft the rare crime short story now and then.

"D.O.A." by Jules Rosenthal (1000 words)★★★

"Thelma's dead—who's responsible" becomes the catch-phrase of this short, but powerful, story about a man searching for Thelma's killer. The tale begins like any other Charles Bronson-esque revenge fantasy but then takes an unexpected and welcome veer into some uncharted territory.

"The Big Bite" by Charles Williams (19,500 words)★★★★

Football star John Harlan has a promising career cut short when his car is sideswiped by an out-of-control motorist. The other driver dies, but Harlan soon learns that there was more to the story than was apparent when a retired insurance agent named Purvis informs him the man was actually murdered by his wife, Joyce. When Purvis winds up dead, Harlan uses the incident as a jumping-off point for blackmail. But Joyce is a tougher cookie than she seems at first sight. A fabulously layered web of sex and murder, "The Big Bite" showcases Charles Williams at the peak of his prowess. An expanded version of the novella was published by Dell in 1956 and was adapted into the French film, *Le Gros Coup* in 1964.

Vol. 4 No. 8 Aug 1956

William Manners takes over as Editor. His biggest change will be to increase the size of the magazine from digest to glossy (quarto) size, believing that the digests were getting lost on the newsstands. The first and only appearance by Harlan Ellison ("Rat Hatter"). Cover by Frank Cozzarelli.

"Cop Killer" by Dan Sontup (4000 words)★

When his partner is stabbed, mean Sergeant Baxter makes it his number one priority to get the guy. Bad cop gets his comeuppance.

"The Man with Two Faces" by Henry Slesar (4000 words)★★

Mrs. Wagner is mugged, but the real terror begins when she looks through the mug books and recognizes her son-in-law. I found the plot to be skimpy and lacking much surprise, but I felt Henry Slesar's adaptation of his own story for *Alfred Hitchcock Presents* to be delightful. That could be, in part, due to the acting talents of Spring Byington (as Mrs. Wagner), and Steve Dunne (as the cop who suspects something is up). Their on-screen time, while the elderly woman looks through mug books, has a realistic energy and the two play well off each other.

"Gruber Corners by Nine" by John R. Starr (2000 words)★★

If he doesn't get to Gruber Corners by nine, Bill Evans will lose his job with the carnival. Lucky for him, a motorist stops to give the hitch-hiker a ride. Unlucky for Bill, the driver wants to play a game of backwoods "Most Dangerous Game." Fair short thriller, but suffers from a telecasted ending.

"Seven Lousy Bucks" by C. L. Sweeney, Jr. (2500 words)★★★★

Joe's got it made: no job, drinks his life away and prostitutes his wife, Clare, for booze money. When his wife fails to bring home more than ten bucks after serving a john, Joe blows his top. Violent, harrowing look at two bottom-of-the-barrel individuals.

"... Puddin' and Pie ..." by De Forbes (2000 words)★★★

A reverend tries to comfort a retarded murderer on the day he's to be hanged. Though the final "twist" ending is not surprising, it's handled well.

"Biggest Risk" by C. B. Gilford (5000 words)★★★

A psychopath kidnaps a woman and tosses her into his trunk. Tired of the same old routine followed by most serial killers, he drives up in front of the victim's house the next day and engages in small talk with police officers while the woman is still in the trunk. She gets the last laugh though by slashing her wrist and bleeding through the trunk. The kind of story that Robert Bloch perfected.

"The Wire Loop" by Steve Harbor (2000 words)★★★

Karl and Norman have been friends since childhood and that irritates Karl's wife, Laura. It bugs her even more when she finds out that Karl and Norman are more than friends. There's a subplot about a strangler here that's wrapped up in a double twist, but the obvious hook is the not-so-subtle homosexual relationship hinted at. There wasn't much of this type of fiction being run in the 1950s, let alone 1950s crime digests. Though I have nothing to prove this, I'd think this story must have drawn some critical feedback from readers.

"Key Witness" by Frank Kane (17,000 words)★★★★

Fred Morrow witnesses three young punks stab a man to death and, without thinking of his own safety or future, agrees to finger the stabber and testify against him in court. When the punk starts making threats against Morrow and his family, the good samaritan begins questioning whether the right thing to do, in the long run, is really the right thing to do.

Frank Kane's masterpiece, "Key Witness" reads like a really good flick, populated with well-casted characters. There are the tough cops, good and bad, with their individual priorities and prejudices; the reporters, with their thirst for sensation, not worrying about the damage they do with their pencils; the lawyers, who see the case as "the one to break a career wide open with"; the thugs, juvenile gang members who rightfully think, so it turns out, they can get away with murder; and of course, the witness, trying to bring justice, and rewarded with suffering for being in the wrong place at the wrong time.

This was filmed in 1960 by director Phil Karlson, starring Dennis Hopper, Pat Crowley, and Jeffrey Hunter as the witness. Kane expanded the story into a novel the same year, released by Dell in paperback.

"Rat Hater" by Harlan Ellison (4000 words)★★★

Lew Greenberg has waited nine long years to avenge the murder of his sister at the hands of Chuckling Harry Kroenfeld. Harry, once a crime bigwig, has gone legit, but that means nothing to Lew who, knowing of Harry's deathly fear of rats, has concocted a nasty avenue of revenge. Good little chiller that would have been welcome in the pages of *Weird Tales*.

This was Harlan Ellison's only story for *Manhunt*, but he did contribute quite a few crime stories to such 1950s digests as *Guilty*, *The Saint*, *Mike Shayne*, and *Web Detective Tales*. Though he's known mostly for his speculative fiction, Ellison has always been a jack of all trades. Collectors who are willing to dig deep can even find a few Ellison stories in the 1950s western fiction digests.

"Thanks for the Drink, Mac" by Philip Weck (3000 words)★

Eddie sits on a barstool, waiting for his past to catch up with him.

"Good-By, World" by Jack Ritchie (1500 words)★★★

A lawyer pulls out all the stops to keep his client from going to the gas chamber ... or does he? Good twist ending.

Peter Enfantino • Jeff Vorzimmer

"The Earrings" by Kermit Shelby (1500 words)★★
Another tale of adultery and farm justice.

"The Playboy" by Claudius Raye (2000 words)★★
Buddy has a way with the girls, but he bites off more than he can chew when he picks up Myreen and takes her back to his place.

Vol. 4 No. 9 Sep 1956

Appearance of "The Last Spin" by Evan Hunter, the only Manhunt story to be nominated for an Edgar Award. First of three consecutive covers by Tom O'Sullivan.

"The Last Spin" by Evan Hunter (2500 words)★★★

Two rival gang members get to know each other as they play a game of Russian Roulette. Though this was probably very powerful in the 1950s, it's very dated now. I can see this being an *American Playhouse*-type live TV show. It's certainly written that way. "The Last Spin" became the only *Manhunt* story to be nominated for an Edgar award (losing to "The Blessington Method" by Stanley Ellin, which appeared in the June 1956 issue of *Ellery Queen*) and later headlined a collection of Hunter's short crime stories.

"Fish-Market Murder" by Robert S. Swenson (1500 words)★

Mistaken identity at the robbery of a fish market.

"Badge of Dishonor" by Norman Struber (4000 words)★★★★

Frank Bulock is assigned to tail Sarillo, a bookkeeper for a big-time mobster. Sarillo has agreed to turn state's evidence against his former boss, but someone gets to him first, leaving him dead and Bulick in big trouble with his lieutenant. I had figured out the twist fairly early in the story (and you will too), but its finale is filled with a couple of good punches regardless.

"Sorry, Mister..." by C. L. Sweeney, Jr. (2500 words)★★

Bess Tinkham has been raped and murdered, and the town naturally suspects the drifter Bess had hired on. Their suspicions wane however when they attempt to dole out some good country justice on the boy and find out, due to his war injury, he doesn't have the necessary equipment to perpetrate such a hideous crime.

"Brusky's Fault" by Robert Plate (2500 words)★

After witnessing a rape/murder, Vincent Melcarth realizes he'd like to commit the same crime.

"The Secret" by Stuart Friedman (5000 words)★★★★

Who got farm girl Agatha pregnant? Her father seems to think that retarded ranch hand Raymond is the culprit but Agatha's claiming it's the second immaculate conception. A chilling, powerful tale of deadly secrets and deceit, capped off with a climax you won't soon forget.

"Anything Goes" by Hal Ellson (5000 words)★★

The misadventures of Ace and Zero, two drugged-out teens who will do anything, and anyone, to get high. What one would call "a cautionary tale."

"The Sealed Envelope" by Allen Lang (9000 words)★★★

Two members of the Air Force steal the base payroll and unexpectedly carry away top secret NATO plans as well. Solid thriller, the kind usually found in the pages of *The Saint* or *The Man From U.N.C.L.E.* (*Manhunt* seldom ran stories of political intrigue), infused with a good sense of humor, but hampered by an abrupt climax.

"The Partners" by Jack Ritchie (3000 words)★★

Harold Romaine, yet another bookkeeper to the mob, decides to do some skimming off the top and ends up six feet under. His father doesn't take the news well and goes after the three mobsters who did in Harold.

"Reach for the Clouds" by Bob Bristow (3500 words)★★★

Nephew Dave decides to endear himself to Uncle Cliff and Uncle's beautiful new wife Anita. Dave wants Uncle Cliff's 20,000 acres and the new wife, so he takes Uncle Cliff out for a spin in his small airplane. A good old-fashioned "last laugh" story with one of those classic H. P. Lovecraft-style final lines that leaves you wondering if Dave (narrator of the story) is telling his story from heaven (or wherever he's gone in the afterlife).

"Invitation to Murder" by Albert Simmons (7000 words)★

Eddie Steele's just served three years for a crime he didn't commit. Shortly after he's released, he's contacted by his lawyer, who informs him that Eddie was framed. Eddie sets out to find out who and why. Really bad mystery reads like something you'd find in one of the 1930s dime pulps.

"Dead People are Never Angry" by C. B. Gilford (3000 words)★★

Paul Melcor is released from prison after a two-year sentence for running down Ann Lambert. Waiting for Melcor is Ann's husband Hugh, who doesn't believe justice was served. He now vows to run Melcor down when the ex-con least expects it. An interesting switch of hunter and hunted towards the climax, but otherwise an ordinary revenge story.

"Webster Street Lush" by James M. Ullman (4000 words)★

Terence McDougall, lawyer, turns state's evidence against the mob and then finds his lovely wife's head in a box on the front porch. He then dedicates his life to find her murderer, a fat man with a small, black mustache and a scar at the left corner of his mouth. He finally finds his killer, much to his surprise. Ho-hum revenger starts off promising and builds to an amazingly laughable expository that would make Angela Lansbury cringe.

Vol. 4 No. 10 Oct 1956

First and only appearances of prolific pulp author Harry Whittington ("Night of Crisis") and Morton Freedgood ("The Lovers"), under his pen name John Godey, who would go on to write the ultimate heist novel, The Taking of Pelham 123 in 1973.

"The Enormous Grave" by Norman Struber (3500 words)★★

Howard helps Anne kill her husband Donald and they bury him under his wine collection in the basement. But then Anne receives a letter from a witness and she panics. Time for Plan B. One of those "the real bad guy is not who you think it is" stories that populate *Alfred Hitchcock Mystery Magazine.*

"Run from the Snakes!" by David Alexander (6000 words)★

A vagrant watches a man kidnap a child from a park bench and follows him throughout New York City. Takes way too long to get to the point.

"Blood and Moonlight" by William R. Cox (4000 words)★★

Harry Jay Wynne, rich and confident, has been getting away with murder all his life. After he murders Betty Lou, he gets the unwanted attention of Detective Langton, who was in love with Betty Lou. Langton can't get the conviction after Harry Jay's wife cops to the killing, so he follows the man, waiting for his next crime. Peyton Place, *Manhunt*-style.

"Ring the Bell Once" by Paul Eiden (3000 words)★★★

Esme D'Artagnan, nineteen year-old "girl about town," commits suicide. Her guilt-ridden sister begins an elaborate revenge scheme against the playboy who got Esme in trouble. The weapon of choice is the playboy's watchdog. Much like an old EC comic book story.

"Matinee" by Gil Brewer (3500 words)★

A sexual predator stalks his latest intended victim. Not one of Brewer's better stories.

"Deadly Beloved" by William Campbell Gault (12,500 words)★★★

Gault's ace P.I. Joe Puma is hired by Grace Engle to find her missing husband, Alan. Puma quickly finds that Engle wasn't the type to consider marriage a hallowed institution and begins to stumble over "other women" left and right. Seems Alan Engle was one of the beautiful people. When Engle's bludgeoned body turns up, Puma must sort through all the people who loved Alan Engle and uncover the one who beat him to death.

Joe Puma had a short, but drawn-out, career, starring in only eight novels beginning with Gault's pseudonymous novel, *Shakedown* (as by Roney Scott; Ace,

1953) and capped off by *The Cana Diversion* (1984), wherein Gault's other P.I., Brock Callahan, investigates Puma's murder. Puma was featured in six short stories, four of which appeared in *Manhunt*, all collected in *Marksman and Other Stories* (Crippen & Landru, 2003).

"Lesson in Murder" by Wally Hunter (1500 words)★

An assassin teaches his son all the fine arts of his trade, including the #1 lesson: always eliminate your competition. This leads to a problem for dad.

"The Lovers" by John Godey (2000 words)★★

Marcia is convinced that her husband, a sculptor, has murdered her lover and hidden his body in one of his sculptures. Author Morton Freedgood wrote several crime novels in the 1940s and 50s under the John Godey pseudonym, including *Killer at His Back*, *The Blue Hour*, and *The Clay Assassin*, but he didn't hit the big time until his 1973 novel, *The Taking of Pelham One Two Three*, became a bestseller and a smash movie starring Walter Matthau and Robert Shaw.

"Night of Crisis" by Harry Whittington (6000 words)★★

Jim Cooper witnesses Arn Crowley murder a bartender. When Cooper goes to the police, they suspect him as an accomplice. Things don't get much better though when he is released. Crowley kidnaps Cooper's wife and baby.

As highly-regarded as any of the seminal crime writers of the 1950s and 1950s, Harry Whittington was a veritable writing factory, pumping out quality pulp stories, crime novels, westerns, and soft-core adult novels under a variety of pseudonyms. As with writers such as Peter Rabe, Jim Thompson, and Gil Brewer, Whittington didn't really become a household name in crime circles until his fiction was reprinted by Barry Gifford's Black Lizard Press in the 1980s. Incredibly, this was Harry's only contribution to *Manhunt*.

"Body in the Rain" by John S. Hill (1500 words)★★

A sheriff is called out to a farm where a man has murdered his father.

"Dangerous Money" by F. J. Smith (2500 words)★★★

Rare humorous tale about a man who finds a wallet stuffed with hundred collar bills and decides he can make the money last longer if only he didn't have to share it with his wife. At the same time, the wife's got similar thoughts.

When "Dangerous Money" showed up on the *Alfred Hitchcock Presents* show the following year (under the title, "Reward to Finder," writer Frank Gabrielson kept most of the story intact, adding only a little padding (the wife goes on a shopping spree, buying furniture, curtains, and even a fur coat), including the effective twist ending. Oscar Homolka and Jo Van Fleet star as the warring couple, with a cameo by a very young Claude Akins.

"Bus to Portland" by L. W. King (3000 words)★★

Carl Rausch boards a bus to Portland shortly after murdering a young babysitter. Rausch's rational mind tells him to be kind, but his paranoia gets the best of him.

"Chicken!" by Phil Perlmutter (2500 words)★★
Juvenile psychotics Bunty and Petey try out their rifle in the city park.

Vol. 4 No. 11 Nov 1956
First and only appearance of Charles Einstein ("Manila Mission"), author of The Bloody Spur.

"Pigeon in an Iron Lung" by Talmage Powell (2500 words)★★★

Entrepreneur Dave catches a bad break when he's left relying on an iron lung due to polio but, at least, he has his young and gorgeous wife, Cindy, to help pass the time. Then Dave becomes convinced Cindy and her new "friend," Arnold, are planning to kill him.

Brilliantly adapted by William Fay for the fifth season of *Alfred Hitchcock Presents*. Essentially, a two-actor play, the re-titled "No Pain" features bravura performances by Brian Keith and a smoldering Joanna Moore. There's a none-too-subtle sexuality (some might call it misogyny) in the way director Norman Lloyd lets the camera linger on Ms. Moore's tight shorts that cannot be ignored. This could be *the* best visualization of a *Manhunt* story.

"Who's Calling?" by Robert Turner (4000 words)★★

Jay Breen is getting phone calls from a man looking for a James Binford. Turns out Binford embezzled a tidy sum and murdered a wise accountant before settling down as Mr. Breen. Now Breen's past has caught up with him and his wife. Fairly obvious twist ending.

"Who's Calling?" has an odd history. It was dramatized on the Studio 57 television show on February 14, 1956, but didn't appear in print until months later. The teleplay was written by TV veteran Lawrence Kimble (who also scripted episodes of *Mike Hammer* and State Trooper) and starred Pat O'Brien as Jay Breen, with Virginia Bruce as his wife, Beth.

"The Tormentors" by Gil Brewer (3000 words)★↙

Unpleasant story about a mentally-challenged man and the thugs who torment him daily. There's an interesting twist at the climax but the surprise doesn't make the tale much better.

"Death Beat" by David C. Cooke (1000 words)★

The musings of a beat cop as the city reels from a series of stranglings.

"Cowpatch Vengeance" by Charles W. Moore (5000 words)★★

Rabbit doesn't know how to tell Pa that Ma is stealing time with neighbor Jud Kimball but it's a moot point once Pa is killed, supposedly, by the family's prize bull. Rabbit is convinced that Jud had a hand in Pa's death and he'll bide his time. "Cowpatch Vengeance" is not a bad story but it's heavily padded and free of any surprises.

"Guts" by John R. Starr (1000 words)★

A punk kid stands up to mob boss Fatso Kelly but, when the time comes to pull the trigger, the kid turns tail and runs. There's a humorous climax, which is appropriate since "Guts" reads more like a padded joke than a story.

"Death Wears a Gray Sweater" by Roy Carroll (6000 words)★★★
Irv Walsh watches in horror as his daughter is killed in a hit-and-run. He chases the car to a nearby field but is then savagely beaten by the driver and his friends. When he comes to, he's taken by the police to the station for questioning and then released. Rather than tell the police all he knows, Irv decides to track down and kill the man responsible for his daughter's death. Fast-paced action-mystery with a down-beat and surprising climax.

"Zero ... Double Zero" by Stuart Friedman (7000 words)★★★⸲
Reno roulette girl Lynne enlists loser Charlie to bust the house. Though the story can dwell on the technical terms at times to the detriment of the pacing, "Zero... Double Zero" is an excellent gambling thriller. Though Stuart Friedman found success with crime fiction, both short and novel-length, he's best known for his string of "erotic" novels published by Monarch, among them *The Revolt of Jill Braddock*, *The Way We Love* (both 1960), *The Fly Girls* (1961), and *Damned are the Meek* (1964).

"Naked Petey" by Jack Q. Lynn (3000 words)★⸲
Three J.D.s attempt to blackmail a beat cop. Bad idea. Lynn inflicts Ellson-style J.D. lingo on the reader.

"Four Hours to Kill" by F. J. Smith (3000 words)★★★
A high-class prostitute has four hours to burn before her next "date." Bored, she plays a game of "tease" with the apartment's custodian, who's working on her bathroom sink. The game gets out of hand when alcohol is introduced and the big man begins to understand he's being made a fool.

"Three's a Crowd" by Joe Grenzeback (3500 words)★★★⸲
Pete and Nita cook up a full-proof scheme to rob J. Martin Fletcher of his jewelry collection but they need a third wheel, someone they can pin the robbery on once the heist is complete. Big, burly Sammy seems to be the perfect dupe and his crush on Nita only helps matters. Things begin to unravel though, once the robbery is underway and it turns out that Fletcher is the mastermind and Pete, Sammy, and Nita are the three stooges. Fast-paced heist thriller has an ironic and satisfying twist in its climax. The best of the four Joe Grenzeback *Manhunt* stories.

"Manila Mission" by Charles Einstein (14,000 words)★★★
Exciting espionage thriller about two cops (one American, one Australian) assigned to help the Manila police force get its house in order shortly after the end of World War II. The duo are assigned the murder of a local chauffeur, who may or may not have been cooperating with the enemy. There are a few too many one-liners but the two cops, Beatty and Heath, are very likable characters and the story

Peter Enfantino • Jeff Vorzimmer

moves along quickly. This was Charles Einstein's only *Manhunt* story but he also had a handful of tales that made their way into *Alfred Hitchcock*. As a novelist, he's best remembered for *The Bloody Spur* (Dell, 1953), filmed by Fritz Lang as *While the City Sleeps*.

Vol. 4 No. 12 Dec 1956

First and only appearance of legendary Western author, Clair Huffaker ("A Couple of Bucks"). First of four consecutive covers by Ray Houlihan.

"High Dive" by Robert Turner (3000 words)★♩
Spencer is sure his wife is fooling around with his wife and he aims to get his revenge. His weapon of choice is the boss's swimming pool.

"Degree of Guilt" by Jack Ritchie (2000 words)★★★
When his daughter is raped, a man takes the law into his own hands... perhaps a bit too soon. "Degree of Guilt" climaxes with a particularly nasty image.

"A Couple of Bucks" by Clair Huffaker (1500 words)★★
George has always bragged to the guys at the bar how he's going to pull the big job someday. Then, one day, he does it. A rare dive into crime fiction from a writer best known for his western novels (*The Cowboy and the Cossack* has developed something of a cult following since its publication in 1973) and screenplays for John Wayne vehicles (*The Comancheros*, *War Wagon*, and *Hellfighters*), "A Couple of Bucks" was Clair Huffaker's only contribution to *Manhunt*.

"I Dig You, Real Cool" by De Forbes (3500 words)★★♩
Deejay Bob Underhill wins the favor of an anonymous admirer, who signs their letters "I Dig You, Real Cool," when he speaks out against juvenile gangs. It quickly becomes apparent the admirer may be a young coquette named Lilly Blane. Bob develops an unhealthy admiration for the teen but his whole world falls apart when he's accused of Lilly's murder. Told mostly as a letter from Bob in prison, "I Dig You, Really Cool" takes a bit of time to work up the suspense but the final act is, literally, a killer.

"Vacation Nightmare" by Roy Carroll (3500 words)★★★
On the way home from vacation, a family is terrorized by three hillbillies in southern Georgia. The mother and daughter are raped and the father is severely beaten. When the women manage to escape and come back with help, the man acts out every he-man's fantasy by refusing a trip to the hospital and instead heads out to hunt down and kill the men who tore apart his family. The ancestor of James Dickey's *Deliverance* and any number of Richard Laymon novels, "Vacation" is a taut little thriller marred only by a predictable and ridiculous outcome. Mind you, it's not the fact that the man goes back to extract his piece of flesh from the hicks, it's the manner in which he delivers that revenge that I found silly.

"The Face of a Killer" by Charles Beaumont (3500 words)★★♩
Deciding he needs a new life, career criminal Frank Lampredi studies Giannini Musso, a very wealthy man for weeks and then approaches a shady plastic sur-

geon with a grim plan: Lampredi will murder Musso and assume his life of splendor. When the time is right, Frank has his operation, recuperates, then sneaks into Musso's mansion one night to murder him. The only problem, Lampredi discovers the next day, is that Musso died a week before and left his estate to his housekeeper.

"G. I. Pigeon" by Joseph F. Karrer (4000 words)★★★
Doc recalls, to a few of his pals, the time he helped one of his barmaids kill her husband with the help of a witless G.I. Engaging thriller with a clever wrap-up.

"Man with a Shiv" by Richard Wormser (11,500 words)★★★
Patrolman Macaley and his partner, Gresham, interrupt a diamond robbery but Gresham is killed and the hoods get away. Wounded, Macaley stashes some of the left-over ice in his shoe and then tends to his partner before passing out. Coming to in the hospital, Macaley is given a choice: he can go up the river for life as an accessory to murder or go undercover in prison and find out who killed his partner.
Once in the penitentiary, Macaley tries to learn what he can but bad luck just seems to come natural to him and the man who may be able to answer his questions ends up dead. Life in the stir hardens him and Mac begins to wonder if he wouldn't be better off behind bars. The most fascinating aspects of "Man with a Shiv" are the see-saw mental state of Mac, and what he has to do in order to stay alive in the pen.
"Man with a Shiv" is the first of four stories Richard Wormser contributed to *Manhunt* and all four were of consistently high quality. Wormser got his start writing Nick Carter, Private Detective stories for the pulp of the same name (under the NC pseudonym) then graduated to novels under his own name. Wormser would bounce back and forth between westerns (*The Lonesome Quarter, Slattery's Range*) and mysteries (*The Late Mrs. Five, Drive East on 66*) his entire career. Wormser's *The Body Looks Familiar* (Dell, 1958) is a fabulously constructed novel about a man framed for murder by a hotshot D.A.

"Payment in Full" by Dave Leigh (1500 words)★★
Cole knows he shouldn't go out in the boat with Markham after sleeping with Markham's wife, Sally, but he just can't help himself. Now he's staring down the barrel of Markham's pistol. The outcome is a bit too predictable.

"Lust Song" by Stuart Friedman (5000 words)★★★
Barton lusts for the wife of his hired hand. She's no good, giving it away nightly to the men in town, but Barton doesn't care. He has to have her no matter what the cost. In the end, Barton gets what he wishes for but it's not exactly how he pictured it. "Lust Song" has a nice, easy Summer-in-the-South vibe to it, avoiding any bursts of violence, but the story has an uneasiness running through its entire length, as if that burst is just around the corner.

"A Clear Day for Hunting" by Jack Q. Lynn (4000 words)★★★⌐

Mrs. Arnold enlists her new boarder, Ralph Karston, to murder her beau for his money. A violent and grim thriller with a soulless protagonist worthy of a Jim Thompson novel. In fact, "A Clear Day For Hunting" begs for an expanded version. Jack Lynn's first two stories for *Manhunt* ("A Helluva Ball" and "Naked Petey") were badly-written and clichéd but none of those habits show their heads here; the writing is crisp and brutal:

> *I stopped breathing and squeezed the trigger. The recoil jarred my shoulder, but I saw the top of Harry Schmidt's head fly off and his brains spray out like the vomit from a sick drunk. And then he was sprawled in the mess, flat on his back. There were empty holes where his eyes had been, His nose was shattered. But his mouth and jaw were intact.*

"So Much Per Body" by Jonathan Craig (1000 words)★★

Eddie Blivens is interviewing for a new job. The questioning leads the reader to believe that the new job's title is "hitman," but author Craig manages to throw a fairly effective curve ball towards the finale of the story.

"A Job for Johnny" by Lawrence Burne (2500 words)★

A mobster's wife is blackmailing him and her former beau is searching for her, only wanting to help. Slow pace and a ludicrous and predictable twist sink this one.

"Showdown at Midnight" by Edward L. Perry (2500 words)★

A beat cop wages war against a J.D. gang after the young thugs rape a teenage girl. The reveal, when it comes, is not much of a surprise.

"The Fast Line" by Art Crockett (1000 words)★★

Chuck has to do some fast thinking to talk Rudy out of ventilating him. There's not much here (due to the word count) but the author wisely saves his best for the climax. Art Crockett may have been king of the "low-budget" crime digests, having placed dozens of stories in titles such as *Keyhole, Off-Beat, Web Detective*, and *Two-Fisted*, but "The Fast Line" was his only appearance in *Manhunt*.

Peter Enfantino • Jeff Vorzimmer

The Best Stories of 1956

"Who Killed Helen?" by Bryce Walton (January)
"Madman" by Roy Carroll (March)
"Hunch" by Helen Nielsen (March)
"Still Screaming" by F. L. Wallace (July)
"Seven Lousy Bucks" by C. L. Sweeney, Jr (August)
"Key Witness" by Frank Kane (August)
"Badge of Dishonor" by Norman Struber (September)
"The Secret" by Stuart Friedman (September)
"Zero… Double Zero" by Stuart Friedman (November)
"Three's a Crowd" by Joe Grenzeback (November)

Vol. 5 No. 1 Jan 1957
First and only appearance of Theodore Pratt ("Stranger in the House").

"The Rabbit Gets a Gun" by John D. MacDonald (2500 words)★★
Daydreaming, Frank heads back to his motel room and accidentally steps into his neighbor's room. Inside are three hoods who have just had a big payday. What to do with Frank?

"Cop for a Day" by Henry Slesar (2500 words)★★★
Phil and his gang pull off a big heist and score eighteen grand, but there's a fatality and, worse, a witness. Now the woman is holed up in a precinct with cops on all sides. Phil is determined to get in the building and silence the one person who could send him to the chair, so he gets his big mitts on a cop's uniform and walks through the doors. The hit goes smoothly, Phil escapes but, ironically, remembers at the last second he forgot to tell the gang about his get-up. Lively short with a laugh-out-loud final paragraph.

Henry Slesar had no one but himself to blame if he didn't like the teleplay for the *Alfred Hitchcock Presents* adaptation of "Cop For a Day." Slesar wrote 18 teleplays for AHP, most from his own stories. The seventh season episode featured Walter Matthau as Phil and Glenn Cannon as Davey (the rest of Phil's gang from the story clearly were not in the budget) and retained that killer of a finish.

"Face of Evil" by David Alexander (3500 words)★★
Lester Ferguson may well be the only man who can identify the Butcher, a serial killer stalking the streets of the city but he's not much help to the police. Lester lies in a hospital bed in shock, after witnessing his wife become the Butcher's latest conquest, and answers every question with a vague "I've seen the face of evil." Not one of David Alexander's best, "Face of Evil" is repetitive and presents a maddeningly vague outcome. Adapted the same year for *The M Squad* TV show starring Lee Marvin.

"Smart Sucker" by Richard Wormser (5000 words)★★★
It's been a bad day for Henry Croft so all he wants is a beer to drown his sorrows but, when he walks into a small tavern on a side street, he finds himself in the middle of something very disturbing. The bar is the hang-out of some very nasty characters who use Henry's weaknesses against him. A very odd story that seems to shift gears every few pages but in a satisfying way.

"A Ride Downtown" by Robert Turner (1000 words)★★↙
Hamilton has decided that he's going to put an end to the affair between Kay and Don so he takes a ride to Don's and strangles him. Short-short does a good job throwing the reader off track and then delivering an effective twist at the climax.

"Somebody's Going to Die" by Talmage Powell (3500 words)★★★
After his business partner catches him embezzling and threatens to go to the police, Enos decides that murder is the only way out. Well, actually, Enos' gorgeous wife, Doreen, talks him into being a man and eliminating any obstacles to their happy future. The foundation of "Somebody's Going to Die" isn't too original but it's the transformation of Doreen that's most intriguing. By the finale, Enos is more afraid of his wife than the repercussions of his violent act.

"His Own Jailor" by Bryce Walton (4000 words)★★★★
Morgan, a diamond seller, is obsessed with the beautiful Rose who, in turn, is obsessed with jewels. Morgan has been selling diamonds for years and has never been ripped off but, shortly after visiting Rose, he's kidnapped and robbed of 70k in diamonds. Sadly, Morgan knows who's behind the heist. Enthralling and unique, "His Own Jailor" is a masterpiece of understatement and suspense. It's odd that the story wasn't snapped up for the *Hitchcock* show.

"Bait for the Red-Head" by Eugene Pawley (11,500 words)★★
When one of his fellow officers is gunned down, rookie cop Ron Jordan is asked to go undercover and use all of his manly skills to bring a witness out of her shell. Though his superiors warn him not to get "too involved," Jordan finds himself falling for the girl big time. Average thriller with not many surprises and a very annoying two-page expository at its climax.

"Stranger in the House" by Theodore Pratt (2000 words)★
Mrs. Belding's cleaning woman may not be what she appears to be. Nineteen hundred words of expository leads to one ludicrous "twist."

"... Into the Parlor" by Paul Eiden (5000 words)★★
Elroy Diener is one of those short-order cooks who just fades into the background; nothing exciting ever happens in his life. Then, on a whim, he calls Linda, a gorgeous model he's seen in a magazine and a date is made. When Elroy gets to the woman's apartment, he's beaten and taken in by a detective named Patterson. There, the cop explains that Linda has been threatened by a psycho and Elroy might be able to help the police in their investigation. Unfortunately, Patterson is running a deadly con and the hapless Elroy has fallen into the spider's web. Needlessly complicated and wordy, "...Into the Parlor" picks up steam only when it reaches its violent and shocking climax.

"Never Kill a Mistress" by Carroll Mayers (1500 words)★★✦
When a wealthy businessman accidentally kills his mistress, he enlists the help of a cabbie to dispose of the body. Fairly average blackmail tale is upped a notch by a nasty twist in the final paragraphs.

"Shoot Them Down" by Bob Bristow (3000 words)★★
Simplistic but fairly exciting melodrama about an attempted prison break.

"On a Sunday Afternoon" by Gil Brewer (5500 words)★★★★

A young couple and their daughter are terrorized by punks while on a Sunday picnic in the woods. "On a Sunday Afternoon" is an odd story, one that begins with, perhaps, a glimpse of infidelity, but soon travels down a completely different path. That path has certainly been done to death by lesser writers, but Brewer subtly builds to an explosively violent showdown, one that allows the reader to exhale only after its final sentence.

"Perfect Getaway" by Henry Petersen (1000 words)★★★

After robbing a bank, a woman decides that fifty grand is much better when it's not split down the middle. Evidently, her partner in crime has decided the same. That rarity, a short-short that works fabulously and makes you wish it had been given more room to breathe.

Vol. 5 No. 2 Feb 1957
First and only appearance of sci-fi writer, Murray Leinster writing as Will F. Jenkins ("Possessed")

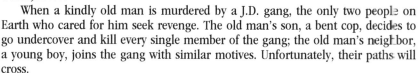

"The Teacher" by Robert Turner (3500 words)★★✦
A young girl, waiting at the bus stop, is offered a ride by a man she believes is one of her teachers. He's not. Harrowing thriller has what some may deem a very misogynistic climax.

"Got a Match?" by David Alexander (4500 words)★★★
When a kindly old man is murdered by a J.D. gang, the only two people on Earth who cared for him seek revenge. The old man's son, a bent cop, decides to go undercover and kill every single member of the gang; the old man's neighbor, a young boy, joins the gang with similar motives. Unfortunately, their paths will cross.

"Troublemakers" by Earl Fultz (3000 words)★★★
Coming back from a business trip in Mexico, a lawyer is harassed on the road by two punks. 1950s road rage in a very suspenseful little drama.

"Possessed" by Will F. Jenkins (2500 words)★★✦
When shopkeeper Tom Kennedy is brutally murdered, the sheriff arrests Tom's employee, Joe Hansford, who happens to be the sheriff's future son-in-law. On the way to the jail, the sheriff picks up an old hitch-hiker who, after only a few minutes, holds a gun to the sheriff's head and confides that he's the actual killer. Will F. Jenkins was better known for the science fiction he wrote under his pseudonym, Murray Leinster.

"Long Distance" by Fletcher Flora (2500 words)★★
With a ten-grand reward in the offing, a gorgeous gal acts as bait for the cops to nab her beau, who's wanted for armed robbery and murder.

"They'll Find Out!" by Richard Hardwick (2000 words)★
Arleigh's been sexually repressed since his folks caught him in the basement with the Watkins girl and put the belt to his rear. Now, six years later, Arleigh's seventeen and a very sexy girl has moved in next door. When the girl catches Arleigh spying on her at night, she seduces the boy and all his pent-up desires explode. Embarrassingly bad psycho-sexual nonsense. This was Richard Hardwick's third published story and the author would place over seventy more in the crime digests (with nine featuring his Sheriff Peavy character), most frequently in *Alfred Hitchcock,* becoming a much more accomplished writer with time.

"Divide and Conquer" by Jack Ritchie (3000 words)★★★
Three grifters ride into town and try to put the strong-arm on nightclub owner

Tommy Harrigan but Tommy uses his wits and good looks to quash the toughies. A thoroughly enjoyable farce starring a character not unlike Richard Deming's Clancy Ross, and peppered with genuinely funny dialogue.

"The 'H' Killer" by Ed McBain (15,500 words)★★★⌁
Detective Steve Carella of the 87th Precinct investigates the apparent suicide of a heroin addict but the deeper he gets the more he becomes convinced the boy was murdered. At the same time, another 87th detective, Peter Byrnes, discovers his son is an addict and may have had something to do with the murder. Carella is tipped off that the kid's pusher is a tough guy named "Gonzo" and, during an undercover meeting, Carella is shot and mortally wounded by the thug. Suddenly, the entire 87th is hunting "Gonzo."

The readers of *Manhunt* get their first look at Ed McBain's 87th Precinct, a series that will change the face of crime fiction and birth dozens (if not hundreds) of copycats. First thing's first, "The 'H' Killer" is a condensed version of the third 87th novel, *The Pusher*, published at the end of 1956. This was Evan Hunter's finale in a three-book deal with Perma and he originally planned to kill off Carella in that book, thinking he could replace the character with another detective. But his editor at Perma intervened and Carella survived.

What's so interesting about "The 'H' Killer" then is that the novella has the original climax where Steve dies, omitting a very important paragraph found in the published novel. Of course, paring down a 160-page novel to a novella means something has to go but the various sub-plots (chiefly, the time Carella spends at home with his wife, Teddy) are well-excised and what we're left with is an exciting and well-written crime drama.

"The Broken Window" by Earle Basinsky, Jr. (1500 words)★
Earle Basinsky, Jr.s three stories for the crime pulps were all short and unremarkable, flawed by outlandish premises and silly expositories. In 'The Broken Window', our nameless narrator is accused by the police of knocking off his rival for the affection of Susan. Our man, however, convinces the police to let him have a go at the crime scene. Once there, he points out to the police a broken window pane which leads to a hidden gun in a trap door in the ceiling (!!). This, of course, as our narrator points out, is exactly how a man would commit suicide and pin it on an innocent man. Basinsky can't leave us stranded in this wild scenario, so he does what any good mystery writer would do: he has his protagonist explain what really happened in the last paragraph.

"Enough Rope for Two" by Clark Howard (4500 words)★★★★
After ten years in the stir, Kedzie is a free man and he's heading to New Mexico to retrieve one hundred grand he dropped into a well just before he went up the river. Before he takes the road trip, he stops and picks up his old partner, Maxie, the guy who fingered him for the job. Maxie wants his share but Kenzie's plan is to keep the whole package for himself and leave an even bigger package, namely Maxie, at the bottom of the well.

A very clever revenge tale with lots of crosses and double-crosses, "Enough

Peter Enfantino • Jeff Vorzimmer

Rope for Two" was adapted for the *Alfred Hitchcock Presents* show and aired November 15, 1957. Howard wrote hundreds of short stories over a nearly six-decade career, most of which appeared in *Alfred Hitchcock* and *Ellery Queen*.

"Run, Carol, Run!" by Talmage Powell (2500 words)★★
Wealthy Donald Norton hires gumshoe Joe Gallagher to bring his daughter back home. Gallagher soon discovers that the young lady is shacking up with an ex-fighter and doesn't necessarily *want* to come home.

"The Cross Forks Incident" by Thomas P. Ramirez (5000 words)★★★
Violent melodrama about racial tension in a small 1950s cannery town.

"The Big Smile" by Stan Wiley (2000 words)★
An elderly dentist is terrorized by a sadistic J.D. Unpleasant bit of rubbish.

Vol. 5 No. 3 Mar 1957

First magazine-size (quarto) issue. The page count for the larger issues would be 64. The spine color is changed from yellow to white. First and only appearance of James Causey with "Deathmate," which would be filmed as an episode of Alfred Hitchcock Presents. That same year he published the novels Killer Take All *and* The Baby Doll Murders.

"Dead as a Mannequin" by Rex Raney (2000 words)★

Dean Jacobs beats his wife to death with a mannequin's arm. He then has to figure out how to move the body, from the clothing store he owns, back to his house. All this trouble on Dean's birthday! When Dean gets home, he gets the surprise of his life.

"Golden Opportunity" by J. W. Aaron (3000 words)★★★

Paul Devore, manager of the Cresthaven department store, happens into a good thing at the right time. He catches Lois Callen shoplifting and blackmails her into helping him bilk his wife out of her fortune. Unfortunately for Paul, he hasn't thought the whole plan through. "Golden Opportunity" was adapted for *Alfred Hitchcock Presents* simply as "The Opportunity" on May 22, 1962, starring Richard Long and Colleen Gray as the two lead characters.

"Victim Number Six" by Robert Plate (1500 words)★★

Fowler's daughter, Alice, is on trial for the "Hatpin" murders, foul deeds wherein five men have had needles plunged into their ears. Fowler is convinced his daughter is guilty and that it's his fault for raising his daughter the wrong way. Is there something he can do to deflect the suspicion from her?

"The Big Hate" by Frank Cetin (3000 words)★

A young J.D. falls for a local whore but she's not buying what he's selling. "The Big Hate" is minimal writing that adds nothing to the J.D. fiction genre.

"Pick-Up" by Richard Deming (3000 words)★★★

Harry and Betty pick up a hitchhiking soldier just outside Fort Bliss and Betty's flirting gets out of hand, culminating in a brutally violent showdown between soldier and Harry. There's not much to "Pick-Up" but its powerful climax and Deming's crisp writing.

"A Place for Emily" by F. J. Smith (4000 words)★★★

Cliff Staley's murdered his big-mouthed wife and he's digging her a grave out back near the barn where her body lies hidden. Well, he's trying to dig a hole but he can't seem to get any work done when neighbor Seth Jacks comes over to ask a million questions about Cliff's yard work. Things get worse when Trooper Jacks drops by and nothing Cliff tells him rings true. Eventually, the trooper is going to find out what's under that blanket in the barn. A very dark comedy almost resembling an Abbott and Costello skit, with poor Cliff Staley interrupted right and left by inquisitive minds.

"Shadowed" by Richard Wormser (2000 words)★★★✔
Gordon Harris is having his wife followed by a P.I. and the gumshoe has distressing news for Harris: Muriel heads to the house of family friend Harvey Melton every day like clockwork. Harris dismisses the P.I. and heads to Melton's place, with no notion he's being set up by his conniving wife. Brilliant and twisty, "Shadowed" also has a very risqué final paragraph where we discover there might be another motive for Muriel wanting Gordon out of the way.

"The Man Who Was Everywhere" by Edward D. Hoch (1000 words)★
Ray is convinced a strange Englishman has been following him.

"War Talk" by Philip Weck (5000 words)★✔
A social worker finds a surly J.D. is after his wife.

"He Never Went Home" by Craig Rice (12,500 words)★★
John J. Malone is called to the aid of a sweet young commercial model who wakes up to find the local gossip columnist in her living room. That would be scandalous on its own but the knife in his chest would make it front page news. John J. does what he does best, including tampering with evidence and lying to the police. It's all very cozy.

"To Save a Body" by Henry Slesar (3500 words)★★★
Tired of slaving his life away while his boss rakes in the millions, Toby plots with his brother to give the man a big scare and put him in Toby's debt. But a twist of fate ruins Toby's plans.

"Deathmate" by James Causey (3500 words)★★
Con artist Ben Conant has his hooks into a sure thing, a tuna cannery heiress with a dope of a husband, but a private investigator forces Ben to change his plans quickly. But for a dandy double cross, "Deathmate" is a weak read, with a clichéd lead character. "Deathmate" was filmed for the *Alfred Hitchcock Presents* show and aired on April 18, 1961.

"The Late Gerald Baumann" by Bob Bristow (5500 words)★✔
Dreary and padded nonsense about a trucker who fakes his own death but may be in for a rude awakening after his wife and her lover plot to escape with the insurance money.

"Next!" by Talmage Powell (1500 words)★
Marty is very nervous about his visit to the barber, the long thin razor making the hair on his arms stand on end.

Vol. 5 No. 4 Apr 1957

The issue that was the subject of the lawsuit United States v. Flying Eagle Publications (see "The History of Manhunt.") Cover by Tom O'Sullivan.

"Body on a White Carpet" by Al James (3000 words)★★★
Mac eyes the lovely broad at the other end of the bar. "Would she be interested in spending time with a small time jewel thief?," he wonders. Well, yes, she would, provided Mac does a very small favor for her. When he follows her back to her ritzy penthouse apartment, he discovers the favor is dumping a body for the babe.
Al James contributed dozens of thrillers for "lower-tier" crime digests such as *Trapped, Guilty, Off Beat,* and *Saturn Web Detective,* but managed to break into the big leagues of *Manhunt* on six occasions. Good writing was in James's DNA; his father was crime writer Day Keene. "Body on a White Carpet," his first, is an amiable read with a very dark, but also very funny, last paragraph.

"Use Five Grand?" by Michael Zuroy (4000 words)★★★
Andy's nothing special, but he *was* a war hero and perhaps that's why the stranger offers him five grand to rub out Ben Fuller. The hit comes off without a hitch and Andy is offered a second job. Murder seems to become easier.

"Night Job" by Robert Plate (2500 words)★★⤴
Detective Sanders is trying to convince Lou Billows to confess to torching his own store but Lou won't budge until he hears the brutal twist Sanders has to throw at him.

"The Percentage" by David Alexander (7000 words)★★
Big Eddie Scarsi has made a success of his life; he's a big-time mobster, he's got a great-looking dame, and his bank account swells every night. There's only one thing Big Eddie doesn't have and that's peace of mind. It all stems from an incident in WWII when, as a Sergeant, Eddie's legs went weak and a pipsqueak named Pete Wladek stepped in and mowed down advancing Germans. If there's one thing Big Eddie hates, it's owing. So, he's been searching for Pete for the last decade so he could somehow even the score but the guy just can't be found. Until Pete's TV set goes out and the Apex repair man is none other than Pete!
Eddie tries to get Pete to take money or favors but Pete is just too honest and hard-working to take charity. When Pete's wife, Louise, begins putting the moves on Eddie, the mob man finally knows how he can wipe out his debt to Pete. If you can look past the whopping coincidence, "The Percentage" is not a bad read but Eddie's ongoing internal strife concerning his debt can be a bit repetitious and the final paragraphs contain a needless twist. "The Percentage" was adapted for the third season of *Alfred Hitchcock Presents* in 1958.

"Was It Worth It, Mr. Markell?" by Lawrence Spingarn (2500 words)★
The owner of a chemical plant hides the fact that several of his assembly line girls are dropping like flies. His just desserts are delivered after he forces himself on one of his employees. Silly pseudo-science fiction.

"Object of Desire" by Paul Swope (1000 words)★
A strangler claims his latest prize.

"Joy Ride" by C. B. Gilford (4000 words)★★★⅃
Two J.D.s heist a car with driver intact. As they enjoy their free ride, the crime escalates and they discuss their options. A riveting and brutal read, not to be confused with the like-titled (and similarly-themed) C. B. Gilford story published in *Ellery Queen* just three months prior to the appearance of *this* "Joy Ride." *That* "Joy Ride," about four J.D.s who terrorize a couple in their home, was filmed in 1958 by Allied Artists.

"You Should Live So Long" by Jack Ritchie (3000 words)★★★
Maylee only wants to leave her life of prostitution but the boss has other ideas. Gritty short story with an effective twist.

"Locker 911" by Richard Wormser (8500 words)★★★
After leaving his wife and draining their bank account, poor schmuck Henry Reynolds is rolled by a prostitute and left penniless in a one-horse town. Shuffling drunken down the main street, Henry stumbles across a locker key and, after some investigating, discovers it opens a locker in a nearby bus station. Opening the locker, he finds a bag containing cash... lots of cash. But since Henry Reynolds is one of the unluckiest guys on the face of the Earth, his dreams of fortune and easy-living are short-lived. A fabulous roller-coaster ride, with a lead character who's easy to root for and a violent and satisfying climax that comes from out of the blue.

"Honey-Child" by Leslie Gordon Barnard (2000 words)★★
George and Clair are on their way to split the heist money with two other partners but Claire's trying to convince George that the whole pie is tastier than a slice.

"Express Stop" by Jason January (2500 words)★★
A young woman is assaulted by five J.D.s on a subway train until the other passengers move, like a wave, onto the youths. "Express Stop" has some interesting ideas but almost capsizes due to its silly climax.

"Death of a Big Wheel" by William Campbell Gault (12,000 words)★★
Tough guy P.I. Joe Puma just wants a nice drink and a quiet night at his favorite bar but when a washed-up actor named John Haskell takes the barstool next to his, the night is anything but peaceful. Haskell wants details about a well-

publicized murder case Puma helped crack and Joe offers to buy the drunk another round and a steak while he tells his story. A cute blonde and her moose bodyguard emerge from the shadows to make a scene and Puma has to deck the big guy. That ruins the mood and Haskell and Puma say their good nights. Two days later, Haskell's body is found with his head caved in and Joe Puma decides he's going to make it his business to solve the murder.

Joe Puma is a dynamic and well-rounded character but, unfortunately, he's stuck in a somewhat padded and boring case. Several bland supporting characters/suspects are introduced but none have the charisma of William Campbell Gault's P.I. The wrap-up comes complete with a long and unsatisfactory expository. The most fascinating aspect of the story is that Haskell wants to drill Puma about the events of "Deadly Beloved" (from the Oct 1956 issue); most P.I. series don't reference previous installments.

Peter Enfantino • Jeff Vorzimmer

Vol. 5 No. 5 May 1957
Last appearance by Henry Slesar. Cover by O. G. Brabbins.

"Prowler!" by Gil Brewer (2500 words)★
Uncharacteristically below-average Brewer short story about a man who's sleeping with his sister-in-law while a killer prowls the streets.

"Bet I Don't Die" by Arnold English (3000 words)★★
A death row inmate bets his comrades he'll miss his date with the executioner.

"College Kill" by Jack Q. Lynn (7000 words)★★★★
Happily married college teacher Matt Lane catches the eye of Edie Jackson, a gorgeous student, and begins flirting with the girl. The flirtation turns into a full-blown affair and a lost weekend filled with booze and sex. Luckily, for Matt, his wife is out of town but, unluckily, he learns Edie has taped their passion-filled nights and plans to use it against him at a later date. While out driving, Edie runs over a man and flees, leaving Matt with just one option: he'll need to kill Edie and ditch the car before the cops trace it back to them.
Matt cracks the girl over the head with a bottle, runs her over a few times for good effect, and then drives her car off a bridge, with Edie behind the wheel. But Matt isn't a professional killer so he inevitably leaves a trail of bread crumbs large enough for the cops to follow. "College Kill" is a gripping thriller with unflinching violence that could very easily have been expanded into an effective novel. Matt Lane begins as a likable guy, becomes someone we empathize with (we all make big mistakes at some point in our lives), but completes his character's arc as a loathsome monster.

"Razor, Razor, Gleaming Bright" by Roy Carroll (2000 words)★
A young girl must walk home after babysitting while the city is terrorized by a mad slasher. There's a positively ludicrous reveal in "Razor's" climax.

"Midnight Blonde" by Talmage Powell (3000 words)★★★
Larry meets the gorgeous, but mysterious, Jeannine in a bar and immediately puts the moves on her. They strike up a conversation but the blonde can't keep her eyes from that clock, now fast approaching midnight. Larry finally talks his prey into going somewhere else and just as the clock strikes midnight, she agrees. When they leave the bar, she screams and tears her own dress as Larry cries out in surprise and runs. The police shoot him down and Jeannine smiles, having scored another run for the girls' side. An intriguing set-up (the reason for Jeannine's clock-watching is a great twist) and a brutal end for Larry.

"40 Detectives Later" by Henry Slesar (3500 words)★★★
P.I. Tyree is hired by Mr. Munro Dean to set in motion a meeting between

Dean and the man who killed his wife several years before. Needing the dough, Tyree agrees and sets the meeting up at a local hotel but, having regrets, heads to the hotel room to prevent Dean from committing murder. Tyree enters the room just as the bullets fly and after both men are mortally wounded, Tyree learns the whole truth: the man is, indeed, the killer of Dean's wife but he was hired to do the deed by... Dean himself!

Tyree is your by-the-numbers P.I. with all the trappings, save a beautiful secretary, but Slesar's story crackles and keeps the reader's interest right up to its genuinely surprising twist. "40 Detectives Later" was adapted (by Slesar) for the sixth season of *Hitchcock*, with Arthur Hiller directing and James Franciscus (always a perfect casting choice for a P.I., I think) starring as Tyree with Jack Weston as the hitman.

"Toward a Grave" by Howard B. Schaeffer (2000 words)★★

Prostitute Helen Johnson is lying on a slab in the morgue but she's not dead yet. How can she get the attendant to realize she's still alive, especially when he seems more interested in making use of her pretty body while he still can? Writer Howard Schaeffer steals the classic hook from Louis Pollock's "Breakdown" and nixes the original's happy ending, opting for a much darker and seedier climax here.

"The Charles Turner Case" by Richard Deming (5500 words)★★★

When a colleague boasts of being seduced by a naked woman living across the courtyard from him, D.A. Frank Garby reminisces about a rape case he worked on—the case that made him a D.A. "The Charles Turner Case" is an engrossing crime drama, told mostly in flashback, with a startling twist in its climax.

"New Girl" by De Forbes (3000 words)★

Sylvia's a very pretty girl but she comes with a high price. Street hustler Patsy swears he's ready to give Sylvia anything she wants.

"The Deadly Dolls" by Henry Kane (23,000 words)★★

Lawyer/gumshoe by night Peter Chambers comes to the aid of Gordon Phelps, a multi-millionaire accused of murdering his blackmailer, Vivian Frayne, a gorgeous exotic dancer at the Nirvana Ballroom. What Phelps didn't know and what Chambers comes to find out is that Vivian is an experienced blackmailer and one of her past marks might be her killer. Antiquated and overlong, "The Deadly Dolls" is a bit of a chore to tread through. Expanded and published as *Death is the Last Lover* by Avon in 1959.

Peter Enfantino • Jeff Vorzimmer

Vol. 5 No. 6 Jun 1957

Hal Walker takes over as Editor. Cover by Ray Houlihan.

"The Woman-Chasers" by Bryce Walton (3500 words)★★

Ella is having a hard time living on her street thanks to the thugs who catcall and ogle her as she walks by. The police won't do a thing but luckily she has strong Mr. Lewis to save her.

"The Amateur" by Richard Deming (4000 words)★★✦

Casino manager Clancy Ross finds his elevator man dead, a fancy bone-handled knife sticking out of his chest. Since Clancy's employee was having an affair with the estranged wife of a mafia goon, Clancy immediately suspects the mobster of foul play. But there may have been another interested party. Even if the plot is dreary, the snappy patter between the headliner and his Man Friday, Sam Black, always makes a Clancy Ross mystery immensely readable.

"He's Never Stopped Running" by Aaron Marc Stein (5000 words)★★★★

Rick's an ex-con but he's pulled himself back up by getting a decent job and keeping his nose clean. Now, he's met Grace, and she seems to be all he's ever wanted. They date and quickly decide to marry but Grace's father doesn't seem very enthusiastic. That's because he's done his homework and hired someone to look into Rick's past. If he has anything to do with it, his daughter won't be marrying a jailbird.

Strong writing grips the reader from the get-go and doesn't let up, with the climax delivering a very powerful blow. Stein, who also wrote several short stories and novels under the pseudonyms of George Bagby and Hampton Stone, usually wrote "cozy" mysteries but "He's Never Stopped Running" is anything but.

"The Geniuses" by Max Franklin (7000 words)★★★★

Two college students, who fancy themselves geniuses, decide to kill a campus football star and dispose of his body to prove they can get away with murder. Engrossing thriller written by Richard Deming, under his Max Franklin alias, and obviously inspired by Leopold and Loeb, builds to an edge-of-the-seat climax, both horrifying and hilarious.

When Robert Bloch adapted the story for *Alfred Hitchcock Presents*, he jettisoned just about every facet of Deming's story but the shock ending. Filmed as "Bad Actor," the TV play stars a very young Robert Duvall as alcoholic actor, Bart Collins, washed up and hoping for that big comeback role in a new play. A younger actor, Jerry Lane, comes along and, when it looks like the new blood will get the prime part, Bart snaps and strangles him. Bart is disposing of the body with acid in his bathtub but is interrupted in his deed by his girlfriend and agent at the door. Jerry's head winds up in the ice bucket and so begins the tension. A well-paced and marvelously acted thriller.

"Blood on the Land" by Hal Ellson (4000 words)★⌐
A padded tale of lust and murder on a small farm.

"The Woman Who Knew Too Much" by Harold Q. Masur (6000 words)★★
When millionaire Matthew Barzun dies in a freak house fire, it kicks off a battle for his estate. Barzun's son, Owen, approaches lawyer Scott Jordan to represent him in what he believes will be a contentious court battle. The lawyer discovers that the old man had drafted his will with Jordan's predecessor, which may be why Owen has come knocking at his office door. It's up to Scott Jordan to uncover the truth.

"Kill the Clown" by Richard S. Prather (22,000 words)★★⌐
Shell Scott is hanging around the office when he's visited by the gorgeous Doris Miller, who's hoping Shell will take her case. Or rather her brother's case, since it's Ross Miller who needs saving from Death Row. Miller supposedly killed K.C. Flagg, a lawyer he'd been feuding with, but a witness has come forward to Ms. Miller and confessed he lied on the stand to save his life. The actual murderer of Flagg was mob boss Frank Quinn. Scott is intrigued by the details and Doris's gams so he takes on the case but very soon finds he may be in over his head.

Despite the fact that Shell Scott shares all the clichéd trappings with the rest of the 1950s P.I.s, I find the character fascinating and never boring. Perhaps it's author Prather's wit and flare for an action scene (such as the highway chase that ends in a rain of bullets) that elevates Scott above Peter Chambers or John J. Malone. Prather expanded "Kill the Clown" into a novel, published by Gold Medal in 1962.

"Decision" by Helen Nielsen (5000 words)★★
A young woman lives under the shadow of her domineering father and weak mother. When her personal life begins to unravel and the walls seem to be closing in on her, she strikes back violently. "Decision" reads more like a Harlequin romance novel than a dark crime story; a rare Nielsen misfire.

Peter Enfantino • Jeff Vorzimmer

Vol. 5 No. 7 Jul 1957
Cover by Dick Shelton.

"On the Sidewalk Bleeding" by Evan Hunter (3500 words)★★★
The last thoughts of a dying boy, stabbed by a rival gang member. Though "On the Sidewalk Bleeding" concerns the J.D. gangs, Evan Hunter wisely avoids the clichéd lingo that sinks so many similar-themed stories.

"Remember Biff Bailey?" by Jonathan Craig (3000 words)★★✔
John Bailey is determined to get revenge on Walt Manning, the newspaperman/fight insider who is responsible for the punch-drunk condition of John's brother, Biff.

"Bothered" by Gil Brewer (2500 words)★★
Little Kenny can't stand next-door neighbor, Mrs. Welch and, one day, gets rid of the woman with her own pruning shears.

"They Came with Guns" by Bruno Fischer (10,500 words)★★★
Jerry Harper awakens one night to the sound of something being dragged in the cellar. He gets up and goes down to the kitchen and finds the door thrown open. His wife, Fay, arrives home and explains she just saw a woman fleeing from the house. Fay, understandably, believes her husband is having an affair, but there's something far more sinister going on.
Jerry's sister Marion, wife of mobster Earle Peer, has set her husband up for a fall and headed out of town with twenty grand. What better place to hide the money than in her estranged brother's house? Unfortunately, Earle's employees know all about Marion and they want the money. Exciting melodrama with one of the oldest plots in the book, the innocent bystanders terrorized by thugs, but Bruno Fischer was a master of crafting great fiction out of the simplest of hooks.

"Lead Cure" by Talmage Powell (2500 words)★✔
Joe Edgerly only wants his new wife to be happy, so they'll work something out. The new bride won't allow Joe to touch her; it brings back memories of that man in the shack on the edge of the swamp. So Joe heads to the shack with his brand new handgun.

"A Piece of Ground" by Helen Nielsen (4000 words)★★★★
They called him "the farmer" because he'd lost his piece of ground and was now working like a slave to save up enough to buy another. Like a ritual, he deposits nearly all his earnings in the bank and writes a letter to his wife every night, assuring her that everything will be all right. That changes when he meets a young girl named Blanche and her "employer," Morrell, who convinces the

farmer" he can invest in the stock market and double his money overnight. Helen Nielsen's masterpiece, "A Piece of Ground" is unrelentingly grim and contains one of the most downbeat climaxes ever to appear in *Manhunt*.

"I Hate Cops" by Henry H. Guild (3500 words)★★
Danny wants to pull just one more big jewelry heist so he makes sweet with Rose, the Vandergrifts' maid, and sets himself up for a really big score. Too bad Rose is thinking along the same lines.

"The Man Who Was Two" by Richard Deming (6000 words)★★
This character study of a young man dealing with Oedipus complex and schizophrenia may have been bold for its time but the story itself really isn't very interesting, a trait not commonly attributed to the work of Richard Deming.

"Bunco" by John R. Starr (2000 words)★★
A moment of intimacy during a boring garment convention turns interesting when the cops show up.

"Movie Night" by Robert Turner (3500 words)★★★
Drive-In family night is ruined when two couples are harassed by juvenile delinquents. When the cops intervene, the folks decline to press charges. Bad move. Effective J.D. shocker with a mild jolt or two in its final paragraphs. Turner's J.D.s seem harmless until pushed and then they become dangerous psychopaths.

"Dead Pigeon" by Frank Kane (8000 words)★★↲
Ann Shields is convinced her old boyfriend, mobster Beau Thomas is going to kill her. Trouble with that notion, Johnny Liddell reminds her, is that Thomas is dead, burned to death in a traffic accident. Despite evidence to the contrary, Ann is steadfast in her denial. When Johnny goes to the investigating detective, he learns that Ann might not be crazy after all.

"The Substitute" by Henry Slesar (2500 words)★★★
Charlie owes five hundred bucks to a local hood and if he doesn't pay pronto, the guy's henchmen are going to cave Charlie's head in. A chance to earn some money in a very dodgy way comes up but Charlie figures beggars can't be choosers. A very funny short with a couple of clever twists.

Peter Enfantino • Jeff Vorzimmer

Vol. 5 No. 8 Sep 1957

Last appearance by Jonathan Craig ("Kitchen Kill"), who contributed 27 stories to the magazine. Cover by Dick Shelton.

"One Summer Night" by Bryce Walton (4000 words)★↲

Teenage Leo takes a shine to the woman who lives upstairs but she thinks Leo's too young. Tedious melodrama that takes a sudden and violent turn.

"Business as Usual" by Arnold English (3000 words)★★↲

Tension at the whorehouse when an escaped con comes to exact revenge on the prostitute who helped send him up the river.

"Say It With Flowers" by Craig Rice (9000 words)★★↲

Beautiful Miss McIlhenny begs John J. Malone to find her uncle, Jabez, missing for two weeks. Though Malone is about to catch a boat to Cuba for some RnR, he eventually caves in and agrees to look into the disappearance. Malone discovers that, as usual, there is no shortage of suspects. Though I always question why a lawyer is putting on a P.I. suit (or why anyone would come to his office to hire him for those services), it's easy to get lost in the "cozy" world of John J. Malone, thanks mostly to the breezy writing style of Craig Rice and the characters that populate Malone's world. There's also a very clever reveal in the final paragraph that is sure to bring a smile to a reader's face.

"Trespasser" by Fletcher Flora (3000 words)★★★

Agnew uses some information he's gathered to blackmail Mrs. Fenimore, a very beautiful and very rich woman with a sordid past. The joke's on him when he discovers the woman who shows up for the meeting is actually Mrs. Fenimore's secretary, who has been blackmailing her employer for years and can't stand the competition.

"Death of a Stripper" by Sherry La Verne (4000 words)★★★

Showgirl Mimi Love has fallen hard for her manager, Dave Exeter, but Dave has eyes for another stripper and plans to pop the question. A well-timed letter from a number-one-fan gives Mimi an idea of how to eliminate her competition. I can find no trace of an exotic dancer named Sherry La Verne so there's a good chance "Death of a Stripper" was written under an alias.

"Fly-By-Night" by Robert Gold (5000 words)★★★↲

With only a decade-old picture and minimal information, a P.I. takes on what he hopes will be his last case and then becomes obsessed with the girl he's searching for. A thoroughly absorbing drama, one that draws the reader in with each page turned. Devoid of sex, guns, or murder, it's not the usual cup of tea for

Manhunt. The wrap-up is a bit of a letdown but Gold's primary character, the weathered and tiring investigator, is so richly-delineated that you can't help but become immersed in each step of his journey.

"The Favor" by Talmage Powell (3500 words)★★
After he's tossed from a moving boxcar, Lonnie is rescued by a kind woman and her alcoholic husband but his presence in their house stirs up tension.

"Kitchen Kill" by Jonathan Craig (7500 words)★★
The gorgeous girl on the couch died from gas poisoning but Selby and Rayder are too smart to fall for the suicide trappings. The killer made a few errors and it's only a matter of time before the super detectives get their man (or woman). A by-the-numbers "Police Files" installment that left me cold.

Scripted by Lawrence Kimble (who also did several teleplays for *Mike Hammer*), "Kitchen Kill" was dramatized in the second season of *State Trooper* (airing on April 20, 1958), with Nevada trooper Lt. Rod Blake (played by western movie veteran Rod Cameron) standing in for Selby and Rayder. Kimble does a good job emphasizing characterization and minimizing the tools

"The Crying Target" by James McKimmey (11,000 words)★★★
Clintock is searching for the three men who murdered his brother but he discovers the story is a little more complicated than that. Seems Clint's brother, Bud, was involved with the three in a bank robbery and then hoofed it, money bags and all. Clintock is a fascinating anti-hero in the vein of Richard Stark's Parker, but with a conscience.

"Girl Friend" by Mark Mallory (3000 words)★★★
A powerful short, told mostly through police Q&As, about a fourteen-year-old girl driven into prostitution by her mother and facing jail time for a more serious crime. Mark Mallory is one of those mystery writers I can't seem to find much info on. This was his only story for *Manhunt* and he sold only a few more stories to digests such as *Alfred Hitchcock, Trapped* and *Double-Action Detective.* Though "Girl Friend" is a quick read, it's full of very good writing: "One of the hard things about being a cop is that you can excuse the bad in most people because it's in you, too…"

Peter Enfantino • Jeff Vorzimmer

Vol. 5 No. 9 Oct 1957

The last original Richard Prather story to appear in Manhunt is the only one that's not a Shell Scott story. Cover by O. G. Brabbins.

"Cut-Throat World" by J. W. Aaron (3000 words)★★
Wealthy businessman C.J. Victor is in trouble with the police; his mistress has just been found murdered and he's the number one suspect. He goes to his assistant, Barney, and asks the man to lie for him but the hole keeps getting deeper. A ludicrous climax ruins what might have been a decent thriller.

"Flesh" by Meyer Levin (4000 words)★
Though Meyer Levin was a respected novelist (his novel, *Compulsion*, inspired by Leopold and Loeb won an Edgar Award and was adapted into a well-received film in 1959), "Flesh" is an unreadable mish-mash about a butcher named Andreas, who has trouble with his new wife and then trouble with his cleaver.

"Top Dog" by Max Franklin (9500 words)★★✓
Rackets boss Marty DeCola gets wind of a takeover attempt by one of his guys. He's lucky to have a loyal right-hand man like Joel to handle the dirty work. "Top Dog" gets a bit complicated and the reveal is not very surprising, but the writing is crisp and engaging.

"Knife in His Hand" by Mike Brett (3500 words)★★✓
A peeping tom decides to elevate his game but picks the wrong woman as his first conquest. Michael Brett later went on to author the Pete McGrath, P.I. series of novels (ten novels total, beginning with *Kill Him Quickly, It's Raining*, published by Pocket) and several stories for *Alfred Hitchcock's Mystery Magazine*.

"The Rival Act" by Richard S. Prather (2000 words)★★✓
Pamela is running a con on racketeer Johnny Martin, using her boyfriend, Carl, to make the mobster jealous. The idea is that Johnny will shower her with gifts just to keep her. He does that, but he also eliminates the competition. A rare non-Shell Scott crime drama from Prather.

"Omit Flowers" by Arnold English (3000 words)★★
In an effort to convince the parole board he's a changed man, life-long con Rusty has, for years, been sending flowers to the grave of the man he murdered. Now an old man, Rusty discovers he's forgotten the deceased's name only weeks before he's up before the board. A nasty inmate decides to take advantage of Rusty's bad memory for kicks.

"Secondary Target" by Richard Deming (6500 words)★★★
The gorgeous and, evidently wealthy, Marie Carr walks into the Rotunda and

immediately catches the eye of owner Clancy Ross, who allows Marie to cash a check when she runs out of dough at the roulette wheel. When the check bounces, Clancy calls the woman and she invites him over to the hotel to pay her debt. Clancy arrives at the hotel to find Marie and her husband, George, waiting outside. A man approaches from behind, calls out Ross's name and pulls a gun. Clancy gets off a shot and blows the man's head off, but not before a stray bullet hits Marie's husband, killing him.

Who is the dead assassin, who hired him, and was Clancy the target? Plot is trivial in a Clancy Ross story; the joy is in spending time with the casino owner and his supporting cast and "Secondary Target" is no exception. The reader pretty much knows who the target is from the get-go but Deming's characterizations keep us intrigued.

"Fat Chance" by Wayne Hyde (5500 words)★★
Ed and Carley have the perfect partnership; Ed is the "World's Fattest Man" and Carley is the world's best barker. But that all changes when they add Gloria to the act and Carley falls hard for the young and beautiful dancer. Very soon Carley and Gloria are planning Ed's death.

"The Wife-Beater" by George Bagby (12,500 words)★★⌿
When Millie Bronson, a pregnant housewife, is brutally murdered in her own kitchen, it's up to Inspector Schmidt to bring the culprit to justice. But is it the woman's jealous husband? Or the plumber who carries a torch? Or could it be that strange and quiet man at the back of Hogan's Bar, the man who may or may not have been Millie's lover? Though "The Wife-Beater" has a convoluted wrap-up, the case and Schmidt's dogged approach to sifting through clues make for an absorbing read.

"A Beautiful Babe and Money" by Talmage Powell (1500 words)★⌿
After robbing and killing a big time bookie, Greene arrives at an old acquaintance's house to ride out the heat.

Vol. 5 No. 10 Nov 1957

The first and only appearance of Steve Allen, co-creator and first host of The Tonight Show. Scott Meredith returns as Editor under the name of Francis X. Lewis. Cover by O. G. Brabbins.

"The Blood of the Lamb" by Steve Allen (5000 words)★★★

It's seems like the beginning of a typical flight until the guy next to Slater begins quoting passages from the bible and claiming that all aboard are about to meet God. When pressed, the religious fanatic claims he's got a bomb in his luggage and it's set to go off in fifteen minutes. Can the pilot land the plane in time? When the name Steve Allen is attached to a short story, the natural inclination is to assume it has comedic elements (if not an outright comedy) but "The Blood of the Lamb" is a white-knuckled thriller that eases up only at the climax.

"Kill Joy" by Jack Ritchie (2000 words)★★★

A bent cop recognizes the driver of a getaway car from the scene of a bank heist and decides to cut himself in on the action. About as hardboiled as it gets.

"Cheese It, The Corpse!" by Craig Rice (8000 words)★↲

John J. Malone receives a call in the middle of the night from a gorgeous secretary. She's arrived in her hotel room to find a dead man in her bed. Well, that's not exactly how it happened. The dead man, the wealthy Gil Perry, was about to enter into divorce proceedings and his soon-to-be-ex wanted some leverage to use against him in court. Like unflattering pictures. Of course, it wasn't the dame that offed poor Perry, and Malone spits the goods in another obligatory last page expository.

"Shimmy" by Mike Brett (1200 words)★

Aggressive sex is the only way to turn Shimmy on.

"Compensation" by Helen Nielsen (5000 words)★★★↲

After his daughter is raped and beaten by a rich punk, Don Vickers struggles with his need for revenge amidst a sea of doubters who just tell Don to "give it time." A dense, well-written tale that almost begs to be expanded into novel length.

"The Closed Door" by Walt Frisbie (3500 words)★★★

Felsen and Cass are looking at an open and shut case. Phil Torbal was found beside his dead wife's body, her blood all over him. So why is Torbal denying the crime and, further, why is he denying the woman is his wife? Cass seems to think a good beating is the answer but that brings no confession. The truth becomes clear a few hours later when a beat cop calls in to report he's had to kill a crazy man with a knife.

"Setup" by Fletcher Flora (10,000 words)★★★↙
Jude is a simple farmer, trying to keep his marriage alive but his wife, Hester, tells him she feels like she's rotting inside and she's sick to her soul of him. Jude's farm sits on a huge amount of acreage belonging to the Hobart family and, one night, he sees young Alix Hobart drive in to the main house with the front of her convertible busted up good. Alix explains that she's accidentally run over and killed one of the Bromwitch boys on the highway. Is there something Jude could do to help hide the accident?

Jude does, indeed, abet in the crime and his mind begins working overtime, plotting a way to get ahold of the Hobart millions through blackmail. Another knockout by Fletcher Flora, "Setup" is an almost perfect (its climax is a bit of a letdown) cocktail of engaging plot, smart dialogue, and almost poetic prose:

> *Strangely, the moment she put it into words, her trouble and her fear, she became quiet at once, as if expression were a miraculous catharsis that reduced the magnitude and menace of her act.*

"I'll Handle This" by Al James (2500 words)★★
Sheriff Collins discovers that Ira Menson has shot her husband dead. Problem is, the sheriff was carrying on in private with Mrs. Menson and had unceremoniously dumped her not long before. A woman scorned...

"The Big Fish" by Hal Ellson (4500 words)★
Creel has stolen a very large amount of dope and the word spreads quick on the streets. Suddenly, everyone on the street wants a piece. Another tedious Hal Ellson J.D. tale filled with hip lingo ("Man, you real stupid. How come? I'll tell you how, cause you snatched Willie's stuff. Let the word get to him and you get your head shrunk for nothing.") and silly nicknames.

"Stolen Star" by William Campbell Gault (8000 words)★★★★
When Hollywood star, Laura Spain, is kidnapped, her agent pays P.I. Joe Puma two grand to deliver the dough to an isolated desert spot. Puma hires a friend to ride shotgun and heads for the California desert. The drop goes as planned and, miles away, Laura Spain is released, but the thugs decide that Puma and his hired gun are witnesses and need to be dealt with. Puma's buddy is killed and Joe hospitalized but, once he's on the mend, the gumshoe is out for blood.

Riveting thriller actually reads as though it were written for the screen in the late sixties, with its fast-paced action scenes and tough guy dialogue (think *Bullitt*), rather than in 1957. The fourth and final appearance of Gault and Joe Puma is also the best.

"Repeat Performance" by Robert Turner (2000 words)★
Pervert gets his kicks in jammed concert halls. Goofy and sleazy.

Vol. 5 No. 11 Dec 1957
First appearance of Joe Gores with "Chain Gang".
Cover by Walter Benke.

"The Merry, Merry Christmas" by Evan Hunter (2500 words)★★
An altercation in a bar on Christmas Eve turns deadly. Though the cover advertises "a hard, tough story," this simplistic tale is far from Hunter's best work.

"Bad Word" by David Alexander (5000 words)★
A meandering and pretentious character study of a young man whose mind is destroyed by Southern religion.

"The Scavengers" by Richard Harper (2500 words)★
A pair of thugs comes across a wrecked car and, ignoring the dying passengers, scavenge the vehicle.

"Chain Gang" by Joe Gores (3500 words)★★★
Fresh off a freight train, Larkie and Dale are looking for work in a small town but all they find is the law. Thrown onto a chain gang, Dale meets with a grim end and Larkie uses his Haitian background to exact revenge on the guard who murdered his friend.

"Out of Business" by C. B. Gilford (5000 words)★★★
When working girl, Fern Smith, arrives in town, it shakes the populace to its core. Engagements are broken, the sheriff discovers his son is a client, and Mrs. Karnes insists Fern's lease be voided. At the initial meeting of the "Citizen's Committee for the Eradication of Unsavory Women," it's decided that the only solution is murder and the obvious man for the job is Willy Dolfin, the town "simpleton." A borderline cozy (not necessarily a derogatory term), "Out of Business" is the type of story that *Alfred Hitchcock Mystery Magazine* excelled at, not quite gruesome or overly violent but well-written and gripping. Not surprising since C. B. Gilford was a regular of *AHMM*.

"Duel in the Pit" by Rick Sargent (5000 words)★
In what could be the nadir of J.D. gang fiction, two girls try to iron out their differences with guns in a pit. "Duel in the Pit" is worse than any of the Grade-Z J.D. exploitation movies of the 1950s and stocked full of clichéd, laughable dialogue.

"Time to Kill" by Jack Webb (7500 words)★★✓
A Los Angeles police sergeant goes undercover when a contract is put out on a Phoenix judge. The cop heads to the "Valley of the Sun" and discovers the natives are not that friendly. A good plot is hampered by unexciting prose but there's a

genuinely surprising twist at the climax when we discover the true origin of the contract.

"They're Going to Kill Me" by Bob Bristow (3000 words)★⌐
After his brother is killed in the line of duty by the mob, Carl Polcyn gets his day in court.

"First Nighter" by Richard Hardwick (1000 words)★
Morey discovers that life with a J.D. gang isn't all it's cracked up to be when the boys try to threaten a couple in the park.

"The Doubles" by Richard Deming (5000 words)★★⌐
Wade Harmon had been trying to figure a way to murder his rich uncle when he bumped into Harry Meadows on the street. Harry and Wade could be twins! Wade quickly talks Harry into flying overseas and being his alibi while he takes care of some business in the States. But then Wade doesn't plan on his wife flying over to surprise him. The set-up for "The Doubles" is quirky and enjoyable but the mid-section, where the two men discuss the plan, is overly-complicated and dull.

"Dead Set" by Frank Kane (10,000 words)★★
Before she was a Hollywood starlet, Lydia Johnson was a call girl. Now, some-one from her past has sent her pictures from that past, poses she'd rather not get out into Hollywood tattle rags. She calls Johnny Liddell in to smoke out the blackmailer and Johnny recognizes a few faces around Lydia. Could the blackmail be mob-related? A thoroughly pedestrian Johnny Liddell mystery with a laughable reveal at story's end (you'll never guess who the leech behind the pictures is!).

"Clay Pigeon" by Joseph Cummings (1500 words)★⌐
A hitman tasked with taking out a Union leader gets too close to the man and can't perform the act when the time comes. But the Union guy certainly can!

Peter Enfantino • Jeff Vorzimmer

The Best Stories of 1957

"His Own Jailor" by Bryce Walton (January)
"On a Sunday Afternoon" by Gil Brewer (January)
"Enough Rope for Two" by Clark Howard (February)
"College Kill" by Jack Q. Lynn (May)
"He's Never Stopped Running" by Aaron Marc Stein (June)
"The Geniuses" by Max Franklin (June)
"A Piece of Ground" by Helen Nielsen (July)
"Fly-By-Night" by Robert Gold (September)
"Compensation" by Helen Nielsen (November)
"Stolen Star" by William Campbell Gault (November)

Vol. 6 No. 1 Jan 1958

The first issue of seven consecutive issues to use recycled cover art. This issue reuses the cover art by "Michael" from Jan 1955. First and only appearance of the writing team of Bob Wade and Bill Miller ("Midnight Caller") writing as Wade Miller.

"The Hitchhiker" by Al James (2500 words)★★
 A mental patient escapes from the asylum and makes his way down the highway, murdering anyone who crosses his path. A thoroughly unpleasant story redeemed slightly by a clever last paragraph twist.

"Jungle" by Hal Ellson (4000 words)★★
 After ripping off the local mob, a man awaits his punishment.

"Return No More" by Talmage Powell (2500 words)★★
 After serving a twenty-year stretch, an ex-con has a hard time dealing with the new world.

"The New Girl" by Max Franklin (8000 words)★★★
 Jimmy Harrod is a pimp and his "main girl" is showing the effects of heroin abuse and being used on a nightly basis. It's time for Jimmy to find a new girl. Author Richard Deming doesn't seem to know whether "The New Girl" is a harrowing thriller (it succeeds) or a semi-documentary on the machinery of heroin addiction and prostitution (not as successful), but the story still delivers its shocks.

"Midnight Caller" by Wade Miller (1000 words)★★ⵊ
 Nina wakes up in the middle of the night to find a man in her room. But is he dangerous?
 Robert Wade and Bill Miller delivered several tough crime novels under a variety of pseudonyms, including Wade Miller (*Devil May Care, Kiss Her Goodbye*), Dale Widmer (*Dead Fall, Memo for Murder*), Whit Masterson (*Dead, She Was Beautiful, The Dark Fantastic*). Their classic novel, *Badge of Evil* (1956) was filmed as the equally classic, *Touch of Evil,* directed and co-starring Orson Welles. When Miller died in 1961, Wade continued on under the Masterson alias.

"Moon Bright, Moon Fright" by Warren J. Shanahan (4500 words)★ⵊ
 A small bayou town is rocked by a string of vicious murders every full moon. The only *Manhunt* story by Warren J. Shanahan is a silly thriller filled with psychological claptrap designed to give the reader an insight into the diseased brain of a killer.

"Togetherness" by Aaron Marc Stein (7500 words)★ⵊ
 A meandering and overlong melodrama about a boy, raised by his prostitute

mother, searching for the man she claims is his father.

"The Spinner" by Avram Davidson (3500 words)★★★
Dr. Elsa Anders is an "arachnologist," an expert in spiders who is also bordering on becoming an old maid. When she receives obscene phone calls, Elsa decides to experiment. "The Spinner" is a chiller with a blackly humorous ending.

"The Town Says Murder" by Cornell Woolrich (18,000 words)★★
The cover cries out, "a great new novel," but that's not what the readers got.
"The Town Says Murder" is a rewriting of Woolrich's "The Hopeless Defense of
Mrs Dellford" from the Dec 1942 issue of *Dime Detective*. This was the second
time Woolrich tried to pull a fast one on the editors of *Manhunt* (see "The Hunted" in Jan 1953) and, according to Woolrich's biographer, Frances Nevins, they
demanded their money back. Woolrich never appeared in *MH* again. In hindsight,
it's hard to understand how the editor of *Manhunt* could have been fooled by
"The Town..." since it has all the trappings and purple prose of a 1940s pulp
thriller.

"Arrest" by Donald E. Westlake (2000 words)★★
William Winthrop contemplates suicide as he awaits the arrival of the police.

Vol. 6 No. 2 Feb 1958

The last appearance of Robert Turner ("Hooked"), who contributed 21 stories to the magazine. Cover by Michael. Reuses the art from Sep 1954.

"The Painter" by Michael Zuroy (2000 words)★★↲

Anton Druller is a sign painter by trade and he takes pride in his work. But is sign painting the vocation he daydreams about? Anton pats himself on the back that he hasn't killed anyone in at least twenty years, but his new client, the pompous Mr. Packer, is pushing our protagonist to the limit. An odd and ambiguous short-short, one that might elicit several reactions in its reader. I liked the deliberately vague backstory in which we're told Druller has committed murder in some fashion but others might see those missing details as necessary for an enjoyable read. The climax, in which Anton opens Mr. Parker up with a blade and uses his blood to craft a new sign, is certainly not ambiguous.

"A Real Quiet Guy" by Tom Phillips (3500 words)★↲

Arne's a slow-witted, but likable, guy who works down at the quarry and he's a target for local hussy, Carol. Since Arne makes a good salary and Carol has a bun in the oven, she figures the big dope is an easy mark. Arne's buddies try to warn him but he violently disagrees with their assessment of Carol and very soon the two are married. After the baby arrives, Carol goes back to bedding every man who strikes her fancy, including some of the guys down at the quarry. When Arne comes home from work early one day and catches his wife in the sack with one of his co-workers, he uses his stone-cutting skills instead of divorce papers. There's nothing original here and the twists are obvious but the tale is slightly redeemed by its laughably gruesome finale.

"Pressure" by Arnold English (3000 words)★★★

Dapper Phil Rand knows a lot about the local mobsters. Now, picked up on a small-time gambling charge, the cops are squeezing Phil for info on his bosses. Phil scoffs, knowing that if he talks, he's a dead man. But Detective Coffee, the cop in charge of getting Phil to talk, has a dirty plan up his sleeve after Phil refuses to sing. He invites all the local reporters in and gives them the scoop they've been waiting for: Dapper Phil Rand is co-operating in full with the authorities! After Coffee springs his surprise, Phil still refuses and the detective releases him. As Phil walks the street, he hears footsteps approaching from behind. A gripping tale with a nasty climax, "Pressure" reminds us that, in the *Manhunt* world, it's not just the "bad guys" that are bad.

"Meet Me in the Dark" by Gil Brewer (10,000 words)★★↲

After an accident leaves his wife temporarily blind, Guy Dennison finds his life turned upside down. But Guy isn't the wonderful, caring husband most men would be in his situation. While on vacation, Guy sneaks out of their hotel room to a local bar on the beach and it's only a matter of time before he's in the sack with a gorgeous blonde nicknamed Bunny. Very shortly after, Guy discovers that Bunny has a partner and a plan to divest Guy of his fortune. Guy see-saws between contemplating the murder of his invalid wife or the murder of his blackmailers and, in the end, gets just what he deserves.

"Meet Me in the Dark" has all the earmarks of a Gil Brewer story: the easy mark, the gorgeous (but dark-hearted) dame, and the downbeat ending. The climax is a tad predictable but at least we have some fabulous noir-ish writing before we get there:

> *Her name was Janine Bonney. She was maybe nineteen, and beautiful in a way that got a man where it was tender.*
> *He looked at her, shaking his head slightly.*
> *She gave a tiny nod, then began writing in the sand four feet from his side with a crimson-tipped toe.*
> *"BAR—" she wrote. "NOW."*

Brewer keeps the suspense at a high level as Dennison attempts to talk his wife into a swim (so that he can drown her) and, a page later, contemplates the murder of Bunny, all the while keeping his calm.

"The Helping Hand" by Avram Davidson (4500 words)★↲

Dr. Harold Marmon is a quack who stocks his faux cancer clinic with gorgeous "nurses" so that he'll have something to do in his spare time. But Dr. Marmon slips up and hires the wrong girl. Thin-bare plot with ho-hum results. Avram Davidson may be well-known for his fantasy and science fiction, but he placed several stories in the crime digests and also wrote two mystery novels under the Ellery Queen pen name.

"Be a Man!" by Talmage Powell (2500 words)★★

Unremarkable short-short about a man who bullies his son one time too many.

"Hooked" by Robert Turner (8500 words)★★★

Ray Marchand has it made, married to a woman much older and much richer, but he's got a roving eye and expensive tastes. Luckily, his wife Gladys loves to fish and doesn't mind her husband's indiscretions as long as he's discreet. Ray's got a new babe all lined up: Nila, the coquette who works with her father down at the dock where Gladys rents her small fishing boats. Ray falls hard for Nila, but she wants to live lavishly as well so, before long, the two hatch a plan to toss Gladys in the drink (even though a rabid fisher, Gladys can't swim!) and reap the benefits. Unfortunately, for Ray, Gladys has the same plan for her husband (who can't swim either!).

Often, I'll compare these novelettes to a short Gold Medal novel but, perhaps, "Hooked!" might have been picked up by a lesser paperback company such as Monarch or Midwood. It's certainly got the tame sex required for those two companies:

She was wearing white sharkskin shorts, the kind, buckled at the sides so tightly that the edge of the material bites into the flesh and so snug all around that a man wonders how the girl ever got into them and why they don't split with her slightest movement.

Gladys's counterpoint scheme (which, we discover, hinged on the involvement of lovely Nila), is a fabulous twist and one I never saw coming. I would question why someone so avid about fishing in a little boat would never learn how to swim. When the time came to adapt "Hooked" for the fifth season of Alfred Hitchcock Presents, writer Thomas Grant tamed down the sexual side a tad but, otherwise, adhered to the storyline. The adaptation is greatly enhanced by a fabulous performance by Anne Francis as the devious Nila.

"You Can't Lose" by Lawrence Block (2500 words)★★✔
A young con man explains how he survives, day to day, off small robberies and swindles but a call from a mobster may prove to be a big pay day. Nothing more than small vignettes tied together but the shame here is that the real story is beginning at the climax. This was Lawrence Block's first professional short story sale and, of course, he would go on to hundreds more and also best-seller success with his Matt Scudder novels.

"Black Cat in the Snow" by John D. MacDonald (2000 words)★★
Martin Wadaslaw was a tyrant and was probably molesting his daughter but the question is: was his death the result of a shooting accident or was it murder? "Black Cat" does not have the usual snap and crackle of a John D. MacDonald thriller, due to both its length and tired hook.

"The Portraits of Eve" by Bruno Fischer (10,500 words)★★★
After serving a ten-year sentence for murdering a model he was painting, an artist comes back to the apartment where the crime was committed to make sense of that night. With the help of a look-alike model, he's able to reconstruct the crime and reveal the identity of the actual killer. Enthralling psychological thriller.

"The Babe and the Bum" by Mike Brett (2000 words)★
Rose feels stifled by her obese aunt Midge so she picks up a hammer and does something about it.

Peter Enfantino • Jeff Vorzimmer

Vol. 6 No. 3 Apr 1958
Last glossy-size (quarto) issue. Reuses cover art of Jan 1954 by "Michael".

"Don't Twist My Arm" by Jack Ritchie (3500 words)★★★
As a young boy, Freddie is hit by a car driven by a senator and Freddie's worthless father cashes in. But now, years later, with Freddie's arm useless, Pop gets it into his head the Senator should be paying a lot more. "Don't Twist My Arm" (a terrible title) is a nightmarish slice of ghetto life amongst the alcoholics and thieves that has a great plot but disappointing climax.

"Fifteen Grand" by Jack Q. Lynn (4000 words)★★✔
After serving a stint in stir, Duke is looking forward to digging up the fifteen grand he stashed from the heist. But bent cop Harry Dill and his girl, Mavis, want that dough as well. Who will get there first?

"Colby's Monster" by Stuart Friedman (4500 words)★★★★
Colby created the screen goddess known as Mary Maine from the ground floor up. Mary's gimmick is that she exudes pure sex while also giving off a good-girl image. Now the empire that Colby created is in jeopardy as Mary has found a new man, John St. Garland, a crackpot who quotes poetry and delivers philosophical rantings. Colby needs to get rid of this guy fast before his cash cow gets rid of *him*.
"Colby's Monster" is a fascinating study of three sociopaths of varying degree. Mary loves herself and perhaps no one else but is willing to be drawn into the web of anyone who holds her to such high esteem as her new "number one fan." Colby couldn't care about anything but money and power, not even his princess. And St. Garland who, at first glance, seems to be just an obsessed fan but may be something even more sinister under the skin. As in "Zero… Double Zero" (from Nov 1956), Stuart Friedman proves he's an unsung master of character development and nasty twists.

"The Hit" by Alson J. Smith (9500 words)★★★✔
Mike LiMandri is nervous as all hell, but that's only natural since this is his first hit. As for the hit, that would be mob *capo* Paulo Marchese, who has insulted rival gangster Momo Masseria and must be done away with. Unfortunately, Mike falls in love with Marchese's beautiful daughter and that brings complications. Momo pressures Mike to do the hit *now* rather than later.
"The Hit" is a wonderful little "epic" mafia drama with hints of what would come a decade later with *The Godfather*. Only the epilogue, which fills readers in on what happened to the survivors after Mike finally gets around to that hit seems rushed.

"The Dame Across the River" by Talmage Powell (2500 words)★★↲

After a lucrative heist, two men hold up in a small Mexican village until the heat is off. Across the river, a gorgeous woman beckons and all the carefully-laid plans begin to erode.

"One More Clue" by Craig Rice (7500 words)★↲

John J. Malone takes the case of a writer who allegedly committed suicide, but his fiancé doesn't buy it. The writer was in a locked room with the gas turned on full. How could it be murder? To make a really long story short, it was murder, and the solution is a very silly one (the murderer trained a pigeon to turn the gas on!).

Ironically, Craig Rice had died of a drug overdose about six months prior to the publishing of "One More Clue" and the cover of this issue notes "Craig Rice's last story." "One More Clue" almost feels of another age and its "cozyness" is particularly stark in contrast to the harder-edged fiction that was becoming *Manhunt*'s mainstay. There would be several posthumous appearances by Rice, including a "collaboration" between Rice and Evan Hunter, *The April Robin Murders*, which was actually a partial manuscript finished up by Hunter. "One More Clue" was the sole *Manhunt* story from 1958 to make it into David C. Cooke's *Best Detective Stories of the Year* (14th Annual, Dutton, 1959)

"Zeke's Long Arm" by C. B. Gilford (2000 words)★★

Olen is annoyed that his brother, Zeke, is marrying the rich widow, Carrie, so he blows a hole in Zeke and buries the corpse in a shallow grave. But the long arm of Zeke refuses to let his brother live in peace.

"Trouble in Town" by Richard Deming (7000 words)★★★

Bix Lawson is not easily flustered, so Clancy Ross is very interested when the local mobster demands an audience with our favorite casino owner. Clancy is prepared for the "semi-annual-join-my-mob-and-sell-me-the-Club Rotunda" speech but what he gets is far more interesting. Lawson reveals that an out-of-town syndicate is rolling in to St. Stephens to muscle in on Bix and crowd out Clancy.

Sadly, "Trouble in Town" was the final Clancy Ross story to grace the pages of *Manhunt* and, if I'd been a faithful reader, I'd have been sad to see him go. Deming's intelligent but easy-flowing prose and full-bodied characters always made for entertaining reading. Luckily, for those who want more of the formula, Deming carried the cast over into a series of stories for *Mike Shayne Mystery Magazine* (and at least one for *Man's Magazine*) and the novel, *She'll Hate Me Tomorrow* (Monarch Books, 1963).

"You're Dead" by Helen Nielsen (10,000 words)★★

Sebastian Granada is an up-and-coming dancer but he's also an illegal immigrant. Charlie Pal is a blackmailer who may be looking for an easy payday with the dancer but, when Charlie winds up murdered, there are plenty of suspects to go around. A meandering and padded mystery with very little to keep the interest.

"Goodbye, Charlie" by Bob Prichard (2500 words)★★★

Charlie just wants to have a good time but Beth wants wedding bells. When he calls the relationship off she screams "rape" to her father, who's quick with a gun. A very short, very compact thriller that uses its space wisely.

Vol. 6 No. 4 Jun 1958
First issue back at digest-size. Page count back to 128. Cover by Michael. Reuses cover art of Feb 1955.

"The Threat" by Max Franklin (5000 words)★★★
P.I. Harold Stander is contacted by Marie Wolfendon, wife of multi-millionaire (and ex-playboy) Joshua Wolfendon, and Wolfendon confidante George Harbor, when Marie is threatened by an ex-beau. Stander moves in to the mansion to act as bodyguard and overhears a late night phone call from the ex-lover, threatening to kill Marie right then and there. Joshua rushes to his wife's room and is shot in the head by Marie for his troubles. The police naturally write the killing off as an accident but Stander smells a rat. He does some digging and, sure enough, discovers the ex-boyfriend committed suicide months before.

When he confronts Marie and George with his theory about what's really going on, they confess they are lovers and plotted the killing of Joshua. What's Stander going to do about it? The P.I. smiles and tells them his price for silence is a cool million. They agree. Though the reveal is much too predictable, I thought it was supremely ballsy and *un*predictable to leave the story off with Stander accepting the bribe and entering in an unholy alliance with the murderers. Most P.I.s are much too moral to be swayed.

"Pro" by Joe Gores (3000 words)★★★★
Hit man Falkoner is hired to murder a dame in the California desert who may or may not have witnessed a mob hit. The killing goes fine but the getaway goes south when Falkoner is betrayed. Pissed off, he heads for San Fran to take out his boss. Intense and gritty, Joe Gores's "Pro" almost lays the foundation for similar tough guys to follow, be they thieves like Richard Stark's Parker or Max Allan Collins's hitman, Quarry. It's a shame Gores chose to kill off the Falkoner character as he would have made for a very readable series character, but the author concentrated his energies in the 1970s on the well-received Dan Kearney novels.

"Give Me a Break!" by Norman Struber (2500 words)★★
The adventures of J.D.s Punchy and Rick as they graduate to armed robbery and murder.

"Say a Prayer for the Guy" by Nelson Algren (1500 words)★★★
Very funny short-short about five old men playing poker. One of them drops dead and the other four try to figure out how to carry on. The only contribution to *Manhunt* by author Nelson Algren, who had rocketed into the public eye via his best-selling *The Man with the Golden Arm* in 1949.

"Deadly Charm" by Stuart Friedman (5000 words)★★↙
Colby discovers that his wife has been raped by a junior partner in his law

firm. But was it really rape? Odd that Friedman would choose "Colby" as his main protagonist's surname since he used it previously, just last issue, in "Colby's Monster."

"The Sight of Blood" by C. B. Gilford (3000 words)★↙
The mildly humorous tale of Miles, who gets deathly ill at the sight of blood, and his foolproof plan for murdering his uncle.

"A Fire at Night" by Lawrence Block (1000 words)★★★
Lawrence Block's short-short about an arsonist delivers suspense and shock very few stories this brief can achieve.

"Stage Fright" by D. E. Forbes (2500 words)★★★
Caroline Fincher knows from the moment her daughter, Margot, is born that she's destined to be a star. Things go their way and Margot climbs the ladder to success but then, when the precocious tot doesn't get the plum role in a hit play, she takes on another role... a real life "Bad Seed."

"The Chips are Down" by Wilfried Alexander (3000 words)★★
Ace has ripped off Raven, owner of the Conga Club and Casino for eight Gs. Now, Raven has sent his goons out to retrieve Ace and his girlfriend, Anna, so that he can voice his displeasure in person.

"It Never Happened" by William O'Farrell (13,500 words)★★★↙
Successful drive-in owner Dick Hammett discovers his wife is sleeping with his business partner. During a drinking binge, Hammett tosses his wife off their balcony, embezzles the company account, and flees to Acapulco to lie low for a while. His life devolves into a grim haze of murder and booze, with reality see-sawing with alcohol-fueled hallucinations.
"It Never Happened" is a fabulously complex crime drama, with so many surprising twists and turns and a bleak outcome that never once cheats the reader. A lesser writer would have woven in silly plots (did Dick really kill his wife or was it the evil business partner?) but O'Farrell keeps the narrative on track and doesn't deviate from the main point: Dick Hammett, thanks to alcohol, is an evil and dangerous character, despite all his charm.
O'Farrell was a successful author with several novels under his belt by this time, including *Repeat Performance* (1942), *Brandy for a Hero* (1948), and *Doubles in Death* (1953), the latter of which was filmed for *Boris Karloff's Thriller*. O'Farrell's 1963 novel, *The Golden Key*, has a plot hook similar to "It Never Happened."

"Killer Cop" by Arnold English (2500 words)★↙
A cop kills his wife and his Captain, wishing to avoid controversy, covers up the crime. Clumsily written thriller with a ludicrous climax.

"Blackmailers Don't Take Chances" by David C. Cooke (3000 words)★★⌐

Norm Bennett has been having an affair with a gorgeous young woman while he's separated from his wife. Everything's legal but if his estranged wife were to get wind of the affair, she'd demand more in the settlement. Then, one day, Norm gets some compromising pics in the mail and the blackmail begins. "Blackmailers" is a bit predictable but it's got a darkly humorous twist in its finale that makes it a winner.

Vol. 6 No. 5 Aug 1958

John Underwood takes over as Editor for the rest of the magazine's run. Cover by Michael. Reuses the cover art of April 1955.

"Dead Cats" by Henry Marksbury (2500 words)★
A man murders his wife and then must contend with the feral cat she loved so much. Unlike any other story published in *Manhunt*, "Dead Cats" is a ludicrous horror story more suited to *Weird Tales* than a crime digest.

"The Jacket" by Jack Q. Lynn (4000 words)★
More J.D. rumbles, this time with the Swans and their main chick, Tammy. As with Hal Ellson's J.D. fiction, "The Jacket" is a nearly unreadable mess littered with "cool" nicknames like Zing and Big Moe and foreign-language dialogue ("Get the hen in the house.") that tests the reader's patience to no end.

"Big Hands" by L. J. Krebs (1000 words)★
A nasty tale of a very large man who finally tires of being called names and molests a woman. The kind of story that turned up in the later years of *MH* that never would have been published in prior years. Bottom-of-the-barrel drivel.

"The Murder Pool" by Robert Stephens (2500 words)★✓
Every night, at the same local bar, a group of men bet on how many murders have been committed that day. When Jim Crane discovers he's going to be one killing shy of a win, he heads out on the streets with a butcher knife.

"Caught in the Act" by Niel Franklin (1500 words)★
A woman finds herself paralyzed and helpless in her home.

"Poor Sherm" by Ruth Chessman (4500 words)★★
Living under his sister's thumb isn't much of a life, but the day she's murdered Sherman begins to blossom. Years later, he marries and a frightening pattern emerges. There's no denying that "Poor Sherm" has a powerful climax but too much of the narrative is written in almost a true-crime style.

"A Friend of Stanley's" by Guy Crosby (4000 words)★★✓
Stanley's not one to be made fun of so when a local girl plays a trick on him and Stanley is made the laughing stock of the town, he uses his big and slow friend to get his revenge.

"Loose Ends" by Fletcher Flora (21,000 words)★★★✓
The beautiful Faith Salem is about to marry the very-rich Graham Markley but there are a few question marks in his past that need to be looked into. So Faith hires P.I. Percy Hand to find out why Graham's previous wife up and disappeared.

in the middle of the night with her boyfriend and has never been heard from since. Percy digs and digs and raises the ire of some very important people before getting to the truth of the matter.

"Loose Ends" is enthralling detective fiction by a master storyteller. The usual private dick clichés apply (no one likes a P.I., Percy gets roughed up a few times, all the dames seem to like him, etc.) but they're also handled well, with some of the old standbys turned upside down. There's also a whopper of a twist towards the climax that the reader won't see coming and leads to a very satisfying outcome. It's a shame Fletcher Flora didn't utilize Percy Hand for further adventures.

"Cabin 13" by Edward Perry (1000 words)★

A short-short about an industrious motel owner who sets up two-way mirrors in his cabins and then sells the photos to a local pervert.

"The Real Thing" by Fritz Dugan (2500 words)★★

On an army base, a troubled soldier is accused of raping an officer's daughter. The reader isn't given much information about the crime or the true identity of the rapist and the climax certainly leaves the mystery open for interpretation.

Vol. 6 No. 6 Oct 1958
Cover by "Michael." Reuses cover art of Jul 1955. All but two original stories are by first-time contributors.

"Dope to Kill" by Edward Wellen (6500 words)★★★
Harrowing thriller about a dope dealer administered pure heroin by a vengeful couple. The dealer must escape and then attempt to stay alive. This is the first *Manhunt* appearance by Edward Wellen (with four more to follow); Wellen was a prolific dual-genre author, writing both mystery and science fiction (his novel *Hijack* is a hybrid of the two genres). From 1958 through 1986, Wellen was also a regular in *Ellery Queen*, *Alfred Hitchcock*, and *Mike Shayne*.

"Rivals" by Talmage Powell (2000 words)★★✦
Lissa's not about to share Carl with new girl in town, Jocelin, so when the three take a boat ride out to a sunken ship, Lissa decides Jocelin will become a deep sea-diving statistic. "Rivals" is too short, I'd have preferred it double the length, as the story is definitely intriguing, but there's a sly, clever twist in its wrap-up.

"The Nude Next Door" by Ivan Lyons-Pleskow (1000 words)★
Sleazy short about a peeping tom who bites off more than he can chew. Not surprisingly, this was Lyons-Pleskow's only published fiction.

"My Pal Isaac" by David Lee (4000 words)★★★
Isaac Sweeney swiftly rises from mousey elevator op to hired assassin and the only man who really knows him is his best friend, Pete. Engrossing character study with a predictable. but still effective, twist ending.

"I'd Die for You" by Charles Burgess (2000 words)★★
Dawson gets a call from old flame Angela one night, telling him she misses him and asking if he can come pick her up. Angela had eloped with a very rich guy named Richard Emory several months before, but now she's not so much in love with him and wants out. When Dawson meets Angela, she proposes a get-rich-quick scheme involving her staged murder by Richard and blackmail to the tune of a hundred grand. Being a dope in love, Dawson agrees to the plan and, of course, regrets it in the end when Angela double-crosses him.

"Time to Kill" by Bryce Walton (6500 words)★★★★
Traveling to the desert town of Ten Palms ("the place where rich people go to die") with six months to live, Allan Barton makes quick friends with a neighbor named Steve but, one night, he trips over Steve's body outside his cabin and Allan's life changes for the good. Allan pulls clues from a conversation he had with

Steve that evening and begins "investigating." Suddenly, his life is exciting again. He's pushing around bad guys, bedding bad girls and, in an ultra-violent climax, piling up the corpses.

Allan's transformation from boring, death-bed zombie ("formerly of Johnson Belt and Dye") to murderous lunatic is jarring but also oddly humorous; the finale is tantamount to that of *Taxi Driver*, in that Allan is pinballing from shooting to shooting and the reader roots for him to make that one last kill before he himself expires.

"Surprise" by Don Lombardy (2000 words)★★★

It's just another boring commute home on the subway for accountant Jason Bartlett. When he opens the newspaper and reads about a man who found a box filled with cash on the subway, Bartlett dreams of a similar fate. Bartlett nods off but is awakened when the train comes to a stop. Across from him sits a cardboard box and images of unclaimed tens and twenties dance in his brain.

He leaves the train, box in hand, but panics and flees when a conductor calls to him. When the chase goes above ground, the police intercede and Bartlett surrenders, thinking his wonderful payday just went South. When the police open the box, however, it's not money they find. "Surprise" is a snake in the grass, lulling the reader into a semi-comatose state and then springing with a humdinger of a reveal at the climax. The utter randomness of the final event only deepens the dread.

"Deadline Murder" by Jack Ritchie (5000 words)★★★⫶

Publishing a tattle magazine can make a man many enemies and Roy Tenney seems to have hundreds. The only person he can call "friend" is his bodyguard, Eddie, and that's a one-way friendship. Celebrities who've had their name dragged through the mud approach Eddie, offering him thousands to kill the schmuck, but Eddie is biding his time until the offers add up to a princely sum. When a twist of fate takes him out of the role of murderer, he has to think fast or lose his big payday. Black comedy has all the Ritchie trademarks: lively characters, rich dialogue, and an engrossing plot.

"The Shooter" by Craig Mooney (2000 words)★

Tedious trip into the mind of a man holding a gun on an assailant. The entire story only takes place across a few seconds but, to the reader, it seems like hours.

"I'm Not Dead" by Carl Milton (12,000 words)★

Mike Harmon comes home after a hard day at the gas station to find a dead man in his living room. Since this is the 1950s, that wasn't so rare but what strikes Mike odd is that the man has his face! When the police arrive, Mike tells his story but the cops aren't buying it, and when Mike's wife, Gloria, shows up, she insists the dead guy is her husband! In the end, we discover that Gloria just happened to take up with a guy who looks just like Mike and the pair decide to off the real Mike for his life insurance policy.

Strictly amateur hour at *Manhunt*, "I'm Not Dead" could very well be the most ludicrous nonsense the magazine ever ran but, to add insult to injury, someone at *Manhunt* thought this bad bit of typing was worth thirty pages. Not surprisingly, this was Carl Milton's only appearance in *MH* but he did manage to score space in *Alfred Hitchcock, Terror Detective, Killers,* and *Guilty.*

"Murder by Appointment" by Al James (2500 words)★↙

Blake's career as a architect takes a header when the dam he designed bursts, killing several and setting up lawsuits in the millions. He hires a gunman to kill him so that his wife might be left with a good sum of money. Or is that the motive?

Vol. 6 No. 7 Dec 1958

Page count reduced to 128 pages, the lowest for the digest-size issues. Reuses the cover art of the August 1953 edition of Verdict, another Flying Eagle publication.

"A Little Variety" by Richard Hardwick (2000 words)★★★⁄

A quiet day in suburbia turns violent when working stiff Everett Sheldon decides his friend's wife is for the taking. A brutal and shocking short thriller; its violent events almost seem everyday occurrences to those living in the 21st Century.

"The Strangler" by Richard Deming (6000 words)★⁄

Popular newspaper photographer Linda Martin is shocked when her brother, Tommy, is arrested for the stranglings of three women. Though Linda is certain her brother is a sweet kid, her fiancé, Lt. Sam Terrill, isn't so sure. Linda decides to do some investigating on her own and becomes the Strangler's next target. Weak, pedestrian material from a writer who usually contributes strong fiction.

"Flowers for Barney" by Ovid Demaris (4000 words)★★★

Barney Lester used ta be a contenda but then he fell in love with and married Edna Nowicki and gave up boxing. He was drafted and she started posing nude. The photos led to Hollywood and before Barney knew it, he was ogling his wife on the covers of Hollywood tattlers. For the last ten years, Barney has lived off Edna (now Gloria Miles) and his own guilt. A crazy scheme comes to Barney after a run-in with two hopheads on Sunset Blvd., but the plan goes awry thanks to some unpredictable detours.

By 1958, Ovid Demaris was already a best-selling novelist for Gold Medal (*Ride the Gold Mare* and *The Hoods Take Over*) but this was the writer's entry into crime digests (he would have only one more short story published before concentrating on novels). "Flowers for Barney" is a wild ride, both violent and humorous, with a sad, sardonic climax.

"Gigolo" by C. B. Gilford (5000 words)★★

Dion Landess refuses to be owned by any woman—not even his clinging wife, Merle. One night, while Dion is at a party, his wife calls to tell him she's coming over to shoot him in front of his friends and romantic interests. Dion slips out the back door and heads for his apartment. When he gets there, his wife pulls a gun on him, they tussle and Merle is killed. Dion thinks he can use the party as an alibi but one of those romantic interests decides it's high time that Dion become *her* property!

"Ride a White Horse" by Lawrence Block (3500 words)★★★★

Andy is a nothing schmuck until he wanders into the White Horse for the first time and meets Sara. They immediately fall in love and Andy moves into Sara's place for what seems like domestic bliss. Every day, Andy runs down to the library to pick up a package for Sara and, after several weeks, he becomes interested in what's inside the boxes. While she's out one day, Andy opens one of the packages and discovers it's filled with heroin. Sara comes clean; she's a small time dope dealer and she sells H to addicts on the street.

At first, Andy is horrified but, eventually, Sara whittles away at his fears. As a result, Andy becomes hooked on the product and begins dreaming of taking over all narcotics trafficking in the city. Sara is in the way. Harrowing, if a bit dated in its representation of the "horrors of marijuana," "Ride a White Horse" shows just how unglamorous the drug world can be, capped off with Andy's final descent into madness and murder.

"Desert Chase" by Thurber Jensen (20,500 words) ★ ✔

On a deserted highway just south of Las Vegas, two thugs kidnap Mike Bruce's wife and son and leave him with their car, the front seat soaked with blood. The hoods tell Mike his family will be safe as long as he stays away from the cops. A further inspection of the vehicle turns up a pistol so Mike does what any rational man would do: he flags down the next oncoming car, points his gun at the driver, and takes off in the man's car. Oh, and he kidnaps the guy's daughter as well.

The girl ends up accepting her role as hostage with elan and very soon, the pair are tracking the bad guys into Arizona for a deadly showdown. A completely ridiculous, padded and, worst of all, boring chase thriller with the requisite happy ending. Mike Bruce seems to go from meek husband (he practically begs his wife to go with the men) to hardboiled gun-toter in about three paragraphs; his female companion on the trip does likewise. I've not been able to dig up any information for writer Thurber Jensen but this appears to be his only published work (in the crime genre at least); how he was able to land a gig this big with such a weak plot would be a more interesting read than "Desert Chase" itself.

"Wait for Death" by Karl Kramer (6000 words) ★★★

Paul Miller is pulled from a river by mobster Vance Jensen after he attempts suicide. Vance has a proposition for the bedraggled Miller: come to work for him for four hundred a week until a particular job is done and then he can try suicide again if he likes. Miller agrees but life gets complicated by his feelings for Vance's wife, Judith, who's known to stray into the beds of other men now and then. Turns out that Vance has had enough of the carousing when Judith takes up with young hood, Johnny Hunter, and Paul assumes Hunter's murder is his ultimate task. Unfortunately for Miller, Hunter is not the target.

A hardboiled delight from start to finish (although that first chapter is a bit confusing), "Wait for Death" has two great male leads and a saucy dame who might be the most evil of the three. The climax, which details Paul's decision to run away with, rather than execute, Judith has a very nasty bite to it.

The Best Stories of 1958

"Pressure" by Arnold English (February)
"Colby's Monster" by Stuart Friedman (April)
"The Hit" by Alson J. Smith (April)
"Pro" by Joe Gores (June)
"It Never Happened" by William O'Farrell (June)
"Loose Ends" by Fletcher Flora (August)
"Deadline Murder" by Jack Ritchie (October)
"Time to Kill" by Bryce Walton (October)
"A Little Variety" by Richard Hardwick (December)
"Ride a White Horse" by Lawrence Block (December)

Vol. 7 No. 1 Feb 1959
The last new story ("Killer's Wedge") by Evan Hunter, who contributed 46 stories to the magazine.

"Second Chance" by Joe Grenzeback (11,500 words)★★★✈

Monk Holly's just a working grunt with his own gas station when local club owner and big shot Tabscott comes in for a fill-up. Monk recognizes the gorgeous blonde in the front seat as his old flame Marcia and, while Tabscott isn't looking, she slips Monk her number. Tabscott slips Monk a twenty and tells him in gruff terms that he never saw the blonde in the car. Later, Monk pays Marcia a visit and lets her know he's still not happy about the way they parted company; the girl swears she'll make it up to him. Soon after, Marcia tells Monk that Tabscott is in financial straits and he's going to stage a robbery, stealing his rich wife's savings out of the safe in the den. Monk sees this as an opportunity and talks Marcia into a heist. Unfortunately, Mrs. Tabscott takes a header off a cliff and suddenly robbery becomes murder. Only Monk knows how Mr. Tabscott did it and he's going to make the man pay.

A white-knuckle ride that twists and detours to keep the reader guessing but never veers into ridiculous territory. Author Grenzeback delights in teasing us with Marcia and Monk's backstory; there's some illegal business in the past but the events are hinted at rather than detailed. An extraordinarily graphic burst of violence at the climax, when Monk discovers he's being played by all parties concerned, is tantamount to a literary slap in the face.

"Killer in the Ring" by Paul Johnson (4500 words)★★✈

A boxer discovers his wife has been having an affair with the guy he's going toe-to-toe with in his next match. When the bout begins, it suddenly occurs to him that his opponent is going to kill him in the ring. An interesting and unique angle to the standard "murderous spouse" plot but the climax is a bit too hurried.

"Lovers" by R. J. Hochkins (2000 words)★★

A gorgeous blonde forces a hitch-hiker to go along with the murder of a sadistic cop.

"Night of Death" by Bob Bristow (3000 words)★✈

Fred Merrill's just looking for a place to stay after a long drive on a rainy night, so he stops at the small motel along the side of the road. He walks in and finds the owner bleeding and a woman standing over him with a gun. She's obviously hopped up and, she explains, the wounded old man was her peddler. Now, how does Fred manage to talk an addict out of blowing him away too?

"Killer's Wedge" by Ed McBain (27,000 words)★★★★

Virginia Dodge walks into the 87th Precinct and holds a gun on the boys in the office. "I'm here to kill Steve Carella," she confesses. To prove she means business, Virginia pulls a bottle of what she claims is Nitro-Glycerin out of the bag she's carrying and sits down to wait for Carella to return. The wanted man, meanwhile, is investigating that rarest of mysteries, the locked-door suicide. Problem is, after Carella interviews the victim's family and discovers the man was a wealthy businessman with plenty of vultures circling, he's convinced it wasn't suicide despite evidence to the contrary.

Either one of these storylines would be enough to fill a novel but Evan Hunter brilliantly juggles the tension at the station house with the Agatha Christie-esque whodunit investigated by Carella. The irony, of course, is that Steve never actually makes it to the Precinct before Virginia is foiled. It's odd (and risky) that *Manhunt* would devote so much space to what is the eighth book in the series. Yes, the 87th Precinct novels were big sellers but you run the risk of turning off those readers not familiar with the now-iconic characters of the McBain world. With some rewriting and expanding (there's quite a bit of pre-Virginia Dodge banter between the boys in the office), Evan Hunter packaged this as the aforementioned 8th novel (same title), released by Perma in August of 1959. To this day, *Killer's Wedge* is considered by many to be among the best of the 87ths.

Vol. 7 No. 2 Apr 1959
Reuses the Maguire cover art of Nov 1955.

"The Runaway" by Bryce Walton (3500 words)★★↲
A bank manager embezzles 250,000 bucks and hides out in a slum. He befriends a small girl in the neighborhood but when the child is found murdered, the police come calling. A taut little thriller with a likable character; oddly, the girl's murder is left unsolved.

"Road to Samarra" by Jane Roth (3000 words)★★★
Vic and Velma are going to rob and kill fortune teller Madame Futura, who keeps her life savings inside her crystal ball. Just before Vic does the deed, Velma asks the swami to tell her fortune. Futura sees the "two Vees" involved in a nasty crash. Fortune teller dead, Vic and Velma high tail it but both are still haunted by the woman's prediction. Velma comes up with a great idea: if Vic would crash the car into a tree at a safe speed, they could put the crash behind them and live their lives right. So Vic wraps the car around a tree and both survive, thinking they've beaten the odds. However, Velma receives a nasty head injury and the two are loaded into an ambulance to be taken to a hospital. The ambulance hits a parked car around the next bend and bursts into flames. Jane Roth's only published crime story has a fabulously twisted climax and two slightly daffy, unpredictable lead characters.

"Fair Play" by Jack Ritchie (2000 words)★★
There's no love left in the marriage so Henry and Edna play a game of "I can kill you better than you can kill me!"

"The Double Take" by Edward Wellen (7500 words)★★★↲
Unemployed actor Denis Omrat tries to get a few bucks and laughs out of the fact that he resembles mega-movie star Rick Bishop. He flies to Vegas, begins signing checks with Bishop's signature and impressing the ladies with his million-dollar smile. But two people see right through Omrat's disguise: Bishop's ex-press agent, who hates Bishop for dumping him and gives Omrat some tips to better his ploy, and the star's wife, who Denis stumbles upon at a casino.

She invites Denis back to her apartment and gives him the whole awful story, how Rick Bishop left her to marry his current wife, and now she lives on the blackmail money. There are at least three effective twists in "The Double Take," two delivered on the last page, and in the hands of a lesser writer, that could be a problem. Here, each new turn brings a smile to the reader's face.

"Mr. Big Nose" by Martin Suto (5500 words)★★
Once Norman breaks out of prison, he focuses on getting to Leggett, a man who will get him out of the country. Norman encounters a few bumps along the road.

"Tie Score" by Carroll Mayers (1000 words)★
Two youths decide to rob a working girl outside of a bar.

"Awake to Fear" by Robert Camp (3000 words)★
A young couple awakens to find an escaped convict at their bedside. A night of very awkwardly-written terror ensues.

"One Hour Late" by William O'Farrell (21,000 words)★★★★
There's a new coquette strolling the beach of Palisades City; she's a sixteen-year-old fireball named Thelma, and she has all the local men begging for her time. Failing artist Dave Russell, whose marriage to wife Helen is also failing, is captivated by this young girl, enough to begin sketching her. Then there's her "cousin," Lu, who might not be the kin everyone thinks he is. And perhaps deadliest of all, Deputy Tommy Riggs, a sociopath who's already taken a liking to beating his wife and is spending late night hours with Thelma.

When Thelma ends up dead on the beach, her head bashed in and lungs full of water, Palisades City police Lt. Morgan turns to Russell for answers, while Riggs attempts to frame the artist for the murder. The real identity of the killer is saved until the final pages, but author O'Farrell does a superb job of keeping the lid on the pressure cooker until then. All of his characters are superbly mapped out; we know there's a dead girl coming because she's got her own illustration on the title page but when the event occurs, it's a shock. "One Hour Late" is a spellbinder in the John D. MacDonald tradition.

Vol. 7 No. 3 Jun 1959

Last original story by Henry Kane ("A Corpse That Didn't Die") and the only one that's not a Peter Chambers story. Reuses cover art of May 1955.

"Down and Out" by Joe Gores (5000 words)★★★★

Rick gives a few bucks to an aged alcoholic one cold night, but regrets his act of kindness when two toughs pick him up for info on the bum. The hoods let Rick go when they realize he knows nothing but our hapless hero just can't let the incident go so he tracks the derelict to a nearby flophouse and confronts him with news of the incident. Turns out the old man has a nasty secret about the two tough guys and a key to a safe deposit box holding eighty thousand dollars. A gripping and exciting noir chase thriller that keeps the reader guessing right up to its cliffhanging finale.

"The Bargainmaster" by Bob Bristow (3000 words)★★

A kindly pawn shop owner buys a gun from a teenager and then discovers the weapon was used to kill a policeman.

"The Blonde in Room 320" by William Hurst (9000 words)★★

A hotel manager finds a dead man in Room 302 and becomes a target when he witnesses the killer escaping.

"Some Play with Matches" by Dick Ellis (2500 words)★★★

A newspaper columnist finds he's made some very nasty enemies when he pokes fun at a teen idol. Deceptive drama simmers and then boils over in a violent finale.

"Absinthe for Superman" by Robert Edmond Alter (4000 words)★★★★

Mason reports to duty as a deck hand and discovers Captain Gann has a penchant for literature. Being a reader himself, Mason soon finds himself drawn into deep discussions of the world with Gann. Unfortunately, for all aboard, the Captain also has a yen for absinthe and, very soon, the addiction drives the man to madness.

Robert Edmond Alter may be best known to crime fiction readers as the author of two classic Gold Medal novels, *Swamp Sister* and *Carny Kill* (both published in 1966), but Alter was a master of suspense and adventure in the short form as well. He excelled at thrillers set on the high sea (as in his numerous tales published in *Argosy* and *Adventure*) but also found time to dabble in various other genres Mostly due to his paucity of full-length work (only five novels published), Alter remains a mostly-undiscovered treasure.

"Bronco" by Roy Koch (2500 words)★★

Willie "Bronco" Texas is on a shooting spree. Now's he's murdered two men and kidnapped their female companion. What drives "Bronco?" Murky thriller (which opens with startling violence like that of a Jim Thompson novel), open to several interpretations, none of which I found satisfying.

"The Cop Hater" by Floyd Wallace (4000 words)★★✔

A cop is robbed and murdered and Dover is called in to catch the kids who knifed him, but Dover is more interested in recovering the loot than bringing killers to justice.

"A Corpse That Didn't Die" by Henry Kane (16,500 words)★★★✔

From the moment he sees Flame Cortez stripping in a nightclub, med student Don Reed knows he has to have her all to himself. Flame insists she's not the marrying kind, she's "rotten," but Don won't be dissuaded and, after several months of dating, he convinces her to take the plunge. Things are hot at the start but, very soon, Don knows he's in over his head when Flame's flirting with other men forces Don's hand and he commits murder. "A Corpse That Didn't Die"; is a grim ride that climaxes in a shocking and ironic finale. This could be Henry Kane's best *Manhunt* contribution.

Peter Enfantino • Jeff Vorzimmer

Vol. 7 No. 4 Aug 1959
Second and last appearance of Ovid Demaris. Reuses cover art of Feb 1957.

"Nickel Machine" by Neil Boardman (5000 words)★★
No one can understand why Bennie smashed up the pinball machine over at Fleener's Grill; not Eddie Fleener, nor the police, nor Bennie's abusive wife. Probably not even Bennie. Except for a sudden explosion of violence in its climax, "Nickel Machine" is a slow and unrewarding read.

"Crossed and Double-Crossed" by Carroll Mayers (1500 words)★★↲
Gil is hoping to muscle out Frankie as Big Max's number one right hand man but Frankie has other ideas.

"Dead on Arrival" by Bob Bristow (3000 words)★↲
After a fall from a high platform, Zack Rogers is pronounced dead and taken to the morgue. Only problem is that Zack isn't actually dead and now he has to find a way to alert the mortician before he begins the embalming process. Highly derivative of Louis Pollock's "Breakdown" but with a humorous climax.

"The Return of Joey Dino" by Elwood Corley (9000 words)★
Johnny Wade made something of himself when it seemed he'd grow up a gangster like his father. Mob boss Joey Dino helped him buy a grocery store and become a success story. But everything comes with a price and, after a ten-year-stint in stir, Joey Dino has returned, hoping Wade will come in on one last big heist with Dino and the gang. By-the-numbers mobster nonsense has a promising opening act but quickly descends into a silly and predictable mess.

"The Bird Watcher" by Frank Sisk (2500 words)★↲
Mr. Doxius has been sending alimony checks to his ex-wife's address and they're being cashed. Which is odd, since he tossed her off a cliff months before. Doxius discovers a nosy neighbor with high-powered binoculars has appreciated the donations and expects them to keep coming.

"Sunday Killer" by Al James (2500 words)★
A stranger in town picks up a woman in a bar and takes her out for a thrill ride.

"The Extortioners" by Ovid Demaris (22,500 words)★★★↲
Hugh DeWitt has transformed himself from two-bit gambler to millionaire oil tycoon in only a few years time but now he's the target of a mobster named Jimmy Grazio, who wants a piece of Hugh's latest goldmine. DeWitt scoffs at first until the hood starts using his goons to get his message across.
A rollicking and thoroughly enjoyable pulp thriller, stocked with involving

characters and plenty of action. Standing out amidst the cast is the goon who turns Grazio on to DeWitt's good fortune; picture Ernest Borgnine as the half-witted Joe Rizzola explaining the deal to DeWitt's business partner:

> *"Look, I wouldn't have gone to this man if I'd thought DeWitt was gonna welsh. This is a big man and otherwise I wouldn't have gone to him and said, 'look, let's have this so we can have this, and then the man is gonna expect this, this and this from us. If he's got any beefs, we have to represent him, and we will. So we're all right, you're all right. The big guy is DeWitt."*
> *"I swear, Joe. You're a mental case."*

If "The Extortioners" has one drawback, it's a rushed and chaotic finish but since Demaris expanded the story into a novel (published by Gold Medal in 1960), perhaps the author smoothed out the rough spots eventually.

"A Matter of Judgement" by Jordan Bauman (1000 words)★★
A young couple are attacked while necking in a lovers' lane.

Vol. 7 No. 5 Oct 1959

Reuses Tom O'Sullivan cover art of Mar 1956. First and only appearance by Ray Russell, who was Playboy's Executive Editor at the time.

"Mad Dog—Beware" by J. W. Aaron (3500 words)★★✔
Amusing tale of an alcoholic cop who solves the murder of a racketeer found dead in his car with his dog.

"The Nude Killer" by K. McCaffrey (1000 words)★★
An American falls in love with the daughter of a Chinese businessman but then tosses her aside for an English woman. On a return trip to China, he meets up with her again and she delivers him a potent dose of revenge. Very odd that a short-short would receive lead billing on the cover.

"The Sword of Laertes" by Ray Russell (2000 words)★★✔
A veteran Shakespearean stage actor decides to murder his up-and-coming rival while the two perform on stage. A rare African poison applied to a fencing sword will provide the weapon. Things don't go as planned. Ray Russell, Playboy editor and screenwriter (*Mr. Sardonicus*), only wrote a handful of short stories for the crime digests and "The Sword of Laertes" was his single contribution to *Manhunt*.

"Snow Job" by Carroll Mayers (1000 words)★★
Two thugs use a gorgeous stripper to get to her mobster boyfriend.

"Big Brother" by Robert M. Hodges (3500 words)★★★
Lawyer Rodney Wilby has a new client, his sister-in-law, Linda, who's left her husband, Bronson, and seeks divorce. Rodney knows that he's courting trouble with his brother but he can't tell Linda no and, minutes after she leaves his office bound for a hotel, Bronson calls Rodney to bully him. Bronson promises he's on his way. Sections of "Big Brother" seem over-written and flowery but the plot is engaging and the climax is right out of left field.

"A Weakness for Women" by Arthur Kaplan (5500 words)★★✔
Lonely little Charlie meets beautiful blonde Sonia down at Dopey Norman's, buys her a drink, and falls madly in love with the woman. Sonia, for her part, likes Charlie but she likes lots of men. Eventually, the two get married, but Charlie objects to Sonia's late nights. One day, Charlie comes home from work to find Sonia, battered and bloody in the bedroom, claiming she was raped. Despite his doubts, Charlie promises his wife he'll track the assailant down and kill him. Though "A Weakness for Women" is needlessly padded, the third act, Charlie's quest for the rapist and the deliberately nebulous climax, are very powerful.

"The Death of Me" by Anne Smith Ewing (4500 words)★✈

Clara Willoughby has had enough of her husband's womanizing ways and hires a killer to off the new girlfriend. Contrived and overlong, "The Death of Me" is, worst of all, predictable.

"Curses" by Koller Ernst (4000 words)★★★✈

Redmond shuts the door of the Arctic shack he shares with his prospecting partner, Wylie, and sets off alone for the nearest village, one hundred miles away. Just before he leaves, his partner, sick and dying, curses Redmond to a similar fate. The trek is arduous and supplies dwindle while, all around him, a pack of wolves closes in.

Author Koller Ernst was a mainstay in the "lower rent" crime and science fiction digests of the 1950s (*Super Science Fiction, Guilty, Trapped, Terror Detective*, etc.) but this was his only *Manhunt* appearance. That's a shame because "Curses" is a harrowing, white-knuckled ride that never lets up, a tale that could just as easily have wound up in *Weird Tales* or *Adventure* as *Manhunt*.

"Escape Route" by Richard Deming (16,000 words)★★✈

When Pedro Bianca steals four million of Fidel Castro's money and hightails it out of Cuba, mercenary Casey Denver and his right-hand man, Sam McCabe, are hired to track the man, believed to be hidden away in Los Angeles. Denver stages a fake assassination attempt, claiming to be anti-Castro, hoping Bianca will extend an invite to sanctuary. Unfortunately, Denver and McCabe are kidnapped by some of Castro's own men and become embroiled in a murder. An odd, but satisfying, mixture of espionage, adventure, and whodunit, with more than a heaping of humor thrown in as well. Denver and McCabe are a very charismatic pair of "heroes" and this particular adventure was expanded into the novel, *This is My Night*, for Monarch Books in 1961.

"Wrong Alibi" by Roy Carroll (2000 words)★★

Alec Volpitto wants to make sure his boss, Verney, leaves him his boat but the old man's wife is back and that spells trouble. Time for murder.

"Check Out" by Edward Wellen (1500 words)★★

When Lt. Barend questions a hit-and-run suspect and discovers the guy was involved with the cop's fiancé, Barend blows his stack and murders her.

Peter Enfantino • Jeff Vorzimmer

Vol. 7 No. 6 Dec 1959

First and only appearance of writing teacher, Burley "Bud" Hendricks and of Alice Wernherr, who wrote a lot of nationally-syndicated short fiction that appeared in newspapers across the country.

"Free to Die" by Bryce Walton (8000 words)★★★★

Gino Ricci takes a leave of absence from his job as a detective to investigate, on his own time, the murder of his brother, Candela. Gino has a reputation as a tough bull so it's a foregone conclusion someone is going to die. A maniacally macho, full shot of adrenalin (and I'm not normally given over to hype), delivered in a very addictive style. Bryce Walton was very obviously influenced by Spillane while writing "Free to Die"; the characters speak in a strange clipped manner (such as the gorgeous dame who continually addresses Gino by his full name or the bad guy who uses Gino's nickname "Il Martello"—The Hammer) and every event seems to be escalated to a fever pitch. Not everyone's cup of tea and certainly a stand out in style from most of the fiction *Manhunt* was running at the time, but "Free to Die" is a thoroughly enjoyable and memorable read.

"Red Blood Bend" by Burley Hendricks (3000 words)★★★

Red Blood Bend is a particularly dangerous sharp turn on the highway. Accidents occur there frequently. When our narrator is discharged from the Navy, he soups up his hot rod and attempts to tame that corner. A gripping drama with a very edgy twist.

"The Simian Suspect" by Frank Sisk (4000 words)★★

A slow-as-molasses "cozy" about a St. Petersburg hotel dick called in to soothe an eccentric old lady's nerves; the woman is convinced that another resident of the hotel is holding her monkey hostage.

"Dead Reckoning" by Frank Kane (6500 words)★★

Johnny Liddell is hired by shady nightclub owner Tony Russo, who's getting threatening letters in the mail. It doesn't take long for Johnny to figure the pen pal is one of Maxie's dancing girls, Chilly Conover. When Russo finds out, he blows his top and throws Chilly out, threatening her with bodily harm. But later that day, it's Russo who turns up dead and Chilly is the prime suspect. It's up to Johnny Liddell to clear her good name. One of the weaker of the Johnny Liddell stories and that may be due to its brevity; there's not much meat on its bone. "Dead Reckoning" was later reprinted in the Liddell collection, *Stacked Deck* (Dell, 1961).

"Cat's Meow" by Jordan Bauman (1000 words)★★★

Emma can't stand the stray cat that Paul has brought home but then she's never liked any of the animals she's been forced to live with. When the cat breaks a very expensive vase, Emma decides it's got to go. But permanently. An extremely nasty short-short that won't find much favor with animal lovers but the most shocking moment is saved for the final paragraph when we discover the true identity of Paul.

"Stand In" by Albert Simmons (4000 words)★★
Tony and Rita have been a very popular dancing act for years but Rita is starting to look her thirty-five years. With a little prodding from Rita's beautiful, and very young, stand-in, Tony decides to break up the act in a violent way. Unfortunately, Tony's plans hit a bump in the road when Rita finds out what's on his mind.

"You Pay Your Money" by Lawrence Harvey (1000 words)★
A very young girl uses extortion to force a man to pay her a hundred bucks.

"Confession" by C. B. Gilford (4500 words)★★★
Sarah and Joe Beiser have owned the local confectionary for years but it's Sarah who profits from the business. Tired of his wife's bullying, Joe looks elsewhere for comfort and finds it in the pretty young May. When Sarah dies in a bizarre robbery at the store, Detective Magarian believes it was Joe cutting strings in order to inherit the business. Magarian becomes a pain in Beiser's ass, following him around and tracking all of his business dealings. Intriguing cat-and-mouse drama with a jarring twist climax.

"On Second Thought" by Carroll Mayers (1000 words)★✈
After discovering his wife is sleeping with his best friend, Mark Better decides to kill them both and blame it on a rash of neighborhood break-ins. But Mark loses his nerve at the last second and ditches the idea. Too late, he realizes that his wife and her lover think it was a great idea.

"The Swizzle Stick" by Alice Wernherr (4000 words)★★
Augustus Brimble has been the chief accountant at the Hirsh Teddybear Company for 22 years but the boss thinks it time that Augustus got himself an assistant. Enter the very eccentric Robert Wellesley, part-time playwright and would-be murderer.

The Best Stories of 1959

"Second Chance" by Joe Grenzeback (February)
"Killer's Wedge" by Ed McBain (February)
"The Double Take" by Edward Wellen (April)
"One Hour Late" by William O'Farrell (April)
"Down and Out" by Joe Gores (June)
"Absinthe for Superman" by Robert Edmond Alter (June)
"A Corpse That Didn't Die" by Henry Kane (June)
"The Extortioners" by Ovid Demaris (August)
"Curses" by Koller Ernst (October)
"Free to Die" by Bryce Walton (December)

Vol. 8 No. 1 Feb 1960
First and only appearance by Raymond Chandler and his P.I. Philip Marlowe.

"Wrong Pigeon" by Raymond Chandler (10,500 words)★★↲

Ikky Rosenstein is tired of being a hood for the mob; he wants out. Problem is, the mob won't let you retire. So, Ikky comes to Philip Marlowe to keep him alive. When Marlowe gets wind that two hit men have come calling, he helps Ikky get out of town. The next day, the dick watches as the two assassins gun down a man they believe to be Rosenstein. That pushes Marlowe into contacting his buddy, Detective Bernie Ohls. What follows is a clever set of twists and turns, leading Marlowe into some very dangerous alleys.

Previously published, just a few weeks after Chandler's death, in the British newspaper, *The Daily Mail*, in Apr 1959, "Wrong Pigeon" was retitled "Philip Marlowe's Last Case" when it was reprinted in *Ellery Queen* in 1962.

"A Killer's Witness" by Dick Ellis (3500 words)★★

Bob Brandeis witnesses his boss at the bank gunned down and robbed, and now the murderer is threatening to do the same to Bob's wife. How can he tell the cops the truth when it could mean Joan's life?

"Miser's Secret" by Richard Hardwick (3000 words)★★

Ike and Clay head out to ol' man Wolfe's shack on the bayou to rob him of his life savings, but Wolfe is a mean old cuss and he aims to fight back.

"The Twelve-Grand Smoke" by Frank Sisk (4500 words)★↲

A hotel dick must catch the man who committed a robbery on the 21st floor and then changed costumes to blend in with the hotel guests. The kind of mannered, stuffy detective fiction, centered around a peculiar gumshoe (à la Poirot), that was more prevalent in *Ellery Queen* than *Manhunt*.

"The Worm Turns" by R. D'Ascoli (2500 words)★★★

Al is losing his wife, Marianne, to his best buddy, Phil, but he won't go down without a fight. When Phil pushes Al to sell dope on the street, Al murders Marianne and pins it on his friend. A twisted triangle with a brutal outcome.

"The Grateful Corpse" by Bob Bristow (3500 words)★★

Phil Melton makes a big mistake and allows the mob to buy into his night club. When an associate is gunned down, Phil is the lead suspect. The mob makes him an offer: take the fall and his family will be taken care of. The D.A. offers a better idea: witness protection for all the info Phil has on his bosses. Phil's biggest problem, he learns, is that the Mob is playing on both sides. Author Bob Bristow spends too much time rehashing the build-up and the predictable finale is a letdown.

"The Lost Key" by Hal Ellson (1500 words)★↗
A sleazy Lothario discovers, too late, that he's made the wrong choice in women.

"Death at Full Moon" by Al James (8500 words)★↗
Three women have been murdered, all during a full moon and all strangled with a red scarf. The chief suspect is Professor Philip Henderson, an astronomy teacher who knew all three girls. But when Henderson turns up dead, Detective Mike Redden has to expand his suspect base. "Death at Full Moon" (which is retitled "Death *by* Full Moon" on the cover) begins compellingly enough but soon descends into silliness and an inane twist.

"Switch-Blade" by Paul Daniels (2000 words)★
The journey of one switchblade as it travels from crime to crime.

"The Idiot's Tale" by Leo Ellis (3000 words)★
Emmett Proule wakes from a months-long stupor to find himself in a mental hospital. But why is he here and why can't he remember his recent past? The answers are predictable.

"An Empty Threat" by Donald E. Westlake (2000 words)★★★
A thug breaks into the house of Frederick and Louise Leary and demands that Frederick return to work and empty the safe or Louise will die. On his way, Frederick ponders a life without Louise.

"No Place to Run" by Carroll Mayers (1500 words)★★
After he rips off the mob for sixty grand, Tallon hides out in a little town far from the action but Eddie and Al are good at what they do and it's not long before they track Tallon down and put the muscle on him. After Al pistol whips Tallon, he rapes the dope's girlfriend and says his goodbyes. But the girl doesn't like the treatment she received and manages to drive a wedge between Al and his partner. "No Place to Run" has a swell hardboiled build-up that's just itching for a great fade-out but what the reader gets is a clumsy, and quite unbelievable, expository.

Vol. 8 No. 2 Apr 1960

Last issue to feature an original Johnny Liddell story by Frank Kane, which was the longest running series in the magazine since its appearance in the first issue.

"Shakedown" by C. L. Sweeney, Jr. (2000 words)★★
A con man has over seventy prostitutes paying him fifty dollars a month thanks to his fake police badge and a little intimidation. One very smart girl turns the tables on her assailant.

"Please Believe Me!" by Jess Shelton (2500 words)★★
"Slim" is down at Uncle Al's tavern, crowing to the boys that he just stabbed his wife in the belly but no one will believe the poor slob. Not until the police come calling.

"Time for Revenge" by Dick Ellis (4000 words)★★★★
Halloran has been double-crossed by his two partners in crime, Al and Frank. Halloran smuggled in the diamonds and, for his trouble, got a bullet through the head. But the bullet didn't kill him; unfortunately, his former comrades decided Halloran's girl, Helen, was in the way as well and they put a bullet in her as well. That shooting was fatal. Now, only hours from death, Halloran scours the city looking for Al and Frank for some last-minute revenge. A wholly absorbing story with a shockingly brutal climax.

Though Dick Ellis only wrote three stories for *Manhunt*, he was a popular author in the crime digests, in particular *Alfred Hitchcock*, where he saw 45 stories, published between 1963 and 1974, under various pseudonyms.

"Pass the Word Along" by Frank Kane (7000 words)★⌐
A gorgeous Asian girl interrupts P.I. Johnny Liddell's precious drinking time, hiring him to hold an envelope for her. All very mysterious, but minutes after the girl leaves the bar, two heavies work Johny over and steal the envelope. Now Liddell has to find the girl before the thugs get to her. "Pass the Word Along" operates on a threadbare plot and lacks the usual Johnny Liddell humor.

"Lovers Quarrel" by Kelly Reynolds (3000 words)★
Harvey loves to belittle his most prized possession, the gorgeous Fran but when she gets hold of a pistol and aims it at Harvey's head, he has to learn how to praise.

"Life Sentence" by Talmage Powell (1500 words)★★
On his way to the big house, Hervie Taylor tells his guard the story of how he came to chop his wife into small pieces.

"The Challenge" by John Carnegie (5000 words)★★★

Casino is a highly sought-after paid assassin but he won't be considered "top dog" until colleague Parker is out of the way. When Casino decides it's time to climb the ladder, the two hitmen play a game of "Hunted and Hunter," with the roles switching constantly. Gripping thriller stumbles a bit towards the end but still makes an impression.

"Rub Out the Past" by Robert S. Aldrich (3000 words)★★★

Movie producer Nate Klohn has sunk a bundle of dough into rising movie star, Dice Thorne, but suddenly that investment is at risk. A blackmailer named "Gus" contacts Nate, demanding two million bucks or he'll unearth some dirty secrets about Nate's cash cow. That's when Dice calls in a fixer. Aldrich does such a good job building up his central character, the "fixer," that the reader wishes this could have been the novella this issue. "Rub Out the Past" finishes with a twist no one saw coming.

"Don't Clip My Wings" by David W. Maurer (5500 words)★★★⭩

Moonshine mules Skid and Tom lead the police on a harrowing chase in their souped-up Ford. A definite change of pace for *Manhunt*, "Don't Clip My Wings" is an exhilarating thrill-ride that never lets up. David W. Maurer was predominately a non-fiction crime writer (he sued Universal in the 1970s, claiming they'd pilfered his study, *The Big Con*, for the film *The Sting*) but managed to eke out two stories for *Manhunt*.

"The Nude in the Subway" by Arne Mann (1000 words)★

A married couple are terrified when they stumble across a woman in the subway who's been abused by several J.D.s. The last line is mildly amusing but this really is a gimmick without substance.

"Wharf Rat" by Robert Page Jones (7500 words)★★★

When a well-liked derelict is murdered on a nearby pier, P.I. Johnny Chance takes it upon himself to find out who the guilty party is. Though nothing distinguishes Chance from any other of the dozens of P.I.s that dotted the crime fiction landscape in the 1950s and 1960s, the writing of Robert Page Jones at least keeps the action and dialogue entertaining. There's a meta-moment when Chance mentions that he rents a garage to park his Corvette "and stack old copies of *Nugget*" (which was a men's magazine published by Flying Eagle).

"Mother's Waiting" by Murray Klater (1500 words)★

Hawkins waits in dirty bars and picks up girls so he can strangle them. There's an odd atmosphere to this unpleasant bit of drivel as if author Klater imagines an audience of readers too dumb to know what's going on from the start.

"The Safe Kill" by Kenneth Moore (1500 words)★★

Dirty cop takes assignment as hit man on the side. One of three 1960 *Man-*

hunt stories selected by Brett Halliday for *Best Detective Stories of the Year, 16th Annual Edition* (Dutton, 1961). The other two stories picked were "A Question of Values" by C. L. Sweeney, Jr. (June) and "Shatter Proof" by Jack Ritchie (Oct).

Vol. 8 No. 3 Jun 1960

"A Question of Values" by C. L. Sweeney from this issue is chosen for the annual Best Detective Stories of the Year anthology and would be his last contribution to the magazine.

"Right Thing to Do" by Robert Leon (3000 words)★
A young assassin is given the target only he can successfully hit: his own brother!

"Pics for Sale" by Ben Satterfield (1000 words)★★
Life among the seedy on a Mexico street corner.

"A Question of Values" by C. L. Sweeney, Jr. (1500 words)★★
A jilted husband invites his wife's new lover, a concert pianist, to his mountain cabin to discuss the future. The husband explains that the lover is the only one in this triangle who has nothing to lose and, to make the playing field even, he handcuffs the man, hands him a knife and lights fire to the cabin. The real question here is why the lover would ever agree to meet, with the man who hates him most, at a remote location.

"Bodyguard" by Richard Hardwick (4500 words)★★★⌐
When the bar he owns goes under, Vinnie Pratt accepts an invite from mobster Mack Silverman to work at the Zebra Club. Shortly after arriving, Mack shows his skill with a gun when a couple of out-of-town hoods try to put Mack six feet under. The boss's grateful and makes Vinnie his bodyguard. There's only one problem with the set-up and that's Mack's girl, Fran, who's not all that enamored of her beau and looking for a way out. Vinnie seems to be the way out. Tough, energetic prose that never lets up, with a shocking climax that begs a sequel.

"The Faithless Woman" by Carroll Mayers (1500 words)★★⌐
A cop questions whether his partner is ready for duty again after troubling domestic problems.

"Mis-fire" by Norman Struber (6500 words)★★
Predictable tale of a veteran cop who's told his wife has been murdered and demands to be lead detective on the case. Turns out the woman was seeing someone on the side and her husband was well aware of that fact.

"Set-Up for Two" by Norman Anthony (21,000 words)★★★
Barry and Connie Middleton were once ideal for each other but now Barry is a struggling novelist and Connie can't find a stage director who will hire her. Both have hit rock bottom with alcohol and marital woes. Now, Barry has decided to use his novelist's smarts to concoct the perfect murder... of Connie. Unfortunately, for Barry, his wife has hit on the same idea. Their plans merge on one deadly night. "Set-Up For Two" is overlong by about half but both lead characters are

well-composed and their personal drama, and how they manipulate each other, is oddly compelling.

"Nightmare" by James Walz (1500 words)★
Silly short-short about a woman trapped in a remote cabin with a madman on the loose.

"Harmless" by Mildred Jordan Brooks (2500 words)★★
A mentally-ill young man is being transported to a hospital when his driver stops at a gas station and all hell breaks loose.

"The Loving Victim" by Lottie Belle Davis (3500 words)★⅃
Bill Powers is carrying on an affair with his secretary. No great sin there, except that his wife holds the purse strings and the company Bill runs. A scandal would ruin all of Bill's plans for the future. So, Bill plans what he thinks is the perfect crime. Unfortunately for Bill, his secretary has a habit of writing lots of notes. Ludicrous climax reminiscent of a Lovecraft story where the writer keeps on typing out his manuscript as the nameless horror beats down his door.

Vol. 8 No. 4 Aug 1960

Last appearances of Fletcher Flora (18 stories) and David Alexander (13 stories). Reuses the cover art of Dec 25, 1954.

"Goodbye" by Charles Carpentier (1000 words)★★ᛎ
Helen and Frank discuss the murder of Frank's wife between a steel-mesh divider in a prison visiting room. But which one is in prison and which one is free? Carpentier pulls off the deception right until the final line.

"She's Nothing But Trouble" by Glenn Canary (2500 words)★★★
Paul really doesn't want the girl coming into his bar but she does so every night. She orders a Pink Lady and waits for a man to take her home. A different man every night. Tonight, the girl gets more than she bargained for when five hoods come in for a drink and decide to have a party. "She's Nothing But Trouble" starts out innocently enough but an atmosphere of dread enters halfway through and escalates, with the story ending on a decidedly downbeat note. Glenn Canary went on to write a trio of "sleaze" novels for Monarch Books: *The Trailer Park Girls*, *The Sadist* (both 1962), and *The Damned and the Innocent* (1964).

"The Deserter" by Hal Ellson (3500 words)★
Tedious thriller about a military cop searching a pier for a deserter.

"The Accuser" by Robert Wallsten (4000 words)★★★ᛎ
A young man is detained by police on suspicion of rape charges but, when he's brought to the girl's house, he's cleared of charges. A harrowing examination of both sides of the crime, with the alleged rapist knowing anything he says or does will look like an admission of guilt, and the victim's endless terror and humiliation adding to her wish to "just get this all over with."

"She Asked for It" by Fletcher Flora (10,000 words)★★★
When Faye Bratton is found dead on a burning haystack, Sheriff Colby has a long list of suspects. Faye was married, but to what you might call a "wanderer," and several of the men in town had spent time with her. One of those men rises to number one on Colby's "Most Wanted" list and that's Fergus Cast, Faye's latest lover. Now, Colby has to find Fergus. A gripping whodunit with a marvelous cast of characters, especially Colby and his deputy, the dim-witted Virgil. Imagine a dour Andy Taylor and a more stupid Barney Fife. This was Fletcher Flora's 18th and final story for *Manhunt*.

"Kill One Kill Two" by H. A. DeRosso (4000 words)★★
When her husband is killed during a jewelry heist, Laura moves to a remote cabin to get away from "all the questions," but a stubborn insurance investigator tracks her down, believing she has the hot jewels. Standard thriller with a predic-

able twist ending.

Henry Andrew DeRosso was a writing machine from 1947 through 1960 (the year of his death at the age of 43), selling crime stories to *Mobsters*, *Thrilling Detective*, *Hunted*, and *Alfred Hitchcock* (under his own name and as by John Cortez) but the writer is best known for his tough, noir-ish westerns. His four novels, *Tracks in the Sand*, *The Gun Trail*, *End of the Gun*, and (his masterpiece) *.44* eschew the trappings of the prototypical western, instead emphasizing the darker and pessimistic nature of the Old West. Perhaps author/historian Bill Pronzini summed up DeRosso's fiction best in his introduction to the DeRosso collection, *Under the Burning Sun* (Five Star, 1997): "An aura of melancholy pervades even those of his stories which have upbeat resolutions."

"Survival" by David Alexander (3000 words)★★★

When an avalanche leaves them stranded in a small shack a mile up a Swiss mountain, a writer, his wife, and their guide must ration what little food they have until the weather permits a rescue. When the food is gone, other options will be explored.

"Deadly Error" by Avram Davidson and Chester Cohen (2000 words)★★

Grover Blain discovers his wife is having an affair and wants to teach her lover a lesson really quick, so he visits a man who specializes in such business.

"The Prisoner" by Lawrence Harvey (1000 words)★★↲

The sheriff of a small town is holding a wanted prisoner in his jail, awaiting the arrival of a cop from Atlanta. Though short-shorts aren't usually effective, "The Prisoner" has a very good, unexpected twist.

"Heat Crazy" by Virgie F. Shockley (2000 words)★★

Sheriff Bruce always has problems when the heat of summer arrives. This time it's Link Slover, who's taking shots at the mailman and pert near anyone who comes near his farm. But when the Sheriff gets to Link's place, he discovers something more sinister.

"New Year's Party" by Alson J. Smith (10,000 words)★↲

Lt. Steve O'Hara, second in charge of the newly formed Criminal Investigation Division, investigates a series of jewelry robberies in North Chicago. O'Hara and his squad of detectives are obviously an attempt by author Smith to duplicate the success of the Ed McBain 87th Precinct. Though there are a few flashes of imagination (O'Hara drives a Porsche), Smith's fascination with the minutiae of police investigation leaves little room for character development.

"Busybody" by J. Simmons Scheb (1500 words)★★

Karl murders his wife and hopes the busybody (who listens in through paper thin walls) next door will provide a perfect alibi. He's wrong.

Peter Enfantino • Jeff Vorzimmer

"Frustration" by Anne Smith Ewing (1500 words)★ʲ

Samuel has been dreaming of that ice-cooled watermelon all day, working hard at the stiflingly hot factory, but his dreams are shattered when he gets home and discovers his wife has had guests.

Vol. 8 No. 5 Oct 1960
First of six issues to use new original cover art. The magazine's circulation is 189,745.

"Too Much to Prove" by Glenn Canary (2500 words)★★★

Hitch-hiker Carley is picked up by a couple on the way to Vegas. The driver picks at Carley, telling him he's a bum and should get some guts, while his wife tries to calm him. At last, the man pulls a gun from his glovebox, pops in a bullet, spins the cylinder, and tells Carley he'll give him five grand to play Russian Roulette with him. A taut, riveting short play, with all the action taking place in the front seat of the car.

"Dead Beat" by Hayden Howard (4000 words)★

Murder in a flophouse filled with alcoholics and drug addicts. With its beatnik slang and incomprehensible plot, "Dead Beat" is my choice for the single worst story to run in *Manhunt* magazine. If Jack Kerouac had known what the consequences would entail, perhaps he never would have written *On the Road*.

"White Lightning" by David Maurer (4500 words)★★½

If you run liquor in the hills and want to dodge the law, then you need to see Tinker. Tonight, Jock and Lefty have brought their '53 Olds in for Tinker to work his magic. He can make the car do 120 but he can't help the boys when they take that dangerous curve doing 90.

"Name Unknown, Subject Murder" by Sheila S. Thompson (2000 words)★★

A woman finds the "diary" of a rapist/murderer and becomes so obsessed with the killer she begins adding details to the book as he continues his work.

"The Trouble Shooters" by Dan Brennan (5000 words)★★

All the hoods in Cereal City are on the lookout for Johnny Skidmore, the lousy collector who put a bullet in the head of mafia chief Ed Morgan, but Skidmore is too smart for these bums. That is, until he's not smart anymore and the hoods catch up to him. Too much of "The Trouble Shooters" reads like a non-fiction essay on the mafia in the early 1960s. Not much excitement, save for the brutal final scene.

"Shatter Proof" by Jack Ritchie (1500 words)★★★

Mr. Williams is about to be shot to death by an assassin hired by his own greedy wife. But Williams won't go quietly and, by the end of the evening, he's not only talked his way out of death but talked his would-be killer into setting his sights on Mrs. Williams. A clever short-short with a brilliant twist ending.

"The Fugitives" by Marc Perry Winters (7000 words)★★

After killing a cop during a routine traffic stop, two gunrunners must hide in a field while, all around them, the police close in. "The Fugitives" certainly has some interesting moments, but it's padded, and author Winters foregoes telling a really good story to write what he feels is an American tragedy.

"Protection" by Hal Ellson (1500 words)★★

Amato is being shaken down by some hoods who want part of the dock worker's check. Amato refuses and is slashed for it; he refuses again and his wife is raped. Wising up, he goes to "the Circle," a group his friend recommends, and airs his beef. The Circle take care of Amato's problem but now he has to pay *them* every week for protection.

"To Catch a Spy" by Philip Freund (18,000 words)★↲

Snail's-pace espionage thriller about an agent named Stephen Pardus who is sent into West Berlin to catch a "master spy." Espionage was never one of the genres that *Manhunt* excelled in and "To Catch a Spy" is a prime example. The story was later re-titled "Spymaster" and published in a collection under that name by Ives Washburn.

Vol. 8 No. 6 Dec 1960

Two stories from this issue would be used as the basis for Alfred Hitchcock *episodes, H. A. DeRosso's "The Old Pro" and Charles Runyon's "Hangover", the latter would be the last* Manhunt *story to be used in that series, which was then in its eighth season and titled* The Alfred Hitchcock Hour. *First of four consecutive covers by Dick Shelton.*

"Carnival Con" by David Zinman (3000 words)★★↲
When the con game that carnival illusionist, Zanda the Magnificent, and his lovely assistant, Ida, run begins making serious coin, Zanda decides he wants 100% of the take. That doesn't go over well with Ida.

"The Old Pro" by H. A. DeRosso (4000 words)★★★
A retired assassin hires a hit man to take out a blackmailer for him but, it turns out, the blackmailer has the same idea. Engrossing character study of a killer who just wants to enjoy some peace and quiet with his wife after a long career.

When the story was dramatized in the seventh season of *Alfred Hitchcock Presents*, Frank Burns, the retired assassin, was perfectly realized by Richard Conte. Perhaps best known for his role as Don Barzini in *The Godfather*, Conte plays Burns like a quiet storm.

"Dead Heat" by Tom Phillips (3500 words)★★
How could the county's best hot rod driver, Skit Costello, roll his '54 Merc on a straight stretch of highway? Ask Bart and Charlie, who both had good reason to see Skit dead.

"Hangover" by Charles Runyon (4000 words)★★★↲
Greg Maxwell wakes from an all-night drinking binge to find a blonde named Sandy lying in the bed next to him. Unable to piece together the events of the night before, Greg wakes the girl and quizzes her. After she tells him her name is Sandy, she lets on that Greg has been on a bender for five days and he's pledged undying love to this stranger. The house is a disaster, he's told off his boss, the neighbor's dog is in his backyard, and he can't reach his estranged wife (Greg threw Marian out after discovering she's having an affair with the guy who's building their patio); it's all like some bad dream.

The dream gets worse though when Sandy mentions that Marian showed up to the house the night before. "Hangover" is a fabulously constructed tale, a snake in the grass that spends most of its running time selling you a black comedy; the mess Greg has made unfolds a little at a time and the reader can't help but laugh while simultaneously grimacing.

Oddly enough, when "Hangover" was bought for the first season of *The Alfred Hitchcock Hour*, it was welded together with another story (coincidentally or not) titled "Hangover." Written by John D. MacDonald and appearing in the Jul 1956 issue of *Cosmopolitan*, this "Hangover" was, in ways, quite similar to Runyon's story. Ad executive Hadley Purvis has a drinking problem and it ruins his job and his family life. As in Runyon's version, the downward spiral leads to murder. MacDonald, in the introduction to his story collection, *End of the Tiger*, praises actor Tony Randall "exceptional job as the lead," but I found Randall's performance to be histrionic and forced. Writer Lou Rambeau does a good job stitching these two very similar stories together for a cohesive whole but there's a lot of padding here. Still, that final shot, of the corpse of Purvis's wife in the closet, is unnerving.

"Tee Vee Murder" by Harold R. Daniels (6000 words)★★★

A pretty young girl named Peggy Coken is found dead in an alleyway near her home. The only clues hardboiled detective Ed Tanager has to go on is a unique pack of matches and that the girl was on a local dance TV show. Using good detective work, Ed narrows his search to twenty local bars and begins his stake-out. Since most of the patrons are leering sexual deviates, Ed discovers it will be harder to narrow down the list of suspects. "Tee Vee Murder" is a solid murder mystery, with a gritty lead character, marred only by a rushed climax.

Daniels wrote six well-received crime novels: *In His Blood* (1955), *The Girl in 304* (1956), *The Accused* (1958), *The Snatch* (1958), *For the Asking* (1962), and *The House on Greenapple Road* (1966). The latter became the TV-movie of the same name in 1970; that film morphed into *Dan August*, the TV series starring Burt Reynolds.

"Death and the Blue Rose" by William O'Farrell (5000 words)★★★★

Tired of being a fragile flower with no life, Mildred sees a psychologist who hypnotizes her and solves her problem. She only has to say two words, "blue rose," and Mildred becomes a happy, assertive woman. Ricky has just robbed and murdered a mobster and is running from two goons who want to put him six feet under and retrieve that stolen dough. The two collide at just the right time and become entangled.

A thoroughly engrossing novella about two disparate personalities that somehow meet in the middle for a fleeting moment, "Death and the Blue Rose" has a heartbreaking climax that will stay with the reader for quite a while.

"Jail Break" by Dan Sontup (3000 words)★★⁁

After a bank heist goes wrong, Carl and Jerry have to break Lila out of a small-town jailhouse. Good action thriller with a startling jolt or two.

Dan Sontup is best remembered for the dozens of "Portrait of a Killer" profiles he wrote for *Manhunt*. Though Sontup only saw two fiction pieces published in the magazine (this and "Cop Killer" back in Aug 1956), the writer was a mainstay in the other crime digests (*Trapped, Guilty, Off Beat, Mike Shayne*) of the day.

"The Model Dies Naked" by Harry Widmer (11,000 words)★★⁁

Roger Falconer's wife, Adele, has been having an affair with Roger's friend,

Joe Beck. Roger discovers that the affair may go back as far as four years, during the time Roger was serving overseas. In a bit of a revenge mood, Roger sleeps with a gorgeous woman name Majel, who poses nude for fun and profit. Immediately following the coupling, Roger spies Majel putting something in his drink. Turning the tables, Falconer pours the drink down the beauty's throat and watches as she passes out. Convinced that Adele and Joe Beck had something to do with this, Roger heads to a local bar and makes a threatening phone call to Beck. He then returns to Majel's apartment for a second helping. Unfortunately, the girl is dead, suffocated with a pillow. Who killed the model?

"The Model Dies Naked" certainly contains some entertaining passages but, overall, it's nothing more than a *Peyton Place*-esque soap opera with a murder as its centerpiece. The four-page expository is clunky and complicated, but Harry Widmer's dialogue is spry, like that of a 1930s screwball comedy. Widmer had a long career in the pulps and is probably best known for his P.I., "Blackie" Blackmoor, a character that appeared in *Ten Detective Aces* in the mid-1930s.

"A Long Wait" by Richard L. Sargent (6000 words)★★★

Accountant Harold Jennings discovers his boss, R.K. Adams, has embezzled twenty grand from the Philips Toy Company. When Harold confronts his boss about the theft, R.K. offers him a bribe to keep quiet. The next day, R.K. has Harold go to the bank and withdraw fifty thousand, an amount, Harold knows, that will bankrupt the company. Suddenly, Harold gets a bright idea: why should he stand in a bread line while R.K. enjoys "retirement?" He gets to plotting. An amusing and enjoyable little crime fantasy with an ironic twist.

"Desperation" by Joachim H. Woos (1000 words)★★★

John has just done a stint for robbery but, cold and desperate, he uses a gun he's found in a box car to rob a pawn shop. That's the idea anyway. "Desperation" isn't so much a crime story as a well-told joke with a very funny punchline.

The Best Stories of 1960

"Time for Revenge" by Dick Ellis (April)
"Rub Out the Past" by Robert S. Aldrich (April)
"Don't Clip My Wings" by David W. Maurer (April)
"Bodyguard" by Richard Hardwick (June)
"The Accuser" by Robert Wallsten (August)
"She Asked For It" by Fletcher Flora (August)
"Shatter Proof" by Jack Ritchie (October)
"The Old Pro" by H. A. DeRosso (December)
"Hangover" by Charles Runyon (December)
"Death and the Blue Rose" by William O'Farrell (December)

Vol. 9 No. 1 Feb 1961
The debut of the column "It's the Law."

"Hold-Up" by Jess Shelton (3000 words)★
After watching a young boy come out of a liquor store wielding a knife, a good samaritan gives chase but is beaten badly for his troubles. To add insult to injury, he later discovers that the theft was staged.

"Please Find My Sister!" by David H. Ross (11,000 words)★
Eunice Blair has a job for P.I. Al Delaney; she wants him to find her missing sister, Mavis. With nothing to go on, Delaney refuses and tells the girl to go to the cops. Minutes after Eunice leaves, two goons come into Delaney's office, rough him up, and tell him that if he looks in to the Mavis Blair disappearance, he'll be the next one to vanish into thin air. As with most P.I.s, this is a challenge that Al Delaney won't walk away from.
"Please Find My Sister" seems horribly dated, but then I assume it was horribly dated in 1961 since P.I. fiction was on the wane in the pages of *Manhunt* and Delaney is just a cheap copy of Shell Scott, Mike Shayne, and Peter Chambers. Like many of the "novels" that appeared in the second half of *Manhunt*'s life, "Please Find" is slow-paced, padded, and written by an author who would never be seen in these pages again.

"Last Payment" by Ron Boring (2000 words)★
A newspaperman is fired for being drunk and must work up his courage before getting home to tell his wife. But she's with a John when he comes in. A complete and utter waste of precious space.

"Vengeance" by Robert Page Jones (3500 words)★★★
A holocaust survivor recognizes a man in his neighborhood as the Nazi who tortured him in a concentration camp, and plans his revenge. Well-constructed short story that leaves more than a touch of ambiguity after its climax. Is this man really a Nazi? With his nine appearances in *Manhunt* in the 1960s, Robert Page Jones became the closest thing to a "regular" the magazine would have in this era. Novels by the author include: *The Heisters* (1963) and *Operation: Countdown* (1970).

"Body-Snatcher" by C. B. Gilford (5000 words)★★★
Poor Anton has been slaving away as Mrs. Kopping's gardener for years but now his back is giving out and he wants to retire. His wife, Stella, who doubles as Mrs. Kopping's housemaid, won't hear of it and she threatens her much-smaller husband with police action if he should quit. In a rage, Anton strangles Stella and buries her in the rose garden. Unfortunately for Anton, Mrs. Kopping is a light sleeper and she sees everything. Entertaining and almost darkly humorous, with a clever twist in its finale.

"How Much to Kill?" by Michael Zuroy (4000 words)★★★

Sheldon Cummins is about to invest every dollar in a get-rich-quick scheme that involves land in a flood zone. He'll need good P.R. so he wants to pay journalist Sam Tuttle a tidy sum to get him that great press. While Cummins is giving Tuttle a grand tour of the land, a storm hits and the two flee for higher ground, but they spot two kids stranded on an island in the middle of the raging water. Cummins rescues the boys but may come to regret the decision later. A thrilling adventure with several effective twists.

Only two stories from 1961 issues of *Manhunt* were selected by Brett Halliday for *The Best Detective Stories of the Year 17th Annual Edition*. Both were written by Michael Zuroy (the other story picked was "Retribution" from the April issue).

"The Alarmist" by Donald Tothe (2000 words)★★↲

Ed Manson goes to quite a bit of expense building a bomb shelter under his house; his neighbors think he's nuts but Ed is convinced doomsday is coming. When an explosion rocks the town, Ed heads below-ground to wait out the apocalypse. His neighbors bang on the door, insisting the explosion was just a laboratory accident on the edge of town, but Ed holds fast. Doubt begins to creep in and, eventually, Ed unbolts the door to see what's up. Bad decision. Even though the climax is a bit predictable (to be fair, there are only two possible outcomes), "The Alarmist" delivers the claustrophobic, fatalistic, and terrifying goods.

"The Master Mind" by Walter Monaghan (16,500 words)★↲

An insurance investigator attempts to infiltrate a gang of clever jewel thieves before they pull their next job. "The Master Mind" works up a bit of excitement initially but it's apparent very quickly that this is a short story padded out to novella length.

Peter Enfantino • Jeff Vorzimmer

Vol. 9 No. 2 Apr 1961
The debut of "Manhunt's Gun Rack" which would run fairly consistently through Mar 1965.

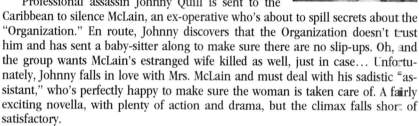

"Deadly Triangle" by Les Collins (3000 words)★★

An unhappy woman convinces her lover that he should do away with the woman's husband in a hunting "accident."

"The Last Kill" by Charles Runyon (13,500 words)★★ꜜ

Professional assassin Johnny Quill is sent to the Caribbean to silence McLain, an ex-operative who's about to spill secrets about the "Organization." En route, Johnny discovers that the Organization doesn't trust him and has sent a baby-sitter along to make sure there are no slip-ups. Oh, and the group wants McLain's estranged wife killed as well, just in case... Unfortunately, Johnny falls in love with Mrs. McLain and must deal with his sadistic "assistant," who's perfectly happy to make sure the woman is taken care of. A fairly exciting novella, with plenty of action and drama, but the climax falls short of satisfactory.

Charles Runyon wrote several crime novels throughout the 1960s (*The Anatomy of Violence* (1960), *The Death Cycle* (1963), *Color Him Dead* (1963) and *The Prettiest Girl I Ever Killed* (1965) among them) before switching gears and becoming a science fiction writer. In an interview with Ed Gorman, Runyon revealed the switch came after his younger brother was murdered in 1967 and he found the similar elements in his novels to be unsavory.

"Blizzard, Brother, Blood" by Lewis Banci (2000 words)★★

An eight year-old girl writes in her diary about her strange brother and their disappearing family during a blizzard. The final entry is laughable in that the girl writes about her brother coming in the room with an axe as in those old Lovecraft stories.

"Grudge Fight" by Frank Hardy (4000 words)★ꜜ

Darky, the toughest man in a small Australian mining town, must face Jimmy Younger, an upstart kid who wants to steal Darky's reputation by beating him in a street fight. "Grudge Fight" has a six-page blow-by-blow description of the brawl and not much else.

"To Kill a Cop" by D. M. Downing (4500 words)★

After ten long years in the stir, Jim Cole is back in town. To Johnny Manse, that means only one thing: the cop who put Cole away, kindly Pop Mahoney, has to die. And Johnny knows, he'll be the one called on for the job. Slow-moving and padded, "To Kill a Cop" is tough to get through and comes equipped with a nauseatingly maudlin fade-out.

"The Knife" by Glenn Canary (3000 words)★★★✦
On a whim, Paul Talent buys a switchblade in a small shop while he's trying to keep warm. Though he's not sure why, the knife changes his life, transforms him into an emboldened thrill-seeker. When he takes his wife to a local bar and she's hit on by another man, Paul pulls out the knife, feeling unstoppable, but his adversary has a gun. A clever little thriller with multiple subtle metaphors and observations. Size matters.

"Retribution" by Michael Zuroy (1000 words)★★
An audit reveals that a handsome bank clerk has embezzled forty grand. The fact that the clerk had affairs with the auditor's wife and bank manager's daughter might have something to do with the charges.

"The Evidence of Murder" by Kenneth McCaffrey (1000 words)★✦
Even though she's left him for another man, Helen asks Tom for five thousand dollars. Tom refuses. Helen claims she has dirt on her ex-beau and is not above blackmail. Tom kills her.

"Patsy" by Paul Fairman (9000 words)★★✦
Larry Bowman has a simple business, supplying and servicing jukeboxes in and around Central City, but it's a good living and he has no complaints. Not until the day his life falls apart. It begins when Larry picks up a pretty young blonde, standing along the highway next to her flat tire, and gives her a ride into town. Little does Larry know the woman is involved with Gus Largo, a rival jukebox-man who's about to be brought in by the FBI for his questionable business tactics. The only witness the FBI has is Largo's secretary, Gloria Dane, so is it a coincidence that Dane's car ends up in Larry's possession just before she goes missing?
There are a few too many loose ends but also a few too many coincidences explained away in the rushed finale but, for the first half of the story, "Patsy" is very entertaining. Paul W. Fairman's career spanned five decades, countless novels and short stories, and several genres, including science fiction (*Starhaven*) and horror (*Rest in Agony, The Frankenstein Wheel*). Fairman also sat in the editor's chair at *If, Amazing*, and *Fantastic* for a short while.

"Fair Warning" by James Holding (2500 words)★★
Mobster Virgil Paoli oversteps his boundaries with a rival Chicago mob and now he's convinced they've sent a hitman to teach him a lesson. A humorous reveal saves "Fair Warning" from tedium.

"The Pain Killer" by Charles Carpentier (1000 words)★
A doctor administers care to a couple who've been in a car crash. A silly waste of space with a last paragraph that adds a ludicrous cherry on top.

Peter Enfantino • Jeff Vorzimmer

Vol. 9 No. 3 Jun 1961
Last appearance of Charles Runyon, who contributed three stories to the magazine.

"The Honest John" by Martin Suto (4500 words)★★✓
After he hits rock bottom, Grimes is offered an easy job by his friend, the Greek. Fly to Florida, pick up a box from an airport locker, and bring it to a man named Brewer. When he tells the Greek he wants to know what's in a box he's carrying, the Greek tells him to open it if he likes. He knows that should run up the red flags, but Grimes needs the job badly. The trip goes off without a hitch but, on the flight back, the plane explodes and he's the only survivor. Grimes is mad and he wants answers. An exciting little thriller that changes gears midway and throws the reader a welcome curve.

"Lady Killer" by Herbert Kastle (4000 words)★★✓
Marvin has a great business going. He answers personal ads from people selling appliances, then robs and murders them. But what happens when Marvin answers an ad belonging to the *other* serial killer in the city?

"Hangover Alley" by Robert Page Jones (10,000 words)★★
Johnny Phelan plays a mean piano down at a local blues club but he's not very good when it comes to finances. He owes Sonny Mergel a large sum of money and Sonny's a shylock who isn't shy about breaking bones. Arnie Gold, one of Sonny's top goons, comes down one night to collect from Johnny but the two men get into a tussle in the alley out back of the club and Arnie is killed. But was Gold already dying when Johnny entered the alley? With his girlfriend, Johnny attempts to find the real killer before either the cops or Sonny Mergel get their hands on him. Familiar plot and familiar padding.

"Cheap Kicks" by William Brothers (5000 words)★★★✓
Three J.D.s kidnap a young waitress, take her into the woods, and rape and murder her. Though the framework of the story is not much more than that simple synopsis, the effect of this brutal and unflinching short story is like a slap in the face. "Cheap Kids" is a story that will, unfortunately, never seem dated.

"The Girl Friend" by David Dwyer (2500 words)★★
A lot of disreputable people stay at the Hotel Astor but when a wanted thief and murderer checks in, co-proprietor Elfreda figures a way to get rid of her no-good husband and latch on to the guest's fortune as well.

"Wrong Victim" by W. Delos (2000 words)★
Ike Baker confesses to the murder of his wife but the coroner claims the woman died of natural causes. Regardless, Ike continues to confess.

"Taste of Terror" by Paul Fairman (1500 words)★★

After a lifetime of cowardice, Billy Wayne must face his fears when he's taken prisoner in war and tortured for military secrets.

"The Possessive Female" by Charles Runyon (5500 words)★★ⵏ

After killing a man in a bar, Paul flees to the Caribbean plantation owned by his army buddy, Greg, and his exotic wife, Marie. While Greg is off on business, Paul and Marie get *down* to business and Marie grows attached to her new man. Paul plans to break off the affair when his friend gets home but, that same evening, Marie comes to him and explains that Greg died accidentally while drinking. The accident, Paul discovers, included a pair of scissors to the jugular. Soon after, Marie confesses that her first husband died similarly and Paul realizes he has a problem.

"In Memoriam" by Charles Boeckman (2500 words)★★

Wilber is expected not to last the night and so, his wife Hortensia begins funeral arrangements and informing the family. But what happens when Wilber outlives his expectancy?

"Smuggler's Monkey" by Arne Mann (5000 words)★

A man wakes up from a drunk to find a beautiful woman in his living room, pointing a gun at him. An abstract farce involving drugs, stolen jewels and lots of quotes from *Alice in Wonderland.*

"Sales Pitch" by Mark Starr (2000 words)★ⵏ

Door-to-door salesman Webb discovers his wife is having an affair with one of his colleagues, the amorous Mark, who spends quite a lot of time in the homes of beautiful women. Webb murders Mark at the home of his latest sale and then kills the woman as well, discovering later that Mark was actually making a stop home to see his *own* wife for a little afternoon delight.

"Dead Letter" by Don Tothe (1000 words)★

Smiley is waiting for a very important letter, one that might stop him from receiving a bullet to the gut. Meanwhile, the mailman is having a hard time getting onto the street.

Peter Enfantino • Jeff Vorzimmer

Vol. 9 No. 4 Aug 1961
Cover by Dick Shelton is the last painted cover.

"Decay" by Michael Zuroy (2000 words)★★
Shock jock Vance Taggart has made a lot of enemies due to his radio gossip show, but Vance soon learns that perhaps the worst mistake you can make is to alienate your dentist.

"Death by the Numbers" by Ed Lacy (3000 words)★★
A woman is found strangled, her farm hand is the chief suspect, but an out-of-town inspector suspects the sheriff may be involved. This was Ed Lacy's first of four appearances in *Manhunt*. He would later become the well-respected author of over 25 crime novels, including the series of mysteries featuring African-American P.I., "Touie" Moore. Lacy was also a mainstay in the crime digests, with stories published in *Mike Shayne, Alfred Hitchcock, Ellery Queen,* and *The Saint*.

"Finger-Man" by John Connolly (17,000 words)★★★
Robert Donaldson has gone missing. The ex-Mrs. Donaldson couldn't care less other than the fact that Robert is behind on his alimony payments. The gorgeous blonde (aren't they all?) hires P.I. Bill Sweeney to find Roger and Bill always finds his man. Trouble is, when Sweeney catches up to the elusive Donaldson, the man claims he's not married. Further, he explains to Sweeney, he's in hiding because he accidentally got mixed up in an elaborate drug-smuggling ring and there have been two attempts on his life. Sweeney hates to be had, so he agrees to protect Donaldson and get to the bottom of this mess. Sweeney is an amiable character and the action and drama move along at a nice clip despite its length. John Connolly should not be confused with the Irish crime writer best known for his series of books featuring cop-turned-private-eye Charlie Parker.

"Bugged" by Bruno Fischer (4000 words)★★★
Mobster Lew Angel meets the love of his life, teacher Esther Hunt, and has an epiphany: he's going to go straight, marry Esther, and retire to a legitimate lifestyle. This doesn't sit well with two of Lew's henchmen and they hatch a plot to drive a wedge between Lew and Esther. Unbeknownst to these two dopes, the FBI has been bugging Lew's house.

"Die, Die, Die!" by Rosemary Johnson (4000 words)★
Joe Adams sits on his barstool, fantasizing out loud different methods of killing his mother-in-law. So when the old bag is found murdered, with the weapon in Joe's hand, the case is open and shut, right?

"The Big Haul" by Robert Page Jones (17,000 words)★★★★
When his big rig breaks down in a one-horse town, trucker Johnny Womack has to figure out how to stay alive on twenty-three bucks. He meets a gorgeous

woman at a truck stop diner and they head out to a bar to have a drink, but he's pulled over by a couple deputies and has the shit kicked out of him. Unbeknownst to Womack, a big heist is being planned involving the armored car that delivers payroll to the local army base. One of the three men in on the plot is the town sheriff and he immediately recognizes that Womack is down on his luck and may provide that fourth wheel the trio needs.

"The Big Haul" is an exhilarating and unpredictable thrill-ride that sits with the best of the 1950s heist novels. Womack is that rarity, a protagonist who's propelled into a bad deed, not by force but by circumstance, and still holds the reader's compassion. Robert Page Jones builds the tension so expertly that when the lid blows and the graphic violence arrives, we're completely unready. "The Big Haul" was expanded into the novel, *The Heisters*, published in 1963 by Monarch, and adapted into the 1967 French Film, *That Man George*. Later in his career, Jones wrote a trio of suspense novels (*The Man Who Killed Hitler*, *The Wine of the Generals*, *The Coventry Code*) involving Nazis and espionage.

Peter Enfantino • Jeff Vorzimmer

Vol. 9 No. 5 Oct 1961

First photo cover (would continue through 1965). Last appearance of Charles Beckman, Jr. who appeared in the first issue and eight times subsequently.

"Pure Vengeance" by Michael Zuroy (4000 words)★★★

George Raber moves into a quiet neighborhood, builds a gallows in his front room, and keeps the blinds open for all to see. What's George's game? Suicide in public display? Or is there something more sinister involved?

"Dear Sir" by Talmage Powell (3000 words)★★

Trudy Singleton is arrested for the murder of her husband but she finds a sympathetic ear in attorney Phil Carrington. After her acquittal, Trudy grows closer to Phil, despite his advanced age and marriage. A predictable story told through a series of letters sent from Trudy to Phil. Though the entire situation is laughable, particularly ridiculous is the timeline (each letter is dated), wherein Trudy is arrested, put on trial, acquitted, and falls in and out of love with Phil all in a space of under two months.

"The Death of El Indio" by Ed Lacy (10,000 words)★★★

P.I. Sam Eggers is called down to Mexico City and hired by the very wealthy Mrs. Grace Lupe-Varon, who is convinced Mexico's most popular matador, El Indio, murdered her husband. Mr. Lupe-Varon, a reporter, had been digging into El Indio's business practices and silenced before he could blow the whistle. Sam Eggers is an involving character and his observations of those around him and his devil-may-care attitude keep the reader turning pages.

"The Deadly Affair" by Charles Carpentier (1500 words)★

Very predictable affair about a mob goon who's extorting money from a married woman to pay his debt to his boss. Guess who the woman is married to.

"Chain Reaction" by Charles Boeckman (1500 words)★↓

A black cat sets off a chain reaction of bad events.

"Sea Widow" by William P. Brothers (4000 words)★★

George Matthews has a perfect life… well, almost. He's got a gorgeous wife, a cozy position at the office, two great kids, and a fabulous boat any mariner would swoon over. But then George's wandering eye gets the best of him and he enters into an illicit affair with young and precocious Lola, who soon shows her hand and demands big bucks for her silence. George knows there's only one way out of this trap.

"The Novelty Shop" by Donald Tothe (1500 words)★★✔
Jake has been selling novelty items to Morton for years. He's also been sleeping with the man's wife. Now Morton has a new skull in the window of his novelty shop. Black comedy with a reveal worthy of Robert Bloch.

"Break Down" by Robert Edmond Alter (1500 words)★★✔
Two men, working alone on an island in the South Pacific, go stir crazy. Author Alter builds the suspense perfectly, then lands the climax with a smile.

"Cop in a Frame" by Dick Ellis (7500 words)★★
Detective David Weldon is a good cop, so why is he accused of police brutality? The man making the accusation was arrested for attempted rape on Weldon's girlfriend, so everyone assumes David took advantage of his badge to get in a little revenge but that's not the case. Weldon never touched the guy. After he's suspended, Weldon digs deeper and discovers his partner, Pete Branden, might not be as lily-white as he imagined. Padded and predictable.

"A Woman's Wiles" by Ray T. Davis (1000 words)★★
A death row inmate becomes pregnant while in prison. Her lawyer argues successfully that an unborn child cannot be punished for the sins of its mother. But who is the father?

"The Nude Above the Bar" by Marvin Larson (4500 words)★★★
Gil just wants to have a beer and stare at the painting of the naked woman above Percy's bar, but mobster Temper Riley takes an immediate dislike to Gil. Temper does all he can to ruin Gil's life (and even sets up a murder attempt on the man) but Gil just won't be persuaded: "there's something about a naked woman, Percy!" Light and amusing, with a genuinely surprising twist.

"An Aspect of Death" by James L. Liverman (1000 words)★
Pointless short-short about a man who murders his wife's lover.

"Night Out" by Joe Gores (1000 words)★★✔
A gorgeous barfly has a unique way of saying "no" to the men hitting on her.

"The Sure Things" by Bernard Epps (1000 words)★
Broke and smelling "a sure thing," a gambler holds up his bookie.

Peter Enfantino • Jeff Vorzimmer

Vol. 9 No. 6 Dec 1961

Michael Zuroy's fourth story for Manhunt for the year of 1961 appears in this issue. Two of them would be chosen for the Seventh Annual Best Detective Stories anthology. All but two original stories are by first-time contributors.

"Killer Dog" by M. R. James (2500 words)★★↲

After Virgil buys his new dog, the previous owner lets Virgil in on a secret: feed the dog an animal's heart before each fight and nothing will stop the canine. Virgil uses chicken and pig hearts and the dog goes undefeated but, when Virgil's wife announces she's leaving with another man, he broadens the menu.

"Blackmail" by Eugene Gaffney (3500 words)★★↲

When gorgeous Ellen McKinley is the target of a blackmailer, she turns to her favorite "Uncle" Riegel for help. Riegel inadvertently ends up in bed with the young girl and then takes care of her blackmailing problem with the aid of a metal pipe. "Blackmail" has a sleazy, uncomfortable edge and climaxes on a decidedly downbeat note.

"The Queer Deal" by Jack Ritchie (3500 words)★★★

Three men kidnap syndicate man, Pete Fargo, and ransom him for two hundred thousand. The payday comes, they let Fargo go, but while counting the dough they realize they got conned—the dough is counterfeit. Entertaining thriller featuring more than one big con.

"The Huntress" by Gordon T. Allred (7500 words)★★★

Mountain guide Cam Cowley is hired by Freddy and Victoria Ravell to track a mountain lion for sport. The long outing brings out the worst in both men and Victoria seems to know how best to throw logs on that fire. "The Huntress" is a gripping adventure tale that seems to be going down a certain (clichéd) path, but actually strays onto a darker course, much to the delight of this reader.

"Sweets to the Sweet" by J. Simmons Scheb (1000 words)★★

Ludicrous short about a man who poisons his wife with insecticide, knowing she won't grant him a divorce.

"Brother's Keeper" by Brian Lowe (3000 words)★↲

Reporter Carl Lindsay witnesses a mob hit and is sequestered in a local jail for protection until his day to testify in court. His brother, Dan, arrives and acts as bodyguard. But does he have another objective?

"The Prey" by Daniel De Paola (3500 words)★★★↲

Stopping in a small Arizona town while drifting, Forster witnesses a mob murder and tries to do the right thing. A strange, simmering drama that seems to be leading to an explosion but keeps its top from blowing, "The Prey" reminded me of David Morrell's *First Blood* in several ways. The climax almost hints at the same kind of violent outburst but author De Paola wisely leaves that to the imagination.

"The Kangaroo Court" by Frank Ward (22,500 words)★★★

After a long absence, George Bryan returns to his hometown of Martinvale to find a welcoming party of his three best friends, Tom Buck, Johnny Lederer, and Fred Sedgely. George had returned to open up a new business and settle down with his new wife (who would arrive on a train the next night) but his three friends convince him that a hunting party is just the ticket.

The four men drive to a distant cabin on a lake and then Tom, Johnny, and Fred tell George what the trip is really all about. Lederer's daughter has committed suicide after leaving a note that George had gotten her pregnant and then dumped her unceremoniously; this is all news to George. He claims the child was not his and that he and the girl had never had cross words. Tom, Johnny, and Fred hold a mock trial and declare George guilty. They plan to arm him with one gun and one bullet and let him free before they hunt him down.

Meanwhile, Mrs. George Bryan arrives and finds her husband missing; she heads to the local police precinct where she finds a sympathetic ear in veteran cop, Arthur Dulane, who immediately suspects that there's something untoward happening. Dulane reopens the suicide case and discovers that the girl actually didn't take her own life. She was murdered.

A thoroughly enjoyable thriller (albeit with a fairly predictable reveal) that actually seems like two novels combined into one. The action section, with the four men in the cabin, is exciting, but I found author Ward's strength to be in the building of Dulane's character. This is a character I wanted to read more about.

The Best Stories of 1961

"How Much to Kill?" by Michael Zuroy (February)
"The Knife" by Glenn Canary (April)
"Cheap Kicks" by William Brothers (June)
"The Big Haul" by Robert Page Jones (August)
"Finger-Man" by John Connolly (August)
"The Death of El Indio" by Ed Lacy (October)
"The Nude Above the Bar" by Marvin Larson (October)
"The Prey" by Daniel De Paola (December)
"The Huntress" by Gordon T. Allred (December)
"The Kangaroo Court" by Frank Ward (December)

Peter Enfantino • Jeff Vorzimmer

Vol. 10 No. 1 Feb 1962

First and only appearance of the writing team of Robert Weaver & Samuel Rubinstein who write under the pseudonym Lancaster Salem. All but two original stories are by first-time contributors.

"The Bloodless Bayonet" by Thomas Milstead (3500 words)★
Tedious tale of a self-loathing drill instructor who's never seen combat and suspects that everyone around him is mocking him.

"Found and Lost" by T. E. Brooks (4000 words)★
Herregat has a grudge against Ratch, a small-time "burlesque manager" (read that as pimp), and he's orchestrated a convoluted plan involving a postal heist guaranteed to land Ratch in the slammer. An unpleasant story that excels only in its increasingly ridiculous revelations.

"Dog Eat Dog" by Georges Carousso (2500 words)★★
Snow-bound in the wilds of Canada, a murderer depends on a pack of unfriendly dogs to get him back to civilization through a blizzard.

"Little Napoleon" by Leo Ellis (2000 words)★★
Black comedy about power struggles between the main attractions at a carnival freak show.

"S. O. P. Murder" by Rick Rubin (4500 words)★✔
Private Mosconi discovers that Corporal Dixon has it out for him. Then when Mosconi witnesses Dixon selling army supplies in a back alley, the grudge becomes something more dangerous. There's not much plot here and the events seem to be analyzed time and again, much to the detriment of the pace.

"The Devereaux Monster" by Jack Ritchie (5000 words)★★★
The Devereauxs have lived on the moors for centuries and their name is associated with the gorilla-like monster that roams through the countryside. But is the creature some throwback to prehistory or simply a legend designed to bolster the Devereaux name? A delightful farce, obviously an homage to "The Hound of the Baskervilles," that keeps the reader guessing until the final paragraphs. Leave it to veteran Jack Ritchie to salvage an otherwise below-average issue of *Manhunt*.

"Bail Out!" by Lancaster Salem (22,000 words)★
When two "fly boys" are tasked, by their General, with driving down to Mexico to pick up a load of booze for a base party, they naturally ask the kindly Lt. Jennings to drive them. But the party is a bust when the booze they bought turns out to be rotgut and several of the attendees come down with Montezuma's Revenge. The Colonel is livid but the boys point their fingers at Jennings and it seems he'll

be the target of much rage. Not to worry though, since the Colonel soon ends up dead and Jennings suspects the two pesky fly boys are to blame. A snail's pace, endless padding, and eye-rolling one-liners make "Bail Out" one long, empty read.

"Hot Furs" by David Kasanof (2000 words)★★
 Ex-con Ryan, just out of the stir, decides to take on a big job: hauling stolen furs in a tanker truck. The boss wants to see how Ryan does under the stress so he sends one of his henchmen along for the ride, which doesn't exactly calm the driver's nerves.

Vol. 10 No. 2 Apr 1962

Last appearance of Hal Ellson ("Set-up"), who contributed 23 stories to the magazine and the last appearance of the "It's the Law" column, which, besides "Manhunt's Gun Rack" is the last feature to appear in the magazine.

"Obsession" by Robert Page Jones (6000 words)★★
A concentration camp prisoner, being transported by train, keeps his hopes alive by fantasizing his escape to the woman he loves.

"Half Past Eternity" by Robert Leon (4500 words)★★★
Shamed and disgraced by medical errors, and anticipating the loss of his job, Dr. Geet decides life is not worth living. Taking out a quickie insurance policy, he boards a plane with a bomb in his medical bag. Unfortunately for Dr. Geet, his practice isn't the only thing he fumbles.

"Gun Lover" by Charles Carpentier (2500 words)★⌐
A woman and her young daughter are kidnapped by a gun-toting murderer and forced to drive to Mexico.

"Academic Freedom" by Glenn Canary (2500 words)★★⌐
Dean Warner is being blackmailed by Professor Martin, who has been tailing the Dean and knows the man has been stepping out with teenage student, Elaine Darma. Now Martin wants to be head of the English Department and five grand to keep his mouth shut. The Dean has other ideas.

"The Assassin" by Peter Marks (4500 words)★★★★
After embezzling twenty-five grand from his bank, William Hawkins flees to a South American country, where he believes he can hide out safely. Unfortunately, for Hawkins, a shadow faction within the government discovers who is in their midst and blackmail the man into taking part in a phony assassination of the "Generalissimo." The day of the event arrives and, too late, Hawkins discovers he's been set up; there's a second gunman who will perform the killing… for real.
Though there's not much action to "The Assassin," Peter Marks does a fine job building tension and then delivers a memorably downbeat climax. It's hard, of course, not to draw parallels between the events depicted in "The Assassin" and JFK's murder the following year. Peter Marks was the pseudonym of children's book writer, Robert Kimmel Smith.

"Set-Up" by Hal Ellson (3000 words)★
After a fumbled assassination attempt, Tony has to hide from the mobsters who are out to get him.

"Last Job" by Raymond Dyer (4000 words)★★↓
Big Frank keeps promising Rita that the next job is "the last job," but she's getting impatient now that she and Frank have had a baby and Frank's partner, Moss, keeps giving her the eye. Now, the latest job has gone belly-up, Big Frank is dead, and she's stuck in a cabin deep in the woods with an obviously-very-happy Moss. An average crime story elevated by an effective twist ending.

"The Righteous" by Talmage Powell (2500 words)★★★
An old man meets a very young girl in the park and a "friendship" begins. Each day, they meet and talk innocently enough but the man's neighbors soon begin to murmur and gossip. When the little girl goes missing, the crowd becomes rabid. "The Righteous" is a gripping read in the tradition of an EC *Shock Suspen-Stories* comic book where the innocent are punished and the guilty walk away free.

"Double Payment" by Max F. Harris (1500 words)★
Barry's got 'til four to get get Hoak his five grand or Hoak is going to ventilate him. Barry keeps pleading with the man, telling him his dad will come through for him, but the clock keeps ticking.

"The Kidnappers" by Edward Charles Bastien (4000 words)★★★
Two young hoods attempt to roll an old man but he's ready for them. Gun drawn, the old codger, who introduces himself as Humphrey Nortwick, offers Mike and Jack a chance to make an easy ten grand. Humphrey explains he's a very rich man but his money is wrapped up in stocks, so he wants the boys to kidnap him and then he'll send a ransom note to his wife. Once Humphrey gets the dough, he'll give the boys their cut and then head to South America to grow old without his shrewish wife. The kidnapping goes as planned but things take a turn for the weird when Humphrey disappears and the police show up. "The Kidnappers" is an intricately designed delight with several smile-inducing twists in its climax.

"Poor Widow" by Madeline M. Fraser (4500 words)★★
It's only after Henry decides he wants to buy a farm that Nell decides to kill her husband. She's even got it all figured out. That tricky coffee pot that boils over and kills the flame but leaves the gas on. Now she just needs to establish an alibi.

"The Fix" by Max Van Derveer (4000 words)★
When college basketball star, Candy Kane, refuses to throw a game, his life becomes a series of near-misses and near-fatalities. A sluggish read; the theme of fixed basketball was handled much better in Fletcher Flora's novel, *The Hot Shot* (Avon, 1956). This was Max Van Derveer's one and only short story written for *Manhunt* but the author would go on to become a staple of the mystery digests in the 1960s and 1970s, including a stint as ghost writer for Brett Halliday in *Mike Shayne's Mystery Magazine*.

Vol. 10 No. 3 Jun 1962
Last appearance of Lawrence Block, who contributed
four stories to the magazine.

"Motive to Kill" by James Ullman (1500 words)★
Even with a "thrill killer" terrorizing the town, Ruth finds herself in a singles bar, looking for Mister Right. When he shows up and asks her to go home with him, she agrees. Utterly predictable. Ullman was the author of *The Neon Haystack* (1965), *Good Night, Irene* (1967), and *The Venus Trap* (1968), all published by Pocket.

"Sucker Bait" by Norm Kent (4500 words)★★⅟
Joe Jarrett attempts to rob Mr. Lloyd Bierdham in an alley but the portly gentleman gets the best of Joe. Amazingly, instead of calling the cops Lloyd invites Joe to dinner and a friendship develops. After both of the men lose their jobs, Bierdham suggests a vacation at a remote lodge where they can recharge their batteries. The boys become involved in a con involving a gorgeous woman who beds and then robs her targets. Lloyd and Joe spin the con around and manage to pocket some serious coin. An amusing, light-hearted comedy-crime tale that doesn't try to be anything more than it is.

"Fly by Night" by Dick Moore (4000 words)★★
Two army buddies pool their resources and buy an old cargo plane to use in a shipping business. Times are tough, money gets tight, and the boys end up taking on some shady work. During one of these runs, they are double-crossed and commit murder. But the real trouble occurs on the trip home when the plane catches on fire. "Fly by Night" is all over the place; Dick Moore seemingly could not decide whether to write a crime drama or an adventure thriller. Neither pans out in the long run.

"The Greatest" by Hollis Gale (1500 words)★
Honeyboy is the greatest boxer there is, but during his title bout he can't remember what happened to his girl, Verna. Flashes come back to him during the fight and the cop waiting for him after Round Ten brings back events vividly.

"According to Plan" by Seymour Richin (4500 words)★★
Exotic dancer Mona sees her payday in retired boxer Charlie Forbes. His new line of work is security for a vault full of payroll, so Mona uses her charm to worm her way into Charlie's heart and, very soon, into that vault.

"Stay of Execution" by Al Martinez (3000 words)★
Paul is suddenly released from his stay on Death Row in San Quentin; he's a free man. But why was he released? And why does he keep having flashes back to the night he allegedly murdered a prostitute? Convoluted and predictable, "Stay of

Execution" is awash with clichés and bad writing.

"Family Argument" by Neal Curtis (1500 words)★
A hitchhiker is happy to be picked up by an older couple until he realizes the woman in the front passenger seat is dead. A ludicrous short-short, padded with descriptions designed to make the reader believe the woman is alive but, on second glance, are cheats.

"The Fallen Cop" by Robert Anthony (5500 words)★✔
Night club singer Leona Brett knows quite a lot about the local mobsters. Now the D.A. has Leona under protective custody before she testifies at a trial. Cop Ralph Adams is tasked to protect Leona before her big day in court but he finds himself, slowly but surely, falling in love with the beautiful torch singer.

"Cry Wolf!" by C. B. Gilford (4000 words)★★✔
Stanley Bingham's life is in turmoil. He's really beginning to hate his brother-in-law, who's come to stay with him and Stanley's wife, but more importantly, he suspects he's become a werewolf. Stanley decides to use one problem to solve the other. Odd and slow-paced, "Cry Wolf!" has an amusing twist ending.

"Frozen Stiff" by Lawrence Block (2000 words)★★★
A butcher finds he has cancer and, in order to leave his wife a healthy insurance payoff, plans suicide via meat locker. When his wife visits the shop with a tough guy, he learns she's planned his murder. That changes everything.

"Price of Life" by Michael Zuroy (4000 words)★★★
Successful businessman Nat Jacobs has been threatened by the mob and his lawyer recommends he get himself a bodyguard. So Nat goes to a "professional agency" and he's assigned a goon named Angelo, who proceeds to save Nat's life on several occasions. Problem is, Angelo loves sardines and onions and demands the company of a very loud hi-fi stereo. Over time, Nat begins to wish for death. A very funny little black comedy.

"The Crime Broker" by Steve Frazee (9500 words)★★
A group of big businessmen decide they're going to murder the leaders of a narcotics ring, but a debate grows about the moral ramifications of such acts. The writing, unfortunately, is as cold and sterile as the characters and nothing seems to happen. That's quite a surprise since Frazee is usually a master of plotting and characterization.

Vol. 10 No. 4 Aug 1962

First and only appearance of William W. Stuart, who was primarily a science fiction writer.

"Lifeline" by John Conner (1000 words)★
A barely coherent conversation between a man and his wife after a rough day at the office. There is, literally, no plot (nor idea, for that matter) running through "Lifeline."

"Heroes are Made" by Ben Mahnke (3000 words)★★★
Roy Harrison is the best college basketball player in America but his skill still doesn't land him the State Championship. He can't block a last-second shot by rival (and long-time buddy) Johnny Farris and Western State takes home another trophy. Later, Roy accepts his payment from Johnny's dad just like he's been doing for the last two years. Despite the absence of anything resembling serious crime (unless point shaving qualifies), "Heroes are Made" is an enthralling character study that might have been even better given a little more room.

"Blackmail, Inc." by Michael Dedina (7500 words)★
After spending four years in a Parisian asylum, Frank Lorris barely has a chance to breathe in the air before he finds a dead woman in his apartment. Knowing the police will throw Frank back in the asylum and lose the keys, he sets out to prove he's innocent of the crime. What follows is a crazed kaleidoscope of murder, prostitution, forced abortion, mistaken identity, and the beneficiaries of a contested will. Nothing makes sense but the climactic twist almost makes the preceding nonsense worth reading. The title, by the way, does not come into play until the final paragraph!

"Protect Us!" by Don Tothe (1000 words)★
One thousand word stories are nothing more than fragments and "Protect Us!" (about a mean boozer who constantly threatens to kill his wife and son) is no exception. We all know how this is going to end and Don Tothe does little to surprise us.

"A Man Called" by George Burke (2000 words)★½
Living a life filled with boredom, a waitress begins enjoying the obscene phone calls she receives every night. George Burke seems to want to say something profound about the loneliness of the average woman but what he churns out is a story with an obviously misogynistic bent.

"Summer Heat" by Constance Pike (1000 words)★
A little boy recounts his summer day with his friend. There's a murder involved but the vignette itself is not involving. In fact, not one of the three short-shorts this issue is readable, begging the question, "Why did the editors accept

stories this brief?"

"Red for Murder" by Rod Barker (8000 words)★★

A newspaper writer conducts an interview with author Oliver Crawford and then wakes the next morning to the shocking news that the scribe was murdered, shortly after their session, during a bungled robbery. Smelling a rat, the writer does some investigating and connects Crawford's death with a Communist organization called SAFE. The most disturbing fact in our hero's notebook is that Crawford's daughter is a key figure in SAFE.

What begins as an interesting whodunit devolves quickly into a ridiculous commie espionage "thriller" in which our main protagonist is conked over the head several times, (each time we're graced with a clichéd description of the injury such as *All at once everything around me exploded and I pitched into a black, bottomless well*), involved in a fatal car crash, and shot.

"A License to Kill" by Charles Carpentier (4000 words)★★

Frank Doria asks the chief if he can be involved in catching the guy who murdered his next-door neighbor. Doria is given the thumbs-up and he finds himself partnering up with by-the-book Lt. Keats. We discover about halfway through "A License to Kill" that Frank is the murderer. He was having an affair with the deceased's wife and she conned him into offing the guy. Author Carpentier does a good job unfurling the reveal but his final twist is ludicrous and a cheat.

"Friend in Deed" by Shelby Harrison (4000 words)★★★

Golf pro Frank Nieman decides he hasn't got what it takes to be number one so he quits the circuit and takes his war pal, Bill Mallory, up on an offer to work at the course Bill owns. Complications ensue when Frank meets Bill's wife, Shari, and the two hit it off immediately. The only thing standing in their way is Bill. "Friend in Deed" seems like it's heading down the *Double Indemnity* road but veers off into a (welcomed) different territory altogether.

"The Woman Hater" by Leo Ellis (3000 words)★★✦

Willie Keener might hate women but when a nasty fellow at the flat begins harassing poor Miss McCready, down the hall, Willie finds it in his heart to defend her.

"Going Straight" by Rick Rubin (3000 words)★★★

A two-time loser swears he'll go straight but then his buddy comes up with a bank heist that just can't miss. The main character, Howard, is a poor schmuck you can't help but root for even while you know this guy's no good.

"False Bait" by Don Sollars (3000 words)★

A tedious tale of adultery and a cat-and-mouse game between neighboring farmers, ends on an indecipherable note.

Peter Enfantino • Jeff Vorzimmer

"The Final Solution" by William W. Stuart (3000 words) ★ ⌐

Mr. and Mrs. Tupple visit a marriage counselor when they come to the conclusion they can't stand each other. While Mr. Tupple is being interviewed, his counselor, Mr. Hartwell, lets it slip that his firm can arrange "accidents" on their client's behalf for a "donation."

Vol. 10 No. 5 Oct 1962
Manhunt's circulation has fallen to 178,145.

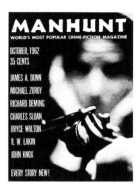

"A Reasonable Doubt" by James A. Dunn (7500 words)★↲
Young Debbie is raped and her father, a hard-nose lawyer wants to know who's responsible. When he finds out, he grabs his gun and heads out for some old west retribution. Unfortunately for pop, he only has half the story. A slow, way too slow, simmer that culminates in a truly ludicrous reveal, seemingly tacked on to elicit shock after such a calm build-up. None of it works.

"Jump Chicken!" by R. W. Lakin (2000 words)★★↲
Freddy wakes to find his troubled sister, Mildred, has climbed out onto her window ledge and is threatening to jump. Freddy ponders whether it might be a good thing to bring her back in or not.

"Welcome Mother" by Bryce Walton (3500 words)★★★
Norman has convinced his mother he's in New York living the life of a beatnik, partying and making art. Mom, thinking that's so cool, keeps sending her son those checks every month to keep him going, never knowing those parties she hears over the phone are actually recordings. Now, mom calls to let Norman know she's in the city and wants to meet all his friends and, especially, Norman's girlfriend, Betty. Norman scrambles to make his apartment just right and then goes out looking for a Betty. What starts out almost as an unmade Jerry Lewis film ends very, very darkly.

"Eye-Witness" by Charles Sloan (10,500 words)★★★★
Tough cop Dave Fleers has only one thing in the world he cares about and that's his gorgeous wife, Myra. Dave runs afoul of a local mob, run by brothers Chris and John Cartello, with Chris threatening to get Dave "where it hurts most." Chris schemes to assault Myra and have a syndicate porn photographer take pictures to spread them around town, but something goes wrong and Chris ends up dead, shot six times. Myra is arrested for the murder but Dave is convinced that John Cartello, who's always wanted to be head of the syndicate, murdered his own brother.

Myra's trial is swift and she's found guilty and sentenced to the gas chamber. Only one person can save Myra now: the photographer, who's hiding from the surviving Cartello. With only hours to spare, Dave finds the shutterbug but the footage he watches sheds new light on the murder. To call "Eye-Witness" dark would be an understatement; this is pitch black. Dave is a misogynistic brute who has no problem beating confessions out of suspects or roughing up prostitutes when they don't give him the right answers. The events in the final paragraphs, Dave watching in disbelief as his wife has unforced sex with a mobster, and then

Dave turning to the photographer and shooting him in cold blood, are jarring even after the brutality detailed in the previous pages.

"Inside Story" by Edward Wellen (1000 words)★

Pete Richards, editor of the *Chronicle*, sends Harry Stevens into an asylum, disguised as an inmate, for an inside story. Turns out Pete only wants to steal away Harry's wife and, when the asylum calls to check on Harry's story, he disavows any knowledge. A bit too complicated a plot for such a short story.

"For the Sake of Love" by Hilda Cushing (1000 words)★

Otto doesn't like his wife's new nose job so he stabs her to death.

"Good at Heart" by John Knox (5000 words)★★

Bittner is a jewel thief who goes after Mrs. Duquesne's ice but is caught redhanded in the act. Instead of calling the cops, the rich widow makes Bittner her new pet project.

"The Old Guard" by Michael Zuroy (4000 words)★★

Kin Fo Shoo has outlived his usefulness as the leader of the Chinatown tong, at least according to three of his henchmen. They hire an assassin to murder Kin but that doesn't go as planned. Shoo may be sharper than his men think.

"Reward" by Richard Deming (11,000 words)★★✦

Actress Cherry Graves has her valuable jewelry stolen from her at the hotel she lives in, and offers a reward of 25 grand. Very soon after, Connie Stewart shows up at the office of P.I. Matt Gannon and confesses she thinks her boyfriend is the thief. She wants to hire Gannon to recover the jewelry so she can cash in on the reward. But Matt's case gets more complicated as he digs deeper. By 1962, the book racks were literally flooded with P.I. thrillers so it can't be said that Matt Gannon is unique, but he is in that class with Johnny Liddell known as "likable." The "gimmick" Deming uses with Gannon is a forelock on the P.I.'s head that constantly falls over his eyes and makes women swoon. Gannon will return in the following issue.

Vol. 10 No. 6 Dec 1962

The Last Appearance of Richard Deming, who contributed 37 stories to the magazine, with "The Red Herring," which would be chosen for inclusion in The Eighteenth Annual Best Detective Stories of the Year. All but two stories are by first-time contributors.

"Hot Shot" by Robert Goodney (4500 words)★★★
Someone is killing the junkies of Brooklyn with "hot shots," heroin laced with strychnine, and the cops don't seem to be bothered. Three junkies decide they need to find the man responsible before one of them gets a hot shot.

"Spot of Color" by Edith Fitzgerald Golden (3000 words)★★
Maggie lives out in the middle of nowhere, on a sheep farm with her husband, Ernest. Every day, she cooks, cleans, and mends Ernest's clothes and asks for nothing. The lack of color in and around her house depresses her. One day, when Ernest hitches up the wagon and gets ready to go into town for supplies, Maggie asks him to bring her some cocoa and then spends the next 24 hours, until Ernest gets back from town, dreaming about that cocoa. When her husband admits he forgot to get it and that they "don't need it anyway," Maggie gets down the shotgun and adds a little color to the landscape. For most of its running time, "Spot of Color" is an interesting enough portrait of a crumbling soul until author Golden remembers that she's writing for *Manhunt* magazine and adds that last-second burst of violence to the mix.

""H' Run" by Alex Pong (10,000 words)★★★
Carl has two loves in his life: his fishing boat, the Pelican, and his lady love, Anna. When Anna leaves Carl and takes up with a no-gooder named Mansfield, Carl turns his attention back to the Pelican and the heroin runs he makes to Mexico for his boss, Hale Riverman. Anna returns to Carl and accompanies him on his latest run as his "good luck charm." When the Pelican pulls into Mexico, Carl knows there's something up when Riverman's best hired thug, Mac, comes on board, accompanied by a clearly hang-dog Mansfield.
Mac explains to Carl that Mansfield has been blackmailing Riverman and the boss wants him taken out and dumped at sea. Forty miles out, when Carl drops his anchor, Anna comes from below deck with a shotgun. It's then that Carl knows his "goddess" is far from his "good luck charm." An exciting, unpredictable thriller with strong characters, marred only by a maudlin epilogue, transforming Anna from noir bitch into misunderstood pawn.

"Party Pooper" by Dundee McDole (2000 words)★★✓
Elvera pesters her husband into building her a bomb shelter. After two weeks of steady and grueling work, Jack finishes the shelter only to receive a brusque, "it looks like a tomb" from Elvera. Agreeing, he decides to make it hers.

"The Deceiver" by Lucy Spears Griffin (5000 words)★

Tedious and overlong story of a woman who puts her violent past (and equally violent husband) behind her and starts her life over when she marries a rich entrepreneur. Then, one day while out driving, she pulls into a gas station and stumbles upon her ex. Knowing things could get complicated, she plots to kill him.

"Overnight Guest" by Frederick Chamberlain (3000 words)★★✔

Fresh out of prison and looking for easy prey, Ray thumbs a ride with a farmer and then smiles to himself as the man invites him to stay the night at his place. Turns out the farmer has been waiting for an easy mark himself.

"Clear Conscience" by Lawrence Harvey (1000 words)★✔

A thief has second thoughts about robbing a safe and breaks back into a building to return the dough. The twist is an interesting one but, as with most of these 1000-word vignettes, as soon as the interest is sparked, the ride is over.

"The Red Herring" by Richard Deming (10,500 words)★★

In his sophomore case, Matt Gannon (he of the "falling forelock") is hired by Holt and Bancroft, the partners in a mechanical firm who have been threatened by a former business associate named Gerald Greene. The man thinks Holt and Bancroft cheated him out of a fortune. Gannon doesn't give the case much credence until Bancroft's wife is killed by a mail bomb. Suddenly everything looks serious, but Gannon has doubts as to the actual identity of the bomb-builder when Greene turns up dead at a beach house owned by the firm. It all leads to a contrived climax where all the characters meet at the Holt and Bancroft office, while Gannon holds court and runs down the motives and guilty parties.

"A Sweet Deal" by Jack Lemmon (4500 words)★★

Eddie's just a poor dope who buys a pretty girl a drink and then can't believe his luck when she asks him back to her place. Despite a 9–5 job and a wife and kid, Eddie makes the best of his nights with Doris until the other shoe drops and Eddie discovers he's in a whole lot of trouble. Mildly amusing con game tale.

"Mother Love" by Marion Duckworth (1000 words)★★★

Edna wants her brand new baby to remain just as beautiful as the day she was born and her husband won't be back from the war for a year. So she puts the baby in her freezer. A very sick little bit of nastiness but "Mother Love" manages to do something very few of the short-shorts can do: make the reader give it a second thought.

The Best Stories of 1962

"The Devereaux Monster" by Jack Ritchie (February)
"The Assassin" by Peter Marks (April)
"The Righteous" by Talmage Powell (April)
"Price of Life" by Michael Zuroy (June)
"Friend in Deed" by Shelby Harrison (August)
"Heroes are Made" by Ben Mahnke (August)
"Eye-Witness" by Charles Sloan (October)
"Welcome, Mother" by Bryce Walton (October)
"Hot Shot" by Robert Goodney (December)
"The 'H' Run" by Alex Pong (December)

Vol. 11 No. 1 Feb 1963
The last issue to have spot color illustrations. All but one original story are by first-time contributors.

"Avenging Angel" by Mark Del Franco (2500 words)★★

After losing quite a bit of weight, Eve Sadreski heads back to her hometown of Meriton to exact revenge on those who had tortured her.

"Prison Break" by Duane Clark (4000 words)★★★

A daring escape from Alcatraz ends in a hail of bullets. Though a simple idea, "Prison Break" manages to grip you from the first sentence right up to its violent climax.

"Ripper Moon" by Jack Ritchie (5000 words)★★

A psychiatrist, thinking about murdering his wife for her money, uses the happy coincidence that a patient of his thinks he's Jack the Ripper, to his advantage.

"The Sea-Gull" by J. Heidloff (1500 words)★★

When a quarter-million in heroin goes missing, the men in charge come looking for Hegan.

"Shake-Down" by Dean Ball (3500 words)★★✓

Things get violent when club owner Jay refuses to pay the muscle strongarming him. Well-done little violent thriller.

"The Absent Professor" by Robert Weaver (26,000 words)★★

Professor Wilson, who is just about to put his university on the map with a stunning formula that will ensure a doubling of livestock population, goes missing. Initially, the President of the campus thinks Wilson has been kidnapped, or headed for Russia and a big payday, but he tasks one of his underlings, Jack Ober, with finding Wilson.

Ober, once a P.I. (or something tantamount to a private dick, he claims) and now just an office guy, does his best to track down the absent professor but his leads are slim. Then a body is found in a car on campus. It's not Wilson, but rather a man he had a heated argument with on more than one occasion. Did the man know something about Wilson that necessitated his murder? And are the Russians really involved?

At 26,000 words, "The Absent Professor" is one of the longest tales ever to appear in *Manhunt* and also one of the most padded. Jack Ober is a likable enough character but he's just not given enough to do. The events seem to go on for pages at a time and lead nowhere. The final reveal (disclosed during a laborious three-page expository) is lazy and feels like a cheat to those who invested in the time to read a sixty-six page crime story.

"Exile" by Martin Kelly (3500 words)★★★

The very involving story of Luis Miguel Perez, a former dictator now living in exile on the French Riviera. Perez lives in seclusion, with the constant fear of assassination, but has a penchant for gambling and pretty young girls. The latter becomes his downfall. Happily, author Kelly does not go down the well-traveled road the climax seems heading onto and, rather, ends the tale in a surprising fashion. Since the writing is so strong, I find it odd that, like most of the authors in this issue (and the era, frankly), Kelly never placed any other stories in the crime digests.

Vol. 11 No. 2 Apr 1963
The last appearance of Talmadge Powell with "Precious Pigeon."

"Precious Pigeon" by Talmadge Powell (1500 words)★★★
Constantine and Cary stand to make a fortune once they murder Cary's wife but, at the last moment, Cary decides he actually loves the woman and takes evasive measures.

"Dear Edie" by Pat Macmillan (1500 words)★
A man writes to the "Dear Edie" newspaper column, complaining about his treatment at the hands of his wife. The story is told in letter form between the reader and the columnist. The final letter tells Edie he's decided to kill his wife and the twist, of course, is that Edie *is* his wife. Extremely silly short-short even climaxes with Edie typing her response as her husband comes into the office to kill her.

"The Price of Lust" by Joe Gores (10,500 words)★★✓
P.I. Bartholomew Drew is witness to the murder of a dirty pictures photographer on the steps of a San Francisco Turkish bath. The next day, an old friend named Edie comes to call on Bart at his office; she's being blackmailed by someone who's gotten hold of some pictures of Edie and a man in a motel room in compromising positions. Are the two incidents connected? It's up to Bart Drew to find out.

Though the plot isn't necessarily anything new, Gores keeps the pace moving rapidly and the reader smiling with his constant analogies and descriptive phrases:

> *Violent death, like a night with a virgin, leaves too many regrets... She squeezed her eyes shut as if scanning the lids for guidance... She concentrated over my card like a chimp with an Einstein equation...*

"Conned" by Bernard Epps (1000 words)★
A bartender tells one of his stories, this one about a con artist named Jerry "the Pup," a guy who tried to pass bad twenties, but got shut down instead.

"Kiloman" by Don Lowry (6500 words)★★★✓
The rise and fall of hophead Marty Bello, a small-time pusher who works his way up through the ranks of a major drug organization and then watches it all fall apart after a few minor mistakes. "Kiloman" is a variant on the *Scarface* story (with a prescient view of what Brian DePalma would do with the fable two decades later) but at a much smaller level. Bello is a fascinating character and Lowry a smart enough writer to avoid all the clichés inherent in a plot like this.

"Kiloman" was the first of 14 stories by Don Lowry to appear in *Manhunt*;

Lowry seems to have made this magazine his only market as I can find no reference to his work elsewhere.

"A Patient Man" by Dave Hill (1500 words)★★✦
When Marty Valentine gets out of the stir after doing eleven years for embezzlement, the cops are waiting for him, pressuring him to hand over the million he took. But Marty is a very patient man and he's playing his cards close to the vest.

"Gambler's Cross" by Robert McKay (4500 words)★★★
Jack's a small time bookie when he meets Kathy and falls completely in love. She wants no part of life with a bookie so Jack immediately changes vocations and Kathy agrees to marry him. But then Jack gets a visit from his future father-in-law who's up to his ears in debt to a local bookie and asks Jack for his help. No problem, thinks Jack, and he rips off his former boss.

"For the Defense" by Terry McCormick (1000 words)★
Short-short about a lawyer who will do anything to get his client out of jail.

"The Outfit" by Richard Stark (17,500 words)★★★★
Parker, a thief by trade, has run afoul of a syndicate known as the Outfit, and now they're sending assassins out to end his career. Parker has tried to make peace with the Outfit in the past but decides enough is enough and declares war. He writes to all the thief/buddies he knows and asks them to hit any Outfit-owned businesses they can, hoping the dent in business will teach the organization a lesson. At the same time, he heads for Buffalo to take out the Outfit's head man, Bronson, after making a deal with the second-in-charge, Karns. Parker meets up with old partner, Handy McKay, and they descend on Bronson's Buffalo mansion.

No one wrote better crime fiction in the 1960s than Richard Stark (Donald E.Westlake) and there was never a more intriguing nor exciting lead character in a series than Parker, the star of 24 novels published from 1962 through 2008 (the year of Westlake's death). The brilliant, elaborate heists, the clipped dialogue, the brutal violence, the vast and reappearing supporting cast, the ultimate anti-hero. All adding up to a "formula" that worked over and over again and never seemed to get old.

It's odd that *Manhunt* decided to run what amounts to a severely condensed version of the third Parker novel (which would be published by Perma only a few months later) but, though it is a bit scattershot at times, the story clearly shows why this character is so compelling and why his universe drew in so many crime fans over the years. What's missing from the shorter version, mostly, is a heist perpetrated by one of Parker's pals and quite a bit of Bronson's character development. Still, full version or truncated, "The Outfit" is a dazzler.

Vol. 11 No. 3 Jun 1963

Only appearance by Neil M. Clark, western and mystery author and, at 73, one of the oldest contributors to Manhunt.

"No Escape" by Glenn Canary (3000 words)★★★
A reporter follows a sheriff and his deputies into a snow-covered field to smoke out an armed robber who's escaped from the local jail.

"Deadly Cuckold" by F. S. Landstreet (3000 words)★★
Joe Dunlop thinks of his new farm hand, Harry, as the son he never had but Mrs. Dunlop sure doesn't treat Harry like a son when her husband isn't around.

"Bad Magic" by Robert Page Jones (1500 words)★★✓
Korner the Great was once a magnificent magician but now he spends most of his time on a barstool. Legend has it that he chopped his wife's head off after he caught her with another man. Now, fifty years later, he's remarried to a very young and very pretty girl who's his show assistant. She's also stepping out on Korner and he knows about it. Time for the great "saw the girl in half" trick! Though it's a bit reminiscent of Robert Bloch's classic "The Sorcerer's Apprentice," "Bad Magic" is still a lot of fun, akin to a EC Comics horror story.

"One Big Pay-Off" by Charles Sloan (4000 words)★★★✓
Ex-strongarm, Wies Miller, returns to Reno to work for his one-time boss, casino owner, Mike Cassle. Mike's brother, Phil, had been kidnapped and ransomed; Mike had paid but the snatchers had murdered Phil anyway. Now Mike wants Miller to get him his money back and put the 'nappers six feet under. Extremely violent and dark, with a nasty twist in its climax.

"The Punk" by Herbert Leslie Greene (1500 words)★
A beat cop has a particular punk he likes to hassle constantly. Turns out the cop is sleeping with the punk's girl.

"The Pervert" by T. K. Fitzpatrick (1500 words)★✓
Two little girls accuse an old man who lives across the street of fondling them. The neighbors have gathered like a mob as the police arrive. But was a crime committed?

"The Loners" by Clark Howard (7000 words)★
After a stick-up goes sideways and leaves two of his friends and a cop dead, Cory takes a young girl hostage in her apartment and waits out the police. After only a few hours, the girl relaxes and the two grow close. Maudlin and unbelievable, with sappy dialog, "The Loners" is like bad TV.

"Finders, Keepers" by B. A. Cody (1000 words)★

Jake Lantz is constantly in trouble with the police and his older brother, Ralph, is always there to bail him out. This time, the roles are reversed.

"Vegas ... And Run" by Don Lowry (18,500 words)★★★★

Larry and Billy have been buddies since doing a long stretch together at Leavenworth. While in the can, they cook up a foolproof con, utilizing Larry's skills as a counterfeiter. Printing up a bundle of funny traveler's checks, the boys head to Vegas and scam ten casinos out of fifty thousand. The con comes off without a hitch until one casino manager becomes a problem and Larry has to murder him in the parking lot. Suddenly, the guys have to get out of Vegas quick.

It's only a matter of hours before the Feds and the casino men are hot on their tail and the duo have to flee the country. Thanks to a network of underground contacts, Larry and Billy buy phony passports and make it to Hong Kong on a freighter but soon discover that, even in a foreign country, someone is always on the lookout for a payday.

There are obvious comparisons between "Vegas... And Run" and *Ocean's Eleven* but, thankfully, once we get past the multiple casino scam, this story sets off on a much darker path than the Rat Pack blockbuster. As in Don Lowry's first *Manhunt* story, "Kiloman," plot is necessary but seemingly secondary to rich characterization. Larry, Billy, and their old prison buddies feel like real people; the two men never turn on each other (as most protagonists in these crime stories do) and remain tight right up to the open-ended climax. As with "Kiloman," I would have liked to have seen this story expanded into novel-length. It's that good.

"The Guilty Dead" by Neil M. Clark (4500 words)★★★

Small-town sheriff, George Day, asks his city cop brother, Ben to help him with a curious fatality. A ranch hand, Harry Marr, has been found drowned inside a water tank. No possible way this could have been an accident but George is hard put to come up with a list of suspects. The more the brothers dig, though, the more they discover that Marr had more than a few enemies and it might not be to the town's advantage to close the case. Enthralling whodunit with an ambiguous, but satisfying, ending; the type of story that would have been found in the pages of *Alfred Hitchcock* in the early 1960s.

Vol. 11 No. 4 Aug 1963

Last appearance by John Jakes and the only appearance of Arthur Porges, who was mainly a science fiction writer.

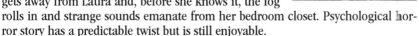

"Change of Heart" by Arthur Porges (2000 words)★★ꞌ

A rapist/killer is terrorizing the houses of a California beach town; every time the fog rolls in, the killer strikes. Dick has to go into San Fran on business and may be away until the next day so he makes Laura promise him she'll stay with friends overnight. The day gets away from Laura and, before she knows it, the fog rolls in and strange sounds emanate from her bedroom closet. Psychological horror story has a predictable twist but is still enjoyable.

Though Arthur Porges placed hundreds of short stories in the science fiction and crime digests, this was his one and only appearance in *Manhunt*.

"One Thousand Steps" by John Channing Carter (2000 words)★

The boys down at the gym have no idea why McGinniss trains so oddly. He lifts weights, walks around the gym and then drops the bars. He adds a few pounds every day until he can do the routine with 250 pounds. But why is he doing it? When the boys remark that McGinniss has a shrew of a wife and she weighs about 250, the aim is all too clear.

"Strange Triangle" by Ray Stewart (2000 words)★★★

"Strange Triangle" is that rare bird that would be completely ruined by anything more than a cursory synopsis. Celia is a love-hungry 16-year-old, just off the bus, who is taken in and taught the finer aspects of sex by our narrator. The reveal is a shocker and may be the earliest example of this twist.

"Hard-Rocks" by Robert McKay (5000 words)★★

Warden Carmichael contemplates a change of vocation when a full-scale riot breaks out. A well-worn plot with the obligatory maudlin finale.

"No Dice!" by Bernard Epps (1000 words)★ꞌ

The story of barfly Johnny and his descent from high-roller to married and miserable.

"Nite Work" by Frank Sisk (1500 words)★★

First-timer Conrad Dibble is questioned by veteran cop, Emmet Boylan, who feels there must be some good deep down in this boy.

"Bad Habit" by G. F. McLennan (4000 words)★★ꞌ

After a stint in stir, career drunk Larry Keller takes a chauffeur job with rich man, J.B. Farrell, and begins to put his life back in some semblance of order. Enter J.B.'s black sheep daughter, Betty, who takes an immediate shine to "Kel" and the two find themselves drunk and married in no time. J.B. casts them both out and the marriage lasts just as long as the money. Betty decides to head back to daddy but Kel has other ideas; he drinks a bottle of gin and carves Betty up with a butcher knife. After a five-year sentence (California was certainly more lenient on murderers back in the day), Larry is back on the street but at least he's sober. Enter future second wife, Lucille. "Bad Habit" has some high points (Betty's murder is stark and violent) but most of the narrative is meandering and unfocused.

"Bounty" by Ray T. Davis (1500 words)★★↩
A bank robber holds an old man hostage in his snow-bound cabin but the old guy is much too smart for the villain. Amiable fable with a very amusing last line.

"Sister's Keeper" by John Lower (2500 words)★★★
Quasi-P.I. Richard Hammond accepts a job from pretty Lorna Garner: she broke up with her lover but he's stolen a bracelet Lorna's husband bought her. The job is to get the bracelet back so Hammond heads to the lover's house and finds him there, two bullets holes in his head. Who killed the Romeo? A thoroughly enjoyable thriller that should have been given more room to breathe.

"Suspect" by John Jakes (4500 words)★★★
Tom Ford finds himself at the mercy of a sadistic small-town sheriff who's convinced Tom murdered a local banker. Things like evidence and alibis mean nothing to this sheriff and Tom begins to fear for his life.

Decades before he became the best-selling author of the Kent Family Chronicles and North and South series of novels, John Jakes honed his craft in the crime digest field, contributing dozens of hard-hitting tales to such titles as *Web Terror, Hunted, Terror Detective, Mike Shayne*, and *Guilty*. "Suspect," a compelling slice of small-town "justice," was Jakes' final contribution to *Manhunt*.

"The Star Boarder" by Charles Miron (2000 words)★
Silly short-short about a trio of misfit teens boarding at the house of Mrs. Zurn.

"The Scoop" by Ort Louis (12,000 words)★★
Mike picks up a hitchhiker on the road to his mountain cabin; the girl tells him someone is trying to kill her. He scoffs, and they stop at a bar for a drink. As they're leaving, two goons grab them. Mike is seriously hurt and the girl is murdered. Why would anyone want to murder a pretty young girl? Mike makes it his job to find out. Confusing and overly complicated, "The Scoop" is also hampered by an ambiguous climax.

"Speedtrap" by David Elgar (2500 words)★★
After ripping off the mob, Riker leads them on a chase to Florida. Well, Riker hopes to make it to Florida, but things are not looking up in that department, especially when he gets stopped in Georgia by a couple of trigger-happy cops.

Peter Enfantino • Jeff Vorzimmer

"A Little Loyalty" by Larry Powell (2500 words)★★✔

Sheriff Johnson is constantly called up to the Laney lodge, home to the area's richest couple. Trouble is, Mrs. Laney keeps trying to off her husband and Mr. Laney wants no publicity, even if the attempts continue. What's an elected small-town sheriff to do? The twist is predictable but the read is entertaining.

Vol. 11 No. 5 Oct 1963
Last issue with four-color cover and last issue for that year. Stephen Marlowe's last appearance with a Chester Drum story "Wanted—Dead and Alive," which would be the last Manhunt story to appear in the Best Detective of the Year anthologies. No "Manhunt's Gun Rack" in this issue.

"The Duchess" by Charles Miron (1000 words)★
A stripper commits suicide after finding out her boyfriend has dumped her. Maudlin, but mercifully short.

"Wanted—Dead and Alive" by Stephen Marlowe (4000 words)★★
Drunk and depressed, director Sebastian Spinner hires an Italian goon to murder his wife, superstar Carole Frazer, after she threatens to ruin his latest mega-budget production. Immediately regretting his action, Spinner hires ace P.I., Chester Drum, to accompany the crew on a cruise to Greece, where the murder is set to take place. Enjoyable enough set-up but the payoff is ludicrous. The action takes place between the Drum novels, *Francesca* (which is referenced in the story) and *Drumbeat: Berlin*, the latter of which began Marlowe's shift in focus from P.I. to more of an espionage-tinged character.

"Retirement" by Robert Edmond Alter (2500 words)★★★ɟ
A war criminal hides amongst the Aborigines, convinced if he shows his face he'll be found out. He cowers in the jungle with a shrewish wife, who spouts orders at him and denounces the man to all who surround him. To say much more would be to ruin the delightful climax (yes, it does go there) but, suffice to say, "Retirement" is suffused with the same sense of adventure and foreign spice found in Alter's other fiction.

"The Good Citizen" by Bernard Epps (1000 words)★
Silly short-short about a derelict brought in for questioning when he witnesses the murder of a reporter who's working on a story about police corruption.

"The Suitcase" by N. E. Jaeger (1500 words)★
Abbie and Matt have had a perfectly orchestrated marriage for 12 years. Matt goes off to work, Abbie cleans the house. She's always ignored that small suitcase at the bottom of his underwear drawer... until today.

"A Grave Affair" by Roswell B. Rohde (1500 words)★
Rupert Green is notoriously thrifty and when he hears that one of his friends has amassed a small fortune, he murders the man and buries him in a recently dug grave.

"Home Free" by Robert Goodney (6000 words)★★★
Grady joins up with a couple of his pals to rob a bank but the heist goes wrong and a cop ends up dead. The police are immediately onto Grady's trail and he has to find somewhere to hide... fast! Author Robert Goodney seems to have more in mind than just a good, quick, thrilling read but that's all "Home Free" turns out to be. Goodney has something to say about how vets are used and then cast aside but doesn't have the tools to make it much deeper than that. Anything else might be labeled pretension.

"Confidant" by Bob Anis (1000 words)★
Jackson has been carrying on with Peter's wife, Carla, and now Peter has come to his house to let him know that Carla is dead. Ridiculous short-short with a very predictable climactic twist.

"The Prospect" by Milt Woods, Jr. (3000 words)★★
Deep in the Superstition Mountains, Prager follows the old man, hoping to discover where the old timer keeps his cache of gold. Tedious drama never seems to get where it's supposed to go.

"One Way—Out" by Gene Jones (3000 words)★✓
A traveling salesman descend into madness, obsessing over the placement of a chair in his hotel room. "One Way—Out" is less a story in a professional crime fiction magazine and more a beginner's exercise in creative writing.

"Final Reckoning" by Pat Collins (3000 words)★★★
A college student finds his whole world turned upside down when a man accuses him of adultery. Author Collins does a fine job of keeping the reader guessing right up to the last line.

"Liberty" by Tom O'Malley (4000 words)★
Tired of his drunken, lazy wife, a man plans her murder, unaware that the target feels exactly the same way about him. Like Robert Goodney, with "Home Free," Tom O'Malley obviously was reaching for something more than just a mystery story in a seedy crime digest but the results are less than satisfactory. Worse, "Liberty" comes off as pretentious and clichéd.

"Interference" by Glenn Canary (2000 words)★★★
Alan is standing on the platform when a pretty young woman tries to step out in front of an approaching train. Alan saves her but then spends quite a bit of time trying to talk the girl out of another attempt. She's just been dumped by her boyfriend and life is not worth living. Alan tries to explain that everyone goes through this experience at some time in their life, but the girl insists this is different. When Alan takes the woman home to her apartment, he discovers why this situation is different. The bulk of "Interference" is given over to the calm dialogue between Alan and the (unnamed) young lady but it's the climax, and its shocking

reveal, that gives this short-short its emotional power.

"Fence Wanted" by Don Lowry (8500 words) ★★★✓
Former cons Tom and Art return to their lives of crime and violence once they get out of the stir but life is looking a little rosier when an ordinary home safe heist becomes a really big deal. Turns out the home owner is a jeweler who had brought his stock home with him and stashed it in his wall safe. Tom and Art had hoped for a few thousand in jewels and cash but what they get is a few hundred thousand in very hot ice.

Suddenly, no fence will take the jewels and there's a target on their backs. The insurance companies and the Feds are right behind the boys no matter where they go. Another enthralling crime classic from author Don Lowry that echoes several of the elements that made "Vegas… and Run" such a page-turner. In Lowry's world, the ex-cons have an underground friendship and bond that is everything, anyone else outside that circle is disposable (as in "Vegas….," there is murder committed with no remorse nor regret). There's a moral code to the two men reminiscent of the protagonists of Sam Peckinpah's *Ride the High Country*; their partnership ends only in death.

"Mother's Day" by Donald Emerson (2000 words) ★★★
Two assassins have a conversation about life, business, and golf while setting up a double hit.

The Best Stories of 1963

"Prison Break" by Duane Clark (February)
"Exile" by Martin Kelly (February)
"The Outfit" by Richard Stark (April)
"Kiloman" by Don Lowry (April)
"One Big Pay-Off" by Charles Sloan (June)
"Vegas ... And Run" by Don Lowry (June)
"Strange Triangle" by Ray Stewart (August)
"Suspect" by John Jakes (August)
"Fence Wanted" by Don Lowry (October)
"Retirement" by Robert Edmond Alter (October)

Vol. 12 No. 1 Jan 1964

First issue photo cover with only one spot color. Number of pages increases to 160 for the rest of the rest of the magazine's run, but many stories are reprints from earlier issues. The first reprinted stories from the 1950s appear as "Manhunt Classics." Newsstand price raised from 35¢ to 50¢. A year subscription is raised to $5.

"Hot" by Don Lowry (4000 words)★★★

After serving a stint in stir, Tom Canto robs a bank and lands on the FBI's Ten Most Wanted list. Suddenly, the mobsters who palled with Tom consider him a pariah, won't hire him, and order him to leave the country. After one more plea for a job goes wrong, Tom is forced into killing a mob boss and hiding in South America, where he ponders his life as a "free man."

"The Grass Cage" by Robert Edmond Alter (4000 words)★★★★

When a thrill-seeker on a safari botches a Cape Buffalo kill, four members of the hunting party head into a narrow thicket to finish the job. A white-knuckle thrill-ride that has absolutely no elements of a *Manhunt* story (much like the rest of Alter's contributions to the magazine) other than a wildly good read. Alter wisely ignores the heist, the drunken husband, the serial killer, and the kidnapper, and focuses on what he does best: adventure and exoticism. The claustrophobia that paralyzes our white hunter can also be felt by the reader, thanks to Alter's vividly descriptive prose:

> *He's hiding in there somewhere with a gut like red pulp, and every time he breathes the pain rips through him like he'd swallowed barbed wire, and he's waiting with his pig-eyes all bright with hate and he's concentrating his libido on one purpose: Us. He's going to charge when we're right on top of him and we won't see him until it's too late and he's going to use his bone helmet-head as a battering ram and he's going to use his horns to do the things to our guts that I've done to his and it's going to be hell on a pogo-stick.*

"Accident Prone" by A. M. Mathews (2000 words)★★

Mae Clohessy has had enough of her husband's drunken ways, drinking up the money and coming home at all hours. Now, the man has a brain tumor and Mae can just imagine the bills piling up. The long, steep staircase to their apartment's front door presents a solution but Pat Clohessy seems to have nine lives.

"Love for Hate" by Xavier San Luis Rey (7000 words)★★

Unrelentingly grim and distasteful study of Jaime Caballero, a young Cuban man who hates women so much that he drugs them and takes unflattering pictures in order to blackmail them. Though I found "Love for Hate" to be a misogynistic waste of paper, I couldn't ignore the fact that author Xavier San Luis Rey (in his first of five *Manhunt* appearances) could produce some memorable writing:

> *Jaime Caballero, or so people said, had been born with a forked tongue and horns protruding from his forehead. He didn't carry a pitchfork or wear a tail because he was by nature fastidious and conservative and didn't like to weigh down his appearance with non-essentials.*

"Bum Rap" by James L. Little (3000 words)★↲
Harold has been sent up the river on what he claims is a "bum rap," but luckily his parole officer is on his side and does what he can to get the man released. The story is so filled with sunshine that it's no surprise when the predictable twist arrives in the climax.

"Last Dime" by Charles Miron (2000 words)★
The mob is after Hughie for ripping them off. He's stuck in a phone booth, waiting for a rain of bullets and, with his last dime, he calls a girl he knew back in school.

"Tap-A-San" by Daniel Walker (5000 words)★
During the Korean War, an American soldier somehow finds a friend on the other side of the trenches and the two "enemies" tap out a dialogue until the war interferes. Padded and maudlin.

"The Eight Ball" by Charles Dilly (2500 words)★★
Pool shark Arnie discovers another player who looks exactly like he does so Arnie hatches a plot to murder the newcomer, have the body identified as Arnie, and then collect on multiple life insurance polices. It's a foolproof plan until Arnie's wife takes a shine to the new guy.

"Fugitive" by Robert McKay (4500 words)★
Lifer Boyd Kimbrough escapes from a chain gang and holds up at the small cottage belonging to a beautiful young girl named Frances. Slowly, but surely, the two fall in love and Fran talks Boyd into giving himself up. Schmaltzy, near-unreadable romance story that would have made a great "Hallmark Movie of the Week", but fails in every other regard.

"I Came to Kill You" by Mickey Spillane
(Reprint of "Everybody's Watching Me." See Vol. 1 No. 1)

Peter Enfantino • Jeff Vorzimmer

Vol. 12 No. 2 Mar 1964

Edward D. Hoch's second and last appearance with an Al Darlan story. This issue would feature the most first-time contributors in the magazine's 14-year history. No "Manhunt's Gun Rack" in this issue.

"Rape!" by Alex Pong (7000 words)★★
Linda Rearwin is very young and pretty but she's also the new teacher at Emmettsville High, a town run and owned by millionaire John Emmett. Though she's warned by her fellow teachers, Linda takes one of her students, Roger Emmett, under her wing when she sees potential in his writing ability. But when the relationship goes sour and Roger rapes and humiliates her, Linda discovers that money will buy anyone a free pass. "Rape!" is an odd story in that Linda makes bad decisions (while explaining a scene in a book to Roger, Linda kisses him) that most right-headed women would avoid; author Pong seems to at least hint that the woman deserves her fate. The climax is lachrymose and bogus.

"The Brothers" by Jim Mueller (1500 words)★
Contrived and ridiculous tale of twin brothers, one accused of murder. But which twin is which? A simple matter of fingerprinting would certainly eliminate any doubt but obviously the police were too inept in 1964 to think of such procedures.

"Video Vengeance" by Pat MacMillan (2000 words)★★✔
Blakely's daughter, Sally, has become obsessed with a TV character named Lieutenant Lollipop, a clown who seems hell bent on selling his viewers every toy known to man. When the Lt. advertises a "replacement daddy" and Sally begs for one, Blakely has had enough and he sends a nice little parcel to the Lt. Very amusing climax.

"To Kill a Cop" by Robert Camp (4000 words)★★✔
Detective Sam Belton gets a call from Vince Rebas, a con he threw in the slammer a few years before, a psycho who's escaped and swears he'll get Sam. When Sam's partner traces the call, both cops are horrified to discover Rebas is calling from Sam's house. Knowing his wife is home, Sam immediately heads for the precinct door but his captain wants well-thought-out strategy. Unfortunately, that plan costs precious time. "To Kill a Cop" is nothing new, but it's a fairly entertaining thrill ride with a memorably nasty finale.

"Losing Streak" by Bernard Epps (2000 words)★★
Side-Bet Benny owes Lew the Shank five large and he's dead broke. Luckily, he's got a high class dame who's worth a million, so he cooks up a fake kidnapping to pry the dough from her gorgeous hands. The scheme doesn't come off as planned but Lew the Shank is arrested and Side-Bet Benny breathes a sigh of re-

lief. Humorous short-short has a vaudeville feel to it.

"The Deadly Bore" by Roswell B. Rohde (1000 words)★★
Martin Cambridge loves to demonstrate the game of Russian Roulette to his friends; only Martin knows the lone bullet is a blank. When his wife, Muriel, demands a divorce and Martin refuses, he dramatically grabs the gun and begins the game, unaware that Muriel has discovered his trick.

"Death's Head" by Richard Prather
(Reprint of "The Best Motive." See Vol. 1 No. 1)

"The Junkie Trap" by Clark Howard (4000 words)★★✔
Public defender Lester Talman had a sister who died with a needle in her arm and he's fought to defend junkies ever since, believing that the addicted are sick, rather than felons. So why has he never had an acquittal in 43 attempts? Could it be that his sister's death has affected him in a different way? A well-told tale, filled with the intricacies of a courtroom drama, but the expository epilogue really wasn't needed. We got it.

"Where There's Smoke" by Edward D. Hoch (6500 words)★★★
Semi-retired P.I. Al Darlin, fresh out of the hospital and nursing a bum ticker, is enticed into "one last case" by Magger Museum curator Wilmer Browse, who is afraid international painting thief Laura Fain is in town to rob his gallery of priceless art. Al reluctantly agrees to tackle the case but he quickly wonders why he bothered. When Al catches up to Fain, she tells him that the paintings hanging in the Magger are fakes and Wilmer is planning a huge heist, with Fain taking the blame. Who's telling the truth? Lots of fun twists and double-crosses highlight this excellent detective tale.
Private Eye Al Darlin began his fictional life as "Al Diamond" and appeared in nineteen stories between 1957 and 2008. According to author Ed Hoch, Darlin was to be killed off in "Where There's Smoke," but he "kept popping up." What, with Darlin, Simon Ark, Nick Velvet, Captain Leopold, Ben Snow, and Alexander Swift, among many others, Hoch must own some kind of record for most continuing series characters.

"Guilt Complex" by Carroll Mayers (1500 words)★✔
The police are called by a landlord when a husband finds his wife hanging in their apartment and the man locks himself in his bathroom with a gun. What begins promisingly enough ends with a ridiculous pay-off, owing to several outlandish coincidences.

"Two Seconds Late" by Harold Rolseth (2000 words)★
Why are there seventeen vehicle accidents within a span of minutes at the same intersection, when there have been none reported there in ages? The answer is a very silly one.

Peter Enfantino • Jeff Vorzimmer

"Fratricide" by John Hanford (4500 words)★★
Ted Lauren covets his brother's fortune and his brother's wife, Laurrie. She's had enough of Jack Lauren so she happily makes a pact with Ted to murder Jack and make it look like a boating accident. But Laurrie might be running two plots at the same time.

"*Omerta!*" by Don Lowry (12,500 words)★★★
Mob boss Frank Cast sees something in the young sociopath, Benny Jack, and he takes him under his wing, molding him into the mob's number one hit man. But the mafia is at a turning point and, suddenly, the five dons are at each other's throats. Benny Jack finds himself very busy. Intricately plotted and populated with characters complemented with Lowry's usual flourishes, "Omerta" is an exciting and unpredictable short novel of the mafia five years before Mario Puzo released *The Godfather*. Benny sees himself as an indestructible force of nature but, in the end, he's just a disposable pawn. Lowry does a nice job juggling two perspectives: that of Benny and that of the Feds, closing in on him.

"Self-Preservation" by Russell W. Lake (2000 words)★★
Tony Lambeth is involved in a serious car accident when a drunk forces the car he's riding in off a cliff. The man driving is seriously hurt but Tony isn't in a rush to get him aid. He stews at the side of the road, thinking about what his college professor would do and then finally hikes to a nearby gas station to call for help. Turns out Tony is a prisoner being transported to the state pen. The reveal is no surprise, there are too many unsubtle clues, but Tony's inner conflict makes for interesting reading.

"The Little Black Book" by Xavier San Luis Rey (3000 words)★★★★
El Tigre, Cuba's most feared and hated policeman, cleans the streets of what he perceives to be evil influence. Tonight, he and his men apprehend Miguel Suarez, a boy who dabbles in the sale of cocaine and marijuana, and spends his idle time beating his girlfriend. Miguel knows he will never see another day. A bleak and hopeless culture breeds violence and, in answer, more violence, cautions San Luis Rey, who presents us with a story that couldn't possibly have anything but a pessimistic climax.

Vol. 12 No. 3 May 1964
This issue would feature stories by eight first time authors.

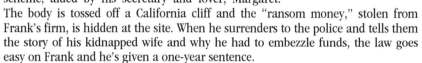

"On the Street" by Lucille Williams (7000 words)★
This awful bit of rubbish isn't so much a story as a series of uninteresting incidents.

"Dead End" by Lawrence E. Orin (4500 words)★★★⤸
Frank Darrow murders his wife, Irene, and then sets into motion an intricately-plotted kidnapping scheme, aided by his secretary and lover, Margaret. The body is tossed off a California cliff and the "ransom money," stolen from Frank's firm, is hidden at the site. When he surrenders to the police and tells them the story of his kidnapped wife and why he had to embezzle funds, the law goes easy on Frank and he's given a one-year sentence.

Released from prison, Frank collects Margaret and they head for the stashed bag of loot. Leaning over the cliff to grab the suitcase, Frank sees the ghost of his dead wife and he and Margaret and the loot tumble into the sea. An enthralling thriller with (a first for *Manhunt*) what appears to be a genuinely supernatural twist. Author Orin offers up no other solution for the appearance of Irene and the specter is a jolt not only for Frank but for the reader as well.

"The Hole Card" by Bernard Epps (1500 words)★
There's a rat in Little Joe's organization. But is the mouth singing to the cops?

"The Dead and the Dying" by Evan Hunter
(Reprint of "Dead Men Don't Dream." See Vol. 1 No.3)

A Deadly Nuisance by Maeva Park (3000 words)★★★
Poor old Mrs. Saunder lives next door to the second cousin of The Bad Seed, a boy whose cruelty grows from mere pranks to dangerous acts of violence. But what can Mrs. Saunder do when she can't prove a thing to the police. Solid "cozy" with a brilliant twist.

"Cosa Mia" by Lee Costa (2000 words)★
The story of a Mexican sheriff and all the terrible things he loves to do comes off as more of a stream of consciousness; a greatest hits of this man's sadistic past. There's no flow, just sadism.

"Divorce ... New York Style" by Kennan Hourwich (2500 words)★⤸
Gary Mason divorces his wife in order to move up the food chain; he's found a very rich woman who's begging him to marry her. A very confusing story.

"The Silent Dead" by Don Lowry (11,000 words)★★★⤸
After being fingered for a robbery, Mike Paco spends his years on Alcatraz as a

model prisoner, earning an early release. But his days of civility are now behind him and Mike spends the next several years racking up bank robberies, diamond holdups, even supermarket heists, but never leaving any witnesses. Any accomplices Mike works with end up dead in a ditch or, like one unfortunate ex-con, buried alive.

Mike finally retires and buys himself a nice house, investing his money well, but finds domestic life a total bore. Deciding to "widen his scope," Mike hunts down anyone in his past who betrayed him and puts a bullet in their head. That draws the attention of the FBI.

An odd short novel, with a see-saw pace. The first half is given over to Paco's heists and murders (at one point, the text almost becomes the equivalent of a 1970s men's adventure novel, with each crime becoming more and more gruesome), while the second dwells on the law enforcement and how they compare notes. By now, I'm convinced that Don Lowry was patterning his work after the Parker novels written by Richard Stark, filling his tales with the same type of intricate heist details and staccato dialogue. Fortunately, Lowry's doing it at the same level Stark did.

"The Switch" by R. C. Stimers (1500 words)★★
Leslie and Bill think they've put one over on the mob, swapping out counterfeit dough for the real thing. Then the masters come calling.

"Buddies" by A. M. Staudy (2000 words)★
Lt. Jud Renton tries to choke a confession out of a guy who's clearly shot his best friend over a game of cards. But, as the Lieutenant discovers, the killing wasn't that simple. A tired, stupid, padded bit of nonsense with a reveal that would not have passed the editor's desk ten years earlier.

"The Easiest Way" by Charles Dilly (3000 words)★★
After a scandal ruins his career, a doctor climbs over the rail of a bridge and readies himself for the fall. Just then, a voice from further down the bridge alerts him that he's not alone in his suicide jump. There's a clever twist, but then a silly epilogue.

"Easy Money" by Thomas Rountree (3000 words)★↙
When a traveling salesman breaks down and leaves his car in the yard of hillbillies, Louis and Verbena, they can't believe their luck. In a bag in the back seat, they find ten grand. But their luck has never been that good and the man swiftly comes back for his dough and he's packing a heater.

"The Singing Pigeon" by John Ross Macdonald
(Reprint of "The Imaginary Blonde." See Vol. 1 No. 2)

Vol. 12 No. 4 Jul 1964
Last appearance of Joe Gores, who contributed six stories to the magazine.

"Sweet Vengeance" by Joe Gores (7500 words)★★✓
Uneven action-thriller about a professor who goes after the four teenagers who raped his wife. The set-up is unnerving but the pay-off is trite, though Gores' revenge fantasy seemingly paved the way for *Death Wish* and its plethora of imitators. The basic plot of "Sweet Vengeance" was rebooted as Gores' first published novel, *A Time of Predators*, which won the Edgar Award for Best First Novel in 1969.

"What Could I Do?" by James R. Hall (3500 words)★★★
Eddie Moore decides to rob a convenience store, just to put some spending money in his pocket, but he ends up killing the watchman. Not understanding the options handed to him by his court-appointed lawyer (one of which is a sure-fire guilty verdict and a possible death penalty sentence), Eddie pleads guilty and heads to prison for a life sentence. A sober vignette about wrong decisions and their consequences.

"Epitaph" by Hilda Cushing (2000 words)★★✓
Vera Leach is arrested for first-degree murder after her husband dies of a heart attack. But it's not her husband's death she was arrested for.

"Commitment to Death" by John E. Lower (4000 words)★★★
A writer opens his door to find an old flame, down on her luck, who's looking for a bit of help. She's become a dancer and pregnant with a Senator's child. The politician is married and he's sent goons out to kill her. Our hero tries valiantly to keep the girl alive. "Commitment to Death" (a very bad, generic title) takes a worn-out theme and gives it a bit of spark; the second half of the story is an exciting car chase that leads to a violent climax.

"The Right Man" by William Engeler (1500 words)★★✓
Assassin Gerald Madden is hired by millionaire Howard Parker to kill his wife, who's been planning to murder Howard for his money. Dirty deed complete, Gerald decides to double his payday by taking out the old man as well.

"A Deadly Proposition" by Pat MacMillan (3500 words)★
Elmo has had enough of his wife (who he has nicknamed "Mouth" in honor of her fondness for talking) and, after a chance meeting with a stranger in a restaurant, decides now is the time to get rid of her. Slow-paced black comedy that strays a little too close to *Strangers on a Train*.

"Circle of Jeopardy" by Henry Kane
(Reprint of "One Little Bullet." See Vol. 1 No. 4)

"Craving" by Nel Rentub (2000 words)★
Irma plays with fire by teasing the gentle giant known as Hector. Sleazy short-short, lacking anything worth note.

"A Cruise to Hell" by Ed Lacy (21,000 words)★★★↲
TV writer Harry flies out to Hawaii to meet with action star Buzz Roberts, who's looking to add a TV series to his resume. Roberts is cagey and keeps Harry on pins and needles, waiting to hear if he's got the gig. Buzz suggests a cruise to get the juices flowing and three friends join the trip: K.K., an exotic, beautiful island girl who may or may not be carrying Buzz's baby; the mysterious Jimmy Turo, who might have a secret or two to hide; and Captain Will Howell, a WWII vet, who's gotten used to Buzz's strange cruise demands.

When trip plans are made, Will suggests visiting Suran, a desolate small island; as a captain of a PT boat, Will and his crew stopped at Suran for repairs and were attacked by a small group of Japanese soldiers. Most of the crew were killed and Will was left with a "million dollar wound," running the length of his face. The boat arrives at the island and, immediately, Buzz wants to investigate. While walking with Harry, Buzz is shot and killed by a mystery sniper. Will claims to have seen the Japanese lieutenant who made pizza of his face, but the others scoff. When K.K. is kidnapped, Harry and Jimmy have to admit there's something weird going on here. Could the Japanese soldier have survived on this small island for twenty years?

An exciting page-turner, "A Cruise to Hell" takes a page from Charles Williams's playbook, that of the adventure on the high seas. The mystery is explained away in satisfying fashion but what may be more important to a lengthy story such as this is that Ed Lacy nails these characters; all five are rich and textured. Buzz's death is a shock, coming out of nowhere. I'm amazed Lacy never expanded this into a novel-length thriller.

"Jail-Bait" by C. Ashley Lousignont (1500 words)★
Another in a seemingly endless series of reprehensible short-shorts, this one about a twice-arrested pedophile who gets sent up the river for a murder he didn't commit. Composed of staccato sentences à la Hal Ellson.

Vol. 12 No. 5 Sep 1964
Last appearance by Michael Zuroy with "The Mule."
No "Manhunt's Gun Rack" in this issue.

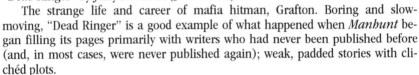

"Death Begins..." by Herbert Leslie Greene (2000 words)★
A man picks up a woman in a bar and talks her into a nighttime stroll on the beach. There, he tries to rape her. It's as simple as that. Truly no redeeming qualities to this nasty vignette.

"Dead Ringer" by Jerry Newman (3000 words)★
The strange life and career of mafia hitman, Grafton. Boring and slow-moving, "Dead Ringer" is a good example of what happened when *Manhunt* began filling its pages primarily with writers who had never been published before (and, in most cases, were never published again); weak, padded stories with clichéd plots.

"Cross and Double Cross" by B. D. Dupont (1500 words)★
A detective has to explain to his lieutenant why his partner committed suicide. About as predictable as they come.

"Don't Tempt Me" by Robert Page Jones (14,500 words)★★★✦
After serving a two-year stint for a rape he didn't commit, Johnny Scchapov tries to start a new life in a small town in a crap job, delivering booze to rich pricks. Then, one day, Johnny meets Lara, a sexy box of fire, who seems to be the property of a gruff man named Harry. Lara makes a move on Johnny but Harry interrupts and the delivery man hoofs a quick exit. The next day, Lara calls for another delivery but this time she has a surprise for Johnny: Harry, in the bathtub, a gaping hole in his throat.
Lara spills the beans: Harry was jealous of Johnny and about to toss Lara out on her shapely behind so she showed him who was boss. The upside, Lara tells Johnny, is that Harry left behind plans for a major bank heist, a job she wants to pull with Johnny. It takes a bit of sweet-talking but, eventually, Johnny is in. "Don't Tempt Me" is another winner for Robert Page Jones; it has the same winning elements that made "The Big Haul" so mesmerizing. Jones' greatest creation might not be the heist plot or the small-town sheriff who knows something's up, or even Johnny, who begins his odyssey as an innocent man. No, the greatest piece of Jones' puzzle here is Lara, who might be one of fiction's greatest female sociopaths, devoid of anything resembling a conscience or morals. When Johnny wants to come clean and tells Lara about his stint in prison for rape, Jones pulls no punches:

> *She was watching me. Impulsively, she slid across the seat toward me, and I smelled her perfume. She was breathing funny.*
> *"Show me," she said.*

"Queer Siren" by C. L. Roderman (1000 words)★
Warren is tempted by his secretary but it turns out the woman may be plotting something with Warren's wife.

"Two-Way Patsy" by John H. Goeb (15,000 words)★✦
"Popeye" Pedderson, owner of the Medusa party boat, takes pretty Rita Corsico out for a spin and regrets it when the babe pulls a gun on him and orders him to head out to sea. Turns out Rita is working with the Cuban underground and is to meet up with a submarine. "Popeye" is to be killed and the Medusa gutted but the sailor manages to get away after a fierce struggle. Now, he must deal with the police, who claim he murdered Rita and dumped her body overboard. Padded and plodding, with a ridiculous expository at the climax.

"Sore Loser" by Frank Sisk (2000 words)★★✦
Humorous fable about a fight manager and his estranged wife.

"Kill and Run" by Floyd Mahannah
(Reprint of "Backfire." See Vol. No. 1)

"The Mule" by Michael Zuroy (2000 words)★★
When the business he owns with his partner goes belly-up, Wallace hires a hitman to make it a one-owner business. Then the hitman gets an idea and contacts the partner. This is a twist that has been done to death but "The Mule" does have a laugh-out-loud last line.

Vol. 12 No. 6 Nov 1964

The only issue after Jan 1964 that doesn't have at least one reprinted story. Last appearance by Bernard Epps, who contributed seven stories to the magazine.

"Courier" by Don Lowry (4000 words)★★★

Dons Benito Rainone and Anthony Garmoni ponder the continued losses they face in the heroin market. The Feds keep busting their operations and they can't get enough product onto the streets. The answer to their problems arrives in South American embassy Attaché, Jules Hernandez, a man who can smuggle heroin into America under diplomatic immunity. Rainone works at Hernandez's love for gambling and pretty blondes and, very soon, the man is running 'H' for the mob.

Another gritty and violent fable from Don Lowry, "Courier" takes place within the same world as Lowry's other mob tales (Rainone's lakeside residence, which can be accessed "only by plane," is very similar to the mob hangout in Lowry's "*Omerta!*"). Also like Lowry's other *Manhunt* stories, "Courier" is completely unpredictable. At one point in the story, Hernandez decides to commit suicide but shoots his lover in the head first. A mob photographer, in the closet to snap dirty pics, prevents Hernandez from following through on his wish.

"Whitemail" by Edward Wellen (1000 words)★★

An old friend comes to call on the vet but it's not good times he wants to discuss.

"One Hungry Pigeon" by Patrick Connolly (2000 words)★★★

A very funny story about two dimwits who plan a double-murder.

"The Slayer" by Robert Page Jones (11,500 words)★★★⤴

Serial killer Johnny Polichek murders a cop and hops aboard a bus bound for Tampa, unaware that the vehicle is heading into the path of a hurricane. When a local cop pulls the bus over and tells the six passengers the roads are impassable and they'll have to take shelter in a bar up the road, Polichek sees this as a wonderful opportunity to add "points to his score." He plans to murder everyone when the time is right. Though "The Slayer" suffers a bit from a rushed climax, the backstory to each character is fascinating as is the shift in tone from crime to thriller back to crime. "The Slayer" would benefit greatly from an expansion to novel-length as in the case of Jones's "The Big Haul"/*The Heisters* but, sadly, that never happened.

"Eyes in the Night" by Nel Rentub (2000 words)★★

When she can't get any men to notice her, Lucy turns to a dangerous game of exhibition.

"The Stud" by James Harvey (27,000 words)★★

Unemployed actor Vic Harper pressures his agent into getting him a job… any job. Faster than you can say "Roll 'em!," the agent has Vic a job but our hero discovers too late that the role is in a stag film, bankrolled by the New York mob. Disgusted, Vic moves to the West Coast to try his hand at a legit career but "real work" eludes him and he finds himself working in a porn factory owned by L.A. mobster, Archie Saks. Before long, Vic finds himself bedding Hollywood superstar, Sara Summers, an actress set up by Saks for blackmail. Add to this the escalating war between Saks and the East Coast mobsters, who desperately want Vic Harper back as their star humper.

A terribly written but mildly entertaining bit of nonsense, undoubtedly the oddest choice of fiction ever to be found within the pages of *Manhunt* magazine. What was the motivation behind publishing what was essentially a soft-core porn novel with flashes of violence? And what could the reaction be from *Manhunt*'s loyal (and dwindling) audience? Proving that no idea should be wasted, author Harvey explored virtually the same territory in his soft-core novel, *Stag Model* (Midwood, 1960).

"The Pro Beau" by R. A. Gardner (1500 words)★

Harry is a "professional husband"; he marries rich women, has them sign over all the valuables, and then tosses the radio into their bath water to get rid of them. It's worked nine times already but Harry is getting bored. He wants to find a woman he can fall in love with. He finds her in gorgeous blonde, Linda, who's there at the crap table the night he wins seventy grand. It's love at first sight for Harry. Very predictable comedy/mystery with a too on-the-nose punchline.

"Astral Body" by Maeva Park (2500 words)★★↲

Everything in Cyrus Wilson's life is decided by his daily horoscope. So, when his astrologer, Mina, tells Cyrus he should divorce his wife, Pamela, naturally he's going to follow her instructions. But Pamela refuses to divorce, so Cyrus has to come up with another plan.

"Two for the Show" by Bernard Epps (3500 words)★★

Ernie the Apples is looking for a bride; he's made a boatload of money but now he wants to be noticed and he feels the only way he can be deemed a success is to be married. The boys down at the Paradise cook up a scheme to determine which of the two girls Ernie likes the most will win "the prize." Ernie will play dead (funeral and all) and the dame that frets most over his coffin gets the ring. Mildly amusing quasi-crime-sitcom.

"Banker's Trust" by Paul Curtis (4000 words)★★★

Bank manager Jim Glenning receives a disturbing phone call at his desk just before closing. A man is holding Jim's wife and young son hostage and is demanding one hundred thousand in small bills. Jim is booked on a plane to Mexico City and there he is to hand over the suitcase of dough to a man at the Vista Hotel. If all goes well, wife and kid will be freed.

But, when Jim arrives at the Vista, the police nab him and extradite him back to the States, where he's taken to a room and questioned by Feds. Jim is accused of stealing three hundred grand from his bank and his wife denies ever being held hostage. What's the real story? An ingenious heist tale that only falters in its TV drama-esque neat wrap-up.

The Best Stories of 1964

"The Grass Cage" by Robert Edmond Alter (January)
"Hot" by Don Lowry (January)
"Where There's Smoke" by Edward D. Hoch (March)
"The Little Black Book" by Xavier San Luis Rey (March)
"Dead End" by Lawrence E. Orin (May)
"The Silent Dead" by Don Lowry (May)
"A Cruise to Hell" by Ed Lacy (July)
"Don't Tempt Me" by Robert Page Jones (September)
"The Slayer" by Robert Page Jones (November)
"Courier" by Don Lowry (November)

Peter Enfantino • Jeff Vorzimmer

Vol. 13 No. 1 Jan 1965

All but one original story—"The Specialists" by Ed Lacy in his last appearance—are by first-time contributors. No "Manhunt's *Gun Rack*" in this issue.

"The Sweet Taste" by David Goodis
(Reprint of "Black Pudding." See Vol.1 No. 12)

"Man's Man" by Charles A. Freylin (1000 words)★★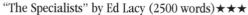
The Weymouth-Bright Hospital is like a second home to Colonel Kelmont. Whenever his old war wound flares up, he comes round to pinch the prettier nurses and spin battle yarns. But for some reason, he refuses to allow the staff to extricate the bullet from his back. The twist, revealing why the Colonel keeps his wound intact, is a good one.

"The Specialists" by Ed Lacy (2500 words)★★★
All the money is in Maddy's name so there's no way James Warren is filing for divorce. So he cooks up an intricate kidnapping scheme, including a ransom note, and then murders Maddy and dumps her body in the forest. The only problem is that the cop in charge of the case, the one Warren is so sure is a boob, is pretty darn smart. A clever little crime story with a strong cast; along the lines of a good episode of *Columbo*, where we know the identity of the murderer, but have to learn where he screwed up.

"Conviction" by Will Cotton (6000 words)★★
Detective Blaine has an itch for crime boss, Zellers, but he can't seem to get up enough evidence to put the murdering scum behind bars. So Blaine goes outside the parameters of the law and uses Zellers' girlfriend to bring the big man down. "Conviction" has a 1950s vibe to it, with its gangster moll and questionable police tactics.

"The Last Freedom" by W. Sherwood Hartman (1500 words)★★
Lifer Ervie finds it hard to live in prison; his cellmates spit on him and his life is constantly threatened. So he decides to escape in a garbage can one day, knowing that the only stop for him will be an incinerator. Nasty little shocker.

"Blood Money" by Gary Jennings (15,500 words)★★
"Doc" was a skilled surgeon until his wife died tragically; then he turned to the bottle. Years later, as a skid row bum, Doc sells his blood for booze money but one day a stranger approaches him with an odd, but attractive, offer: four walls and all the booze and food he needs to survive if he'll give blood privately to one party now and then. Doc agrees but, a few weeks later, the arrangement begins smelling fishy and he starts doing a little private eye work to gain the identity of his benefactor. "Blood Money" starts strong but becomes anemic by the second half. Gary Jennings would go on to write the bestseller, *Aztec*.

"The Wrong Man" by Stanley Mohr (7500 words)★✈

After a seven-year stint in prison for a job he didn't pull, Martin Sheen is out to clear his name and sue the city for false imprisonment. A series of red herrings and ludicrous expository (one of which comes from the POV of a man who wasn't even witness to the events) sinks "The Wrong Man," which could have used a good editing and proofreading.

"The Explosive Triangle" by Frank Gay (1500 words)★★✈

Barbara Catcher is caught between her lover and her husband in a complicated con but, after much thought, she's not sure which one she'd rather see dead. In a clever twist, she has her cake and eats it too.

"Alien Hero" by John Chancellor (16,000 words)★✈

After his date for the evening jilts him, Jeff drives off to a pub in the English countryside to drown his sorrows. Along the way, his tire throws a hubcap and, when he exits the car to retrieve it, Jeff hears gunshots and a bullet grazes him. Before he knows it, he's involved with a beauty named Trudi, who claims the bullets are meant for her. She's a member of a secret organization from Germany, in England to capture a Nazi war criminal named Wolfgang Skager. When Trudi shows Jeff a photo of Skager, he immediately recognizes the man as Preez, the proprietor of a local hotel called the Polish Volunteer. At first skeptical, ensuing events convince Jeff that Trudi is telling the truth. A low-rent espionage thriller that revisits territory explored several times before.

Vol. 13 No. 2 Mar 1965
Last appearance of "Manhunt's Gun Rack". All but two original stories are by first-time contributors.

"Play Tough" by Frank Kane
(Reprint of "The Icepick Artists." See Vol. 1 No. 12)

"The Gate" by Walter E. Handsaker (3000 words)★↵
After forty years, Henry Carruthers is being released from prison. He's been a model prisoner and the warden shakes his hand as he leaves his office. Henry tells the warden he has to get outside the gate quickly as Henry's wife, Edith, should be waiting for him. When he finally gets outside the prison, Edith is nowhere in sight. Where is she? A maudlin set-up leads to a predictable twist.

"The Dead Sell" by George Beall (4500 words)★
Pauline opens a string of ritzy dress shops that offer a little something extra on the side at the right price.

"A Con's Code" by William P. Perry (3000 words)★★↵
New con Angelo considers guard Charlie to be a kind and generous man but those sentiments can get you killed in the yard. "A Con's Code" is a solid read but it really doesn't say much about anything. It's just a series of events within a prison yard.

"Shenanigans" by Rod Barker (6000 words)★★★
A good, old-fashioned whodunit with a newspaper publisher and editor playing Sherlock and Watson, investigating the murder of a Hollywood TV writer.

"Bad Risk" by Jack Farrell (3500 words)★★
With the help of his brother, Bert breaks out of prison and heads up the swamp towards his dying father's farm. Realizing that's the first place the cops will check, Bert talks his brother into heading in the opposite direction. But Bert is an impetuous hothead and trouble comes to the two brothers when they try to board a train and a gunfight ensues. What begins as an exciting chase yarn devolves into psychological nonsense.

"The Men from the Boys" by Allyn Dennis (8500 words)★
A mother tries to keep her son away from bad influences by murdering the loose hussy he's been seeing. Truly awful soap opera masquerading as hard-hitting crime drama.

"Trans-Atlantic Lam" by Don Lowry (1500 words)★★
Two American thieves, stuck in London, pull a job and then hop onto a luxury liner bound for New York.

"5 Days to Kill" by Jerry Bailey (21,000 words)★

An American serviceman in Japan becomes amateur detective when his buddy is murdered. "5 Days to Kill" is way too long and filled with silly espionage clichés and offensive stereotypes; worse, it's boring.

Vol. 13 No. 3 May 1965
Last of two stories by author Thomas Millstead.

"Kill or Die" by Charles A. Freylin (4500 words)★★★
An assassin readies his equipment and his mind as the target approaches. Less than two years after the assassination of JFK, "Kill or Die" must have been a tough read; it's an involving look into the mind of a killer and what makes him tick.

"The Seduction" by Frank Gay (1500 words)★
A man hires a P.I. to seduce his estranged wife (for monetary reasons), but when the dick sees how gorgeous the woman is, he adopts a different strategy.

"Hijack" by Don Pep (5000 words)★★★
Five washed-up and out of work mafia hitmen converge upon a small motel and plan a heist. Engaging and clever "buddy" thriller where the buddies eventually turn on each other.

"Virtue's Prize" by H. Rayburn (3500 words)★★
A good samaritan quickly rues saving a young lady from her ex-boyfriend when the nut comes after him.

"Clean-Up" by Frank Kane
(Reprint of "Finish the Job." See Vol. 2 No. 1)

"Decoy for a Pigeon" by Herb Hartman (2000 words)★★
Prison is tough on Corky but at least he's got the beautiful Thelma visiting him. Now, the two have cooked up something for getting Corky out on the sly but the con better watch his back; Thelma is playing both sides. A routine prison break tale with quite a bit of soft-core sex to spice things up.

"Nightmare's Edge" by Robert Page Jones (5500 words)★★★
A jazz musician wakes up, covered in blood, convinced he's murdered his ex-wife after a long night of drinking. When he arrives at her apartment and finds her alive, he breathes a sigh of relief, until he digs into his pocket and finds a woman's stocking. "Nightmare's Edge" is not a bad story but it doesn't have the full-blooded characters found in Jones's longer work and the constant "did he do it/didn't he do it" see-saw is tiring.

"The Big Fall" by Don Lowry (14,000 words)★★
New York mobster Max Beaver has been having a hard time making ends meet and his West Coast counterparts believe all it would take is a change of scenery. So Max trades business with his comrades, grabs his gorgeous moll, and plants roots in Los Angeles. Things go sour quickly. Unlike any of Don Lowry's previous short

novels, "The Big Fall" is padded, meandering and, except for a white-knuckle finish, a chore to wade through.

"The Helpmate" by E. A. Bogart (2500 words)★

At the funeral of her husband, European film star Gina Galaire de Neve reflects on the "perfect marriage" she shared with the deceased. Then Gina's family doctor lets on he knows she fed the old man too many pills. And only the companionship of Gina will buy his silence. What looked like freedom suddenly becomes hell again.

"The Death Maker" by Nelson Adcock (7500 words)★★★⌐

Former moll Elsie Kane hires hitman Slant Edwards to murder Monk Callahan and John Clement, two men who beat her to a pulp some years before. Slant's fee is five grand and he never turns a job down, but Elsie insists on being there when the assassin pulls the trigger.

What follows could best be described as a darkly comic road trip to hell. The two exchange miserable stories of past injustices while they travel to the farm owned by Clement and, if anything, Elsie's hatred for the man multiplies as the miles roll away. The hit transforms from easy job for Slant into a bloodbath initiated by Elsie herself. The final pages are harrowing. An impressive *Manhunt* debut for Nelson Adcock.

"Blood is Thicker" by Dave Hill (1500 words)★

Two siblings plan the murder of their father but neither can help double-crossing the other.

"The Helpful Cop" by Thomas Millstead (2000 words)★★

Two cops investigate a missing gardener at a posh estate. The owner of the estate, an eccentric old bird, confesses he was convinced his gardener was a vampire.

Vol. 13 No. 4 Jul 1965
Last appearance of Jack Ritchie, who contributed 22 stories to the magazine.

"Hunt the Hunter" by Patrick Connolly (2500 words)★★

Lorraine finally leaves husband, Ralph, just as she's always promised, and heads right into the arms of her lover Mitch. But desertion isn't enough for Lorraine so she begins phoning Ralph's mother and threatening her. The woman dies of a heart attack and Ralph heads out, searching for Lorraine and Mitch, swearing he'll even the score.

"Going Down?" by Jack Ritchie (1000 words)★★

Sergeant Morgan is tasked with talking the prospective jumper off the ledge but the more the guy talks, the more Morgan wants him to jump.

"Mata Seguro" by Xavier San Luis Rey (5000 words)★★★

Police Captain Manolo Alvarez stumbles across a plot to murder the president of Cuba via an extremely rare and toxic poison called Mata Seguro ("clearly dead"). El Capitan has arrested and interrogated Señor Castillo in an attempt to learn more about the assassination attempt, but the old man may know more than he's letting on. Intricately detailed and suspenseful, "Mata Seguro" is a gem with a maddeningly abstract climax.

"Lamster War" by Don Lowry (5000 words)★★★﹤

Prince Montio has become a safe haven for any shady character wishing to flee the States. For a fee, Chico Winters and his band of entrepreneurs will set a lamster up with new ID and a place to live. Chico's paradise thrives until a group of Nazi war criminals, also hiding out in Prince Montio, start wiping out Chico's "guests." The Germans are afraid the lamsters will draw the attention of Federales and so will do anything to keep the heat off. A riotous and completely original hodgepodge of genres, "Lamster War" is akin to a 1960s low-budget horror film, shot in black-and-white, and featuring memorable dialogue and loads of action.

"Travelin' Man" by Rod Bryant (3000 words)★★★

On the run from the law, white trader Max Blessing relies on the kindness of strangers when his car conks out in the swamp. Con artists Dawson and Luke (who had fooled with the road in order to drum up business) agree to fix Max's car for a steep price and Max is about to balk when he sees Dawson's daughter, Opal. Smitten from the start, Max starts plotting a way to get the beauty out of the swamp and into the hands of one of his customers. Clever swamp drama with a nasty twist.

"Aversion" by Miriam Allen deFord (4000 words)★★★

A quartet plan to rob a Spanish money exchange but their petty squabbles might be the downfall of all of them. A multi-genre author and veteran of pulps such as *Weird Tales, Startling Stories, Real Detective*, and *The Shadow*, Miriam Allen deFord was a frequent contributor to the major crime digests. "Aversion" was, surprisingly, deFord's only contribution to *Manhunt*.

"Alias: Trouble" by Craig Rice
(Reprint of "I'm a Stranger Here Myself," See Vol. 2 No. 2))

"Loser's Choice" by Nelson Adcock (9500 words)★★

George Creese was once a feared mob leader, but a downfall and a twenty-year stint in the pen have left him a penniless alcoholic. A letter from his ex-wife, asking for his help, leads George to the kind of penthouse apartment he once owned. Wendy has re-married in the years since George went away, to a newspaper publisher who's made some very influential enemies. When the paperman's life is threatened, Wendy naturally reaches out to the only person she knows who can use violence to get a point across.

There's an intriguing story buried under the page upon page of ponderous self-examination and regret but, alas, that tale only surfaces occasionally and, by the time the violent climax arrives, the reader might have drifted off.

"Tough Boy" by Richard Welles (1000 words)★★★

Ben has an altercation with a gang of hoods at a diner and they follow him down the highway after he leaves. Realizing they'll be a nuisance, he pulls over to the side of the road and one of the boys charges him with a switchblade. Ben pulls out his gun, blows the kid's head off, and then muses he'll have to get another gun for the hit he's on the way to performing. A surprisingly effective little tale with a burst of graphic violence and a thinly veiled publishing taboo (at one point one of the kids uses Pig Latin to tell Ben, "uckfay ouyay!").

"No Future" by Donald Lee (3000 words)★★⅃

Ex-cons Jim and Fat sit in a bar, discussing their lives since being released. No one will hire them, the police treat them like dogs, and the only place they're received warmly is in a pub. Both decide that pulling a job is their only way out of this life. "No Future" is an involving look at the ex-con and how hopeless life can be once you're branded a "bad guy."

"The Other Side" by Daniel Depaolo (11,000 words)★★★

Well-paced novella about four inmates planning a prison break. Whereas most breakout stories concentrate on the after-effects, "The Other Side" shows us the intricate prep work and everything that can go wrong, in this case, a stoolie amongst the quartet of escapees.

Peter Enfantino • Jeff Vorzimmer

"Double or Nothing" by W. Sherwood Hartman (2000 words)★★
Identical twin thieves beat a gas station robbery rap by messing with the system.

Vol. 13 No. 5 Sep 1965
All original stories in this issue are by first-time contributors.

"Bury Me Proper" by George H. Bennett (3500 words)★★ℐ
Aubrey is afraid of dying and not receiving a proper burial so, after his wife and young son die tragically, he approaches ex-lover, Dolly Freeman, to marry him. A weird, atmospheric horror story that's a bit too long, but still very unnerving.

"Fair Exchange" by Patrick Sherlock (3000 words)★★★
A thief plans an ingenious caper involving an airport currency exchange office but, in the excitement of the moment, the dimwit grabs the foreign currency out of the vault rather than the greenbacks.

"Blood Brother" by Jerry Spafford (7000 words)★★
Three years after his brother meets with a suspicious death aboard a merchant vessel, Dunlop boards the boat and investigates the men he's been told had something to do with the incident. Slow-moving and, ultimately, unsatisfying, "Blood Brother" has one interesting aspect: the climax revisits the violent scene we come into at the onset and gives us a "bigger picture."

"The Virile Image" by Gerald Pearce (3000 words)★★★
An important Hollywood producer marries a woman three decades younger and, after three years, her adultery has pushed him to contemplate murder. "The Virile Image" takes a very simple plot, one used countless times before, and crafts it into an engrossing vignette about power, money, and love.

"The Fixer" by Robert Turner
(Reprint of "Be My Guest." See Vol. 1 No. 4)

"Portrait in Blood" by Bob Temmey (10,000 words)★
Buddy Merrill hasn't seen his friend, P.I. Steve McCann, in years, so their reunion on the train station platform means a lot to the painter. Unfortunately, a thick atmosphere of tension hangs over the happy occasion when Buddy finds out Steve is in trouble with the CIA. A slow-moving catalog of espionage clichés concerning spies and missing microfilm.

"Beneficiary" by Natalie Jenkins Bond (4500 words)★★ℐ
Mary McCall has had some bad luck in the last ten years; both her husbands die in freak accidents and now her baby girl ends up dead in her crib. Thank goodness all deceased were insured. Naturally, the police suspect Mary but they question her boyfriend and her two children as well. Could Mary have murdered her own daughter? An involving (and grim) murder mystery resolves itself with a

tad too much inspiration from *The Bad Seed*; which wouldn't be so bad if we didn't have to suffer through a ludicrous two-page expository.

"Turnabout" by Billy Gill (3000 words)★

After twelve long years in prison, Jake Harlan is released and the only thing on his mind is murdering the cop that framed him all those years ago.

"After the Fact" by Harold Q. Masur
(Reprint of "The Mourning After." See Vol. 1 No. 3)

"Tennis Bum" by G. L. Tassone (4000 words)★★★

Ex-tennis pro, Barry Cole, is hired by the Milburn Racquet Club to teach tennis to its rich, spoiled members. One of those members is Mrs. Milburn herself, recently widowed and bound to a wheelchair. Mrs. Milburn takes a liking to Barry's svelte figure and makes him an offer: she is dying and wants to make her last year special so if Barry will be her private sex toy, she will leave him her immense fortune in his will.

Barry agrees but finds out from the woman's doctor that she's not dying; in fact, she's on the mend. Feeling trapped, Barry wheels Mrs. Milburn off the lake dock and then relaxes, awaiting the reading of the will. Unfortunately for Barry, Mrs. Milburn had many friends who lived in the same complex and one of them loves to take amateur footage of the lake every day. A fun read, with a climax that actually leaves the reader feeling sorry for Barry.

"Middle-Man" by Raymond Crooks (7500 words)★★

P.I. Krag is contacted by a gang of kidnappers to act as go-between for the ransom. Krag arrives at the home of the Jackridges, parents of the young boy who's been kidnapped, and immediately suspects something's not right. He accepts the fifty thousand in ransom money, drops the briefcase off at the train station and decides to forget about this job. That's easier said than done when a thug arrives at his place a couple nights later and beats the hell out of Krag, explaining that the ransom money they received was marked bills from a bank robbery six months before. So, who's the kidnapper's true identity? Mr. or Mrs. Jackbridge? The premise draws the reader in but the wrap-up is weak.

"The Payment is Death" by John E. Cameron (3000 words)★★

Explosives expert/mafia hitman Jack Colmar does a number on his boss, Sam Effron and, suddenly, he's at the top of Effron's "kill list." Jack is about to be iced when he's saved by the righthand man of Effron's rival, Ned Lattic. Colmar is "persuaded" to kill his old boss but he knows as soon as the job is over, Lattic will put him six feet under.

Vol. 13 No. 6 Dec 1965

Last appearance of Robert Patrick Wilmot, the longest-running author with original stories, the first of which appeared in the third issue.

"Means to an End" by Robert Edmond Alter (5000 words)★★★
In the early days of the Wall. a conscience proves to be a sympathetic guard's undoing. Though "Means to an End" is certainly a thoughtful drama, *Manhunt* seems to be a strange place for the story to have been placed; perhaps *The Saturday Evening Post* would have been more appropriate.

"Do-Gooder" by Roy Carroll
(Reprint of "Wife Beater." See Vol. 1 No. 12)

"The Loyal" by Lawrence E. Orin (2500 words)★★★
June Bowman has been murdered, right in her own living room and next-door neighbor, Martha Donovan tells her husband, Mark, that she saw Mr. Bowman leave the house right about the time the police say June was bashed in the skull with one of her golf clubs. The news devastates Mark as he was having an affair with June but, as the day wears on, Mark becomes convinced that Martha found out about his adultery and murdered June. What appears to be a predictable soap opera/whodunit culminates in a satisfying double-twist.

"Collection" by Nelson Adcock (6500 words)★★↲
Myra Cade believes her brother-in-law is planning to kill her in order to gain her half of the family inheritance, an art collection worth millions. To prevent her untimely demise, she hires Oliver Short of the Cosmopolitan Detective Agency to act as a "bodyguard." Once Oliver looks into the case, he discovers that all is not what it seems to be with Mrs. Cade. Enjoyable mystery akin to an Agatha Christie short story, a whodunit with a few clever twists. Short is a likable character and would appear two more times in *Manhunt*.

"Man of the People" by Xavier San Luis Rey (4500 words)★★★↲
As Castro comes closer to overthrowing the Cuban government, factions within that government attempt desperate measures to win back the loyalty of the people. Senator Castanello meets with high-ranking military officers and puts forth a plan to bring down Castro, but the plot involves the murder of hundreds of innocents. The sideways coup seems to be going well until Castro's army takes over the palace and the Senator is burned to death by an angry mob. As with all of San Luis Rey's stories, "Man of the People" is more of a vignette or snippet of a bigger story; there's no real beginning, middle, or end, just powerful observations on Cuba circa early 1960s.

"A Second Chance" by C. G. Cunningham (3500 words)★★★↙

A hitchhiker is picked up by a beautiful motorist but his paradise turns to hell when the car is stopped by the local sheriff and the drifter is accused of murder. A sly and sexy short story with a noir twist.

"Two Grand and a Bullet" by Robert Patrick Wilmot
(Reprint of "The G-Notes." See Vol. 1 No. 4)

"The Nebulous Lover" by Jerry Hopkins (3000 words)★★

Alicia Bennett is found murdered in her apartment. The police suspect the man that Alicia had been involved with may have committed the deed but, the more they investigate, the closer they come to the realization that there was no man. Alicia invented a lover; spread men's clothing through the apartment, kept men's toiletries in the bathroom. But there was no man. So who murdered Alicia?

"Busman's Holiday" by Jerry Jacobson (3000 words)★★

Humorous tale about a con trying to clear his debts and, into his cell block walks a Grade-A baseball pitcher. Suddenly, the joint is buzzing about a tournament between cell blocks worth thousands. The day of the game, the pitcher pulls a prison break.

"To Each His Own" by Tom Cox (4000 words)★★

His old mob boss hot on his tail. Dixon packs his girl up and tries to leave the city but the showdown is inevitable. Standard mafia revenge yarn.

"Night Bus" by Don Lowry (4000 words)★★↙

Ex-con Ted Sloan is in the wrong place at the wrong time, waiting outside a bar for his girl, Nita, to get off work, when a robbery goes down in the neighborhood and an APB goes out for a man fitting his description. Knowing he won't get a fair shake, Ted decides to rob a supermarket and head out of town with his girl. Nita gets cold feet and heads back home, while Ted hops a flight to Los Angeles and goes on a crime spree. Ironically, just after being caught during a robbery, his name is cleared in the initial heist.

"Damn You, Die" by Jeremiah Sommers (5000 words)★★★

Harley and his uncle have built their farm up to be the most productive in the area, but now Uncle Hobart has taken a wife, Mercy, a girl nearly thirty years younger than himself and only a few years older than Harley. Inevitably, Harley and Mercy begin seeing each other out at the barn and Mercy lets on that Uncle Hobart has been a little creative during their evenings alone. Harley, jealous and angry, shoots his uncle in the throat, expecting to spend the rest of his life with Mercy. But Mercy has other plans. What starts out as just another reworking of a tired formula takes a detour and ends, satisfyingly, with a twist.

"Fraternity" by Frank Gay (2500 words)★
Our narrator tells us exactly how his brother came to die in a street fight.

The Best Stories of 1965

"The Specialists" by Ed Lacy (January)
"The Death Maker" by Nelson Adcock (May)
"Mata Seguro" by Xavier San Luis Rey (July)
"Lamster War" by Don Lowry (July)
"The Virile Image" by Gerald Pearce (September)
"Fair Exchange" by Patrick Sherlock (September)
"The Other Side" by Daniel De Paola (September)
"Means to an End" by Robert Edmond Alter (December)
"Man of the People" by Xavier San Luis Rey (December)
"A Second Chance" by C. G. Cunningham (December)

Vol. 14 No. 1 Feb/Mar 1966

First issue to use only line art and one spot color on cover. These would be used for the rest of the run of the magazine. Last appearance by Robert Edmond Alter who contributed six stories to the magazine.

"The Anonymous Body" by Nancy A. Black (6500 words)★★
When a woman's body is found in a grain silo, a small town photographer aids the local sheriff in ID'ing the victim. Inexplicably, when the girl is identified, her brother is arrested for the murder. This doesn't sit well with the photo-man and he digs deeper in order to get to the truth. Engaging and likable characters but the plot is pedestrian.

"Wrath" by Peter Brandt (3000 words)★★↵
Night club singer Cathy Rain is asked to dinner by three of the mob's finest. When she declines, they kidnap and rape her, and she ends up in a mental institution. Later, someone hunts down each man, one by one, and evens the score.

"The Last Fix" by Jack Belck (4000 words)★★
A young girl is brutally murdered and the sheriff tracks down the man responsible. When he finds him and locks him up, the young man smiles at the sheriff and tells him he'll plead insanity and avoid the death penalty. Knowing the kid is right, the sheriff stages a breakout and murders his prisoner. The finale's twist, that the kid was the sheriff's son, is ludicrous and unnecessary.

"The (Deadly) Ad-Man" by Hayes Rabon (1000 words)★★
Ralph's biggest account is Greater Airlines but after a horrific crash, no one wants to ride Greater anymore. Greater gives Ralph and his advertising staff one month to get the customers back or they'll ditch the company. Ralph uses his head and gets right to work.

"Deadly Star-Dust" by Larry Dane (8500 words)★↵
A stranger comes in to Sam's diner on the same day a bank was robbed down the road. When Sam learns the thief made off with twelve thousand, he begins to see dollar signs and concocts a plan to take the money away from the stranger.

"Predator" by Robert Edmond Alter (4000 words)★★★
Harris and Ramsay, two fish and game patrolmen go hunting a pair of deadly pumas in the Florida everglades, unaware that they are the hunted. Coz Tanner has sworn he'll get Harris for reporting him to the cops for poaching 'gators and, sure enough, the man is waiting in the reeds for the perfect chance.

"Murder, Though It Have No Tongue" by Maeva Park (3000 words)★ᛃ
Retired movie star Cora Ransome has opened a boarding house for fellow retired actors and actresses. Cora and the tenants live a quiet but happy life filled with memories and evening viewings of their old films. Then Conrad Dillingham, once a co-star of Cora's, enters the picture and requests a room at the "Mon Repos." Immediately, the elan turns to stress and Cora knows she has to do something quick.

"Stiff Competition" by Frank Sisk (8000 words)★★
Police Captain McFate investigates the shooting of harmless drunk, Tippy Welinski. What does the shooting have to do with *Evening Express* obituary editor, Martin Mulcahy, and mobster Anthony Iacobucci? There's not much action and the hook is a bit too complicated. "Stiff Competition" is slow and padded but it does have a clever twist ending.

"In Self Defense" by Richard Deming
(Reprint of "Mugger Murder." See Vol. 1 No. 4)

"The 'N' Man" by Don Lowry (10,500 words)★★
Undercover narcotics agent Chris Padgett goes after the biggest fish in the West Coast heroin trade, Karl Gortoff, by gaining the trust of the drug king and becoming his right hand man. Limp, uneventful, and lacking his usual flourish, "The 'N' Man" is Don Lowry's weakest *Manhunt* work; though it's set in Lowry's fictional universe (for the third time, a drug man's surname is Bello), the author doesn't seem to have much interest this time out.

"Past Imperfect" by Frank Gay (1000 words)★ᛃ
Widget recognizes the doctor's wife as the stripper he once had a crush on. He approaches the woman, telling her he doesn't want money, simply a roll in the hay. If he doesn't get what he wants, he'll go public. Widget has picked the wrong woman to blackmail.

"The Anniversary Murder" by Craig Rice
(Reprint of "The Tears of Evil." See Vol. 1 No. 3)

Vol. 14 No. 2 Apr/May 1966

Only appearance by Michael Collins under his Dennis Lynds pseudonym with the story "Viking Blood," which would serve as the basis for the novel Act of Fear, that appeared the following year.

"Scandal Anyone?" by Frank Gay (2000 words)★★↲
Reporter Tom Ballard convinces his editor to go front-page with a bombshell report on political shenanigans perpetrated by the city's mayor. The special edition hits the stands and the *Banner*'s publisher quickly discovers the story is bogus. Why would Tom drag the paper through the wringer?

"The Proof is In" by S. K. Snedegar (2500 words)★★
Methodical accountant Harry Pulver believes his wife is having an affair so he uses his intricate skills to murder her.

"The Hand" by Charles A. Freylin (5000 words)★
A group of female nurses play a trick on a fellow employee, using an amputated hand, but the prank backfires.

"The Lonesome Bride" by Nelson Adcock (12,000 words)★★★
Susan McCrory wakes up in the hotel she's staying at with her husband on their honeymoon and finds no John McCrory. She inquires at the desk but they answer that they never saw a Mr. McCrory and the same question elicits the same answer from anyone else she encountered in the small town bordering Mexico. When a trip to the local sheriff brings her no satisfaction, Susan calls the Cosmopolitan Detective Agency and they send up their best man, Oliver Short.
Short suspects something's up immediately (everyone around him is acting "cagey") but he can't figure out why one unimportant musician named John McCrory would warrant such a cover-up. The more Short digs though, the more dirt is uncovered. Oliver Short's sophomore case is a delight, taking what appears to be a standard plot and adding several layers of mystery and intrigue. It's a shame Adcock never applied himself (and Short) to novel-length fiction as his personable P.I. (who manages to avoid most of the P.I. clichés) might have proved to be most popular.

"Southern Comfort" by Shirley Dunbar (1500 words)★
Laurie Lee just loves her country estate but her husband prefers their city apartment so Lauri Lee poisons his tea. No more discussion.

"Needle Street" by J. Kenneth O'Street (3000 words)★★★
Jim and Carol are in love and they experiment with everything, including sex and drugs. But then Carol's habit gets out of hand and Jim has to deal horse to pay for her habit. Carol's supposed to be Jim's lookout, to let him know when the

narcs are nosing around, but Carol starts hooking instead, leaving Jim vulnerable. When he goes up for three years, the fantasy that holds him together is strangling his wife. When he makes parole, Jim goes looking for his wife and finds her on Needle Street. A nasty, no-holds-barred slice of drug life, with a jarring final scene.

"A Deadly Secret" by Beatrice S. Smith (8500 words)★↲

Marta Hale begins her new job as school secretary but discovers that her predecessor met with an untimely end. Putting her amateur sleuth hat on, Marta begins grilling her co-workers and neighbors, attempting to find out if poor Aggie Drury committed suicide or was murdered. A swirling cocktail of *Peyton Place*-esque soap opera and mystery that never quite gels. The reveal is head-scratching.

"Double Damned" by C. G. Cunningham (3500 words)★★★

A young couple plot the death of the girl's mother. A nasty gem with a brilliantly dark final sentence.

"City Cop" by Jack Belck (2000 words)★

A cop means to spend a peaceful weekend at his country cabin but a knock on his door at three a.m. bring him into a local murder investigation. The outcome is wholly predictable.

"An Angle on Death" by Roy Carroll
(Reprint of "Shakedown." See Vol. 1 No. 4)

"Viking Blood" by Dennis Lynds (14,000 words)★★★

One-armed P.I. "Slot Machine" Kelly is almost elbowed into the case of Jo-Jo Olsen, a very popular boy in the neighborhood who disappears shortly after the mugging of a beat cop. The cops suspect Jo-Jo of the mugging and also of murder, but Kelly believes the boy was on the straight-and-narrow and he aims to prove it.

Well-paced and involving, "Viking Blood" was the 13th and final "Slot Machine" Kelly story and the only one to appear in the pages of *Manhunt*. The other tales all appeared in *Mike Shayne's Mystery Magazine*. Dennis Lynds was a pseudonym for author Michael Collins, who used Kelly as a prototype for his very popular Dan Fortune series.

Vol. 14 No. 3 Jun/Jul 1966
All but two original stories are by first-time contributors.

"Leopard Man" by Russell W. Lake (6500 words)★★⌐
When an American woman is viciously murdered in the Congo, a news magazine sends reporter David McKenzie in to investigate a strange cult called "The Society of Leopard Men." McKenzie encounters interference right from the get-go, surviving a knife attack but, with the help of a local cop, our hero gets his story.
Author Lake does a superb job of evoking the atmosphere of a "shudder pulp," with "Leopard Man" teetering between horror story and adventure.

"Sin of Omission" by Pat Airey (5500 words)★★★
Fashion designer Claire Paterson, in London to pick up her canine, accidentally cuts open her hand. The hotel manager suggests a G.P. down the road and Claire calls upon him with her little dog. While the doctor is bandaging the woman's hand, the dog is violently scratching at rolls of carpet in the doctor's hall. Hand bandaged, Claire leaves for Paris.
Months later, Claire is visited in Paris by a Scotland Yard detective, explaining that the kindly doctor has been arrested and is on trial for murdering his wife. Claire is asked to testify about her morning at the physician's. A slow but clever little cozy, "Sin of Omission" is that rarity in short crime fiction: a murder mystery where the act of violence actually takes a back seat to the characters.

"Ace in the Hole" by Don Lee (2500 words)★⌐
Attorney Waldo Schmidt is on trial for jury tampering but he's confident he'll win; he bribed this jury as well. Most of "Ace in a Hole" reads like a trial summation; only the final line brings a smile.

"Bloody Reformation" by Grover Brinkman (3000 words)★★★
Four young boys pick the wrong day to kill hornets out at the abandoned swamp church. While they're having their fun, in walks a badly-wounded man who hands them a sack of money and tells them to go fetch his friends. While they're gone, the dying man rigs a bomb in the church as a welcome for his partners. Very atmospheric and involving, "Bloody Reformation" begs to be expanded to novella length.
Though Grover Brinkman had dozens of stories published in the "lower-tier" crime digests such as *Off Beat* ("Hell's Lovely Gravedigger!"), *Web Detective* ("Bodies Won't Sink!"), and *Two-Fisted* ("My Love's a Tramp!"), this was Brinkman's only story for *Manhunt*.

"Deadly Outpost" by Robert Armpriest (5000 words)★★★

On a desolate island in the Pacific during World War II, a bomb in the mess hall during the officers' meal makes Sgt. Nelson Atkins the number one man on the base. Was the terrorism courtesy of the Japanese or was this an inside job? A suspenseful adventure tale.

"Tough Chippie" by Jonathan Craig
(Reprint of "The Quiet Room." See Vol. 1 No. 12)

"A Widow's Word" by George B. Scanlan (3500 words)★★

Fresh out of jail, Blake Canslow receives a letter from his sister-in-law, Lillian, inviting Blake to come live with her and Blake's brother, Matt. But Blake knows something's up immediately when Matt gives him a less than brotherly welcome. At least Lillian is more than affectionate towards her brother-in-law, that is until Matt turns up dead. Standard "black widow" tale, with no surprising twists.

"The Conspirators" by Robert Street Aldrich (3000 words)★★⅃

Bank teller Bert Wilson meets ex-con Gus Hunniker and the two men strike up an immediate friendship. Gus draws Bert into his life of betting on horses and high-stakes poker games and, before he knows it, Bert is in debt to some very shady characters. But, luckily, Gus has a plan handy: he'll rob Bert on a Friday when they'll be sure to make enough to erase Bert's debts. The job goes well except for one minor detail: the female teller next to Bert who takes in every detail but will keep quiet, providing she's the next Mrs. Wilson.

"Twice a Patsy" by Floyd Mahannah
(Reprint of "The Hero." See Vol. 2 No. 10)

"The Matriarch" by James B. Kittell (2500 words)★

Amelia Wentworth has written a slightly fictionalized version of her wealthy, greedy family as a novel entitled "The Matriarch," and sent it off to a literary agent. As Amelia lies in bed, reading the agent's notes, she hears someone prowling outside her bedroom door. Could this be the final chapter she's been looking for?

"Graveyard Shift" by Henry Kane
(Reprint of "Precise Moment." See Vol. 2 No. 11)

"Missile Missing" by S. K. Snedegar (5000 words)★★

When a new experimental missile goes missing at the Vulcan Rocket Works, Inspector Truitt must weed out the guilty party from a host of scientists and management. There's an interesting plot here but it's buried under all the technical jargon.

Vol. 14 No. 4 Augt/Sep 1966

All but one original story are by first-time contributors. This issue, along with the Sep 1965 issue, had the most appearances (10) of authors who contributed only once to the magazine.

"A Weakness ... For Women" by Craig Rice
(Reprint of "Flowers to the Fair." See Vol. 2 No. 11)

"One Man's Meat" by Jif Frank (2000 words)★
A group of young thugs hitchhike a ride with a meek, quiet man. When the youths become too much, he pulls to the side of the road and shoots each one of them. Nothing original nor thought-provoking here.

"Reluctant Witness" by Duff Howard (7500 words)★↙
Using binoculars through his picture window, Mike Younger witnesses a murder in the canyon across from his house. Not wanting to be involved, Mike calls in anonymously to the local police chief but the cop recognizes his voice. The next day, a gruff state trooper comes calling at Mike's workplace and questions him, but Mike denies any knowledge of the call. When Mike threatens a call to his lawyer, the trooper heads out but returns the same night to continue his questioning with his fists. Only Mike is dumb enough not to get what the "twist" is in "Reluctant Witness."

"Venom" by Guy Gowen (6000 words)★
Dr. Davis suspects a deadly Strep virus is responsible for his patients dying shortly after common surgeries. Another first for *Manhunt*: a medical mystery, taking place mostly within hospital walls and containing loads of dry pharmaceutical terms.

"Baby ... Don't Cry" by Marie Elston Collamore (1500 words)★
When his wife becomes unstable after being told she cannot bear children, a man murders a couple and kidnaps their child. A miserable bit of nastiness.

"The Past is Dead" by Jonathan Craig
(Reprint of "Man From Yesterday." See Vol. 2 No. 9)

"The Hot One" by J. Robert Carroll (4500 words)★↙
Two strangers sit in a bar, shooting the bull about everything under the sun. A strange betting game ensues. "The Hot One" spends a lot of time setting up an event that is handled "off screen" on the final page. An interminable amount of unimportant dialogue bogs this story down.

"One Fingerprint" by Bob Russell (1500 words)★★
A Soviet defector is captured by Russians in Washington and faces a choice:

become a double-spy or die!

"Dude Sheriff" by Richard Hill Wilkinson (4500 words)★★⌐
Hank Douglas is sheriff in a town where the primary business is a dude ranch, and now one of the cowpunchers has been found dead, a bullet in his head. Who would have wanted to see Barney Aaron dead? As Hank investigates, the question is: who *wouldn't* want to see the man dead? This contemporary western is an entertaining read but the *who* in whodunit is easy to guess.

Richard Hill Wilkinson wrote quite a few stories for the pulps before gravitating towards radio scripts for shows such as *Murder is My Hobby*. Wilkinson returned to print in the early 1960s with a series of stories for *Alfred Hitchcock's*; "Dude Sheriff" was his only *Manhunt* appearance.

"Killer Instinct" by David Chandler
(Reprint of "The Coyote." See Vol. 1 No. 12)

"Frustration" by Ruth Aldrich Gray (1500 words)★
Mary's life is coming apart; her marriage is quickly unraveling and her doctor wants her committed. The solution, she decides, is to shoot her husband in the head.

"Blonde Bait" by Norm Kent (4000 words)★★
A charter boat Captain gets pulled into a deadly heroin smuggling ring. Charles Williams-lite.

"The Deceiver" by Lawrence Orin (2000 words)★
An accident leaves Laura Jamison temporarily paralyzed and confined to a wheelchair. Growing comfortable with the attention, she doesn't want to let her husband, Don, know when her ability to walk returns. Then the notorious rapist/murderer terrorizing her town attempts to come through Laura's bedroom window, while Don is at work, and she belts him with a bowling trophy. Don seems genuinely concerned about the close call until, later that week, when the couple head for their cabin in the woods and author Lawrence Orin introduces a clichéd and silly reveal.

"Big Score" by Don Lowry (2000 words)★★⌐
Amusing comedy starring two very inept bank robbers.

"The Hard Way" by C. Durbin (5500 words)★★★
On his way to dinner, a wealthy businessman picks up a vagrant on the street and treats him to a meal. The two men tell each other about their lives. Essentially a 4,000-word monologue with bumpers, "The Hard Way" is a compelling tale, even though it lacks the requisite chases, molls, or murders.

Peter Enfantino • Jeff Vorzimmer

Vol. 14 No. 5 Oct/Nov 1966

All but one—Nelson Adcock's last appearance with an Oliver Short story—are original stories by first-time contributors. Four of the stories are reprints from previous issues.

"Fernando's Return" by Vic Hendrix (2500 words)★★

Carmelita awaits the return of her beloved husband, Fernando, who's otherwise engaged with another woman in the neighboring town. Carmelita does not want to believe the rumors but must face facts when Fernando comes home, tail between his legs, to ask for more money from his wife. Hell hath no fury and all that.

"Obie's Girl" by Fletcher Flora
(Reprint of "Two Little Hands." See Vol. 2 No. 10)

"The Prisoner" by David Daheim (9500 words)★★✓

In Belgium, at the onset of the Battle of the Bulge, German spies have been infiltrating Allied forces in a small town called Romain. The spies, dressed as American soldiers are being rounded up, tried, and executed but one prisoner raises flags. Lt. Thomas is sure the young man (who has a German accent but a very good backstory) may be a deserter, but not a spy. Colonel Simms orders the man shot immediately but Thomas begs his Colonel to allow the man a proper trial. The Colonel agrees but orders Thomas to be the prisoner's counsel. A rare *Manhunt* period piece, "The Prisoner" has an engrossing set-up, with some excellent twists but, in the end, it's a tad too contrived and complicated.

"A Friend of a Friend" by Morris F. Baughman (1000 words)★

Two men on a plane discuss a bank robbery. One of them is the thief.

"Bomb Scare" by Robert Slaughter (8000 words)★

A maniac has mailed bomb threats to three utility companies and a bank president. Lt. Johnny Stain of the Bomb Squad disagrees with his Captain that the sender is crazy. Some sixth sense tells Johnny there's something else at work here. Then the bank president gets blown to bits in his Caddy and the man's son-in-law is the prime suspect. Could this dolt have been smart enough to rig a complicated explosive? If "Bomb Scare" weren't so damned serious, it could almost be perceived as parody (with Johnny Stain being one of the most unfortunate monikers in crime literature), but its smart-assed lead character and ludicrous twist ending are hard to bear.

"Two Weeks with Pay" by Ernest Chamberlain (2500 words)★

Frank Wichita "borrows" a hundred grand from his bank, murders his shrewish wife, and heads out for two weeks of vacation—all expenses paid.

"Sitting Duck" by Robert Turner
(Reprint of "A Life for a Life." See Vol. 2 No. 10)

"Willful Murder" by Harold Q. Masur
(Reprint of "Dead Issue." See Vol. 2 No. 11)

"The Misplaced Star" by Nelson Adcock (20,500 words)★★
When Chief Harry Zorn has a particularly rough case handed to the Cosmopolitan Detective Agency, he counts on Oliver Short to come through. But Oliver is on his way out the door to vacation and only the juicier aspects of this case (and a $500 bonus) keep Short from hopping a plane. World class physicist Luigi Boltini (author of the famous theory on calculating the changing parameters of complex interrelated fields) has misplaced his wife, #1 international movie star, Maria Tarella, and he fears something untoward has occurred. Unlike the previous Oliver Short mysteries, "The Misplaced Star" (Short's final adventure) is overlong, slow, and unengaging.

"All the Loose Women" by Jonathan Craig
(Reprint of "The Dead Darling." See Vol. 2 No. 8)

Vol. 14 No. 6 Dec 1966/Jan 1967
Seven stories in this issue are by authors appearing for the first time.

"Hot Pilot" by Alex Pong (4500 words)★
Annoying, near-soft core nonsense about a flight school owner whose wife is sleeping with all his pilots.

"The Recluse" by James R. Franz (2000 words)★
Two men run out of gas in Henry Tate's driveway. The old miser only has his vicious dogs to keep him company and never has anyone round. After grilling the strangers, Tate allows them to stay the night but the newcomers have something up their sleeve.

"Alacran" by Jack Kelsey (5500 words)★★✓
A pompous retired American living in a small Mexican village tangles with a scorpion and his ex-gardener. The two might be related.

"Ricochet" by W. Sherwood Hartman (3000 words)★★✓
A businessman believes his new son-in-law is out to kill him in order to inherit the family business. Since he has no proof, he rigs a trap in order to catch the young man out. Though the climax leaves a few questions unanswered, the twist is very effective.

"A Time to Live" by Vic Hendrix (8000 words)★
Anna Rankin discovers that her abusive husband, Zack, has been spending time with a stripper who lives in town. To add insult to injury, Zack decides to build a small house on the farm, paid for with Anna's money, in order for his mistress to live closer to him. Anna will not take this lying down.

"Love, a Thief and Salvation" by Xavier San Luis Rey (2000 words)★★
Jose Sosa has no idea how his money keeps disappearing from his apartment and his fiancé won't marry Jose until he's earned enough for both of them to be comfortable. Not even a new door and window can stop what seems to be a ghostly thief. The true thief is quite a bit more down to earth. Final (and weakest) *Manhunt* contribution by San Luis Rey.

"Whiz Cop" by Jim Robinson (1000 words)★
Two old friends who haven't seen each other since school meet on the train one day. In small conversation, it's revealed that one is a cop assigned to pickpocket duty. The other, we discover as the story ends, is a grifter who just picked his buddy's pocket.

"Sucker Play" by Wilfred C. Vroman (2500 words)★★★
A kindly man, helping a down-on-her-luck young lady and her son, becomes

the victim of a con game. Or is it the other way around? Funny short with a clever twist.

"Lust or Honor" by William Vance
(Reprint of "Clean Getaway." See Vol. 2 No. 8)

"Burst of Glory" by Joseph Brophy (2000 words) ★★★

Poor, forgetful Irving Murphy loses his job, his wife, and his self-respect. Deciding to kill himself and take several others along with him, Irving types up suicide notes to be mailed, just before the big event, to all the major newspapers and steals 60 pounds of dynamite. He lugs the suitcase filled with TNT to Grand Central Station and settles back, confident that the next day his name will be known throughout the land. Just as the bomb goes off, Irving sees his letters, the ones he forgot to mail, tumble out of his briefcase. Hilarious and ironic, "Burst of Glory" is a welcome gem amongst the overly serious crime dramas.

"Kill Him for Me" by John G. Allen (10,000 words) ★✒

A lovely lass named Laura offers to pay British P.I. Frank McGrath one thousand pounds to kill her blackmailer. McGrath declines but is contacted by the woman a couple weeks later after the blackmailer's demands have increased. McGrath agrees to investigate and what he finds is a perverted world of prostitution and dirty old rich men. "Kill Him For Me" is a rarity, a British hardboiled tale that evokes the 1950s, but *that* might be its main problem. The tale never seems to work up any originality, instead coming off as a thinly-veiled rip-off of Spillane's Mike Hammer, over a decade after that formula had run its course.

"Death on the Make" by Ort Louis (9000 words) ★

Linc Keller comes into possession of a very valuable apartment building and now someone wants Linc dead. Is it his former boss, Steve Black, who's behind the hit? An unintelligible mess, jammed full of bad crime clichés and heaving breasts.

"Death in the Mirror" by Lee Russell (2500 words) ★

Ridiculous "thriller" about a woman terrorized by a goon she helped put in prison years before.

Vol. 15 No. 1 Feb/Mar 1967

Last story by Don Lowry who contributed 14 stories to the magazine and also the last appearance by future inventor, Alex Pong, who made his first of four contributions to Manhunt in the Dec 1962 issue at the age of 22.

"Big Time Carly" by Ernest Chamberlain (5000 words)★★
Carly Bryan was tough the moment he was born. Father murdered by a rival moonshiner, mother a whore, and Carly robbing grocery stores at the age of twelve. Then Carly falls in love with Sally, a prostitute who works at Rosie's, and proposes to her. He believes his life is going to change. "Big Time Carly" is one tough read, more like a reading of a "priors" sheet than a flowing narrative. By the end, the reader wonders, "why bother?"

"No Riders" by Shirley Dunbar (1000 words)★
A traveling salesman picks up a girl on a backwoods highway and immediately regrets it.

"Dog Days" by Clayton Matthews (5000 words)★★★
Ex-baseball player Jerry Hand is now a semi-P.I.; he investigates small matters but doesn't like to identify himself as a detective. A woman approaches Jerry with a job: someone shot her dog while robbing her liquor store. She loved her dog and she wants to know who the guy was, really bad. "Dog Days" is an amiable, near-cozy, mystery with a likable central character, and what almost seems to be a game-by-game commentary on the 1965 World Series as background noise.

"Fair Game" by Russell B. Rohde (2500 words)★★
Tension between a city man, and his guide, while hunting for big game in Africa.

"Indian Giver" by Harold Q. Masur
(Reprint of "Richest Man in the Morgue." See Vol. 1 No. 12)

"Breakout" by John G. Allen (10,500 words)★
P.I. Frank McGrath investigates the murder of his old partner in this awful British whodunit, a pastiche of every tough guy P.I. cliché *Manhunt* ever published. Absolute bottom-of-the-barrel.

"The Fifty Grand Stretch" by Richard Marsten
(Reprint of "Switch Ending." See Vol. 1 No. 12)

"Modus Operandi" by Edward Y. Breese (3000 words)★✓
Pop and his buddy are convinced the drunk upstairs is the guy who robbed the

local bank and killed two tellers. Now how do they prove it?,

"Hot Wheels" by Don Lowry (4500 words)★★⌐
Burns and Ray have a great gig, running hot cars across the border into Mexico, but cockiness leads to their downfall.

"Out on a Wing" by Alex Pong (4500 words)★★
A stunt pilot falls in love with an ex-beauty queen. "Out on a Wing" is a readable story but it is, by no means, a *Manhunt* story. There's a fistfight and some crude language and that's about as criminal as it gets.

"The Party Line" by E. F. Golden (3000 words)★
Years ago, Clem refused to get off the party line even though poor Lettie had to get a doctor out to her place for her sick baby. The child died and Lettie came after Clem with a butcher knife. Her first attempt was foiled by the police but now, years later, Lettie has escaped the asylum and is coming for Clem. "The Party Line" seems to take forever to get to an unsatisfying finish.

"Impulse" by Paul Curtis
(Reprint of "Banker's Trust." See Vol. 12 No. 6)

"Golden Opportunity" by Clayton Matthews (4000 words)★★⌐
When Mr. Fairchild falls under the wheels of a truck, George Reardon becomes bank manager, which makes George's plans to embezzle thousands that much easier. With "Dog Days" and "Golden Opportunity," Clayton Matthews becomes the only author ever to have two stories in a single issue of *Manhunt* under the same name. Matthews became a regular in *Alfred Hitchcock* and *Mike Shayne* throughout the 1960s and 70s, with several of the better *Shayne* stories collected in *Hager's Castle* (Powell, 1969).

Peter Enfantino • Jeff Vorzimmer

Vol. 15 No. 2 Apr/May 1967

Fittingly an Evan Hunter story appears in this, the last issue, albeit with a reprint of an earlier story. Although he contributed 46 stories in all, not a single original story of his appeared in the 1960s.

"Bad Blood" by John Ross Macdonald
(Reprint of "Guilt-Edged Blonde." See Vol. 1 No. 5)

"A Good Man is Hard to Find" by Lawrence E. Brin
(1000 words)★↲
Martha watches out the kitchen window as her husband digs a grave for his beloved dog. She never meant to kill the mongrel but he'd made her very angry. Soon, Martha wonders why her husband is digging such a big hole.

"The Lesson" by Gene Wilson (4000 words)★★
When seventeen-year-old Paul Morrow heists a car with his friends and gets busted, his father refuses to bail him out, instead opting to teach his son a "lesson." Paul gets to know his new cellmates intimately. "The Lesson" was probably considered risqué and harrowing in 1967 but fifty years later it's tame and predictable.

"Blow-Up" by Jack Lynch (3500 words)★
Someone has blown photographer Ronnie Haspurtin to kingdom come with a whole lot of dynamite. Could it be due to the sleazy pictures Ronnie's been selling of underage girls in various stages of undress?

"Flood" by Jackson Bowling (4500 words)★
Tension runs high when some bad guys try to take over a small diner during a driving rainstorm. Interminably long and talky.

"The Scavengers" by J. Bachman (4000 words)★★★
Special agent Castle is sent to an airplane crash site in the woods of Pennsylvania to recover an attaché case containing top secret government papers. His boss thinks the plane was downed by enemy agents who might be sifting through the wreckage at that very moment. Castle gets to the site but discovers the plane has been ransacked by scavengers. Assuming it's someone local, Castle enlists a couple of deputies to help him search the nearby farms. He finds the scavenger but so does the enemy agent. An exciting espionage story, with an involving plot and a charismatic lead character, let down only by a rushed and predictable climax.

"The Lucky Prey" by Dale L. Gilbert (3000 words)★★★
After much practice, Harry is convinced he's got a formula for winning at the roulette table. He heads to Vegas and, sure enough, wins eleven grand. Problem is,

he becomes the target of every goon in town; Harry can't make it to the airport to save his life. Very grim action tale.

"The Dead Undertaker" by Craig Rice
(Reprint of "Murder Marches On!" See Vol. 1 No. 12)

"The Cool One" by George Antonich (2500 words)★★⌐
Claude Johnson discovers his gorgeous wife is having an affair so he cracks her over the head with a cake of ice. Turns out Claude may have discovered the perfect murder weapon as, when the cops show up, they're perplexed! A variation on Roald Dahl's "Lamb to the Slaughter," but enjoyable nonetheless.

"Circumstantial Evidence" by Hunt Collins
(Reprint of "Sucker." See Vol. 1 No. 12)

"Two-Sided Triangle" by Larry Dane (3000 words)★
Pedestrian tale of a man who discovers his wife is having an affair so he kills her with his bowling ball. A unique weapon but not a standout story.

"The Snatchers" by M. G. Wesleder (17,000 words)★
Two ex-cons kidnap the daughter of a wealthy doctor and lock her in an abandoned building in San Francisco. Through ingenuity (and a lot of coincidences), the girl is able to alert the FBI to her predicament and they swoop in to save her. Very long and padded, "The Snatchers" has a lot of wrong steps: the dialogue is, at times, childish, the set-up is ridiculous, and there's no sense that this girl is in any kind of danger. It's hard to believe a story this bad and this long could have been stamped "Fit to Publish" by a capable editor.

"No Fair" by B. J. Starr (1500 words)★★
Mr. Carver is held up in his office by a mystery man who seems to know quite a lot about him. Carver is ordered to open his wall safe and then he recognizes the thief as someone who danced with his wife at a party. Suddenly, the picture becomes very clear. "No Fair" is a fun quickie but it contains a twist too many.

"Buddies" by Herbert Leslie Greene (2000 words)★★★
After a gas station stick-up goes south and buddy Hap is gut-shot, Curt has to drive them as far away from the city as he can. His thoughts see-saw from how much he loves this dying man in his backseat to how he wishes Hap would just die already. Grim and tinged with black comedy, "Buddies" is an excellent short-short and a fitting way to close out *Manhunt*'s run.

Peter Enfantino • Jeff Vorzimmer

The Best Stories of 1966/67

"Predator" by Robert Edmond Alter (February/Mar 1966)
"The Lonesome Bride" by Nelson Adcock (April/May 1966)
"Needle Street" by J. Kenneth O'Street (April/May 1966
"Deadly Outpost" by Robert Armpriest (June/Jul 1966)
"Bloody Reformation" by Grover Brinkman (June/Jul 1966)
"The Hard Way" by C. Durbin (August/Sep 1966)
"Burst of Glory" by Joseph Brophy (Dec 1966/Jan 1967)
"Dog Days" by Clayton Matthews (February/Mar 1967)
"Buddies" by Herbert Leslie Greene (April/May 1967)
"The Scavengers" by J. Bachman (April/May 1967)

Stories and Articles by Issue

Key for Story/Article Types BR=book review, MR=movie review, NA=novella, NV=novelette, SF=special feature, SS=short story, TC=true crime, PZ=puzzle, QZ=quiz and RP=reprint.

Jan 1953	v. 1 n. 1	35¢	144 Pages	Editor: John McCloud	
Story/Article	**Pg Series**	**Author**	**Pseudonym**	**Type**	
Everybody's Watching Me [Part 1 of 4]	1	Mickey Spillane		NA	
Die Hard	16 Matt Cordell	Evan Hunter		SS	
I'll Make the Arrest	30	Charles Boeckman	Charles Beckman, Jr.	SS	
The Hunted	39	Cornell Woolrich	William Irish	NV	
The Best Motive	59 Shell Scott	Richard S. Prather		SS	
Shock Treatment	71	Kenneth Millar		SS	
The Frozen Grin	81 Johnny Liddell	Frank Kane		SS	
Backfire	98	Floyd Mahannah		NV	
The Set-Up	142	Stanley L. Colbert	Sam Cobb	SS	

Feb 1953	v. 1 n. 2	35¢	144 Pages	Editor: John McCloud	
Story/Article	**Pg Series**	**Author**	**Pseudonym**	**Type**	
The Imaginary Blonde	1 Lew Archer	Kenneth Millar	John Ross Macdonald	NV	
Sex Murder in Cameron	28	Michael Fessier		SS	
Dirge for a Nude	37	Frank E. Smith	Jonathan Craig	SS	
Stabbing in the Streets	51 David Wiley	Eleazar Lipsky		SS	
Carrera's Woman	65	Evan Hunter	Richard Marsten	SS	
Attack	77	Evan Hunter	Hunt Collins	SS	
Everybody's Watching Me [Part 2 of 4]	81	Mickey Spillane		NA	
So Dark for April	94 Paul Pine	Howard Browne	John Evans	NV	
The Lesser Evil	113 Manville Moon	Richard Deming		SS	
As I Lie Dead	131	Fletcher Flora		SS	

Mar 1953	v. 1 n. 3	35¢	144 Pages	Editor: John McCloud	
Story/Article	**Pg Series**	**Author**	**Pseudonym**	**Type**	
The Sleeper Caper	1 Shell Scott	Richard S. Prather		NV	
Dead Men Don't Dream	21 Matt Cordell	Evan Hunter		SS	
Stop Him!	34	Bruno Fischer		SS	
Triple-Cross	46	Robert Patrick Wilmot		SS	
The Loaded Tourist	55 The Saint	Leslie Charteris		NV	
Payoff	71 Johnny Liddell	Frank Kane		SS	
The Tears of Evil	85 John J. Malone	Georgiana Craig	Craig Rice	SS	
The Mourning After	95 Scott Jordan	Harold Q. Masur		SS	
Everybody's Watching Me [Part 3 of 4]	107	Mickey Spillane		NA	
Teaser	118	William Lindsay Gresham		SS	
Prognosis Negative	129	Floyd Mahannah		SS	
Against the Middle	140	Evan Hunter	Richard Marsten	SS	

Apr 1953	v. 1 n. 4	35¢	144 Pages	Editor: John McCloud	
Story/Article	**Pg Series**	**Author**	**Pseudonym**	**Type**	
One Little Bullet	1 Peter Chambers	Henry Kane		NV	

Peter Enfantino • Jeff Vorzimmer   295

Story/Article	Pg	Series	Author	Pseudonym	Type
Big Talk	31		Kris Neville		SS
Be My Guest	39		Robert Turner		SS
Fan Club	48	Steve Drake	Richard Ellington		SS
Shakedown	57		Robert Turner	Roy Carroll	SS
The G-Notes	65		Robert Patrick Wilmot		NV
Mugger Murder	85		Richard Deming		SS
Kid Kill	93		Evan Hunter		SS
Crime and Punishment	100		Shepherd Kole		SF
The Blue Sweetheart	102		David Goodis		NV
Everybody's Watching Me [Part 4 of 4]	120		Mickey Spillane		NA

May 1953		**v. 1**	**n. 5**	**35¢**		**144 Pages**	**Editor: John McCloud**

Story/Article	Pg	Series	Author	Pseudonym	Type
The Guilty Ones	1	Lew Archer	Kenneth Millar	John Ross Macdonald	NV
Services Rendered	22		Frank E. Smith	Jonathan Craig	SS
Crime Cavalcade	32		Vincent H. Gaddis		C
Stakeout	35		Robert Patrick Wilmot		SS
Graveyard Shift	46		Steve Frazee		SS
Now Die in It	58	Matt Cordell	Evan Hunter		NV
Portrait of a Killer No. 01 — Warren Lincoln	83		Dan Sontup		F
Cigarette Girl	85		James M. Cain		SS
Nice Bunch of Guys	95		Michael Fessier		SS
Old Willie	101		William P. McGivern		SS
Build Another Coffin	107	Scott Jordan	Harold Q. Masur		SS
Manhunt's Movie of the Month: I Confess	120				AR
Don't Go Near	121	John J. Malone	Georgiana Craig	Craig Rice	NV
Assault	142		Grant Colby		SS

Jun 1953		**v. 1**	**n. 6**	**35¢**		**144 Pages**	**Editor: John McCloud**

Story/Article	Pg	Series	Author	Pseudonym	Type
Far Cry	1	Peter Chambers	Henry Kane		NV
Small Homicide	30		Evan Hunter		SS
Ybor City	40		Charles Boeckman	Charles Beckman, Jr.	SS
Manhunt's Movie of the Month: The Hitch-Hiker	51				MR
The Loyal One	52		Richard Deming		SS
The Faceless Man	64		Michael Fessier		SS
Crime Cavalcade	75		Vincent H. Gaddis		C
The Double Frame	78	Scott Jordan	Harold Q. Masur		SS
The Caller	90		Emmanuel Winters		SS
Hot-Rock Rumble	104	Shell Scott	Richard S. Prather		NV
One Down	142		Evan Hunter	Hunt Collins	SS

Jul 1953		**v. 1**	**n. 7**	**35¢**		**144 Pages**	**Editor: John McCloud**

Story/Article	Pg	Series	Author	Pseudonym	Type
The Wench Is Dead	1		Fredric Brown		NV
Quiet Day in the County Jail	23		Georgiana Craig	Craig Rice	SS

The Manhunt Companion

Story/Article	Pg	Series	Author	Pseudonym	Type
I'll Kill for You	34		Fletcher Flora		SS
Day's Work	44		Evan Hunter	Jonathan Lord	SS
Good and Dead	47	Matt Cordell	Evan Hunter		SS
Say Goodby to Janie	62		Bruno Fischer		NV
The Follower	83		Evan Hunter	Hunt Collins	SS
Crime Cavalcade	90		Vincent H. Gaddis		TC
I'm Getting Out	92		Elliot West		SS
Evidence	101	Johnny Liddell	Frank Kane		SS
Portrait of a Killer No. 02 — Charles Henry Schwartz	112		Dan Sontup		SF
The Double Take	114	Shell Scott	Richard S. Prather		NV
Heirloom	142		Arnold Marmor		SS

Aug 1953	**v. 1**	**n. 8**	**35¢**	**144 Pages**	**Editor: John McCloud**
Story/Article	**Pg**	**Series**	**Author**	**Pseudonym**	**Type**
The Collector Comes After Payday	1		Fletcher Flora		NV
Still Life	16		Evan Hunter		SS
The Little Lamb	27		Fredric Brown		SS
Slay Belle	37	Johnny Liddell	Frank Kane		SS
The Crime of My Wife	48		Robert Turner		SS
Portrait of a Killer No. 03 — Robert W. Buchanan, M.	56		Dan Sontup		SF
The End of Fear	58	John J. Malone	Georgiana Craig	Craig Rice	NV
Crime Cavalcade	76		Vincent H. Gaddis		TC
Less Perfect	81		Frances Carfi Matranga		SS
The Two O'Clock Blonde	84		James M. Cain		SS
The Ripper	92	Steve Drake	Richard Ellington		SS
Kayo	104		Roy Carroll	Roy Carroll	SS
Rhapsody in Blood	108	Scott Jordan	Harold Q. Masur		NV
Throwback	131		Donald Hamilton		SS
The Innocent One	140		Evan Hunter	Richard Marsten	SS

Sep 1953	**v. 1**	**n. 9**	**35¢**	**144 Pages**	**Editor: John McCloud**
Story/Article	**Pg**	**Series**	**Author**	**Pseudonym**	**Type**
The Death of Me	1	Matt Cordell	Evan Hunter		NV
Fair Game	26		Fletcher Flora		SS
What Am I Doing?	36		William Vance		SS
Accident Report	48		Evan Hunter	Richard Marsten	SS
Bonus Cop	59		Richard Deming		NV
Portrait of a Killer No. 04 — Chester Jordan	82		Dan Sontup		SF
The Motive	85		Erskine Caldwell		SS
Chase by Night	92		Jack M. Bagby		SS
The Millionth Murder	99		Ray Bradbury		NV
Crime Cavalcade	116		Vincent H. Gaddis		TC
The Molested	118		Evan Hunter	Hunt Collins	SS
Life Can Be Horrible	121	John J. Malone	Georgiana Craig	Craig Rice	NV
The Scrapbook	137		Frank E. Smith	Jonathan Craig	SS

Peter Enfantino • Jeff Vorzimmer

Oct 1953	v. 1 n. 10	35¢	144 Pages	Editor: John McCloud	
Story/Article	Pg	Series	Author	Pseudonym	Type
The Girl Behind the Hedge	1		Mickey Spillane		NV
Squeeze Play	12	Shell Scott	Richard S. Prather		SS
Balanced Account	24		Richard Deming		SS
Dead Heat	35		Robert Turner		SS
The Idiot	47		Harold Cantor		SS
Professional Man	54		David Goodis		NV
Crime Cavalcade	57		Vincent H. Gaddis		TC
Summer Is a Bad Time	81		Sam S. Taylor		SS
Response	93		Arnold Marmor		SS
Portrait of a Killer No. 05 — Louise Peete	97		Dan Sontup		SF
Where's the Money?	99		Floyd Mahannah		SS
The Beat-Up Sister	110	Lew Archer	Kenneth Millar	John Ross Macdonald	NV
The Bobby-Soxer	141		Frank E. Smith	Jonathan Craig	SS

Nov 1953	v. 1 n. 11	35¢	144 Pages	Editor: John McCloud	
Story/Article	Pg	Series	Author	Pseudonym	Type
The Big Touch	1	Peter Chambers	Henry Kane		NV
The Watcher	37		Peter Paige		SS
The Bells Are Ringing	42	John J. Malone	Georgiana Craig	Craig Rice	SS
Case History	52		Charles Boeckman	Charles Beckman, Jr.	SS
The Right Hand of Garth	62		Evan Hunter		SS
Crime Cavalcade	75		Vincent H. Gaddis		TC
Six Stories Up	81		Raymond Dyer		SS
Classification: Dead	87		Evan Hunter	Richard Marsten	SS
A Long Way to KC	100		Fletcher Flora		SS
Portrait of a Killer No. 06 — Pat Mahon	113		Dan Sontup		SF
Coney Island Incident	116		Bruno Fischer		NV
Kid Stuff	138		Frank E. Smith	Jonathan Craig	SS

Dec 1953	v. 1 n. 12	35¢	144 Pages	Editor: John McCloud	
Story/Article	Pg	Series	Author	Pseudonym	Type
Black Pudding	1		David Goodis		NV
Switch Ending	22		Evan Hunter	Richard Marsten	SS
Killing on Seventh Street	33		Charles Boeckman	Charles Beckman, Jr.	SS
Murder Marches On!	39	John J. Malone	Georgiana Craig	Craig Rice	SS
Sucker	51		Evan Hunter	Hunt Collins	SS
Portrait of a Killer No. 07 — Tillie Gburek	58		Dan Sontup		SF
The Wife of Riley	61		Evan Hunter		SS
Richest Man in the Morgue	81	Scott Jordan	Harold Q. Masur		SS
The Quiet Room	94		Frank E. Smith	Jonathan Craig	SS
The Coyote	102		David Chandler		SS
Wife Beater	108		Roy Carroll	Roy Carroll	SS
The Icepick Artists	117	Johnny Liddell	Frank Kane		NV

298   The Manhunt Companion

| Crime Cavalcade | 133 | | Vincent H. Gaddis | | TC |
| The Insecure | 138 | | R. Van Taylor | | SS |

Jan 1954	v. 2 n. 1	35¢	160 Pages	Editor: John McCloud	
Story/Article	**Pg**	**Series**	**Author**	**Pseudonym**	**Type**
Guilt-Edged Blonde	1	Lew Archer	Kenneth Millar	John Ross Macdonald	SS
The Six-Bit Fee	13	Manville Moon	Richard Deming		SS
Finish the Job	24	Johnny Liddell	Frank Kane		SS
Over My Dead Body	39	Scott Jordan	Harold Q. Masur		SS
The Wrong Touch	51	Peter Chambers	Henry Kane		NV
Crime Cavalcade	85		Vincent H. Gaddis		TC
And Be Merry	88	John J. Malone	Georgiana Craig	Craig Rice	SS
Pattern for Panic	91	Shell Scott	Richard S. Prather		NA

Feb 1954	v. 2 n. 2	35¢	144 Pages	Editor: John McCloud	
Story/Article	**Pg**	**Series**	**Author**	**Pseudonym**	**Type**
Runaway	1		Evan Hunter	Richard Marsten	NV
The Rope Game	26		Bryce Walton		SS
Deadlier Than the Mail	39	Matt Cordell	Evan Hunter		SS
The Disaster	52		Emmanuel Winters		SS
Crime Cavalcade	57		Vincent H. Gaddis		TC
I'm a Stranger Here Myself	60	John J. Malone	Georgiana Craig	Craig Rice	NV
Heels Are for Hating	83		Fletcher Flora		SS
The Murder Market	99		William A. P. White	H. H. Holmes	BR
The Onlooker	103		Robert Turner		SS
Comeback	107		R. Van Taylor		SS
Portrait of a Killer No. 08 — William Coffey	114		Dan Sontup		SF
Mr. Chesley	117		Robert Zacks		SS
Shadow Boxer	121	Steve Drake	Richard Ellington		NV
Holdup Man	136		Leonard S. Gray		PZ
The Man Who Found the Money	138		James E. Cronin		SS

May 1954	v. 2 n. 3	35¢	144 Pages	Editor: John McCloud	
Story/Article	**Pg**	**Series**	**Author**	**Pseudonym**	**Type**
The Blonde in the Bar	1		Richard Deming		NV
Murder of a Mouse	18		Fletcher Flora		SS
The Woman on the Bus	29		R. Van Taylor		SS
The Murder Market	41		William A. P. White	H. H. Holmes	BR
Broken Doll	45	Airport Detail	Jack Webb		NV
Portrait of a Killer No. 09 — Theodore Durrant	61		Dan Sontup		SF
... or Leave It Alone	64		Evan Hunter		SS
Crime Cavalcade	77		Vincent H. Gaddis		TC
Lead Ache	81	Johnny Liddell	Frank Kane		NV
The Right One	110		Frank E. Smith	Jonathan Craig	SS
Footprints	115		Fred L. Anderson		TC
The Old Flame	117		James T. Farrell		NV

Peter Enfantino • Jeff Vorzimmer

Story/Article	Pg	Series	Author	Pseudonym	Type
A Clear Picture	131		Sam S. Taylor		SS
You Know What I Did?	136		Charles Boeckman	Charles Beckman, Jr.	SS

Jun 1954	v. 2	n. 4	35¢	144 Pages	Editor: John McCloud	
Story/Article	**Pg**	**Series**	**Author**	**Pseudonym**	**Type**
Skip a Beat	1	Peter Chambers	Henry Kane		NA
Points South	43		Fletcher Flora		SS
My Enemy, My Father	53		John M. Sitan		SS
The Murder Market	58		Hal Walker	H. H. Holmes	BR
The Choice	62		Richard Deming		SS
Homicide, Suicide or Accident	76		Fred L. Anderson		TC
Double	82		Bruno Fischer		SS
Butcher	101	Shell Scott	Richard S. Prather		SS
Crime Cavalcade	111		Vincent H. Gaddis		TC
No Vacancies	114	John J. Malone	Georgiana Craig	Craig Rice	NV
Portrait of a Killer No. 10 — Rose Palmer	131		Dan Sontup		SF
Die Like a Dog	133		David Alexander		SS

Jul 1954	v. 2	n. 5	35¢	144 Pages	Editor: John McCloud	
Story/Article	**Pg**	**Series**	**Author**	**Pseudonym**	**Type**
Chinese Puzzle	1		Evan Hunter	Richard Marsten	NV
My Game, My Rules	14		John G. Reitci	Jack Ritchie	SS
Association Test	21		Evan Hunter	Hunt Collins	SS
Two Grand	25		Charles Boeckman	Charles Beckman, Jr.	SS
The Judo Punch	35		V. E. Thiessen		SS
Crime Cavalcade	39		Vincent H. Gaddis		TC
Sanctuary	42		W. W. Hatfield		SS
Return	47	Matt Cordell	Evan Hunter		SS
Portrait of a Killer No. 11 — Vernon Booher	60		Dan Sontup		SF
I Want a French Girl	63		James T. Farrell		NV
The Innocent	74		Muriel Berns		SS
Burglaries	78		Fred L. Anderson		TC
Confession	81		John M. Sitan		SS
Find a Victim	90	Lew Archer	Kenneth Millar	John Ross Macdonald	NA
Helping Hand	142		Arnold Marmor		SS

Aug 1954	v. 2	n. 6	35¢	144 Pages	Editor: John McCloud	
Story/Article	**Pg**	**Series**	**Author**	**Pseudonym**	**Type**
Identity Unknown	1		Frank E. Smith	Jonathan Craig	SS
Necktie Party	13		Robert Turner		SS
Crime Cavalcade	20		Vincent H. Gaddis		TC
The Old Man's Statue	23		R. Van Taylor		SS
Effective Medicine	31		B. Traven		NV
Accident	43		John M. Sitan		SS
I Don't Fool Around	50		Charles Jackson		SS
What's Your Verdict? No. 01 — The Cooperative Corp	59		Sam Ross		PZ

300   The Manhunt Companion

Story/Article	Pg	Series	Author	Pseudonym	Type
Frame	61	Johnny Liddell	Frank Kane		NV
Portrait of a Killer No. 12 — Jesse Walker	84		Dan Sontup		SF
And Share Alike	87		Charles Williams		NA
Yard Bull	141		Frank Selig		SS

Sep 1954	v. 2	n. 7	35¢	144 Pages	Editor: John McCloud
Story/Article	**Pg**	**Series**	**Author**	**Pseudonym**	**Type**
The Witness	1		John Sabin		SS
Bedbug	10		Evan Hunter		SS
State Line	14		Sam S. Taylor		NV
Night Watch	31		Frank E. Smith	Jonathan Craig	SS
What's Your Verdict? No. 02 — The Uncooperative Wi	43		Sam Ross		PZ
Tin Can	46		B. Traven		SS
Ambition	57		Patrick Madden		SS
Crime Cavalcade	61		Vincent H. Gaddis		TC
A Moment's Notice	64		Jerome Weidman		NV
Every Morning	88		Evan Hunter	Richard Marsten	SS
Some Things Never Change	93		Robert Patrick Wilmot		SS
Portrait of a Killer No. 13 — Leon Peltzer	101		Dan Sontup		SF
The Empty Fort	104		Basil Heatter		NA
The Promise	141		Richard Welles		SS

Oct 1954	v. 2	n. 8	35¢	144 Pages	Editor: John McCloud
Story/Article	**Pg**	**Series**	**Author**	**Pseudonym**	**Type**
The Beatings	1	Matt Cordell	Evan Hunter		SS
The Bargain	11		Charles Boeckman	Charles Beckman, Jr.	SS
Clean Getaway	20		William Vance		NV
Laura and the Deep, Deep Woods	35		William B. Hartley		SS
What's Your Verdict? No. 03 — The Drinking Man	41		Sam Ross		PZ
Second Cousin	44		Erskine Caldwell		SS
Love Affair	50		Richard Deming		SS
Lady Killer	57		Evan Hunter	Richard Marsten	SS
The Dead Darling	64	18th Precinct	Frank E. Smith	Jonathan Craig	NV
Crime Cavalcade	78		Vincent H. Gaddis		TC
That Stranger, My Son	81		C. B. Gilford		SS
One of a Kind	90		Ben Smith		SS
The Famous Actress	94		Harry Roskolenko		SS
Portrait of a Killer No. 14 — Albert Van Dyke	99		Dan Sontup		SF
Candlestick	102	Peter Chambers	Henry Kane		NA

Nov 1954	v. 2	n. 9	35¢	144 Pages	Editor: John McCloud
Story/Article	**Pg**	**Series**	**Author**	**Pseudonym**	**Type**
Pistol	1		Hal Ellson		NV
Replacement	12		John G. Reitci	Jack Ritchie	SS
Shy Guy	22		Robert Turner		SS
What's Your Verdict? No. 04 — The Anxious Friend	28		Sam Ross		PZ

Story/Article	Pg	Series	Author	Pseudonym	Type
Man from Yesterday	31		Frank E. Smith	Jonathan Craig	V
Crime Cavalcade	45		Vincent H. Gaddis		C
A Bull to Kill	47		Evan Hunter	Richard Marsten	S
The Stalkers	57		Grant Colby		S
Portrait of a Killer No. 15 — Joseph McElroy	61		Dan Sontup		F
The Wet Brain	64		David Alexander		V
The Man Who Had Too Much to Lose	84 Jeremiah X. Gibson		Aaron Marc Stein	Hampton Stone	A

Dec 1954   v. 2   n. 10   35¢   144 Pages   Editor: John McCloud

Story/Article	Pg	Series	Author	Pseudonym	Type
Pretty Boy	1		Hal Ellson		S
Two Little Hands	9		Fletcher Flora		S
The Red Tears	15	18th Precinct	Frank E. Smith	Jonathan Craig	V
To a Wax Doll	29		Arnold Marmor		S+
What's Your Verdict? No. 05 — The Angry Man	33		Sam Ross		Z
A Bachelor in the Making	36		Charles Jackson		S
A Life for a Life	42		Robert Turner		S
Twilight	49		Hal Harwood		S
For a Friend	53		Bob McKnight		S
Crime Cavalcade	57		Vincent H. Gaddis		C
The Hero	61		Floyd Mahannah		V
Diary of a Devout Man	76		Richard Deming	Max Franklin	S
Opportunity	85		Russell E. Bruce		S
The Housemother Cometh	87		Hayden Howard		S
Manslaughter	92		Henry Ewald		S
Portrait of a Killer No. 16 — Vernon Oldaker	95		Dan Sontup		F
Hit and Run	98		Richard Deming		A
No Half Cure	138		Robert E. Murray		S
Judgment	141		G. H. Williams		S

Dec 1954   v. 2   n. 11   35¢   144 Pages   Editor: John McCloud

Story/Article	Pg	Series	Author	Pseudonym	Type
Crime of Passion	1	Shell Scott	Richard S. Prather		S
The Purple Collar	11	18th Precinct	Frank E. Smith	Jonathan Craig	V
What's Your Verdict? No. 06 — The Young Lovebirds	27		Sam Ross		Z
Flowers to the Fair	29	John J. Malone	Georgiana Craig	Craig Rice	V
The Scarlet King	45		Evan Hunter		S
Crime Cavalcade	55		Vincent H. Gaddis		C
The Pickpocket	57		Mickey Spillane		S
Big Steal	61	Johnny Liddell	Frank Kane		V
Dead Issue	82	Scott Jordan	Harold Q. Masur		S
Death Sentence	93	Manville Moon	Richard Deming		S
Portrait of a Killer No. 17 — Arthur Eggers	105		Dan Sontup		F
Precise Moment	108	Peter Chambers	Henry Kane		A
YOU, Detective No. 01 — The Bathing Beauty	136		Wilson Harman		Z

302   The Manhunt Companion

Six Fingers	138		Hal Ellson		SS

Jan 1955	**v. 3 n. 1**	**35¢**	**144 Pages**	**Editor: John McCloud**	
Story/Article	**Pg**	**Series**	**Author**	**Pseudonym**	**Type**
The Killer	1		John D. MacDonald		NV
You Can't Trust a Man	14		Helen Nielsen		SS
May I Come In?	25		Fletcher Flora		SS
The Blood Oath	31	Manville Moon	Richard Deming		SS
Panic	43		Grant Colby		SS
The Floater	47		Frank E. Smith	Jonathan Craig	NV
Green Eyes	63		Hal Ellson		SS
Crime Cavalcade	73		Vincent H. Gaddis		TC
Morning Movie	77		Muriel Berns		SS
What's Your Verdict? No. 07 — The Loving Wife	81		Sam Ross		PZ
Epitaph	83		Erskine Caldwell		SS
YOU, Detective No. 02 — The Green Beard	89		Wilson Harman		QZ
The Drifter	91		Robert S. Swenson		SS
Portrait of a Killer No. 18 — Evan Thomas	96		Dan Sontup		SF
The Death-Ray Gun	100		Evan Hunter		NA
Kiss Me, Dudley	139		Evan Hunter	Hunt Collins	SS

Feb 1955	**v. 3 n. 2**	**35¢**	**144 Pages**	**Editor: John McCloud**	
Story/Article	**Pg**	**Series**	**Author**	**Pseudonym**	**Type**
The Revolving Door	1		Sam Merwin, Jr.		SS
Hot	12		Evan Hunter		SS
Return Engagement	25	Johnny Liddell	Frank Kane		NV
What's Your Verdict? No. 08 — The Legal Mind	45		Sam Ross		PZ
The Pigeons	47		Hal Ellson		SS
The Competitors	53		Richard Deming		SS
Rendezvous	64		James T. Farrell		NV
Crime Cavalcade	78		Vincent H. Gaddis		TC
Self-Defense	81	Scott Jordan	Harold Q. Masur		SS
Portrait of a Killer No. 19 — Herbert Mills	94		Dan Sontup		SF
Classification: Homicide	97	Police File	Frank E. Smith	Jonathan Craig	NA
YOU, Detective No. 03 — The Sweet Death	142		Wilson Harman		QZ

Mar 1955	**v. 3 n. 3**	**35¢**	**160 Pages**	**Editor: John McCloud**	
Story/Article	**Pg**	**Series**	**Author**	**Pseudonym**	**Type**
I Didn't See a Thing	1		Hal Ellson		NV
The Punisher	14	Police File	Frank E. Smith	Jonathan Craig	SS
What's Your Verdict? No. 09 — The Domestic Killer	29		Sam Ross		PZ
First Case	32		David Alexander		SS
Moonshine	42		Gil Brewer		SS
The Bite	51		Edward D. Radin		TC
Welcome Home	62		G. T. Fleming-Roberts		NA
The Jury	102		Kenneth Fearing		SS

Peter Enfantino • Jeff Vorzimmer

303

Crime Cavalcade	112		Vincent H. Gaddis		TC
The First Fifty Thousand	116	Airport Detail	Jack Webb		NV
Memento	133		Erskine Caldwell		SS
Portrait of a Killer No. 20 — Everett Appelgate	139		Dan Sontup		SF
Sweet Charlie	142	Peter Chambers	Henry Kane		SS
Incident in August	155		G. H. Williams		SS

Apr 1955 v. 3 n. 4	**35¢**		**160 Pages**	**Editor: John McCloud**	
Story/Article	**Pg**	**Series**	**Author**	**Pseudonym**	**Type**
Blood Brothers	1		Hal Ellson		NV
The Movers	22		Bryce Walton		SS
The Day It Began Again	31		Fletcher Flora		SS
The Meek Monster	38		Edward D. Radin		TC
His Own Hand	49	Alphabet Hicks	Rex Stout		SS
Mug Shot	62	Inspector Schmidt	Aaron Marc Stein	George Bagby	NA
Crime Cavalcade	114		Vincent H. Gaddis		TC
The General Slept Here	116	Neal Cotten	Sam S. Taylor		NV
Portrait of a Killer No. 21 — James Crawford	141		Dan Sontup		SF
Sylvia	144		Ira Levin		SS
What's Your Verdict? No. 10 — The Murdered Divorcé	154		Sam Ross		PZ
The Imposters	157		Frank E. Smith	Jonathan Craig	SS

May 1955 v. 3 n. 5	**35¢**		**160 Pages**	**Editor: John McCloud**	
Story/Article	**Pg**	**Series**	**Author**	**Pseudonym**	**Type**
Wrong Way Home	1		Hal Ellson		SS
I'll Never Tell	9		Bryce Walton		SS
Mama's Boy	20		David Alexander		NV
What's Your Verdict? No. 11 — The Escaping Man	36		Sam Ross		PZ
Shake-Up	38		Kenneth Fearing		SS
Tex	50		John Jakes		SS
I'll Get Even	58		Michael Zuroy		SS
We Are All Dead	64		Bruno Fischer		NA
Crime Cavalcade	94		Vincent H. Gaddis		TC
Protection	98		Erle Stanley Gardner		SS
Hold Out	109		John G. Reitci	Jack Ritchie	SS
Double Trouble	113		Edward D. Radin		TC
The Lady in Question	124	Police File	Frank E. Smith	Jonathan Craig	NV
The Goldfish	145		Roy Carroll	Roy Carroll	SS
Portrait of a Killer No. 22 — Bill Lovett	154		Dan Sontup		SF
El Rey	156		William Logan		SS

Jun 1955 v. 3 n. 6	**35¢**		**192 Pages**	**Editor: John McCloud**	
Story/Article	**Pg**	**Series**	**Author**	**Pseudonym**	**Type**
The Reluctant Client	1	Mike Shayne	Davis Dresser	Brett Halliday	SS
Interrogation	11		John G. Reitci	Jack Ritchie	SS
What's Your Verdict? No. 12 — The Protected Killer	18		Sam Ross		PZ

Body Snatcher	21		Aaron Marc Stein	George Bagby	SS
Code 197	27	Shell Scott	Richard S. Prather		NV
The Locked Room	42		Edward D. Radin		TC
Decoy	51		Hal Ellson		SS
The Careful Man	56		Richard Deming	Max Franklin	NA
Crime Cavalcade	100		Vincent H. Gaddis		TC
The Makeshift Martini	102	Airport Detail	Jack Webb		SS
The Dead Grin	115	Johnny Liddell	Frank Kane		SS
YOU, Detective No. 04 — The Mixed Drink	120		Wilson Harman		QZ
Everybody's Watching Me	122		Mickey Spillane		RP
Portrait of a Killer No. 23 — Mildred Bolton	185		Dan Sontup		SF
The Vicious Young	188		Pat Stadley		SS

Jul 1955	v. 3	n. 7	35¢	160 Pages	Editor: John McCloud
Story/Article	**Pg**	**Series**	**Author**	**Pseudonym**	**Type**
See Him Die	1		Evan Hunter		NV
Solitary	14		John G. Reitci	Jack Ritchie	SS
The Repeater	21		Edward D. Radin		TC
The Baby Sitter	31	Police File	Frank E. Smith	Jonathan Craig	SS
Scarecrow	47		David Alexander		SS
The Watch	58		Wally Hunter		SS
What's Your Verdict? No. 13 — The Sympathetic Frie	62		Sam Ross		PZ
Juvenile Delinquent	64	Manville Moon	Richard Deming		NA
Crime Cavalcade	116		Vincent H. Gaddis		TC
The Big Score	120		Sam Merwin, Jr.		NV
Portrait of a Killer No. 24 — Oliver Bishop	139		Thomas O'Connor		SF
You Can't Kill Her	142		C. B. Gilford		SS
YOU, Detective No. 05 — The Timed Murder	153		Wilson Harman		QZ
The Death of Arney Vincent	155		C. L. Sweeney, Jr.		SS

Aug 1955	v. 3	n. 8	35¢	144 Pages	Editor: John McCloud
Story/Article	**Pg**	**Series**	**Author**	**Pseudonym**	**Type**
Red Hands	1		Bryce Walton		SS
The Happy Marriage	12		Richard Deming		NV
Bug Doctor	26		Edward D. Radin		TC
Make It Neat	32	Johnny Liddell	Frank Kane		SS
Pass the Word	46	A Casebook Story	Jack Sword		SS
Crime Cavalcade	55		Vincent H. Gaddis		TC
Shot in the Dark	57	John J. Malone	Georgiana Craig	Craig Rice	NV
What's Your Verdict? No. 14 — The Buried Fortune	80		Sam Ross		PZ
Nudists Die Naked	82	Shell Scott	Richard S. Prather		NA
YOU, Detective No. 06 — The Burgled Apartment	136		Wilson Harman		QZ
Try It My Way	138		John G. Reitci	Jack Ritchie	SS

Peter Enfantino • Jeff Vorzimmer

Sep 1955 v. 3 n. 9	35¢		144 Pages	Editor: John McCloud	
Story/Article	Pg	Series	Author	Pseudonym	Type
Uncle Tom	1		David Alexander		SS
Cast Off	14	Police File	Frank E. Smith	Jonathan Craig	SS
The Big Day	25		Evan Hunter	Richard Marsten	NV
Mass Production	40		Andrew J. Burris		TC
Pickup	44		Hal Ellson		SS
Side Street	50		James T. Farrell		SS
Crime Cavalcade	55		Vincent H. Gaddis		TC
The Muscle	57		Philip Weck		SS
What's Your Verdict? No. 15 — The Good Time	62		Sam Ross		PZ
The War	64	Clancy Ross	Richard Deming		NV
YOU, Detective No. 07 — The Outside Job	90		Wilson Harman		QZ
Flight to Nowhere	92		Charles Williams		NA

Oct 1955 v. 3 n. 10	35¢		144 Pages	Editor: John McCloud	
Story/Article	Pg	Series	Author	Pseudonym	Type
The Spoilers	1	Police File	Frank E. Smith	Jonathan Craig	NV
Field of Honor	19		Robert Turner		SS
Sales Resistance	25		Andrew J. Burris		TC
In Memory of Judith Courtright	28		Erskine Caldwell		SS
I Saw Her Die	37		Gil Brewer		SS
Crime Cavalcade	44		Vincent H. Gaddis		TC
Blonde at the Wheel	47		Stephen Marlowe		NV
Experts in Crime: Forgery	61		Edward Clark		SF
Tell Them Nothing	64		Hal Ellson		NV
The Hunter	85		John A. Sentry		SS
What's Your Verdict? No. 16 — The Whole Truth	92		Sam Ross		PZ
A Stranger in Town	94	Mike Shayne	Davis Dresser	Brett Halliday	NA
YOU, Detective No. 08 — The Metal Finger	142		Wilson Harman		QZ

Nov 1955 v. 3 n. 11	35¢		144 Pages	Editor: John McCloud	
Story/Article	Pg	Series	Author	Pseudonym	Type
Big Frank	1		Bryce Walton		SS
I'll Do Anything	13		Charles Beaumont		SS
One at a Time	23		Andrew J. Burris		TC
Time to Kill	26		Evan Hunter	Richard Marsten	NV
Fat Boy	52		Hal Ellson		SS
Crime Cavalcade	60		Vincent H. Gaddis		TC
Vanishing Act	64		W. R. Burnett		NV
Woman Hater	86		Sam Merwin, Jr.		SS
What's Your Verdict? No. 17 — The Wild Shot	99		Sam Ross		PZ
The Trap	101		Robert Turner		SS
The Man Between	108	Police File	Frank E. Smith	Jonathan Craig	NA
The Alligator Man	134		Tom Beach		TC

Story/Article	Pg	Series	Author	Pseudonym	Type
YOU, Detective No. 09 — The Obliging Fire	137		Wilson Harman		QZ
Low Tide	139		Cole Price		SS

Dec 1955	v. 3	n. 12	35¢	128 Pages	Editor: John McCloud
Story/Article	**Pg**	**Series**	**Author**	**Pseudonym**	**Type**
First Offense	3		Evan Hunter		NV
My Son and Heir	18	Chester Drum	Stephen Marlowe		SS
The Good Boy	29		Andrew J. Burris		TC
Custody	32		Richard Deming		SS
Crime Cavalcade	41		Vincent H. Gaddis		TC
Outside the Cages	43		Jack Webb		NV
The Jokers	55		Robert Turner		SS
What's Your Verdict? No. 18 — The Complete Failure	62		Sam Ross		PZ
The High Trap	64		Floyd Mahannah		NV
YOU, Detective No. 10 — The Many Motives	85		Wilson Harman		QZ
Kill Me Tomorrow	87		Fletcher Flora		NA
Surprise! Surprise!	115		David Alexander		SS

Jan 1956	v. 4	n. 1	35¢	128 Pages	Editor: John McCloud
Story/Article	**Pg**	**Series**	**Author**	**Pseudonym**	**Type**
Who Killed Helen?	2		Bryce Walton		SS
Dangerous	14		Hal Ellson		NV
The Boiler	31		Andrew J. Burris		TC
Fight Night	35		Robert Turner		SS
It's Hot Up Here	41		Arnold Marmor		SS
The Cheater	45	Police File	Frank E. Smith	Jonathan Craig	NV
Breaking Point	58		Eleanor Roth		SS
Spectator Sport	64		Roy Carroll	Roy Carroll	SS
The Dead Stand-In	68	Johnny Liddell	Frank Kane		NA
YOU, Detective No. 11 — The Rich Corpse	122		Wilson Harman		QZ
You Want Her?	124		Pat Stadley		SS

Feb 1956	v. 4	n. 2	35¢	144 Pages	Editor: N. F. King
Story/Article	**Pg**	**Series**	**Author**	**Pseudonym**	**Type**
Block Party	1		Sam Merwin, Jr.		NV
Sauce for the Gander	13	Clancy Ross	Richard Deming		NV
Dead Soldier	40	A Casebook Story	Jack Sword		SS
Fog	50		Gil Brewer		SS
Marty	58		Robert S. Swenson		SS
Cool Cat	63		Hal Ellson		NV
Terror in the Night	85		Robert Bloch		SS
Handy Man	90		Fletcher Flora		SS
They're Chasing Us!	98		Herbert D. Kastle		SS
The Watchers	110		Wally Hunter		SS
Killer	115		William Logan		SS
Job with a Future	122		Richard Welles		SS

Peter Enfantino • Jeff Vorzimmer

Story/Article	Pg	Series	Author	Pseudonym	Type
Sleep Without Dreams	127	Johnny Liddell	Frank Kane		:S
Shot	140		Gil Brewer	Roy Carroll	:S

Mar 1956	v. 4	n. 3	35¢	144 Pages	Editor: N. F. King	
Story/Article	**Pg**	**Series**	**Author**	**Pseudonym**	**Type**
The Temptress	1	Police File	Frank E. Smith	Jonathan Craig	IV
Split It Three Ways	19		Walter Kaylin		:S
Lend Me Your Gun	26		Hal Ellson		:S
An Eye for an Eye	36		Philip Weck		:S
Madman	43		Roy Carroll	Roy Carroll	:S
His Own Petard	54		Daniel O'Shea		:S
.38	60		Joe Grenzeback		:S
Hunch	64		Helen Nielsen		:S
Crime Cavalcade	78		Vincent H. Gaddis		:C
Suffer Little Children	82		Deloris Staton Forbes	De Forbes	:S
Two Hours to Midnight	91	Mike Shayne	Davis Dresser	Brett Halliday	IA

Apr 1956	v. 4	n. 4	35¢	144 Pages	Editor: N. F. King	
Story/Article	**Pg**	**Series**	**Author**	**Pseudonym**	**Type**
First Kill	1		Helen Nielsen		IV
Strictly Business	15		Hamilton Frank		:S
Pat Hand	20		J. W. Aaron		IV
Widow's Choice	36		Cole Price		:S
The Better Bargain	43		Richard Deming		:S
Come Across	52		Gil Brewer		:S
Line of Duty	62		Fredric Brown		IA
Room Service	108		Robert Turner		:S
Dry Run	112		Norman Struber		:S
One Way or the Other	120		John R. Starr		:S
A Trophy for Bart	124		James Charles Lynch		:S
Open Heart	132		Bryce Walton		:S
One-Way Ticket	137		Duane Yarnell		:S

May 1956	v. 4	n. 5	35¢	144 Pages	Editor: N. F. King	
Story/Article	**Pg**	**Series**	**Author**	**Pseudonym**	**Type**
Squealer	1		John D. MacDonald		:S
The Man Who Never Smiled	10		Robert S. Swenson		:S
Preacher's Tale	17		Max Kane		:S
Kill Fever	24		Rey Isely		:S
The Unholy Three	36	Joe Puma	William Campbell Gault		:S
Ten Minutes to Live	51		George Fielding Eliot		:S
Lenore	64		Frederick C. Davis		IV
Devil Eyes	94		John G. Reitci	Jack Ritchie	:S
Oedipus	100		Walt Sheldon		:S
The Strangler	112		A. I. Schutzer		:S
City Hunters	127		George Lange		:S

308   The Manhunt Companion

Story/Article	Pg	Series	Author	Pseudonym	Type
The Red of Bourgainvillea	131		Grove Hughes		SS
The Pigeon	140		Claudius Raye		SS

Jun 1956	v. 4	n. 6	35¢	144 Pages	Editor: N. F. King
Story/Article	**Pg**	**Series**	**Author**	**Pseudonym**	**Type**
Circle for Death	1		Pat Stadley		SS
A Helluva Ball	9		Jack Q. Lynn		SS
Hitch-Hiker	15		Roland F. Lee		SS
One More Mile to Go	19		F. J. Smith		SS
Addict	27		W. E. Douglas		SS
Dead Man's Cat	31		Sylvie Pasche		SS
Three, Four, Out the Door	42		Robert S. Swenson		SS
The Canary	47		John G. Reitci	Jack Ritchie	SS
Lipstick	53		Wenzell Brown		SS
The Squeeze	62	Clancy Ross	Richard Deming		NV
Vigil by Night	81		James W. Phillips		SS
The Prisoners	85		Evans Harrington		NA

Jul 1956	v. 4	n. 7	35¢	144 Pages	Editor: N. F. King
Story/Article	**Pg**	**Series**	**Author**	**Pseudonym**	**Type**
Still Screaming	1		F. L. Wallace		SS
Terminal	9		William L. Jackson		SS
Pal with a Switch Blade	20		Norman Struber		SS
Rumble	32		Edward Perry		SS
Stay Dead, Julia!	36		Peter Georgas		SS
Office Party	42		Austin Hamel		SS
Terror in the Night	52		Carl G. Hodges		SS
Fall Guy	64		Joe Grenzeback		NV
A Date with Harry	79		George Lange		SS
Change for a C-Note	84		Jerry Sohl		SS
D. O. A.	91		Jules Rosenthal		SS
The Big Bite	95		Charles Williams		NA

Aug 1956	v. 4	n. 8	35¢	144 Pages	Editor: William Manners
Story/Article	**Pg**	**Series**	**Author**	**Pseudonym**	**Type**
Cop Killer	1		Dan Sontup		SS
The Man with Two Faces	12		Henry Slesar		SS
Gruber Corners by Nine	23		John R. Starr		SS
Seven Lousy Bucks	29		C. L. Sweeney, Jr.		SS
"Puddin' and Pie"	36		Deloris Staton Forbes	De Forbes	SS
Biggest Risk	43		C. B. Gilford		NV
The Wire Loop	57		Steve Harbor		SS
Key Witness	64		Frank Kane		NA
Rat Hater	108		Harlan Ellison		SS
Thanks for the Drink, Mac	119		Philip Weck		SS
Good-By, World	128		John G. Reitci	Jack Ritchie	SS

Peter Enfantino • Jeff Vorzimmer

Story/Article	Pg	Series	Author	Pseudonym	Type
The Earrings	133		Kermit Shelby		SS
The Playboy	138		Claudius Raye		SS

Sep 1956	v. 4	n. 9	35¢	144 Pages	Editor: William Manners
Story/Article	**Pg**	**Series**	**Author**	**Pseudonym**	**Type**
The Last Spin	1		Evan Hunter		SS
Fish-Market Murder	8		Robert S. Swenson		SS
Badge of Dishonor	13		Norman Struber		SS
"Sorry, Mister ..."	24		C. L. Sweeney, Jr.		SS
Brusky's Fault	31		Robert Plate		SS
The Secret	38		Stuart Friedman		SS
Anything Goes	51		Hal Ellson		SS
The Sealed Envelope	64		Allen Lang		NV
The Partners	87		John G. Reitci	Jack Ritchie	SS
Reach for the Clouds	95		Bob Bristow		SS
Invitation to Murder	105		Albert Simmons		NV
Dead People Are Never Angry	125		C. B. Gilford		SS
Webster Street Lush	133		James M. Ullman		SS

Oct 1956	v. 4	n. 10	35¢	144 Pages	Editor: William Manners
Story/Article	**Pg**	**Series**	**Author**	**Pseudonym**	**Type**
The Enormous Grave	1		Norman Struber		SS
Run from the Snakes!	11		David Alexander		SS
Blood and Moonlight	27		William R. Cox		SS
Ring the Bell Once	38		Paul Eiden		SS
Matinee	47		Gil Brewer		SS
Deadly Beloved	57	Joe Puma	William Campbell Gault		NV
The Lovers	89		Morton Freedgood	John Godey	SS
Lesson in Murder	89		Wally Hunter		SS
Night of Crisis	101		Harry Whittington		SS
Body in the Rain	117		John S. Hill		SS
Dangerous Money	122		F. J. Smith		SS
Bus to Portland	129		L. W. King		SS
Chicken!	138		Phil Perlmutter		SS

Nov 1956	v. 4	n. 11	35¢	144 Pages	Editor: William Manners
Story/Article	**Pg**	**Series**	**Author**	**Pseudonym**	**Type**
Pigeon in an Iron Lung	1		Talmage Powell		SS
Who's Calling?	7		Robert Turner		SS
The Tormentors	19		Gil Brewer		SS
Death Beat	27		David C. Cooke		SS
Cowpatch Vengeance	31		Charles W. Moore		SS
Guts	45		John R. Starr		SS
Death Wears a Gray Sweater	48		Roy Carroll	Roy Carroll	SS
Zero ... Double Zero	64		Stuart Friedman		NV
Naked Petey	83		Jack Q. Lynn		SS

The Manhunt Companion

Four Hours to Kill	91	F. J. Smith		SS
Three's a Crowd	99	Joe Grenzeback		SS
Manila Mission	109	Charles Einstein		NA

Dec 1956	v. 4	n. 12	35¢	144 Pages	Editor: William Manners

Story/Article	Pg	Series	Author	Pseudonym	Type
High Dive	1		Robert Turner		SS
Degree of Guilt	9		John G. Reitci	Jack Ritchie	SS
A Couple of Bucks	15		Clair Huffaker		SS
I Dig You, Real Cool	20		Deloris Staton Forbes	De Forbes	SS
Vacation Nightmare	30		Robert Turner	Roy Carroll	SS
The Face of a Killer	40		Charles Beaumont		SS
G.I. Pigeon	50		Joseph F. Karrer		SS
Man with a Shiv	62		Richard Wormser		NV
Payment in Full	92		Dave Leigh		SS
Lust Song	97		Stuart Friedman		SS
A Clear Day for Hunting	110		Jack Q. Lynn		SS
So Much Per Body	121		Frank E. Smith	Jonathan Craig	SS
A Job for Johnny	125		Lawrence Burne		SS
Showdown at Midnight	133		Edward L. Perry		SS
The Fast Line	141		Art Crockett		SS

Jan 1957	v. 5	n. 1	35¢	144 Pages	Editor: William Manners

Story/Article	Pg	Series	Author	Pseudonym	Type
The Rabbit Gets a Gun	1		John D. MacDonald		SS
Cop for a Day	8		Henry Slesar		SS
Face of Evil	15	Lieutenant Romano	David Alexander		SS
Smart Sucker	25		Richard Wormser		SS
A Ride Downtown	39		Robert Turner		SS
Somebody's Going to Die	43		Talmage Powell		SS
His Own Jailor	53		Bryce Walton		SS
Bait for the Red Head	64		Eugene Pawley		NV
Stranger in the House	95		Theodore Pratt		SS
... Into the Parlor	101		Paul Eiden		SS
Never Kill a Mistress	115		Carroll Mayers		SS
Shoot Them Down	120		Bob Bristow		SS
On a Sunday Afternoon	128		Gil Brewer		SS
Perfect Getaway	142		Henry Petersen		SS

Feb 1957	v. 5	n. 2	35¢	144 Pages	Editor: William Manners

Story/Article	Pg	Series	Author	Pseudonym	Type
The Teacher	1		Robert Turner		SS
"Got a Match?"	11		David Alexander		SS
Troublemakers	23		Earl Fultz		SS
Possessed	32		Murray Leinster	Will F. Jenkins	SS
Long Distance	39		Fletcher Flora		SS

Peter Enfantino • Jeff Vorzimmer

Story/Article	Pg	Series	Author	Pseudonym	Type
They'll Find Out!	46		Richard Hardwick		SS
Divide and Conquer	53		John G. Reitci	Jack Ritchie	SS
The "H" Killer	61	87th Precinct	Evan Hunter	Ed McBain	NV
The Broken Window	101		Earle Basinsky, Jr.		SS
Enough Rope for Two	106		Clark Howard		SS
Run, Carol, Run!	118		Talmage Powell		SS
The Cross Forks Incident	126		Thomas P. Ramirez		SS
The Big Smile	139		Stan Wiley		SS

Mar 1957	v. 5	n. 3	35¢	64 Pages	Editor: William Manners

Story/Article	Pg	Series	Author	Pseudonym	Type
Dead as a Mannequin	1		Rex Raney		SS
Golden Opportunity	4		J. W. Aaron		SS
Victim Number Six	8		Robert Plate		SS
The Big Hate	11		Frank Cetin		SS
Pick-Up	15		Richard Deming		SS
A Place for Emily	19		F. J. Smith		SS
Shadowed	24		Richard Wormser		SS
The Man Who Was Everywhere	27		Edward D. Hoch		SS
War Talk	29		Philip Weck		SS
He Never Went Home	35	John J. Malone	Georgiana Craig	Craig Rice	NV
To Save a Body	48		Henry Slesar		SS
Deathmate	52		James Causey		SS
The Late Gerald Baumann	56		Bob Bristow		SS
Next!	62		Talmage Powell		SS

Apr 1957	v. 5	n. 4	35¢	64 Pages	Editor: William Manners

Story/Article	Pg	Series	Author	Pseudonym	Type
Body on a White Carpet	1		Albert James Hjertstedt	Al James	SS
"Use Five Grand?"	5		Michael Zuroy		SS
Night Job	10		Robert Plate		SS
The Percentage	13		David Alexander		SS
Was It Worth It, Mr. Markell?	21		Lawrence Spingarn		SS
Object of Desire	25		Paul Swope		SS
Joy Ride	27		C. B. Gilford		SS
You Should Live So Long	32		John G. Reitci	Jack Ritchie	SS
Locker 911	36		Richard Wormser		NV
Honey-Child	45		Leslie Gordon Barnard		SS
Express Stop	48		Jason January		SS
Death of a Big Wheel	52	Joe Puma	William Campbell Gault		NV

May 1957	v. 5	n. 5	35¢	64 Pages	Editor: William Manners

Story/Article	Pg	Series	Author	Pseudonym	Type
Prowler!	1		Gil Brewer		SS
Bet I Don't Die	4		Arnold English		SS
College Kill	8		Jack Q. Lynn		SS

Story/Article	Pg	Series	Author	Pseudonym	Type
Razor, Razor, Gleaming Bright	16		Roy Carroll	Roy Carroll	SS
Midnight Blonde	19		Talmage Powell		SS
40 Detectives Later	23		Henry Slesar		SS
Toward a Grave	27		Howard B. Shaeffer		SS
The Charles Turner Case	30		Richard Deming		SS
New Girl	37		Deloris Staton Forbes	De Forbes	SS
The Deadly Dolls	41	Peter Chambers	Henry Kane		NV

Jun 1957	**v. 5**	**n. 6**	**35¢**	**64 Pages**	**Editor: Hal Walker**	
Story/Article	**Pg**	**Series**	**Author**	**Pseudonym**	**Type**
The Woman-Chasers	1		Bryce Walton		SS
The Amateur	5	Clancy Ross	Richard Deming		SS
He's Never Stopped Running	10		Aaron Marc Stein		SS
The Geniuses	16		Richard Deming	Max Franklin	NV
Blood on the Land	24		Hal Ellson		SS
The Woman Knew Too Much	29	Scott Jordan	Harold Q. Masur		SS
Kill the Clown	36	Shell Scott	Richard S. Prather		NA
Decision	59		Helen Nielsen		SS

Jul 1957	**v. 5**	**n. 7**	**35¢**	**64 Pages**	**Editor: Hal Walker**	
Story/Article	**Pg**	**Series**	**Author**	**Pseudonym**	**Type**
On the Sidewalk, Bleeding	1		Evan Hunter		SS
Remember Biff Bailey?	5		Frank E. Smith	Jonathan Craig	SS
Bothered	9		Gil Brewer		SS
They Came with Guns	12		Bruno Fischer		NV
Lead Cure	23		Talmage Powell		SS
A Piece of Ground	27		Helen Nielsen		SS
I Hate Cops	32		Henry H. Guild		SS
The Man Who Was Two	37		Richard Deming		SS
Bunco	44		John R. Starr		SS
Movie Night	47		Robert Turner		SS
Dead Pigeon	52	Johnny Liddell	Frank Kane		NV
The Substitute	61		Henry Slesar		SS

Sep 1957	**v. 5**	**n. 8**	**35¢**	**64 Pages**	**Editor: Hal Walker**	
Story/Article	**Pg**	**Series**	**Author**	**Pseudonym**	**Type**
One Summer Night	1		Bryce Walton		SS
Business as Usual	6		Arnold English		SS
Say It with Flowers	10	John J. Malone	Georgiana Craig	Craig Rice	NV
Trespasser	20		Fletcher Flora		SS
Death of a Stripper	24		Sherry La Verne		SS
Fly-By-Night	29		Robert Gold		SS
The Favor	35		Talmage Powell		SS
Kitchen Kill	40	Police File	Frank E. Smith	Jonathan Craig	SS
The Crying Target	49		James McKimmey		SS
Girl Friend	61		Morris Hershman	Mark Mallory	SS

Peter Enfantino • Jeff Vorzimmer

Oct 1957	v. 5	n. 9	35¢	64 Pages	Editor: Hal Walker	
Story/Article	**Pg**	**Series**	**Author**		**Pseudonym**	**Type**
Cut-Throat World	1		J. W. Aaron			SS
Flesh	5		Meyer Levin			SS
Top Dog	16		Richard Deming		Max Franklin	NV
Knife in His Hand	21		Mike Brett			SS
The Rival Act	26		Richard S. Prather			SS
Omit Flowers	29		Morris Hershman		Arnold English	SS
Secondary Target	33	Clancy Ross	Richard Deming			SS
Fat Chance	41		Wayne Hyde			SS
The Wife-Beater	48	Inspector Schmidt	Aaron Marc Stein		George Bagby	NV
A Beautiful Babe and Money	62		Talmage Powell			SS

Nov 1957	v. 5	n. 10	35¢	64 Pages	Editor: Francis X. Lewis	
Story/Article	**Pg**	**Series**	**Author**		**Pseudonym**	**Type**
The Blood of the Lamb	1		Steve Allen			SS
Kill Joy	7		John G. Reitci		Jack Ritchie	SS
Cheese It, the Corpse	10	John J. Malone	Georgiana Craig		Craig Rice	NV
Shimmy	19		Mike Brett			SS
Compensation	21		Helen Nielsen			SS
The Closed Door	27		Walt Frisbie			SS
Setup	32		Fletcher Flora			NV
I'll Handle This	43		Albert James Hjertstedt		Al James	SS
The Big Fish	47		Hal Ellson			SS
Stolen Star	53	Joe Puma	William Campbell Gault			NV
Repeat Performance	62		Robert Turner			SS

Dec 1957	v. 5	n. 11	35¢	64 Pages	Editor: Francis X. Lewis	
Story/Article	**Pg**	**Series**	**Author**		**Pseudonym**	**Type**
The Merry, Merry Christmas	1		Evan Hunter			SS
Bad Word	5		David Alexander			SS
The Scavengers	11		Richard Harper			SS
Chain Gang	14		Joe Gores			SS
Out of Business	19		C. B. Gilford			SS
Duel in the Pit	25		Rick Sargent			SS
Time to Kill	31	Airport Detail	Jack Webb			NV
They're Going to Kill Me	39		Bob Bristow			SS
First Nighter	43		Richard Hardwick			SS
The Doubles	45		Richard Deming			SS
Dead Set	51	Johnny Liddell	Frank Kane			NV
Clay Pigeon	62		Joseph Commings			SS

Jan 1958	v. 6	n. 1	35¢	64 Pages	Editor: Francis X. Lewis	
Story/Article	**Pg**	**Series**	**Author**		**Pseudonym**	**Type**
The Hitchhiker	1		Albert James Hjertstedt		Al James	SS
Jungle	4		Hal Ellson			SS

Story/Article	Pg	Series	Author	Pseudonym	Type
Return No More	9		Talmage Powell		SS
The New Girl	13		Richard Deming	Max Franklin	NV
Midnight Caller	22		Bob Wade & Bill Miller	Wade Miller	SS
Moon Bright, Moon Fright	24		Warren J. Shanahan		SS
Togetherness	29		Aaron Marc Stein		NV
The Spinner	38		Avram Davidson		SS
The Town Says Murder	43		Cornell Woolrich		NA
Arrest	62		Donald E. Westlake		SS

Feb 1958	**v. 6**	**n. 2**	**35¢**	**64 Pages**	**Editor: Francis X. Lewis**
Story/Article	**Pg**	**Series**	**Author**	**Pseudonym**	**Type**
The Painter	1		Michael Zuroy		SS
A Real Quiet Guy	4		Tom Phillips		SS
Pressure	9		Morris Hershman	Arnold English	SS
Meet Me in the Dark	13		Gil Brewer		NV
The Helping Hand	24		Avram Davidson		SS
Be a Man	29		Talmage Powell		SS
Hooked	33		Robert Turner		NV
You Can't Lose	43		Lawrence Block		SS
Black Cat in the Snow	47		John D. MacDonald		SS
The Portraits of Eve	50		Bruno Fischer		NV
The Babe and the Bum	62		Mike Brett		SS

Apr 1958	**v. 6**	**n. 3**	**35¢**	**64 Pages**	**Editor: Francis X. Lewis**
Story/Article	**Pg**	**Series**	**Author**	**Pseudonym**	**Type**
Don't Twist My Arm	1		John G. Reitci	Jack Ritchie	SS
Fifteen Grand	6		Jack Q. Lynn		SS
Colby's Monster	11		Stuart Friedman		SS
The Hit	17		Alson J. Smith		NV
The Dame Across the River	28		Talmage Powell		SS
One More Clue	31	John J. Malone	Georgiana Craig	Craig Rice	SS
Zeke's Long Arm	39		C. B. Gilford		SS
Trouble in Town	42	Clancy Ross	Richard Deming		NV
You're Dead!	50		Helen Nielsen		NV
Goodbye, Charlie	61		Bob Prichard		SS

Jun 1958	**v. 6**	**n. 4**	**35¢**	**128 Pages**	**Editor: Francis X. Lewis**
Story/Article	**Pg**	**Series**	**Author**	**Pseudonym**	**Type**
The Threat	1		Richard Deming	Max Franklin	NV
Pro	14		Joe Gores		SS
"Give Me a Break!"	23		Norman Struber		SS
Say a Prayer for the Guy	31		Nelson Algren		SS
Deadly Charm	36		Stuart Friedman		NV
The Sight of Blood	50		C. B. Gilford		SS
A Fire at Night	59		Lawrence Block		SS
Stage Fright	63		Deloris Staton Forbes	D. E. Forbes	SS

Peter Enfantino • Jeff Vorzimmer

Story/Article	Pg	Series	Author	Pseudonym	Type
The Chips Are Down	71		Wilfred Alexander		SS
It Never Happened	79		William O'Farrell		NA
Killer Cop	114		Morris Hershman	Arnold English	SS
Blackmailers Don't Take Chances	121		David C. Cooke		SS

Aug 1958	v. 6	n. 5	35¢	128 Pages	Editor: John Underwood
Story/Article	**Pg**	**Series**	**Author**	**Pseudonym**	**Type**
Dead Cats	1		Henry Marksbury		SS
The Jacket	8		Jack Q. Lynn		SS
Big Hands	20		L. J. Krebs		SS
The Murder Pool	24		Robert Stephens		SS
Caught in the Act	31		Niel Franklin		SS
Poor Sherm	36		Ruth Chessman		SS
A Friend of Stanley's	48		Guy Crosby		NV
Loose Ends	60		Fletcher Flora		NV
Cabin 13	114		Edward Perry		SS
The Real Thing	121		Fritz Dugan		SS

Oct 1958	v. 6	n. 6	35¢	128 Pages	Editor: John Underwood
Story/Article	**Pg**	**Series**	**Author**	**Pseudonym**	**Type**
Dope to Kill	1		Edward Wellen		SS
Rivals	18		Talmage Powell		SS
The Nude Next Door	25		Ivan Lyons-Pleskow		TC
My Pal Isaac	29		David Lee		SS
I'd Die for You	41		Charles Burgess		SS
Time to Kill	47		Bryce Walton		SS
Surprise	64		Don Lombardy		TC
Deadline Murder	70		John G. Reitci	Jack Ritchie	SS
The Shooter	83		Craig Mooney		SS
I'm Not Dead	91		Carl Milton		NA
Murder by Appointment	122		Albert James Hjertstedt	Al James	SS

Dec 1958	v. 6	n. 7	35¢	128 Pages	Editor: John Underwood
Story/Article	**Pg**	**Series**	**Author**	**Pseudonym**	**Type**
A Little Variety	1		Richard Hardwick		SS
The Strangler	8		Richard Deming		SS
Flowers for Barney	24		Ovid Demaris		SS
Gigolo	35		C. B. Gilford		SS
Ride a White Horse	48		Lawrence Block		SS
Desert Chase	58		Thurber Jensen		NA
Wait for Death	113		Karl Kramer		SS

Feb 1959	v. 7	n. 1	35¢	128 Pages	Editor: John Underwood
Story/Article	**Pg**	**Series**	**Author**	**Pseudonym**	**Type**
Second Chance	3		Joe Grenzeback		NV
Killer in the Ring	31		Paul H. Johnson, Jr.		SS
Lovers	43		R. J. Hochkins		SS

| Night of Death | 49 | | Bob Bristow | | SS |
| Killer's Wedge | 58 87th Precinct | | Evan Hunter | Ed McBain | NA |

Apr 1959	v. 7	n. 2	35¢	128 Pages	Editor: John Underwood
Story/Article	**Pg**	**Series**	**Author**	**Pseudonym**	**Type**
The Runaway	1		Bryce Walton		SS
Road to Samarra	11		Jane Roth		SS
Fair Play	20		John G. Reitci	Jack Ritchie	SS
The Double Take	26		Edward Wellen		NV
Mr. Big Nose	46		Martin Suto		SS
The Score	61		Carroll Mayers		SS
Awake to Fear	65		Robert Camp		SS
One Hour Late	76		William O'Farrell		NA

Jun 1959	v. 7	n. 3	35¢	128 Pages	Editor: John Underwood
Story/Article	**Pg**	**Series**	**Author**	**Pseudonym**	**Type**
Down and Out	1		Joe Gores		SS
The Bargainmaster	15		Bob Bristow		SS
The Blonde in Room 320	24		William Hurst		NV
Some Play with Matches	48		Dick Ellis		SS
Absinthe for Superman	55		Robert Edmond Alter		SS
Bronco	66		Roy Koch		SS
The Cop Hater	76		Floyd Wallace		SS
A Corpse That Didn't Die	87		Henry Kane		NA

Aug 1959	v. 7	n. 4	35¢	128 Pages	Editor: John Underwood
Story/Article	**Pg**	**Series**	**Author**	**Pseudonym**	**Type**
Nickel Machine	1		Neil Boardman		SS
Crossed and Double-Crossed	14		Carroll Mayers		SS
Dead on Arrival	19		Bob Bristow		SS
The Return of Joey Dino	28		Elwood Corley		NV
The Bird Watcher	52		Frank Sisk		SS
Sunday Killer	62		Albert James Hjertstedt	Al James	SS
The Extortioners	69		Ovid Demaris		NA
A Matter of Judgment	126		Jordan Bauman		SS

Oct 1959	v. 7	n. 5	35¢	128 Pages	Editor: John Underwood
Story/Article	**Pg**	**Series**	**Author**	**Pseudonym**	**Type**
Mad Dog Beware!	1		J. W. Aaron		SS
The Nude Killer	11		K. McCaffrey		SS
The Sword of Laertes	15		Ray Russell		SS
Snow Job	21		Carroll Mayers		SS
Big Brother	25		Robert M. Hodges		SS
A Weakness for Women	35		Arthur Kaplan		NV
The Death of Me	50		Anne Smith Ewing		SS
Curses	63		Koller Ernst		SS
Escape Route	75		Richard Deming		NA

Peter Enfantino • Jeff Vorzimmer

Story/Article	Pg	Series	Author	Pseudonym	Type
Wrong Alibi	117		Roy Carroll	Roy Carroll	SS
Check Out	123		Edward Wellen		SS

Dec 1959	v. 7 n. 6	35¢	128 Pages	Editor: John Underwood	
Story/Article	Pg	Series	Author	Pseudonym	Type
Free to Die	1		Bryce Walton		SS
Red Blood Bend	22		Burley Hendricks		SS
The Simian Suspect	32		Frank Sisk		SS
Dead Reckoning	42	Johnny Liddell	Frank Kane		NV
Cat's Meow	62		Jordan Bauman		SS
End of an Era	68		James Malone		TC
Stand In	88		Albert Simmons		SS
You Pay Your Money	99		Lawrence Harvey		SS
Confession	102		C. B. Gilford		SS
On Second Thought	114		Carroll Mayers		SS
The Swizzle Stick	118		Alice Wernherr		SS

Feb 1960	v. 8 n. 1	35¢	128 Pages	Editor: John Underwood	
Story/Article	Pg	Series	Author	Pseudonym	Type
Wrong Pigeon	1	Philip Marlowe	Raymond Chandler		NV
A Killer's Witness	28		Dick Ellis		SS
Miser's Secret	38		Richard Hardwick		SS
The Twelve-Grand Smoke	46		Frank Sisk		SS
The Worm Turns	58		R. D'Ascoli		SS
The Grateful Corpse	66		Bob Bristow		SS
The Lost Key	75		Hal Ellson		SS
Death at Full Moon	80		Albert James Hjertstedt	Al James	NV
Switch-Blade	103		Paul Daniels		SS
The Idiot's Tale	109		Leo Ellis		SS
An Empty Threat	118		Donald E. Westlake		SS
No Place to Run	124		Carroll Mayers		SS

Apr 1960	v. 8 n. 2	35¢	128 Pages	Editor: John Underwood	
Story/Article	Pg	Series	Author	Pseudonym	Type
Shakedown	1		C. L. Sweeney, Jr.		SS
Please Believe Me!	7		Jess Shelton		SS
Time for Revenge	14		Dick Ellis		SS
Pass the Word Along	25	Johnny Liddell	Frank Kane		NV
Lovers Quarrel	44		Kelly Reynolds		SS
Life Sentence	52		Talmage Powell		SS
The Challenge	57		John Carnegie		SS
Rub Out the Past	70		Robert S. Aldrich		SS
Don't Clip My Wings	79		David W. Maurer		SS
The Nude in the Subway	94		Arne Mann		SS
Wharf Rat	98		Robert Page Jones		NV
Mother's Waiting	118		Murray Klater		SS

| The Safe Kill | 124 | | Kenneth Moore | | SS |

Jun 1960 · v. 8 · n. 3 · 35¢ · 128 Pages · Editor: John Underwood

Story/Article	Pg	Series	Author	Pseudonym	Type
Right Thing to Do	1		Robert Leon		SS
Pics for Sale	10		Ben Satterfield		SS
A Question of Values	14		C. L. Sweeney, Jr.		SS
Bodyguard	18		Richard Hardwick		SS
The Faithless Woman	30		Carroll Mayers		SS
Mis-Fire	34		Norman Struber		SS
Set-Up for Two	51		Norman Anthony		NA
Nightmare	106		James Walz		SS
Harmless	111		Mildred Jordan Brooks		SS
The Loving Victim	118		Lotte Belle Davis		SS

Aug 1960 · v. 8 · n. 4 · 35¢ · 128 Pages · Editor: John Underwood

Story/Article	Pg	Series	Author	Pseudonym	Type
Goodbye	1		Charles Carpentier		SS
She's Nothing but Trouble	4		Glenn Canary		SS
The Deserter	11		Hal Ellson		SS
The Accuser	20		Robert Wallsten		SS
She Asked for It	31		Fletcher Flora		NV
Kill One Kill Two	57		H. A. DeRosso		SS
Survival	68		David Alexander		SS
Deadly Error	77		Avram Davidson & Chester Cohen		SS
The Prisoner	84		Lawrence Harvey		SS
Heat Crazy	87		Virgie F. Shockley		SS
New Year's Party	93	Lieutenant O'Hara	Alson J. Smith		NV
Busybody	119		J. Simmons Scheb		SS
Frustration	124		Anne Smith Ewing		SS

Oct 1960 · v. 8 · n. 5 · 35¢ · 128 Pages · Editor: John Underwood

Story/Article	Pg	Series	Author	Pseudonym	Type
Too Much to Prove	1		Glenn Canary		SS
Dead Beat	8		Hayden Howard		SS
White Lightning	20		David Maurer		SS
Name Unknown, Subject Murder	32		Sheila S. Thompson		SS
The Trouble Shooters	38		Dan Brennan		SS
Shatter Proof	53		John G. Reitci	Jack Ritchie	SS
The Fugitives	58		Marc Penry Winters		NV
Protection	77		Hal Ellson		SS
To Catch a Spy	83		Philip Freund		NA

Dec 1960 · v. 8 · n. 6 · 35¢ · 128 Pages · Editor: John Underwood

Story/Article	Pg	Series	Author	Pseudonym	Type
Carnival Con	1		David Zinman		SS
The Old Pro	9		H. A. DeRosso		SS

Peter Enfantino • Jeff Vorzimmer

Story/Article	Pg	Series	Author	Pseudonym	Type
Dead Heat	21		Tom Phillips		S
Hangover	31		Charles Runyon		S
Tee Vee Murder	43		Harold R. Daniels		S
Death and the Blue Rose	59		William O'Farrell		S
Jail Break	72		Dan Sontup		S
The Model Dies Naked	81		Harry Widmer		S
A Long Wait	110		Richard L. Sargent		S
Desperation	126		Joachim H. Woos		S

Feb 1961   v. 9   n. 1   35¢   128 Pages   Editor: John Underwood

Story/Article	Pg	Series	Author	Pseudonym	Type
Hold-Up	1		Jess Shelton		S
Please Find My Sisters!	10		David H. Ross		V
Last Payment	34		Ron Boring		S
Vengeance	44		Robert Page Jones		S
Body-Snatcher	54		C. B. Gilford		S
How Much to Kill?	68		Michael Zuroy		S
It's the Law	80		Floyd Hurl		F
The Alarmist	81		Donald Tothe		S
The Master Mind	87		Walter Monaghan		V

Apr 1961   v. 9   n. 2   35¢   128 Pages   Editor: John Underwood

Story/Article	Pg	Series	Author	Pseudonym	Type
Deadly Triangle	1		Les Cole	Les Collins	S
It's the Law	9		Floyd Hurl		F
The Last Kill	10		Charles Runyon		V
Buzzard, Brother, Blood	46		Lewis Banci		S
Grudge Fight	52		Frank Hardy		S
To Kill a Cop	63		D. M. Downing		S
The Knife	75		Glenn Canary		S
Retribution	84		Michael Zuroy		S
Manhunt's Gun Rack: S&W .357 Magnum	88				F
The Evidence of Murder	89		Kenneth McCaffrey		S
Patsy	93		Paul Fairman		V
Fair Warning	117		James Holding		S
The Pain Killer	125		Charles Carpentier		S

Jun 1961   v. 9   n. 3   35¢   128 Pages   Editor: John Underwood

Story/Article	Pg	Series	Author	Pseudonym	Type
The Honest John	1		Martin Suto		S
Lady Killer	14		Herbert D. Kastle		S
Manhunt's Gun Rack: S&W .38 Terrier	25				F
Hangover Alley	26		Robert Page Jones		V
Cheap Kicks	52		William Brothers		S
The Girl Friend	65		David Dwyer		S
It's the Law	72		Floyd Hurl		F

Story/Article	Pg	Series	Author	Pseudonym	Type
Wrong Victim	73		W. Delos		SS
Taste of Terror	79		Paul Fairman		SS
The Possessive Female	84		Charles Runyon		SS
In Memoriam	99		Charles Boeckman	Charles Beckman, Jr.	SS
Smuggler's Monkey	106		Arne Mann		SS
Sales Pitch	120		Mark Starr		SS
Dead Letter	125		Don Tothe		SS

Aug 1961	v. 9	n. 4	35¢	128 Pages	Editor: John Underwood	
Story/Article	**Pg**	**Series**	**Author**	**Pseudonym**	**Type**	
Decay	1		Michael Zuroy		SS	
Manhunt's Gun Rack: S&W .357 Magnum	7				SF	
Death by the Numbers	8		Leonard S. Zinberg	Ed Lacy	SS	
It's the Law	16		Floyd Hurl		SF	
Finger-Man	17		John Connolly		NV	
Bugged	61		Bruno Fischer		SS	
Die, Die, Die!	72		Rosemary Johnston		SS	
The Big Haul	84		Robert Page Jones		NV	

Oct 1961	v. 9	n. 5	35¢	128 Pages	Editor: John Underwood	
Story/Article	**Pg**	**Series**	**Author**	**Pseudonym**	**Type**	
Pure Vengeance	1		Michael Zuroy		SS	
Dear Sir	12		Talmage Powell		SS	
It's the Law	21		Harold Helfer		SF	
The Death of El Indio	22		Leonard S. Zinberg	Ed Lacy	NV	
The Deadly Affair	49		Charles Carpentier		SS	
Chain Reaction	54		Charles Boeckman	Charles Beckman, Jr.	SS	
Sea Widow	58		William P. Brothers		SS	
The Novelty Shop	69		Donald Tothe		SS	
Manhunt's Gun Rack: Colt .45 Automatic	75				SF	
Break Down	76		Robert Edmond Alter		SS	
Cop in a Frame	80		Dick Ellis		SS	
A Woman's Wiles	101		Ray T. Davis		SS	
The Nude Above the Bar	105		Marvin Larson		SS	
An Aspect of Death	118		James L. Liverman		SS	
Night Out	121		Joe Gores		SS	
The Sure Things	125		Bernard Epps		SS	

Dec 1961	v. 9	n. 6	35¢	128 Pages	Editor: John Underwood	
Story/Article	**Pg**	**Series**	**Author**	**Pseudonym**	**Type**	
Killer Dog	1		M. R. James		SS	
Blackmail	9		Eugene Gaffney		SS	
The Queer Deal	19		John G. Reitci	Jack Ritchie	SS	
The Huntress	29		Gordon T. Allred		SS	
Sweets to the Sweet	49		J. Simmons Scheb		SS	
It's the Law	52		Floyd Hurl		SF	

Peter Enfantino • Jeff Vorzimmer

Story/Article	Pg	Series	Author	Pseudonym	Type
Brother's Keeper	53		Brian Lowe		SS
Manhunt's Gun Rack: S&W .357 Magnum (short-barr	62				SF
The Prey	63		Daniel DePaola		SS
The Kangaroo Court	72		Frank Ward		NA

Feb 1962	v. 10 n. 1	35¢	128 Pages	Editor: John Underwood	
Story/Article	**Pg**	**Series**	**Author**	**Pseudonym**	**Type**
The Bloodless Bayonet	1		Thomas Millstead		SS
It's the Law	11		Floyd Hurl		SF
Found and Lost	12		T. E. Brooks		SS
Dog Eat Dog	25		Georges Carousso		SS
Little Napoleon	32		Leo Ellis		SS
S.O.P. Murder	37		Rick Rubin		SS
The Deveraux Monster	52		John G. Reitci	Jack Ritchie	SS
Bail Out!	66		Robert Weaver & Samuel Rubinstein	Lancaster Salem	NA
Manhunt's Gun Rack: Ruger .44 Magnum Blackhawk	122				SF
Hot Furs	123		David Kasanof		SS

Apr 1962	v. 10 n. 2	35¢	128 Pages	Editor: John Underwood	
Story/Article	**Pg**	**Series**	**Author**	**Pseudonym**	**Type**
Obsession	1		Robert Page Jones		SS
It's the Law	17		Floyd Hurl		SF
Half Past Eternity	18		Robert Leon		SS
Gun Lover	31		Charles Carpentier		SS
Academic Freedom	39		Glenn Canary		SS
The Assassin	46		Robert Kimmel Smith	Peter Marks	SS
Set-Up	58		Hal Ellson		SS
Manhunt's Gun Rack: The Frontier Derringer	67				SF
Last Job	70		Raymond Dyer		SS
The Righteous	81		Talmage Powell		SS
Double Payments	89		Max F. Harris		SS
The Kidnappers	95		Edward Charles Bastien		SS
Poor Widow	106		Madeline Fraser		SS
The Fix	118		Max Van Derveer		SS

Jun 1962	v. 10 n. 3	35¢	128 Pages	Editor: John Underwood	
Story/Article	**Pg**	**Series**	**Author**	**Pseudonym**	**Type**
Motive to Kill	1		James Ullman		SS
Sucker Bait	6		Norm Kent		SS
Fly by Night	18		Dick Moore		SS
The Greatest	32		Hollis Gale		SS
According to Plan	37		Seymour Richin		SS
Stay of Execution	49		Al Martinez		SS
Family Argument	57		Neal Curtis		SS
Manhunt's Gun Rack: S&W .44 Military	61				SF
The Fallen Cop	62		Robert Anthony		SS

Story/Article	Pg	Series	Author	Pseudonym	Type
Cry Wolf!	76		C. B. Gilford		SS
Frozen Stiff	87		Lawrence Block		SS
Price of Life	93		Michael Zuroy		SS
The Crime Broker	104		Steve Frazee		NV

Aug 1962	v. 10 n. 4	35¢	128 Pages	Editor: John Underwood	
Story/Article	**Pg**	**Series**	**Author**	**Pseudonym**	**Type**
Lifeline	1		John Conner		SS
Heroes Are Made	5		Ben Mahnke		SS
Blackmail, Inc.	14		Michel Dedina		NV
Protect Us!	35		Don Tothe		SS
A Man Called	38		George Burke		SS
Summer Heat	45		Constance Pike		SS
Red for Murder	49		Rod Barker		NV
Manhunt's Gun Rack: Colt Police Positive Special	71				SF
A License to Kill	74		Charles Carpentier		SS
Friend in Deed	85		Shelby Harrison		SS
The Woman Hater	97		Leo Ellis		SS
Going Straight	105		Rick Rubin		SS
False Bait	113		Don Sollars		SS
The Final Solution	121		William W. Stuart		SS

Oct 1962	v. 10 n. 5	35¢	128 Pages	Editor: John Underwood	
Story/Article	**Pg**	**Series**	**Author**	**Pseudonym**	**Type**
A Reasonable Doubt	1		James A. Dunn		SS
Jump Chicken!	21		R. W. Lakin		SS
Welcome Mother	31		Bryce Walton		SS
Eye-Witness	40		Charles Sloan		NV
Inside Story	68		Edward Wellen		SS
Manhunt's Gun Rack: Colt Detective Special	71				SF
For the Sake of Love	72		Hilda Cushing		SS
Good at Heart	75		John Knox		SS
The Old Guard	88		Michael Zuroy		SS
Reward	100	Matt Gannon	Richard Deming		NV

Dec 1962	v. 10 n. 6	35¢	128 Pages	Editor: John Underwood	
Story/Article	**Pg**	**Series**	**Author**	**Pseudonym**	**Type**
Hot Shot	1		Robert Goodney		SS
Spot of Color	14		Edith Fitzgerald Golden		SS
"H" Run	24		Alex Pong		NV
Party Pooper	51		Dundee McDole		SS
The Deceiver	60		Lucy Spears Griffin		SS
Overnight Guest	73		Frederick Chamberlain		SS
Clear Conscience	82		Lawrence Harvey		SS
The Red Herring	86	Matt Gannon	Richard Deming		NV
Manhunt's Gun Rack: S&W .44 Magnum	113				SF

Peter Enfantino • Jeff Vorzimmer

A Sweet Deal	114	Jack Lemmon		SS
Mother Love	125	Marion Duckworth		SS

Feb 1963	v. 11 n. 1	35¢	128 Pages	Editor: John Underwood	
Story/Article	Pg	Series	Author	Pseudonym	Type
Avenging Angel	1		Mark Del Franco		SS
Prison Break	8		Duane Clark		SS
Ripper Moon!	19		John G. Reitci	Jack Ritchie	SS
The Sea-Gull	34		J. Heidloff		SS
Shake-Down	39		Dean Ball		SS
The Absent Professor	50		Robert Weaver		NA
Manhunt's Gun Rack: Llama .45 Automatic	117				SF
Exile	118		Martin Kelly		SS

Apr 1963	v. 11 n. 2	35¢	128 Pages	Editor: John Underwood	
Story/Article	Pg	Series	Author	Pseudonym	Type
Precious Pigeon	1		Talmage Powell		SS
Dear Edie	6		Pat Macmillan		SS
The Price of Lust	10		Joe Gores		NV
Conned	40		Bernard Epps		SS
Kiloman	43		Don Lowry		SS
Manhunt's Gun Rack: Colt Woodsman	60				SF
A Patient Man	61		Dave Hill		SS
Gambler's Cross	65		Robert McKay		SS
For the Defense	78		Terry McCormick		SS
The Outfit	82		Donald E. Westlake	Richard Stark	NV

Jun 1963	v. 11 n. 3	35¢	128 Pages	Editor: John Underwood	
Story/Article	Pg	Series	Author	Pseudonym	Type
No Escape	1		Glenn Canary		SS
Deadly Cuckold	9		F. S. Landstreet		SS
Bad Magic	18		Robert Page Jones		SS
Manhunt's Gun Rack: The Trailsman-snub	23				SF
One Big Pay-Off	24		Charles Sloan		SS
The Punk	35		Herbert Leslie Greene		SS
The Pervert	42		T. K. Fitzpatrick		SS
The Loners	46		Clark Howard		SS
Finders, Keepers	64		B. A. Cody		SS
Vegas . . . And Run	68		Don Lowry		NV
The Guilty Dead	117		Neil M. Clark		SS

Aug 1963	v. 11 n. 4	35¢	128 Pages	Editor: John Underwood	
Story/Article	Pg	Series	Author	Pseudonym	Type
Change of Heart	1		Arthur Porges		SS
One Thousand Steps	7		John Channing Carter		SS
Strange Triangle	12		Ray Stewart		SS
Hard-Rocks	18		Robert McKay		SS

The Manhunt Companion

No Dice!	31	Bernard Epps	SS
Nite Work	34	Frank Sisk	SS
Manhunt's Gun Rack: S&W Auto Pistol	39		SF
Bad Habit	40	G. F. McLennan	SS
Bounty	52	Ray T. Davis	SS
Sister's Keeper	56	John Lower	SS
Suspect	63	John Jakes	SS
The Star Boarder	75	Charles Miron	SS
The Scoop	82	Ort Louis	NV
Speedtrap	114	David Edgar	SS
A Little Loyalty	122	Larry Powell	SS

Oct 1963 v. 11 n. 5	35¢		128 Pages	Editor: John Underwood	
Story/Article	**Pg**	**Series**	**Author**	**Pseudonym**	**Type**
The Duchess	1		Charles Miron		SS
Wanted — Dead and Alive	4	Chester Drum	Stephen Marlowe		SS
Retirement	15		Robert Edmond Alter		SS
The Good Citizen	22		Bernard Epps		SS
The Suitcase	26		N. E. Jaeger		SS
A Grave Affair	33		Roswell B. Rohde		SS
Home Free	38		Robert Goodney		SS
Confidant	54		Bob Anis		SS
The Prospect	58		Milt Woods, Jr.		SS
One Way — Out	66		Gene Jones		SS
Final Reckoning	75		Pat Collins		SS
Liberty	83		Tom O'Malley		SS
Interference	94		Glenn Canary		SS
Fence Wanted	100		Don Lowry		NV
Mother's Day	123		Donald Emerson		SS

Jan 1964 v. 12 n. 1	50¢		160 Pages	Editor: John Underwood	
Story/Article	**Pg**	**Series**	**Author**	**Pseudonym**	**Type**
Hot	1		Don Lowry		SS
The Grass Cage	12		Robert Edmond Alter		SS
Accident Prone	25		A. M. Mathews		SS
Love for Hate	32		Xavier San Luis Rey		NV
Bum Rap	51		James L. Little		SS
Last Dime	59		Charles Miron		SS
Tap-a-San	65		Daniel Walker		SS
The Eight Ball	78		Charles Dilly		SS
Fugitive	85		Robert McKay		SS
Manhunt's Gun Rack: Ruger Mark 1 Target Pistol	97				SF
I Came to Kill You	100		Mickey Spillane		RP

Peter Enfantino • Jeff Vorzimmer

Mar 1964 v. 12 n. 2	50¢		160 Pages	Editor: John Underwood	
Story/Article	Pg	Series	Author	Pseudonym	Type
Rape!	2		Alex Pong		SS
The Brothers	21		Jim Mueller		SS
Video Vengeance	25		Pat Macmillan		SS
To Kill a Cop	31		Robert Camp		SS
Losing Streak	42		Bernard Epps		SS
The Deadly Bore	48		Roswell B. Rohde		SS
Death's Head	52	Shell Scott	Richard S. Prather		NP
The Junkie Trap	65		Clark Howard		SS
Where There's Smoke	75	Al Darlan	Edward D. Hoch		SS
Guilt Complex	92		Carroll Mayers		SS
Two Seconds Late	97		Harold Rolseth		SS
Fratricide	103		John Hanford		SS
Omerta!	114		Don Lowry		NV
Self-Preservation	147		Russell W. Lake		SS
The Little Black Book	153		Xavier San Luis Rey		SS

May 1964 v. 12 n. 3	50¢		160 Pages	Editor: John Underwood	
Story/Article	Pg	Series	Author	Pseudonym	Type
On the Street	2		Lucille Williams		SS
Dead End	21		Lawrence E. Orin		SS
The Hole Card	34		Bernard Epps		SS
The Dead and the Dying	38		Evan Hunter		RP
Manhunt's Gun Rack: .44 Remington	52				SF
A Deadly Nuisance	53		Maeva Park		SS
Cosa Mia	61		Lee Costa		SS
Divorce . . . New York Style	68		Kennan Hourwich		SS
The Silent Dead	76		Don Lowry		NV
The Switch	105		R. C. Stimers		SS
Buddies	112		A. M. Staudy		SS
The Easiest Way	117		Charles Dilly		SS
Easy Money	125		Thomas Rountree		SS
The Singing Pigeon	134	Lew Archer	Kenneth Millar	John Ross Macdonald	RP

Jul 1964 v. 12 n. 4	50¢		160 Pages	Editor: John Underwood	
Story/Article	Pg	Series	Author	Pseudonym	Type
Sweet Vengeance	2		Joe Gores		SS
What Could I Do?	22		James R. Hall		SS
Epitaph	32		Hilda Cushing		SS
Commitment to Death	38		John E. Lower		SS
The Right Man	49		William Engeler		SS
A Deadly Propositon	55		Pat Macmillan		SS
Circle of Jeopardy	66	Peter Chambers	Henry Kane		RP
Craving	97		Nel Rentub		SS

The Manhunt Companion

| A Cruise to Hell | 102 | | Leonard S. Zinberg | Ed Lacy | NA |
| Jail-Bait | 156 | | C. Ashley Lousignont | | SS |

Sep 1964	v. 12 n. 5	50¢	160 Pages	Editor: John Underwood	
Story/Article	**Pg**	**Series**	**Author**	**Pseudonym**	**Type**
Death Begins	2		Herbert Leslie Greene		SS
Dead Ringer	9		Jerry Newman		SS
Cross and Double Cross	17		B. D. Dupont		SS
Don't Tempt Me	22		Robert Page Jones		NV
Queer Siren	59		C. L. Roderman		SS
Two-Way Patsy	62		John H. Goeb		NV
Sore Loser	103		Frank Sisk		SS
Kill and Run	110		Floyd Mahannah		RP
The Mule	155		Michael Zuroy		SS

Nov 1964	v. 12 n. 6	50¢	160 Pages	Editor: John Underwood	
Story/Article	**Pg**	**Series**	**Author**	**Pseudonym**	**Type**
Courier	1		Don Lowry		SS
Whitemail	13		Edward Wellen		SS
One Hungry Pigeon	17		Patrick Connolly		SS
The Slayer	22		Robert Page Jones		NV
Eyes in the Night	54		Nel Rentub		SS
The Stud	60		James Harvey		NA
The Pro Beau	65		R. A. Gardner		SS
Astral Body	70		Maeva Park		SS
Two for the Show	77		Bernard Epps		SS
Banker's Trust	86		Paul Curtis		SS

Jan 1965	v. 13 n. 1	50¢	160 Pages	Editor: John Underwood	
Story/Article	**Pg**	**Series**	**Author**	**Pseudonym**	**Type**
The Sweet Taste	2		David Goodis		RP
Man's Man	24		Charles A. Freylin		SS
The Specialists	28		Leonard S. Zinberg	Ed Lacy	SS
Conviction	35		Will Cotton		SS
The Last Freedom	51		W. Sherwood Hartman		SS
Blood Money	56		Gary Jennings		NV
The Wrong Man	96		Stanley Mohr		SS
The Explosive Triangle	116		Frank Gay		SS
Alien Hero	120		John Chancellor		NV

Mar 1965	v. 13 n. 2	50¢	160 Pages	Editor: John Underwood	
Story/Article	**Pg**	**Series**	**Author**	**Pseudonym**	**Type**
Play Tough	2	Johnny Liddell	Frank Kane		RP
The Gate	18		Walter E. Handsaker		SS
The Dead Sell	28		George Beall		SS
A Con's Code	41		William P. Perry		SS
Shenanigans	50		Rod Barker		SS

Peter Enfantino • Jeff Vorzimmer

Bad Risk	65		Jack Farrell		SS
The Men from the Boys	75		Allyn Dennis		SS
Manhunt's Gun Rack: North & Cheney Flintlock	97				SF
Trans-Atlantic Lam	100		Don Lowry		SS
Five Days to Kill	106		Jerry Bailey		NA

May 1965	**v. 13 n. 3**	**50¢**		**160 Pages**	**Editor: John Underwood**	
Story/Article	**Pg**	**Series**	**Author**		**Pseudonym**	**Type**
Kill or Die	2		Charles A. Freylin			SS
The Seduction	15		Frank Gay			SS
Hijack	19		Don Pep			SS
Virtue's Prize	34		H. Rayburn			SS
Clean-Up	44	Johnny Liddell	Frank Kane			RP
Decoy for a Pigeon	60		Herb Hartman			SS
Nightmare's Edge	68		Robert Page Jones			SS
The Big Fall	84		Don Lowry			NV
The Helpmate	121		E. A. Bogert			SS
The Death Maker	128		Nelson Adcock			SS
Blood Is Thicker	150		Dave Hill			SS
The Helpful Cop	155		Thomas Millstead			SS

Jul 1965	**v. 13 n. 4**	**50¢**		**160 Pages**	**Editor: John Underwood**	
Story/Article	**Pg**	**Series**	**Author**		**Pseudonym**	**Type**
Hunt the Hunter	2		Patrick Connolly			SS
Going Down?	9		John G. Reitci		Jack Ritchie	SS
Mata Seguro	16		Xavier San Luis Rey			SS
Lamster War	30		Don Lowry			SS
Travelin' Man	45		Rod Bryant			SS
Aversion	54		Miriam Allen deFord			SS
Alias: Trouble	65	John J. Malone	Georgiana Craig		Craig Rice	RP
Loser's Choice	88		Nelson Adcock			NV
Tough Boy	114		Richard Welles			SS
No Future	118		Donald Lee			SS
The Other Side	126		Daniel DePaola			NV
Double or Nothing	156		W. Sherwood Hartman			SS

Sep 1965	**v. 13 n. 5**	**50¢**		**160 Pages**	**Editor: John Underwood**	
Story/Article	**Pg**	**Series**	**Author**		**Pseudonym**	**Type**
Bury Me Proper	2		George H. Bennett			SS
Fair Exchange	11		Patrick Sherlock			SS
Blood Brother	20		Jerry Spafford			SS
The Virile Image	40		Gerald Pearce			SS
The Fixer	49		Robert Turner			RP
Portrait in Blood	58		Bob Temmey			NV
Beneficiary	85		Natalie Jenkins Bond			SS
Turnabout	100		Billy Gill			SS

Story/Article	Pg	Series	Author	Pseudonym	Type
After the Fact	108 Scott Jordan		Harold Q. Masur		RP
Tennis Bum	120		G. L. Tassone		SS
Middle-Man	132		Raymond Crooks		NV
The Payment Is Death	152		John E. Cameron		SS

Dec 1965	v. 13 n. 6		50¢		160 Pages		Editor: John Underwood	
Story/Article	Pg	Series	Author	Pseudonym	Type
Means to an End	2		Robert Edmond Alter		SS
Do-Gooder	16		Roy Carroll	Roy Carroll	RP
The Loyal	25		Lawrence E. Orin		SS
Collection	33 Oliver Short		Nelson Adcock		NV
Man of the People	52		Xavier San Luis Rey		SS
A Second Chance	65		C. G. Cunningham		SS
Two Grand . . . and a Bullet	76		Robert Patrick Wilmot		RP
The Nebulous Lover	97		Jerry Hopkins		SS
Busman's Holiday	105		Jerry Jacobson		SS
To Each His Own	114		Tom Cox		SS
Night Bus	125		Don Lowry		SS
Damn You, Die	138		Jeremiah Sommers		SS
Fraternity	154		Frank Gay		SS

Feb-Mar 1966	v. 14 n. 1		50¢		160 Pages		Editor: John Underwood	
Story/Article	Pg	Series	Author	Pseudonym	Type
The Anonymous Body	2		Nancy A. Black		SS
Wrath	21		Peter Brandt		SS
The Last Fix	29		Jack Belck		SS
The Deadly Ad-Man	39		Hayes Rabon		SS
Deadly Star-Dust	43		Larry Dane		SS
Predator	68		Robert Edmond Alter		SS
Murder, Though It Have No Tongue	80		Maeva Park		SS
Stiff Competition	88		Frank Sisk		NV
In Self Defense	112		Richard Deming		RP
The "N" Man	120		Don Lowry		NV
Past Imperfect	148		Frank Gay		SS
The Anniversary Murder	151		Georgiana Craig	Craig Rice	RP

Apr-May 1966	v. 14 n. 2		50¢		160 Pages		Editor: John Underwood	
Story/Article	Pg	Series	Author	Pseudonym	Type
Scandal Anyone?	2		Frank Gay		SS
The Proof Is In	9		S. K. Snedegar		SS
The Hand	16		Charles A. Freylin		SS
The Lonesome Bride	30 Oliver Short		Nelson Adcock		NV
Southern Comfort	61		Shirley Dunbar		SS
Needle Street	65		J. Kenneth O'Street		SS
A Deadly Secret	74		Beatrice S. Smith		NV
Double Damned	97		C. G. Cunningham		SS

Peter Enfantino • Jeff Vorzimmer

Story/Article	Pg		Series	Author	Pseudonym	Type
City Cop	108			Jack Belck		SS
An Angle on Death	116			Robert Turner	Roy Carroll	RP
Viking Blood	125	Slot Machine Kelly		Michael Collins	Dennis Lynds	NV

Jun-Jul 1966	v. 14 n. 3	50¢	160 Pages	Editor: John Underwood	
Story/Article	**Pg**	**Series**	**Author**	**Pseudonym**	**Type**
Leopard Man	2		Russell W. Lake		SS
Sin of Omission	22		Pat Airey		SS
Ace in the Hole	37		Don Lee		SS
Bloody Reformation	45		Grover Brinkman		SS
Deadly Outpost	54		Robert Armpriest		SS
Tough Chippie	67		Frank E. Smith	Jonathan Craig	RP
A Widow's Word	75		George B. Scanlan		SS
The Conspirators	86		Robert Streeter Aldrich		SS
Twice a Patsy	95		Floyd Mahannah		RP
The Matriarch	112		James B. Kittell		SS
Graveyard Shift	118	Peter Chambers	Henry Kane		RP
Missile Missing	148		S. K. Snedegar		SS

Aug-Sep 1966	v. 14 n. 4	50¢	160 Pages	Editor: John Underwood	
Story/Article	**Pg**	**Series**	**Author**	**Pseudonym**	**Type**
A Weakness for . . . Women	2	John J. Malone	Georgiana Craig	Craig Rice	RP
One Man's Meat	20		Jif Frank		SS
Reluctant Witness	26		Duff Howard		SS
Venom	48		Guy Gowen		SS
Baby . . . Don't Cry	65		Marie Elston Collamore		SS
The Past Is Dead	70		Frank E. Smith	Jonathan Craig	RP
The Hot One	85		J. Robert Carroll		SS
One Fingerprint	97		Bob Russell		SS
Dude Sheriff	102		Richard Hill Wilkinson		SS
Killer Instinct	114		David Chandler		RP
Frustration	120		Ruth Aldrich Gray		SS
Blonde Bait	125		Norm Kent		SS
The Deceiver	135		Lawrence Orin		SS
Big Score	140		Don Lowry		SS
The Hard Way	146		C. Durbin		SS

Oct-Nov 1966	v. 14 n. 5	50¢	160 Pages	Editor: John Underwood	
Story/Article	**Pg**	**Series**	**Author**	**Pseudonym**	**Type**
Fernando's Return	2		Vic Hendrix		SS
Obie's Girl	10		Fletcher Flora		RP
The Prisoner	16		David Daheim		NV
A Friend of a Friend	41		Morris F. Baughman		SS
Bomb Scare	46		Robert Slaughter		SS
Two Weeks with Pay	67		Ernest Chamberlain		SS
Sitting Duck	76		Robert Turner		RP

Story/Article	Pg	Series	Author	Pseudonym	Type
Willful Murder	83	Scott Jordan	Harold Q. Masur		RP
The Misplaced Star	95	Oliver Short	Nelson Adcock		NA
All the Loose Women	147	18th Precinct	Frank E. Smith	Jonathan Craig	RP

Dec-Jan 1967   v. 14 n. 6   50¢   160 Pages   Editor: John Underwood

Story/Article	Pg	Series	Author	Pseudonym	Type
Hot Pilot	2		Alex Pong		SS
The Recluse	14		James R. Frantz		SS
Alacran	20		Jack Kelsey		SS
Ricochet	36		W. Sherwood Hartman		SS
A Time to Live	45		Vic Hendrix		SS
Love, A Thief and Salvation	65		Xavier San Luis Rey		SS
Whiz Cop	71		Jim Robinson		SS
Sucker Play	75		Wilfred C. Vroman		SS
Lust or Honor	82		William Vance		RP
Burst of Glory	97		Joseph Brophy		SS
Kill Him for Me	104		John G. Allen		NV
Death on the Make	130		Ort Louis		NV
Death in the Mirror	154		Lee Russell		SS

Feb-Mar 1967   v. 15 n. 1   50¢   160 Pages   Editor: John Underwood

Story/Article	Pg	Series	Author	Pseudonym	Type
Big Time Carly	2		Ernest Chamberlain		SS
No Riders	16		Shirley Dunbar		SS
Dog Days	22		Clayton Matthews		SS
Fair Game	36		Roswell B. Rohde		SS
Indian Giver	43	Scott Jordan	Harold Q. Masur		RP
Breakout	56		John G. Allen		NV
The Fifty Grand Stretch	86		Evan Hunter	Richard Marsten	RP
Modus Operandi	97		Edward Y. Breese		SS
Hot Wheels	106		Don Lowry		SS
Out on a Wing	118		Alex Pong		SS
The Party Line	131		E. F. Golden		SS
Impulse	139		Paul Curtis		RP
Golden Opportunity	150		Clayton Matthews		SS

Apr-May 1967   v. 15 n. 2   50¢   160 Pages   Editor: John Underwood

Story/Article	Pg	Series	Author	Pseudonym	Type
Bad Blood	2	Lew Archer	Kenneth Millar	John Ross Macdonald	RP
A Good Man Is Hard to Find	16		Lawrence E. Orin		SS
The Lesson	20		Gene Wilson		SS
Blow-Up	31		Jack Lynch		SS
Flood	40		Jackson Bowling		SS
The Scavengers	54		J. Bachman		SS
The Lucy Prey	65		Dale L. Gilbert		SS
The Dead Undertaker	74	John J. Malone	Georgiana Craig	Craig Rice	RP

Peter Enfantino • Jeff Vorzimmer

The Cool One	85	George Antonich		ES
Circumstantial Evidence	91	Evan Hunter	Hunt Collins	FP
Two-Sided Triangle	98	Larry Dane		ES
The Snatchers	106	M. G. Wealeder		FV
No Fair	151	B. J. Starr		ES
Buddies	156	Herbert Leslie Greene		ES

Alphabetical Index by Story
*Denotes full-length novel. †Denotes Name of television episode.

Story/Article	Alt. Title	Author	Issue	Page
.38		Joe Grenzeback	Mar 1956	60
40 Detectives Later	Forty Detectives Later†	Henry Slesar	May 1957	23
Absent Professor, The		Robert Weaver	Feb 1963	50
Absinthe for Superman		Robert Edmond Alter	Jun 1959	55
Academic Freedom		Glenn Canary	Apr 1962	39
Accident		John M. Sitan	Aug 1954	43
Accident Prone		A. M. Mathews	Jan 1964	25
Accident Report		Evan Hunter	Sep 1953	48
According to Plan		Seymour Richin	Jun 1962	37
Accuser, The		Robert Wallsten	Aug 1960	20
Ace in the Hole		Don Lee	Jun-Jul 1966	37
Addict		W. E. Douglas	Jun 1956	27
After the Fact	The Mourning After	Harold Q. Masur	Sep 1965	108
Against the Middle		Evan Hunter	Mar 1953	140
Alacran		Jack Kelsey	Dec-Jan 1967	20
Alarmist, The		Donald Tothe	Feb 1961	81
Alias: Trouble	I'm a Stranger Here Myself	Georgiana Craig	Jul 1965	65
Alien Hero		John Chancellor	Jan 1965	120
All the Loose Women	The Dead Darling	Frank E. Smith	Oct-Nov 1966	147
Alligator Man, The		Tom Beach	Nov 1955	134
Amateur, The		Richard Deming	Jun 1957	5
Ambition		Patrick Madden	Sep 1954	57
And Be Merry		Georgiana Craig	Jan 1954	88
And Share Alike	A Touch of Death*	Charles Williams	Aug 1954	87
Angle on Death, An	Shakedown	Robert Turner	Apr-May 1966	116
Anniversary Murder, The	The Tears of Evil	Georgiana Craig	Feb-Mar 1966	151
Anonymous Body, The		Nancy A. Black	Feb-Mar 1966	2
Anything Goes		Hal Ellson	Sep 1956	51
Arrest		Donald E. Westlake	Jan 1958	62
As I Lie Dead		Fletcher Flora	Feb 1953	131
Aspect of Death, An		James L. Liverman	Oct 1961	118
Assassin, The		Robert Kimmel Smith	Apr 1962	46
Assault		Grant Colby	May 1953	142
Association Test		Evan Hunter	Jul 1954	21
Astral Body		Maeva Park	Nov 1964	70
Attack		Evan Hunter	Feb 1953	77
Avenging Angel		Mark Del Franco	Feb 1963	1
Aversion		Miriam Allen deFord	Jul 1965	54
Awake to Fear		Robert Camp	Apr 1959	65
Babe and the Bum, The		Mike Brett	Feb 1958	62

Peter Enfantino • Jeff Vorzimmer

Story/Article	Alt. Title	Author	Issue	Page
Baby . . . Don't Cry		Marie Elston Collamore	Aug-Sep 1966	65
Baby Sitter, The		Frank E. Smith	Jul 1955	31
Bachelor in the Making, A		Charles Jackson	Dec 1954	36
Backfire		Floyd Mahannah	Jan 1953	98
Bad Blood	Guilt-Edged Blonde	Kenneth Millar	Apr-May 1967	2
Bad Habit		G. F. McLennan	Aug 1963	40
Bad Magic		Robert Page Jones	Jun 1963	18
Bad Risk		Jack Farrell	Mar 1965	65
Bad Word		David Alexander	Dec 1957	5
Badge of Dishonor		Norman Struber	Sep 1956	13
Bail Out!		Robert Weaver & Samuel Rubi	Feb 1962	66
Bait for the Red Head		Eugene Pawley	Jan 1957	64
Balanced Account		Richard Deming	Oct 1953	24
Banker's Trust	Impulse	Paul Curtis	Nov 1964	86
Bargain, The		Charles Boeckman	Oct 1954	11
Bargainmaster, The		Bob Bristow	Jun 1959	15
Be a Man		Talmage Powell	Feb 1958	29
Be My Guest	The Fixer	Robert Turner	Apr 1953	39
Beatings, The		Evan Hunter	Oct 1954	1
Beat-Up Sister, The		Kenneth Millar	Oct 1953	110
Beautiful Babe and Money, A		Talmage Powell	Oct 1957	62
Bedbug		Evan Hunter	Sep 1954	10
Bells Are Ringing, The		Georgiana Craig	Nov 1955	42
Beneficiary		Natalie Jenkins Bond	Sep 1965	85
Best Motive, The	Death's Head	Richard S. Prather	Jan 1953	59
Bet I Don't Die		Arnold English	May 1957	4
Better Bargain, The		Richard Deming	Apr 1956	43
Big Bite, The		Charles Williams	Jul 1956	95
Big Brother		Robert M. Hodges	Oct 1959	25
Big Day, The		Evan Hunter	Sep 1955	25
Big Fall, The		Don Lowry	May 1965	84
Big Fish, The		Hal Ellson	Nov 1957	47
Big Frank		Bryce Walton	Nov 1955	1
Big Hands		L. J. Krebs	Aug 1958	20
Big Hate, The		Frank Cetin	Mar 1957	11
Big Haul, The	The Heisters*	Robert Page Jones	Aug 1961	84
Big Score, The		Sam Merwin, Jr.	Jul 1955	120
Big Score		Don Lowry	Aug-Sep 1966	140
Big Smile, The		Stan Wiley	Feb 1957	139
Big Steal		Frank Kane	Dec 1954	61
Big Talk		Kris Neville	Apr 1953	31
Big Time Carly		Ernest Chamberlain	Feb-Mar 1967	2
Big Touch, The		Henry Kane	Nov 1953	1

334   The Manhunt Companion

Story/Article	Alt. Title	Author	Issue	Page
Biggest Risk		C. B. Gilford	Aug 1956	43
Bird Watcher, The		Frank Sisk	Aug 1959	52
Bite, The		Edward D. Radin	Mar 1955	51
Black Cat in the Snow		John D. MacDonald	Feb 1958	47
Black Pudding	The Sweet Taste	David Goodis	Dec 1953	1
Blackmail		Eugene Gaffney	Dec 1961	9
Blackmail, Inc.		Michel Dedina	Aug 1962	14
Blackmailers Don't Take Chances		David C. Cooke	Jun 1958	121
Block Party		Sam Merwin, Jr.	Feb 1956	1
Blonde at the Wheel		Stephen Marlowe	Oct 1955	47
Blonde Bait		Norm Kent	Aug-Sep 1966	125
Blonde in Room 320, The		William Hurst	Jun 1959	24
Blonde in the Bar, The		Richard Deming	May 1954	1
Blood and Moonlight		William R. Cox	Oct 1956	27
Blood Brother		Jerry Spafford	Sep 1965	20
Blood Brothers		Hal Ellson	Apr 1955	1
Blood Is Thicker		Dave Hill	May 1965	150
Blood Money		Gary Jennings	Jan 1965	56
Blood Oath, The		Richard Deming	Jan 1955	31
Blood of the Lamb, The		Steve Allen	Nov 1957	1
Blood on the Land		Hal Ellson	Jun 1957	24
Bloodless Bayonet, The		Thomas Millstead	Feb 1962	1
Bloody Reformation		Grover Brinkman	Jun-Jul 1966	45
Blow-Up		Jack Lynch	Apr-May 1967	31
Blue Sweetheart, The		David Goodis	Apr 1953	102
Bobby-Soxer, The		Frank E. Smith	Oct 1953	141
Body in the Rain		John S. Hill	Oct 1956	117
Body on a White Carpet		Albert James Hjertstedt	Apr 1957	1
Body Snatcher		Aaron Marc Stein	Jun 1955	21
Bodyguard		Richard Hardwick	Jun 1960	18
Body-Snatcher		C. B. Gilford	Feb 1961	54
Boiler, The		Andrew J. Burris	Jan 1956	31
Bomb Scare		Robert Slaughter	Oct-Nov 1966	46
Bonus Cop		Richard Deming	Sep 1953	59
Bothered		Gil Brewer	Jul 1957	9
Bounty		Ray T. Davis	Aug 1963	52
Break Down		Robert Edmond Alter	Oct 1961	76
Breaking Point		Eleanor Roth	Jan 1956	58
Breakout		John G. Allen	Feb-Mar 1967	56
Broken Doll		Jack Webb	May 1954	45
Broken Window, The		Earle Basinsky, Jr.	Feb 1957	101
Bronco		Roy Koch	Jun 1959	66
Brothers, The		Jim Mueller	Mar 1964	21

Peter Enfantino • Jeff Vorzimmer

Story/Article	Alt. Title	Author	Issue	Page
Brother's Keeper		Brian Lowe	Dec 1961	53
Brusky's Fault		Robert Plate	Sep 1956	31
Buddies		A. M. Staudy	May 1964	112
Buddies		Herbert Leslie Greene	Apr-May 19☛7	156
Bug Doctor		Edward D. Radin	Aug 1955	26
Bugged		Bruno Fischer	Aug 1961	61
Build Another Coffin		Harold Q. Masur	May 1953	107
Bull to Kill, A		Evan Hunter	Nov 1954	47
Bum Rap		James L. Little	Jan 1964	51
Bunco		John R. Starr	Jul 1957	44
Burglaries		Fred L. Anderson	Jul 1954	78
Burst of Glory		Joseph Brophy	Dec-Jan 19☛7	97
Bury Me Proper		George H. Bennett	Sep 1965	2
Bus to Portland		L. W. King	Oct 1956	129
Business as Usual		Arnold English	Sep 1957	6
Busman's Holiday		Jerry Jacobson	Dec 1965	105
Busybody		J. Simmons Scheb	Aug 1960	119
Butcher		Richard S. Prather	Jun 1954	101
Buzzard, Brother, Blood		Lewis Banci	Apr 1961	46
Cabin 13		Edward Perry	Aug 1958	114
Caller, The		Emmanuel Winters	Jun 1953	90
Canary, The		John G. Reitci	Jun 1956	47
Candlestick		Henry Kane	Oct 1954	102
Careful Man, The		Richard Deming	Jun 1955	56
Carnival Con		David Zinman	Dec 1960	1
Carrera's Woman		Evan Hunter	Feb 1953	65
Case History		Charles Boeckman	Nov 1953	52
Cast Off		Frank E. Smith	Sep 1955	14
Cat's Meow		Jordan Bauman	Dec 1959	62
Caught in the Act		Niel Franklin	Aug 1958	31
Chain Gang		Joe Gores	Dec 1957	14
Chain Reaction		Charles Boeckman	Oct 1961	54
Challenge, The		John Carnegie	Apr 1960	57
Change for a C-Note		Jerry Sohl	Jul 1956	84
Change of Heart		Arthur Porges	Aug 1963	1
Charles Turner Case, The		Richard Deming	May 1957	30
Chase by Night		Jack M. Bagby	Sep 1953	92
Cheap Kicks		William Brothers	Jun 1961	52
Cheater, The		Frank E. Smith	Jan 1956	45
Check Out		Edward Wellen	Oct 1959	123
Cheese It, the Corpse		Georgiana Craig	Nov 1957	10
Chicken!		Phil Perlmutter	Oct 1956	138
Chinese Puzzle		Evan Hunter	Jul 1954	1

Story/Article	Alt. Title	Author	Issue	Page
Chips Are Down, The		Wilfred Alexander	Jun 1958	71
Choice, The		Richard Deming	Jun 1954	62
Cigarette Girl		James M. Cain	May 1953	85
Circle for Death		Pat Stadley	Jun 1956	1
Circle of Jeopardy	One Little Bullet	Henry Kane	Jul 1964	66
Circumstantial Evidence	Sucker	Evan Hunter	Apr-May 1967	91
City Cop		Jack Belck	Apr-May 1966	108
City Hunters		George Lange	May 1956	127
Classification: Dead		Evan Hunter	Nov 1953	87
Classification: Homicide		Frank E. Smith	Feb 1955	97
Clay Pigeon		Joseph Commings	Dec 1957	62
Clean Getaway		William Vance	Oct 1954	20
Clean-Up	Finish the Job	Frank Kane	May 1965	44
Clear Conscience		Lawrence Harvey	Dec 1962	82
Clear Day for Hunting, A		Jack Q. Lynn	Dec 1956	110
Clear Picture, A		Sam S. Taylor	May 1954	131
Closed Door, The		Walt Frisbie	Nov 1957	27
Code 197		Richard S. Prather	Jun 1955	27
Colby's Monster		Stuart Friedman	Apr 1958	11
Collection		Nelson Adcock	Dec 1965	33
Collector Comes After Payday, The		Fletcher Flora	Aug 1953	1
College Kill		Jack Q. Lynn	May 1957	8
Come Across		Gil Brewer	Apr 1956	52
Comeback		R. Van Taylor	Feb 1954	107
Commitment to Death		John E. Lower	Jul 1964	38
Compensation		Helen Nielsen	Nov 1957	21
Competitors, The		Richard Deming	Feb 1955	53
Coney Island Incident	So Wicked My Love*	Bruno Fischer	Nov 1953	116
Confession		John M. Sitan	Jul 1954	81
Confession		C. B. Gilford	Dec 1959	102
Confidant		Bob Anis	Oct 1963	54
Conned		Bernard Epps	Apr 1963	40
Con's Code, A		William P. Perry	Mar 1965	41
Conspirators, The		Robert Streeter Aldrich	Jun-Jul 1966	86
Conviction		Will Cotton	Jan 1965	35
Cool Cat		Hal Ellson	Feb 1956	63
Cool One, The		George Antonich	Apr-May 1967	85
Cop for a Day		Henry Slesar	Jan 1957	8
Cop Hater, The		Floyd Wallace	Jun 1959	76
Cop in a Frame		Dick Ellis	Oct 1961	80
Cop Killer		Dan Sontup	Aug 1956	1
Corpse That Didn't Die, A		Henry Kane	Jun 1959	87
Cosa Mia		Lee Costa	May 1964	61

Peter Enfantino • Jeff Vorzimmer

Story/Article	Alt. Title	Author	Issue	Page
Couple of Bucks, A		Clair Huffaker	Dec 1956	15
Courier		Don Lowry	Nov 1964	1
Cowpatch Vengeance		Charles W. Moore	Nov 1956	31
Coyote, The		David Chandler	Dec 1953	102
Craving		Nel Rentub	Jul 1964	97
Crime and Punishment		Shepherd Kole	Apr 1953	100
Crime Broker, The		Steve Frazee	Jun 1962	104
Crime Cavalcade		Vincent H. Gaddis	May 1953	32
Crime Cavalcade		Vincent H. Gaddis	Jun 1953	75
Crime Cavalcade		Vincent H. Gaddis	Jul 1953	90
Crime Cavalcade		Vincent H. Gaddis	Aug 1953	76
Crime Cavalcade		Vincent H. Gaddis	Sep 1953	116
Crime Cavalcade		Vincent H. Gaddis	Oct 1953	57
Crime Cavalcade		Vincent H. Gaddis	Nov 1953	75
Crime Cavalcade		Vincent H. Gaddis	Dec 1953	133
Crime Cavalcade		Vincent H. Gaddis	Jan 1954	85
Crime Cavalcade		Vincent H. Gaddis	Feb 1954	57
Crime Cavalcade		Vincent H. Gaddis	May 1954	77
Crime Cavalcade		Vincent H. Gaddis	Jun 1954	111
Crime Cavalcade		Vincent H. Gaddis	Jul 1954	39
Crime Cavalcade		Vincent H. Gaddis	Aug 1954	20
Crime Cavalcade		Vincent H. Gaddis	Sep 1954	61
Crime Cavalcade		Vincent H. Gaddis	Oct 1954	78
Crime Cavalcade		Vincent H. Gaddis	Nov 1954	45
Crime Cavalcade		Vincent H. Gaddis	Dec 1954	57
Crime Cavalcade		Vincent H. Gaddis	Dec 1954	55
Crime Cavalcade		Vincent H. Gaddis	Jan 1955	73
Crime Cavalcade		Vincent H. Gaddis	Feb 1955	78
Crime Cavalcade		Vincent H. Gaddis	Mar 1955	112
Crime Cavalcade		Vincent H. Gaddis	Apr 1955	114
Crime Cavalcade		Vincent H. Gaddis	May 1955	94
Crime Cavalcade		Vincent H. Gaddis	Jun 1955	100
Crime Cavalcade		Vincent H. Gaddis	Jul 1955	116
Crime Cavalcade		Vincent H. Gaddis	Aug 1955	55
Crime Cavalcade		Vincent H. Gaddis	Sep 1955	55
Crime Cavalcade		Vincent H. Gaddis	Oct 1955	44
Crime Cavalcade		Vincent H. Gaddis	Nov 1955	60
Crime Cavalcade		Vincent H. Gaddis	Dec 1955	41
Crime Cavalcade		Vincent H. Gaddis	Mar 1956	78
Crime of My Wife, The		Robert Turner	Aug 1953	48
Crime of Passion		Richard S. Prather	Dec 1954	1
Cross and Double Cross		B. D. Dupont	Sep 1964	17
Cross Forks Incident, The		Thomas P. Ramirez	Feb 1957	126

Story/Article	Alt. Title	Author	Issue	Page
Crossed and Double-Crossed		Carroll Mayers	Aug 1959	14
Cruise to Hell, A		Leonard S. Zinberg	Jul 1964	102
Cry Wolf!		C. B. Gilford	Jun 1962	76
Crying Target, The		James McKimmey	Sep 1957	49
Curses		Koller Ernst	Oct 1959	63
Custody		Richard Deming	Dec 1955	32
Cut-Throat World		J. W. Aaron	Oct 1957	1
D. O. A.		Jules Rosenthal	Jul 1956	91
Dame Across the River, The		Talmage Powell	Apr 1958	28
Damn You, Die		Jeremiah Sommers	Dec 1965	138
Dangerous		Hal Ellson	Jan 1956	14
Dangerous Money	Reward to Finder†	F. J. Smith	Oct 1956	122
Date with Harry, A		George Lange	Jul 1956	79
Day It Began Again, The		Fletcher Flora	Apr 1955	31
Day's Work		Evan Hunter	Jul 1953	44
Dead and the Dying, The	Dead Men Don't Dream	Evan Hunter	May 1964	38
Dead as a Mannequin		Rex Raney	Mar 1957	1
Dead Beat		Hayden Howard	Oct 1960	8
Dead Cats		Henry Marksbury	Aug 1958	1
Dead Darling, The	All the Loose Women	Frank E. Smith	Oct 1954	64
Dead End		Lawrence E. Orin	May 1964	21
Dead Grin, The		Frank Kane	Jun 1955	115
Dead Heat		Robert Turner	Oct 1953	35
Dead Heat		Tom Phillips	Dec 1960	21
Dead Issue	Willful Murder	Harold Q. Masur	Dec 1954	82
Dead Letter		Don Tothe	Jun 1961	125
Dead Man's Cat		Sylvie Pasche	Jun 1956	31
Dead Men Don't Dream	The Dead and the Dying	Evan Hunter	Mar 1953	21
Dead on Arrival		Bob Bristow	Aug 1959	19
Dead People Are Never Angry		C. B. Gilford	Sep 1956	125
Dead Pigeon		Frank Kane	Jul 1957	52
Dead Reckoning		Frank Kane	Dec 1959	42
Dead Ringer		Jerry Newman	Sep 1964	9
Dead Sell, The		George Beall	Mar 1965	28
Dead Set		Frank Kane	Dec 1957	51
Dead Soldier		Jack Sword	Feb 1956	40
Dead Stand-In, The		Frank Kane	Jan 1956	68
Dead Undertaker, The	Murder Marches On!	Georgiana Craig	Apr-May 1967	74
Deadlier Than the Mail		Evan Hunter	Feb 1954	39
Deadline Murder		John G. Reitci	Oct 1958	70
Deadly Ad-Man, The		Hayes Rabon	Feb-Mar 1966	39
Deadly Affair, The		Charles Carpentier	Oct 1961	49
Deadly Beloved		William Campbell Gault	Oct 1956	57

Peter Enfantino • Jeff Vorzimmer

Story/Article	Alt. Title	Author	Issue	Page
Deadly Bore, The		Roswell B. Rahde	Mar 1964	48
Deadly Charm		Stuart Friedman	Jun 1958	36
Deadly Cuckold		F. S. Landstreet	Jun 1963	9
Deadly Dolls, The	Death is the Last Lover*	Henry Kane	May 1957	41
Deadly Error		Avram Davidson & Chester Co	Aug 1960	77
Deadly Nuisance, A		Maeva Park	May 1964	53
Deadly Outpost		Robert Armpriest	Jun-Jul 1966	54
Deadly Propositon, A		Pat Macmillan	Jul 1964	55
Deadly Secret, A		Beatrice S. Smith	Apr-May 1966	74
Deadly Star-Dust		Larry Dane	Feb-Mar 1966	43
Deadly Triangle		Les Cole	Apr 1961	1
Dear Edie		Pat Macmillan	Apr 1963	6
Dear Sir		Talmage Powell	Oct 1961	12
Death and the Blue Rose		William O'Farrell	Dec 1960	59
Death at Full Moon		Albert James Hjertstedt	Feb 1960	80
Death Beat		David C. Cooke	Nov 1956	27
Death Begins		Herbert Leslie Greene	Sep 1964	2
Death by the Numbers		Leonard S. Zinberg	Aug 1961	8
Death in the Mirror		Lee Russell	Dec-Jan 1967	154
Death Maker, The		Nelson Adcock	May 1965	128
Death of a Big Wheel		William Campbell Gault	Apr 1957	52
Death of a Stripper		Sherry La Verne	Sep 1957	24
Death of Arney Vincent, The		C. L. Sweeney, Jr.	Jul 1955	155
Death of El Indio, The		Leonard S. Zinberg	Oct 1961	22
Death of Me, The		Evan Hunter	Sep 1953	1
Death of Me, The		Anne Smith Ewing	Oct 1959	50
Death on the Make		Ort Louis	Dec-Jan 1967	130
Death Sentence		Richard Deming	Dec 1954	93
Death Wears a Gray Sweater		Roy Carroll	Nov 1956	48
Deathmate		James Causey	Mar 1957	52
Death-Ray Gun, The		Evan Hunter	Jan 1955	100
Death's Head	The Best Motive	Richard S. Prather	Mar 1964	52
Decay		Michael Zuroy	Aug 1961	1
Deceiver, The		Lucy Spears Griffin	Dec 1962	60
Deceiver, The		Lawrence Orin	Aug-Sep 1966	135
Decision		Helen Nielsen	Jun 1957	59
Decoy		Hal Ellson	Jun 1955	51
Decoy for a Pigeon		Herb Hartman	May 1965	60
Degree of Guilt		John G. Reitci	Dec 1956	9
Desert Chase		Thurber Jensen	Dec 1958	58
Deserter, The		Hal Ellson	Aug 1960	11
Desperation		Joachim H. Woos	Dec 1960	126
Deveraux Monster, The		John G. Reitci	Feb 1962	52

Story/Article	Alt. Title	Author	Issue	Page
Devil Eyes		John G. Reitci	May 1956	94
Diary of a Devout Man		Richard Deming	Dec 1954	76
Die Hard		Evan Hunter	Jan 1953	16
Die Like a Dog		David Alexander	Jun 1954	133
Die, Die, Die!		Rosemary Johnston	Aug 1961	72
Dirge for a Nude		Frank E. Smith	Feb 1953	37
Disaster, The		Emmanuel Winters	Feb 1954	52
Divide and Conquer		John G. Reitci	Feb 1957	53
Divorce . . . New York Style		Kennan Hourwich	May 1964	68
Dog Days		Clayton Matthews	Feb-Mar 1967	22
Dog Eat Dog		Georges Carousso	Feb 1962	25
Do-Gooder	Wife Beater	Roy Carroll	Dec 1965	16
Don't Clip My Wings		David W. Maurer	Apr 1960	79
Don't Go Near		Georgiana Craig	May 1953	121
Don't Tempt Me		Robert Page Jones	Sep 1964	22
Don't Twist My Arm		John G. Reitci	Apr 1958	1
Dope to Kill		Edward Wellen	Oct 1958	1
Double		Bruno Fischer	Jun 1954	82
Double Damned		C. G. Cunningham	Apr-May 1966	97
Double Frame, The		Harold Q. Masur	Jun 1953	78
Double or Nothing		W. Sherwood Hartman	Jul 1965	156
Double Payments		Max F. Harris	Apr 1962	89
Double Take, The		Richard S. Prather	Jul 1953	114
Double Take, The		Edward Wellen	Apr 1959	26
Double Trouble		Edward D. Radin	May 1955	113
Doubles, The		Richard Deming	Dec 1957	45
Down and Out	South of Market	Joe Gores	Jun 1959	1
Drifter, The		Robert S. Swenson	Jan 1955	91
Dry Run		Norman Struber	Apr 1956	112
Duchess, The		Charles Miron	Oct 1963	1
Dude Sheriff		Richard Hill Wilkinson	Aug-Sep 1966	102
Duel in the Pit		Rick Sargent	Dec 1957	25
Earrings, The		Kermit Shelby	Aug 1956	133
Easiest Way, The		Charles Dilly	May 1964	117
Easy Money		Thomas Rountree	May 1964	125
Effective Medicine		B. Traven	Aug 1954	31
Eight Ball, The		Charles Dilly	Jan 1964	78
El Rey		William Logan	May 1955	156
Empty Fort, The	A Night Out*	Basil Heatter	Sep 1954	104
Empty Threat, An		Donald E. Westlake	Feb 1960	118
End of an Era		James Malone	Dec 1959	68
End of Fear, The		Georgiana Craig	Aug 1953	58
Enormous Grave, The		Norman Struber	Oct 1956	1

Peter Enfantino • Jeff Vorzimmer

Story/Article	Alt. Title	Author	Issue	Page
Enough Rope for Two		Clark Howard	Feb 1957	106
Epitaph		Erskine Caldwell	Jan 1955	83
Epitaph		Hilda Cushing	Jul 1964	32
Escape Route	This is My Night*	Richard Deming	Oct 1959	75
Every Morning		Evan Hunter	Sep 1954	88
Everybody's Watching Me	I Came to Kill You	Mickey Spillane	Jun 1955	122
Everybody's Watching Me [Part 1 of 4]	I Came to Kill You	Mickey Spillane	Jan 1953	1
Everybody's Watching Me [Part 2 of 4]	I Came to Kill You	Mickey Spillane	Feb 1953	81
Everybody's Watching Me [Part 3 of 4]	I Came to Kill You	Mickey Spillane	Mar 1953	107
Everybody's Watching Me [Part 4 of 4]	I Came to Kill You	Mickey Spillane	Apr 1953	120
Evidence		Frank Kane	Jul 1953	101
Evidence of Murder, The		Kenneth McCaffrey	Apr 1961	89
Exile		Martin Kelly	Feb 1963	118
Experts in Crime: Forgery		Edward Clark	Oct 1955	61
Explosive Triangle, The		Frank Gay	Jan 1965	116
Express Stop		Jason January	Apr 1957	48
Extortioners, The		Ovid Demaris	Aug 1959	69
Eye for an Eye, An		Philip Weck	Mar 1956	36
Eyes in the Night		Nel Rentub	Nov 1964	54
Eye-Witness		Charles Sloan	Oct 1962	40
Face of a Killer, The		Charles Beaumont	Dec 1956	40
Face of Evil		David Alexander	Jan 1957	15
Faceless Man, The		Michael Fessier	Jun 1953	64
Fair Exchange		Patrick Sherlock	Sep 1965	11
Fair Game		Fletcher Flora	Sep 1953	26
Fair Game		Roswell B. Rohde	Feb-Mar 1957	36
Fair Play		John G. Reitci	Apr 1959	20
Fair Warning		James Holding	Apr 1961	117
Faithless Woman, The		Carroll Mayers	Jun 1960	30
Fall Guy		Joe Grenzeback	Jul 1956	64
Fallen Cop, The		Robert Anthony	Jun 1962	62
False Bait		Don Sollars	Aug 1962	113
Family Argument		Neal Curtis	Jun 1962	57
Famous Actress, The		Harry Roskolenko	Oct 1954	94
Fan Club		Richard Ellington	Apr 1953	48
Far Cry		Henry Kane	Jun 1953	1
Fast Line, The		Art Crockett	Dec 1956	141
Fat Boy		Hal Ellson	Nov 1955	52
Fat Chance		Wayne Hyde	Oct 1957	41
Favor, The		Talmage Powell	Sep 1957	35
Fence Wanted		Don Lowry	Oct 1963	100
Fernando's Return		Vic Hendrix	Oct-Nov 1966	2
Field of Honor	The Violent Ones	Robert Turner	Oct 1955	19

342   The Manhunt Companion

Story/Article	Alt. Title	Author	Issue	Page
Fifteen Grand		Jack Q. Lynn	Apr 1958	6
Fifty Grand Stretch, The	Switch Ending	Evan Hunter	Feb-Mar 1967	86
Fight Night		Robert Turner	Jan 1956	35
Final Reckoning		Pat Collins	Oct 1963	75
Final Solution, The		William W. Stuart	Aug 1962	121
Find a Victim		Kenneth Millar	Jul 1954	90
Finders, Keepers		B. A. Cody	Jun 1963	64
Finger-Man		John Connolly	Aug 1961	17
Finish the Job	Clean-up	Frank Kane	Jan 1954	24
Fire at Night, A		Lawrence Block	Jun 1958	59
First Case		David Alexander	Mar 1955	32
First Fifty Thousand, The		Jack Webb	Mar 1955	116
First Kill		Helen Nielsen	Apr 1956	1
First Nighter		Richard Hardwick	Dec 1957	43
First Offense	Number Twenty-Two†	Evan Hunter	Dec 1955	3
Fish-Market Murder		Robert S. Swenson	Sep 1956	8
Five Days to Kill		Jerry Bailey	Mar 1965	106
Fix, The		Max Van Derveer	Apr 1962	118
Fixer, The	Be My Guest	Robert Turner	Sep 1965	49
Flesh		Meyer Levin	Oct 1957	5
Flight to Nowhere	Scorpian Reef*	Charles Williams	Sep 1955	92
Floater, The		Frank E. Smith	Jan 1955	47
Flood		Jackson Bowling	Apr-May 1967	40
Flowers for Barney		Ovid Demaris	Dec 1958	24
Flowers to the Fair		Georgiana Craig	Dec 1954	29
Fly by Night		Dick Moore	Jun 1962	18
Fly-By-Night		Robert Gold	Sep 1957	29
Fog		Gil Brewer	Feb 1956	50
Follower, The		Evan Hunter	Jul 1953	83
Footprints		Fred L. Anderson	May 1954	115
For a Friend		Bob McKnight	Dec 1954	53
For the Defense		Terry McCormick	Apr 1963	78
For the Sake of Love		Hilda Cushing	Oct 1962	72
Found and Lost		T. E. Brooks	Feb 1962	12
Four Hours to Kill		F. J. Smith	Nov 1956	91
Frame		Frank Kane	Aug 1954	61
Fraternity		Frank Gay	Dec 1965	154
Fratricide		John Hanford	Mar 1964	103
Free to Die		Bryce Walton	Dec 1959	1
Friend in Deed		Shelby Harrison	Aug 1962	85
Friend of a Friend, A		Morris F. Baughman	Oct-Nov 1966	41
Friend of Stanley's, A		Guy Crosby	Aug 1958	48
Frozen Grin, The		Frank Kane	Jan 1953	81

Peter Enfantino • Jeff Vorzimmer

Story/Article	Alt. Title	Author	Issue	Page
Frozen Stiff		Lawrence Block	Jun 1962	87
Frustration		Anne Smith Ewing	Aug 1960	124
Frustration		Ruth Aldrich Gray	Aug-Sep 1968	120
Fugitive		Robert McKay	Jan 1964	85
Fugitives, The		Marc Penry Winters	Oct 1960	58
G.I. Pigeon		Joseph F. Karrer	Dec 1956	50
Gambler's Cross		Robert McKay	Apr 1963	65
Gate, The		Walter E. Handsaker	Mar 1965	18
General Slept Here, The		Sam S. Taylor	Apr 1955	116
Geniuses, The	Bad Actor†	Richard Deming	Jun 1957	16
Gigolo		C. B. Gilford	Dec 1758	35
Girl Behind the Hedge, The	The Lady Says Die!	Mickey Spillane	Oct 1953	1
Girl Friend		Morris Hershman	Sep 1957	61
Girl Friend, The		David Dwyer	Jun 1761	65
"Give Me a Break!"		Norman Struber	Jun 1758	23
G-Notes, The	Two Grand ... and a Bullet	Robert Patrick Wilmot	Apr 1753	65
Going Down?		John G. Reitci	Jul 1965	9
Going Straight		Rick Rubin	Aug 1962	105
Golden Opportunity	The Opportunity†	J. W. Aaron	Mar 1957	4
Golden Opportunity		Clayton Matthews	Feb-Mar 1967	150
Goldfish, The		Roy Carroll	May 1955	145
Good and Dead	So That's Who That Is?†	Evan Hunter	Jul 1953	47
Good at Heart		John Knox	Oct 1962	75
Good Boy, The		Andrew J. Burris	Dec 1955	29
Good Citizen, The		Bernard Epps	Oct 1963	22
Good Man Is Hard to Find, A		Lawrence E. Orin	Apr-May 1967	16
Good-By, World		John G. Reitci	Aug 1956	128
Goodbye		Charles Carpentier	Aug 1960	1
Goodbye, Charlie		Bob Prichard	Apr 1958	61
"Got a Match?"		David Alexander	Feb 1957	11
Grass Cage, The		Robert Edmond Alter	Jan 1964	12
Grateful Corpse, The		Bob Bristow	Feb 1960	66
Grave Affair, A		Roswell B. Rohde	Oct 1963	33
Graveyard Shift		Steve Frazee	May 1953	46
Graveyard Shift	Precise Moment	Henry Kane	Jun-Jul 1965	118
Greatest, The		Hollis Gale	Jun 1962	32
Green Eyes		Hal Ellson	Jan 1955	63
Gruber Corners by Nine		John R. Starr	Aug 1956	23
Grudge Fight		Frank Hardy	Apr 1961	52
Guilt Complex		Carroll Mayers	Mar 1964	92
Guilt-Edged Blonde	Bad Blood	Kenneth Millar	Jan 1954	1
Guilty Dead, The		Neil M. Clark	Jun 1963	117
Guilty Ones, The	The Sinister Habit	Kenneth Millar	May 1953	1

Story/Article	Alt. Title	Author	Issue	Page
Gun Lover		Charles Carpentier	Apr 1962	31
Guts		John R. Starr	Nov 1956	45
"H" Killer, The	The Pusher*	Evan Hunter	Feb 1957	61
"H" Run		Alex Pong	Dec 1962	24
Half Past Eternity		Robert Leon	Apr 1962	18
Hand, The		Charles A. Freylin	Apr-May 1966	16
Handy Man		Fletcher Flora	Feb 1956	90
Hangover		Charles Runyon	Dec 1960	31
Hangover Alley		Robert Page Jones	Jun 1961	26
Happy Marriage, The		Richard Deming	Aug 1955	12
Hard Way, The		C. Durbin	Aug-Sep 1966	146
Hard-Rocks		Robert McKay	Aug 1963	18
Harmless		Mildred Jordan Brooks	Jun 1960	111
He Never Went Home		Georgiana Craig	Mar 1957	35
Heat Crazy		Virgie F. Shockley	Aug 1960	87
Heels Are for Hating		Fletcher Flora	Feb 1954	83
Heirloom		Arnold Marmor	Jul 1953	142
Helluva Ball, A		Jack Q. Lynn	Jun 1956	9
Helpful Cop, The		Thomas Millstead	May 1965	155
Helping Hand		Arnold Marmor	Jul 1954	142
Helping Hand, The		Avram Davidson	Feb 1958	24
Helpmate, The		E. A. Bogert	May 1965	121
Hero, The		Floyd Mahannah	Dec 1954	61
Heroes Are Made		Ben Mahnke	Aug 1962	5
He's Never Stopped Running		Aaron Marc Stein	Jun 1957	10
High Dive		Robert Turner	Dec 1956	1
High Trap, The		Floyd Mahannah	Dec 1955	64
Hijack		Don Pep	May 1965	19
His Own Hand		Rex Stout	Apr 1955	49
His Own Jailor		Bryce Walton	Jan 1957	53
His Own Petard		Daniel O'Shea	Mar 1956	54
Hit, The		Alson J. Smith	Apr 1958	17
Hit and Run		Richard Deming	Dec 1954	98
Hitchhiker, The		Albert James Hjertstedt	Jan 1958	1
Hitch-Hiker		Roland F. Lee	Jun 1956	15
Hold Out		John G. Reitci	May 1955	109
Hold-Up		Jess Shelton	Feb 1961	1
Holdup Man		Leonard S. Gray	Feb 1954	136
Hole Card, The		Bernard Epps	May 1964	34
Home Free		Robert Goodney	Oct 1963	38
Homicide, Suicide or Accident		Fred L. Anderson	Jun 1954	76
Honest John, The		Martin Suto	Jun 1961	1
Honey-Child		Leslie Gordon Barnard	Apr 1957	45

Peter Enfantino • Jeff Vorzimmer

Story/Article	Alt. Title	Author	Issue	Page
Hooked		Robert Turner	Feb 1958	33
Hot		Evan Hunter	Feb 1955	12
Hot		Don Lowry	Jan 1964	1
Hot Furs		David Kasanof	Feb 1962	123
Hot One, The		J. Robert Carroll	Aug-Sep 1966	85
Hot Pilot		Alex Pong	Dec-Jan 1967	2
Hot Shot		Robert Goodney	Dec 1962	1
Hot Wheels		Don Lowry	Feb-Mar 1967	106
Hot-Rock Rumble		Richard S. Prather	Jun 1953	104
Housemother Cometh, The		Hayden Howard	Dec 1954	87
How Much to Kill?		Michael Zuroy	Feb 1961	68
Hunch		Helen Nielsen	Mar 1958	64
Hunt the Hunter		Patrick Connolly	Jul 1965	2
Hunted, The	Death in Yoshiwara	Cornell Woolrich	Jan 1953	39
Hunter, The		John A. Sentry	Oct 1955	85
Huntress, The		Gordon T. Allred	Dec 1961	29
I Came to Kill You	Everybody's Watching Me	Mickey Spillane	Jan 1964	100
I Didn't See a Thing		Hal Ellson	Mar 1955	1
I Dig You, Real Cool		Deloris Staton Forbes	Dec 1956	20
I Don't Fool Around		Charles Jackson	Aug 1954	50
I Hate Cops		Henry H. Guild	Jul 1957	32
I Saw Her Die		Gil Brewer	Oct 1955	37
I Want a French Girl		James T. Farrell	Jul 1954	63
Icepick Artists, The	Play Tough	Frank Kane	Dec 1953	117
I'd Die for You		Charles Burgess	Oct 1958	41
Identity Unknown		Frank E. Smith	Aug 1954	1
Idiot, The		Harold Cantor	Oct 1953	47
Idiot's Tale, The		Leo Ellis	Feb 1961	109
I'll Do Anything	A Point of Honor	Charles Beaumont	Nov 1955	13
I'll Get Even		Michael Zuroy	May 1955	58
I'll Handle This		Albert James Hjertstedt	Nov 1957	43
I'll Kill for You		Fletcher Flora	Jul 1953	34
I'll Make the Arrest		Charles Boeckman	Jan 1953	30
I'll Never Tell		Bryce Walton	May 1956	9
I'm a Stranger Here Myself		Georgiana Craig	Feb 1954	60
I'm Getting Out		Elliot West	Jul 1953	92
I'm Not Dead		Carl Milton	Oct 1958	91
Imaginary Blonde, The	Gone Girl	Kenneth Millar	Feb 1953	1
Imposters, The		Frank E. Smith	Apr 1955	157
Impulse	Banker's Trust	Paul Curtis	Feb-Mar 1967	139
In Memoriam		Charles Boeckman	Jun 1961	99
In Memory of Judith Courtright		Erskine Caldwell	Oct 1953	28
In Self Defense	Mugger Murder	Richard Deming	Feb-Mar 1966	112

346   The Manhunt Companion

Story/Article	Alt. Title	Author	Issue	Page
Incident in August		G. H. Williams	Mar 1955	155
Indian Giver	Richest Man in the Morgue	Harold Q. Masur	Feb-Mar 1967	43
Innocent, The		Muriel Berns	Jul 1954	74
Innocent One, The		Evan Hunter	Aug 1953	140
Insecure, The		R. Van Taylor	Dec 1953	138
Inside Story		Edward Wellen	Oct 1962	68
Interference		Glenn Canary	Oct 1963	94
Interrogation		John G. Reitci	Jun 1955	11
... Into the Parlor		Paul Eiden	Jan 1957	101
Invitation to Murder		Albert Simmons	Sep 1956	105
It Never Happened		William O'Farrell	Jun 1958	79
It's Hot Up Here		Arnold Marmor	Jan 1956	41
It's the Law		Floyd Hurl	Feb 1961	80
It's the Law		Floyd Hurl	Apr 1961	9
It's the Law		Floyd Hurl	Jun 1961	72
It's the Law		Floyd Hurl	Aug 1961	16
It's the Law		Harold Helfer	Oct 1961	21
It's the Law		Floyd Hurl	Dec 1961	52
It's the Law		Floyd Hurl	Feb 1962	11
It's the Law		Floyd Hurl	Apr 1962	17
Jacket, The		Jack Q. Lynn	Aug 1958	8
Jail Break		Dan Sontup	Dec 1960	72
Jail-Bait		C. Ashley Lousignont	Jul 1964	156
Job for Johnny, A		Lawrence Burne	Dec 1956	125
Job with a Future		Richard Welles	Feb 1956	122
Jokers, The		Robert Turner	Dec 1955	55
Joy Ride		C. B. Gilford	Apr 1957	27
Judgment		G. H. Williams	Dec 1954	141
Judo Punch, The		V. E. Thiessen	Jul 1954	35
Jump Chicken!		R. W. Lakin	Oct 1962	21
Jungle		Hal Ellson	Jan 1958	4
Junkie Trap, The		Clark Howard	Mar 1964	65
Jury, The		Kenneth Fearing	Mar 1955	102
Juvenile Delinquent		Richard Deming	Jul 1955	64
Kangaroo Court, The		Frank Ward	Dec 1961	72
Kayo		Roy Carroll	Aug 1953	104
Key Witness		Frank Kane	Aug 1956	64
Kid Kill		Evan Hunter	Apr 1953	93
Kid Stuff		Frank E. Smith	Nov 1953	138
Kidnappers, The		Edward Charles Bastien	Apr 1962	95
Kill and Run	Backfire	Floyd Mahannah	Sep 1964	110
Kill Fever		Rey Isely	May 1956	24
Kill Him for Me		John G. Allen	Dec-Jan 1967	104

Peter Enfantino • Jeff Vorzimmer

347

Story/Article	Alt. Title	Author	Issue	Page
Kill Joy		John G. Reitci	Nov 1957	7
Kill Me Tomorrow		Fletcher Flora	Dec 1955	87
Kill One Kill Two		H. A. DeRosso	Aug 1960	57
Kill or Die		Charles A. Freylin	May 1965	2
Kill the Clown		Richard S. Prather	Jun 1957	36
Killer, The		John D. MacDonald	Jan 1955	1
Killer		William Logan	Feb 1956	115
Killer Cop		Morris Hershman	Jun 1958	114
Killer Dog		M. R. James	Dec 1961	1
Killer in the Ring		Paul H. Johnson, Jr.	Feb 1959	31
Killer Instinct	The Coyote	David Chandler	Aug-Sep 1966	114
Killer's Wedge		Evan Hunter	Feb 1959	58
Killer's Witness, A		Dick Ellis	Feb 1960	28
Killing on Seventh Street		Charles Boeckman	Dec 1953	33
Kiloman		Don Lowry	Apr 1963	43
Kiss Me, Dudley		Evan Hunter	Jan 1955	139
Kitchen Kill		Frank E. Smith	Sep 1957	40
Knife, The		Glenn Canary	Apr 1961	75
Knife in His Hand		Mike Brett	Oct 1957	21
Lady in Question, The		Frank E. Smith	May 1955	124
Lady Killer		Evan Hunter	Oct 1954	57
Lady Killer		Herbert D. Kastle	Jun 1961	14
Lamster War		Don Lowry	Jul 1965	30
Last Dime		Charles Miron	Jan 1964	59
Last Fix, The		Jack Belck	Feb-Mar 1966	29
Last Freedom, The		W. Sherwood Hartman	Jan 1965	51
Last Job		Raymond Dyer	Apr 1962	70
Last Kill, The		Charles Runyon	Apr 1961	10
Last Payment		Ron Boring	Feb 1961	34
Last Spin, The		Evan Hunter	Sep 1956	1
Late Gerald Baumann, The		Bob Bristow	Mar 1957	56
Laura and the Deep, Deep Woods		William B. Hartley	Oct 1954	35
Lead Ache		Frank Kane	May 1954	81
Lead Cure		Talmage Powell	Jul 1957	23
Lend Me Your Gun		Hal Ellson	Mar 1956	26
Lenore		Frederick C. Davis	May 1956	64
Leopard Man		Russell W. Lake	Jun-Jul 1966	2
Less Perfect		Frances Carfi Matranga	Aug 1953	81
Lesser Evil, The		Richard Deming	Feb 1953	113
Lesson, The		Gene Wilson	Apr-May 1967	20
Lesson in Murder		Wally Hunter	Oct 1956	89
Liberty		Tom O'Malley	Oct 1963	83
License to Kill, A		Charles Carpentier	Aug 1962	74

Story/Article	Alt. Title	Author	Issue	Page
Life Can Be Horrible		Georgiana Craig	Sep 1953	121
Life for a Life, A	Sitting Duck	Robert Turner	Dec 1954	42
Life Sentence		Talmage Powell	Apr 1960	52
Lifeline		John Conner	Aug 1962	1
Line of Duty	The Lenient Beast*	Fredric Brown	Apr 1956	62
Lipstick		Wenzell Brown	Jun 1956	53
Little Black Book, The		Xavier San Luis Rey	Mar 1964	153
Little Lamb, The		Fredric Brown	Aug 1953	27
Little Loyalty, A		Larry Powell	Aug 1963	122
Little Napoleon		Leo Ellis	Feb 1962	32
Little Variety, A		Richard Hardwick	Dec 1958	1
Loaded Tourist, The		Leslie Charteris	Mar 1953	55
Locked Room, The		Edward D. Radin	Jun 1955	42
Locker 911		Richard Wormser	Apr 1957	36
Loners, The		Clark Howard	Jun 1963	46
Lonesome Bride, The		Nelson Adcock	Apr-May 1966	30
Long Distance		Fletcher Flora	Feb 1957	39
Long Wait, A		Richard L. Sargent	Dec 1960	110
Long Way to KC, A		Fletcher Flora	Nov 1953	100
Loose Ends		Fletcher Flora	Aug 1958	60
Loser's Choice		Nelson Adcock	Jul 1965	88
Losing Streak		Bernard Epps	Mar 1964	42
Lost Key, The		Hal Ellson	Feb 1960	75
Love Affair		Richard Deming	Oct 1954	50
Love for Hate		Xavier San Luis Rey	Jan 1964	32
Love, A Thief and Salvation		Xavier San Luis Rey	Dec-Jan 1967	65
Lovers, The		Morton Freedgood	Oct 1956	89
Lovers		R. J. Hochkins	Feb 1959	43
Lovers Quarrel		Kelly Reynolds	Apr 1960	44
Loving Victim, The		Lotte Belle Davis	Jun 1960	118
Low Tide		Cole Price	Nov 1955	139
Loyal, The		Lawrence E. Orin	Dec 1965	25
Loyal One, The		Richard Deming	Jun 1953	52
Lucy Prey, The		Dale L. Gilbert	Apr-May 1967	65
Lust or Honor	Clean Getaway	William Vance	Dec-Jan 1967	82
Lust Song		Stuart Friedman	Dec 1956	97
Mad Dog Beware!		J. W. Aaron	Oct 1959	1
Madman		Roy Carroll	Mar 1956	43
Make It Neat		Frank Kane	Aug 1955	32
Makeshift Martini, The		Jack Webb	Jun 1955	102
Mama's Boy		David Alexander	May 1955	20
Man Between, The		Frank E. Smith	Nov 1955	108
Man Called, A		George Burke	Aug 1962	38

Peter Enfantino • Jeff Vorzimmer

349

Story/Article	Alt. Title	Author	Issue	Page
Man from Yesterday	The Past Is Dead	Frank E. Smith	Nov 1954	31
Man of the People		Xavier San Luis Rey	Dec 1965	52
Man Who Found the Money, The		James E. Cronin	Feb 1954	138
Man Who Had Too Much to Lose, The		Aaron Marc Stein	Nov 1954	84
Man Who Never Smiled, The		Robert S. Swenson	May 1956	10
Man Who Was Everywhere, The		Edward D. Hoch	Mar 1957	27
Man Who Was Two, The		Richard Deming	Jul 1957	37
Man with a Shiv		Richard Wormser	Dec 1956	62
Man with Two Faces, The		Henry Slesar	Aug 1956	12
Manhunt's Gun Rack: .44 Remington			May 1964	52
Manhunt's Gun Rack: Colt .45 Automatic			Oct 1961	75
Manhunt's Gun Rack: Colt Detective Special			Oct 1962	71
Manhunt's Gun Rack: Colt Police Positive Special			Aug 1962	71
Manhunt's Gun Rack: Colt Woodsman			Apr 1963	60
Manhunt's Gun Rack: Llama .45 Automatic			Feb 1963	117
Manhunt's Gun Rack: North & Cheney Flintlock			Mar 1965	97
Manhunt's Gun Rack: Ruger .44 Magnum Blackhawk			Feb 1962	122
Manhunt's Gun Rack: Ruger Mark 1 Target Pistol			Jan 1964	97
Manhunt's Gun Rack: S&W .357 Magnum			Apr 1961	88
Manhunt's Gun Rack: S&W .357 Magnum			Aug 1961	7
Manhunt's Gun Rack: S&W .357 Magnum (short-barrel)			Dec 1961	62
Manhunt's Gun Rack: S&W .38 Terrier			Jun 1961	25
Manhunt's Gun Rack: S&W .44 Magnum			Dec 1962	113
Manhunt's Gun Rack: S&W .44 Military			Jun 1962	61
Manhunt's Gun Rack: S&W Auto Pistol			Aug 1963	39
Manhunt's Gun Rack: The Frontier Derringer			Apr 1962	67
Manhunt's Gun Rack: The Trailsman-snub			Jun 1963	23
Manhunt's Movie of the Month: I Confess			May 1953	120
Manhunt's Movie of the Month: The Hitch-Hiker			Jun 1953	51
Manila Mission		Charles Einstein	Nov 1956	109
Man's Man		Charles A. Freylin	Jan 1965	24
Manslaughter		Henry Ewald	Dec 1954	92
Marty		Robert S. Swenson	Feb 1956	58
Mass Production		Andrew J. Burris	Sep 1955	40
Master Mind, The		Walter Monaghan	Feb 1961	87
Mata Seguro		Xavier San Luis Rey	Jul 1965	16
Matinee		Gil Brewer	Oct 1956	47
Matriarch, The		James B. Kittell	Jun-Jul 1966	112
Matter of Judgment, A		Jordan Bauman	Aug 1959	126
May I Come In?		Fletcher Flora	Jan 1955	25
Means to an End		Robert Edmond Alter	Dec 1965	2
Meek Monster, The		Edward D. Radin	Apr 1955	38
Meet Me in the Dark		Gil Brewer	Feb 1958	13

The Manhunt Companion

Story/Article	Alt. Title	Author	Issue	Page
Memento		Erskine Caldwell	Mar 1955	133
Men from the Boys, The		Allyn Dennis	Mar 1965	75
Merry, Merry Christmas, The		Evan Hunter	Dec 1957	1
Middle-Man		Raymond Crooks	Sep 1965	132
Midnight Blonde		Talmage Powell	May 1957	19
Midnight Caller		Bob Wade & Bill Miller	Jan 1958	22
Millionth Murder, The		Ray Bradbury	Sep 1953	99
Miser's Secret		Richard Hardwick	Feb 1960	38
Mis-Fire		Norman Struber	Jun 1960	34
Misplaced Star, The		Nelson Adcock	Oct-Nov 1966	95
Missile Missing		S. K. Snedegar	Jun-Jul 1966	148
Model Dies Naked, The		Harry Widmer	Dec 1960	81
Modus Operandi		Edward Y. Breese	Feb-Mar 1967	97
Molested, The		Evan Hunter	Sep 1953	118
Moment's Notice, A		Jerome Weidman	Sep 1954	64
Moon Bright, Moon Fright		Warren J. Shanahan	Jan 1958	24
Moonshine		Gil Brewer	Mar 1955	42
Morning Movie		Muriel Berns	Jan 1955	77
Mother Love		Marion Duckworth	Dec 1962	125
Mother's Day		Donald Emerson	Oct 1963	123
Mother's Waiting		Murray Klater	Apr 1960	118
Motive, The		Erskine Caldwell	Sep 1953	85
Motive to Kill		James Ullman	Jun 1962	1
Mourning After, The	After the Fact	Harold Q. Masur	Mar 1953	95
Movers, The		Bryce Walton	Apr 1955	22
Movie Night		Robert Turner	Jul 1957	47
Mr. Big Nose		Martin Suto	Apr 1959	46
Mr. Chesley		Robert Zacks	Feb 1954	117
Mug Shot	Death's Doorway	Aaron Marc Stein	Apr 1955	62
Mugger Murder		Richard Deming	Apr 1953	85
Mule, The		Michael Zuroy	Sep 1964	155
Murder by Appointment		Albert James Hjertstedt	Oct 1958	122
Murder Marches On!		Georgiana Craig	Dec 1953	39
Murder Market, The		William A. P. White	Feb 1954	99
Murder Market, The		William A. P. White	May 1954	41
Murder Market, The		Hal Walker	Jun 1954	58
Murder of a Mouse		Fletcher Flora	May 1954	18
Murder Pool, The		Robert Stephens	Aug 1958	24
Murder, Though It Have No Tongue		Maeva Park	Feb-Mar 1966	80
Muscle, The		Philip Weck	Sep 1955	57
My Enemy, My Father		John M. Sitan	Jun 1954	53
My Game, My Rules		John G. Reitci	Jul 1954	14
My Pal Isaac		David Lee	Oct 1958	29

Peter Enfantino • Jeff Vorzimmer

Story/Article	Alt. Title	Author	Issue	Page
My Son and Heir		Stephen Marlowe	Dec 1955	18
"N" Man, The		Don Lowry	Feb-Mar 1966	120
Naked Petey		Jack Q. Lynn	Nov 1956	83
Name Unknown, Subject Murder		Sheila S. Thompson	Oct 1960	32
Nebulous Lover, The		Jerry Hopkins	Dec 1965	97
Necktie Party		Robert Turner	Aug 1954	13
Needle Street		J. Kenneth O'Street	Apr-May 1966	65
Never Kill a Mistress		Carroll Mayers	Jan 1957	115
New Girl		Deloris Staton Forbes	May 1957	37
New Girl, The		Richard Deming	Jan 1958	13
New Year's Party		Alson J. Smith	Aug 1960	93
Next!		Talmage Powell	Mar 1957	62
Nice Bunch of Guys		Michael Fessier	May 1953	95
Nickel Machine		Neil Boardman	Aug 1955	1
Night Bus		Don Lowry	Dec 1963	125
Night Job		Robert Plate	Apr 1957	10
Night of Crisis		Harry Whittington	Oct 1956	101
Night of Death		Bob Bristow	Feb 1955	49
Night Out	A Time of Predators*	Joe Gores	Oct 1961	121
Night Watch		Frank E. Smith	Sep 1954	31
Nightmare		James Walz	Jun 1960	106
Nightmare's Edge		Robert Page Jones	May 1965	68
Nite Work		Frank Sisk	Aug 1965	34
No Dice!		Bernard Epps	Aug 1965	31
No Escape		Glenn Canary	Jun 1963	1
No Fair		B. J. Starr	Apr-May 1967	151
No Future		Donald Lee	Jul 1965	118
No Half Cure		Robert E. Murray	Dec 1954	138
No Place to Run		Carroll Mayers	Feb 1960	124
No Riders		Shirley Dunbar	Feb-Mar 1967	16
No Vacancies		Georgiana Craig	Jun 1954	114
Novelty Shop, The		Donald Tothe	Oct 1961	69
Now Die in It		Evan Hunter	May 1953	58
Nude Above the Bar, The		Marvin Larson	Oct 1961	105
Nude in the Subway, The		Arne Mann	Apr 1962	94
Nude Killer, The		K. McCaffrey	Oct 1955	11
Nude Next Door, The		Ivan Lyons-Pleskow	Oct 1955	25
Nudists Die Naked		Richard S. Prather	Aug 1955	82
Obie's Girl	Two Little Hands	Fletcher Flora	Oct-Nov 1966	10
Object of Desire		Paul Swope	Apr 1957	25
Obsession		Robert Page Jones	Apr 1962	1
Oedipus		Walt Sheldon	May 1955	100
Office Party		Austin Hamel	Jul 1956	42

352   The Manhunt Companion

Story/Article	Alt. Title	Author	Issue	Page
Old Flame, The		James T. Farrell	May 1954	117
Old Guard, The		Michael Zuroy	Oct 1962	88
Old Man's Statue, The		R. Van Taylor	Aug 1954	23
Old Pro, The		H. A. DeRosso	Dec 1960	9
Old Willie		William P. McGivern	May 1953	101
Omerta!		Don Lowry	Mar 1964	114
Omit Flowers		Morris Hershman	Oct 1957	29
On a Sunday Afternoon		Gil Brewer	Jan 1957	128
On Second Thought		Carroll Mayers	Dec 1959	114
On the Sidewalk, Bleeding		Evan Hunter	Jul 1957	1
On the Street		Lucille Williams	May 1964	2
One at a Time		Andrew J. Burris	Nov 1955	23
One Big Pay-Off		Charles Sloan	Jun 1963	24
One Down		Evan Hunter	Jun 1953	142
One Fingerprint		Bob Russell	Aug-Sep 1966	97
One Hour Late		William O'Farrell	Apr 1959	76
One Hungry Pigeon		Patrick Connolly	Nov 1964	17
One Little Bullet	Circle of Jeopardy	Henry Kane	Apr 1953	1
One Man's Meat		Jif Frank	Aug-Sep 1966	20
One More Clue		Georgiana Craig	Apr 1958	31
One More Mile to Go		F. J. Smith	Jun 1956	19
One of a Kind		Ben Smith	Oct 1954	90
One Summer Night		Bryce Walton	Sep 1957	1
One Thousand Steps		John Channing Carter	Aug 1963	7
One Way or the Other		John R. Starr	Apr 1956	120
One Way — Out		Gene Jones	Oct 1963	66
One-Way Ticket		Duane Yarnell	Apr 1956	137
Onlooker, The		Robert Turner	Feb 1954	103
Open Heart		Bryce Walton	Apr 1956	132
Opportunity		Russell E. Bruce	Dec 1954	85
... or Leave It Alone		Evan Hunter	May 1954	64
Other Side, The		Daniel DePaola	Jul 1965	126
Out of Business		C. B. Gilford	Dec 1957	19
Out on a Wing		Alex Pong	Feb-Mar 1967	118
Outfit, The		Donald E. Westlake	Apr 1963	82
Outside the Cages		Jack Webb	Dec 1955	43
Over My Dead Body		Harold Q. Masur	Jan 1954	39
Overnight Guest		Frederick Chamberlain	Dec 1962	73
Pain Killer, The		Charles Carpentier	Apr 1961	125
Painter, The		Michael Zuroy	Feb 1958	1
Pal with a Switch Blade		Norman Struber	Jul 1956	20
Panic		Grant Colby	Jan 1955	43
Partners, The		John G. Reitci	Sep 1956	87

Peter Enfantino • Jeff Vorzimmer

Story/Article	Alt. Title	Author	Issue	Page
Party Line, The		E. F. Golden	Feb-Mar 1957	131
Party Pooper		Dundee McDole	Dec 1962	51
Pass the Word		Jack Sword	Aug 1955	46
Pass the Word Along		Frank Kane	Apr 1960	25
Past Imperfect		Frank Gay	Feb-Mar 1956	148
Past Is Dead, The	Man from Yesterday	Frank E. Smith	Aug-Sep 1956	70
Pat Hand		J. W. Aaron	Apr 1956	20
Patient Man, A		Dave Hill	Apr 1963	61
Patsy		Paul Fairman	Apr 1961	93
Pattern for Panic		Richard S. Prather	Jan 1954	91
Payment in Full		Dave Leigh	Dec 1956	92
Payment Is Death, The		John E. Cameron	Sep 1965	152
Payoff		Frank Kane	Mar 1953	71
Percentage, The		David Alexander	Apr 1957	13
Perfect Getaway		Henry Petersen	Jan 1957	142
Pervert, The		T. K. Fitzpatrick	Jun 1963	42
Pickpocket, The		Mickey Spillane	Dec 1954	57
Pickup		Hal Ellson	Sep 1955	44
Pick-Up		Richard Deming	Mar 1957	15
Pics for Sale		Ben Satterfield	Jun 1960	10
Piece of Ground, A		Helen Nielsen	Jul 1957	27
Pigeon, The		Claudius Raye	May 1956	140
Pigeon in an Iron Lung	No Paint	Talmage Powell	Nov 1956	1
Pigeons, The		Hal Ellson	Feb 1955	47
Pistol		Hal Ellson	Nov 1954	1
Place for Emily, A		F. J. Smith	Mar 1957	19
Play Tough	The Icepick Artists	Frank Kane	Mar 1965	2
Playboy, The		Claudius Raye	Aug 1956	138
Please Believe Me!		Jess Shelton	Apr 1960	7
Please Find My Sisters!		David H. Ross	Feb 1961	10
Points South		Fletcher Flora	Jun 1954	43
Poor Sherm		Ruth Chessman	Aug 1958	36
Poor Widow		Madeline Fraser	Apr 1962	106
Portrait in Blood		Bob Temmey	Sep 1965	58
Portrait of a Killer No. 01 — Warren Lincoln		Dan Sontup	May 1953	83
Portrait of a Killer No. 02 — Charles Henry Schwartz		Dan Sontup	Jul 1953	112
Portrait of a Killer No. 03 — Robert W. Buchanan, M.D.		Dan Sontup	Aug 1953	56
Portrait of a Killer No. 04 — Chester Jordan		Dan Sontup	Sep 1953	82
Portrait of a Killer No. 05 — Louise Peete		Dan Sontup	Oct 1953	97
Portrait of a Killer No. 06 — Pat Mahon		Dan Sontup	Nov 1953	113
Portrait of a Killer No. 07 — Tillie Gburek		Dan Sontup	Dec 1953	58
Portrait of a Killer No. 08 — William Coffey		Dan Sontup	Feb 1954	114
Portrait of a Killer No. 09 — Theodore Durrant		Dan Sontup	May 1954	61

354   The Manhunt Companion

Story/Article	Alt. Title	Author	Issue	Page
Portrait of a Killer No. 10 — Rose Palmer		Dan Sontup	Jun 1954	131
Portrait of a Killer No. 11 — Vernon Booher		Dan Sontup	Jul 1954	60
Portrait of a Killer No. 12 — Jesse Walker		Dan Sontup	Aug 1954	84
Portrait of a Killer No. 13 — Leon Peltzer		Dan Sontup	Sep 1954	101
Portrait of a Killer No. 14 — Albert Van Dyke		Dan Sontup	Oct 1954	99
Portrait of a Killer No. 15 — Joseph McElroy		Dan Sontup	Nov 1954	61
Portrait of a Killer No. 16 — Vernon Oldaker		Dan Sontup	Dec 1954	95
Portrait of a Killer No. 17 — Arthur Eggers		Dan Sontup	Dec 1954	105
Portrait of a Killer No. 18 — Evan Thomas		Dan Sontup	Jan 1955	96
Portrait of a Killer No. 19 — Herbert Mills		Dan Sontup	Feb 1955	94
Portrait of a Killer No. 20 — Everett Appelgate		Dan Sontup	Mar 1955	139
Portrait of a Killer No. 21 — James Crawford		Dan Sontup	Apr 1955	141
Portrait of a Killer No. 22 — Bill Lovett		Dan Sontup	May 1955	154
Portrait of a Killer No. 23 — Mildred Bolton		Dan Sontup	Jun 1955	185
Portrait of a Killer No. 24 — Oliver Bishop		Thomas O'Connor	Jul 1955	139
Portraits of Eve, The		Bruno Fischer	Feb 1958	50
Possessed		Murray Leinster	Feb 1957	32
Possessive Female, The		Charles Runyon	Jun 1961	84
Preacher's Tale		Max Kane	May 1956	17
Precious Pigeon		Talmage Powell	Apr 1963	1
Precise Moment	Graveyard Undertaking†	Henry Kane	Dec 1954	108
Predator		Robert Edmond Alter	Feb-Mar 1966	68
Pressure		Morris Hershman	Feb 1958	9
Pretty Boy		Hal Ellson	Dec 1954	1
Prey, The		Daniel DePaola	Dec 1961	63
Price of Life		Michael Zuroy	Jun 1962	93
Price of Lust, The		Joe Gores	Apr 1963	10
Prison Break		Duane Clark	Feb 1963	8
Prisoner, The		Lawrence Harvey	Aug 1960	84
Prisoner, The		David Daheim	Oct-Nov 1966	16
Prisoners, The		Evans Harrington	Jun 1956	85
Pro		Joe Gores	Jun 1958	14
Pro Beau, The		R. A. Gardner	Nov 1964	65
Professional Man		David Goodis	Oct 1953	54
Prognosis Negative		Floyd Mahannah	Mar 1953	129
Promise, The		Richard Welles	Sep 1954	141
Proof Is In, The		S. K. Snedegar	Apr-May 1966	9
Prospect, The		Milt Woods, Jr.	Oct 1963	58
Protect Us!		Don Tothe	Aug 1962	35
Protection		Erle Stanley Gardner	May 1955	98
Protection		Hal Ellson	Oct 1960	77
Prowler!		Gil Brewer	May 1957	1
"Puddin' and Pie"		Deloris Staton Forbes	Aug 1956	36

Peter Enfantino • Jeff Vorzimmer

Story/Article	Alt. Title	Author	Issue	Page
Punisher, The		Frank E. Smith	Mar 1955	14
Punk, The		Herbert Leslie Greene	Jun 1963	35
Pure Vengeance		Michael Zuroy	Oct 1961	1
Purple Collar, The		Frank E. Smith	Dec 1954	11
Queer Deal, The		John G. Reitci	Dec 1961	19
Queer Siren		C. L. Roderman	Sep 1964	59
Question of Values, A		C. L. Sweeney, Jr.	Jun 1960	14
Quiet Day in the County Jail		Georgiana Craig	Jul 1953	23
Quiet Room, The	Tough Chippie	Frank E. Smith	Dec 1953	94
Rabbit Gets a Gun, The		John D. MacDonald	Jan 1957	1
Rape!		Alex Pong	Mar 1964	2
Rat Hater		Harlan Ellison	Aug 1956	108
Razor, Razor, Gleaming Bright		Roy Carroll	May 1957	16
Reach for the Clouds		Bob Bristow	Sep 1956	95
Real Quiet Guy, A		Tom Phillips	Feb 1958	4
Real Thing, The		Fritz Dugan	Aug 1958	121
Reasonable Doubt, A		James A. Dunn	Oct 1962	1
Recluse, The		James R. Frantz	Dec-Jan 1967	14
Red Blood Bend		Burley Hendricks	Dec 1959	22
Red for Murder		Rod Barker	Aug 1962	49
Red Hands		Bryce Walton	Aug 1955	1
Red Herring, The		Richard Deming	Dec 1962	86
Red of Bourgainvillea, The		Grove Hughes	May 1956	131
Red Tears, The		Frank E. Smith	Dec 1954	15
Reluctant Client, The		Davis Dresser	Jun 1955	1
Reluctant Witness		Duff Howard	Aug-Sep 1964	26
Remember Biff Bailey?		Frank E. Smith	Jul 1957	5
Rendezvous		James T. Farrell	Feb 1955	64
Repeat Performance		Robert Turner	Nov 1957	62
Repeater, The		Edward D. Radin	Jul 1955	21
Replacement		John G. Reitci	Nov 1954	12
Response		Arnold Marmor	Oct 1953	93
Retirement		Robert Edmond Alter	Oct 1963	15
Retribution		Michael Zuroy	Apr 1961	84
Return	Love and Blood†	Evan Hunter	Jul 1954	47
Return Engagement	Death Takes an Encore†	Frank Kane	Feb 1955	25
Return No More		Talmage Powell	Jan 1958	9
Return of Joey Dino, The		Elwood Corley	Aug 1959	28
Revolving Door, The		Sam Merwin, Jr.	Feb 1955	1
Reward		Richard Deming	Oct 1962	100
Rhapsody in Blood		Harold Q. Masur	Aug 1953	108
Richest Man in the Morgue	Indian Giver	Harold Q. Masur	Dec 1953	81
Ricochet		W. Sherwood Hartman	Dec-Jan 1967	36

Story/Article	Alt. Title	Author	Issue	Page
Ride a White Horse		Lawrence Block	Dec 1958	48
Ride Downtown, A		Robert Turner	Jan 1957	39
Right Hand of Garth, The		Evan Hunter	Nov 1953	62
Right Man, The		William Engeler	Jul 1964	49
Right One, The		Frank E. Smith	May 1954	110
Right Thing to Do		Robert Leon	Jun 1960	1
Righteous, The		Talmage Powell	Apr 1962	81
Ring the Bell Once		Paul Eiden	Oct 1956	38
Ripper, The	Final Curtain†	Richard Ellington	Aug 1953	92
Ripper Moon!		John G. Reitci	Feb 1963	19
Rival Act, The		Richard S. Prather	Oct 1957	26
Rivals		Talmage Powell	Oct 1958	18
Road to Samarra		Jane Roth	Apr 1959	11
Room Service		Robert Turner	Apr 1956	108
Rope Game, The		Bryce Walton	Feb 1954	26
Rub Out the Past		Robert S. Aldrich	Apr 1960	70
Rumble		Edward Perry	Jul 1956	32
Run from the Snakes!		David Alexander	Oct 1956	11
Run, Carol, Run!		Talmage Powell	Feb 1957	118
Runaway	Runaway Black*	Evan Hunter	Feb 1954	1
Runaway, The		Bryce Walton	Apr 1959	1
S.O.P. Murder		Rick Rubin	Feb 1962	37
Safe Kill, The		Kenneth Moore	Apr 1960	124
Sales Pitch		Mark Starr	Jun 1961	120
Sales Resistance		Andrew J. Burris	Oct 1955	25
Sanctuary		W. W. Hatfield	Jul 1954	42
Sauce for the Gander		Richard Deming	Feb 1956	13
Say a Prayer for the Guy		Nelson Algren	Jun 1958	31
Say Goodby to Janie		Bruno Fischer	Jul 1953	62
Say It with Flowers		Georgiana Craig	Sep 1957	10
Scandal Anyone?		Frank Gay	Apr-May 1966	2
Scarecrow		David Alexander	Jul 1955	47
Scarlet King, The		Evan Hunter	Dec 1954	45
Scavengers, The		Richard Harper	Dec 1957	11
Scavengers, The		J. Bachman	Apr-May 1967	54
Scoop, The		Ort Louis	Aug 1963	82
Score, The		Carroll Mayers	Apr 1959	61
Scrapbook, The		Frank E. Smith	Sep 1953	137
Sea Widow		William P. Brothers	Oct 1961	58
Sea-Gull, The		J. Heidloff	Feb 1963	34
Sealed Envelope, The		Allen Lang	Sep 1956	64
Second Chance		Joe Grenzeback	Feb 1959	3
Second Chance, A		C. G. Cunningham	Dec 1965	65

Peter Enfantino • Jeff Vorzimmer

Story/Article	Alt. Title	Author	Issue	Page
Second Cousin		Erskine Caldwell	Oct 1954	44
Secondary Target		Richard Deming	Oct 1957	33
Secret, The		Stuart Friedman	Sep 1956	38
Seduction, The		Frank Gay	May 1963	15
See Him Die		Evan Hunter	Jul 1955	1
Self-Defense		Harold Q. Masur	Feb 1955	81
Self-Preservation		Russell W. Lake	Mar 1964	147
Services Rendered		Frank E. Smith	May 1953	22
Setup		Fletcher Flora	Nov 1957	32
Set-Up, The		Stanley L. Colbert	Jan 1953	142
Set-Up		Hal Ellson	Apr 1962	58
Set-Up for Two		Norman Anthony	Jun 1960	51
Seven Lousy Bucks		C. L. Sweeney, Jr.	Aug 1956	29
Sex Murder in Cameron		Michael Fessier	Feb 1953	28
Shadow Boxer	A Detective Tail†	Richard Ellington	Feb 1954	121
Shadowed		Richard Wormser	Mar 1957	24
Shakedown	An Angle on Death	Robert Turner	Apr 1953	57
Shakedown		C. L. Sweeney, Jr.	Apr 1960	1
Shake-Down		Dean Ball	Feb 1963	39
Shake-Up		Kenneth Fearing	May 1955	38
Shatter Proof		John G. Reitci	Oct 1960	53
She Asked for It		Fletcher Flora	Aug 1960	31
Shenanigans		Rod Barker	Mar 1965	50
She's Nothing but Trouble		Glenn Canary	Aug 1960	4
Shimmy		Mike Brett	Nov 1957	19
Shock Treatment		Kenneth Millar	Jan 1953	71
Shoot Them Down		Bob Bristow	Jan 1957	120
Shooter, The		Craig Mooney	Oct 1958	83
Shot		Gil Brewer	Feb 1956	140
Shot in the Dark		Georgiana Craig	Aug 1955	57
Showdown at Midnight		Edward L. Perry	Dec 1956	133
Shy Guy		Robert Turner	Nov 1954	22
Side Street		James T. Farrell	Sep 1955	50
Sight of Blood, The		C. B. Gilford	Jun 1958	50
Silent Dead, The		Don Lowry	May 1964	76
Simian Suspect, The		Frank Sisk	Dec 1959	32
Sin of Omission		Pat Airey	Jun-Jul 1956	22
Singing Pigeon, The	The Imaginary Blonde	Kenneth Millar	May 1964	134
Sister's Keeper		John Lower	Aug 1963	56
Sitting Duck	A Life for a Life	Robert Turner	Oct-Nov 1966	76
Six Fingers		Hal Ellson	Dec 1954	138
Six Stories Up		Raymond Dyer	Nov 1955	81
Six-Bit Fee, The		Richard Deming	Jan 1954	13

Story/Article	Alt. Title	Author	Issue	Page
Skip a Beat		Henry Kane	Jun 1954	1
Slay Belle		Frank Kane	Aug 1953	37
Slayer, The		Robert Page Jones	Nov 1964	22
Sleep Without Dreams		Frank Kane	Feb 1956	127
Sleeper Caper, The		Richard S. Prather	Mar 1953	1
Small Homicide		Evan Hunter	Jun 1953	30
Smart Sucker		Richard Wormser	Jan 1957	25
Smuggler's Monkey		Arne Mann	Jun 1961	106
Snatchers, The		M. G. Wealeder	Apr-May 1967	106
Snow Job		Carroll Mayers	Oct 1959	21
So Dark for April		Howard Browne	Feb 1953	94
So Much Per Body		Frank E. Smith	Dec 1956	121
Solitary		John G. Reitci	Jul 1955	14
Some Play with Matches		Dick Ellis	Jun 1959	48
Some Things Never Change		Robert Patrick Wilmot	Sep 1954	93
Somebody's Going to Die		Talmage Powell	Jan 1957	43
Sore Loser		Frank Sisk	Sep 1964	103
"Sorry, Mister ..."		C. L. Sweeney, Jr.	Sep 1956	24
Southern Comfort		Shirley Dunbar	Apr-May 1966	61
Specialists, The		Leonard S. Zinberg	Jan 1965	28
Spectator Sport		Roy Carroll	Jan 1956	64
Speedtrap		David Edgar	Aug 1963	114
Spinner, The		Avram Davidson	Jan 1958	38
Split It Three Ways		Walter Kaylin	Mar 1956	19
Spoilers, The		Frank E. Smith	Oct 1955	1
Spot of Color		Edith Fitzgerald Golden	Dec 1962	14
Squealer		John D. MacDonald	May 1956	1
Squeeze, The		Richard Deming	Jun 1956	62
Squeeze Play		Richard S. Prather	Oct 1953	12
Stabbing in the Streets		Eleazar Lipsky	Feb 1953	51
Stage Fright		Deloris Staton Forbes	Jun 1958	63
Stakeout		Robert Patrick Wilmot	May 1953	35
Stalkers, The		Grant Colby	Nov 1954	57
Stand In		Albert Simmons	Dec 1959	88
Star Boarder, The		Charles Miron	Aug 1963	75
State Line		Sam S. Taylor	Sep 1954	14
Stay Dead, Julia!		Peter Georgas	Jul 1956	36
Stay of Execution		Al Martinez	Jun 1962	49
Stiff Competition		Frank Sisk	Feb-Mar 1966	88
Still Life		Evan Hunter	Aug 1953	16
Still Screaming		F. L. Wallace	Jul 1956	1
Stolen Star		William Campbell Gault	Nov 1957	53
Stop Him!		Bruno Fischer	Mar 1953	34

Peter Enfantino • Jeff Vorzimmer

Story/Article	Alt. Title	Author	Issue	Page
Strange Triangle		Ray Stewart	Aug 1963	12
Stranger in the House		Theodore Pratt	Jan 1957	95
Stranger in Town, A		Davis Dresser	Oct 1955	94
Strangler, The		A. I. Schutzer	May 1956	112
Strangler, The		Richard Deming	Dec 1958	8
Strictly Business		Hamilton Frank	Apr 1956	15
Stud, The		James Harvey	Nov 1964	60
Substitute, The		Henry Slesar	Jul 1957	61
Sucker	Circumstantial Evidence	Evan Hunter	Dec 1953	51
Sucker Bait		Norm Kent	Jun 1962	6
Sucker Play		Wilfred C. Vroman	Dec-Jan 1957	75
Suffer Little Children		Deloris Staton Forbes	Mar 1956	82
Suitcase, The		N. E. Jaeger	Oct 1963	26
Summer Heat		Constance Pike	Aug 1962	45
Summer Is a Bad Time		Sam S. Taylor	Oct 1953	81
Sunday Killer		Albert James Hjertstedt	Aug 1959	62
Sure Things, The		Bernard Epps	Oct 1961	125
Surprise		Don Lombardy	Oct 1958	64
Surprise! Surprise!		David Alexander	Dec 1955	115
Survival		David Alexander	Aug 1960	68
Suspect		John Jakes	Aug 1963	63
Sweet Charlie		Henry Kane	Mar 1955	142
Sweet Deal, A		Jack Lemmon	Dec 1962	114
Sweet Taste, The	Black Pudding	David Goodis	Jan 1965	2
Sweet Vengeance		Joe Gores	Jul 1964	2
Sweets to the Sweet		J. Simmons Scheb	Dec 1961	49
Switch, The		R. C. Stimers	May 1964	105
Switch Ending	The Fifty Grand Stretch	Evan Hunter	Dec 1953	22
Switch-Blade		Paul Daniels	Feb 1960	103
Swizzle Stick, The		Alice Wernherr	Dec 1959	118
Sword of Laertes, The		Ray Russell	Oct 1959	15
Sylvia		Ira Levin	Apr 1955	144
Tap-a-San		Daniel Walker	Jan 1964	65
Taste of Terror		Paul Fairman	Jun 1961	79
Teacher, The		Robert Turner	Feb 1957	1
Tears of Evil, The		Georgiana Craig	Mar 1955	85
Teaser		William Lindsay Gresham	Mar 1955	118
Tee Vee Murder		Harold R. Daniels	Dec 1960	43
Tell Them Nothing		Hal Ellson	Oct 1955	64
Temptress, The		Frank E. Smith	Mar 1956	1
Ten Minutes to Live		George Fielding Eliot	May 1955	51
Tennis Bum		G. L. Tassone	Sep 1965	120
Terminal		William L. Jackson	Jul 1956	9

360   The Manhunt Companion

Story/Article	Alt. Title	Author	Issue	Page
Terror in the Night		Robert Bloch	Feb 1956	85
Terror in the Night		Carl G. Hodges	Jul 1956	52
Tex		John Jakes	May 1955	50
Thanks for the Drink, Mac		Philip Weck	Aug 1956	119
That Stranger, My Son		C. B. Gilford	Oct 1954	81
They Came with Guns		Bruno Fischer	Jul 1957	12
They'll Find Out!		Richard Hardwick	Feb 1957	46
They're Chasing Us!		Herbert D. Kastle	Feb 1956	98
They're Going to Kill Me		Bob Bristow	Dec 1957	39
Threat, The		Richard Deming	Jun 1958	1
Three, Four, Out the Door		Robert S. Swenson	Jun 1956	42
Three's a Crowd		Joe Grenzeback	Nov 1956	99
Throwback		Donald Hamilton	Aug 1953	131
Time for Revenge		Dick Ellis	Apr 1960	14
Time to Kill		Evan Hunter	Nov 1955	26
Time to Kill		Jack Webb	Dec 1957	31
Time to Kill		Bryce Walton	Oct 1958	47
Time to Live, A		Vic Hendrix	Dec-Jan 1967	45
Tin Can		B. Traven	Sep 1954	46
To a Wax Doll		Arnold Marmor	Dec 1954	29
To Catch a Spy		Philip Freund	Oct 1960	83
To Each His Own		Tom Cox	Dec 1965	114
To Kill a Cop		D. M. Downing	Apr 1961	63
To Kill a Cop		Robert Camp	Mar 1964	31
To Save a Body		Henry Slesar	Mar 1957	48
Togetherness		Aaron Marc Stein	Jan 1958	29
Too Much to Prove		Glenn Canary	Oct 1960	1
Top Dog		Richard Deming	Oct 1957	16
Tormentors, The		Gil Brewer	Nov 1956	19
Tough Boy		Richard Welles	Jul 1965	114
Tough Chippie	The Quiet Room	Frank E. Smith	Jun-Jul 1966	67
Toward a Grave		Howard B. Shaeffer	May 1957	27
Town Says Murder, The	The Hopeless Defense of Mrs. Dellfor	Cornell Woolrich	Jan 1958	43
Trans-Atlantic Lam		Don Lowry	Mar 1965	100
Trap, The		Robert Turner	Nov 1955	101
Travelin' Man		Rod Bryant	Jul 1965	45
Trespasser		Fletcher Flora	Sep 1957	20
Triple-Cross		Robert Patrick Wilmot	Mar 1953	46
Trophy for Bart, A		James Charles Lynch	Apr 1956	124
Trouble in Town		Richard Deming	Apr 1958	42
Trouble Shooters, The		Dan Brennan	Oct 1960	38
Troublemakers		Earl Fultz	Feb 1957	23
Try It My Way		John G. Reitci	Aug 1955	138

Peter Enfantino • Jeff Vorzimmer

Story/Article	Alt. Title	Author	Issue	Page
Turnabout		Billy Gill	Sep 1965	100
Twelve-Grand Smoke, The		Frank Sisk	Feb 1960	46
Twice a Patsy	The Hero	Floyd Mahannah	Jun-Ju 1966	95
Twilight		Hal Harwood	Dec 1954	49
Two for the Show		Bernard Epps	Nov 1964	77
Two Grand		Charles Boeckman	Jul 1954	25
Two Grand . . . and a Bullet	The G-Notes	Robert Patrick Wilmot	Dec 1965	76
Two Hours to Midnight	The Blonde Cried Murder	Davis Dresser	Mar 1956	91
Two Little Hands	Obie's Girl	Fletcher Flora	Dec 1954	9
Two O'Clock Blonde, The		James M. Cain	Aug 1953	84
Two Seconds Late		Harold Rolseth	Mar 1964	97
Two Weeks with Pay		Ernest Chamberlain	Oct-Nov 196■	67
Two-Sided Triangle		Larry Dane	Apr-May 196❼	98
Two-Way Patsy		John H. Goeb	Sep 1964	62
Uncle Tom		David Alexander	Sep 1955	1
Unholy Three, The		William Campbell Gault	May 1956	36
"Use Five Grand?"		Michael Zuroy	Apr 1957	5
Vacation Nightmare		Robert Turner	Dec 1956	30
Vanishing Act		W. R. Burnett	Nov 1955	64
Vegas . . . And Run		Don Lowry	Jun 1963	68
Vengeance		Robert Page Jones	Feb 1961	44
Venom		Guy Gowen	Aug-Sep 1956	48
Vicious Young, The		Pat Stadley	Jun 1955	188
Victim Number Six		Robert Plate	Mar 1957	8
Video Vengeance		Pat Macmillan	Mar 1964	25
Vigil by Night		James W. Phillips	Jun 1956	81
Viking Blood	Act of Fear*	Michael Collins	Apr-May 1966	125
Virile Image, The		Gerald Pearce	Sep 1965	40
Virtue's Prize		H. Rayburn	May 1965	34
Wait for Death		Karl Kramer	Dec 1958	113
Wanted — Dead and Alive		Stephen Marlowe	Oct 1963	4
War, The		Richard Deming	Sep 1955	64
War Talk		Philip Weck	Mar 1957	29
Was It Worth It, Mr. Markell?		Lawrence Spingarn	Apr 1957	21
Watch, The		Wally Hunter	Jul 1955	58
Watcher, The		Peter Paige	Nov 1953	37
Watchers, The		Wally Hunter	Feb 1956	110
We Are All Dead		Bruno Fischer	May 1955	64
Weakness for . . . Women, A	Flowers to the Fair	Georgiana Craig	Aug-Sep 1966	2
Weakness for Women, A		Arthur Kaplan	Oct 1959	35
Webster Street Lush		James M. Ullman	Sep 1956	133
Welcome Home		G. T. Fleming-Roberts	Mar 1955	62
Welcome Mother		Bryce Walton	Oct 1962	31

Story/Article	Alt. Title	Author	Issue	Page
Wench Is Dead, The		Fredric Brown	Jul 1953	1
Wet Brain, The		David Alexander	Nov 1954	64
Wharf Rat		Robert Page Jones	Apr 1960	98
What Am I Doing?		William Vance	Sep 1953	36
What Could I Do?		James R. Hall	Jul 1964	22
What's Your Verdict? No. 01 — The Cooperative Corpse		Sam Ross	Aug 1954	59
What's Your Verdict? No. 02 — The Uncooperative Wife		Sam Ross	Sep 1954	43
What's Your Verdict? No. 03 — The Drinking Man		Sam Ross	Oct 1954	41
What's Your Verdict? No. 04 — The Anxious Friend		Sam Ross	Nov 1954	28
What's Your Verdict? No. 05 — The Angry Man		Sam Ross	Dec 1954	33
What's Your Verdict? No. 06 — The Young Lovebirds		Sam Ross	Dec 1954	27
What's Your Verdict? No. 07 — The Loving Wife		Sam Ross	Jan 1955	81
What's Your Verdict? No. 08 — The Legal Mind		Sam Ross	Feb 1955	45
What's Your Verdict? No. 09 — The Domestic Killer		Sam Ross	Mar 1955	29
What's Your Verdict? No. 10 — The Murdered Divorcé		Sam Ross	Apr 1955	154
What's Your Verdict? No. 11 — The Escaping Man		Sam Ross	May 1955	36
What's Your Verdict? No. 12 — The Protected Killer		Sam Ross	Jun 1955	18
What's Your Verdict? No. 13 — The Sympathetic Friend		Sam Ross	Jul 1955	62
What's Your Verdict? No. 14 — The Buried Fortune		Sam Ross	Aug 1955	80
What's Your Verdict? No. 15 — The Good Time		Sam Ross	Sep 1955	62
What's Your Verdict? No. 16 — The Whole Truth		Sam Ross	Oct 1955	92
What's Your Verdict? No. 17 — The Wild Shot		Sam Ross	Nov 1955	99
What's Your Verdict? No. 18 — The Complete Failure		Sam Ross	Dec 1955	62
Where There's Smoke		Edward D. Hoch	Mar 1964	75
Where's the Money?		Floyd Mahannah	Oct 1953	99
White Lightning		David Maurer	Oct 1960	20
Whitemail		Edward Wellen	Nov 1964	13
Whiz Cop		Jim Robinson	Dec-Jan 1967	71
Who Killed Helen?		Bryce Walton	Jan 1956	2
Who's Calling?		Robert Turner	Nov 1956	7
Widow's Choice		Cole Price	Apr 1956	36
Widow's Word, A		George B. Scanlan	Jun-Jul 1966	75
Wife Beater	Do-Gooder	Roy Carroll	Dec 1953	108
Wife of Riley, The		Evan Hunter	Dec 1953	61
Wife-Beater, The		Aaron Marc Stein	Oct 1957	48
Willful Murder	Dead Issue	Harold Q. Masur	Oct-Nov 1966	83
Wire Loop, The		Steve Harbor	Aug 1956	57
Witness, The		John Sabin	Sep 1954	1
Woman Hater		Sam Merwin, Jr.	Nov 1955	86
Woman Hater, The		Leo Ellis	Aug 1962	97
Woman Knew Too Much, The		Harold Q. Masur	Jun 1957	29
Woman on the Bus, The		R. Van Taylor	May 1954	29
Woman-Chasers, The		Bryce Walton	Jun 1957	1

Peter Enfantino • Jeff Vorzimmer

Story/Article	Alt. Title	Author	Issue	Page
Woman's Wiles, A		Ray T. Davis	Oct 1961	101
Worm Turns, The		R. D'Ascoli	Feb 1960	58
Wrath		Peter Brandt	Feb-Mar 1966	21
Wrong Alibi		Roy Carroll	Oct 1959	117
Wrong Man, The		Stanley Mohr	Jan 1965	96
Wrong Pigeon	Marlowe Takes on the Syndicate	Raymond Chandler	Feb 1960	1
Wrong Touch, The		Henry Kane	Jan 1954	51
Wrong Victim		W. Delos	Jun 1961	73
Wrong Way Home		Hal Ellson	May 1952	1
Yard Bull		Frank Selig	Aug 1954	141
Ybor City		Charles Boeckman	Jun 1953	40
You Can't Kill Her		C. B. Gilford	Jul 1955	142
You Can't Lose		Lawrence Block	Feb 1958	43
You Can't Trust a Man		Helen Nielsen	Jan 1955	14
You Know What I Did?		Charles Boeckman	May 1954	136
You Pay Your Money		Lawrence Harvey	Dec 1955	99
You Should Live So Long		John G. Reitci	Apr 1957	32
You Want Her?		Pat Stadley	Jan 1956	124
YOU, Detective No. 01 — The Bathing Beauty		Wilson Harman	Dec 1954	136
YOU, Detective No. 02 — The Green Beard		Wilson Harman	Jan 1955	89
YOU, Detective No. 03 — The Sweet Death		Wilson Harman	Feb 1955	142
YOU, Detective No. 04 — The Mixed Drink		Wilson Harman	Jun 1955	120
YOU, Detective No. 05 — The Timed Murder		Wilson Harman	Jul 1955	153
YOU, Detective No. 06 — The Burgled Apartment		Wilson Harman	Aug 1955	136
YOU, Detective No. 07 — The Outside Job		Wilson Harman	Sep 1952	90
YOU, Detective No. 08 — The Metal Finger		Wilson Harman	Oct 1955	142
YOU, Detective No. 09 — The Obliging Fire		Wilson Harman	Nov 1955	137
YOU, Detective No. 10 — The Many Motives		Wilson Harman	Dec 1955	85
YOU, Detective No. 11 — The Rich Corpse		Wilson Harman	Jan 1955	122
You're Dead!		Helen Nielsen	Apr 1956	50
Zeke's Long Arm		C. B. Gilford	Apr 1953	39
Zero ... Double Zero		Stuart Friedman	Nov 1954	64

Manhunt Alphabetical Index by Author

Author/Pseudonym	Story/Article	Issue	Page
Aaron, J. W.			
	Cut-Throat World	Oct 1957	1
	Golden Opportunity	Mar 1957	4
	Mad Dog Beware!	Oct 1959	1
	Pat Hand	Apr 1956	20
Adcock, Nelson			
	Collection	Dec 1965	33
	Death Maker, The	May 1965	128
	Lonesome Bride, The	Apr-May 1966	30
	Loser's Choice	Jul 1965	88
	Misplaced Star, The	Oct-Nov 1966	95
Airey, Pat			
	Sin of Omission	Jun-Jul 1966	22
Aldrich, Robert S.			
	Rub Out the Past	Apr 1960	70
Aldrich, Robert Streeter			
	Conspirators, The	Jun-Jul 1966	86
Alexander, David			
	Bad Word	Dec 1957	5
	Die Like a Dog	Jun 1954	133
	Face of Evil	Jan 1957	15
	First Case	Mar 1955	32
	"Got a Match?"	Feb 1957	11
	Mama's Boy	May 1955	20
	Percentage, The	Apr 1957	13
	Run from the Snakes!	Oct 1956	11
	Scarecrow	Jul 1955	47
	Surprise! Surprise!	Dec 1955	115
	Survival	Aug 1960	68
	Uncle Tom	Sep 1955	1
	Wet Brain, The	Nov 1954	64
Alexander, Wilfred			
	Chips Are Down, The	Jun 1958	71
Algren, Nelson			
	Say a Prayer for the Guy	Jun 1958	31
Allen, John G.			
	Breakout	Feb-Mar 1967	56
	Kill Him for Me	Dec-Jan 1967	104
Allen, Steve			
	Blood of the Lamb, The	Nov 1957	1
Allred, Gordon T.			
	Huntress, The	Dec 1961	29
Alter, Robert Edmond			
	Absinthe for Superman	Jun 1959	55
	Break Down	Oct 1961	76
	Grass Cage, The	Jan 1964	12

Peter Enfantino • Jeff Vorzimmer

Author/Pseudonym	Story/Article	Issue	Page
	Means to an End	Dec 1965	2
	Predator	Feb-Mar 1966	68
	Retirement	Oct 1963	15
Anderson, Fred L.			
	Burglaries	Jul 1954	78
	Footprints	May 1954	115
	Homicide, Suicide or Accident	Jun 1954	76
Anis, Bob			
	Confidant	Oct 1963	54
Anthony, Norman			
	Set-Up for Two	Jun 1960	51
Anthony, Robert			
	Fallen Cop, The	Jun 1962	62
Antonich, George			
	Cool One, The	Apr-May 1967	85
Armpriest, Robert			
	Deadly Outpost	Jun-Jul 1966	54
Bachman, J.			
	Scavengers, The	Apr-May 1967	54
Bagby, Jack M.			
	Chase by Night	Sep 1953	92
Bailey, Jerry			
	Five Days to Kill	Mar 1965	106
Ball, Dean			
	Shake-Down	Feb 1963	39
Banci, Lewis			
	Buzzard, Brother, Blood	Apr 1961	46
Barker, Rod			
	Red for Murder	Aug 1962	49
	Shenanigans	Mar 1965	50
Barnard, Leslie Gordon			
	Honey-Child	Apr 1957	45
Basinsky, Jr., Earle			
	Broken Window, The	Feb 1957	101
Bastien, Edward Charles			
	Kidnappers, The	Apr 1962	95
Baughman, Morris F.			
	Friend of a Friend, A	Oct-Nov 1966	41
Bauman, Jordan			
	Cat's Meow	Dec 1959	62
	Matter of Judgment, A	Aug 1959	126
Beach, Tom			
	Alligator Man, The	Nov 1955	134
Beall, George			
	Dead Sell, The	Mar 1965	28
Beaumont, Charles			
	Face of a Killer, The	Dec 1956	40
	I'll Do Anything	Nov 1955	13

366

The Manhunt Companion

Author/Pseudonym	Story/Article	Issue	Page
Belck, Jack			
	City Cop	Apr-May 1966	108
	Last Fix, The	Feb-Mar 1966	29
Bennett, George H.			
	Bury Me Proper	Sep 1965	2
Berns, Muriel			
	Innocent, The	Jul 1954	74
	Morning Movie	Jan 1955	77
Black, Nancy A.			
	Anonymous Body, The	Feb-Mar 1966	2
Bloch, Robert			
	Terror in the Night	Feb 1956	85
Block, Lawrence			
	Fire at Night, A	Jun 1958	59
	Frozen Stiff	Jun 1962	87
	Ride a White Horse	Dec 1958	48
	You Can't Lose	Feb 1958	43
Boardman, Neil			
	Nickel Machine	Aug 1959	1
Boeckman, Charles			
	Charles Beckman, Jr.	Bargain, The	Oct 1954	11
	Charles Beckman, Jr.	Case History	Nov 1953	52
	Charles Beckman, Jr.	Chain Reaction	Oct 1961	54
	Charles Beckman, Jr.	I'll Make the Arrest	Jan 1953	30
	Charles Beckman, Jr.	In Memoriam	Jun 1961	99
	Charles Beckman, Jr.	Killing on Seventh Street	Dec 1953	33
	Charles Beckman, Jr.	Two Grand	Jul 1954	25
	Charles Beckman, Jr.	Ybor City	Jun 1953	40
	Charles Beckman, Jr.	You Know What I Did?	May 1954	136
Bogert, E. A.			
	Helpmate, The	May 1965	121
Bond, Natalie Jenkins			
	Beneficiary	Sep 1965	85
Boring, Ron			
	Last Payment	Feb 1961	34
Bowling, Jackson			
	Flood	Apr-May 1967	40
Bradbury, Ray			
	Millionth Murder, The	Sep 1953	99
Brandt, Peter			
	Wrath	Feb-Mar 1966	21
Breese, Edward Y.			
	Modus Operandi	Feb-Mar 1967	97
Brennan, Dan			
	Trouble Shooters, The	Oct 1960	38
Brett, Mike			
	Babe and the Bum, The	Feb 1958	62
	Knife in His Hand	Oct 1957	21

Peter Enfantino • Jeff Vorzimmer   367

Author/Pseudonym	Story/Article	Issue	Page
	Shimmy	Nov 1957	19
Brewer, Gil			
	Bothered	Jul 1957	9
	Come Across	Apr 1956	52
	Fog	Feb 1956	50
	I Saw Her Die	Oct 1955	37
	Matinee	Oct 1956	47
	Meet Me in the Dark	Feb 1958	13
	Moonshine	Mar 1955	42
	On a Sunday Afternoon	Jan 1957	128
	Prowler!	May 1957	1
Roy Carroll	Shot	Feb 1956	140
	Tormentors, The	Nov 1956	19
Brinkman, Grover			
	Bloody Reformation	Jun-Jul 1966	45
Bristow, Bob			
	Bargainmaster, The	Jun 1959	15
	Dead on Arrival	Aug 1959	19
	Grateful Corpse, The	Feb 1960	66
	Late Gerald Baumann, The	Mar 1957	56
	Night of Death	Feb 1959	49
	Reach for the Clouds	Sep 1956	95
	Shoot Them Down	Jan 1957	120
	They're Going to Kill Me	Dec 1957	39
Brooks, Mildred Jordan			
	Harmless	Jun 1960	111
Brooks, T. E.			
	Found and Lost	Feb 1962	12
Brophy, Joseph			
	Burst of Glory	Dec-Jan 1967	97
Brothers, William			
	Cheap Kicks	Jun 1961	52
Brothers, William P.			
	Sea Widow	Oct 1961	58
Brown, Fredric			
	Line of Duty	Apr 1956	62
	Little Lamb, The	Aug 1953	27
	Wench Is Dead, The	Jul 1953	1
Brown, Wenzell			
	Lipstick	Jun 1956	53
Browne, Howard			
John Evans	So Dark for April	Feb 1953	94
Bruce, Russell E.			
	Opportunity	Dec 1954	85
Bryant, Rod			
	Travelin' Man	Jul 1965	45
Burgess, Charles			
	I'd Die for You	Oct 1958	41

Author/Pseudonym	Story/Article	Issue	Page
Burke, George			
	Man Called, A	Aug 1962	38
Burne, Lawrence			
	Job for Johnny, A	Dec 1956	125
Burnett, W. R.			
	Vanishing Act	Nov 1955	64
Burris, Andrew J.			
	Boiler, The	Jan 1956	31
	Good Boy, The	Dec 1955	29
	Mass Production	Sep 1955	40
	One at a Time	Nov 1955	23
	Sales Resistance	Oct 1955	25
Cain, James M.			
	Cigarette Girl	May 1953	85
	Two O'Clock Blonde, The	Aug 1953	84
Caldwell, Erskine			
	Epitaph	Jan 1955	83
	In Memory of Judith Courtright	Oct 1955	28
	Memento	Mar 1955	133
	Motive, The	Sep 1953	85
	Second Cousin	Oct 1954	44
Cameron, John E.			
	Payment Is Death, The	Sep 1965	152
Camp, Robert			
	Awake to Fear	Apr 1959	65
	To Kill a Cop	Mar 1964	31
Canary, Glenn			
	Academic Freedom	Apr 1962	39
	Interference	Oct 1963	94
	Knife, The	Apr 1961	75
	No Escape	Jun 1963	1
	She's Nothing but Trouble	Aug 1960	4
	Too Much to Prove	Oct 1960	1
Cantor, Harold			
	Idiot, The	Oct 1953	47
Carnegie, John			
	Challenge, The	Apr 1960	57
Carousso, Georges			
	Dog Eat Dog	Feb 1962	25
Carpentier, Charles			
	Deadly Affair, The	Oct 1961	49
	Goodbye	Aug 1960	1
	Gun Lover	Apr 1962	31
	License to Kill, A	Aug 1962	74
	Pain Killer, The	Apr 1961	125
Carroll, J. Robert			
	Hot One, The	Aug-Sep 1966	85

Peter Enfantino • Jeff Vorzimmer

Author/Pseudonym	Story/Article	Issue	Page
Carroll, Roy			
Roy Carroll	Death Wears a Gray Sweater	Nov 1956	48
Roy Carroll	Do-Gooder	Dec 1965	16
Roy Carroll	Goldfish, The	May 1955	145
Roy Carroll	Kayo	Aug 1953	104
Roy Carroll	Madman	Mar 1956	43
Roy Carroll	Razor, Razor, Gleaming Bright	May 1957	16
Roy Carroll	Spectator Sport	Jan 1956	64
Roy Carroll	Wife Beater	Dec 1953	108
Roy Carroll	Wrong Alibi	Oct 1959	117
Carter, John Channing			
	One Thousand Steps	Aug 1963	7
Causey, James			
	Deathmate	Mar 1957	52
Cetin, Frank			
	Big Hate, The	Mar 1957	11
Chamberlain, Ernest			
	Big Time Carly	Feb-Mar 1967	2
	Two Weeks with Pay	Oct-Nov 1966	67
Chamberlain, Frederick			
	Overnight Guest	Dec 1962	73
Chancellor, John			
	Alien Hero	Jan 1965	120
Chandler, David			
	Coyote, The	Dec 1953	102
	Killer Instinct	Aug-Sep 1966	114
Chandler, Raymond			
	Wrong Pigeon	Feb 1960	1
Charteris, Leslie			
	Loaded Tourist, The	Mar 1953	55
Chessman, Ruth			
	Poor Sherm	Aug 1958	36
Clark, Duane			
	Prison Break	Feb 1963	8
Clark, Edward			
	Experts in Crime: Forgery	Oct 1955	61
Clark, Neil M.			
	Guilty Dead, The	Jun 1963	117
Cody, B. A.			
	Finders, Keepers	Jun 1963	64
Cohen, Avram Davidson & Chester			
	Deadly Error	Aug 1960	77
Colbert, Stanley L.			
Sam Cobb	Set-Up, The	Jan 1953	142
Colby, Grant			
	Assault	May 1953	142
	Panic	Jan 1955	43
	Stalkers, The	Nov 1954	57

370

The Manhunt Companion

Author/Pseudonym	Story/Article	Issue	Page
Cole, Les			
Les Collins	Deadly Triangle	Apr 1961	1
Collamore, Marie Elston			
	Baby . . . Don't Cry	Aug-Sep 1966	65
Collins, Michael			
Dennis Lynds	Viking Blood	Apr-May 1966	125
Collins, Pat			
	Final Reckoning	Oct 1963	75
Commings, Joseph			
	Clay Pigeon	Dec 1957	62
Conner, John			
	Lifeline	Aug 1962	1
Connolly, John			
	Finger-Man	Aug 1961	17
Connolly, Patrick			
	Hunt the Hunter	Jul 1965	2
	One Hungry Pigeon	Nov 1964	17
Cooke, David C.			
	Blackmailers Don't Take Chances	Jun 1958	121
	Death Beat	Nov 1956	27
Corley, Elwood			
	Return of Joey Dino, The	Aug 1959	28
Costa, Lee			
	Cosa Mia	May 1964	61
Cotton, Will			
	Conviction	Jan 1965	35
Cox, Tom			
	To Each His Own	Dec 1965	114
Cox, William R.			
	Blood and Moonlight	Oct 1956	27
Craig, Georgiana			
Craig Rice	Alias: Trouble	Jul 1965	65
Craig Rice	And Be Merry	Jan 1954	88
Craig Rice	Anniversary Murder, The	Feb-Mar 1966	151
Craig Rice	Bells Are Ringing, The	Nov 1953	42
Craig Rice	Cheese It, the Corpse	Nov 1957	10
Craig Rice	Dead Undertaker, The	Apr-May 1967	74
Craig Rice	Don't Go Near	May 1953	121
Craig Rice	End of Fear, The	Aug 1953	58
Craig Rice	Flowers to the Fair	Dec 1954	29
Craig Rice	He Never Went Home	Mar 1957	35
Craig Rice	I'm a Stranger Here Myself	Feb 1954	60
Craig Rice	Life Can Be Horrible	Sep 1953	121
Craig Rice	Murder Marches On!	Dec 1953	39
Craig Rice	No Vacancies	Jun 1954	114
Craig Rice	One More Clue	Apr 1958	31
Craig Rice	Quiet Day in the County Jail	Jul 1953	23
Craig Rice	Say It with Flowers	Sep 1957	10

Peter Enfantino • Jeff Vorzimmer

Author/Pseudonym	Story/Article	Issue	Page
Craig Rice	Shot in the Dark	Aug 1955	57
Craig Rice	Tears of Evil, The	Mar 1953	85
Craig Rice	Weakness for . . . Women, A	Aug-Sep 1966	2
Crockett, Art			
	Fast Line, The	Dec 1956	141
Cronin, James E.			
	Man Who Found the Money, The	Feb 1954	138
Crooks, Raymond			
	Middle-Man	Sep 1965	132
Crosby, Guy			
	Friend of Stanley's, A	Aug 1958	48
Cunningham, C. G.			
	Double Damned	Apr-May 1966	97
	Second Chance, A	Dec 1965	65
Curtis, Neal			
	Family Argument	Jun 1962	57
Curtis, Paul			
	Banker's Trust	Nov 1964	86
	Impulse	Feb-Mar 1967	139
Cushing, Hilda			
	Epitaph	Jul 1964	32
	For the Sake of Love	Oct 1962	72
D'Ascoli, R.			
	Worm Turns, The	Feb 1960	58
Daheim, David			
	Prisoner, The	Oct-Nov 1966	16
Dane, Larry			
	Deadly Star-Dust	Feb-Mar 1966	43
	Two-Sided Triangle	Apr-May 1967	98
Daniels, Harold R.			
	Tee Vee Murder	Dec 1960	43
Daniels, Paul			
	Switch-Blade	Feb 1960	103
Davidson, Avram			
	Helping Hand, The	Feb 1958	24
	Spinner, The	Jan 1958	38
Davis, Frederick C.			
	Lenore	May 1956	64
Davis, Lotte Belle			
	Loving Victim, The	Jun 1960	118
Davis, Ray T.			
	Bounty	Aug 1963	52
	Woman's Wiles, A	Oct 1961	101
Dedina, Michel			
	Blackmail, Inc.	Aug 1962	14
deFord, Miriam Allen			
	Aversion	Jul 1965	54

Author/Pseudonym	Story/Article	Issue	Page
Delos, W.			
	Wrong Victim	Jun 1961	73
Demaris, Ovid			
	Extortioners, The	Aug 1959	69
	Flowers for Barney	Dec 1958	24
Deming, Richard			
	Amateur, The	Jun 1957	5
	Balanced Account	Oct 1953	24
	Better Bargain, The	Apr 1956	43
	Blonde in the Bar, The	May 1954	1
	Blood Oath, The	Jan 1955	31
	Bonus Cop	Sep 1953	59
Max Franklin	Careful Man, The	Jun 1955	56
	Charles Turner Case, The	May 1957	30
	Choice, The	Jun 1954	62
	Competitors, The	Feb 1955	53
	Custody	Dec 1955	32
	Death Sentence	Dec 1954	93
Max Franklin	Diary of a Devout Man	Dec 1954	76
	Doubles, The	Dec 1957	45
	Escape Route	Oct 1959	75
Max Franklin	Geniuses, The	Jun 1957	16
	Happy Marriage, The	Aug 1955	12
	Hit and Run	Dec 1954	98
	In Self Defense	Feb-Mar 1966	112
	Juvenile Delinquent	Jul 1955	64
	Lesser Evil, The	Feb 1953	113
	Love Affair	Oct 1954	50
	Loyal One, The	Jun 1953	52
	Man Who Was Two, The	Jul 1957	37
	Mugger Murder	Apr 1953	85
Max Franklin	New Girl, The	Jan 1958	13
	Pick-Up	Mar 1957	15
	Red Herring, The	Dec 1962	86
	Reward	Oct 1962	100
	Sauce for the Gander	Feb 1956	13
	Secondary Target	Oct 1957	33
	Six-Bit Fee, The	Jan 1954	13
	Squeeze, The	Jun 1956	62
	Strangler, The	Dec 1958	8
Max Franklin	Threat, The	Jun 1958	1
Max Franklin	Top Dog	Oct 1957	16
	Trouble in Town	Apr 1958	42
	War, The	Sep 1955	64
Dennis, Allyn			
	Men from the Boys, The	Mar 1965	75

Author/Pseudonym	Story/Article	Issue	Page
DePaola, Daniel			
	Other Side, The	Jul 1965	126
	Prey, The	Dec 1961	63
DeRosso, H. A.			
	Kill One Kill Two	Aug 1960	57
	Old Pro, The	Dec 1960	9
Derveer, Max Van			
	Fix, The	Apr 1962	118
Dilly, Charles			
	Easiest Way, The	May 1964	117
	Eight Ball, The	Jan 1964	78
Douglas, W. E.			
	Addict	Jun 1956	27
Downing, D. M.			
	To Kill a Cop	Apr 1961	63
Dresser, Davis			
Brett Halliday	Reluctant Client, The	Jun 1955	1
Brett Halliday	Stranger in Town, A	Oct 1955	94
Brett Halliday	Two Hours to Midnight	Mar 1956	91
Duckworth, Marion			
	Mother Love	Dec 1962	125
Dugan, Fritz			
	Real Thing, The	Aug 1958	121
Dunbar, Shirley			
	No Riders	Feb-Mar 1967	16
	Southern Comfort	Apr-May 1966	61
Dunn, James A.			
	Reasonable Doubt, A	Oct 1962	1
Dupont, B. D.			
	Cross and Double Cross	Sep 1964	17
Durbin, C.			
	Hard Way, The	Aug-Sep 1966	146
Dwyer, David			
	Girl Friend, The	Jun 1961	65
Dyer, Raymond			
	Last Job	Apr 1962	70
	Six Stories Up	Nov 1953	81
Edgar, David			
	Speedtrap	Aug 1963	114
Eiden, Paul			
	... Into the Parlor	Jan 1957	101
	Ring the Bell Once	Oct 1956	38
Einstein, Charles			
	Manila Mission	Nov 1956	109
Eliot, George Fielding			
	Ten Minutes to Live	May 1956	51
Ellington, Richard			
	Fan Club	Apr 1953	48

374

The Manhunt Companion

Author/Pseudonym	Story/Article	Issue	Page
	Ripper, The	Aug 1953	92
	Shadow Boxer	Feb 1954	121
Ellis, Dick			
	Cop in a Frame	Oct 1961	80
	Killer's Witness, A	Feb 1960	28
	Some Play with Matches	Jun 1959	48
	Time for Revenge	Apr 1960	14
Ellis, Leo			
	Idiot's Tale, The	Feb 1960	109
	Little Napoleon	Feb 1962	32
	Woman Hater, The	Aug 1962	97
Ellison, Harlan			
	Rat Hater	Aug 1956	108
Ellson, Hal			
	Anything Goes	Sep 1956	51
	Big Fish, The	Nov 1957	47
	Blood Brothers	Apr 1955	1
	Blood on the Land	Jun 1957	24
	Cool Cat	Feb 1956	63
	Dangerous	Jan 1956	14
	Decoy	Jun 1955	51
	Deserter, The	Aug 1960	11
	Fat Boy	Nov 1955	52
	Green Eyes	Jan 1955	63
	I Didn't See a Thing	Mar 1955	1
	Jungle	Jan 1958	4
	Lend Me Your Gun	Mar 1956	26
	Lost Key, The	Feb 1960	75
	Pickup	Sep 1955	44
	Pigeons, The	Feb 1955	47
	Pistol	Nov 1954	1
	Pretty Boy	Dec 1954	1
	Protection	Oct 1960	77
	Set-Up	Apr 1962	58
	Six Fingers	Dec 1954	138
	Tell Them Nothing	Oct 1955	64
	Wrong Way Home	May 1955	1
Emerson, Donald			
	Mother's Day	Oct 1963	123
Engeler, William			
	Right Man, The	Jul 1964	49
English, Arnold			
	Bet I Don't Die	May 1957	4
	Business as Usual	Sep 1957	6
Epps, Bernard			
	Conned	Apr 1963	40
	Good Citizen, The	Oct 1963	22

Peter Enfantino • Jeff Vorzimmer

Author/Pseudonym	Story/Article	Issue	Page
	Hole Card, The	May 1964	34
	Losing Streak	Mar 1964	42
	No Dice!	Aug 1963	31
	Sure Things, The	Oct 1961	125
	Two for the Show	Nov 1964	77
Ernst, Koller			
	Curses	Oct 1959	63
Ewald, Henry			
	Manslaughter	Dec 1954	92
Ewing, Anne Smith			
	Death of Me, The	Oct 1959	50
	Frustration	Aug 1960	124
Fairman, Paul			
	Patsy	Apr 1961	93
	Taste of Terror	Jun 1961	79
Farrell, Jack			
	Bad Risk	Mar 1965	65
Farrell, James T.			
	I Want a French Girl	Jul 1954	63
	Old Flame, The	May 1954	117
	Rendezvous	Feb 1955	64
	Side Street	Sep 1955	50
Fearing, Kenneth			
	Jury, The	Mar 1955	102
	Shake-Up	May 1955	38
Fessier, Michael			
	Faceless Man, The	Jun 1953	64
	Nice Bunch of Guys	May 1953	95
	Sex Murder in Cameron	Feb 1953	28
Fischer, Bruno			
	Bugged	Aug 1961	61
	Coney Island Incident	Nov 1953	116
	Double	Jun 1954	82
	Portraits of Eve, The	Feb 1958	50
	Say Goodby to Janie	Jul 1953	62
	Stop Him!	Mar 1953	34
	They Came with Guns	Jul 1957	12
	We Are All Dead	May 1955	64
Fitzpatrick, T. K.			
	Pervert, The	Jun 1963	42
Fleming-Roberts, G. T.			
	Welcome Home	Mar 1955	62
Flora, Fletcher			
	As I Lie Dead	Feb 1953	131
	Collector Comes After Payday, The	Aug 1953	1
	Day It Began Again, The	Apr 1955	31
	Fair Game	Sep 1953	26
	Handy Man	Feb 1956	90

Author/Pseudonym	Story/Article	Issue	Page
	Heels Are for Hating	Feb 1954	83
	I'll Kill for You	Jul 1953	34
	Kill Me Tomorrow	Dec 1955	87
	Long Distance	Feb 1957	39
	Long Way to KC, A	Nov 1953	100
	Loose Ends	Aug 1958	60
	May I Come In?	Jan 1955	25
	Murder of a Mouse	May 1954	18
	Obie's Girl	Oct-Nov 1966	10
	Points South	Jun 1954	43
	Setup	Nov 1957	32
	She Asked for It	Aug 1960	31
	Trespasser	Sep 1957	20
	Two Little Hands	Dec 1954	9
Forbes, Deloris Staton			
De Forbes	I Dig You, Real Cool	Dec 1956	20
De Forbes	New Girl	May 1957	37
De Forbes	"Puddin' and Pie"	Aug 1956	36
D. E. Forbes	Stage Fright	Jun 1958	63
De Forbes	Suffer Little Children	Mar 1956	82
Franco, Mark Del			
	Avenging Angel	Feb 1963	1
Frank, Hamilton			
	Strictly Business	Apr 1956	15
Frank, Jif			
	One Man's Meat	Aug-Sep 1966	20
Franklin, Niel			
	Caught in the Act	Aug 1958	31
Frantz, James R.			
	Recluse, The	Dec-Jan 1967	14
Fraser, Madeline			
	Poor Widow	Apr 1962	106
Frazee, Steve			
	Crime Broker, The	Jun 1962	104
	Graveyard Shift	May 1953	46
Freedgood, Morton			
John Godey	Lovers, The	Oct 1956	89
Freund, Philip			
	To Catch a Spy	Oct 1960	83
Freylin, Charles A.			
	Hand, The	Apr-May 1966	16
	Kill or Die	May 1965	2
	Man's Man	Jan 1965	24
Friedman, Stuart			
	Colby's Monster	Apr 1958	11
	Deadly Charm	Jun 1958	36
	Lust Song	Dec 1956	97
	Secret, The	Sep 1956	38

Peter Enfantino • Jeff Vorzimmer

Author/Pseudonym	Story/Article	Issue	Page
	Zero ... Double Zero	Nov 1956	64
Frisbie, Walt			
	Closed Door, The	Nov 1957	27
Fultz, Earl			
	Troublemakers	Feb 1957	23
Gaddis, Vincent H.			
	Crime Cavalcade	Aug 1954	20
	Crime Cavalcade	May 1953	32
	Crime Cavalcade	Jul 1954	39
	Crime Cavalcade	Dec 1955	41
	Crime Cavalcade	Oct 1955	44
	Crime Cavalcade	Nov 1954	45
	Crime Cavalcade	Dec 1954	55
	Crime Cavalcade	Sep 1955	55
	Crime Cavalcade	Aug 1955	55
	Crime Cavalcade	Dec 1954	57
	Crime Cavalcade	Feb 1954	57
	Crime Cavalcade	Oct 1953	57
	Crime Cavalcade	Nov 1955	60
	Crime Cavalcade	Sep 1954	61
	Crime Cavalcade	Jan 1955	73
	Crime Cavalcade	Nov 1953	75
	Crime Cavalcade	Jun 1953	75
	Crime Cavalcade	Aug 1953	76
	Crime Cavalcade	May 1954	77
	Crime Cavalcade	Oct 1954	78
	Crime Cavalcade	Feb 1955	78
	Crime Cavalcade	Mar 1956	78
	Crime Cavalcade	Jan 1954	85
	Crime Cavalcade	Jul 1953	90
	Crime Cavalcade	May 1955	94
	Crime Cavalcade	Jun 1955	100
	Crime Cavalcade	Jun 1954	111
	Crime Cavalcade	Mar 1955	112
	Crime Cavalcade	Apr 1955	114
	Crime Cavalcade	Jul 1955	116
	Crime Cavalcade	Sep 1953	116
	Crime Cavalcade	Dec 1953	133
Gaffney, Eugene			
	Blackmail	Dec 1961	9
Gale, Hollis			
	Greatest, The	Jun 1962	32
Gardner, Erle Stanley			
	Protection	May 1955	98
Gardner, R. A.			
	Pro Beau, The	Nov 1964	65

Author/Pseudonym	Story/Article	Issue	Page
Gault, William Campbell			
	Deadly Beloved	Oct 1956	57
	Death of a Big Wheel	Apr 1957	52
	Stolen Star	Nov 1957	53
	Unholy Three, The	May 1956	36
Gay, Frank			
	Explosive Triangle, The	Jan 1965	116
	Fraternity	Dec 1965	154
	Past Imperfect	Feb-Mar 1966	148
	Scandal Anyone?	Apr-May 1966	2
	Seduction, The	May 1965	15
Georgas, Peter			
	Stay Dead, Julia!	Jul 1956	36
Gilbert, Dale L.			
	Lucy Prey, The	Apr-May 1967	65
Gilford, C. B.			
	Biggest Risk	Aug 1956	43
	Body-Snatcher	Feb 1961	54
	Confession	Dec 1959	102
	Cry Wolf!	Jun 1962	76
	Dead People Are Never Angry	Sep 1956	125
	Gigolo	Dec 1958	35
	Joy Ride	Apr 1957	27
	Out of Business	Dec 1957	19
	Sight of Blood, The	Jun 1958	50
	That Stranger, My Son	Oct 1954	81
	You Can't Kill Her	Jul 1955	142
	Zeke's Long Arm	Apr 1958	39
Gill, Billy			
	Turnabout	Sep 1965	100
Goeb, John H.			
	Two-Way Patsy	Sep 1964	62
Gold, Robert			
	Fly-By-Night	Sep 1957	29
Golden, E. F.			
	Party Line, The	Feb-Mar 1967	131
Golden, Edith Fitzgerald			
	Spot of Color	Dec 1962	14
Goodis, David			
	Black Pudding	Dec 1953	1
	Blue Sweetheart, The	Apr 1953	102
	Professional Man	Oct 1953	54
	Sweet Taste, The	Jan 1965	2
Goodney, Robert			
	Home Free	Oct 1963	38
	Hot Shot	Dec 1962	1
Gores, Joe			
	Chain Gang	Dec 1957	14

Peter Enfantino • Jeff Vorzimmer   379

Author/Pseudonym	Story/Article	Issue	Page
	Down and Out	Jun 1959	1
	Night Out	Oct 1961	121
	Price of Lust, The	Apr 1963	10
	Pro	Jun 1958	14
	Sweet Vengeance	Jul 1964	2
Gowen, Guy			
	Venom	Aug-Sep 1966	48
Gray, Leonard S.			
	Holdup Man	Feb 1954	136
Gray, Ruth Aldrich			
	Frustration	Aug-Sep 1966	120
Greene, Herbert Leslie			
	Buddies	Apr-May 1967	156
	Death Begins	Sep 1964	2
	Punk, The	Jun 1963	35
Grenzeback, Joe			
	.38	Mar 1956	60
	Fall Guy	Jul 1956	64
	Second Chance	Feb 1959	3
	Three's a Crowd	Nov 1956	99
Gresham, William Lindsay			
	Teaser	Mar 1953	118
Griffin, Lucy Spears			
	Deceiver, The	Dec 1962	60
Guild, Henry H.			
	I Hate Cops	Jul 1957	32
Hall, James R.			
	What Could I Do?	Jul 1964	22
Hamel, Austin			
	Office Party	Jul 1956	42
Hamilton, Donald			
	Throwback	Aug 1953	131
Handsaker, Walter E.			
	Gate, The	Mar 1965	18
Hanford, John			
	Fratricide	Mar 1964	103
Harbor, Steve			
	Wire Loop, The	Aug 1956	57
Hardwick, Richard			
	Bodyguard	Jun 1960	18
	First Nighter	Dec 1957	43
	Little Variety, A	Dec 1958	1
	Miser's Secret	Feb 1960	38
	They'll Find Out!	Feb 1957	46
Hardy, Frank			
	Grudge Fight	Apr 1961	52
Harman, Wilson			
	YOU, Detective No. 01 — The Bathing Beauty	Dec 1954	136

380   The Manhunt Companion

Author/Pseudonym	Story/Article	Issue	Page
	YOU, Detective No. 02 — The Green Beard	Jan 1955	89
	YOU, Detective No. 03 — The Sweet Death	Feb 1955	142
	YOU, Detective No. 04 — The Mixed Drink	Jun 1955	120
	YOU, Detective No. 05 — The Timed Murder	Jul 1955	153
	YOU, Detective No. 06 — The Burgled Apartment	Aug 1955	136
	YOU, Detective No. 07 — The Outside Job	Sep 1955	90
	YOU, Detective No. 08 — The Metal Finger	Oct 1955	142
	YOU, Detective No. 09 — The Obliging Fire	Nov 1955	137
	YOU, Detective No. 10 — The Many Motives	Dec 1955	85
	YOU, Detective No. 11 — The Rich Corpse	Jan 1956	122
Harper, Richard			
	Scavengers, The	Dec 1957	11
Harrington, Evans			
	Prisoners, The	Jun 1956	85
Harris, Max F.			
	Double Payments	Apr 1962	89
Harrison, Shelby			
	Friend in Deed	Aug 1962	85
Hartley, William B.			
	Laura and the Deep, Deep Woods	Oct 1954	35
Hartman, Herb			
	Decoy for a Pigeon	May 1965	60
Hartman, W. Sherwood			
	Double or Nothing	Jul 1965	156
	Last Freedom, The	Jan 1965	51
	Ricochet	Dec-Jan 1967	36
Harvey, James			
	Stud, The	Nov 1964	60
Harvey, Lawrence			
	Clear Conscience	Dec 1962	82
	Prisoner, The	Aug 1960	84
	You Pay Your Money	Dec 1959	99
Harwood, Hal			
	Twilight	Dec 1954	49
Hatfield, W. W.			
	Sanctuary	Jul 1954	42
Heatter, Basil			
	Empty Fort, The	Sep 1954	104
Heidloff, J.			
	Sea-Gull, The	Feb 1963	34
Helfer, Harold			
	It's the Law	Oct 1961	21
Hendricks, Burley			
	Red Blood Bend	Dec 1959	22
Hendrix, Vic			
	Fernando's Return	Oct-Nov 1966	2
	Time to Live, A	Dec-Jan 1967	45

Peter Enfantino • Jeff Vorzimmer

Author/Pseudonym	Story/Article	Issue	Page
Hershman, Morris			
Mark Mallory	Girl Friend	Sep 1957	61
Arnold English	Killer Cop	Jun 1958	114
Arnold English	Omit Flowers	Oct 1957	29
Arnold English	Pressure	Feb 1958	9
Hill, Dave			
	Blood Is Thicker	May 1965	150
	Patient Man, A	Apr 1963	61
Hill, John S.			
	Body in the Rain	Oct 1956	117
Hjertstedt, Albert James			
Al James	Body on a White Carpet	Apr 1957	1
Al James	Death at Full Moon	Feb 1960	80
Al James	Hitchhiker, The	Jan 1958	1
Al James	I'll Handle This	Nov 1957	43
Al James	Murder by Appointment	Oct 1958	122
Al James	Sunday Killer	Aug 1959	62
Hoch, Edward D.			
	Man Who Was Everywhere, The	Mar 1957	27
	Where There's Smoke	Mar 1964	75
Hochkins, R. J.			
	Lovers	Feb 1959	43
Hodges, Carl G.			
	Terror in the Night	Jul 1956	52
Hodges, Robert M.			
	Big Brother	Oct 1959	25
Holding, James			
	Fair Warning	Apr 1961	117
Hopkins, Jerry			
	Nebulous Lover, The	Dec 1965	97
Hourwich, Kennan			
	Divorce . . . New York Style	May 1964	68
Howard, Clark			
	Enough Rope for Two	Feb 1957	106
	Junkie Trap, The	Mar 1964	65
	Loners, The	Jun 1963	46
Howard, Duff			
	Reluctant Witness	Aug-Sep 1966	26
Howard, Hayden			
	Dead Beat	Oct 1960	8
	Housemother Cometh, The	Dec 1954	87
Huffaker, Clair			
	Couple of Bucks, A	Dec 1956	15
Hughes, Grove			
	Red of Bourgainvillea, The	May 1956	131
Hunter, Evan			
Richard Marsten	Accident Report	Sep 1953	48
Richard Marsten	Against the Middle	Mar 1953	140

The Manhunt Companion

Author/Pseudonym	Story/Article	Issue	Page
Hunt Collins	Association Test	Jul 1954	21
Hunt Collins	Attack	Feb 1953	77
	Beatings, The	Oct 1954	1
	Bedbug	Sep 1954	10
Richard Marsten	Big Day, The	Sep 1955	25
Richard Marsten	Bull to Kill, A	Nov 1954	47
Richard Marsten	Carrera's Woman	Feb 1953	65
Richard Marsten	Chinese Puzzle	Jul 1954	1
Hunt Collins	Circumstantial Evidence	Apr-May 1967	91
Richard Marsten	Classification: Dead	Nov 1953	87
Jonathan Lord	Day's Work	Jul 1953	44
	Dead and the Dying, The	May 1964	38
	Dead Men Don't Dream	Mar 1953	21
	Deadlier Than the Mail	Feb 1954	39
	Death of Me, The	Sep 1953	1
	Death-Ray Gun, The	Jan 1955	100
	Die Hard	Jan 1953	16
Richard Marsten	Every Morning	Sep 1954	88
Richard Marsten	Fifty Grand Stretch, The	Feb-Mar 1967	86
	First Offense	Dec 1955	3
Hunt Collins	Follower, The	Jul 1953	83
	Good and Dead	Jul 1953	47
Ed McBain	"H" Killer, The	Feb 1957	61
	Hot	Feb 1955	12
Richard Marsten	Innocent One, The	Aug 1953	140
	Kid Kill	Apr 1953	93
Ed McBain	Killer's Wedge	Feb 1959	58
Hunt Collins	Kiss Me, Dudley	Jan 1955	139
Richard Marsten	Lady Killer	Oct 1954	57
	Last Spin, The	Sep 1956	1
	Merry, Merry Christmas, The	Dec 1957	1
Hunt Collins	Molested, The	Sep 1953	118
	Now Die in It	May 1953	58
	On the Sidewalk, Bleeding	Jul 1957	1
Hunt Collins	One Down	Jun 1953	142
	. . . or Leave It Alone	May 1954	64
	Return	Jul 1954	47
	Right Hand of Garth, The	Nov 1953	62
Richard Marsten	Runaway	Feb 1954	1
	Scarlet King, The	Dec 1954	45
	See Him Die	Jul 1955	1
	Small Homicide	Jun 1953	30
	Still Life	Aug 1953	16
Hunt Collins	Sucker	Dec 1953	51
Richard Marsten	Switch Ending	Dec 1953	22
Richard Marsten	Time to Kill	Nov 1955	26
	Wife of Riley, The	Dec 1953	61

Peter Enfantino • Jeff Vorzimmer

Author/Pseudonym	Story/Article	Issue	Page
Hunter, Wally			
	Lesson in Murder	Oct 1956	89
	Watch, The	Jul 1955	58
	Watchers, The	Feb 1956	110
Hurl, Floyd			
	It's the Law	Apr 1961	9
	It's the Law	Feb 1962	11
	It's the Law	Aug 1961	16
	It's the Law	Apr 1962	17
	It's the Law	Dec 1961	52
	It's the Law	Jun 1961	72
	It's the Law	Feb 1961	80
Hurst, William			
	Blonde in Room 320, The	Jun 1959	24
Hyde, Wayne			
	Fat Chance	Oct 1957	41
Isely, Rey			
	Kill Fever	May 1956	24
Jackson, Charles			
	Bachelor in the Making, A	Dec 1954	36
	I Don't Fool Around	Aug 1954	50
Jackson, William L.			
	Terminal	Jul 1956	9
Jacobson, Jerry			
	Busman's Holiday	Dec 1965	105
Jaeger, N. E.			
	Suitcase, The	Oct 1963	26
Jakes, John			
	Suspect	Aug 1963	63
	Tex	May 1955	50
James, M. R.			
	Killer Dog	Dec 1961	1
January, Jason			
	Express Stop	Apr 1957	48
Jennings, Gary			
	Blood Money	Jan 1965	56
Jensen, Thurber			
	Desert Chase	Dec 1958	58
Johnson, Jr., Paul H.			
	Killer in the Ring	Feb 1959	31
Johnston, Rosemary			
	Die, Die, Die!	Aug 1961	72
Jones, Gene			
	One Way—Out	Oct 1963	66
Jones, Robert Page			
	Bad Magic	Jun 1963	18
	Big Haul, The	Aug 1961	84
	Don't Tempt Me	Sep 1964	22

Author/Pseudonym	Story/Article	Issue	Page
	Hangover Alley	Jun 1961	26
	Nightmare's Edge	May 1965	68
	Obsession	Apr 1962	1
	Slayer, The	Nov 1964	22
	Vengeance	Feb 1961	44
	Wharf Rat	Apr 1960	98
Kane, Frank			
	Big Steal	Dec 1954	61
	Clean-Up	May 1965	44
	Dead Grin, The	Jun 1955	115
	Dead Pigeon	Jul 1957	52
	Dead Reckoning	Dec 1959	42
	Dead Set	Dec 1957	51
	Dead Stand-In, The	Jan 1956	68
	Evidence	Jul 1953	101
	Finish the Job	Jan 1954	24
	Frame	Aug 1954	61
	Frozen Grin, The	Jan 1953	81
	Icepick Artists, The	Dec 1953	117
	Key Witness	Aug 1956	64
	Lead Ache	May 1954	81
	Make It Neat	Aug 1955	32
	Pass the Word Along	Apr 1960	25
	Payoff	Mar 1953	71
	Play Tough	Mar 1965	2
	Return Engagement	Feb 1955	25
	Slay Belle	Aug 1953	37
	Sleep Without Dreams	Feb 1956	127
Kane, Henry			
	Big Touch, The	Nov 1953	1
	Candlestick	Oct 1954	102
	Circle of Jeopardy	Jul 1964	66
	Corpse That Didn't Die, A	Jun 1959	87
	Deadly Dolls, The	May 1957	41
	Far Cry	Jun 1953	1
	Graveyard Shift	Jun-Jul 1966	118
	One Little Bullet	Apr 1953	1
	Precise Moment	Dec 1954	108
	Skip a Beat	Jun 1954	1
	Sweet Charlie	Mar 1955	142
	Wrong Touch, The	Jan 1954	51
Kane, Max			
	Preacher's Tale	May 1956	17
Kaplan, Arthur			
	Weakness for Women, A	Oct 1959	35
Karrer, Joseph F.			
	G.I. Pigeon	Dec 1956	50

Peter Enfantino • Jeff Vorzimmer

Author/Pseudonym	Story/Article	Issue	Page
Kasanof, David			
	Hot Furs	Feb 1962	123
Kastle, Herbert D.			
	Lady Killer	Jun 1961	14
	They're Chasing Us!	Feb 1956	98
Kaylin, Walter			
	Split It Three Ways	Mar 1956	19
Kelly, Martin			
	Exile	Feb 1963	118
Kelsey, Jack			
	Alacran	Dec-Jan 1967	20
Kent, Norm			
	Blonde Bait	Aug-Sep 1966	125
	Sucker Bait	Jun 1962	6
King, L. W.			
	Bus to Portland	Oct 1956	129
Kittell, James B.			
	Matriarch, The	Jun-Jul 1966	112
Klater, Murray			
	Mother's Waiting	Apr 1960	118
Knox, John			
	Good at Heart	Oct 1962	75
Koch, Roy			
	Bronco	Jun 1959	66
Kole, Shepherd			
	Crime and Punishment	Apr 1953	100
Kramer, Karl			
	Wait for Death	Dec 1958	113
Krebs, L. J.			
	Big Hands	Aug 1958	20
Lake, Russell W.			
	Leopard Man	Jun-Jul 1966	2
	Self-Preservation	Mar 1964	147
Lakin, R. W.			
	Jump Chicken!	Oct 1962	21
Landstreet, F. S.			
	Deadly Cuckold	Jun 1963	9
Lang, Allen			
	Sealed Envelope, The	Sep 1956	64
Lange, George			
	City Hunters	May 1956	127
	Date with Harry, A	Jul 1956	79
Larson, Marvin			
	Nude Above the Bar, The	Oct 1961	105
Lee, David			
	My Pal Isaac	Oct 1958	29
Lee, Don			
	Ace in the Hole	Jun-Jul 1966	37

Author/Pseudonym	Story/Article	Issue	Page
Lee, Donald			
	No Future	Jul 1965	118
Lee, Roland F.			
	Hitch-Hiker	Jun 1956	15
Leigh, Dave			
	Payment in Full	Dec 1956	92
Leinster, Murray			
Will F. Jenkins	Possessed	Feb 1957	32
Lemmon, Jack			
	Sweet Deal, A	Dec 1962	114
Leon, Robert			
	Half Past Eternity	Apr 1962	18
	Right Thing to Do	Jun 1960	1
Levin, Ira			
	Sylvia	Apr 1955	144
Levin, Meyer			
	Flesh	Oct 1957	5
Lipsky, Eleazar			
	Stabbing in the Streets	Feb 1953	51
Little, James L.			
	Bum Rap	Jan 1964	51
Liverman, James L.			
	Aspect of Death, An	Oct 1961	118
Logan, William			
	El Rey	May 1955	156
	Killer	Feb 1956	115
Lombardy, Don			
	Surprise	Oct 1958	64
Louis, Ort			
	Death on the Make	Dec-Jan 1967	130
	Scoop, The	Aug 1963	82
Lousignont, C. Ashley			
	Jail-Bait	Jul 1964	156
Lowe, Brian			
	Brother's Keeper	Dec 1961	53
Lower, John			
	Sister's Keeper	Aug 1963	56
Lower, John E.			
	Commitment to Death	Jul 1964	38
Lowry, Don			
	Big Fall, The	May 1965	84
	Big Score	Aug-Sep 1966	140
	Courier	Nov 1964	1
	Fence Wanted	Oct 1963	100
	Hot	Jan 1964	1
	Hot Wheels	Feb-Mar 1967	106
	Kiloman	Apr 1963	43
	Lamster War	Jul 1965	30

Peter Enfantino • Jeff Vorzimmer

Author/Pseudonym	Story/Article	Issue	Page
	"N" Man, The	Feb-Mar 1966	120
	Night Bus	Dec 1965	125
	Omerta!	Mar 1964	114
	Silent Dead, The	May 1964	76
	Trans-Atlantic Lam	Mar 1965	100
	Vegas . . . And Run	Jun 1963	68
Lynch, Jack			
	Blow-Up	Apr-May 1967	31
Lynch, James Charles			
	Trophy for Bart, A	Apr 1956	124
Lynn, Jack Q.			
	Clear Day for Hunting, A	Dec 1956	110
	College Kill	May 1957	8
	Fifteen Grand	Apr 1958	6
	Helluva Ball, A	Jun 1956	9
	Jacket, The	Aug 1958	8
	Naked Petey	Nov 1956	83
Lyons-Pleskow, Ivan			
	Nude Next Door, The	Oct 1958	25
MacDonald, John D.			
	Black Cat in the Snow	Feb 1958	47
	Killer, The	Jan 1955	1
	Rabbit Gets a Gun, The	Jan 1957	1
	Squealer	May 1956	1
Macmillan, Pat			
	Deadly Propositon, A	Jul 1964	55
	Dear Edie	Apr 1963	6
	Video Vengeance	Mar 1964	25
Madden, Patrick			
	Ambition	Sep 1954	57
Mahannah, Floyd			
	Backfire	Jan 1953	98
	Hero, The	Dec 1954	61
	High Trap, The	Dec 1955	64
	Kill and Run	Sep 1964	110
	Prognosis Negative	Mar 1953	129
	Twice a Patsy	Jun-Jul 1966	95
	Where's the Money?	Oct 1953	99
Mahnke, Ben			
	Heroes Are Made	Aug 1962	5
Malone, James			
	End of an Era	Dec 1959	68
Mann, Arne			
	Nude in the Subway, The	Apr 1960	94
	Smuggler's Monkey	Jun 1961	106
Marksbury, Henry			
	Dead Cats	Aug 1958	1

Author/Pseudonym	Story/Article	Issue	Page
Marlowe, Stephen			
	Blonde at the Wheel	Oct 1955	47
	My Son and Heir	Dec 1955	18
	Wanted — Dead and Alive	Oct 1963	4
Marmor, Arnold			
	Heirloom	Jul 1953	142
	Helping Hand	Jul 1954	142
	It's Hot Up Here	Jan 1956	41
	Response	Oct 1953	93
	To a Wax Doll	Dec 1954	29
Martinez, Al			
	Stay of Execution	Jun 1962	49
Masur, Harold Q.			
	After the Fact	Sep 1965	108
	Build Another Coffin	May 1953	107
	Dead Issue	Dec 1954	82
	Double Frame, The	Jun 1953	78
	Indian Giver	Feb-Mar 1967	43
	Mourning After, The	Mar 1953	95
	Over My Dead Body	Jan 1954	39
	Rhapsody in Blood	Aug 1953	108
	Richest Man in the Morgue	Dec 1953	81
	Self-Defense	Feb 1955	81
	Willful Murder	Oct-Nov 1966	83
	Woman Knew Too Much, The	Jun 1957	29
Mathews, A. M.			
	Accident Prone	Jan 1964	25
Matranga, Frances Carfi			
	Less Perfect	Aug 1953	81
Matthews, Clayton			
	Dog Days	Feb-Mar 1967	22
	Golden Opportunity	Feb-Mar 1967	150
Maurer, David			
	White Lightning	Oct 1960	20
Maurer, David W.			
	Don't Clip My Wings	Apr 1960	79
Mayers, Carroll			
	Crossed and Double-Crossed	Aug 1959	14
	Faithless Woman, The	Jun 1960	30
	Guilt Complex	Mar 1964	92
	Never Kill a Mistress	Jan 1957	115
	No Place to Run	Feb 1960	124
	On Second Thought	Dec 1959	114
	Score, The	Apr 1959	61
	Snow Job	Oct 1959	21
McCaffrey, K.			
	Nude Killer, The	Oct 1959	11

Peter Enfantino • Jeff Vorzimmer

Author/Pseudonym	Story/Article	Issue	Page
McCaffrey, Kenneth			
	Evidence of Murder, The	Apr 1961	89
McCormick, Terry			
	For the Defense	Apr 1963	78
McDole, Dundee			
	Party Pooper	Dec 1962	51
McGivern, William P.			
	Old Willie	May 1953	101
McKay, Robert			
	Fugitive	Jan 1964	85
	Gambler's Cross	Apr 1963	65
	Hard-Rocks	Aug 1963	18
McKimmey, James			
	Crying Target, The	Sep 1957	49
McKnight, Bob			
	For a Friend	Dec 1954	53
McLennan, G. F.			
	Bad Habit	Aug 1963	40
Merwin, Jr., Sam Merwin,			
	Big Score, The	Jul 1955	120
	Block Party	Feb 1956	1
	Revolving Door, The	Feb 1955	1
	Woman Hater	Nov 1955	86
Millar, Kenneth			
John Ross Macdonald	Bad Blood	Apr-May 1967	2
John Ross Macdonald	Beat-Up Sister, The	Oct 1953	110
John Ross Macdonald	Find a Victim	Jul 1954	90
John Ross Macdonald	Guilt-Edged Blonde	Jan 1954	1
John Ross Macdonald	Guilty Ones, The	May 1953	1
John Ross Macdonald	Imaginary Blonde, The	Feb 1953	1
	Shock Treatment	Jan 1953	71
John Ross Macdonald	Singing Pigeon, The	May 1964	134
Miller, Bob Wade & Bill			
Wade Miller	Midnight Caller	Jan 1958	22
Millstead, Thomas			
	Bloodless Bayonet, The	Feb 1962	1
	Helpful Cop, The	May 1965	155
Milton, Carl			
	I'm Not Dead	Oct 1958	91
Miron, Charles			
	Duchess, The	Oct 1963	1
	Last Dime	Jan 1964	59
	Star Boarder, The	Aug 1963	75
Mohr, Stanley			
	Wrong Man, The	Jan 1965	96
Monaghan, Walter			
	Master Mind, The	Feb 1961	87

Author/Pseudonym	Story/Article	Issue	Page
Mooney, Craig			
	Shooter, The	Oct 1958	83
Moore, Charles W.			
	Cowpatch Vengeance	Nov 1956	31
Moore, Dick			
	Fly by Night	Jun 1962	18
Moore, Kenneth			
	Safe Kill, The	Apr 1960	124
Mueller, Jim			
	Brothers, The	Mar 1964	21
Murray, Robert E.			
	No Half Cure	Dec 1954	138
Neville, Kris			
	Big Talk	Apr 1953	31
Newman, Jerry			
	Dead Ringer	Sep 1964	9
Nielsen, Helen			
	Compensation	Nov 1957	21
	Decision	Jun 1957	59
	First Kill	Apr 1956	1
	Hunch	Mar 1956	64
	Piece of Ground, A	Jul 1957	27
	You Can't Trust a Man	Jan 1955	14
	You're Dead!	Apr 1958	50
O'Connor, Thomas			
	Portrait of a Killer No. 24 — Oliver Bishop	Jul 1955	139
O'Farrell, William			
	Death and the Blue Rose	Dec 1960	59
	It Never Happened	Jun 1958	79
	One Hour Late	Apr 1959	76
O'Malley, Tom			
	Liberty	Oct 1963	83
O'Shea, Daniel			
	His Own Petard	Mar 1956	54
O'Street, J. Kenneth			
	Needle Street	Apr-May 1966	65
Orin, Lawrence			
	Deceiver, The	Aug-Sep 1966	135
Orin, Lawrence E.			
	Dead End	May 1964	21
	Good Man Is Hard to Find, A	Apr-May 1967	16
	Loyal, The	Dec 1965	25
Paige, Peter			
	Watcher, The	Nov 1953	37
Park, Maeva			
	Astral Body	Nov 1964	70
	Deadly Nuisance, A	May 1964	53
	Murder, Though It Have No Tongue	Feb-Mar 1966	80

Peter Enfantino • Jeff Vorzimmer

Author/Pseudonym	Story/Article	Issue	Page
Pasche, Sylvie			
	Dead Man's Cat	Jun 1956	31
Pawley, Eugene			
	Bait for the Red Head	Jan 1957	64
Pearce, Gerald			
	Virile Image, The	Sep 1965	40
Pep, Don			
	Hijack	May 1965	19
Perlmutter, Phil			
	Chicken!	Oct 1956	138
Perry, Edward			
	Cabin 13	Aug 1958	114
	Rumble	Jul 1956	32
Perry, Edward L.			
	Showdown at Midnight	Dec 1956	133
Perry, William P.			
	Con's Code, A	Mar 1965	41
Petersen, Henry			
	Perfect Getaway	Jan 1957	142
Phillips, James W.			
	Vigil by Night	Jun 1956	81
Phillips, Tom			
	Dead Heat	Dec 1960	21
	Real Quiet Guy, A	Feb 1958	4
Pike, Constance			
	Summer Heat	Aug 1962	45
Plate, Robert			
	Brusky's Fault	Sep 1956	31
	Night Job	Apr 1957	10
	Victim Number Six	Mar 1957	8
Pong, Alex			
	"H" Run	Dec 1962	24
	Hot Pilot	Dec-Jan 1967	2
	Out on a Wing	Feb-Mar 1967	118
	Rape!	Mar 1964	2
Porges, Arthur			
	Change of Heart	Aug 1963	1
Powell, Larry			
	Little Loyalty, A	Aug 1963	122
Powell, Talmage			
	Be a Man	Feb 1958	29
	Beautiful Babe and Money, A	Oct 1957	62
	Dame Across the River, The	Apr 1958	28
	Dear Sir	Oct 1961	12
	Favor, The	Sep 1957	35
	Lead Cure	Jul 1957	23
	Life Sentence	Apr 1960	52
	Midnight Blonde	May 1957	19

Author/Pseudonym	Story/Article	Issue	Page
	Next!	Mar 1957	62
	Pigeon in an Iron Lung	Nov 1956	1
	Precious Pigeon	Apr 1963	1
	Return No More	Jan 1958	9
	Righteous, The	Apr 1962	81
	Rivals	Oct 1958	18
	Run, Carol, Run!	Feb 1957	118
	Somebody's Going to Die	Jan 1957	43
Prather, Richard S.			
	Best Motive, The	Jan 1953	59
	Butcher	Jun 1954	101
	Code 197	Jun 1955	27
	Crime of Passion	Dec 1954	1
	Death's Head	Mar 1964	52
	Double Take, The	Jul 1953	114
	Hot-Rock Rumble	Jun 1953	104
	Kill the Clown	Jun 1957	36
	Nudists Die Naked	Aug 1955	82
	Pattern for Panic	Jan 1954	91
	Rival Act, The	Oct 1957	26
	Sleeper Caper, The	Mar 1953	1
	Squeeze Play	Oct 1953	12
Pratt, Theodore			
	Stranger in the House	Jan 1957	95
Price, Cole			
	Low Tide	Nov 1955	139
	Widow's Choice	Apr 1956	36
Prichard, Bob			
	Goodbye, Charlie	Apr 1958	61
Rabon, Hayes			
	Deadly Ad-Man, The	Feb-Mar 1966	39
Radin, Edward D.			
	Bite, The	Mar 1955	51
	Bug Doctor	Aug 1955	26
	Double Trouble	May 1955	113
	Locked Room, The	Jun 1955	42
	Meek Monster, The	Apr 1955	38
	Repeater, The	Jul 1955	21
Ramirez, Thomas P.			
	Cross Forks Incident, The	Feb 1957	126
Rarey, Rex			
	Dead as a Mannequin	Mar 1957	1
Rayburn, H.			
	Virtue's Prize	May 1965	34
Raye, Claudius			
	Pigeon, The	May 1956	140
	Playboy, The	Aug 1956	138

Peter Enfantino • Jeff Vorzimmer

393

Author/Pseudonym	Story/Article	Issue	Page
Reitci, John G.			
Jack Ritchie	Canary, The	Jun 1956	47
Jack Ritchie	Deadline Murder	Oct 1958	70
Jack Ritchie	Degree of Guilt	Dec 1956	9
Jack Ritchie	Deveraux Monster, The	Feb 1962	52
Jack Ritchie	Devil Eyes	May 1956	94
Jack Ritchie	Divide and Conquer	Feb 1957	53
Jack Ritchie	Don't Twist My Arm	Apr 1958	1
Jack Ritchie	Fair Play	Apr 1959	20
Jack Ritchie	Going Down?	Jul 1965	9
Jack Ritchie	Good-By, World	Aug 1956	128
Jack Ritchie	Hold Out	May 1955	109
Jack Ritchie	Interrogation	Jun 1955	11
Jack Ritchie	Kill Joy	Nov 1957	7
Jack Ritchie	My Game, My Rules	Jul 1954	14
Jack Ritchie	Partners, The	Sep 1956	87
Jack Ritchie	Queer Deal, The	Dec 1961	19
Jack Ritchie	Replacement	Nov 1954	12
Jack Ritchie	Ripper Moon!	Feb 1963	19
Jack Ritchie	Shatter Proof	Oct 1960	53
Jack Ritchie	Solitary	Jul 1955	14
Jack Ritchie	Try It My Way	Aug 1955	138
Jack Ritchie	You Should Live So Long	Apr 1957	32
Rentub, Nel			
	Craving	Jul 1964	97
	Eyes in the Night	Nov 1964	54
Rey, Xavier San Luis			
	Little Black Book, The	Mar 1964	153
	Love for Hate	Jan 1964	32
	Love, A Thief and Salvation	Dec-Jan 1967	65
	Man of the People	Dec 1965	52
	Mata Seguro	Jul 1965	16
Reynolds, Kelly			
	Lovers Quarrel	Apr 1960	44
Richin, Seymour			
	According to Plan	Jun 1962	37
Robinson, Jim			
	Whiz Cop	Dec-Jan 1967	71
Roderman, C. L.			
	Queer Siren	Sep 1964	59
Rohde, Roswell B.			
	Deadly Bore, The	Mar 1964	48
	Fair Game	Feb-Mar 1967	36
	Grave Affair, A	Oct 1963	33
Rolseth, Harold			
	Two Seconds Late	Mar 1964	97

Author/Pseudonym	Story/Article	Issue	Page
Rosenthal, Jules			
	D. O. A.	Jul 1956	91
Roskolenko, Harry			
	Famous Actress, The	Oct 1954	94
Ross, David H.			
	Please Find My Sisters!	Feb 1961	10
Ross, Sam			
	What's Your Verdict? No. 01 — The Cooperative Corpse	Aug 1954	59
	What's Your Verdict? No. 02 — The Uncooperative Wife	Sep 1954	43
	What's Your Verdict? No. 03 — The Drinking Man	Oct 1954	41
	What's Your Verdict? No. 04 — The Anxious Friend	Nov 1954	28
	What's Your Verdict? No. 05 — The Angry Man	Dec 1954	33
	What's Your Verdict? No. 06 — The Young Lovebirds	Dec 1954	27
	What's Your Verdict? No. 07 — The Loving Wife	Jan 1955	81
	What's Your Verdict? No. 08 — The Legal Mind	Feb 1955	45
	What's Your Verdict? No. 09 — The Domestic Killer	Mar 1955	29
	What's Your Verdict? No. 10 — The Murdered Divorcé	Apr 1955	154
	What's Your Verdict? No. 11 — The Escaping Man	May 1955	36
	What's Your Verdict? No. 12 — The Protected Killer	Jun 1955	18
	What's Your Verdict? No. 13 — The Sympathetic Friend	Jul 1955	62
	What's Your Verdict? No. 14 — The Buried Fortune	Aug 1955	80
	What's Your Verdict? No. 15 — The Good Time	Sep 1955	62
	What's Your Verdict? No. 16 — The Whole Truth	Oct 1955	92
	What's Your Verdict? No. 17 — The Wild Shot	Nov 1955	99
	What's Your Verdict? No. 18 — The Complete Failure	Dec 1955	62
Roth, Eleanor			
	Breaking Point	Jan 1956	58
Roth, Jane			
	Road to Samarra	Apr 1959	11
Rountree, Thomas			
	Easy Money	May 1964	125
Rubin, Rick			
	Going Straight	Aug 1962	105
	S.O.P. Murder	Feb 1962	37
Rubinstein, Robert Weaver & Samuel Lancaster Salem	Bail Out!	Feb 1962	66
Runyon, Charles			
	Hangover	Dec 1960	31
	Last Kill, The	Apr 1961	10
	Possessive Female, The	Jun 1961	84
Russell, Bob			
	One Fingerprint	Aug-Sep 1966	97
Russell, Lee			
	Death in the Mirror	Dec-Jan 1967	154
Russell, Ray			
	Sword of Laertes, The	Oct 1959	15
Sabin, John			
	Witness, The	Sep 1954	1

Author/Pseudonym	Story/Article	Issue	Page
Sargent, Richard L.			
	Long Wait, A	Dec 1960	110
Sargent, Rick			
	Duel in the Pit	Dec 1957	25
Satterfield, Ben			
	Pics for Sale	Jun 1960	10
Scanlan, George B.			
	Widow's Word, A	Jun-Jul 1966	75
Scheb, J. Simmons			
	Busybody	Aug 1960	119
	Sweets to the Sweet	Dec 1961	49
Schutzer, A. I.			
	Strangler, The	May 1956	112
Selig, Frank			
	Yard Bull	Aug 1954	141
Sentry, John A.			
	Hunter, The	Oct 1955	85
Shaeffer, Howard B.			
	Toward a Grave	May 1957	27
Shanahan, Warren J.			
	Moon Bright, Moon Fright	Jan 1958	24
Shelby, Kermit			
	Earrings, The	Aug 1956	133
Sheldon, Walt			
	Oedipus	May 1956	100
Shelton, Jess			
	Hold-Up	Feb 1961	1
	Please Believe Me!	Apr 1960	7
Sherlock, Patrick			
	Fair Exchange	Sep 1965	11
Shockley, Virgie F.			
	Heat Crazy	Aug 1960	87
Simmons, Albert			
	Invitation to Murder	Sep 1956	105
	Stand In	Dec 1959	88
Sisk, Frank			
	Bird Watcher, The	Aug 1959	52
	Nite Work	Aug 1963	34
	Simian Suspect, The	Dec 1959	32
	Sore Loser	Sep 1964	103
	Stiff Competition	Feb-Mar 1966	88
	Twelve-Grand Smoke, The	Feb 1960	46
Sitan, John M.			
	Accident	Aug 1954	43
	Confession	Jul 1954	81
	My Enemy, My Father	Jun 1954	53
Slaughter, Robert			
	Bomb Scare	Oct-Nov 1966	46

Author/Pseudonym	Story/Article	Issue	Page
Slesar, Henry			
	40 Detectives Later	May 1957	23
	Cop for a Day	Jan 1957	8
	Man with Two Faces, The	Aug 1956	12
	Substitute, The	Jul 1957	61
	To Save a Body	Mar 1957	48
Sloan, Charles			
	Eye-Witness	Oct 1962	40
	One Big Pay-Off	Jun 1963	24
Smith, Alson J.			
	Hit, The	Apr 1958	17
	New Year's Party	Aug 1960	93
Smith, Beatrice S.			
	Deadly Secret, A	Apr-May 1966	74
Smith, Ben			
	One of a Kind	Oct 1954	90
Smith, F. J.			
	Dangerous Money	Oct 1956	122
	Four Hours to Kill	Nov 1956	91
	One More Mile to Go	Jun 1956	19
	Place for Emily, A	Mar 1957	19
Smith, Frank E.			
Jonathan Craig	All the Loose Women	Oct-Nov 1966	147
Jonathan Craig	Baby Sitter, The	Jul 1955	31
Jonathan Craig	Bobby-Soxer, The	Oct 1953	141
Jonathan Craig	Cast Off	Sep 1955	14
Jonathan Craig	Cheater, The	Jan 1956	45
Jonathan Craig	Classification: Homicide	Feb 1955	97
Jonathan Craig	Dead Darling, The	Oct 1954	64
Jonathan Craig	Dirge for a Nude	Feb 1953	37
Jonathan Craig	Floater, The	Jan 1955	47
Jonathan Craig	Identity Unknown	Aug 1954	1
Jonathan Craig	Imposters, The	Apr 1955	157
Jonathan Craig	Kid Stuff	Nov 1953	138
Jonathan Craig	Kitchen Kill	Sep 1957	40
Jonathan Craig	Lady in Question, The	May 1955	124
Jonathan Craig	Man Between, The	Nov 1955	108
Jonathan Craig	Man from Yesterday	Nov 1954	31
Jonathan Craig	Night Watch	Sep 1954	31
Jonathan Craig	Past Is Dead, The	Aug-Sep 1966	70
Jonathan Craig	Punisher, The	Mar 1955	14
Jonathan Craig	Purple Collar, The	Dec 1954	11
Jonathan Craig	Quiet Room, The	Dec 1953	94
Jonathan Craig	Red Tears, The	Dec 1954	15
Jonathan Craig	Remember Biff Bailey?	Jul 1957	5
Jonathan Craig	Right One, The	May 1954	110
Jonathan Craig	Scrapbook, The	Sep 1953	137

Peter Enfantino • Jeff Vorzimmer

Author/Pseudonym	Story/Article	Issue	Page
Jonathan Craig	Services Rendered	May 1953	22
Jonathan Craig	So Much Per Body	Dec 1956	121
Jonathan Craig	Spoilers, The	Oct 1955	1
Jonathan Craig	Temptress, The	Mar 1956	1
Jonathan Craig	Tough Chippie	Jun-Jul 1966	67
Smith, Robert Kimmel			
Peter Marks	Assassin, The	Apr 1962	46
Snedegar, S. K.			
	Missile Missing	Jun-Jul 1966	148
	Proof Is In, The	Apr-May 1966	9
Sohl, Jerry			
	Change for a C-Note	Jul 1956	84
Sollars, Don			
	False Bait	Aug 1962	113
Sommers, Jeremiah			
	Damn You, Die	Dec 1965	138
Sontup, Dan			
	Cop Killer	Aug 1956	1
	Jail Break	Dec 1960	72
	Portrait of a Killer No. 01 — Warren Lincoln	May 1953	83
	Portrait of a Killer No. 02 — Charles Henry Schwartz	Jul 1953	112
	Portrait of a Killer No. 03 — Robert W. Buchanan, M.D.	Aug 1953	56
	Portrait of a Killer No. 04 — Chester Jordan	Sep 1953	82
	Portrait of a Killer No. 05 — Louise Peete	Oct 1953	97
	Portrait of a Killer No. 06 — Pat Mahon	Nov 1953	113
	Portrait of a Killer No. 07 — Tillie Gburek	Dec 1953	58
	Portrait of a Killer No. 08 — William Coffey	Feb 1954	114
	Portrait of a Killer No. 09 — Theodore Durrant	May 1954	61
	Portrait of a Killer No. 10 — Rose Palmer	Jun 1954	131
	Portrait of a Killer No. 11 — Vernon Booher	Jul 1954	60
	Portrait of a Killer No. 12 — Jesse Walker	Aug 1954	84
	Portrait of a Killer No. 13 — Leon Peltzer	Sep 1954	101
	Portrait of a Killer No. 14 — Albert Van Dyke	Oct 1954	99
	Portrait of a Killer No. 15 — Joseph McElroy	Nov 1954	61
	Portrait of a Killer No. 16 — Vernon Oldaker	Dec 1954	95
	Portrait of a Killer No. 17 — Arthur Eggers	Dec 1954	105
	Portrait of a Killer No. 18 — Evan Thomas	Jan 1955	96
	Portrait of a Killer No. 19 — Herbert Mills	Feb 1955	94
	Portrait of a Killer No. 20 — Everett Appelgate	Mar 1955	139
	Portrait of a Killer No. 21 — James Crawford	Apr 1955	141
	Portrait of a Killer No. 22 — Bill Lovett	May 1955	154
	Portrait of a Killer No. 23 — Mildred Bolton	Jun 1955	185
Spafford, Jerry			
	Blood Brother	Sep 1965	20
Spillane, Mickey			
	Everybody's Watching Me	Jun 1955	122
	Everybody's Watching Me [Part 1 of 4]	Jan 1953	1

Author/Pseudonym	Story/Article	Issue	Page
	Everybody's Watching Me [Part 2 of 4]	Feb 1953	81
	Everybody's Watching Me [Part 3 of 4]	Mar 1953	107
	Everybody's Watching Me [Part 4 of 4]	Apr 1953	120
	Girl Behind the Hedge, The	Oct 1953	1
	I Came to Kill You	Jan 1964	100
	Pickpocket, The	Dec 1954	57
Spirgarn, Lawrence			
	Was It Worth It, Mr. Markell?	Apr 1957	21
Stacley, Pat			
	Circle for Death	Jun 1956	1
	Vicious Young, The	Jun 1955	188
	You Want Her?	Jan 1956	124
Starr, B. J.			
	No Fair	Apr-May 1967	151
Starr, John R.			
	Bunco	Jul 1957	44
	Gruber Corners by Nine	Aug 1956	23
	Guts	Nov 1956	45
	One Way or the Other	Apr 1956	120
Starr, Mark			
	Sales Pitch	Jun 1961	120
Staudy, A. M.			
	Buddies	May 1964	112
Stein, Aaron Marc			
George Bagby	Body Snatcher	Jun 1955	21
	He's Never Stopped Running	Jun 1957	10
Hampton Stone	Man Who Had Too Much to Lose, The	Nov 1954	84
George Bagby	Mug Shot	Apr 1955	62
	Togetherness	Jan 1958	29
George Bagby	Wife-Beater, The	Oct 1957	48
Stephens, Robert			
	Murder Pool, The	Aug 1958	24
Stewart, Ray			
	Strange Triangle	Aug 1963	12
Stimers, R. C.			
	Switch, The	May 1964	105
Stout, Rex			
	His Own Hand	Apr 1955	49
Struser, Norman			
	Badge of Dishonor	Sep 1956	13
	Dry Run	Apr 1956	112
	Enormous Grave, The	Oct 1956	1
	"Give Me a Break!"	Jun 1958	23
	Mis-Fire	Jun 1960	34
	Pal with a Switch Blade	Jul 1956	20
Stuart, William W.			
	Final Solution, The	Aug 1962	121

Author/Pseudonym	Story/Article	Issue	Page
Suto, Martin			
	Honest John, The	Jun 1961	1
	Mr. Big Nose	Apr 1959	46
Sweeney, Jr., C. L.			
	Death of Amey Vincent, The	Jul 1955	155
	Question of Values, A	Jun 1960	14
	Seven Lousy Bucks	Aug 1956	29
	Shakedown	Apr 1960	1
	"Sorry, Mister ..."	Sep 1956	24
Swenson, Robert S.			
	Drifter, The	Jan 1955	91
	Fish-Market Murder	Sep 1956	8
	Man Who Never Smiled, The	May 1956	10
	Marty	Feb 1956	58
	Three, Four, Out the Door	Jun 1956	42
Swope, Paul			
	Object of Desire	Apr 1957	25
Sword, Jack			
	Dead Soldier	Feb 1956	40
	Pass the Word	Aug 1955	46
Tassone, G. L.			
	Tennis Bum	Sep 1965	120
Taylor, R. Van			
	Comeback	Feb 1954	107
	Insecure, The	Dec 1953	138
	Old Man's Statue, The	Aug 1954	23
	Woman on the Bus, The	May 1954	29
Taylor, Sam S.			
	Clear Picture, A	May 1954	131
	General Slept Here, The	Apr 1955	116
	State Line	Sep 1954	14
	Summer Is a Bad Time	Oct 1953	81
Temmey, Bob			
	Portrait in Blood	Sep 1965	58
Thiessen, V. E.			
	Judo Punch, The	Jul 1954	35
Thompson, Sheila S.			
	Name Unknown, Subject Murder	Oct 1960	32
Tothe, Don			
	Dead Letter	Jun 1961	125
	Protect Us!	Aug 1962	35
Tothe, Donald			
	Alarmist, The	Feb 1961	81
	Novelty Shop, The	Oct 1961	69
Traven, B.			
	Effective Medicine	Aug 1954	31
	Tin Can	Sep 1954	46

Author/Pseudonym	Story/Article	Issue	Page
Turner, Robert			
Roy Carroll	Angle on Death, An	Apr-May 1966	116
	Be My Guest	Apr 1953	39
	Crime of My Wife, The	Aug 1953	48
	Dead Heat	Oct 1953	35
	Field of Honor	Oct 1955	19
	Fight Night	Jan 1956	35
	Fixer, The	Sep 1965	49
	High Dive	Dec 1956	1
	Hooked	Feb 1958	33
	Jokers, The	Dec 1955	55
	Life for a Life, A	Dec 1954	42
	Movie Night	Jul 1957	47
	Necktie Party	Aug 1954	13
	Onlooker, The	Feb 1954	103
	Repeat Performance	Nov 1957	62
	Ride Downtown, A	Jan 1957	39
	Room Service	Apr 1956	108
Roy Carroll	Shakedown	Apr 1953	57
	Shy Guy	Nov 1954	22
	Sitting Duck	Oct-Nov 1966	76
	Teacher, The	Feb 1957	1
	Trap, The	Nov 1955	101
Roy Carroll	Vacation Nightmare	Dec 1956	30
	Who's Calling?	Nov 1956	7
Ullman, James			
	Motive to Kill	Jun 1962	1
Ullman, James M.			
	Webster Street Lush	Sep 1956	133
Vance, William			
	Clean Getaway	Oct 1954	20
	Lust or Honor	Dec-Jan 1967	82
	What Am I Doing?	Sep 1953	36
Verne, Sherry La			
	Death of a Stripper	Sep 1957	24
Vroman, Wilfred C.			
	Sucker Play	Dec-Jan 1967	75
Walker, Daniel			
	Tap-a-San	Jan 1964	65
Walker, Hal			
H. H. Holmes	Murder Market, The	Jun 1954	58
Wallace, F. L.			
	Still Screaming	Jul 1956	1
Wallace, Floyd			
	Cop Hater, The	Jun 1959	76
Wallsten, Robert			
	Accuser, The	Aug 1960	20

Peter Enfantino • Jeff Vorzimmer

Author/Pseudonym	Story/Article	Issue	Page
Walton, Bryce			
	Big Frank	Nov 1955	1
	Free to Die	Dec 1959	1
	His Own Jailor	Jan 1957	53
	I'll Never Tell	May 1955	9
	Movers, The	Apr 1955	22
	One Summer Night	Sep 1957	1
	Open Heart	Apr 1956	132
	Red Hands	Aug 1955	1
	Rope Game, The	Feb 1954	26
	Runaway, The	Apr 1959	1
	Time to Kill	Oct 1958	47
	Welcome Mother	Oct 1962	31
	Who Killed Helen?	Jan 1956	2
	Woman-Chasers, The	Jun 1957	1
Walz, James			
	Nightmare	Jun 1960	106
Ward, Frank			
	Kangaroo Court, The	Dec 1961	72
Wealeder, M. G.			
	Snatchers, The	Apr-May 1967	106
Weaver, Robert			
	Absent Professor, The	Feb 1963	50
Webb, Jack			
	Broken Doll	May 1954	45
	First Fifty Thousand, The	Mar 1955	116
	Makeshift Martini, The	Jun 1955	102
	Outside the Cages	Dec 1955	43
	Time to Kill	Dec 1957	31
Weck, Philip			
	Eye for an Eye, An	Mar 1956	36
	Muscle, The	Sep 1955	57
	Thanks for the Drink, Mac	Aug 1956	119
	War Talk	Mar 1957	29
Weidman, Jerome			
	Moment's Notice, A	Sep 1954	64
Wellen, Edward			
	Check Out	Oct 1959	123
	Dope to Kill	Oct 1958	1
	Double Take, The	Apr 1959	26
	Inside Story	Oct 1962	68
	Whitemail	Nov 1964	13
Welles, Richard			
	Job with a Future	Feb 1956	122
	Promise, The	Sep 1954	141
	Tough Boy	Jul 1965	114

Author/Pseudonym	Story/Article	Issue	Page
Wernherr, Alice			
	Swizzle Stick, The	Dec 1959	118
West, Elliot			
	I'm Getting Out	Jul 1953	92
Westlake, Donald E.			
	Arrest	Jan 1958	62
	Empty Threat, An	Feb 1960	118
Richard Stark	Outfit, The	Apr 1963	82
White, William A. P.			
H. H. Holmes	Murder Market, The	May 1954	41
H. H. Holmes	Murder Market, The	Feb 1954	99
Whittington, Harry			
	Night of Crisis	Oct 1956	101
Widmer, Harry			
	Model Dies Naked, The	Dec 1960	81
Wiley, Stan			
	Big Smile, The	Feb 1957	139
Wilkinson, Richard Hill			
	Dude Sheriff	Aug-Sep 1966	102
Williams, Charles			
	And Share Alike	Aug 1954	87
	Big Bite, The	Jul 1956	95
	Flight to Nowhere	Sep 1955	92
W lliams, G. H.			
	Incident in August	Mar 1955	155
	Judgment	Dec 1954	141
Williams, Lucille			
	On the Street	May 1964	2
Wilmot, Robert Patrick			
	G-Notes, The	Apr 1953	65
	Some Things Never Change	Sep 1954	93
	Stakeout	May 1953	35
	Triple-Cross	Mar 1953	46
	Two Grand . . . and a Bullet	Dec 1965	76
Wilson, Gene			
	Lesson, The	Apr-May 1967	20
Winters, Emmanuel			
	Caller, The	Jun 1953	90
	Disaster, The	Feb 1954	52
Winters, Marc Penry			
	Fugitives, The	Oct 1960	58
Woods, Jr., Milt Woods,			
	Prospect, The	Oct 1963	58
Woolrich, Cornell			
William Irish	Hunted, The	Jan 1953	39
	Town Says Murder, The	Jan 1958	43
Woos, Joachim H.			
	Desperation	Dec 1960	126

Peter Enfantino • Jeff Vorzimmer

Author/Pseudonym	Story/Article	Issue	Page
Wormser, Richard			
	Locker 911	Apr 1957	36
	Man with a Shiv	Dec 1956	62
	Shadowed	Mar 1957	24
	Smart Sucker	Jan 1957	25
Yarnell, Duane			
	One-Way Ticket	Apr 1956	137
Zacks, Robert			
	Mr. Chesley	Feb 1954	117
Zinberg, Leonard S.			
Ed Lacy	Cruise to Hell, A	Jul 1964	102
Ed Lacy	Death by the Numbers	Aug 1961	8
Ed Lacy	Death of El Indio, The	Oct 1961	22
Ed Lacy	Specialists, The	Jan 1965	28
Zinman, David			
	Carnival Con	Dec 1960	1
Zuroy, Michael			
	Decay	Aug 1961	1
	How Much to Kill?	Feb 1961	68
	I'll Get Even	May 1955	58
	Mule, The	Sep 1964	155
	Old Guard, The	Oct 1962	88
	Painter, The	Feb 1958	1
	Price of Life	Jun 1962	93
	Pure Vengeance	Oct 1961	1
	Retribution	Apr 1961	84
	"Use Five Grand?"	Apr 1957	5

Alphabetical Index by Series

Series/Author	Story	Issue	Page
18th Precinct			
Jonathan Craig	The Dead Darling	Oct 1954	64
Jonathan Craig	The Red Tears	Dec 1954	15
Jonathan Craig	The Purple Collar	Dec 1954	11
Jonathan Craig	All the Loose Women	Oct 1966	147
87th Precinct			
Ed McBain	The "H" Killer	Feb 1957	61
Ed McBain	Killer's Wedge	Feb 1959	58
A Casebook Story			
Jack Sword	Pass the Word	Aug 1955	46
Jack Sword	Dead Soldier	Feb 1956	40
Airport Detail			
Jack Webb	Broken Doll	May 1954	45
Jack Webb	The First Fifty Thousand	Mar 1955	116
Jack Webb	The Makeshift Martini	Jun 1955	102
Jack Webb	Time to Kill	Dec 1957	31
Al Dorlan			
Edward D. Hoch	Where There's Smoke	Mar 1964	75
Alphabet Hicks			
Rex Stout	His Own Hand	Apr 1955	49
Chester Drum			
Stephen Marlowe	My Son and Heir	Dec 1955	18
Stephen Marlowe	Wanted — Dead and Alive	Oct 1963	4
Clancy Ross			
Richard Deming	The War	Sep 1955	64
Richard Deming	Sauce for the Gander	Feb 1956	13
Richard Deming	The Squeeze	Jun 1956	62
Richard Deming	The Amateur	Jun 1957	5
Richard Deming	Secondary Target	Oct 1957	33
Richard Deming	Trouble in Town	Apr 1958	42
David Wiley			
Eleazar Lipsky	Stabbing in the Streets	Feb 1953	51
Inspector Schmidt			
George Bagby	Mug Shot	Apr 1955	62
George Bagby	The Wife-Beater	Oct 1957	48
Jeremiah X. Gibson			
Hampton Stone	The Man Who Had Too Much to Lose	Nov 1954	84
Joe Puma			
William Campbell Gault	The Unholy Three	May 1956	36
William Campbell Gault	Deadly Beloved	Oct 1956	57
William Campbell Gault	Death of a Big Wheel	Apr 1957	52
William Campbell Gault	Stolen Star	Nov 1957	53
John J. Malone			
Craig Rice	The Tears of Evil	Mar 1953	85
Craig Rice	Don't Go Near	May 1953	121
Craig Rice	The End of Fear	Aug 1953	58
Craig Rice	Life Can Be Horrible	Sep 1953	121

Peter Enfantino • Jeff Vorzimmer

Series/Author	Story	Issue	Page
Craig Rice	The Bells Are Ringing	Nov 1953	42
Craig Rice	Murder Marches On!	Dec 1953	39
Craig Rice	And Be Merry	Jan 1954	88
Craig Rice	I'm a Stranger Here Myself	Feb 1954	60
Craig Rice	No Vacancies	Jun 1954	114
Craig Rice	Flowers to the Fair	Dec 1954	29
Craig Rice	Shot in the Dark	Aug 1955	57
Craig Rice	He Never Went Home	Mar 1957	35
Craig Rice	Say It with Flowers	Sep 1957	10
Craig Rice	Cheese It, the Corpse	Nov 1957	10
Craig Rice	One More Clue	Apr 1958	31
Craig Rice	Alias: Trouble	Jul 1965	65
Craig Rice	A Weakness for . . . Women	Aug 1966	2
Craig Rice	The Dead Undertaker	Apr 1967	74
Johnny Liddell			
Frank Kane	The Frozen Grin	Jan 1953	81
Frank Kane	Payoff	Mar 1953	71
Frank Kane	Evidence	Jul 1953	101
Frank Kane	Slay Belle	Aug 1953	37
Frank Kane	The Icepick Artists	Dec 1953	117
Frank Kane	Finish the Job	Jan 1954	24
Frank Kane	Lead Ache	May 1954	81
Frank Kane	Frame	Aug 1954	61
Frank Kane	Big Steal	Dec 1954	61
Frank Kane	Return Engagement	Feb 1955	25
Frank Kane	The Dead Grin	Jun 1955	115
Frank Kane	Make It Neat	Aug 1955	32
Frank Kane	The Dead Stand-In	Jan 1956	68
Frank Kane	Sleep Without Dreams	Feb 1956	127
Frank Kane	Dead Pigeon	Jul 1957	52
Frank Kane	Dead Set	Dec 1957	51
Frank Kane	Dead Reckoning	Dec 1959	42
Frank Kane	Pass the Word Along	Apr 1960	25
Frank Kane	Play Tough	Mar 1965	2
Frank Kane	Clean-Up	May 1965	44
Lew Archer			
John Ross Macdonald	The Imaginary Blonde	Feb 1953	1
John Ross Macdonald	The Guilty Ones	May 1953	1
John Ross Macdonald	The Beat-Up Sister	Oct 1953	110
John Ross Macdonald	Guilt-Edged Blonde	Jan 1954	1
John Ross Macdonald	Find a Victim	Jul 1954	90
John Ross Macdonald	The Singing Pigeon	May 1964	134
John Ross Macdonald	Bad Blood	Apr 1967	2
Lieutenant O'Hara			
Alson J. Smith	New Year's Party	Aug 1960	93
Lieutenant Romano			
David Alexander	Face of Evil	Jan 1957	15
Manville Moon			
Richard Deming	The Lesser Evil	Feb 1953	113

Series/Author	Story	Issue	Page
Richard Deming	The Six-Bit Fee	Jan 1954	13
Richard Deming	Death Sentence	Dec 1954	93
Richard Deming	The Blood Oath	Jan 1955	31
Richard Deming	Juvenile Delinquent	Jul 1955	64
Matt Cordell			
Evan Hunter	Die Hard	Jan 1953	16
Evan Hunter	Dead Men Don't Dream	Mar 1953	21
Evan Hunter	Now Die in It	May 1953	58
Evan Hunter	Good and Dead	Jul 1953	47
Evan Hunter	The Death of Me	Sep 1953	1
Evan Hunter	Deadlier Than the Mail	Feb 1954	39
Evan Hunter	Return	Jul 1954	47
Evan Hunter	The Beatings	Oct 1954	1
Matt Gannon			
Richard Deming	Reward	Oct 1962	100
Richard Deming	The Red Herring	Dec 1962	86
Mike Shayne			
Brett Halliday	The Reluctant Client	Jun 1955	1
Brett Halliday	A Stranger in Town	Oct 1955	94
Brett Halliday	Two Hours to Midnight	Mar 1956	91
Neal Cotten			
Sam S. Taylor	The General Slept Here	Apr 1955	116
Oliver Short			
Nelson Adcock	Collection	Dec 1965	33
Nelson Adcock	The Lonesome Bride	Apr 1966	30
Nelson Adcock	The Misplaced Star	Oct 1966	95
Paul Pine			
John Evans	So Dark for April	Feb 1953	94
Peter Chambers			
Henry Kane	One Little Bullet	Apr 1953	1
Henry Kane	Far Cry	Jun 1953	1
Henry Kane	The Big Touch	Nov 1953	1
Henry Kane	The Wrong Touch	Jan 1954	51
Henry Kane	Skip a Beat	Jun 1954	1
Henry Kane	Candlestick	Oct 1954	102
Henry Kane	Precise Moment	Dec 1954	108
Henry Kane	Sweet Charlie	Mar 1955	142
Henry Kane	The Deadly Dolls	May 1957	41
Henry Kane	Circle of Jeopardy	Jul 1964	66
Henry Kane	Graveyard Shift	Jun 1966	118
Philip Marlowe			
Raymond Chandler	Wrong Pigeon	Feb 1960	1
Police File			
Jonathan Craig	Classification: Homicide	Feb 1955	97
Jonathan Craig	The Punisher	Mar 1955	14
Jonathan Craig	The Lady in Question	May 1955	124
Jonathan Craig	The Baby Sitter	Jul 1955	31
Jonathan Craig	Cast Off	Sep 1955	14
Jonathan Craig	The Spoilers	Oct 1955	1

Peter Enfantino • Jeff Vorzimmer

Series/Author	Story	Issue	Page
Jonathan Craig	The Man Between	Nov 1955	08
Jonathan Craig	The Cheater	Jan 1956	45
Jonathan Craig	The Temptress	Mar 1956	1
Jonathan Craig	Kitchen Kill	Sep 1957	40
Scott Jordan			
Harold Q. Masur	The Mourning After	Mar 1953	75
Harold Q. Masur	Build Another Coffin	May 1953	147
Harold Q. Masur	The Double Frame	Jun 1953	78
Harold Q. Masur	Rhapsody in Blood	Aug 1953	108
Harold Q. Masur	Richest Man in the Morgue	Dec 1953	81
Harold Q. Masur	Over My Dead Body	Jan 1954	39
Harold Q. Masur	Dead Issue	Dec 1954	82
Harold Q. Masur	Self-Defense	Feb 1955	8
Harold Q. Masur	The Woman Knew Too Much	Jun 1957	28
Harold Q. Masur	After the Fact	Sep 1965	105
Harold Q. Masur	Willful Murder	Oct 1966	83
Harold Q. Masur	Indian Giver	Feb 1967	43
Shell Scott			
Richard S. Prather	The Best Motive	Jan 1953	55
Richard S. Prather	The Sleeper Caper	Mar 1953	1
Richard S. Prather	Hot-Rock Rumble	Jun 1953	104
Richard S. Prather	The Double Take	Jul 1953	114
Richard S. Prather	Squeeze Play	Oct 1953	12
Richard S. Prather	Pattern for Panic	Jan 1954	91
Richard S. Prather	Butcher	Jun 1954	101
Richard S. Prather	Crime of Passion	Dec 1954	1
Richard S. Prather	Code 197	Jun 1955	27
Richard S. Prather	Nudists Die Naked	Aug 1955	82
Richard S. Prather	Kill the Clown	Jun 1957	36
Richard S. Prather	Death's Head	Mar 1964	52
Slot Machine Kelly			
Dennis Lynds	Viking Blood	Apr 1966	125
Steve Drake			
Richard Ellington	Fan Club	Apr 1953	48
Richard Ellington	The Ripper	Aug 1953	92
Richard Ellington	Shadow Boxer	Feb 1954	121
The Saint			
Leslie Charteris	The Loaded Tourist	Mar 1953	55

TV Episodes Based on Manhunt Stories

Story	Title (If Different)	Author	Pseudonym	Series	Air Date
The Better Bargain		Richard Deming		Alfred Hitchcock Presents	2/9/1956
Who's Calling?		Robert Turner		Studio 57	2/14/1956
I'll Make the Arrest		Charles Boeckman	Charles Beckman, Jr.	Celebrity Playhouse	5/22/1956
First Offense	Number Twenty-Two	Evan Hunter		Alfred Hitchcock Presents	2/17/1957
One More Mile to Go		F. J. Smith		Alfred Hitchcock Presents	4/7/1957
Face of Evil		David Alexander		M Squad	10/18/1957
The Face of a Killer		Charles Beaumont		Studio 57	11/5/1957
Dangerous Money	Reward to Finder	F. J. Smith		Alfred Hitchcock Presents	11/10/1957
Enough Rope for Two		Clark Howard		Alfred Hitchcock Presents	11/15/1957
The Percentage		David Alexander		Alfred Hitchcock Presents	1/5/1958
Sylvia		Ira Levin		Alfred Hitchcock Presents	1/19/1958
Good and Dead	So That's Who That Is	Evan Hunter		Mike Hammer	2/11/1958
Dead Men Don't Dream		Evan Hunter	Curt Cannon	Mike Hammer	2/18/1958
Return Engagement	Death Takes an Encore	Frank Kane		Mike Hammer	3/7/1958
Lead Ache		Frank Kane		Mike Hammer	3/14/1958
Precise Moment	Grave Undertaking	Henry Kane		Mike Hammer	3/28/1958
Kitchen Kill		Frank E. Smith	Jonathan Craig	State Trooper	4/20/1958
My Son and Heir		Stephen Marlowe		Mike Hammer	7/5/1958
The Ripper	Final Curtain	Richard Ellington		Mike Hammer	7/12/1958
Shadow Boxer	A Detective Tail	Frank Kane		Mike Hammer	7/19/1958
Mugger Murder		Richard Deming		M Squad	2/13/1959
Now Die in It		Evan Hunter	Curt Cannon	Mike Hammer	7/17/1959
Pigeon in an Iron Lung	No Pain	Talmage Powell		Alfred Hitchcock Presents	10/25/1959
Dry Run		Norman Struber		Alfred Hitchcock Presents	11/8/1959
40 Detectives Later	Forty Detectives Later	Henry Slesar		Alfred Hitchcock Presents	4/24/1960
Hooked		Robert Turner		Alfred Hitchcock Presents	9/25/1960
The Man With Two Faces		Henry Slesar		Alfred Hitchcock Presents	12/13/1960
The Man Who Found the Mon		James E. Cronin		Alfred Hitchcock Presents	12/27/1960
Deathmate		James Causey		Alfred Hitchcock Presents	4/18/1961
You Can't Trust a Man		Helen Nielsen		Alfred Hitchcock Presents	5/9/1961
Cop for a Day		Henry Slesar		Alfred Hitchcock Presents	10/31/1961
The Old Pro		H. A. DeRosso		Alfred Hitchcock Presents	11/28/1961
The Geniuses	Bad Actor	Richard Deming		Alfred Hitchcock Presents	1/9/1962
The Big Score		Sam Merwin, Jr.		Alfred Hitchcock Presents	3/6/1962
Golden Opportunity	The Opportunity	J. W. Aaron		Alfred Hitchcock Presents	5/22/1962
Hangover		Charles Runyon		Alfred Hitchcock Hour	12/6/1962
The Quiet Room		Frank E. Smith	Jonathan Craig	Fallen Angels	8/29/1993
Return	Love and Blood	Evan Hunter		Fallen Angels	10/8/1995
Professional Man		David Goodis		Fallen Angels	10/15/1995

Peter Enfantino • Jeff Vorzimmer

Also available from Stark House Press:

The Best of *Manhunt*
A Collection of the Best Stories
From *Manhunt* Magazine

Foreword by Lawrence Block
Afterword by Barry N. Malzberg
Edited and Introduction by Jeff Vorzimmer
ISBN: 978-1-944520-68-7 $21.95

The Best of *Manhunt* 2
More of the Best from *Manhunt* Magazine

Foreword by Peter Enfantino
Introduction by Jon Breen
Edited and Introduction by Jeff Vorzimmer
ISBN: 978-1-951473-05-1 $21.95

Lightning Source UK Ltd.
Milton Keynes UK
UKHW022232170821
389016UK00012B/2315